... ces series

"Great fu... ...Prize–winning economist

"Stross brings to fantasy the same kind of sly humor and clear-eyed extrapolation that he previously brought to space opera and horror . . . presented with great wit and high suspense."

—*San Francisco Chronicle*

"Inventive, irreverent, and delightful . . . an alternate world where business is simultaneously low and high tech, and where romance, murder, marriage, and business are hopelessly intertwined—and deadly."   —L. E. Modesitt, Jr., author of the Saga of Recluce

"Fantasies with this much invention, wit, and gusto don't come along every day."   —*SFX*

"Fans of the author's previous work will recognize his trademark skill at world-building—you can almost see the filth on the streets of New England, feel the closeted oppression of the Clan hierarchy, and experience Miriam's terror at the horrifying circumstances she finds herself in."   —*SciFiNow*

"Fast-moving action with a number of interesting characters . . . Stross's ability to combine interesting ideas with solid plotting is one of his great strengths."   —*Asimov's Science Fiction*

"One of the defining phenomena of twenty-first-century SF is Charles Stross, for the quality of his work at its best."   —*Time Out*

"For sheer inventiveness and energy, this cliffhanger-riddled serial remains difficult to top."   —*Publishers Weekly*

Tor Books by Charles Stross

The Merchant Princes

The Bloodline Feud

(Originally published as *The Family Trade* and *The Hidden Family*)

The Traders' War

(Originally published as *The Clan Corporate* and *The Merchants' War*)

The Revolution Trade*

(Originally published as *The Revolution Business* and *The Trade of Queens*)

* forthcoming

THE
TRADERS' WAR

Originally published separately as

THE CLAN CORPORATE and THE MERCHANTS' WAR

Charles Stross

A Tom Doherty Associates Book
New York

This is a work of fiction. All of the characters, organizations, and events portrayed in this novel are either products of the author's imagination or are used fictitiously.

THE TRADERS' WAR

Copyright © 2013 by Charles Stross

All rights reserved.

A Tor Book
Published by Tom Doherty Associates, LLC
175 Fifth Avenue
New York, NY 10010

www.tor-forge.com

Tor® is a registered trademark of Tom Doherty Associates, LLC.

ISBN 978-0-7653-7867-5 (trade paperback)
ISBN 978-1-4668-6394-1 (e-book)

Tor books may be purchased for educational, business, or promotional use. For information on bulk purchases, please contact Macmillan Corporate and Premium Sales Department at 1-800-221-7945, extension 5442, or write specialmarkets@macmillan.com.

Originally published in the United States in somewhat different form, in two separate volumes, as *The Clan Corporate* in 2006 and *The Merchants' War* in 2007.

This revised and updated edition was originally published in Great Britain by Tor, an imprint of Pan Macmillan, a division of Macmillan Publishers Limited.

First U.S. Edition: November 2014

Printed in the United States of America

0 9 8 7 6 5 4 3 2 1

For Andrew, Lorna, James, and Scott

also for Gil, Jane, George, and Leo

Acknowledgments

Thanks are due to James Nicoll, Robert 'Nojay' Sneddon, Cory Doctorow, Andrew Wilson, Caitlin Blasdell, Tom Doherty, and my editors, David Hartwell and Moshe Feder.

TIED DOWN

Nail lacquer, the woman called Helge reflected as she paused in the antechamber, always did two things to her: it reminded her of her mother, and it made her feel like a rebellious little girl. She examined the fingertips of her left hand, turning them this way and that in search of minute imperfections in the early afternoon sunlight slanting through the huge window behind her. There weren't any. The maidservant who had painted them for her had poor nails, cracked and brittle from hard work; her own, in contrast, were pearlescent and glossy, and about a quarter-inch longer than she was comfortable with. There seemed to be a lot of things that she was uncomfortable with these days. She sighed quietly and glanced at the door.

The door opened at that moment. Was it coincidence, or was she being watched? Liveried footmen inclined their heads as another spoke. 'Milady, the duchess bids you enter. She is waiting in the day room.'

Helge swept past them with a brief nod – more acknowledgment of their presence than most of her rank would bother with – and paused to glance back down the hallway as her retinue (a lady-in-waiting, a court butler, and two hard-faced, impassive bodyguards) followed her. 'Wait in the hall,' she told the guards. '*You* can accompany me, but wait at the far end of the room,' she told her attendant ingénue. Lady Kara nodded meekly. She'd been slow to learn that Helge bore an uncommon dislike for having her conversations eavesdropped on: there had been an unfortunate incident some weeks ago, and the lady-in-waiting had not yet recovered her self-esteem.

The hall was perhaps sixty feet long and wide enough for a royal entourage. The walls, paneled in imported oak, were occupied by window bays interspersed with oil paintings and a few more-recent daguerreotypes of noble ancestors, the scoundrels and skeletons cluttering up the family tree. Uniformed servants waited beside each door. Helge paced across the rough marble tiles, her spine rigid and her shoulders set defensively. At the end of the hall an equerry wearing the polished half-armor and crimson breeches of his calling bowed, then pulled the tasseled bell-pull beside the double doors. 'The Countess Helge von Thorold d'Hjorth!'

The doors opened, ushering Countess Helge inside, leaving servants and guards to cool their heels at the threshold.

The day room was built to classical proportions – but built large, in every dimension. Four windows, each twelve feet high, dominated the south wall, overlooking the regimented lushness of the gardens that surrounded the palace. The ornate plasterwork of the ceiling must have occupied a master and his journeymen for a year. The scale of the architecture dwarfed the merely human furniture, so that the chaise longue the duchess reclined on, and the spindly rococo chair beside it, seemed like the discarded toy furniture of a baby giantess. The duchess herself looked improbably fragile: gray hair growing out in intricately coiffed coils, face powdered to the complexion of a china doll, her body lost in a court gown of black lace over burgundy velvet. But her eyes were bright and alert – and knowing.

Helge paused before the duchess. With a little moue of concentration she essayed a curtsey. 'Your grace, I are – am – happy to see you,' she said haltingly in Hochsprache. 'I – I – oh *damn*.' The latter words slipped out in her native tongue. She straightened her knees and sighed. 'Well? How am I doing?'

'Hmm.' The duchess examined her minutely from head to foot, then nodded slightly. 'You're getting better. Well enough to pass tonight. Have a seat.' She gestured at the chair beside her.

Miriam sat down. 'As long as nobody asks me to dance,' she said ruefully. 'I've got two left feet, it seems.' She plucked at her lap. 'And as long as I don't end up being cornered by a drunken backwoods peer who thinks not being fluent in his language is a sign of an imbecile. And as long as I don't accidentally mistake some long-lost third cousin seven times removed for the hat-check clerk and resurrect a two-hundred-year-old blood feud. And as long as – '

2

'Dear,' the duchess said quietly, 'do please shut up.'

The countess, who had grown up as Miriam but whom everyone around her but the duchess habitually called Helge, stopped in mid-flow. 'Yes, Mother,' she said meekly. Folding her hands in her lap she breathed out. Then she raised one eyebrow.

The duchess looked at her for almost a minute, then nodded minutely. 'You'll pass,' she said. 'With the jewelry, of course. And the posh frock. As long as you don't let your mouth run away with you.' Her cheek twitched. 'As long as you remember to be Helge, not Miriam.'

'I feel like I'm acting all the time!'

'Of course you do.' The duchess finally smiled. 'Imposter syndrome goes with the territory.' The smile faded. 'And I didn't do you any favors in the long run by hiding you from all this.' She gestured around the room. 'It becomes harder to adapt, the older you get.'

'Oh, I don't know.' Miriam frowned momentarily. 'I can deal with disguises and a new name and background; I can even cope with trying to learn a new language, it's the sense of permanence that's disconcerting. *I* grew up an only child, but *Helge* has all these – relatives – I didn't grow up with, and they're real. That's hard to cope with. And *you're* here, and part of it! And now this evening's junket. If I thought I could avoid it, I'd be in my rooms having a stomach cramp all afternoon.'

'That would be a Bad Idea.' The duchess still had the habit of capitalizing her speech when she was waxing sarcastic, Miriam noted.

'Yes, I know that. I'm just – there are things I should be doing that are more important than attending a royal garden party. It's all deeply tedious.'

'With an attitude like that you'll go far.' A pause. 'All the way to the scaffold if you don't watch your lip, at least in public. Do I need to explain how sensitive to social niceties your position here is? This is not America – '

'Yes, well, more's the pity.'

'Well, we're stuck with the way things are,' the duchess said sharply, then subsided. 'I'm sorry, dear, I don't mean to snap. I'm just worried for you. The sooner you learn how to mind yourself without

3

mortally offending anyone by accident the happier I'll be.'

'Um.' Miriam chewed on the idea for a while. *She's stressed*, she decided. *Is that all it is, or is there something more?* 'Well, I'll *try*. But I came here to see how you are, not to have a moan on your shoulder. So, how are you?'

'Well, now that you ask . . .' Her mother smiled and waved vaguely at a table behind her chaise longue. Miriam followed her gesture: two aluminum crutches, starkly functional, lay atop a cloisonné stand next to a pill case. 'The doctor says I'm to reduce the prednisone again next week. The Copaxone seems to be helping a lot, and that's just one injection a day. As long as nobody accidentally forgets to bring me next week's prescription I'll be fine.'

'But surely nobody would – '

'Really?' The duchess glanced back at her daughter, her expression unreadable. 'You seem to have forgotten what kind of a place this is. The meds aren't simply costly in dollars and cents: someone has to bring them across from the other world. And courier time is priceless. Nobody gives me a neatly itemized bill, but if I want to keep on receiving them I have to pay. And the first rule of business around here is: Don't piss off the blackmailers.'

Miriam's reluctant nod seemed to satisfy the duchess, because she relented: 'Remember, a lady never unintentionally gives offense – especially to people she depends on to keep her alive. If you can hang on to just one rule to help you survive in the Clan, make it that one. But I'm losing the plot. How are *you* doing? Have there been any after-effects?'

'After-effects?' Miriam caught her hand at her chin and forced herself to stop fidgeting. She flushed, pulse jerking with an adrenaline surge of remembered fear and anger. 'I – ' She lowered her hand. 'Oh, nothing *physical*,' she said bitterly. 'Nothing . . .'

'I've been thinking about him a lot lately, Miriam. He wouldn't have been good for you, you know.'

'I know.' The younger woman – youth being relative: she wouldn't be seeing thirty again – dropped her gaze. 'The political entangle-ments made it a messy prospect at best,' she said. 'Even if you discounted his weaknesses.' The duchess didn't reply. Eventually

Miriam looked up, her eyes burning with emotions she'd experienced only since learning to be Helge. 'I haven't forgiven him, you know.'

'Forgiven *Roland*?' The duchess's tone sharpened.

'No. Your goddamn half-brother. He's meant to be in charge of security! But he – ' Her voice began to break.

'Yes, yes, I know. And do you think he has been sleeping well lately? I'm led to believe he's frantically busy right now. Losing Roland was the least of our problems, if you'll permit me to be blunt, and Angbard has a major crisis to deal with. Your affair with him can be ignored, if it comes to it, by the Council. It's not as if you're a teenage virgin to be despoiled, damaging some aristocratic alliance by losing your honor – and you'd better think about that some more in future, because honor is *the* currency in the circles you move in, a currency that once spent is very hard to regain – but the deeper damage to the Clan that Matthias inflicted – '

'Tell me about it,' Miriam said bitterly. 'As soon as I was back on my feet they told me I could only run courier assignments to and from a safe house. And I'm not allowed to go home!'

'Matthias knows you,' her mother pointed out. 'If he mentioned you to his new employers – '

'I understand.' Miriam subsided, arms crossed before her and back set defensively. After a moment she started tapping her toes.

'Stop that!' Moderating her tone, the duchess added, 'If you do that in public it sends entirely the wrong message. Appearances are everything, you've *got* to learn that.'

'Yes, Mother.'

After a couple of minutes, the duchess spoke. 'You're not happy.'

'No.'

'And it's not just – him.'

'Correct.' Her hem twitched once more before Helge managed to control the urge to tap.

The duchess sighed. 'Do I have to drag it out of you?'

'No, Iris.'

'You shouldn't call me that here. Bad habits of thought and behavior.'

'Bad? Or just inappropriate? Liable to *send the wrong message*?'

5

The duchess chuckled. 'I should know better than to argue with you!' She looked serious. 'The wrong message in a nutshell. *Miriam can't go home, Helge.* Not now, maybe not ever. Thanks to that scum-sucking rat-bastard defector the entire Clan network in Massachusetts is blown wide open and if you even *think* about going – '

'Yeah, yeah, I know, there'll be an FBI SWAT team staking out my backyard and I'll vanish into a supermax prison so fast my feet won't touch the ground. If I'm lucky,' she added bitterly. 'So everything's locked down like a Code Red terrorist alert; the only way I'm allowed to go back to our world is on a closely supervised courier run to an underground railway station buried so deep I don't even see daylight; if I want anything – even a box of tampons – I have to *requisition* it and someone in the Security Directorate has to fill out a risk assessment to see if it's safe to obtain; and, and . . .' Her shoulders heaved with indignation.

'This is what it was like the whole time, during the civil war,' the duchess pointed out.

'So people keep telling me, as if I'm supposed to be grateful! But it's not as if this is my *only* option. I've got another identity over in world three and – '

'Do they have tampons there?'

'Ah.' Helge paused for a moment. 'No, I don't think so,' she said slowly. 'But they've got cotton wool.' She fumbled for a moment, then pulled out a pen-sized voice recorder. 'Memo: business plans. Investigate early patent filings covering tampons and applicators. Also sterilization methods – dry heat?' She clicked the recorder off and replaced it. 'Thanks.' A lightning smile that was pure Miriam flashed across her face. 'I should be over there. World three is my project. I set up the company and I ought to be managing it.'

'Firstly, our dear long-lost relatives are over there,' the duchess pointed out. 'Truce or not, if they haven't got the message yet, you could show your nose over there and get it chopped off. And secondly . . .'

'Ah, yes. Secondly.'

'You know what I'm going to say. So please don't shoot the messenger.'

'Okay.' Helge turned her head to stare moodily out of the nearest window. 'You're going to tell me that the political situation is messy. That if I go over there right now some of the more jumpy first citizens of the Clan will get the idea that I'm abandoning the sinking ship, aided and abetted by my *delightful* grandmother's whispering campaign – '

'Leave the rudeness to me. She's my cross to bear.'

'Yes, but.' Helge stopped.

Her mother took a deep breath. 'The Clan, for all its failings, is a very democratic organization. *Democratic* in the original sense of the word. If enough of the elite voters agree, they can depose the leadership, indict a member of the Clan for trial by a jury of their peers, issue bills of attainder – anything. Which is why appearances, manners, and social standing are so important. Hypocrisy is the grease that lubricates the Clan's machinery.' Her cheek twitched. 'Oh yes. While I remember, love, if you are accused of anything never, *ever*, insist on your right to a trial by jury. Over here, that word does not mean what you think it means. Like the word *secretary*. Pah, but I'm woolgathering! Anyway. My mother, your grandmother, has a constituency, Miri – Helge. Tarnation. Swear at me if I slip again, will you, dear? We need to break each other of this habit.'

Helge nodded. 'Yes, Iris.'

The duchess reached over and swatted her lightly on the arm. 'Patricia! Say my full name.'

'Ah.' Helge met her gaze. 'All right. Your grace is the Honorable Duchess Patricia voh Hjorth d'Wu ab Thorold.' With mild rebellion: 'Also known as Iris Beckstein, of 34 Coffin Street – '

'That's enough!' Her mother nodded sharply. 'Put the rest behind you for the time being. Until – unless – we can ever go back, the memories can do nothing but hurt us. You've got to live in the present. And the present means living among the Clan and deporting yourself as a, a countess. Because if you don't do that, all the alternatives on offer are drastically worse. This isn't a rich world, like America. Most women only have one thing to trade: as a lady of the Clan you're lucky enough to have two, even three if you count the contents of your head. But if you throw away the money and the power that goes with being of the Clan, you'll rapidly find out just what's under the surface – if you survive long enough.'

'But there's no limit to the amount of shit!' the younger woman burst out, then clapped a hand to her face as if to recall the unlady-like expostulation.

'Don't chew your nails, dear,' her mother said automatically.

*

It had started midmorning. Miriam (who still found it an effort of will to think of herself as Helge, outside of social situations where other people expected her to *be* Helge) was tired and irritable, dosed up on ibuprofen and propranolol to deal with the effects of a series of courier runs the day before when, wearing jeans and a lined water-proof jacket heavy enough to survive a northwest passage, she'd wheezed under the weight of a backpack and a walking frame. They'd had her ferrying fifty-kilogram loads between a gloomy cellar of undressed stone and an equally gloomy subbasement of an under-ground car park in Manhattan. There were armed guards in New York to protect her while she recovered from the vicious migraine that world-walking brought on, and there were servants and maids in the palace quarters back home to pamper her and feed her sweetmeats from a cold buffet and apply a cool compress for her head. But the whole objective of all this attention was to soften her up until she could be cozened into making another run. *Two* return trips in eight-een hours. Drugs or no drugs, it was brutal: without guards and flunkies and servants to prod her along she might have refused to do her duty.

She'd carried a hundred kilograms in each direction across the space between two worlds, a gap narrower than atoms and colder than light-years. Lightning Child only knew what had been in those packages. The Clan's mercantilist operations in the United States emphasized high-value, low-weight commodities. Like it or not, there was more money in smuggling contraband than works of art or intel-lectual property. It was a perpetual sore on Miriam's conscience, one that only stopped chafing when for a few hours she managed to stop being Miriam Beckstein, journalist, and to be instead Helge of

Thorold by Hjorth, Countess. What made it even worse for Miriam was that she was acutely aware that such a business model was stupid and unsustainable. Once, mere weeks ago, she'd had plans to upset the metaphorical applecart, designs to replace it with a fleet of milk tankers. But then Matthias, secretary to the Duke Angbard, captain-general of the Clan's Security Directorate, had upset the applecart first, and set fire to it into the bargain. He'd defected to the Drug Enforcement Agency of the United States of America. And whether or not he'd held his peace about the real nature of the Clan, a dynasty of world-walking spooks from a place where the river of history had run a radically different course, he had sure as hell shut down their eastern seaboard operations.

Matthias had blown more safe houses and shipping networks in one month than the Clan had lost in the previous thirty years. His psycho bagman had shot and killed Miriam's lover during an attempt to cover up the defection by destroying a major Clan fortress. Then, a month later, Clan security had ordered Miriam back to Niejwein from New Britain, warning that Matthias's allies in that timeline made it too unsafe for her to stay there. Miriam thought this was bullshit, but bullshit delivered by men with automatic weapons was bullshit best nodded along with, at least until their backs were turned.

Midmorning loomed. Miriam wasn't needed today. She had the next three days off, her corvée paid. Miriam could sleep in, and then Helge would occupy her time with education. Miriam Beckstein had two college degrees, but Countess Helge was woefully uneducated in even the basics of her new life. Just learning how to live among her recently rediscovered extended family was a full-time job. First, language lessons in the Hochsprache vernacular with a most attentive tutor, her lady-in-waiting Kara d'Praha. Then an appointment for a fitting with her dressmaker, whose ongoing fabrication of a suitable wardrobe had something of the quality of a Sisyphean task. Perhaps if the weather was good there'd be a discreet lesson in horsemanship (growing up in suburban Boston, she'd never learned to ride): otherwise, one in dancing, deportment, or court etiquette.

Miriam was bored and anxious, itching to get back to her start-up venture in the old capital of New Britain where she'd established a company to build disk brakes and pioneer automotive technology transfer. New Britain was about fifty years behind the world she'd grown up in, a land of opportunity for a sometime tech journalist turned entrepreneur. Helge, however, was strangely fascinated by the minutiae of her new life. Going from middle-class, middle-American life to the rarefied upper reaches of a barely postfeudal aristocracy meant learning skills she'd never imagined needing before. She was confronting a divide of five hundred years, not fifty, and it was challenging.

She'd taken the early part of the morning off to be Miriam, sitting in her bedroom in jeans and sweater, her seat a folding aluminum camp chair, a laptop balanced on her knees and a mug of coffee cooling on the floor by her feet. *If I can't do, I can at least plan*, she told herself wryly. She had a lot of plans, more than she knew what to do with. The whole idea of turning the Clan's business model around, from primitive mercantilism to making money off technology transfer between worlds, seemed impossibly utopian – especially considering how few of the Clan elders had any sort of modern education. But without plans, written studies, costings and risk analyses, she wasn't going to convince anyone. So she'd ground out a couple more pages of proposals before realizing someone was watching her.

'Yes?'

'Milady.' Kara bent a knee prettily, a picture of instinctive teenage grace that Miriam couldn't imagine matching. 'You bade me remind you last week that this eve is the first of summer twelvenight. There's to be a garden party at the Östhalle tonight, and a ball afterward beside, and a card from her grace your mother bidding you to attend her this afternoon beforehand.' Her face the picture of innocence she added, 'Shall I attend to your party?'

If Kara organized Helge's carriage and guards then Kara would be coming along too. The memories of what had happened the last time Helge let Kara accompany her to a court event nearly made her wince, but she managed to keep a straight face: 'Yes, you do that,' she said evenly. 'Get Mistress Tanzig in to dress me before lunch, and my compliments to her grace my mother and I shall be with her by the second hour of the afternoon.' Mistress Tanzig, the dressmaker, would know what Helge should wear in public and, more important, would be able to alter it to fit if there were any last-minute problems. Miriam hit the save button on her spreadsheet. 'Is that the time? Tell somebody to run me a bath; I'll be out in a minute.'

So much for the day off, thought Miriam as she packed the laptop away. *I suppose I'd better go and be Helge . . .*

*

'Have you thought about marriage?' asked the duchess.

'Mother! As if!' Helge snorted indignantly and her eyes narrowed. 'It's been about, what, ten weeks? Twelve? If you think I'm about to shack up with some golden boy so soon after losing Roland – '

'That wasn't what I meant, dear.'

'What do you mean, then?'

'I meant . . .' The duchess glanced at her sharply, taking stock: 'The, ah, noble institution. Have you thought about what it *means* here? And if so, what did you think?'

'I thought' – puzzlement wrinkled Helge's forehead – 'when I first arrived, Angbard tried to convince me I ought to make an alliance of fortunes, as he put it. Crudely speaking, to tie myself to a powerful man who could protect me.' The wrinkles turned into a full-blown frown. 'I nearly told him he could put his alliance right where the sun doesn't shine.'

'It's a good thing you didn't,' her mother said diplomatically.

'Oh, I know that now! But the whole deal here creeps me out. And then.' Helge took a deep breath and looked at the duchess: 'There's you, your experience. I really don't know how you can stand to be in the same room as her grace your mother, the bitch! How she could – '

'Connive at ending a civil war?'

'Sell off her daughter to a wife-beating scumbag is more the phrase I had in mind.' Helge paused. 'Against her wishes,' she added. A longer pause. 'Well?'

'Well,' the duchess said quietly. 'Well, well. And well again. Would you like to know how she did it?'

'I'm not sure.'

'Well, whether you want to or not, I think you need to know,' Iris – Patricia, the duchess Patricia, said. 'Forewarned is forearmed, and no, when I was your age – and younger – *I* didn't want to know about it, either. But nobody's offering to trade you on the block like a piece of horseflesh. I should think the worst they'll do is drop broad hints your way and make the consequences of noncooperation irritatingly obvious in the hope you'll give in just to make them go away. You've probably got enough clout to ignore them if you want to push it – if it matters to you enough. But whether it would be *wise* to ignore them is another question entirely.'

'Who are "they"?'

'Aha! The right question, at last!' Iris laboriously levered herself upright on her chaise. 'I told you the Clan is democratic, in the classical sense of the word. The marriage market is democracy in action, Helge, and as we all know, Democracy Is Always Right. Yes? Now, can you tell me who, within the family, provides the bride's dowry?'

'Why, the – ' Helge thought for a moment. 'Well, it's the head of the household's wealth, but doesn't the woman's mother have something to do with determining how much goes into it?'

'Exactly.' The duchess nodded. 'Braids cross three families, alternating every couple of generations so that issues of consanguinity don't arise but the Clan gift – the recessive gene – is preserved. To organize a braid takes some kind of continuity across at least three generations. A burden which naturally falls on the eldest women of the Clan. Men don't count: men tend to go and get themselves killed fighting silly duels. Or in wars. Or blood feuds. Or they sire bastards who then become part of the outer families and a tiresome burden. They – the bastards – can't world-walk, but some of their issue might, or their grandchildren. So we must keep track of them and find something useful for them to do – unlike the rest of the nobility here we have an incentive to look after our by-blows. I think we're lucky, in that respect, to have a matrilineal succession – other tribal societies I studied in my youth, patrilineal ones, were generally unpleasant places to be born female. Whichever and whatever, the lineage is preserved largely by the old women acting in concert. A conspiracy of matchmakers, if you like. The 'old bitches', as everyone under sixty tends to call them.' The duchess frowned. 'It doesn't seem quite as funny now I'm sixty-two.'

'Um.' Helge leaned toward her mother. 'You're telling me Hildegarde wasn't acting alone? Or she was being pressured by *her* mother? Or what?'

'Oh, she's an evil bitch in her own right,' Patricia waved off the question dismissively. 'But yes, she was pressured. She and the other ladies of a certain age don't have the two things that a young and eligible Clan lady can bargain with: they can't bear world-walkers, and they can no longer carry heavy loads for the family trade. So they must rely on other, more subtle tools to maintain their position. Like their ability to plait the braids, and to do each other favors, by way of their grandchildren. And when my mother was in her thirties – little older than you are now – she was subjected to much pressure.'

'So there's this conspiracy of old women' – Helge was grasping after the concept – 'who can make everyone's life a misery?'

'Don't underestimate them. They always win in the end, and you'll need to make your peace with them sooner or later. I'm unusual, I managed to evade them for more than three decades. But that almost never happens, and even when it does you can't actually win, because whether you fight them or no, you end up becoming one yourself.' She raised one finger in warning. 'You're relatively safe, kid. You're too old, too educated, and you've got your own power base. As far as I can see they've got no reason to meddle with you *unless* you threaten their honor. Honor is survival here. Don't *ever* do that, Miriam – Helge. Don't ever threaten to dishonor them. If you do, they'll find a way to bring you down. All it takes is leverage, and leverage is the one thing they've got.' She smiled thinly. 'Think of them as Darwin's revenge on us, and remember to smile and curtsey when you pass them because until you've given them grandchildren they *will* regard you as an expendable piece to move around the game board. And if you *have* given them a child, they have a hostage to hold against you. Until you, too, have grandchildren and graduate to playing the game yourself.'

*

13

Midafternoon, Helge returned to her rooms to check briefly on the arrangements for her travel to the Östhalle – it being high summer, with the sun setting well after ten o'clock, she need not depart until close to seven – then turned to Lady Kara. 'I would like to see Lady Olga, if she's available. Will you investigate? I haven't seen her around lately.'

'Lady Olga is in town today. She is down at the battery range,' Kara said without blinking. 'She told me this morning that you'd be welcome to join her.'

Most welcome to – then why didn't you tell *me?* Helge bit her tongue. Kara probably had some reason for withholding the invitation that had seemed valid at the time. Berating her for not passing on trivial messages would only cause Kara to start dropping every piece of trivia to which she was privy on her mistress's shoulders, rather than risk rebuke. 'Then let's go and see her!' Helge said brightly. 'It's not far, is it?'

The battery range was near the outer wall of the palace grounds – the summer palace, owned and occupied by those of the Clan elders who needed accommodation in the capital, Niejwein – and separated from those grounds by its own high stone wall. Miriam strolled slowly behind her guards, taking in the warm air and the scent of the ornamental shrubs planted to either side of the path. Her butler held a silk parasol above her to keep the sunlight off her skin. It still felt strange, the whole noble lady shtick, but there were some aspects of it she could live with. She paused at the gate in the wall. From the other side, she heard a muffled tapping sound. 'Announce us,' she told Kara.

'Yes, milady.' A moment later, the doors opened onto bedlam.

Lady Olga Thorold Arnesen – of Thorold, by Arnesen – was blond, pretty, and on first acquaintance a complete ditz. Her enthusiasms included playing the violin, dancing, and making a good marriage. But first acquaintances could be extremely misleading when dealing with children of the Clan, as Miriam had discovered. Right now the ditz was lying in the grass on the other side of the door, practicing her other great enthusiasm with the aid of a Steyr AUG assault rifle. The more delicately inclined Helge winced and covered her ears as Olga sent a final three-round burst downrange, then safed the gun and bounced to her feet.

'Helge!' Olga beamed widely but refrained from hugging her, settling instead for brushing her cheek. 'How charming to see you! A new creation, I see you're working your seamstress's fingers to the ivory. I suppose you didn't come to join me on the range?'

'If only.' Helge sniffed. 'It's business, I'm afraid.' She took in Olga's camo jacket and trousers. 'Are you coming to tonight's circus?'

'There's enough time to prepare later,' Olga said dismissively. 'I say, Master of Arms! You there! I'm going now, clean this up.' She handed the gun over, then turned back to her visitor. 'It's an excellent device, you really must try it one of these days,' she said, gesturing at the rifle. The range master and his apprentice were fussing with it, unloading the magazine and stripping out the barrel and receiver. 'There's a short version too, chambered for 9mm ammunition: police forces use them a lot. I'm going to get them for my bodyguards.'

'Really?' Helge found it impossible not to smile at Olga's enthusiasm – except when it was pointed right at her, so to speak, a situation that had only happened once, because of an unfortunate misunderstanding she was not keen to repeat. 'Let's walk. Somewhere quiet?' She glanced round, taking in the plethora of servants, from the range master and armorer and their assistants to her own bodyguard and butler and lady-in-waiting, and Olga's two impassive-faced mercenaries from the Kiowa nation.

'I'm hardly dressed for polite company.'

'So let's avoid it. The water garden?'

Olga cocked her head on one side: 'Yes, I do believe it will be nearly empty at this time of year.'

'Let's go. Leave the escort at the edge, I want to talk.'

The water garden began near the far end of the firing range, where a carefully diverted stream ran underground through a steel-barred tunnel in the walls of the grounds and then through sinuous loops around cunningly landscaped mounds and hollows. Trees shaded it, and small conservatories and rustic lodges provided a retreat for visitors tired of the bustle and business of the great estate. However, it was designed for the lush spring or the fiery autumn, not the heat of summer. At this time of year the stream ran sluggishly, yielding barely more than a trickle of water to damp down the mud, and most of the plants were either past their peak or not yet come to it.

Helge and Olga walked alongside the dry streambed on a brick path encrusted in yellow and brown lichen, Olga in her grass-stained camouflage fatigues, Helge in a silk gown fit for a royal garden party. Presently, when they passed the second turn in the path, Olga slowed her pace. 'All right, be you out with it.'

'I'm – ' Helge stopped, an expression of mild puzzlement on her face. 'Let me be Miriam for a bit. Please?'

'My dear, you already are!'

'Huh.' Miriam frowned. 'Well, that's the problem in a nutshell, I suppose. Have you been over to the workshop lately?'

'Have I?' Olga rolled her eyes. 'Your uncle's been running me ragged lately! Me and Brilliana – and everyone else. I think he sent in Morgan du Hjalmar to do the day-to-day stuff in your workshop, and a couple of Henryk's people to audit the organization for security, but honestly, I haven't had time to keep an eye on it. It's been a rat race! I'm lucky to have the time to attend the midsummer season, he's working me like a servant!'

'I see.' Miriam's tone was dry.

Olga looked at her sharply. 'What is it?'

'Oh, nothing much: every time I ask if it's safe for me to go over there and look in on my company I get some excuse from security like, 'We can't go there, the hidden family gangsters may not honor the ceasefire' or 'We think Matthias's little friends may be looking for you there' or 'It isn't safe.' It feels like I'm being cut out, Olga, and they're not even trying very hard to hide it. It's insultingly obvious. I get to sit here in Thorold Palace practicing dance steps and Hochsprache and court etiquette, and every time I try to make myself useful something comes up to divert me. From my own company! The one I set up in New Britain that's showing a higher rate of profit growth than anything else the Clan's seen in thirty years!'

'Profit growth from a very low baseline,' Olga pointed out.

'That's not the *point*!' Miriam managed to keep her temper under control. 'While they're keeping me on the shelf under glass I can't actually meet people and make deals and keep things moving! I'm isolated. I don't know what's going on. Hell, do *you* know what's going on? Is Roger messing around with epoxides again or is he working on the process quality issue? Did Jeremiah sort out the delivery schedules? Who's handling payroll? If it's that man of Bates's it's costing us an arm and a leg. Well? Who's minding the shop?'

Olga shook her head. 'I'm sure Morgan was taking care of all that,' she said slowly, not meeting Miriam's eyes. 'Things are very busy.'

'Well, you're actually going on-site,' Miriam pointed out. 'If you don't know what to look for, how should Morgan know? I'm the only person in the Clan who really knows what the company is good for or where everything goes, and if they're keeping me away from it, there's a good chance that –' She stopped.

Olga busied herself looking around the lower branches of the trees for the mockingbird that had been serenading them only a minute before.

'*Why* am I being frozen out?' asked Miriam.

'I couldn't possibly comment,' Olga sang, almost tonelessly, an odd affectation she sometimes used when forced to deliver bad news, 'because were I to repeat anything I heard from his excellency in the Security Directorate that would be an act of petty treason, not to say a betrayal of his trust in me – but has anything else happened to you lately?'

'Oh, lots.' Miriam's voice sharpened. 'Deportment lessons. Dancing lessons. A daily dossier of relatives and their family trees to memorize. How to ride a horse sidesaddle. How to address a prince, a pauper, or a priest of Sky Father. The use of reflexive verbs in Hochsprache. More clothing than I've ever needed before, all in styles I wouldn't have been seen dead in – or expected to see outside a museum or a movie theater. I've been getting a crash course.' She grimaced, then glanced sidelong at Olga. 'I went to see Ma – Iris, I mean, Her Grace the Duchess Patricia – this afternoon. She's turned almost as stone-faced and Machiavellian as my dear old grandmother.'

'Really?' Olga chirped, just a little too brightly. 'Did she have anything interesting to say?'

17

'Yes, as a matter of fact she did.' Miriam tapped one foot impatiently. 'She asked me what I thought about *marriage*, Olga. She knows damn well what I think about marriage; she was there when I married Ben, and she was still there when the divorce came through, and *that* was over ten years ago. She knows about Roland.' Her voice wobbled slightly as she named him, and for a moment she looked a decade older than her thirty-three years. 'Ma's frightening me, Olga, it's as if something's broken inside her and she's decided it was all a mistake, running away, and she needs to conform to expectations.'

'Well, maybe –' Olga paused. She glanced around. 'Look, Miriam. I *think* it's safe to tell you this, all right? But don't talk about it in front of anybody else.' She took a deep breath. 'You *are* being kept away from your operation in New Britain. It's a security thing, but not, not Matthias. I think her grace was finding out what you think about marriage because that's the fastest way to clear things up. If you were – unambiguously – part of the Clan, there'd be fewer grounds to worry about you.'

'About *me*? What do you think – '

'Hush, it's not what *I* think that's the problem!'

Miriam paused. 'I'm sorry.'

'I accept your apology, dear friend. No, it's – the problem is, you've been too successful too fast. On your own. Think about Roland, think about what *he* tried to do years ago. They're afraid that a lot of young tearaways will look at your example and think, "I could do that,"' and, well, copy everything except the way you came home to face a council hearing and explain what you were doing.'

Miriam looked blank for a moment. 'You mean, they're afraid youngsters would use me as an object lesson and strike out on their own. Defect. Leave the Clan.'

'Yes, Helge. I think that's what they're afraid of. You've handed them a huge opportunity on a plate, but it's also a threat to their very survival as an institution. And there's already a crisis in train for them to worry about. Frightened people act harshly . . . your mother has every reason to be scared witless, on your behalf. Do you see?'

'That's hard to believe.' Eyes downcast, Helge slowly began to walk back along the path. 'Bastards,' she muttered quietly under her breath. 'Lying bastards.'

Olga trotted to catch up. 'Come along to the garden party tonight,' she suggested. 'Try to enjoy it? You'll meet lots of eligible gentles there, I'm sure.' A quiet giggle: 'If they're not overawed by your reputation!'

'Enjoy it?' Helge stopped dead. 'Last time I attended one of those events Matthias tried to blackmail me, his majesty insisted on introducing me to his idiot younger son, and two different factions tried to assassinate me! I'm just hoping that his majesty's too drunk to recognize me, otherwise – '

'This time will be different,' Olga said, offering her hand. 'You'll see!'

TRANSLATED TRANSCRIPT BEGINS

'A most excellent evening, your grace.'

'Any evening at court is a most excellent one, Otto. Blessed by the presence of our royal sun, as it were. Ah, you – a glass for the baron, here!'

(*Pause.*)

'That's very fine, the, ah, Sudten new grape? This year's, fresh from the cask?'

'Absolutely. His majesty's vintners are conscientious as always. I understand we can expect this crop to arrive in our own cellars presently, in perhaps a few weeks – as the ships work their way into port, weather permitting.'

'As the – oh. How *do* they do it?'

'Witchcraft of some description, no doubt, though the how of it hardly matters as much as the *why*, Otto.' (*Pause.*) 'Are you still having problems with your new neighbor?'

'Why that – one-legged whore's son of a bloated tick! I'm sorry, your grace. Sky Father rot his eyes in his head, yes! It continues. As the circuit assizes will attest this high summer. And he's got the sworn men to compurge his case before the justiciars, claiming with their lying hands on the altar that every inch of the forest he's cleared has been in his family since time immemorial.

Which it has *not*, on account of his family being jumped-up peddlers – '

'Not so loudly if you please, Otto. Another glass?'

'My – discreetly! Discreetly does it indeed, sir, I must apologize; it is just that the subject causes me no little inflammation of the senses. My grief is not at the ennoblement of the line, which it must be admitted happened in my grandfather's day, but his attitude is insufferable! To raze the choicest forest is bad enough, but to sow it with weeds, and then to erect fences and bar his fields to the hunt in breach of ancient right is a personal affront. And his claim to be under the instruction of his liege is . . .'

'Quite true, Otto.'

'I most humbly beg your pardon, your grace, but I find that hard to credit.'

(*Pause.*)

'It is entirely true, Otto. The merchants own considerable estates, and fully a tenth of them were turned over to this crop last spring. With considerable hardship to their tenants, I might add; an unseemly lack of care will see many of them starving. Evidently red and purple flowers mean more to them than the health of their peasants, unless by some more of their magic they can transform poppies into bread by midwinter's eve.'

'Idiots.' (*Inarticulate muttering.*) 'It wouldn't be the *first* idiocy they've been guilty of, of course, but to damage the yeomanry adds an insult to the blow.'

'Exactly his thought.'

'He –' (*Pause.*) 'The rising sun is of this thought?'

'Indeed. Even while his father sips his new wine, imported by tinker trickery, and raises them in his esteem without questioning their custody of the lands he's granted them, our future king asks hard questions. He's a born leader, and we are lucky to have his like.'

'I'll drink to that. Long live the king!'

'Long live . . . and long live the prince!'

'Indeed, long live the prince!'

'And may we live to see the day when he succeeds his father to the throne.'

'May we –'(*Coughing.*) (*Pause.*) 'Indeed, my lord. Absolutely, unques-
tionably. Neither too early nor too late nor – ahem. Yes,
I shall treasure your confidence.'
'These are dangerous times, Otto.'
'You can – count on me. Sir. *Should* it come to that – '
'I hope that it will not. We *all* hope that it will not, do you
understand? But youth grows impatient with corruption, as dusk
grows impatient with dawn and as you grow impatient with your
jumped-up peddler of a neighbor. There have been vile rumors
about the succession, even as to the disposition of the young
prince, and the suitability of the lion of the nation for the role of
shepherd . . .'
(*Spluttering.*) 'Insupportable!'
'Yes. I merely mention it to you so that you understand how the land
lies. As one of my most trusted clients . . . Well, Otto, I must be
moving on. People to see, favors to bestow. But if I may leave you
with one observation, it is that it might be to your advantage and
my pleasure for you to present yourself to his grace of Innsford
before the evening is old. In his capacity as secretary to the
prince, you understand, he is most interested in collecting
accounts of insults presented to the old blood by the new.
Against the reckoning of future years, gods willing.'
'Why, thank you, your grace! Gods willing.'
'My pleasure.'

TRANSCRIPT ENDS

RUMORS OF WAR

Meanwhile, a transfinite distance and a split second away, the king-emperor of New Britain was having a bad day.

'Damn your eyes, Farnsworth.' He hunched over his work-glass, tweezers in hand, one intricate gear wheel clasped delicately between its jaws. 'Didn't I tell you not to disturb me at the bench?'

The unfortunate Farnsworth cleared his throat apologetically. A skinny fellow in the first graying of middle age, clad in the knee breeches and tailcoat of a royal equerry, his position as companion of the king's bedchamber made him the first point of contact for anyone who wanted some of the king's time – and also the lightning conductor for his majesty's occasional pique. 'Indeed you did, your majesty.' He stood on the threshold of the royal workshop, flanked on either side by the two soldiers of the Horse Guards who held the door, his attention focused on the royal watchmaker. King John the Fourth of New Britain was clearly annoyed, his plump cheeks florid and his blond curls damp with perspiration from hours of focus directed toward the tiny mechanism clamped to his workbench.

'Then what have you got to say for yourself?' demanded the monarch, moderating his tone very slightly. Farnsworth suppressed a sigh of relief: John Frederick was not his father, blessed with decisiveness but cursed with a whim of steel. Still, he wasn't out of the woods yet. 'I see it is' – the king's eyes swiveled toward a mantel covered from edge to edge in whirring clocks, every one of which he had built with his own hands – 'another thirty-seven minutes before I must withdraw to the Green Room and prepare for the grand opening.'

'I deeply regret the necessity of encroaching upon your majesty's precious time, but' – Farnsworth took a deep breath – 'it's the Ministry for Special Affairs. They've hatched some sort of alarm or excursion, and Sir Roderick says it cannot possibly wait, and the prime minister himself heard Sir Roderick out in private and sent me straight to you forthwith. He apologizes for intruding upon your majesty's business, but says he agrees the news is extremely grave and requests your most urgent attention in your capacity as commander in chief.'

'*News?*' The king snorted. '*Urgent?* It's probably just some jumped-up border fort commander complaining that Milton's been squeezing their bully and biscuit again.' But he carefully lowered the tiny camshaft assembly, placing it back on the velvet cloth beside the rectangular gear mill he was building, and lowered a second cloth atop the work in progress. 'Where's he waiting?'

'In the Gold Office, your Majesty.'

Two footmen of the royal household scurried forward to secure the items on the royal workbench. A third servant bowed deeply, then bent to untie the royal apron, while a fourth approached bearing the king's topcoat. The clockmaker king slid down off his high stool and stretched. At thirty-six years old he was in good health, although his waistline showed the effect of too many state banquets, and his complexion betrayed the choleric blood pressure that so worried his physiopaths and apothecaries. He extended his arms for the coat, of conservative black broadcloth embroidered with gold frogging in the style of the earlier century. 'Take me to Sir Roderick and the prime minister. Let us hear this news that is important enough to drag the royal gearsman away from his analytical engine.'

Farnsworth glanced over his shoulder. 'Make it so,' he snapped. And it was done. The King of New Britain, Emperor of Terra Australis, by grace of God Protector-Regent of the Chrysanthemum Throne, pretender to the Throne of England, and Presider of the Grand Assembly of American States, could go nowhere without an escort of Horse Guards to protect the royal person, majors-domo to announce his presence in advance lest some hapless courtier fail to be alerted and take their cue to pay their respects, household servants to open the doors before him and close them behind him and brush the carpets before his feet fell upon them . . . but John Frederick the man had scant patience when kept waiting, and Farnsworth took considerable pride in ensuring that his lord and master's progress was as frictionless as one of the royal artificer's own jeweled gear trains.

The royal procession paced smoothly through the west wing of the Brunswick Palace, traversing wood-paneled corridors illuminated by the cold, clear brilliance of the electrical illuminants the technocrat-emperor favored. Courtiers and servants scattered before his progress as Farnsworth marched, stony-faced, ahead of the king, aware of the royal eyes drilling speculatively into the back of his high-collared coat. He turned into the North Hall, then through the Hall of Monsters (walled with display cabinets by the king's grandfather, who had taken his antediluvian cryptozoological studies as seriously as the present incumbent took his watchmaker's bench), and then into the New Hall. From there he turned left and paused in a small vestibule before the polished oak doors of the Gold Office.

'Open all and rise for his majesty!' called one of the guards. An answering announcement, muffled by the thickness of wood, reached Farnsworth. He nodded at the nearest footman, who moved smartly to one side and opened the door. Farnsworth stepped forward.

'His Majesty the King bids you good afternoon, and graces you with his presence to enquire of the running of his domains,' he announced. Then he took two steps back, to stand beside the door, as invisible to the powerful occupants as the tape-telegraph on its pillar to one side of the enormous desk or the gigantic map of the world that covered the wall opposite the door.

John Frederick stepped inside, then glanced over his shoulder. 'Shut it. Everyone who isn't cleared, get out,' he said. Two men, one tall and cadaverous in his black suit, the other wizened and stooped with age, waited beside his desk as he strode forward and threw himself down in the wide-armed chair behind it with a grunt of irritation. The stooped man watched impassively, but the tall fellow looked slightly apprehensive, like an errant pupil called into the principal's office. 'Sir Roderick, Lord Douglass. We assume you would not have lightly called us away from our one private hour of the day without good reason. So if you would be good enough to be seated, perhaps you could explain to us what that reason was? You, fetch chairs for my guests.'

Servants cleared for the highest discussions brought chairs for the two ministers. Lord Douglass sat first, creakily lowering himself into his seat. 'Roderick, I believe this is your story,' he said in a thin voice that betrayed no weakness of mind, merely the frailty of extreme old age.

'Yes, your lordship. Majesty. I have the grave duty to report to you that our intelligence confirms that two days ago the Farmers General detonated a corpuscular dissociation petard on their military test range in Northumbria.'

'Shit.' John Frederick closed his eyes and rubbed them with the back of one regal wrist. 'And which of our agents have reported this? Roderick, they were at least six months away from that last week, what-what?'

Sir Roderick cleared his throat. 'I am afraid our intelligence estimates were incorrect, your majesty.' He took a deep breath. 'Our initial information comes from a communicant in Lancaster who has heard eyewitness reports of the flash and a toadstool-shaped cloud from villagers in the Lake District, southwest of the test range. Subsequently a weather ballonet over Iceland detected a radiant plume of corpuscular fragments indicative of a petard of the gun type, using enriched light-kernel cronosium. We've had detailed reports of the progress of the Farmers' jenny-works in Bohemia, which has been taking in shipments of pitchblende from the Cape. If they've got enough highly enriched cronosium to hoist a petard, and if they've also commissioned the crucible complex that was building near Kiev, then according to the revised estimates that my department has prepared we can expect the Frogs to have as many as twelve corpses in service by the end of the year, and production running at two per month through next year, rising to ten per month thereafter.'

The king sighed. 'We cannot afford to ignore this affront. Our credibility will be deeply weakened if we are seen to ignore such a clear challenge by an agency of the French crown. And the insult of using our former territory as a *test range*' – his voice crackled with indignation – 'cannot be other than intentional.' John Frederick straightened up in his chair. 'Lord Douglass. This matter must be addressed by the Imperial Security Council. A new policy is required to deal with the affront. And a public position, lest panic ensue when the Frogs announce their new capability.' He drummed the fingers of his left hand on the intricately lacquered desktop. 'Well. What else to keep us from our workshop?'

Farnsworth focused on the prime minister. Douglass might be old and withered, but there was still a sharp mind behind the wispy white hair and liver-spotted wattles. Moreover, to the extent Farnsworth could claim to know the prime minister at all, he struck the equerry as looking shifty – and Sir Roderick was visibly sweating. *This is going to be very bad indeed*, Farnsworth realized. *They're using the French corpuscular test to soften him up. What on God's earth could be* worse *than Louis XXII with super-weapons?*

'Your majesty.' It was Douglass. Farnsworth focused on him. 'This, ah, led me to question the diligence with which the Ministry for Special Affairs has been discharging its duties abroad. And indeed, Sir Roderick has instigated certain investigations without prompting, investigations which are revealing a very frightening deficit in our understanding of continental machinations against the security of your domain.'

'We . . . see.' The king sounded perplexed and mildly irritated. 'Would you get to the point, please? If the situation is as bad as you say, it would be expedient to draw no attention to our knowledge of it, and to reassure those who know something of it but not the substance – therefore one should depart to dress for the opening as one's progression dictates on time and without sign of turmoil, at least until after the next scheduled ISC meeting. So what exactly are you talking about?'

'Sir Roderick,' Douglass prompted.

Sir Roderick looked like a man about to be hanged. 'Your majesty, it pains me to lay this before you, but in the wake of the disturbances in Boston three weeks ago I instigated certain investigations. To draw a long story short, it appears that certain of our paid agents at large have been in actual fact accepting the coin of a second paymaster, whose livres and francs have added color to their reportage – to say nothing of delaying vital intelligence. We are now trying to ascertain the extent of the damage, but it appears that there has been for some time a French spy ring operating in our very halls, and this ring has suborned at least one network of our agents overseas. My men are now trying to isolate the spies, and discover how far the rot has spread.

'I believe that in addition to perverting the course of incoming intelligence – which they were unable to do with the petard, it would seem, because weather ballonets with scintillation tubes accept no bribes – these enemy agents have been arranging for numerous shipments of gold to arrive in this country. Certainly more gold than usual has been seized on the black market in the past six months, and it appears that certain troublemakers and rabble-rousers have been living high on the hog.'

'The usual?' John Frederick asked coldly.

'Levelers and Ranters,' Douglass said quietly. He looked sad. 'They never learn, although this treason is, I think, unprecedented in recent years. If true.'

The king stood up. 'We do not tolerate slander and libel and anarchism, much less as a front for that *bastard* pretender's machinations!' His cheeks shone; for a moment Farnsworth half-expected him to burst into a denunciation, but after a while the monarch regained control. 'Bring forward the next ISC meeting, as soon as possible,' he ordered. 'Sir Roderick. We expect a daily briefing on the fruits of your investigation. We realize you have had barely nine months to get to grips with your office, but we must insist on holding you responsible for the progress of the ministry. Should you succeed in leeching it back to health you will find us a forgiving ruler, and we appreciate your candor in bringing the disease to our notice – but if this pot boils over, it will not be the Crown who is scalded.' He glanced round. 'Farnsworth, attend to our wardrobe. Lord Douglass, thank you for bringing the situation to our attention. We shall now proceed to appear our regal best for the state opening tonight. If you should care to seek audience with us after the recession of Parliament, we would value your advice.'

'I am at your majesty's service, as always,' murmured the prime minister. He stood, slowly. The minister for Special Affairs rose too, as

Farnsworth moved smoothly to ensure the king's progress back to his dressing room.

*

That evening, after the state opening and the royal progress from Brunswick Palace to the Houses of Parliament at the far end of Manhattan Island, Farnsworth pulled on a heavy overcoat and slipped out through a side door of the palace, to visit an old acquaintance in a public house just off Gloriana Street.

Wooden paneling and a brown, stained ceiling testified to the Dutch origins of the Arend's Nest: the pub's front windows looked out toward the high-rise tenements crowding the inner wall of the bastion that had protected New York from continental aggression as far back as the late eighteenth century. Now a favorite haunt by day of city stock merchants and the upper crust of businessmen who filled the new office blocks behind the administrative complex, by night the Nest was mostly empty. Farnsworth slipped past the bar and stood next to a booth at the back with his coat collar turned up against the chill from the sea and his hat pulled down close to his ears. 'You won't fool 'nay-one like that,' said a familiar voice. 'You look like you're trying to hide and they'll pay attendance on ye when the police come asking. And now what time have you?'

Farnsworth shook himself. 'I'm sorry, but my pocket oyster's broken,' he said in a robotic tone of voice.

'Then ye'll just have to tell me what time it says?'

He hauled out his watch and flipped it open. 'Ten to nine.'

'Jolly good.' With a sigh and a rustle his welcomer moved aside to let him into the cubicle. Farnsworth sat down gratefully. 'I've taken the liberty of ordering your pint already.' He was a plump, slightly shabby man whom Farnsworth knew only as Jack. Farnsworth had studiously suppressed any instinct to dig deeper. Jack wore a dark suit, shiny at the elbows, and a red silk cravat that although clean was clearly in need of ironing. Beside him sat another fellow, unknown to Farnsworth: a long-faced man in early middle age, but with a consumptive pallor about him and a face that seemed to chronicle more

28

insults than any one life should bear. Farnsworth removed his hat and scarf and placed them fastidiously on one of the hooks screwed to the upper rail of the booth. 'Have you anything to report?'

'For whose ears?' Farnsworth picked up his glass. A full one sat untouched before Mr. Long-Face, which seemed an unconscionable waste of a good pint of porter to him. 'No offense.'

'This is, um, Rudolf,' said Jack. 'He's from Head Office. You remember what we spoke about earlier.'

'Ah, yes.' Farnsworth shuffled uneasily in his seat. *Head Office* covered a multitude of sins, most of them capital offenses in the eyes of the Homeland Security Bureau. Far more subversive than any bomb-throwing wild-eyed democrat or fly-by-night unlicensed desktop publisher spreading lies and slanders about her royal highness's enthusiasm for tight-breeched household cavalry officers . . . but the exchange of passwords had gone smoothly. Jack hadn't used the *bail out* challenge. Which meant this was official.

'Nothing new. His majesty is trying to keep a placid face but is mightily exercised over the continental despotism. They've exploded a corpuscular weapon months ahead of what our spies said was possible. Sir Roderick is dusting under chairs and tables in search of a mouse hole, as if his head depends upon it – and indeed it might, if Douglass is of a mind to hold him responsible. There is the usual ongoing crisis over precedence in the royal bedchamber, and My Lady Frazier is vexed to speak of creating a new post of – well, perhaps this is of no interest? In any case, Douglass is exercised, too. He seems much gloomier than normal, and muttered something about fearing war was making virtue of necessity, and we must ensure the French use of the new weapons – corpses, he calls them, a vile contraction – is subjected to prior restraint by a mutual terror of annihilation.' With this, Farnsworth reached into an inner pocket of his jacket and produced a small envelope. He slid it across the table. 'Usual drill.'

Jack passed it to the stranger. It vanished immediately, and at once Farnsworth felt a load off his shoulders. He sighed and drained half his pint. Jack smiled sardonically. 'Pass the noose is what we called this game in Camp Frederick.'

29

The stranger, Rudolf, blinked his rheumy eyes, expressionless. 'We require more detailed economic information,' he said, in an unexpectedly educated accent. 'The V1 and V2 treasury indicators, any information you can obtain about the prevalence of adulterants in the royal mint's stock, confiscations of bullion, the rate of default of debt secured against closed bodies corporate, the proposed repayment terms on the next issue of war bonds, and everything you can discover about the next budget.'

Farnsworth leaned back. 'That's the Exchequer,' he said slowly. 'I don't work there or know anything. Or know anyone who does.'

Rudolf nodded. 'We understand. And we don't expect miracles. All we ask is that you be aware of our needs. Douglass is a not infrequent visitor to the palace, and should he by mistake leave his brief unattended for a few minutes – well.' The hint of a smile came to Rudolf's face. 'Have you ever seen one of these before?' He slid a device barely larger than a box of matches onto the table.

Farnsworth stared at it. 'What is it?'

'It's a camera.'

'Don't be silly' – Farnsworth bent over it – 'nobody could build a camera that small! Could they? And what's it made of, lacquered cardboard?'

'No.' Rudolf pushed it toward him. 'It's made of a material like foramin or cellulate, or a phenolic resin – even the lens. It's waterproof and small enough to conceal in a boot heel. It will take eight pictures, then you must return it to us so that we can remove the sketchplate and downlo – ah, develop it. You aim it with this viewfinder, like so, and take a picture by pressing this button – thus. Yes, it will work without daylight – this is adequate for it. Keep it – no, not that one, this one' – he produced a second camera and handed it to Farnsworth – 'about your person where it will not be found easily but where you can reach it in an instant. Inside your hat ribbon in circumstances like this, perhaps, or in your periwig when paying attendance upon his majesty.'

'I – ' Farnsworth looked at the tiny machine as if it were a live scorpion. 'Did this come from the Frogs?' he heard himself asking as if from a great distance. 'Because if so – '

'No.' Rudolf flushed, and for the first time showed emotion. Anger. 'We aren't pawns of the Bourbon tyranny, sir. We are free democrats all, patriotic Englishmen fighting in the vanguard of the worldwide struggle for the rights of man, for freedom and equality before the law – and we'll liberate France and her dominions as well, when the time comes to join in one great brotherhood of humanity and set the east afire! But we have allies you are unaware of, and hopefully will *remain* unaware of for some time to come, lest you jeopardize the cause.' He fixed Farnsworth with a gimlet stare. 'Do you understand?'

Farnsworth nodded. 'I – yes.' He pocketed the tiny device hastily, then finished his beer. 'Another pint?' he asked Jack. 'In the interests of looking authentic . . .'

'By all means.' Jack stood. 'I'll just go to the bar.'

'And I must make haste to the jakes,' said Rudolf, nodding affably at Farnsworth. 'We won't meet again, I trust. Remember: eight, then to Jack. He will give you a replacement. Good night.' He took his hat and slipped away, leaving Farnsworth to sit alone, lonely and frightened until Jack returned with a fresh glass and a grin of conviviality, to chat about the dog racing and shore up his cover by helping him spend another evening drinking beer with his friend of convenience. Jack the Lad, Jack be Nimble, Jack the Leveler . . .

*

The man Farnsworth knew only as Rudolf was in no particular hurry. First he took his ease in the toilet. It was a cold night for the time of year, and he was old enough to have learned what a chill could do to his bladder. As he buttoned his coat and shuffled out the back door, through the yard with the wooden casks stacked shoulder high, he stifled a rattling cough. Something was moving in his chest again, foreshadowing what fate held in store for him. 'All the more reason to get this over with sooner rather than later, my son,' he mumbled to himself as he unlocked the gate and slid unenthusiastically into the brick-walled alleyway.

The alley was heaped with trash and hemmed in by the tumble-down sheds at the back of the buildings that presented such a fine stone front to the highway. Rudolf picked his way past a rusting fire escape and leaned on a wooden doorway next to a patch of wall streaked with dank slime from a leaky down-pipe. The door opened silently. He ducked inside, then closed and bolted it. The darkness in the cellar was broken only by a faint skylight. Now moving faster, Rudolf crossed over to another door and rapped on it thrice. A second later the inner door opened. 'Ah, it's you.'

'It's me,' Rudolf agreed. The sullen-faced man put away his pistol, looking relieved. 'Coat,' Rudolf snapped, shedding his outer garment. 'Hat.' The new garments were of much better cut than those that he'd removed, suitable for an operagoer of modest means – a ministry clerk, perhaps, or a legal secretary – and as he pulled them on 'Rudolf' forced himself to straighten up, put a spring in his step and a spark in his eye. 'Time to be off, I think. See you later.'

He left by way of a staircase and a dim hallway, an electrical night-light guiding his footsteps. Finally, 'Rudolf' let himself out through the front door, which was itself unlocked. The coat and hat he'd arrived in would be vanishing into the belly of the furnace that heated the law firm's offices by day. In a few minutes there'd be nothing to connect him to the man from the royal household other than a tenuous chain of hearsay – not that it would stop the Homeland Security Bureau's hounds, but with every broken link the chain would become harder to follow.

The main road out front was brightly lit by fizzing gas stands; cabs rumbled up and down it, boilers hissing as their drivers trawled for trade among the late-night crowds who dotted the sidewalk outside cafes and fashionable eating houses. The music hall along the street was emptying out, and knots of men and women stood around chattering raucously or singing the latest ditties from memory – with varying degrees of success, for the bars were awash with genever and scrumpy, and the entertainment was not noted for genteel restraint. Overhead, the neon lights blinked like the promise of a new century, bright blandishments of commerce and a ticker of news running around the outside of the theater's awning. 'Rudolf' stepped off the curb, avoided a cab, and made his way across to the far side of the street. The rumble of an airship's engines echoed off the roadstone paving, a reminder of the royal presence a few miles away. 'Rudolf' forced himself to focus as he walked purposefully along the sidewalk, avoiding the merrymakers and occasional vagrant. *Dear friends*, he thought; *the faces of multitudes*. He glanced around, a frisson of fear running up his spine. *I hope we're in time.*

Passing a penny to a red-cheeked lad yelling the lead from tomorrow's early edition, 'Rudolf' took a copy of *The Times* and scanned the headlines as he walked. *Nader Reasserts Afghan Claim*. Nothing good could ever come from that part of the world, he reflected; especially Shah Nader's thirst for black gold he could sell to the king's navy via the oiling base at Jask. *Saboteurs Apprehended in Breasil*. All part and parcel of the big picture. *Crown Prince James Visits Santa Cruz* made it sound like a grand tour of the nation rather than a desperate hope that the Pacific warmth would do something to ease the child's ailment. 'Rudolf' turned a corner into a narrower street. *Prussian Ambassador Slights French Envoy at Gala Opening*: now *that* didn't sound very clever, did it? As the joke put it, when the French diplomat said 'Frog' the Germanys all croaked in chorus. *Murdock Suit: Malcolm Denies Slur*. All the best barristers arguing the big libel case on a pro bono basis – a faint smile came to the thin man's face as he read the leading paragraph, squinting under the thin glare of the lamps. Then he folded the paper beneath his arm, palming something between the pages, and strode on toward the intersection with New Street. The crowds were thicker here, and as he stepped onto the pavement at the far side a fellow ran straight into him.

'I say, sir, are you all right?' the man asked, dusting himself off. 'You dropped your paper.' He bent and handed a folded broadsheet to 'Rudolf'.

'If you'd been looking where you were going, I wouldn't have.' 'Rudolf' snorted, jammed the paper beneath his arm, and hurried off determinedly. Only when he'd passed the outrageously expensive plate-glass windows of the Store Romanova did he slow, cough once or twice into his handkerchief, and verify with a sidelong glance that the paper clenched in his left hand was a copy of *The Clarion*.

Queen's Counselor Denies Everything, Threatens Libel Suit! screamed the headline. 'Rudolf' smiled to himself. *And so he should,* he thought, *and so he should*. If *Farnsworth* said there was no sub-stance to the rumors then he was almost certainly telling the truth – not that his loyalty was above and beyond question, for nobody was beyond question, but his dislike for her majesty was such that if there had been any substance to the rumors, the dispatches he sent via Jack would almost certainly have confirmed them. 'Rudolf' took a deep, slow, breath, trying not to irritate his chest, and forced himself to relax, slowing to an old man's ambling pace. Every second that passed now meant that the incriminating letter was that much fur-ther from its origin and that much closer to the intelligence cell that would analyze it before making their conclusions known to the Continental Congress.

At the corner with Bread Street, 'Rudolf' paused beside the tram stop for a minute, then waved down a cab. 'Hogarth Villas,' he said tersely. 'On Stepford High Street.'

'Sure, and it's a fine night fir it, sor.' The cabbie grinned knowingly in his mirror as he bled steam into the cylinder and accelerated away from the roadside. His passenger nodded, thoughtfully, but made no attempt to reply.

Hogarth Villas was a broad-fronted stretch of town houses, fronted with iron rails and a gaudy display of lanterns. It stretched for half a block along the high street, between shuttered shop fronts that slept while the villas' residents worked (and vice versa). One of the larger and better-known licensed brothels at the south end of Man-hattan island, it was anything but quiet at this time of night. 'Rudolf' paid off the cabbie with a generous tip, then approached the open vestibule and the two sturdy gentlemen who stood to either side of the glass inner door. 'Name's Rudolf,' he said quietly. 'Ma'am Bishop is expecting me.'

'Aye, sir, if you'd just step this way, please.' The shorter of the two, built like a battleship and with a face bearing the unmistakable spoor of smallpox, opened the door for him and stepped inside. The carpet was red, the lights electric-bright, shining from the gilt-framed mirrors. In the next room, someone was playing a saucy nautical air on the piano; girlish voices chattered and laughed with the gruff undertone of the clientele. This was by no means a lower-class dive.

The doorman led 'Rudolf' along the hallway then through a side door into understairs quarters, where the carpet was replaced by bare teak floorboards and the expensive silk wallpaper by simple sky-blue paint. The building creaked and chattered around them, sounds of partying and other sport carrying through the lath and plaster. They climbed a narrow spiral staircase before arriving on a landing fronted by three doors. The bouncer rapped on one of them. 'Here's where I leave you,' he said, as it began to swing open, and he headed back toward the front of the building.

'Come in, Erasmus.'

Erasmus – Rudolf no more – set his shoulders determinedly and stepped forward. *No avoiding it now*, he told himself, feeling a curious sinking feeling as he met the opening door and the presence behind it.

'Ma'am.' Most of the girls downstairs bared their shoulders and wore their fishtail skirts slit in front to reveal their knees, in an exaggerated burlesque of the latest mode from Nouveau Paris. The woman in the doorway was no girl, and she wore a black crêpe mourning dress. After all, she *was* in mourning. With black hair turning to steel gray at the temples, blue eyes and a face lined with worries, she might have been a well-preserved sixty or a hard-done-by thirty. The truth, like much else about her, lay in between.

'Come in. Sit down. Would you care for a sip of brandy?'

'Don't mind if I do.' The room was furnished with a couple of overstuffed and slightly threadbare chairs, surplus to requirements downstairs: a bed in the corner (too narrow by far to suit the purposes of the house) and a writing desk completed the room. The window opened onto a tiny enclosed square, barely six feet from the side of the next building.

Erasmus waited while his hostess carefully filled two glasses from a brandy decanter sitting atop the bureau, next to a conveniently burning candle – the better to dispose of the desk's contents, should they be interrupted – and handed one to him. Then she sat down. 'How did it go?' she asked tensely.

He took a cautious sip from his glass. 'I made the delivery. And the pickup. I have no reason to believe I was under surveillance and every reason not to.'

'Not that, silly.' She was fairly humming with impatience. 'What word from the palace?'

'Ah.' He smiled. 'They seem to be most obsessed with matters of diplomatic significance.' His smile slipped. 'Like the way the French have pulled the wool over their eyes lately. There's a witch hunt brewing in the Foreign Service, and an arms race in the Ministry of War. The grand strategy of encirclement has not only crumbled, it appears to have backfired. The situation does not sound good, Margaret.'

'A war would suit their purposes.' She nodded to herself, her gaze unfocused. 'A distraction always serves the rascals in charge.' She glanced at the side door to the room. 'And the . . . device? Did you give it to our source?'

'I gave it to him and showed him how to use it. All he knows is that it is a very small camera. And he needs to return it to us to have the, ah, film developed. Or downloaded, as Miss Beckstein's representative calls it.'

Margaret, Lady Bishop, frowned. 'I wish I trusted these alien allies of yours, Erasmus. I wish I understood their motives.'

'What's to understand?' Erasmus shrugged. 'Listen, I'd be dead if not for them and the alibi they supplied. Their gold is pure and their words –' It was his turn to frown. 'I don't know about the aliens, but I trust *Miriam*. Miss Beckstein is a bit like you, milady. There's a sincerity to her that I find more than a little refreshing, although she can be alarmingly open at times. There are strange knots in her thinking – she looks at everything a little oddly. Still, if she doesn't trust her companions, the manner of her mistrust tells me a lot. They're in it for money, pure and simple, Margaret. There's no motive purer than the pig in search of the truffle, is there? And these pigs are very canny indeed, hence the bounteous treasury they've opened to us. They're *our* pigs, at least until it comes time to pay the butcher's bill. As Miss Beckstein says, money talks – bullshit walks.'

She nodded. 'The mint, the national debt, and the ability to debase the currency, has always been the criminal-in-chief's best weapon, Erasmus. He could buy out the bourgeoisie from under our banner in a split second, did he but recognize their importance. It's time *we* recognized that, and acted accordingly.'

'Well.' Erasmus took a sip of brandy. It was fine stuff, liquid fire that warmed his old bag of bones from the inside out. 'Judging from what your "intimate source" told me, even if he recognized its importance he probably wouldn't act on it until it was too late. Indecisive doesn't begin to describe this one, milady. Stranded in a well-stocked kitchen John Frederick could starve himself to death between two cookbooks. He looks solid with the machinery of state behind him, but if he's forced to make tough choices he'll dither and haver until he's half past hanging.'

'Well, that's his look out,' she said tartly. 'Was there anything we can *use*?'

'Yes. If you don't mind risking the source – at least, this week. It's so big that it will leak sooner rather than later; the French have exploded a corpuscular petard. Caught the navy napping, too; they weren't supposed to have that high a command of the new physics. The flash was visible from Blackpool, apparently, and the toadstool cloud from Lancaster.'

'Oh.' Her eyes widened. 'And with wars, and rumors of wars – '

'Yes, milady. I think something is going to have to happen, sooner or later. The situation in Persia if nothing else is a source of friction, and the temptation to *send a message* to the court of the Sun King – I wouldn't place money on it starting this year, but I can't see him lasting out the decade without strife. John Frederick wants to leave his mark on the history books, lest his son is followed rapidly by a nephew or cousin in the line of succession.'

'Then let's start making plans, shall we?' She smiled. It was not a pleasant expression. 'If the leviathan is determined to drink the blood of the people, there's going to be plenty to spare for the ticks.'

Erasmus shivered. 'Indeed, milady.'

'Well then.' She put her glass down. 'Which brings me to another matter I have in mind. I think it's past time you arranged for me to meet this Miss Beckstein, who you say is so like me. I have many questions for her; I'm sure we can trade more than toys once we understand each other better.'

SPOOK SUMMIT

Twelve weeks earlier:

Mike Fleming was on his way home from his office at the DEA, completely exhausted.

Sometimes, when he was extremely tired, he'd lose his sense of smell. It was as if the part of his brain that dealt with scents and stinks and stuff gave up trying to make sense of the world and went to sleep without him. At other times it would come back extra strong, and any passing scent might dredge up a slew of distracting memories. It was a weird kind of borderline synesthesia, and it reminded him uncomfortably of a time a couple of years ago when he'd been on assignment in some scummy mosquito-ridden swamp down in Florida. The hippie asshole he was staking out had made the tail, and instead of doing the usual number with a MAC-10 or running, had spiked his drink with acid. He'd spent a quarter of an hour in the bathroom of his hotel room staring at the amazing colors in the handle of his toothbrush, marveling at the texture of his spearmint dental gel, until he'd thrown up. And now he was so tired it was all coming back to him in unwelcome hallucinatory detail.

Mike worked in Cambridge, but he lived out in the sticks. The T only took him part of the way, and as he stumbled onto the platform he realized fuzzily that he was far too tired to drive. *Did I really just pull a fifty-hour shift in the office?* he wondered. *Or am I imagining an extra day?* Whatever the facts, he was beyond tired. He was at the point where his eyelids were closing on him, randomly trying to fool him into falling asleep on his feet. So he phoned for a cab, nearly zoning out against a concrete pillar just inside the station lobby while he waited. The cab was stuffy and hot and smelled of anonymous cheap sex and furtive medicinal transactions. It was probably his imagination, but he could almost feel the driver watching him in the mirror, the itchy, prickly touch of the guy's eyeballs on his face. It was a relief to get out and slowly climb the steps to his apartment. 'Hello, strange place,' he muttered to himself as he unlocked the door. 'When was I last here?'

Mike knew he was tired, but it was only when he misentered the code to switch off his intruder alarm twice in a row that he got a visceral sense of how totally out of it he was. *Whoa, hold on!* He leaned against the wall and yawned, forced himself to focus, and deliberately held off from fumbling at the manically bleeping control panel until he'd blinked back the fuzz enough to see the numbers. *Two days?* he wondered vaguely as he slouched upstairs, the door banging shut behind him. *Yeah, two days.* A night and most of a day with the SOC team picking over the bones of the buried fortress, then a night and most of the next morning debriefing the paranoid defector in a safe house. Then more meetings all afternoon, trying to get it through Tony Vecchio's head that yes, the source was crazy – in fact, the source was bug-fuck crazy with brass knobs on – but he was an *interesting* crazy, whose every lead had turned over a stone with something nasty scuttling for cover from underneath it, and even the crazy bits were internally consistent.

Mike stumbled past the coat rail and shed his jacket and tie, then fumbled with his shoelaces for a minute. While he was busy unraveling the sacred mysteries of knot theory, Oscar slid out of the living room door, stretched stiffly and cast him a where-have-you-been glare. 'I'll get to you in a minute,' Mike mumbled. He was used to working irregular hours; Helen the cleaner had instructions to keep the cat fed and watered when he wasn't about, though she drew the line at the litter tray. It turned out that unlacing the shoes took the last of his energy. He meant to check Oscar's food and water, but instead he staggered into the bedroom and collapsed on the unmade bed. Sleep came slamming down like a guillotine blade.

A couple of hours later, Oscar dragged Mike back to semiwakefulness. 'Aagh.' Mike opened his eyes. 'Damn. What time is it?' The elderly tom lowered his head and butted his shoulder for attention, purring quietly. *I was dreaming, wasn't I?* Mike remembered. *Something about being in a fancy restaurant with – her.* That ex-girlfriend, the journalist. Miriam. She'd dumped him when he'd explained about The Job. It'd been back during one of his self-hating patches, otherwise he probably wouldn't have been that brutal with the truth, but experience had taught him – 'Damn.' Oscar purred louder and leaned against his stomach. *Why was I naked from the waist down? What the hell is my subconscious trying to tell me?*

It was only about six o'clock in the evening, far too early to turn over and go back to sleep if he wanted to be ready for the office tomorrow. Mike shook his head, trying to dislodge the cobwebs. Then he sat up, gently pushed Oscar out of the way, and began to undress. After ten minutes in the shower with the heat turned right up he felt almost human, although the taste in his mouth and the stubble itching on his jaw felt like curious reminders of a forgotten binge. *Virtual bar-hopping, all the after-effects with none of the fun.* He shook his head disgustedly, toweled himself dry, dragged on sweat pants and tee, then took stock.

The flat was remarkably tidy, considering how little time he'd had to spend on chores in the past week – thank Helen for that. She'd left him a note on the kitchen table, scribbled in her big, childish handwriting: MILK STAIL, BOUT MORE. He smiled at that. Oscar's bowls were half-full, so he ignored the cat's special pleading and went through into what had been a cramped storeroom when he moved in. Now it was an even more cramped gym, or as much of one as there was space for in the bachelor apartment. He flipped the radio on as he climbed wearily onto the exercise bike: *Maybe I should have held the shower?* he wondered as he turned the friction up a notch and began pedaling.

Fifteen minutes on the bike then a round of push-ups and he began to feel a bit looser. It was almost time to start on the punch bag, but as he came up on fifty sit-ups the phone in the living room rang. Swearing, he abandoned the exercise and made a dash for the handset before the answering machine could cut in. 'Yes?' he demanded.

'Mike Fleming? Can you quote your badge number?'

'I – who *is* this?' he demanded, shivering slightly as the sweat began to evaporate.

'Mike Fleming. Badge number. This is an unsecured line.' The man at the other end of the phone sounded impatient.

'Okay.' *More fallout from work. Head office, maybe?* Mike paused for a moment, then recited his number. 'Now, what's this about?'

'Can you confirm that you were in a meeting with Tony Vecchio and Pete Garfinkle this afternoon?'

'I –' Mike's head spun. 'Look, I'm not supposed to discuss this on an open line. If you want to talk about it at the office then you need to schedule an appointment – '

'Listen, Fleming. I'm not cleared for the content of the meeting. Question is, were you in it? Think before you answer, because if you answer wrong you're in deep shit.'

'I – yes.' Mike found himself staring at the wall opposite. 'Now. Who exactly am I talking to?' The CLID display on his phone just said NUMBER WITHHELD. Which was pretty remarkable, on the face of it, because this wasn't an ordinary caller-ID box. And this wasn't an ordinary caller: his line was ex-directory, for starters.

'A minibus will pick you up in fifteen minutes, Fleming. Pack for overnight.' The line went dead, leaving him staring at the phone as if it had just grown fangs.

'What the hell?' Oscar walked past his ankle, leaning heavily. 'Shit.' He tapped the hook then dialed the office. 'Tony Vecchio's line, please, it's Mike Fleming. Oh – okay. He's in a meeting? Can you – yeah, is Pete Garfinkle in? What, he's in a meeting too? Okay, I'll try later. No, no message.' He put the phone down and frowned. 'Fifteen minutes?'

*

Once upon a time, when he was younger, Mike had believed all the myths.

He'd believed that one syringe full of heroin was enough to turn a fine, upstanding family man into a slavering junkie. He'd believed that marijuana caused lung cancer, dementia, and short-term memory loss, that freebase cocaine – crack – could trigger fits of unpredictable rage, and that the gangs of organized criminals who had a lock on the distribution and sale of illegal narcotics in the

United States were about the greatest internal threat that the country faced.

Also, when he was even younger, he'd believed in Santa Claus and the tooth fairy.

Now . . . he still believed in the gangs. Ten years of stalking grade-A scumbags and seeing just what they did to the people around them left precious little room for illusions about his fellow humanity. Some dealers were just ethically impaired entrepreneurs working in a shady, high-risk field, attracted by the potential for high profits. But you had to have a ruthless streak to take that level of risk, or be oblivious to the suffering around you, and the dangers of the field seemed to repel sane people after a while. The whole business of illegal drugs was a magnet for seekers of the only *real* drug, the one that was addictive at first exposure, the one that drove people mad and kept them coming back for more until it killed them: easy money. The promise of quick cash money drew scumbags like flies to a fresh dog turd. Anyone who was in the area inevitably started to smell of shit sooner or later, even if they'd started out clean. Even the cops, and they were supposed to be the good guys.

Ten years ago when he was a fresh-faced graduate with a degree in police science – and still believed in the tooth fairy, so to speak – he'd have arrested his own parents without a second thought if he'd seen them smoking a joint, because it was the right thing to do. But these days, Mike had learned that sometimes it made sense to turn a blind eye to human failings. About six years in, he'd gone through the not-unusual burnout period that afflicted most officers, sooner or later, if they had any imagination or empathy for their fellow citizens. Afterward, he'd clawed his way back to a precarious moral sense, an idea of what was wrong with the world that gave him something to work toward. And now there was only one type of drug addict that he could get worked up over – the kind of enemy that he wanted to lay his hands on so bad he could taste it. He wanted the money addicts; the ones who needed it so bad they'd kill, maim, and wreck numberless other lives to get their fix.

Which was why, a decade after joining up, he was still a dedicated DEA Special Agent – rather than a burned-out GS-12 desk jockey with his third nervous breakdown and his second divorce ahead of him, freewheeling past road marks on the long run down to retirement and the end of days.

When the doorbell chimed exactly twenty-two minutes after the phone rang, the Mike who answered it was dressed again and had even managed to put a comb through his lank blond hair and run an electric razor over his chin. The effect was patchy, and he still felt in need of a good night's sleep. He glanced at the entry phone, then relaxed. It was Pete, his partner on the current case, looking tired but not much worse for wear. Mike picked up his briefcase and opened the door. 'What's the story?'

'C'mon. You think they've bothered to tell me anything?' Mike revised his opinion. Pete didn't simply look tired and overworked, he looked apprehensive. Which was kind of worrying, in view of Pete's usual supreme self-confidence.

'Okay.' Mike armed the burglar alarm and locked his front door. Then he followed Pete toward a big Dodge minivan, waiting at the curb with its engine idling. A woman and two guys were waiting in it, beside the driver, who made a big deal of checking his agency ID. He didn't know any of them except one of the men, who vaguely rang a bell. *FBI office*, Mike realized as he climbed in and sat down next to Pete. 'Where are we going?' he asked as the door closed.

'Questions later,' said the woman sitting next to the driver. She was a no-nonsense type in a gray suit, the kind Mike associated with internal audits and inter-agency joint committees. Mike was about to ask again, when he noticed Pete shake his head very slightly. *Oh*, he thought, and shut up as the van headed for the freeway. *I can take a hint.*

When he realized they were heading for the airport after about twenty minutes, Mike sat up and began to take notice. And when they pulled out of the main traffic stream into the public terminals at Logan and headed toward a gate with a checkpoint and barrier, the sleep seemed to fall away. 'What *is* this?' he hissed at Pete.

The van barely stopped moving as whatever magic charm the driver had got him waved straight through a series of checkpoints and onto the air side of the terminal. 'Look, I don't know either,' Pete whispered. 'Tony said to go with these guys.' He sounded worried.

'Not long now,' the woman in the front passenger seat said apologetically.

They drove past a row of parked executive jets, then pulled in next to a big Gulfstream, painted Air Force gray. 'Okay, change of transport,' called their shepherd. 'Everybody out!'

'Wow.' Mike looked up at the jet. 'They're serious.'

'Whoever they are,' Pete said apprehensively. 'Somehow I don't think we're in Kansas any more, Toto.'

A blue-suiter checked their ID cards again at the foot of the stairs and double-checked them using a sheet of photos. Mike climbed aboard warily. The government executive jet wasn't anything like as luxuriously fitted as the ones you saw in the movies, but that was hardly a surprise – it was a working plane, used for shifting small teams about. Mike strapped himself into a window seat and leaned back as the attendant closed the door, checked to see that everyone was strapped in, and ducked inside the cockpit for a quiet conference. The plane began to taxi, louder than any airliner he'd been on in years. Minutes later they were airborne, climbing steeply into the evening sky. In all, just over an hour had elapsed since he answered the phone.

The seat belt lights barely had time to blink out before the woman was on her feet, her back to the cockpit door, facing Mike and Pete. (A couple of the other guys had to crane their heads round to see her.) 'Okay, you're wondering where you're going and why,' she said matter-of-factly. 'We're going to a small field in Maryland. From there you're going by bus to a secure office in Fort Meade where we wait for another planeload of agents to converge from the west coast. Refreshments *will* be served,' she added dryly, 'although I can't tell you just why you're needed at this meeting because our hosts haven't told me.'

One of the other passengers, a black man with the build of a middleweight boxer, frowned. 'Can you tell us who you are?' he asked in a deep voice. 'Or is that secret, too?'

'Sure. I'm Judith Herz. Boston headquarters staff, FBI, agent responsible for ANSIR coordination. If you guys want to identify yourselves, be my guest.'

44

'I'm Bob Patterson,' said the black man, after a momentary pause. 'I work for DOE,' he added, in tones that said *and I can't tell you any more than that.*

'Rich Wall, FBI.' The thin guy with curly brown hair and a neat goatee flashed a brief grin at Herz. *Undercover?* Mike wondered. *Or specialist?* He didn't look like a special agent, that was for sure, not wearing combat pants and a nose stud.

'Mike Fleming and Pete Garfinkle, Drug Enforcement Agency, Boston SpecOps division,' Mike volunteered.

They all turned to face the last passenger, a portly middle-aged guy with a bushy beard and a florid complexion who wore a pin-striped suit. 'Hey, don't all look at me!' he protested. 'Name's Frank Milford, County Surveyor's Office.' A worried frown crossed his face. 'Just what *is* this, anyway? There's got to be some mistake, here. I don't belong – '

'Yes you do,' said Herz. Mike looked at her. *Five assorted cops and spooks, and a guy from the* County Surveyor's Office? *What in hell's name is going on here?* 'I'm sure all will be revealed when we arrive.'

A minivan with a close-lipped driver met them at the airport. At first it had looked as if he was heading for Baltimore, but then they turned off the parkway, taking an unmarked feeder road that twisted behind a wooded berm and around a slalom course of huge stone blocks, razor-wire fences, and a gauntlet of surveillance cameras on masts. They came to a halt in front of a gatehouse set in a high fence surrounding a complex so vast that Mike couldn't take it in. Members of a municipal police force he'd never heard of carefully checked everyone's ID against a prepared list, then issued red-bordered ID badges with the letters *PV* emblazoned on them. Then the van drove on. The compound was so big there were road signs inside it – and three more checkpoints to stop and present ID at before they finally drew up outside an enormous black-glass tower block. 'Follow me, and do exactly as I say,' their driver told them. The entrance was a separate building, with secured turnstiles and guards who watched inscrutably as Mike followed his temporary companions along a passageway and then out into a huge atrium, dominated by a black marble slab bearing a coat of arms in a golden triangle.

'I've read about this place,' Pete muttered in a slightly overawed tone.

'So when do you think they bring out the dancing girls?' Mike replied.

'When –' Lift doors opened and closed. Pete caught Herz watching him and clammed up.

'Rule one: no questions,' Herz told him, when she was sure she'd got his attention. She glanced at Mike as well. 'Yes?'

'Rule two: no turf wars.' Mike crossed his arms, trying to look self-confident. You worked for the DOJ for years, mucking out the public stables, then suddenly someone sent a car for you and drove you round to the grand palace entrance . . .

'No turf wars.' Herz nodded at him with weary irony. Suddenly he got the picture.

'Whose rules are we playing by?' he asked.

'Probably these guys, NSA. At least for now.' Her eyes flickered at one corner of the ceiling as the elevator came to a halt on the eighth floor. 'I assure you, this is as new to me as it is to you.'

Their escort led them along a carpeted, sound-deadening corridor, through fire doors and then into a reception room. 'Wait here,' he said, and left them under the gaze of a secretary and a security guard. Mike blinked at the huge framed photographs on the walls. *What are they doing, trying to grow the world's biggest puffball mushroom?* All the buildings seemed to have razor-wire fences around them and gigantic white domes sprouting from their roofs.

A head popped out from around a corner. 'This way, please.' Herz led the group as they filed through the door, informatively labeled ROOM 2B8020. Behind the door, Mike blinked with a moment of déjà vu, a flashback to the movie *Dr. Strangelove*. A doughnut-shaped conference table surrounded by rose-colored chairs filled the floor at the near end of the room, but at the other end a series of raised platforms supported a small lecture theater of seats for an audience. Large multimedia screens filled the wall opposite. 'If you'd all take seats in the auditorium, please?' called their guide.

'The film you're about to see is classified. You're not to make notes, or talk about it outside your group. After it's been screened, an officer will brief you in person then take you through a team setup exercise so that you know why you're all here and what's expected of you.'

Pete stuck his hand in the air.

'Yes?' asked the staffer.

'Should I understand that I'm being seconded to some kind of joint operation?' Pete asked quietly. 'Because if so, this is one hell of an odd way to go about it. My superior officer either didn't know or didn't tell. What's going on?'

'He wasn't cleared,' said the staffer – and without saying anything else, he left the room.

'What *is* this?' Frank demanded, looking upset. 'I mean, what is this place?'

The lights dimmed. 'Your attention, please.' The voice came from speakers around the room, slightly breathy as its owner leaned too close to the microphone. 'The following videotape was shot by a closed-circuit surveillance camera yesterday, at a jail in upstate New York.'

Grainy gray-on-white video footage filled the front wall of the theater. It was shot from a camera concealed high up in one corner of the ceiling, with a fish-eye lens staring down at a cell maybe six feet by ten in size.

Mike leaned forward. He could almost smell the disinfectant and sour sweat. This wasn't your ordinary drunk tank. It was a separate cell, with whitewashed cinderblock walls and no window – furnished with a bunk bolted to the floor, a metal toilet and sink bolted to the wall, and not a lot else. Single occupant, high security. *This is important enough to drag me out of bed and fly me six hundred miles?* he wondered.

There was a man in the cell. He was wearing dark pin-striped trousers and a dress shirt, no tie or jacket: he looked like a stockbroker or Wall Street lawyer who'd been picked up for brawling, hair mussed, expression wild. He kept looking at the door.

'This man was arrested yesterday at two-fifteen, stepping off the Acela from Boston with a suitcase that contained some rather interesting items. Agents Fleming and Garfinkle will be pleased to know

47

that information they passed on from the preliminary debriefing of source Greensleeves directly contributed to the bust. Mr. Morgan here was charged with possession of five kilograms of better than ninety-five percent pure cocaine hydrochloride, which goes some way to explain his agitation. There were, ah, other items in the suitcase. I'll get to them later. For now, let's just say that while none of them were contraband they are, if anything, much more worrying than the cocaine.'

Mike focused on the screen. The guy in the cell was clearly uneasy about something – but what? *In solitary.* Knowing he was under surveillance. After a while he stood up and paced back and forth, from the door to the far end of the cell. Occasionally he'd pause halfway, as if trying to remember something.

'Our target here has no previous police record, no convictions, no fingerprints, nothing to draw him to our attention. He hasn't registered to vote. He has a driving license and credit cards but, and here's the interesting bit, some careful digging shows that the name belongs to a child who died thirty-one years ago, aged eleven months. He appears to be the product of a very successful identity theft that established him with a record going back at least a decade. This James Morgan, as opposed to the one who's buried in a family plot near Buffalo, went to college in Minnesota and obtained average grades, majoring in business studies and economics before moving to New York, where he acquired a job with a small import–export company, Livingston and Marks, for whom he has worked for nine years and six months. According to our friends at the IRS, his entry-level salary was $39,605 a year, he takes exactly three days of sick leave every twelve months, and he hasn't had a pay raise, a vacation, or a sabbatical since joining the firm.'

The man on the screen seemed to make up his mind about something. He ceased pacing and, rolling up his sleeve, thrust his left wrist under the hot water faucet on the sink. He seemed to be scrubbing at something – a patch or plaster, perhaps.

'James Morgan lives in an apartment that appears to be owned by a letting agency wholly owned by a subsidiary of Livingston and Marks,' the unseen commentator recited dryly, as if reading from a dossier. 'He pays rent of $630 a month – and you guessed it, he hasn't had a rent rise in nine years. And that's not the only thing that's missing. He isn't a member of a gym or health club or a dating agency or a church or an HMO. He doesn't own an automobile or a pet dog or a television, or subscribe to any newspapers or magazines. He uses his credit card to shop for groceries at the local Safeway twice a week, and here he screwed up – he has a loyalty card for the discounts. It turns out that he never buys toilet paper or light bulbs. However he *does* buy new movie releases on DVD, which is kind of odd for someone who doesn't own a DVD player or a TV or a computer. Once a month, every month, as regular as clockwork, he makes an overnight out of state trip, flying Delta to Dallas–Fort Worth, and while he's away he stays in the Hilton and makes a side trip to buy a Glock 20C, four spare magazines, and four two-hundred-round boxes of ammunition – although he never brings them home. Luckily for him, because he doesn't have a firearms license valid for New York State.'

On the screen, something peeled off Morgan's wrist. He rubbed it some more, then turned the faucet off, raised his arm, and peered at whatever the plaster was concealing.

'Checking our records, it appears that Mr. Morgan has purchased over sixty handguns this way, spending rather more on them than he pays in rent. That's in addition to his other duties, which appear to include smuggling industrial quantities of pharmaceutical-grade narcotics. Now, this is where it gets interesting. Watch the screen.'

Mike blinked. One moment Morgan was standing in front of the washbasin, peering at the inside of his wrist. The next moment, he was nowhere to be seen. The cell was empty.

Off to one side, Frank from the Surveyor's Office started to complain. 'What *is* this? I don't see what this has got to do with me. So you've got a guard taking kickbacks to fool with the videotape in the county jail – '

The lights came up and the door opened. 'Nope.' The man standing in the doorway was slightly built, in his early forties, with receding brown hair cropped short. He smiled easily as he stepped into the room and stood in front of the screen. *It's him*, Mike realized with interest. The commentator with the dry sense of humor. 'That wasn't something we pulled off a tape, that was a live feed. And I assure you, once those data packets arrived here *nobody* tampered with them.'

Mike licked his lips. 'This links in with what Greensleeves was saying, doesn't it?' he asked.

'It does indeed.' The man at the front of the auditorium looked pleased. 'And that's why you're here. All of you, you've been exposed in some way to this business.' He nodded at Mike. 'Some of you more than others – if it wasn't for your quick thinking and the way you escalated it via Boston Special Operations, it might have been another couple of days before we realized what kind of intelligence asset you were sitting on.'

'Greensleeves?' Pete asked, raising a skeptical eyebrow. 'You mean the kook?'

Mike shook his head. *Source Greensleeves*, who called himself Matthias, and who kept yammering on about hidden conspiracies and other worlds in between blowing wholesale rings like they were street-corner crack houses –

'Yes, and I'm afraid he isn't a kook. Let me introduce myself. I'm Lieutenant Colonel Eric Smith, Air Force, on secondment to NSA/CSS, Office of Unconventional Programs. I work for the deputy director of technology. As of an hour ago, you guys are all on secondment from your usual assignments to a shiny new committee that doesn't have a name yet, but that reports to the director of the National Security Council directly, via whoever he puts on top of me – hence all the melted stovepipes and joint action stuff. We've got to break across the usual departmental boundaries if we're going to make this work. One reason you're here is that you've all been vetted and had the security background checks in the course of your ordinary work. In fact, all but one of you are already federal employees working in the national security or crime prevention sectors. The letters have gone out to your managers and you should get independent confirmation when you get back home to Massachusetts and New York after this briefing round and tomorrow's meetings and orientation lectures.' Smith leaned against the wall at the front of the room. 'Any questions?'

The guy from the DOE, Bob, looked up. 'What am *I* doing here?' he rumbled. 'Is the NIRT a stakeholder?'

Smith looked straight at him. 'Yes,' he said softly. 'The Nuclear Incident Response Teams are stakeholders.'

There was a hissing intake of breath: Mike glanced round in time to see Judith Herz look shocked.

'We have reason to believe that theft of fissionable material is involved.'

FERTILE DISCUSSIONS

The Countess Helge and her attendants traveled in convoy with other residents of Thorold Palace that evening, to the Östhalle at the east end of the royal run that formed the artery linking the great houses at the center of Niejwein. Niejwein was the royal capital of the kingdom of Gruinmarkt, which occupied most of the territory of Massachusetts and chunks of New Jersey and New York, over here. As near as Miriam had been able to work out, the first Norse settlements on the eastern seaboard had died out in the eleventh or twelfth centuries, but their replacements – painstakingly carved out by the landless sons of the northern European nobility around the start of the sixteenth century – had flourished, albeit far less so than in her own world. They had no skyscrapers, spacecraft, or steam engines; no United States of America, no Declaration of Independence, no church or Reformation. Rome had fallen on schedule but the dark ages had been darker than in her world. With no Christianity, no Judaism, no Islam, and with no centers of scholarship to preserve the Greek and Roman classics, the climb back up had been correspondingly more painful and protracted.

This was the world the Clan came from, descended from an itinerant tinker who had by accident discovered the ability to walk between worlds – to her own New England, land of dour puritan settlers, to the north of the iron triangle of the sugar and slave trade. *He was lucky not to be hanged as a witch*, Helge thought morosely as she stared out of her carriage window, shielding her face behind a lacquered fan as the contraption jolted along the cobblestone street. *Or institutionalized, like a Kaspar Hauser*. Strange things happened to disoriented adults who appeared as if out of thin air, speaking no known language, bewildered and lost. It had nearly happened to

Miriam, the first time she accidentally world-walked. *But at least now I understand what I'm doing,* she thought.

World-walking appeared to be a recessive-gene-linked trait, one whose carriers far outnumbered those who had the ability. To have the ability in full both parents must at least be carriers: the three-generation-long braids knotted the Clan's six inner families together, keeping the bloodlines strong, while the outer families occasionally threw up a cluster of world-walking siblings. In the past hundred and fifty years – since the world Helge had grown up in as Miriam had industrialized – the Clan had used their ability to claw their way up from poor merchants to the second seat of power in the kingdom. The ability to send messages from one side of the continent to another within a day gave their traders a decisive edge, as did the weapons and luxury goods they were able to import from America.

The maids squeezed into the bench seat opposite Helge giggled as one wheel clattered off a pothole. She glanced at them irritably from behind her fan, unsure what the joke was, her Hochsprache inadequate to follow the conversation. The carriage stank of leather and a faint aroma of stale sweat beneath the cloying toilet waters of the ladies. Helge used no such scents (it was Miriam's habit to bathe daily and wear as little makeup as possible), but Kara was sometimes overenthusiastic, the young Lady Souterne who traveled with them this evening seemed to think that smelling like a brothel would guarantee her a supply of suitors, and as for the last Clan notables to borrow this coach from the livery stable attached to the palace . . .

The four horses harnessed to the coach – not to mention the outriders and the carriages in front – kicked up a fine brown dust, dried out by the hot summer afternoon. It billowed so high that the occupants were forced to keep the windows of the carriage closed. They were thick slabs of rippled green glass, expensive as silver salvers but useful only insofar as they let beams of dusty evening sunlight into the oppressively hot interior. Helge could barely make out the buildings opposite behind their high stone walls, the shacks and lean-tos of the porters and costermongers and pamphleteers thronging the boulevard in front of them.

With a shout from the coachmen up top, the carriage turned off the boulevard and entered the drive up to the front of the Östhalle, passing cottages occupied by royal pensioners, galleries and temporary marquees for holding exhibitions of paintings and tapestries, the wooden fence of a bear pit, and the stone-built walls around the barracks of the Royal Life Guards. People thronged all around, the servants and soldiers and guards and bondslaves of the noble visitors mingling with the royal household in residence and with hawkers and beggars and dipsters and chancers of every kind. A royal party could not transpire without a penumbra of leaky festivities trickling down to the grounds outside.

The carriage stopped. A clatter of steps and the door opened: four brass horns cut through the racket. 'Milady?' Kara asked. Helge rose first and clambered out onto the top step, blinking at the slanting orange sunlight coming over the trees. For a moment she was sure she'd caught her dress on something – a hinge, a protruding nail – and that presently it would tear; then she worried that a gust of wind would render her ridiculous on this exposed platform, until finally she recognized one of the faces looking up at her from below: 'Sieur Huw?' she asked hopefully.

'Milady? If it would please you to take my hand –' he answered in English, accented but comprehensible.

She made it down the steps without embarrassing herself. 'Sieur Huw, how kind of you.' She managed to smile. Huw was another of those interchangeable youngbloods who infested Clan security, hot-headed adolescent duelists who would have been quite intolerable if Angbard had not possessed the means to tame them. When they grew up sufficiently to stop seeking any excuse for a brawl they could be useful; those who had two brain cells to rub together, doubly so. Huw was one of the latter, but Helge had only met him in passing and barely had his measure. Beanpole thin and tall, with brown hair falling freely below his shoulders and a receding chin to spoil what might otherwise have been rugged good looks, Huw moved with a dangerous economy of motion that suggested to those in his path that they had best find business elsewhere. But he wore neither sword nor gun at his belt today. Bearing arms in the presence of the king was a privilege reserved for the royal household and its guards.

'Where's everything happening?' she asked out of the side of her mouth.

'Around the garden at the back. Most notables have arrived already but you are by no means late. We can go through the north wing, if you want to give the impression you've been here discreetly all along,' he offered.

'I suppose you were looking for me,' she said, half-jokingly.

'As a matter of fact' – his gaze slid across the footmen holding the huge doors open for them – 'I was.' He nodded, a minute gesture toward a bow, as he crossed the threshold, then paused to bow fully before the coat of arms displayed above the floor. Miriam – remembering her manners as Helge – dropped a brief curtsey. *Are we being watched?* she wondered. Then, *Who told Huw to wait for me?* Huw waited for her politely, then offered his arm. She took it, and they walked together into the central hall of the north wing of the Östhalle.

The hall was a hollow cube, the walls supporting a wide staircase that meandered upward past three more floors beneath a ceiling glazed with a duke's fortune in lead crystal. Other rooms barely smaller than aircraft hangars opened off to either side, their windows open to admit the last of the evening sunlight. Discreet servants were already moving around the edges, lighting lamps and chandeliers. Others, bearing platters loaded with finger food, moved among the guests. More youngbloods, looking slightly anxious without their swords. Clusters of women in silks and furs, glittering with jewelry, enthusiastic girls shepherded by cynical matrons, higher orders attended by their ladies-in-waiting. Countess Helge paid barely any attention to her own retinue beyond a quick check that Lady Kara and Lady Souterne and Kara's maid Jenny and Souterne's maid whoever-she-was were following. 'I'm sure there are more interesting people for you to wait upon,' she said quietly, pitching her voice so that only Huw might hear it over the chatter of conversations around them. 'I'm just a boring dried-up old countess with poor manners and a sideline in business journalism.'

'Ha-ha. I don't think so. Your ladyship is modest beyond reproach. Would your ladyship care for an aperitif?' He snapped his fingers at a servant bearing a salver laden with glasses.

'Obviously my company is so boring that it's driving you to drink already,' she said with a smile.

'Milady?' He held a glass out for her.

'Thank you.' Helge accepted the offered glass and sniffed. *Sherry*, or something not unlike it. *A slight undertone of honeysuckle. Would they serve fortified wines here?* 'You were looking for me,' she said, gently steering him back toward the far side of the hall and the garden party beyond. 'Are you going to keep me on tenterhooks, wondering why?'

Huw sniffed, his nostrils flaring. 'I do confess that you would have to ask her grace your mother for an explanation,' he said blandly. 'It was at her urging that I made myself available. I'm sure she has her reasons.' He smiled, trying for urbanity and coming dangerously close to a smirk. 'Perhaps she thought that a, ah, "boring dried-up old countess with poor manners and a sideline in business journalism" might need a young beau on whose arm she might lean, thereby inducing paroxysms of jealousy among the youngsters who feel themselves snubbed, or among those pullets who would imagine her a rival for their roosters?'

He repeated me word-perfect, she thought, so astonished that she forgot herself and half-drained her glass instead of sipping from it. (It was a dry sherry, or something very similar. Too dry for her taste.) *He looks like a chinless wonder with a line of witty patter but he's got a memory like a computer.* She raised one eyebrow at him. 'I'm not in the market,' she said, slowly and clearly.

'I beg your pardon?' He sounded genuinely confused, so that for a moment Helge almost relented. But the setup was too perfect.

'I said, I'm not in the marriage market,' she repeated. 'So I'm no threat to anyone.' With some satisfaction she noticed his cheeks flush. 'Nice wine. Fancy another one?' *If I'm going to be a boring dried-up old countess with poor manners I might as well make the most of it*, she resolved. Otherwise the evening promised to drag.

'I think I will,' he said hesitantly. 'I beg your pardon, I intended no disrespect.'

'None taken.' She finished her glass. *Better drink the next one more slowly.*

'Her grace observed that you were looking for gentles with an interest in the sciences,' Huw commented, half-turning to snag a fresh glass so that she had to strain to hear him. 'Is that so?'

Oh. The penny dropped and Miriam felt like kicking Helge for a moment. Trying to be two people at once was so confusing! 'Maybe,' she said guardedly. 'I'm thinking about trying to get a discussion group going. Just people talking to each other. Why do you ask?'

'I was hoping – well, I'm going stale here. You know about the heightened security state, I believe? I don't know much about your background – I was forced to interrupt my studies and return here.' He grimaced. 'It's summer recess on the other side, so I'm not losing much ground – except access to the labs and to the college facilities – but if it goes on much longer I'm going to have to take a year out. And you're right in one supposition, my father's been pressing me to complete my studies and settle down, take a wife, and accept a postal rank. It's only the generosity of the debating society that's allowed me to keep working on my thesis this far.'

'Uh-huh.' Miriam, wearing the Helge identity like a formal dress, steered her interviewee around a small knot of talkative beaux and through a wide-open doorway, through a state dining room where a table set for fifty waited beneath a chandelier loaded with a hundred candles. 'Well, I don't know that I could say anything on your behalf that would help you – but if it's any consolation, I know the feeling. We're cut off and isolated here. For all that we're a social elite, the intellectual climate isn't the most stimulating. I was hoping to find people who'd be interested in helping organize a series of monthly lectures and weekly study group meetings. What were – are – you studying?'

'I'm midway through a master's in media arts and sciences,' Huw admitted, sounding slightly bashful about it. 'Working on fabrication design templates.'

'Oh.' It sounded deathly boring. Miriam switched off as they threaded their way around a gaggle of female courtiers attending on some great lady. 'What does that involve? What college did you say you were studying at?'

'The MIT Media Lab. We're working on a self-contained tool kit for making modern electronic devices in the field – I say! Are you all right?'

Miriam wordlessly passed him her glass then fumbled with a silk handkerchief for a few seconds. 'I'm okay. I think.' *Apart from the after-effects of wine inhalation.* She dabbed at her sleeve, but the worst seemed to have missed it. 'Tell me more . . .'

'Sure. I'm doing a dissertation project on the fab lab – it's a workbench and tool kit that's designed to do for electronics what a blacksmith's forge or a woodworking shop does for ironmongery or carpentry. You'll be able to make a radio, or an oscilloscope, or a protocol analyzer or computer, all in the field. Initially it'll be able to make all of its own principal modules from readily available components like FPGAs and PCB stock – we're working with the printable circuitry team who're trying to use semiconductor inks in bubble-jet printers to print on paper, for example. I was looking into some design modularity issues – to be blunt, I want to be able to take one home with me. But there's a long way to go – '

By the time they fetched up in the huge marquee at the rear of the palace, two drinks and forty-something invitations later, Miriam was feeling more than a little light-headed. But her imagination was running full tilt; Huw had taken to the idea of monthly seminars like a duck to water and suggested half a dozen names of likely participants along the way, all of them young inner family intellects, frustrated and stifled by the extreme conservativism that infused the Clan's structures. Most of them were actively pursuing higher education in America, but had been blocked off from their studies by the ongoing security alert. Most of them were names she'd never heard of, second sons or third daughters of unexceptional lineage – not the best and the brightest whose dossiers Kara was familiarizing her with. Huw knew them by way of something he called the debating society, which seemed to be a group of old drinking buddies who occasionally clubbed together to sponsor a gifted but impecunious student. It was, Miriam reflected, absolutely typical of the Clan that the sons and daughters with an interest in changing the way their society worked were the ones who were furthest from the levers of power, their education left to the grace and charity of dilettantes.

Most of the introductions were not Clan-related in any way, however. As the evening continued, both her smile and her ability to stay in character as the demure blue-blooded Countess Helge became increasingly strained. Huw had other obligations of a social nature to fulfill and took his leave sooner than she'd have liked, leaving her to face the crowds with only occasional support from Kara. Sieur Hyvert of this and Countess Irina of that bowed and curtseyed respectively and addressed her in Hochsprache (and once, in the case of a rural backwoods laird in Loewsprache, confusing her completely), and as the evening wore on she was gripped with a worrying conviction that she was increasingly being greeted with the kindly condescension due an idiot, a mental defective – by those who were willing to speak to her at all. There were political currents here that she was not competent to navigate unaided. English was not the language of the upper class but the tongue the Clan families used among themselves, and her lack of fluency in Hochsprache marked her out as odd, or stupid, or (worst of all) alien. Some of the older established nobility seemed to take the ascendancy of the Clan families as a personal affront. After one particularly pained introduction, she stifled a wince and turned round to hunt for her lady-in-waiting.

'Kara? Where are –' she began, sticking to Hochsprache, that particular phrase coming more easily than most, when she realized that a knot of courtiers standing nearby was coming her way. They were mostly young, and all male, and their loud chatter and raucous laughter caught Miriam's attention in a way that was at once naggingly familiar and unwelcome. *Shit, Kara, you pick your time to go missing beautifully.* She glanced round, ready to retreat, but there was no easy way out of the path of the gaggle of jocks –

One of whom was speaking to her. 'What?' she said blankly, all vestiges of Hochsprache vanishing from her memory like the morning dew.

He glanced over his shoulder and said something: more laughter, with an unfriendly edge to it. 'You are – wrong, the wrong, place,' he said, staring down his nose at her. 'Go home, grovel, bitch.' Someone behind him said something in Hochsprache.

Miriam glared at him. Rudeness needed no translation. And

backing down wouldn't guarantee safety. Her heart hammering, she fumbled for words: 'What dog, are, belong you, do you belong to? I am offense – '

Almost too late she saw his hand tightening on the hilt of his sword. *A sword?* Surprise almost drowned her fear – swords were forbidden in the royal presence, except by the bodyguard. But this wasn't the king's party. The arrogant young asshole began to turn to one side and she realized hazily that he wasn't about to draw on her – not in public – as she got a glimpse past his shoulder of a bored, half-amused golden-boy profile she'd seen once before, saying something to her assailant. *Oh shit, it's him. Egon.* The crown prince, handsome and perfect in form and a spoiled hothead by upbringing. The bottom threatened to drop out of her world: this perfect jock could actually get away with murder, if he was so inclined.

'He says, you bed him, maybe he not kill you when he king, bitch.' Two other bravos, brilliantly dressed, managed to interpose themselves between the self-appointed translator and his pack leader. 'With the others.'

A black fury threatened to cut off Miriam's vision. 'Tell him to get lost,' she said sharply, in English, dropping all pretense of politeness. *If you surrender they'll own you*, she thought bleakly, forcing her momentarily treacherous knees to hold her upright. *And if you won't surrender they'll try to break you.* 'I'm not his – '

'You are the Countess Helge voh Thorold d'Hjorth?' someone behind her shoulder asked in stilted English. She glanced round, her heart hammering in barely suppressed anger. While the jocks made sport she'd completely missed the other group that appeared to want something of her: two gentlemen with the bearing of bodyguards, shepherding four maids who clustered around a stooped figure, moving with exaggerated caution.

'I –' Trapped between the two factions she summoned up Helge, who racked her brain for the correct form of response. 'I am that one,' she managed, flustered.

'Good. You are –' Then she lost him. The guard spoke too fast for her to track his words, syllables sliding into one another.

She forced a smile, tense and ugly, then stole a glance back over her shoulder, lest one of Egon's thugs was about to stick a knife in her back. But they were talking and joking about something else, their attention no longer focused on her like hunting dogs. 'I beg your pardon. Please to repeat this?'

The guard stepped around her. 'I'll take care of the boys,' he said quietly. Louder: 'This is her royal highness, the Queen Mother. She would have words with you.'

'I, ah –' *hope she's not as rude as her eldest grandson.* Numb with surprise, Helge managed a curtsey. 'Am it pleased by your presence, your royal high! Highness,' she managed before she completely lost her ability to stay in character.

The stooped figure reached out a hand to her. 'Rise.'

Damn, Helge swore to herself. *How much worse can it get? The* one *situation where I need backup – a royal audience – comes up* twice, *and what's Kara doing?* 'Your majesty,' she said, bending to kiss the offered hand.

The Queen Mother resembled Mother Theresa of Calcutta – if the latter had ever sported a huge Louis Quinze hairdo and about a hundred yards of black silk taffeta held together with ruby- and sapphire-encrusted lumps of gold. Her eyes were sunken and watery with rheum, and her face was gaunt, the skin drawn tight over her beak of a nose. She looked to be eighty years old, but having been presented before her son, Miriam reckoned she couldn't be much over sixty. 'Rise, I said,' the Queen Mother croaked in Hochsprache. Then in English: 'You shall call me Angelin. And I shall call you Helge.'

'I –' Miriam blanked for a moment. It was just one shock too many. 'Yes, Angelin.' *You're the king's mother – you can call me anything you like and I'm not going to talk back.* (As Roland had put it, his majesty Alexis Nicholau III of the Kingdom of Gruinmarkt liked to collect jokes about his family – he had two dungeons full of them.) 'What can I – I'm at your service – I mean – '

The Queen Mother's face wrinkled. After a moment Miriam realized she was smiling. *At least she isn't howling, 'Off with her head!'* 'What you're wondering is, why do I speak this language?' Miriam nodded mutely, still numb and shaken by the confrontation with

Egon's bravos. 'It's a long story.' The older woman wheezed. 'Walk with me, please.'

Angelin was stooped, her back so bent that she had to crane her neck back to see the ground ahead of her. And she walked at a painful shuffle. Miriam matched her speed, feeling knuckles like walnuts in an empty leather glove clutch at her arm. *I'm being honored*, she realized. Royalty didn't stoop to using just anyone as a walking frame. After a moment a long-dormant part of her memory kicked into life: *Ankylosing spondylitis?* she wondered. If so, it was a miracle Angelin was out of bed without painkillers and anti-inflammatory drugs.

'I knew your mother when she was a little girl,' said the queen. 'Delightful girl, very strong-willed.' *She said 'I.' That means she's talking personally, doesn't it? Or is it only the reigning monarch who says 'we'? If that applies here?* Miriam puzzled as the queen continued: 'Glad to see they haven't drowned it out of her. Have they?'

That seemed to demand a reply. 'I don't think so, your royal highness.' Shuffle.

'Oh, they'll try,' Angelin added unreassuringly. 'Just like last time.'

Like what? Miriam bit her tongue. Her head was spinning with questions, fear and anger demanding attention, and the small of her back was slippery-cold with sweat. Angelin was steering her toward a side door in the palace, and her ladies-in-waiting and guards were screening her most effectively. If Kara had noticed anything – but Kara wasn't in sight and Miriam didn't dare create a scene by looking for her. 'Is there anything I can do for you?' Miriam asked, desperately looking for a tactful formula, something to help her steer the conversation toward waters she was competent to navigate.

'Perhaps.' The door opened before them as if by magic, to reveal a small vestibule. Four more guards waited on either side of a thronelike chair. A padded stool sat before it. 'Please be seated in our presence.' Two of the guards stepped forward to cradle the old queen's shoulders, while a third positioned the stool beneath her. 'Take the chair; I cannot use it.'

Definitely some kind of autoimmune – Miriam forced herself to stop thinking. She sat down carefully, grateful for the support.

'Leave us.' Angelin's gimlet stare sent all but two of the guards packing. The last two stood in front of the door, their faces turned to the woodwork but their hands on the hilts of their swords. The Queen Mother looked back at Miriam. 'It is seven years since Eloise died,' said Angelin. 'And Alexis is not inclined to remarry. He's got his heir, and for all his faults, lack of devotion to his wife's memory is not one of them.'

'Ah.' Miriam realized her fingers were digging into her knees, and she forced herself to let go.

'You can relax. This is not a job interview; nobody is going to offer you the throne,' Angelin added, so abruptly that Miriam almost choked.

'But I didn't want – ' She brought herself up fast. 'I'm sorry. You, uh, speak English very well. The vernacular – '

'I grew up over there,' said Angelin, then was silent for almost a minute.

She grew up *there*? The statement was wholly outrageous, even though the individual words made sense.

Eventually, Angelin began to speak again. 'The six families have aspired to become seven for almost a century now. I was only eighteen, you know. Back in 1942. Last time the council tried to capture the throne. They didn't want me siding with my braid lineage, so they had me brought up in secrecy, in America; it wouldn't be the first time, or the last. They brought me back and civilized me then farmed me out to the third son when I came of age. Both his elder brothers subsequently died, in a hunting accident and of a fever, respectively. The council of landholders – the Landsknee – screamed blue murder and threatened to annul the marriage: but then the six started tearing each other's guts out in civil war, and that was an end to the matter, for a generation.'

The lamplight flickered and Miriam felt an icy certainty clutching at her guts. 'You mean, the Clan?' she asked. 'You're a world-walker?'

'I *was*.' Angelin's eyes were dark hollows in the dim light. 'Pregnancy changes you, you know. I doubt I'd survive if I tried it, today. My old bones are not what they were. And I gather the other world has changed, too. But enough about me.' A withered flicker of a smile: 'I know your grandmother. She swears by you, you know. Well, she swears *about* you, but that's much the same: it means you're in her thoughts. She's pigheaded, too.'

'I don't see eye to eye with her,' Helge said tightly. The Duchess Hildegarde had once sent agents to kill or rape her, thinking her an imposter; since proven wrong, she had subsided into a resentful sulk broken only by expressions of disdain or contempt. *What a loving family we aren't.*

'She told me that herself,' the Queen Mother said dismissively. Her eyes gleamed as she looked directly at Helge. 'I wanted to see you myself before I made my mind up,' she said.

'Made your mind up?' Miriam could hear her voice rising unpleasantly, even though everything she'd learned as Helge told her she must stick to a cultivated awe in the royal personage. 'About *what*? I've just been threatened by your grandson – '

'Don't you worry about that.' Angelin sounded almost amused. 'I'll deal with Egon later. You may leave now. I won't stand on ceremony. Thurman, show the lady out – '

'What *is* this?' Miriam demanded plaintively.

'Later,' said the Queen Mother, as one of the guards – Thurman – urged Helge toward the door. 'The trait is recessive,' she added, slightly louder. 'That means – '

'I know what it means,' Miriam said sharply.

'We'll talk later. Go now.' The Queen Mother looked away dismissively. The door closed behind Helge, stranding the younger woman at one side of a sprung dance floor where couples paced in circles around each other in complex patterns that defied interpretation. Miriam – at this moment she felt herself to be entirely Miriam, not even an echo of the social veneer that formed her alter ego Helge remaining to cover the yawning depths – took a ragged breath. She felt stifled by layers of artifice, suffocated by the social expectations of having to live as a noble lady: and now she had to put up with threats, innuendo, and hints from the royal family? She felt hot and cold at once, and her stomach hurt.

The trait is recessive. The king was a carrier. That meant that each of his sons had a one in four chance of being a carrier. *Have you thought about marriage? Obviously not from the right angle, because you've been too successful, too fast.* Wasn't Prince Egon – golden boy with a thousand-yard stare, watching her with something ugly in his eyes – already engaged to some foreign princess? *Raised in secrecy.* Might *he* be a carrier? *I know your grandmother.*

'Lady Helge!' It was Kara, two maids in tow, looking angry and relieved simultaneously. 'Where have you been? We were so worried!'

'Hold this,' said Miriam, thrusting the empty glass at her. Then she darted outside as fast as she could, in search of a bush to throw up behind.

TRANSLATED TRANSCRIPT BEGINS

'Has the old goose been drinking too much, do you suppose?'

'Hist, now! She'll hear you!'

'Oh don't worry. She only understands one word in ten. It can't be helped, I suppose. She grew up in fairyland, wearing trousers and chopping up dead men to understand how they work. They didn't have time to teach her how to *speak* as well.'

'What, you mean –' (*Shocked giggle.*) '– to the Crone?'

'No, I don't suppose she's *that* stupid. But she's one of the kind such as have a thoughtful temper. You don't want to get on the wrong side of her, you know. Wait, here she comes –' (*English.*) 'Would you like another glass, ma'am?'

(*Click.*)

'Phew, there she goes again, bouncing after some stuffed-pants longhair. This one looks like he swallowed a ferret, look at the way he's twitching.'

'Raw with lust for the old goose.'

'Hist! Is that your third glass?'

'Who's counting, madam? Listen, *you* have that one. Oh, over there! Don't look, don't be so obvious. Himself with the brown hair and the, um, isn't *he* something?'

'He –'

(*Click.*)

'Not as if my lady is stupid, but she is *strange*. Witchy-weird like any of the Six, but more so, if you follow me. Wears breeches and talks the Anglaische all the time except when she's trying to learn. But she does it so badly! Look at the way she carries herself. Wagging tongues have it that she seduced Sieur Roland, but if something like that could seduce anything then *I'm* Queen of Summer Angels. What do you say, Nicky? Dried-up bluestocking or – '

'Don't underestimate her, she's not stupid, even if she doesn't understand much. She may not look like a lizard but she's descended from a long lineage of snakes. Sieur Roland is dead, isn't he, so I'm led to believe? Do you think she had something to do with that? Suck the man dry and cast aside his bones like a spider.'

'Nicky! That's disgusting!'

'Not as disgusting as what that spotty lad wanted with you in the bedchamber when she was away.'

'*Don't* you go talking like that about me – '

'Then don't you go calling me disgusting, *miss.*'

(*Sigh.*) 'I'm not calling you disgusting.'

'Then it's a good thing I didn't call you a whore, isn't it? People might misunderstand.'

'Here, have another – drink while she's not looking. Who *is* that longshanks oddboy, anyway?'

'Him? He's one of the hangers-on at court. Some fancy-boy or other to the king's bedchamber. Dresser-on-of-codpieces or some such.'

'You don't know, do you? She doesn't know!'

'Rubbish, he's Sieur Villem du Praha and he's married to Lady Jain of Cours, and he rides with the king's hunt. And look, there's our missy Kara going all gushy over him.'

'Kara? She's – '

'You just look, whenever she gets within six feet of him she has to tie her knees together with her stay laces to stop them falling apart. Silly little bitch, she hasn't seen the way he looks at his wife.'

'Milady Kara's not one to turn her nose up at a lost cause. But what's with milady the honorable Old Goose? What's *she* doing with him?'

'Who the – knows, pardon my Loewsprache, she's being a witch again. Shamelessly talking to strange men.'

'What's shameless about it? She's got her *chaperone* – '

(*Laughter.*) 'Red-Minge Kara is a chaperone? What color is the sky in your county, and do the fish have feathers to match the birds' scales?'

'I'd like to know what she's talking about, though.'

'I've got an idea. Wait here.'

(*Click.*)

'So? What's the story?'

'Give me that.'

'Must be a long story to wet your throat like that.'

'Long? You haven't heard the first of it – '

'Is she trying to fix Kara up with a paramour?'

'Is she – bah! Even Old Witchy-Goose isn't *that* stupid, what would people say if her lady-in-waiting got pregnant? I'm sorry I asked. I thought it would be something like that. And the promises I had to make!'

'Promises?'

'Yes, I said I'd ask you to meet Oswelt – him with the belly – behind the marquee in half an hour for a midnight promenade.'

'Bitch!'

'Now, now, mind your language! Remember I said you weren't a whore? I didn't *promise* you'd be there, just said I'd ask.'

'You did . . .'

'So if you want . . .'

'What about her ladyship? What did you find out?'

'Well, it's as well I asked because something tells me we'll be dragged hither and back in the next months, or I'm not a household hand.'

'Really? Why? What's she want from him?'

'He's not with the king's wardrobe, he's with the prince's. And you know what that means.'

'Oh!'

'Yes.'

'The slut!'

'Absolutely wanton.'

'We'll be back here three times a night before the month is out.'

'Indeed.'

'Hmm. So what else did you tell master Oswelt about me . . . ?'

(*Click*.)

TRANSCRIPT ENDS

INCORRECT ASSUMPTIONS

Twelve weeks ago (continued):

Mike Fleming leaned back in his chair and tried desperately to stifle a yawn. *This is crazy*, he told himself. *How can you be tired at a time like* this?

The air conditioner in the conference room wheezed, losing the battle to keep the heat of the summer evening at bay. He desperately needed another coffee. Despite the couple of hours' nap he'd caught back home before the spooks from NSA sucked him in, his eyes kept half-closing, threatening him with a sleep-deprivation shutdown.

'Agent Fleming?'

'Oh. Yeah? Sorry, what was the question?'

'How long have you been awake?' It was Smith, his expression unreadable.

Mike shook himself. 'About fifty hours. Got about an hour's sleep before your guys picked me up.'

'Ah – right.' Out of the corner of one eye Mike barely registered Herz from the FBI office looking sympathetic. 'Okay, I'll try not to keep you,' said Smith. 'We need you awake and alert for tomorrow. Meanwhile, can you give us a brief run-through on the background to Greensleeves? I've read Tony's write-up of your report, but everyone else here needs to be put in the frame, and it's probably better if they get it from the horse's mouth first before they get the folder. How do you take your coffee?'

Mike yawned. 'Milk, no sugar.' He stood up. 'Shall I?'

'Be my guest.' Smith waved him toward the podium.

'Okay.' Mike forced himself to breathe deeply, suppressing another yawn, as Colonel Smith quietly picked up a white phone and ordered a round of coffees for the meeting. 'Sorry, folks, but it's been a long couple of days.' Appreciative muttering. 'Source Greensleeves.

Don't ask me who dreams up these stupid names. A couple of weeks ago Greensleeves, whoever he was, casually dropped the hammer on a ring operating out of Cambridge. At this time it was purely a standard narcotics investigation. A low-level wholesaler, name of Ivan Pavlovsk, was handling the supply line for a neighborhood street gang who were shifting maybe a kilo of heroin every month. Greensleeves left a code word and said he'd be back in touch later. I thought at first it was the usual caped-crusader bullshit but it turned out to be solid and the DA up there is nailing down a plea bargain that should put our Ukrainian friend behind bars for the next couple of decades.' He leaned against the podium and glanced at Smith. 'Are you sure you want the whole list?'

'Give us the highlights.' Smith's brow wrinkled. 'Up until yesterday. What you told Tony Vecchio.' Tony was Mike and Pete's boss in the investigation branch.

'Okay. We had two more leads from Greensleeves, at one-week intervals. Both were for intermediate wholesale links supplying cocaine in single-digit kilogram amounts to retail operations. There was no lead on Greensleeves himself. Each time, he used a paid-for-cash or stolen mobile phone, called from somewhere populous – a restroom in the Prudential, the concourse of the Back Bay station – and spent between thirty seconds and three minutes fifteen seconds on the phone before ringing off. He came straight through to my desk extension and left voice mail each time – the third time we had a tap and trace in place but couldn't get any units there in time. He used the same password with each call, and gave no indication as to why he was trying to shop these guys to us. Until yesterday Pete here was betting it was an internal turf war. My money was on an insider wanting to cash out and make a WPP run, but either way the guy was clearly a professional.' Mike paused.

'If anyone wants a recap, we're having copies of the case notes prepared for you,' Smith added. 'Can I ask you all *not* to make any written notes of this briefing,' he added pointedly in the direction of Frank the surveyor. 'We'd only have to incinerate them afterward.'

Like that, is it? Mike wondered. 'Shall I continue?'

'When you're ready.'

'Okay. We got a tip-off from Greensleeves five weeks ago, about Case Phantom's main distribution center for Boston and Cambridge. Case Phantom is Pete's specialty, a really major pipeline we've been trying to crack for months. Greensleeves used the same code word, this time in an envelope along with a sample of merchandise and – this is significant – a saliva sample. Greensleeves wanted to turn himself in, which struck us as noteworthy: but what set the alarm bells going was Greensleeves wanting to turn himself in and enlist in the Witness Protection Program in return for knocking over Case Phantom. And helping us get it right, this time.'

Pete sighed noisily.

'Yeah,' said Mike. 'Operation Phoenix was part of Case Phantom, too. Back before Greensleeves decided to come aboard. It was a really big bust – the wrong kind.'

Now he saw Agent Herz wince. They'd taken up the tip-off and gone in like gangbusters, half the special agents posted at the Boston DEA office with heavy support from the police. But they'd hit a wall – literally. The modern-looking office building had turned out to be a fortress, doors and windows backed by steel barriers and surveillance cameras like a foreign embassy.

Worse, the defenders hadn't been the usual half-assed *Goodfellas* wannabes. Someone with a Russian army-surplus sniper's rifle had taken down two of the backup SWAT team before Lieutenant Smale had pulled them back and called up reinforcements for a siege. Then, four hours into the siege – just as they'd been getting ready to look for alternative ways in – the building had collapsed. Someone had mined its foundations with demolition charges and brought it right down on top of the cellars, which were built like a cold war nuclear bunker. The CSIs and civil engineers were still sieving the wreckage, but Mike didn't expect them to find anything.

'In retrospect, Phoenix should have been a signal that something really weird was happening,' Mike continued. 'It took us a long time to dig our way into the rubble and what we found was disturbing. Bomb shelters, cold stores, closed-circuit air-conditioning . . . and fifty kilograms of pharmaceutical-grade cocaine in a vault. Plus an arsenal like a National Guard depot. But there were no bodies . . .' He trailed off introspectively. *Too tired for this*, he thought dizzily.

'Okay, now fast-forward. You've had a series of tip-offs from source Greensleeves, leading up to Greensleeves turning himself in three days ago,' Colonel Smith stated. 'What about the saliva sample? It's definitely him?'

Mike shrugged. 'The lab says so. Matthias is definitely source Greensleeves. He got us an armored fortress in downtown Cambridge with fifty kilos of pharmaceutical-grade cocaine and a *Twilight Zone* episode to explain, plus a series of crack warehouses and meth labs up and down the coast. Biggest serial bust in maybe a decade. He's –' Mike shook his head. 'I've spent a couple of hours talking to him and it's funny, he doesn't sound crazy, and after watching that video – well. Matt – Greensleeves – *doesn't* sound sane at first, he sounds like a nut. Except that he's right about everything I checked. And the guy vanishing in front of the camera is just icing on the cake. He *predicted* it.' Mike shook his head again. 'Like I said, he sounds crazy – but I'm beginning to believe him.'

'Right.' Colonel Smith broke in just as a buzzer sounded, and a marine guard opened the outer door for a steward, who wheeled in a trolley laden with coffee cups and flasks. 'We'll pause right there for a moment,' Smith said. 'No shop talk until after coffee. Then you and Pete can tell us the rest.'

*

The debriefing room wasn't a cell. It resembled nothing so much as someone's living room, tricked out in cheap sofas, a couple of re-cliners, a coffee table, and a sideboard stocked with soft drinks. The holding suite where they'd stashed Greensleeves for the duration didn't look much like a jail cell, either. It had all the facilities of a rather boring hotel room – beds, desk, compact ensuite bathroom – if the federal government had been in the business of providing motel accommodation for peripatetic bureaucrats.

But the room had two things in common with every jail cell ever built. First, the door was locked on the outside. And second, the windows didn't open. In fact, if you looked at them for long enough you'd realize that they weren't really windows at all. Both the debriefing room and the holding suite were buried in a second-story basement, and to get in you'd have to either prove your identity and sign in through two checkpoints and a pat-down search, or shoot your way past the guards.

Mike and Pete had taken the friendly approach at first, when they'd first started the full debriefing protocol. After all, he was co-operating fully and voluntarily. Why risk pissing him off and making him clam up?

'Okay, let's take it from the top.' Mike smiled experimentally at the thin, hatchet-faced guy on the sofa while Pete hunched over the desk, fiddling with the interview recorder. Hatchet-face – Matt – nodded back, his expression serious. As well it should be, in his situation. Matt was an odd one; mid-thirties in age, with curly black hair and a face speckled with what looked like the remnants of bad acne. He was wiry, all whipcord muscle and bone, and he wore the same leather jacket and jeans he'd had on when he walked through the DEA office door.

'We're going to start the formal debriefing now you're here. When we've got the basics of your testimony down on tape, we'll escalate it to OCDTF and get them to sign off on your WPP participation and then set up a joint liaison team with the usual – us, the FBI, possibly FinCEN, and any other organizations whose turf is directly affected by your testimony. We can't offer you a blanket amnesty for any crimes you've committed, but along the way we'll evaluate your security requirements, and when we've got the prosecutions in train we'll be able to discuss an appropriate plea bargain for you, one that takes your time in secure accommodation here into account as time served. So you should be free to leave with a new identity and a clean record as soon as everything's wrapped up.' He took a breath. 'If there's anything you don't understand, say so. Okay?'

Matt just sat on the sofa, shoulders set tensely, for about thirty seconds, until Mike began to wonder if there was something wrong with him. Then: 'You don't understand,' he said, in a quiet but urgent tone. 'If you treat this as a criminal investigation we will both die. They have agents everywhere and you have no idea what they are capable of.' He had an odd foreign accent, slightly German, but with markedly softened sibilants.

'We've dealt with Mafia families.' Mike smiled encouragingly.

'They are not your Mafia.' Matt stared intimidatingly. 'You are at war. They are a, a shadow government. They will not respond as criminals, but as soldiers and politicians. I am here to defect, but if you are going to insist that they are ordinary criminals, you will lose.'

'Can you point to them on a map?' Mike asked. The informer shook his head. He looked faintly – disappointed? Amused? Annoyed? Mike felt a stab of hot anger. *Stop playing head games with me*, he thought, *or you'll be sorry.*

Pete looked up. 'Are we talking terrorists here? Like al-Qaeda?' he asked.

'I said they are a government. If you do not understand what that means we are both in very deep trouble.' Matt picked up the cigarette packet on the table and unwrapped it carefully. His fingers were long, but his nails were very short. One was cracked, Mike noticed, and his right index finger bore an odd callus: not a shooter's finger, but something similar.

'There is another world,' Matt said carefully as he opened the packet and removed a king-size. 'This world is the world you are familiar with. The world of the United States, and of al-Qaeda. The world of automobiles and airliners and computers and guns and antibiotics. But there is another world, and you know nothing of it.'

He paused for a moment to pick up the table lighter, then puffed once on the cigarette and laid it carefully on the ashtray.

'The other world is superficially like this one. There is a river not far from here, for example, roughly where the Charles River flows. But there is no city. Most of Boston lies under the open sea. Cambridge is heavily forested.

'There are people in the other world. They do not speak your language, this English tongue. They do not worship your tree-slain god. They don't have automobiles or airliners or computers or guns or antibiotics. They don't have a United States. Instead, there are countries up and down this coast, ruled by kings.'

Matt picked up the cigarette and took a deep lungful of smoke.

Mike glanced over at Pete to make sure he was recording, and caught a raised eyebrow. When he looked back at Matt, careful to keep his expression blank, he realized that the informant's hands were shaking slightly.

'It's a nice story. But what does it have to do with the price of cocaine?'

'Everything!' Matthias snapped.

Taken aback, Mike jolted upright. Matt stared at him: he stared right back. 'What do you mean?' He demanded.

After several seconds, Matthias's tension unwound. 'I'm sorry. I will get to the point,' he said. 'The kingdom of Gruinmarkt is dominated by a consortium of six noble houses. Their names are – no, later. The point is, some members of the noble bloodline can walk between the worlds. They can cross over to this world, and cross back again, carrying . . . goods.'

He paused, expectantly.

'Well?' Mike prodded, his heart sinking. *Jesus, just what I need. The hottest lead this year turns out to be a card-carrying tinfoil hat job.*

Matthias sighed. 'Kings and nobles.' He took another drag at his cigarette, and Mike forced himself to stifle a cough. 'Noble houses rise and fall on the basis of their wealth. These six, they are not old. They date their fortunes to the reign of – no, to the, ah, eighteen-fifties. Before then, they were unremarkable merchants – tinkers, really. *Traders.* Today they are the high merchant families, rich beyond comprehension, a law unto themselves. Because they *trade.* They come to this world bearing dispatches and gems and valuables, and ensure that they arrive back in the empire of the Outer Kingdom – in what you would call California, Mexico, and Oregon – the next day. Without risk of disaster, without delay, without theft by the bands of savages who populate the wilderness. And the trade runs on the other side, too.'

'How do they do it?' Mike asked. *Humor him, he may have something useful, after all.* Mentally, he was already working out which forms to submit to request the psychiatric assessment.

'Suppose a broker in Columbia wants half a ton of heroin to arrive in upstate New York.' Matthias ground his cigarette out in the ashtray, even though it was only half-finished. 'He has a choice of distribution channels. He can arrange for an intermediary to buy a fast speedboat, or a light plane, and run the Coast Guard gauntlet in the Caribbean. He can try a false compartment in a truck. Once in the United States, the cargo can be split into shipments and dispatched via other channels – expendable couriers, usually. There is an approximate risk of twenty-five percent associated with this technique. That is, the goods will probably reach the wholesaler – but one time in four, they will not.' His face flickered in a fleeting grin. 'Alternatively, they can contact the Clan. Who will take a commission of ten percent and *guarantee* delivery – or return the cost in full.'

Huh? Mike sat up slightly. Matthias's habit of breaking off and looking at him expectantly was grating, but he couldn't help responding. Even if this sounded like pure baloney, there was something compelling about the way Matt clearly believed his story.

'The Clan is a trading consortium operated by the noble houses,' Matt explained. 'Couriers cross over into this world and collect the cargo, in whatever quantity they can lift – they can only carry whatever they can hold across the gulf between worlds. In the other world, the Clan is invincible. Cargos of heroin or cocaine travel up the coast in wagon trains guarded by the Clan's troops. Local rulers are bribed with penicillin and aluminum tableware and spices for the table. Bandits with crossbows and swords are no match for soldiers with night-vision goggles and automatic weapons. It takes weeks or months, but it's secure – and sooner or later the cargo arrives in a heavily guarded depot in Boston or New York without you ever knowing it's in transit or being able to track it.'

There was a click from across the room. Mike looked round. 'This is bullshit,' complained Pete, stripping off his headphones. He glared at Matt in disgust. 'You're wasting our time, do you realize that?' To Mike, 'Let's just charge him with trafficking on the basis of what we've already got, then commit him for psych – '

'I don't think so –' Mike began, just as Matthias said something guttural in a foreign language the DEA agent couldn't recognize. 'I'm sorry?' he asked.

'I gave you samples,' Matt complained. 'Why not analyze them?'

'What for?' Mike's eyes narrowed. Something about Matthias worried him, and he didn't like that one little bit. Matt wasn't your usual garden-variety dealer's agent or hit man. There was something else about him, some kind of innate sense of his own superiority, which grated. *And* that weird accent. As if – 'What should we look for?'

'The sample I gave you is of heroin, diacetylmorphine, from poppies grown on an experimental farm established by order of the High Duke Angbard Lofstrom, in the estates of King Henryk of Auswjein, which would be in North Virginia of your United States. There has never been an atomic explosion in the other world. I am informed that a device called a mass spectroscope will be able to confirm to you that the sample is depleted of an iso-, um, isotope of carbon that is created by atomic explosions. This is proof that the sample originated in another world, or was prepared at enormous expense to give such an impression, for the mixture of carbon isotopes in this world is different.'

'Uh.' Pete looked as taken aback as Mike felt. 'What? Why haven't you been selling your own here, if you can grow it in this other world?'

'Because it would be obvious where it came from,' Matt explained with exaggerated patience. 'The entire policy of the Clan for the past hundred and seventy years has been to maintain a shroud of secrecy around itself. Its participation in the drug courier business dates back over fifty years. Selling drugs that were clearly harvested on another world would not, ah, contribute to this policy.'

Mike nodded at Pete. 'Switch the goddamn recorder on again.' He turned back to Matthias. 'Summary. There exists a, a parallel world to our own. This world is not industrialized? No. There is a bunch of merchant princes, a *clan*, who can travel between there and here. These guys make their money by acting as couriers for high-value assets which can be transported through the other world without risk of interception because they are not recognized as valuable there. Drugs, in short. Matthias has kindly explained that his last heroin sample contains a, um, carbon isotope balance that will demonstrate it must have been grown on another planet. Either that, or somebody is playing implausibly expensive pranks. Memo: get a mass spectroscopy report on the referenced sample. Okay, so that brings me to the next question.' He leaned toward Matthias. 'Who are *you*, and how come you know all this?'

Matt extracted another cigarette from the packet and lit it. 'I am of the outer families – I cannot world-walk, but must be carried wheresoever I should go. I am – was – private secretary to the head of the Clan's security, Duke Lofstrom. I am here because' – he paused for a deep drag on the cigarette – 'if I was *not* here they would execute me. For treason. Is that clear enough?'

'I, uh, think so.' Pete had walked round behind Matt and was frantically gesturing at Mike, but Mike ignored him. 'Do you have anything else to add?'

'Yes, two things. Firstly, you will find a regular Clan courier on the 14:30 Acela service from Boston to New York. I don't know who they are, so I can't give you a personal description, but standard procedure is that the designated courier arrives at the station no more than five minutes prior to departure. He sits in a reserved seat in carriage B, and he travels with an aluminum Zero Halliburton roll-on case, model ZR-31. He will be conservatively dressed – the idea is to be mistaken for a lawyer or stockbroker, not a gangster – and will be armed with a Glock 20 pistol. You will know you have arrested a courier if he vanishes when confined in a maximum security cell.' He barked a humorless laugh. 'Make sure to videotape it.'

'You said two things?'

'Yes. Here is the second.' Matt reached into his pocket and pulled out a small, silvery metallic cylinder. Mike blinked: on first sight he almost mistook it for a pistol cartridge, but it was solid, with no sign of a percussion cap. And from the way Matt dropped it on the tabletop it looked dense.

'May I?' Mike asked.

Matt waved at it. 'Of course.'

Mike tried to pick it up – and almost dropped it. The slug was *heavy*. It felt slightly oily and was pleasantly warm to the touch. 'Jesus! What is it?'

'Plutonium. From the Duke's private stockpile.' Matt's expression was unreadable as Mike flinched away from the ingot. 'Do not take my word for it; analyze it, then come back here to talk to me.' He crossed his arms. 'I said they were a government. And they have a nuclear weapons program . . .'

*

A lightning discharge always seeks the shortest path to ground. Two days after she discovered Duke Angbard's location to be so secret that nobody would even tell her how to send him a letter, Miriam's wrath ran to ground through the person of Baron Henryk, her mother's favorite uncle and the nearest body to Angbard in age, position, and temperament that she could find.

Later on, it was clear to all concerned that something like this had been bound to happen sooner or later. The dowager Hildegarde was already presumed guilty without benefit of trial, the Queen Mother was out of reach, and Patricia voh Hjorth d'Wu ab Thorold – her mother – was above question. But the consequences of Miriam's anger were something else again. And the trigger that set it off was so seemingly trivial that after the event, nobody could even recall the cause of the quarrel: a torn envelope.

At midmorning Miriam, fresh from yet another fit of obsessive Gantt-chart filing, emerged from her bedroom to find Kara scolding one of the maidservants. The poor girl was almost in tears. 'What's going on here?' Miriam demanded.

'Milady!' Kara turned, eyes wide. 'She's been deliberately slow, is all. If you'd have Bernaard take a switch to her – '

'No. You: go lose yourself for a few minutes. Kara, let's talk.'

The maid scurried away defensively, eager to be gone before the mistress changed her mind. Kara sniffed, offended, but followed Miriam over toward the chairs positioned in a circle around the cold fireplace. 'What troubles you, milady?' asked Kara.

'What day is it?' Miriam leaned casually on the back of a priceless antique.

'Why, it's, I'd need to check a calendar. Milady?'

'It's the fourteenth.' Miriam glanced out the window. 'I'm sick, Kara.'

'Sick?' Her eyes widened. 'Shall I call an apothecary – '

'I'm sick, as in *pissed off*, not sick as in ill.' Miriam's smile didn't reach her eyes. 'I'm being given the runaround. Look.' She held up an envelope bearing the crest of the Clan post. Its wax seal was broken. 'They're returning my letters. "Addressee unknown".'

'Well, maybe they don't know who – '

'Letters to *Duke Angbard*, Kara.'

'Oh.' For a moment the teenager looked guilty.

'Know anything about it?' Miriam asked.

'Oh, but nobody writes to the duke! You write to his secretary.' Kara looked confused for a moment. 'Then he arranges an appointment,' she added hesitantly.

'The duke's last secretary, in case you've forgotten, was Matthias. He isn't answering his correspondence any more, funnily enough.'

'Oh.' A look of profound puzzlement crept over Kara's face.

'I can't get *anywhere*!' Miriam burst out. 'Ma – Patricia – holds formal audiences. Olga's away on urgent business most of the time and on the firing range the rest. I haven't even seen Brill since the – the accident. And Angbard won't answer his mail. What the hell am I meant to do?'

'Weren't you supposed to be going riding this afternoon?' asked the teenager.

'No. I want to talk to someone. Who, of the Clan council, is in town? Who can I get to?'

'There's Baron Henryk, he stays at the Royal Exchange when he's working, but he – '

'He's my great-uncle, he'll have to listen to me. Excellent. He'll do.'

'But, mistress! You can't just – '

Miriam smiled. There was no humor in her expression. 'It has been three weeks since anyone even deigned to tell me how my company is doing, much less answered my queries about when I can go back over and resume managing it. I've been stuck in this oh-so-efficiently doppelgängered suite – secured against world-walking by a couple of hundred tons of concrete piled on the other side – for two months, cooling my heels. If Angbard doesn't want to talk to me, he'll sure as hell listen to Henryk. Right?'

Kara was clearly agitated, bouncing up and down and flapping her hands like a bird. In her green-and-brown camouflage-pattern minidress – like many of the Clan youngsters, she liked to wear imported western fashions at home – she resembled a thrush with one foot caught in a snare. 'But mistress! I can arrange a meeting, if you give me time, but you can't just go barging in – '

'Want to bet?' Miriam stood up. 'Get a carriage sorted, Kara. One hour. We're going round to the Royal Exchange and I'm not leaving until I've spoken to him, and that's an end to the matter.'

Kara protested some more, but Miriam wasn't having it. If Lady Brill had been around she'd have been able to set Miriam straight, but Kara was too young, inexperienced, and unsure of herself to naysay her mistress. Therefore, an hour later, Miriam – with an apprehensive Kara sucked along in her undertow, not to mention a couple of maids and a gaggle of guards – boarded a closed carriage for the journey to the exchange buildings. Miriam had changed for the meeting, putting on her black interview suit. She looked like an attorney or a serious business journalist, sniffing after blood in the corporate watercooler. Kara, ineffectual and lightweight, drifted along passively in the undertow, like the armed guards on the carriage roof.

The Royal Exchange was a forbidding stone pile fronted by Romanesque columns, half a mile up the road from Thorold Palace. Built a century ago to house the lumber exchange (and the tax inspectors who took the royal cut of every consignment making its way down the coast), it had long since passed into the hands of the government and now housed a number of offices. The Gruinmarkt was not long on bureaucracy – it was still very much a marcher kingdom, its focus on the wilderness beyond the mountains to the west – but even a small, primitive country had desks for scores or hundreds of secretaries of this and superintendents of that. Miriam wasn't entirely clear on why the elderly baron might live there, but she was clear on one thing: he'd talk to her.

'Which way?' Miriam asked briskly as she strode across the polished wooden floor of the main entrance.

'I think his offices are in the west wing, mistress, but *please* – '

Miriam found a uniformed footman in her way. 'You. Which way to Baron Henryk's office?' she demanded.

'Er, ah, your business, milady?'

'None of yours.' Miriam stared at him until he wilted. 'Where do I find the baron?'

'On the second floor, west wing, Winter Passage, if it pleases you – '

'Come on.' She turned and marched briskly toward the stairs, scattering a gaggle of robed clerks who stared at her in perplexity. 'Come on, Kara! I haven't got all day.'

'But mistress – '

The second-floor landing featured wallpaper – an expensive luxury, printed on linen – and portraits of dignitaries to either side. Corridors diverged in the pattern of an H. 'West wing,' Miriam muttered. 'Right.' One arm of the H featured tapestries depicting a white, snowbound landscape and scenes of industry and revelry. Miriam nearly walked right into another robed clerk. 'Baron Henryk's office. Which way?' she snapped.

The frightened clerk pointed one ink-blackened fingertip. 'Yonder,' he quavered, then ducked and ran for cover.

Kara hurried to catch up. 'Mistress, if you go shoving in you will upset the order of things.'

'Then it's about time someone upset them,' Miriam retorted, pausing outside a substantial door. 'They've been giving me the runaround, I'm going to give them the bull in a china shop. This the place?'

'What's a Chinese shop?' Kara was even more confused than usual.

'Never mind. He's in here, isn't he?' Not waiting for a reply, Miriam rapped hard on the door.

A twenty-something fellow in knee breeches and an elaborate shirt opened it. 'Yes?'

'I'm here to see Baron Henryk, at his earliest convenience,' Miriam said firmly. 'I assume he's in?'

'Do you have an appointment?'

The youngster didn't get it. Miriam took a deep breath. 'I have, *now*. At his earliest convenience, do you hear?'

'Ah-ahem. Whom should I say . . . ?'

'His great-niece Helge.' Miriam resisted for a moment the urge to tap her toe impatiently, then gave in.

The lad vanished into a large and hideously overdecorated room, and she heard a mutter of conversation. Then: 'Show her in! Show her in by all means, Walther, then make yourself scarce.'

The door opened wider. 'Please come in, the baron will be with you momentarily.' The young secretary stood aside as Miriam walked in, Kara tiptoeing at her heels, then vanished into the corridor. The door closed behind him, and for the first moment Miriam began to wonder if she'd made a mistake.

The room was built to the same vast proportions as most imperial dwellings hereabouts, so that the enormous desk in the middle of it looked dwarfishly short, like a gilded black-topped coffee table covered in red leather boxes. Bookcases lined one wall, filled with dusty ledgers, while the other walls – paneled in oak – were occupied by age-blackened oil paintings or a high window casement looking out over the high street. The plasterwork hanging from the ceiling resembled a cubist grotto, cluttered with gilded cherubim and inedible fruit. Baron Henryk hunched behind the desk, his head bent slightly to one side. His long white hair glowed in the early afternoon light from the window and his face was in shadow; he wore local court dress, hand-embroidered with gold thread, but his fingertips were dark with ink from the array of pens that fronted his desk in carved stone inkwells. 'Ah, great-niece Helge! How charming to see you at such short notice.' He rose slowly and gestured toward a seat. 'This would be your lady-in-waiting, Lady . . . ?'

'Kara,' Miriam supplied.

Kara cringed slightly and smiled ingratiatingly at the baron. 'I tried to explain – '

'Hush, it's perfectly all right, child.' The baron smiled at her. 'Why don't you join Walther outside? Keep the servants out, why don't you. Perhaps you should take tea together in the long hall, I gather that's the custom these days among the young people.'

'But I –' Kara swallowed, dipped a quick curtsey, and fled.

Henryk waited until the door closed behind her, then turned to Miriam with a faint smile on his face. 'Well, well, well. To what emergency do I owe the honor of your presence?'

Miriam pulled the envelope out of her shoulder bag. 'This. Addressee unknown. I was hoping you might be able to explain what's going on.' She took a deep breath. 'I am being given the runaround – nobody's talking to me! I'm sorry I had to barge in on you like this, at short notice. But it's reached the point where any attempt I make to go through channels and find out what's going on is being thrown back in my face.'

'I see.' Henryk gestured vaguely at a chair. 'Please, have a seat. White or red?'

'I'm sorry?'

'Wine?' He walked over to a sideboard that Miriam had barely noticed, beside one of the bookcases. 'An early-afternoon digestif, perhaps.'

'White, if you don't mind. Just a little.' It was one of the things that had taken Miriam by surprise when she first stumbled into the Clan's affairs, the way people hereabouts drank like fishes. Not just the hard liquor, but wine and beer – tea and coffee were expensive imports, she supposed, and the water sanitation was straight out of the dark ages. Diluting it with alcohol killed most parasites.

Henryk fiddled with a decanter, then carried two lead crystal glasses over to his desk. 'Here. Make free with the bottle, you are my guest.'

Miriam raised her glass. 'Your health.'

'Ah.' Henryk sat back down with a sigh. 'Now, where were we?'

'I was trying to reach people.'

'Yes, I can see that,' Henryk nodded. 'Not having much luck,' he suggested.

'Right. Angbard isn't answering his mail. In fact, I can't even get a letter through to him. Same goes for everyone I know in his security operation. Which isn't to say that stuff doesn't come in the other direction, but . . . I've got a company to run, in New Britain, haven't I? They pulled me out two months ago, saying it wasn't safe, and I've been cooling my heels ever since. When *is* it going to be safe? They don't seem to realize business doesn't stop just because they're worried about Matthias having left some surprises behind, or the

Lees are still thinking about signing the papers. I could be going bankrupt over there!'

'Absolutely true.' Henryk took a sip of wine. 'It's incontrovertible. Yes, I think I see what the problem is. You were absolutely right to come to me.' He put his glass down. 'Although next time I would appreciate a little bit more notice.'

'Um, I'm sorry about that.' For the first time Miriam noticed that the top of the desk wasn't leather, it was a black velvet cloth, hastily laid over whatever papers Henryk didn't want her intruding upon. 'I'd exhausted all the regular channels.'

'Yes, well, I'll be having words with Walther.' A brief flicker of smile: 'He needs to learn to be firmer.'

'But you were free to see me at short notice.'

'Not completely free, as you can see.' His languid wave took in the cluttered desk. 'Never mind. If in future you need to see me, have your secretary make an appointment and flag it for my eyes – it will make everything run much more smoothly. In particular, if you attach an agenda it will be dealt with before things reach this state. Your secretary should – '

'You keep saying, have your secretary do this. I don't *have* a secretary, uncle!'

Henryk raised an eyebrow. 'Then who was the young lady who came with you?'

'That's Kara, she's – *oh*. You mean she's supposed to be able to handle appointments?' Miriam covered her mouth.

Baron Henryk frowned. 'No, not her. You were supposed to be assigned an assistant. Who was, ahem, ah – oh yes.' He jerked his chin in an abrupt nod. 'That would be the Lady Brilliana, would it not? And I presume you haven't seen her for some weeks?'

'She's meant to be a secretary?' Miriam boggled at the thought. 'Well, yes, but . . .' Brill probably *would* make a decent administrative assistant, now that she thought about it. Anyone who didn't take her bullet points seriously would find themselves facing real ones, sure enough. Brill was mature, competent, sensible – in the way that Kara was not – and missing, unlike Kara. 'I haven't seen her since I arrived here.'

'That will almost certainly be because of the security flap,' said Henryk. 'I'll try to do something about that. Lady Brilliana is your right hand, Helge. Perhaps her earlier duties – yes, you need her watching your back while you're here more than Angbard needs another sergeant at arms.'

'Another what – oh. Okay.' Miriam nodded. That Angbard had planted Brill in her household as a spy (and bodyguard) wasn't exactly a secret anymore, but it hadn't occurred to her that it was meant to be permanent, or that Brilliana had other duties, as Henryk put it. *Sergeant at arms! Well.* 'That would help.'

'She knows what strings to pull,' Henryk said. 'She can teach you what to do when she's not there to pull them for you. But as a matter of general guidance, it's usually best to tug gently. You never know what might be on the other end,' he added.

Miriam's ears flushed. 'I didn't mean to kick the anthill over,' she said defensively, 'but my business wasn't designed to run on auto-pilot. I've been given the cold shoulder so comprehensively that it feels like I'm being cut out of things deliberately.'

'How do you know you aren't?' asked Henryk.

'But, if I'm –' She stopped. '*Why* would anyone cut me out of running the New Britain operation, when it won't run without me? I'm not doing any good here, I mean, apart from learning to ride a horse and not look a complete idiot on a dance floor. And basic grammar. All I'm asking for is an occasional update. Why is nobody answering?'

'Because they don't trust you,' Henryk replied. He put his glass down and stared at her. 'Why do you think they should let you out where they can't keep an eye on you?'

'I –' Miriam stopped dead. 'They *don't* trust me?' she asked, and even to herself she sounded slightly stupid. 'Well, no shit. They've got my *mother* as a hostage, there's no way I can go back home until we know if Matt's blown my original identity, Angbard knows just where I live on the New Britain side – what do they think I'm going to do? Walk into a Royal Constabulary office and say, "Look, there's a conspiracy of subversives from another world trying to invade you" or something? Ask the DEA to stick me in a witness protection program?' She realized she was getting agitated and tried to control her

86

gestures. 'I'm on side, Henryk! I had this exact same argument with Angbard last year. I chewed it over with, with Roland. Think we didn't discuss the possibility of quietly disappearing on you? Guess what: we didn't! Because in the final analysis, you're family. And I've got no reason good enough to make me run away. It's not like the old days when Patricia had to put up with an abusive husband for the good of the Clan, is it? So yes, they should be able to trust me. About the only way they can expect me to be untrustworthy is if they treat me like this.'

She ran down, breathing heavily. Somewhere in the middle of things, she realized, she'd spilled a couple of drops of wine on the polished walnut top of Henryk's desk. She leaned forward and blotted them up with the cuff of her jacket.

'You make a persuasive case,' Henryk said thoughtfully.

Yes, but do you buy it? Miriam froze inside. *What have I put my foot in here?*

'Personally, I believe you. But you see, I have met you. I can see that you are a lady of considerable personal integrity and completely honorable in all your dealings. But the Clan is *at this moment* battling for its very survival, and the people who make such decisions – *not* Angbard, he directs, his perch is very high up the tree indeed – don't know you from, from your lady-in-waiting out there. All they see is a dossier that says "feral infant, raised by runaway on other side, tendency toward erratic entrepreneurial behavior, feminist, radical, unproven reliability". They *know* you came back to the fold once, of your own accord, and that is marked down in your favor already, isn't it? You're living in the lap of luxury, taking in the social season and pursuing the remedial studies you need in order to learn how to live among us. Expecting anything more, in the middle of a crisis, is pushing things a little hard.'

'You're telling me I'm a prisoner,' Miriam said evenly.

'No!' Henryk looked shocked. 'You're *not* a prisoner! You're –' He paused. 'A probationer. Promising but unproven. If you keep to your studies, cultivate the right people, go through channels, and show the right signs of trustworthiness, then sooner rather than later you'll get exactly what you want. All you need to do is convince the security adjutants charged with your safety that you are loyal and moderately predictable – that you will at least notify them *before* you engage in potentially dangerous endeavors – and they will bow down before you.' He frowned, then sniffed. 'Your glass is empty, my dear. A refill, perhaps?'

'Yes, please.' Miriam sat very still while Henryk paced over to the sideboard and refilled both glasses, her mind whirling. *They see me as a probationer*. It wasn't a nice idea, but it explained a lot of things that had been happening lately. 'If I'm on probation, then what about my mother? What about Patricia?'

'Oh, she's in terrible trouble,' Henryk said reassuringly. 'Absolutely *terrible*! Ghastly beyond belief!' He said it with relish as he passed her the glass. 'Go on, ask me why, you know you're dying to.'

'Um. Is it relevant?'

'Absolutely.' Henryk nodded. 'You know how we normally deal with defectors around here.'

'I –' Miriam stopped. Defection was one of the unforgivable crimes. The Clan's ability to function as an organization devoted to trade between worlds scaled as a function of the number of couriers it could mobilize. Leaving, running away, didn't merely remove the defector from the Clan's control; it reduced the ability of the Clan as a whole to function. Below a certain size, networks of world-walkers were vulnerable and weak, as the Lee family (stranded unknowingly in New Britain two centuries ago) had discovered. 'Go on.'

'Your mother has unusual extenuating circumstances to thank for her predicament. If not for which, she would probably be dead. Angbard swears blind that her disappearance was planned, intended, to draw the faction of murderers out, and that she remained in contact with him at all times. A sleeper agent, in other words.' Henryk's cheek twitched. 'Nobody is going to tell the duke that he's lying to his face. Besides which, if Patricia *hadn't* disappeared when she did, the killing would have continued. When she returned to the fold' – a minute shrug – 'she brought you with her. A life for a life, if you like. Even her mother can see the value of not asking too many pointed questions at this time, of letting sleeping secrets lie. And besides, the story might even be true. Stranger things happened during the war.'

Henryk paused for a sip of wine. 'But as you can see, your background does not inspire trust.'

'Oh.' Miriam frowned. 'But that's not my fault!'

'Of course not.' Henryk put his glass down. 'But you can't escape it. We're a young aristocracy, Helge, rough-cut and uncivilized. This is a marcher kingdom, second sons hunting their fortune on the edges of the great forest. The entire population of this kingdom is perhaps five million, did you know that? You could drop the entire population of Niejwein into Boston and lose them. The Boston you grew up in, that is. Without us, without the Clan, Gruinmarkt culture and high society would make England in the fifteenth century look cosmopolitan and sophisticated. It's true that there are enormous riches on display in the palaces and castles of the aristocracy, but it's superficial – what you see on display is everything there is. Not like America, where wealth is so overwhelming that the truly rich store their assets in enormous bank vaults and amuse themselves by aping the dress and manners of the poor. You're a fish out of water, and you're understandably disoriented. The more so because you had no inkling of your place in the great chain of existence until perhaps six months ago. But you must realize, people here do not labor under your misconceptions. They know you for a child of your parents, your thuggish dead father and your unreliable tearaway mother, and they don't expect any better of you because they *know* that blood will out.'

Miriam stared at her white-haired, hollow-cheeked great-uncle. 'That's all I am, is it?' she asked in a thin voice. 'An ornament on the family tree? And an untrustworthy one, at that?'

'By no means.' Henryk leaned back in his chair. 'But behavior like this, this display of indecorous –' He paused. 'It doesn't help your case. *I* understand. Others would not. It's them you have to convince. But you've chosen the middle of a crisis to do it in – not the best of timing! Some would consider it evidence of guile, to make a bid for independence when all hands are at the breach. I don't for a minute believe you would act in such a manner, but again: it is not me who you must convince. You need to learn to act within the constraints of your position, not against them. Then you'll have something to work with.'

'Um. I should be going, then.' She rubbed the palm of one hand nervously on her thigh. 'I guess I should apologize to you for taking up your time.' She paused for a moment and forced herself to swallow her pride. 'Do you have any specific advice for me, about how to proceed?'

'Hmm.' Baron Henryk stood and slowly walked over to the window casement. 'That's an interesting question.' He turned, so that his face was shadowed against the bright daylight outside. 'What do you want to achieve?'

'What do I –' Miriam's mouth snapped shut. Her eyes narrowed against the glare. 'I think I made myself clear enough at the extraordinary meeting three months ago,' she said.

'That's not what I asked. Why don't you go and think about that question? When you have a better idea, we should talk again. If you'd like to join me for dinner, in a couple of weeks? Have your confidante write to my secretary to arrange things. Meanwhile, I'll try to find out what has happened to your assistant, and I'll ask someone in the security directorate to look into your affairs in New Britain so that you can go back to them as soon as possible. But if you'll excuse me, I have other matters to deal with right now.'

Miriam rose. 'Thank you for finding some time for me,' she said. Halfway to the door she paused. 'By the way, what is it you do exactly?'

Henryk stood. 'Oh, this and that,' he said lightly. 'Remember to write.'

*

Outside in the corridor, Miriam found a nervous Kara shifting from foot to foot impatiently. 'Oh, milady! Can we go now?'

'Sure.' Miriam walked toward the staircase, her expression pensive. 'Kara, do you know what Baron Henryk does here?'

'Milady!' Kara stared at Miriam, her eyes wide. 'I thought you knew!'

'Knew? Knew what?' Miriam shook her head.

Kara scurried closer before whispering loudly. 'The baron is his majesty's master of spies! He collects intelligence for the Crown, from countries far and wide, even from across the eastern ocean! I thought you knew . . .'

Miriam stopped dead, halfway down the first flight of stairs. *I just barged in on the Director of Central Intelligence*, she thought sickly. *And he told me I'm under house arrest.* Then: 'Hang on, you mean he's the *king's* spymaster? Not the Clan's?'

'Well, yes! He's a sworn baron, milady, sworn to his majesty, or hadn't you noticed?' Kara's attempt at sarcasm fell flat, undermined by her frightened expression. 'We're all his majesty's loyal subjects, here, aren't we? *Aren't* we?'

TRANSLATED TRANSCRIPT BEGINS

(*Click.*)
'Ah, your lordship, how good to see you!'
'On the contrary, the honor is mine, your grace.' (*Wheezing.*) 'Here. Walther, a chair for his grace, dammit. And a port for each of us, then make yourself scarce. Yes, the special reserve. I'm sure you've been even busier than I, your grace, this being a tedious little backwater most of the time, but if there's anything I can do for you – '
'Nonsense, Henryk, you never sleep! The boot is on the other foot and the prisoner shrieking his plea as you heat it. You won't get me with that nonsense – ah, thank you, Walther.'
'That will be all.'
(*Sound of door closing.*)
'Sky Father's eye! That's good stuff. Please tell me it's not the last bottle?'
'Indeed not, your grace, and I have it on good authority that there is *at least* a case left in the Thorold Palace cellars.'
(*Pause.*) 'Six?' (*Pause.*) 'Five? Damn your eyes, four and that's my lowest!'
'I'll have them sent over forthwith. Now, what brings you round here in a screaming hurry, nephew, when I'm sure there are plenty of other fires for you to be pissing on? Would I be right in thinking

it's something to do with woman trouble? And if so, which one?'

(*Clink of glassware.*)

'You know perfectly well *which one* could get me out of the office,
pills or no pills. It's the old bitches, Henryk, they are meddling
in that of which they know not, and they are going to blow the
entire powder keg sky-high if I don't find a way to stop them.
And I can't just bang them up in a garret like the young pullet – '

'The shrew?'

'She's not a shrew, she's just overenthusiastic. A New Woman.
They've got lots of them on the other side, I hear. But the old
one, her manners may be good but her poison is of a fine
vintage and she is getting much too close to our corporate
insurance policy. Even if she doesn't know it yet.'

'Your sister – '

'Crone's pawn, uncle, Crone's pawn. Do you think it was coincidence
that it was Helge who came calling on you, and not Patricia?
Patricia is in a cleft stick and dares not even hiss or rattle her tail,
lest the old bitches lop it off. If we could move her back to the
other side things would be different, but it's all I can do to keep
the situation over there from coming apart on us completely –
we've lost more couriers in the past month than in the preceding
decade, and if I can't stop the leakage I fear we will have to shut
the network down completely. Sending Patricia back simply
isn't an option, and now that she's here she's less effective than
we expected. It's that blasted wasting disease. The old bitches
and their quackery have her mewed up like a kitten in a sack.
Meanwhile, Helge isn't much use to us here, either. I've sent her
Lady B to take her in hand, which might begin to repair the
damage to her high esteem among her relatives, in a year or
three – or at least stop her from dancing blind in the minefield –
but you can see how isolated she is. A real disappointment. I had
such high hopes that those two might tackle the bitches, but the
cultural barrier is just too high.'

'Come now, Angbard, there's no need to be so pessimistic! The
best-laid plans, et cetera. So what do you think the old she-devil
is up to?'

'Well, I can't be certain, but she's certainly done *something* to shut
    Patricia up. And I find it somewhat fascinating to see Helge
    outmaneuvered so thoroughly without even knowing who she's
    up against.'
'Do you think Patricia hasn't told her?'
'Do I –' (*Pause.*) 'Henryk, you sly fellow! And here I was thinking
    I was asking *you* for information!'
'The rack cares not who sleeps on it, and – '
'Indeed, yes, all very well and apposite and all that. Henryk, the old
    bitches are turbulent and the she-devil-in-chief is plotting
    something, I feel it in my bowels. *I have more important things
    to worry about right now.* I do not have time to be looking over
    my shoulder for daggers. I do not have time to dance the reel to
    the old bitch's hurdy-gurdy, when I can't sleep at night for fear of
    conspirators. *What do I need to know?*'
'I say – steady on, your grace! Here, let me remedy your glass . . . My
    agents at court opine that the she-devil has carried off a coup.
    Her stroking of the royal ego has come to something, it seems,
    and sparked a passing fancy with the revenant.'
'The – *what*? What's *she* got to do with anything?'
'The royal succession – Oh dear! Here, use my kerchief.'
(*Bell rings.*)
'Walther! Walther, I say!'
(*Sound of door opening.*)
'A towel for his grace! Your grace, if you would care to make use of
    my wardrobe – '
'No need, thank you uncle, I am sure a little wine stain will hurt only
    my dignity.'
'Yes, but – '
(*Sound of door closing.*)
'That's better.'
(*Pause.*)
'The royal succession! Curse me for an imbecile, which one is it, the
    Pervert or the Idiot? Don't tell me, it's the Idiot. More tractable,
    and the Pervert's already promised to the Nordmarkt.'
'That, and the Pervert's bad habits are becoming increasingly

difficult to cover for. Royal privilege is all very well, but if Egon were anyone other than his father's eldest son he'd be learning wisdom from the Tree Father by now. A nastier piece of work hasn't graced the royal court in my memory. If his father is forced to notice his habits . . . remember our ruling dynasty's turbulent origins? Nobody wants to see another civil war, not with Petermann feeling his oats just across our northern border and the backwoods peers staring daggers at our Clan families' newly earned wealth. I believe the old bitches think that the Pervert will go too far one of these days, in which case owning the Idiot would throttle two rabbits with one snare, nailing down Helge and securing the royal bloodline. They're not stupid, they probably think Helge is smart enough to see the advantages, to take what's being offered her, and to play along. One more generation and we – *they* – would be able to splice the monarchy into the Clan for good. Helge's a bit old, but it wouldn't be a first pregnancy – don't look so shocked, we've got her medical records – and she's in good health. Pray for an accident for the Pervert, a single pregnancy, and her payoff is, well, you know how they work.'

'They're crazy!'

'What? You think she'd *refuse*?'

'*Think*? Blue mother, Henryk, did you listen to her *at all*? She is, to all intents and purposes, a modern American woman. They do *not* marry for duty. It was all I could do to stop her eloping with that waste of money, brains, and time, Roland! The old bitches had better hope they've got their claws into her deep, or she will kick back *so* hard – '

'Patricia.'

'Oh. What? That? Hmm, I suppose you're right. She's rather fond of her mother, that's true. But I'm not sure it'll be enough to hold her down in the long run. It raises an interesting question of priorities, doesn't it?'

'You mean, the insurance policy versus the throne? Or . . . ?'

'Yes. I think – hmm. Helge, wearing her Miriam head, would understand the insurance policy. But not the old bitches.

Whereas Patricia, for all her modernity and skeptical ways, probably wouldn't buy it. She was raised by the she-devil, after all. And, ah, Miriam is very *creatively* unreliable. Yes. What do you think?'

'You're hatching one of your plans, your grace, but you forget that I am not a mind reader.'

'Oh, I apologize. Given: we do not want the old bitches to get their hands on the levers of temporal power, are we agreed? They've got too much already. They seem to have decided – well, it's a bit early to be sure, but marrying Helge to the Idiot would simultaneously tie her down and put a spoke in the wheel the reformers are trying to spin, while also tying down Patricia. That debating society . . . Luckily for us, Helge is unreliable in exactly the right sort of way. Right now they've tied her up like a turkey and she hasn't even realized what's going on. That's not very useful to us, is it? I say we should give her enough rope – no reason to tie the noose so tightly she can't escape it, what – and then a little push, and see which way she runs. Yes? Do you think that could work?'

'Angbard – your grace – that verges on criminal irresponsibility! If she *does* hang herself – '

'She'll have only herself to blame. And she'll not be a dagger for her grandmother to hold to our throat.'

'She hates her grandmother! With a passion.'

'I believe you overestimate her vindictiveness; at present it is merely disdain on both sides. The dowager is more than happy to use any weapon that comes to hand without worrying about hurting its feelings. Helge doesn't know enough to turn in her hand, yet. Perhaps if Helge has real reason to hate her grandmother . . .'

'Tell me you wouldn't harm your own half-sister.'

'Mm, no. I wouldn't need to go that far, Henryk. Hildegarde is quite capable of making Helge hate her without any help from me, although admittedly a few choice whispers might fan the flames of misunderstanding. What I need from *you*, uncle, is nothing more than that you play the bad cop to my good, and perhaps the use of your ears at court. We're all loyal subjects of the Crown after all, yes? And it would hardly be in the Crown's best interests to fall into the hands of the old bitches. Or the Pervert, for that matter.'

'I shall pretend I did not hear that last, as a loyal servant of the Crown. Although, come to think of it, perhaps it would be in everyone's best interests if nobody looked too hard for plots against Prince Egon, who is clearly loved by all. The resources can be better used looking for real threats, if you follow my drift. What kind of push do you intend to give Helge?'

(*Glassware on tabletop.*)

'Oh, a perfectly appropriate one, Henryk! A solution of poetic, even beautiful, proportions suggests itself to me. One that meshes perfectly with Helge's background and upbringing, a bait she'll be unable to resist.'

'Bait? What kind of bait?'

'Put your glass down, I don't want you to lose such a fine vintage.'

(*Pause.*)

'I'm going to let her discover the insurance policy.'

TRANSCRIPT ENDS

INSURANCE

Two days after Miriam visited Baron Henryk, the weather broke. Torrential rain streamed across the stone front of Thorold Palace, gurgling through the carved gargoyle waterspouts and down past the windows under the eaves. Miriam, still in a state of mild shock from her meeting with her great-uncle, stayed in her rooms and brooded. A couple of times she hauled out her laptop, plugged it into the solitary electrical outlet in her suite, and tried to write a letter to her mother. After the third attempt she gave up in despair. Patricia was a nut best cracked by Helge, but Miriam wanted nothing to do with her alter ego, the highborn lady. Trying to be Helge had gotten her into a world of hurt, and trying to measure up to their expectations of her was only going to make things worse. Besides, she had an uneasy feeling that her mother was not going to thank her for muddying the waters with Henryk.

Shortly after lunch (a tray of cold cuts delivered by two servants from the great hall below), there came a knock on her dressing-room door. 'Who is it?' she called.

'Me, Miriam! Are you decent?' The door opened. 'What's the matter?' Brilliana d'Ost stepped inside and glanced around. 'Are you hiding from someone? The servants speak of you as if you're a forest troll, lurking in the shadows to bite the next passing trapper's head off.'

'I'm not that bad, surely.' Miriam smiled. 'Welcome back, anyway – it's good to see someone around here who's happy to see me. What have you been up to?' She stood up to embrace the younger woman.

'I could tell you, but then I'd have to kill you,' Brill said lightly, hugging her back. Then her smile faded. 'Don't assume I'm exaggerating. I've been very busy lately. Some things I can't talk about.' She shed her bulky shoulder bag and pushed the door shut behind her.

'Miriam. What do you mean, happy to see you? What on earth has been going on here? I got word by way of the duke's office – '

'Am I in that much trouble, already?' Miriam asked, sitting down again. She saw that Brill had cut her black hair shorter than last time they'd met and was using foundation powder to cover the row of smallpox craters on the underside of her jaw. In her trouser suit she could have been just another office intern on the streets of New York – Miriam's New York.

'Trouble?' Brill shrugged dismissively. 'Trouble is for *little* people. But I hear word, "Brilliana, your mistress needs you, go and look to her side," and I am thinking that perhaps not all is well – and here you are, hiding like a bear with a headache!' She sat down on one of the upholstered stools that served as informal seating. 'Oh, his excellency says, "Tell her to stop making waves and we'll sort everything out."'

'Um. Right.' Miriam closed the lid on her laptop. 'Can I get you anything?' she asked. 'A glass of wine? Coffee?'

'Coffee would be precious, should you have any.' Brill looked wistful as Miriam tugged the bell rope. 'The weather is as impoverished on the other side. Homeful for the ducks, but not enchanting lest your feet be webbed.'

'Nobody told me that Henryk was a palace ogre,' Miriam complained. The door opened: 'Two coffees, cream, no sugar,' she directed. As it closed, she continued. 'I've been stuck here, all isolated, for weeks. It's not easy to fit in. Kara's done her best to help me, but that isn't much – she just isn't perceptive enough to warn me *before* I put my foot in it. Andragh' – the head of her detachment of bodyguards – 'is the strong silent type, not a political advisor. Mom's busy and has her own problems, Olga's in and out but mostly out, and I'm' – she took a deep breath – 'lonely and bored.'

'Yes, well, that's what the boss said.' Brill brooded for a moment, then burst out, 'Miriam, I'm *sorry*!'

'Hey, wait a moment – '

'I mean it! I blame myself. I was supposed to stick to you like glue, but while you were in the hospital I had other tasks to attend to and my – I can't tell you who – needed me elsewhere. High-priority jobs, lots of them – I've been run ragged. Our networks are in tatters, new safe houses must be bought, identities created, safe procedures developed, contacts sanitized and renewed. An underground railroad which took us decades to build has to be scrapped and rebuilt from scratch, and his grace badly needs eyes and ears he can trust. I thought that you'd be all right here on your own, that not much could happen, but I didn't realize – if I had I'd have made a fuss, demanded to be released back to you!'

Brill was upset and Miriam, who hadn't expected any of this, was taken aback. 'Whoa! It's all right. Seriously, we've been in the middle of a real mess and if you had to go fight security fires for Angbard – or whatever – then obviously, there were higher priorities than acting nursemaid for me. And you're here now, which is the main thing, isn't it?'

'Yes, but I *should* have been here earlier.' Brill frowned. 'Not letting you run amok.' For a moment her flashing grin returned. 'So what else have you been up to?'

Miriam sighed. 'Etiquette lessons. Basic Hochsprache.' She began ticking points off on her fingers: 'Learning to ride, memorizing long lists of who's related to who, learning to dance – court dances, over here, that is – endless appointments with the dressmaker. Oh, and getting pissed off about being given the runaround. About when I can get back to my business, that kind of thing. What's missing from this picture?' *Besides brooding over –* She stopped that line of thought dead. Brill hadn't concealed her opinion of Roland very effectively, but she knew better than to pick a fight with Miriam over his memory, especially when Miriam very definitely wasn't over him.

'Let us see. Long lists of who is who – did Kara think to instruct you in their scandals or holdings? Or worse?' Brill raised an eyebrow. 'No? Methought it unlikely. The rest is not unexpected. The travel restrictions . . .' She frowned again. 'I think if it was solely the decision of your uncle you should be able to return from whence you were summoned immediately. He instructed me to tell you to pay your corvée regularly. I think he wishes to shine your loyalty, to demonstrate you are reliable enough as a courier to trust with world-walking. One week or two, he says, and you should be assigned a regular courier duty to the new outposts, with permission to overnight there when not needed here. This would be unofficial, but should anyone ask they can be told you're running errands simple, not looking to your faction. Discretion is the watchword.'

'Uh.' Miriam blinked, taken aback. 'That's – well. That's far too easy. After yesterday, I was expecting the third degree . . .'

'Henryk convinced you that you were under arrest?' Brill tossed her head as the door opened. 'I'll take that.' The maid closed the door and Brill transferred the silver tray to the top of a chest of drawers. 'The baron is jealous of the demands upon his time, whosoever makes them,' she said. 'He wished you subdued for the while. Either that, else there's a discord over how to handle you. Here, this is yours.'

Miriam took the mug. 'I'm confused. Or he *was* trying to lower my expectations. Wasn't he?'

'In all probability.' Brill sat down again. 'I can't believe you bearded the lion in his den, without appointment,' she added with a curious grin.

'I'm not sure I can, either,' Miriam admitted. 'Understand, I'm not going to blame Kara – but if she was up to managing my affairs herself I'd have known better than to go barging in. The whole issue just wouldn't have arisen in the first place. I'm not an idiot, Brill, just – '

'I would never say you were an idiot!'

' – inadequately informed. And I never said you thought I was, but you *know* what I mean, right? I don't like looking stupid, Brill.'

'Well.' Brilliana took a deep breath: 'Be it so little consolation to you, I am supposed to be your confidante, and your honor is mine. It dishonors *me* – directly – should you look stupid. I plead purely out of self-interest, you understand, not at all speaking as your friend who wishes to return the favor you did me in Boston. So if you tell me what you want to achieve, I shall try to find a way to make it happen, if not instantly then certainly as rapidly as possible. How should that go?'

'Okay.' Miriam screwed her eyes shut. 'That's what Baron Henryk told me, you know: to work out what I want, then tell him. Over dinner, maybe next week.' She opened her eyes and focused on Brilliana as if seeing her for the first time. Perhaps she was, for Helge's ghost was prompting her, *Take your allies where you find them*, and Brill was surely the nearest thing to an ally Miriam had within the Clan. 'So. How about it? First, we should arrange for me to dine with the good baron next week – and yourself, I think. Secondly, I want to get back out to see how my company is running, as soon as possible. Thirdly, Ma has been dropping scarily vague hints about marriage, and this crazy old –' She caught herself. 'Sorry. The king's mother. Angelin. She's dropping broad hints. *I need to know what she wants.* Never mind that creepy Prince Egon. And what's got into Ma – Patricia. Can you find out?'

Brill's eyes went very wide at the last confessions. She clenched her hands between her knees and leaned back on her stool: 'The *Queen Mother* bespoke you? About *Egon*?'

'No, Egon threatened me – the Queen Mother just wanted a chat –'

'He *threatened* you? Miriam, that is completely beyond my conscience! Does Duke Angbard know?'

'Why wouldn't he?' It was Miriam's turn to look startled. 'He's head of the Clan's intelligence apparatus! Isn't it his *job* to know things like that?'

'Only if people tell him!' Brill stood up, clearly agitated. 'I imagine I can do something toward your first two desires, but this – this is new to me. I think I had better write to the duke, by your leave. Miriam, you must steer clear of Prince Egon! He's not – he's –'

'Whoa. I got the message, very clearly, that he doesn't like me, or my relatives. Is that it? Or is there something more?'

Brill nodded, vigorously. 'You know their nicknames? The two princes?'

'The . . .' Miriam's forehead creased.

'The Idiot and the Pervert,' Brill said tightly. 'The Idiot is clear enough. The Pervert – there are rumors. Pray you don't come to his attention.'

'Huh?' Miriam stared. 'What are you trying to tell me? He's a rapist? Wouldn't there be some kind of . . .' She trailed off, a sick realization stealing over her.

'He's the *heir* to the *throne*,' Brill said, clearly and slowly, as if talking to a young and rather stupid child. 'He has, as a prince in his own right, the right of summary justice. The only lord with the authority to hear a case against him is his own father. Such a case would depend upon the plaintiffs and the witnesses living long enough to bring suit. This is not America, Miriam. There, if the rich and powerful want to get away with murder, they must pay lawyers and judges. Here, they *are* the judges. Having said that, if the crown prince tried to use such as you or I for sport, he could expect the full weight of the Clan to oppose him. Likely, even his father would disown him. You are not some peasant.'

Miriam shuddered. 'And if he comes to power?'

'He won't move against us.' There was a hard edge to Brilliana's voice. 'He may be wicked, but he isn't stupid. We are like your America in some ways: our king rules by the will of the people – at least, the people who count. The succession has to be ratified by the landsknee, the dukes and barons. If he offends too many of them, he risks his coronation.' Her expression softened. 'But please, make sure someone knows if he menaces you again. Otherwise . . .'

'I get the picture.' Miriam nodded jerkily. *Jesus, is Egon some kind of serial killer? Or am I misunderstanding something, and it's just hardball politics?* Somehow the idea that her encounter with Egon was simply political business as usual didn't make sense. 'What about the Queen Mother?'

'Oh, she's safe,' Brill said dismissively. 'She's family, after a fashion.' She paused, looking thoughtful. 'And she noticed you? Ha. It can't be about Egon, he's already earmarked for an alliance with the Nordmarkt, which means – Creon? She aims to put him into play?' She looked distant for a moment. 'A royal match would seem fantastical, upon its face, but – '

'Not a hope,' Miriam said, tight-lipped. 'I mean that.'

'But are you . . . ?' Brilliana paused, taking in Miriam's expression. 'You would reject it?' she asked, wondering aloud. 'You would reject a match, uncountenanced, to such a high estate?' For a moment she was starry-eyed, before practicality reasserted itself. 'It would hamper your plans, true – '

'In spades,' Miriam said grimly. 'And in case you'd forgotten, we're not talking a prize catch, here, we're talking sloppy seconds. The one everybody calls the Idiot, to his face.' She clenched her hands between her knees. 'Not enough that Roland had to get himself killed, but *this* – '

'I'm sorry, my lady!'

'I don't blame you,' Miriam said, startled out of her gloomy introspection. 'Don't ever think I blame you!' Brilliana had been there when Roland was killed, in that terrible minute in the duke's outer office with Matthias's psychotic bondsman. If Brill had gotten there faster, or if Roland hadn't tried to play the hero, if *she* hadn't been there, a lure for him – 'This is not about you,' she said. Roland she might have married, giving her tacit consent to being bound into the Clan's claustrophobic family structures. 'I'm not planning on marrying anyone, ever again,' Miriam added. Anything else would be too much like an admission that she was absolutely part of the Clan. She had read about Stockholm syndrome once, the tendency of hostages to come to identify with their abductors. It was a concept uncomfortably close to home: sometimes her new life felt like a perpetual struggle not to succumb to it.

Brilliana adroitly changed the subject. 'Would it please you to volunteer for an additional corvée? I can whisper to the duke that it would do you well to walk outside this pit of vipers.'

'If you think he'd go for that,' said Miriam.

'He will, if he believes you are being schemed around.' She frowned. 'One other thing I would suggest.'

'Oh? What's that?'

'That you invite your mother to dine with you in private. As soon as possible.' Brill paused. 'If she refuses, that will tell you everything you need to know.'

'If she refuses –' Miriam stopped dead. 'That's ridiculous!' she burst out. 'I know she's been grumpy since being forced out of isolation, but she already said she didn't blame me. I haven't done anything to offend her, she's my mother! Why wouldn't she come to visit me?'

'She might not, if she is being blackmailed.' Brill stood up. 'Which would fit the other facts of your situation, milady. There's enough of it about.' Her tone was crisp. 'Meanwhile, shall we retire to the morning room? You must tell me all about your encounter with her majesty.'

*

Letters were written and invitations issued. But as events turned out, Miriam did not get the chance to talk to her mother in private – or to dine with the baron – over the next few days. The evening of Brill's arrival, two summonses arrived for her: an invitation to a private entertainment at the royal court, hand-scribed in gold ink on vellum by a second secretary of the honorable lord registrar of nobles, and a formal request for her services, signed by the lord high second chamberlain of the Clan Trade Committee.

Of the two, the court summons was more perplexing. 'This is a dinner invitation,' Brill explained, holding the parchment at arm's length between two fingertips. 'The closed company. It is open to the royal household and their closest hangers-on and friends, only about sixty people, and there will be a private performance by, oh, some entertainers.' A theatrical troupe, or a chamber orchestra, or, if the royal family were feeling particularly avant-garde, a diesel generator, a VCR, and a movie.

'Will the crown prince be there?' Miriam asked tensely.

'I don't know. Possibly not; he hunts a lot in summer. But you need to attend this. To decline the invitation would be most serious.' Brill looked nervous. 'It does not wait upon your disposition, thus attendance is mandatory. I can come along, should you require me.'

'I'd be scared to attend without you,' Miriam admitted. 'How large a retinue can I take?'

'Oh, to escort you there, as many as you like – but inside? One or two, at the most. And' – Brill glanced askance at the doorway – 'Kara would be delighted to go, but might prove less than reliable.' Kara was running some errand or other, arranging an evening meal or scaring up some more servants or perhaps simply taking time by herself.

'Uh-huh. And this other?' Miriam held up the other invitation.

'I was not expecting it so promptly.' Brill's brow wrinkled. 'You would, perhaps, like to return to Boston from time to time? I believe it is probably the baron's little joke on you, to ensure that you see as much of it as you want, with a sore head, in a borrowed cellar.'

'Uh. Right.' Miriam grimaced. 'But the royal – '

'*She* wants to see you,' Brill said firmly. 'What else could it be? You don't ignore the Queen Mother's whim, milady, not unless you are willing to risk the next one being delivered by a company of dragonards.'

'Ah. I see.' Miriam peered at the letter. 'When is it for?'

'Next Sun's Day Eve . . . good. There will be plenty of time to attire you appropriately and prepare you for the company.' Brill frowned. 'But the second chamberlain desires you to present yourself before him tomorrow. Perhaps I should look to your preparations for the royal court while you attend to your corvée?'

Miriam took a deep breath then nodded. 'Do that. Mistress Tanzig has held custody of my wardrobe in your absence, Kara managed to sort me out with the use of one of the livery coaches, and if I'm away you can prepare written notes for me while I'm gone.' She looked at the window pensively. 'I wonder where he wants me to go?'

*

I should have known better, Miriam thought ruefully, as she watched smoke belch across the railway station platform from the shunting locomotive. The breeze blowing under the open cast-iron arches picked up the smuts and dragged them across the early afternoon sky. She held her hat on with one hand and her heavy carpetbag with another as she looked along the platform, hunting for her carriage.

'It's – harrumph! A postal problem we have, indeed,' Lord Brunvig had said, clearing his throat, a trifle embarrassed. 'Every route is in chaos and every identity must be vetted. We have *lost couriers,*' the old buffer had said, in tones of horror. (As well he might, for if a Clan courier went missing in Massachusetts he or she should very well be able to make their own way home eventually unless the worst had happened.) 'So. We need a fallback,' he had added. 'Would you mind awfully . . . ?'

The Clan had plenty of quiet, disciplined men (and some women) who knew the Amtrak timetable inside out and had clean driving licenses, but precious few who had spent time in New Britain – and they weren't about to trust the hidden family with the crown jewels of their shipping service. It took time to acculturate new couriers to the point where they could be turned loose in a strange country with a high-value cargo and expected to reliably deliver it to a destination that might change from day to day, reflecting the realities of where it was safe to make a delivery on the other side of the wall of worlds. Which was why Miriam – a high lady of the Clan, a duchess's eldest child – found herself standing on a suburban railway platform on the outskirts of New London in a gray shalwar suit and shoulder cape, her broad-brimmed hat clasped to her head, tapping her heels as the small shunting engine huffed and panted, shoving a string of three carriages up to the platform. *And all because I already knew how to read a gazetteer*, she thought whimsically.

Not that there was much to be whimsical about, she reflected as she waited for the first-class carriage to screech to a halt in front of her. New Britain was in the grip of a spy fever as intense as the paranoia about terrorism currently gripping the United States, aggravated by the existence of genuine sub rosa revolutionary organizations, some of whom would deal with the devil himself if it would advance their agenda. Things were, in some ways, much simpler here. The machinery of government was autocratic, and the world was polarized between two great superpowers much as it had been during the Cold War. But political simplicity and the absence of sophisticated surveillance technology didn't mean Miriam was safe. What the Constabulary (the special security police, not the common or garden-variety thief-takers) lacked in bugging devices they more than made up for in informers and spies. Her papers were as good as the Clan's fish-eyed forgers could make them, and she was confident she knew her way. But if a nosy thief-taker or weasel-eyed constable decided to finger her, they'd be straight through her bag, and while she wasn't sure what it contained she was certain that it would prove incriminating. If that happened she'd have to world-walk at the drop of a hat – and hope she could make her own way home from wherever she came out. The quid pro quo was itself trivial: a chance to spend some time in New Britain, a chance to replace the paranoia of court life in Niejwein with a different source of stress.

The shunting engine wheezed and clanked, backing off from the carriages. Somewhere down the platform a conductor blew his whistle and waved a green flag, signaling that the train was ready for boarding. Miriam stepped forward, grabbed a door handle, and pulled herself into one of the small, smoke-smelling sleeper compartments in the ladies' first-class carriage. *Alone, I hope*, she told herself. *Let me be alone . . . ?* She pulled the door shut behind her and, grunting quietly, heaved the heavy bag onto the overhead luggage net. With any luck it would stay there undisturbed until Dunedin – near to Joliet, in the United States, there being no such city as Chicago in this timeline. All she had to do was ferry it to a certain suburban address and exchange it for an identical bag, then return to New London. But Dunedin was over a thousand miles from New London. One good thing you could say about the New British railways was that the overnight express service rattled along at seventy miles an hour. But if the train was full she might end up with company, and being kept awake by genteel snoring was not Miriam's idea of fun.

Clank. The carriage bounced, almost throwing her out of her seat. A shrill whistle from the platform, and a distant asthmatic chuffing, followed by a jerk as the newly coupled locomotive began to pull. Miriam relaxed enough to unbutton her cape. *It's going to be all right*, she decided. *No snoring!*

The corridor door opened: 'Carnets, please, ma'am.' The inspector tugged his hat as he scratched her name off on a chalkboard. 'Ah, very good. Bed make-up will be at eight bells, ma'am, and the dining car opens from seven. If you have any requests for breakfast, the cook will be glad to accommodate you.' Miriam smiled as he backed out through the door. First class definitely had some advantages.

Once he'd gone she pulled the slatted wooden shutters across the corridor window, and shot the bolt on the door. *Alone!* It was positively liberating, after weeks spent in the hothouse atmosphere of the Niejwein aristocracy. Her cape went up on the overhead rack first, then she bent down to unbutton her ankle boots. First-class sleeper compartments had carpet and kerosene heaters, not that she'd be needing the latter on this hot, dusty journey. Once the rows of gray, hunchbacked workers' apartments petered out into open countryside, she pulled her Palm Pilot out of her belt-purse. With four hours to go until dinner – and fifteen or sixteen until the train pulled into Dunedin station – she'd have plenty of time for note-taking and reading.

Precisely half an hour later, the machine emitted a strangled squawking noise and switched itself off.

'Bother.' Miriam squeezed the power button without success, then stuck the stylus in the reset hole. *Beep.* The machine switched on again. Miriam breathed a sigh of relief, then tried to open the file she'd been working on. It wasn't there. A couple of minutes of feverish poking proved that the machine had reset itself to factory condition, erasing not only the work she'd already done but all the other files she'd been meaning to read and edit. Miriam stared at it in dismay. 'Fifteen *hours?*' she complained to the empty seat opposite: she hadn't even brought a newspaper. For a moment she was so angry she actually considered throwing the machine out the window. '*Fucking* computers.' She glanced over her shoulder guiltily, but she was alone. Alone with nothing but the parched New Britain countryside rolling past, a faint smoke trail off to one side hinting at the arid wind that seemed to be plaguing the seaboard this summer.

If Miriam had one overwhelming personality flaw it was that she couldn't abide inactivity. After ten minutes of tapping her right toe on the floor she found herself nodding along, trying to make up a syncopated backbeat that followed the rhythm of the wheels as they clattered over the track joints. *Not even a book*, she thought. For a while she thought about leaving her compartment in search of the conductor, but it would look odd, wouldn't it? Single woman traveling alone, no reading matter: that was the sort of funny-peculiar thing that the Homeland Security Directorate might be interested in. The idea of writing on her PDA had lost all its residual charm, in the absence of any guarantee that the faulty device wouldn't consign long hours of work to an electronic limbo. But not doing anything went right against the grain. Worse, it was an invitation to daydream. And when she caught herself daydreaming these days, it tended to be about people she knew. Roland loomed heartbreakingly large in her thoughts. *I'll go out of my mind if I don't do something*, she realized.

And almost without her willing it, her eyes turned upward to gaze at the carpetbag. *It can't do any harm to look, can it?*

COMPANY CONFIDENTIAL

FROM: Director's Office, Gerstein Center for Reproductive Medicine, Stony Brook
TO: Angbard Lofstrom, Director, Applied Genomics Corporation

Here's a summary of the figures for this FY. A detailed breakdown follows this synopsis; I look forward to hearing from you in due course.

Operations continued as scheduled this quarter. I can report that our projected figures are on course to make the Q2 targets in all areas. Demand for ART procedures including IVF, IUI, ICSI, and tubal reversal is up 2% over the same quarter last year, with an aggregate total of 672 clients treated in the Q1 period. Last year's Q2 figures indicate a viable outcome in 598 cases with a total of 661 neonates being delivered.

With reference to AGC subsidized operations, a total of 131 patients were admitted to the program during Q1. A preliminary estimate is that the total cost of subsidized treatment for these individuals during this quarter will incur operation expenses of approximately $397K (detailed breakdown to follow with general quarterly accounts). Confidence-based extrapolation from last year's Q2 crop is that this will result in roughly 125 +/−17 neonates coming to term in next year's Q1 period. Of last year's Q2 crop, PGD and chorionic villus sampling leads me to expect an 87% yield of viable W* heterozygotes.

We were extremely startled when routine screening revealed that one of our patients was a W* heterozygous carrier. As this patient was not an applicant for the AGC program, no follow-on issues arise in this case, although I have taken the liberty of redacting their contact details from all patient-monitoring systems accessible to FDA supervision – copy available on your request. However, I must urgently request policy guidance in dealing with future W*hz clients not referred to the program through your office.

Other than that, it's all business as usual at GCRM! Hope you're having a profitable and successful quarter, and feel free to contact me if you require further supplementary information or a face-to-face inspection of our facility.

Yours sincerely,

DR. ANDREW DARLING, D.O.
Director of Obstetrics

COPS

A lot had happened in twelve weeks. The assorted federal agents who had been sucked into the retreat in Maryland had acquired a name, a chain of command, a mission statement, and a split personality. In fact it was, thought Mike, a classic example of interdepartmental politics gone wrong, or of the blind men and the elephant, or something. Everyone had an idea about how they ought to work on this situation, and most of the ideas were incompatible.

'It's not just Smith,' Pete complained from the other side of his uncluttered desk. 'I am getting the runaround from *everyone*. Judith says she's not allowed to use agency resources to cross-fund my research request without a directive from the Department of Justice – she's ass-covering – Frank says the County Surveyor's Office isn't allowed to release the information without a FOIA, and Smith says he wants to help but he's not allowed to because the regs say that data flows into the NSA, never out.'

Days of running around offices trying to get a consensus together were clearly taking their toll on Pete Garfinkle. Mike nodded wearily. 'Have you tried public sources?'

'What? Architecture websites? Property developers' annual reports, that kind of thing? I could do that, but it'd take me weeks, and there's no guarantee I'd spot everything.' Pete's shoulders were set, tense with frustration. 'We're cops, not intelligence analysts, Mike, isn't that right? I mean, except for you, babysitting source Greensleeves. So we sit here with our thumbs up our asses while the big bad spooks run around pulling their national security cards on everybody. I can't even requisition a goddamned report on underground parking garages in New Jersey that've been fitted with new security doors in the past six months! And this is supposed to be a goddamned joint intelligence task force?'

'Chill out.' It came out more sharply than Mike had intended. 'You've got me doing it too, now. Listen, let's go find a Starbucks and unwind, okay?'

'But that means –' Pete rolled his eyes.

'Yeah, I know, it means checking out of the motel. So what? It's nearly lunchtime. We've *almost certainly* got time to sign out before we have to sign back in again. Come on.'

Mike and Pete cleared their cramped two-man office. It wasn't a simple process: nothing was simple, once you got the FBI and the NSA and the CIA and the DEA all trying to come up with common security standards. First, everything they were reading went into locked desk drawers. Then all the stationery supplies went into another lockable drawer. Then Mike and Pete had to cross-check each other's locked drawers before they could step outside into the corridor, lock the office door, and head for the security station by the elevator bank. FTO – the Family Trade Organization – was big on compartmentalization, big on locks, big on security – big on just about everything except internal cooperation. And big on the upper floors of skyscrapers, where prices were depressed by the post-9/11 hangover and world-walker assassins were considered a greater threat than hijacked jets.

The corridor outside was a blank stretch punctuated by locked doors, some with red lights glowing above them, the walls bare except for security-awareness posters from some weird NSA loose-lips-sink-ships propaganda committee. Mike made sure to lock his door (blue key) and spun the combination dial before he headed toward the elevator bank. The last door on the corridor was ajar. 'Bill?' asked Pete.

'Pete. And Mike.' Bill Swann nodded. 'Got something for me?'

'Sure.' Mike held out his keys, waited for Bill to take them – and Pete's – and make them disappear. 'Going for lunch, probably back in an hour or so,' he said.

'Okay, sign here.' Swann wasn't in uniform – nobody at FTO was, because FTO didn't exist and blue or green suits on the premises might tip some civilian off – but somehow Mike didn't have any trouble seeing him as a marine sergeant. Mike examined the proffered clipboard carefully, then signed to say he'd handed in the keys to his office at 12:27 and witnessed Bill returning them to the automatic key access machine – another NSA-surplus security toy. 'See you later, sirs.'

'Sure thing, I hope.' Pete whistled tunelessly as he scribbled his chop on the clipboard.

'Dangerous places, those Starbucks.'

'You gotta watch those double-chocolate whipped cream lattes,' Pete agreed as they waited at the elevator door. 'They leap out at you and attack you. One mouthful and they'll be rolling you into pre-op for triple bypass surgery. Crack your rib cage just like the alien in, uh, *Alien*.'

'Mine's a turkey club,' said Mike, 'and a long stand. Somewhere where . . .' The elevator arrived as he shrugged. They stood in silence on the way down. The elevator car had seen better days, its plastic trim yellowing and the carpet threadbare in patches: the poster on the back wall was yet another surplus to some super-black NSA security-awareness campaign. *We're at war and the enemy is everywhere.*

'Do you ever get a feeling you've woken up in the wrong company?' he asked Pete as they crossed the lobby.

'Frequently. Usually happens just before her husband gets home.'

'Gross Moral Turpitude 'R' Us, huh? Does Nikki know?'

'Just kidding.'

Pete's marriage was solid enough that he could afford to crack jokes. 'That's not what I meant.'

'I know, I know . . .' Pete paused while they waited at the cross-walk outside. It was a hot day, and Mike wished he'd left his suit coat behind. 'Let's go. Listen, it's the attitude thing that's getting to me. The whole outlook.'

'Cops are from Saturn, spooks are from Uranus?'

'Something like that.' Pete's eyebrows narrowed to a solid black bar when he was angry or tense. 'Over there.' He gestured down a side street lined with shops, in the general direction of Harvard Square. 'It's a cultural thing.'

'You're telling me. Different standards of evidence, different standards on sharing information, different attitudes.'

'I thought it was our job to roll up this supernatural crime syndicate,' Pete complained. 'Collect evidence, build cases, arrange plea bargains and witness support where necessary, observe and induce cooperation, that sort of thing.'

'Right.' Mike nodded. A familiar Starbucks sign; there was no queue round the block, they'd made their break just in time to beat the rush. 'And the management have got other ideas. Is that what you're saying?'

'We're cops. We think of legal solutions to criminal problems. Smith and the entire chain of command above us are national security. They're soldiers and intelligence agents. They work outside the law – I mean, they're governed by international law, the Geneva conventions and so on, but they work outside our domestic framework.' He broke off. 'I'll have a ham-and-cheese sub, large regular coffee no cream, and a danish.' He glanced at Mike. 'I'm buying this time.'

'Okay.' Mike ordered; they waited until a tray materialized, then they grabbed a pair of chairs and a table in the far corner of the shop, backs to the wall and with a good view of the other customers. 'And you figure they're making it difficult because they're not geared up to share national security information with domestic police agencies, at least not without going through Homeland Security.'

'Home of melted stovepipes.' Pete regarded his coffee morosely. 'It's frustrating, sure, but what really worries me is the policy angle. I'm not sure we're getting enough input into this. NSC grabbed the ball and the AG is too busy looking for pornographers under the bed and jailing bong dealers to have time for the turf war. Wouldn't surprise me if they've classified it so he doesn't even know we exist, or thinks we're just another drug ring roundup embedded in some sort of counter-terrorist operation Wolf Boy and Daddy Warbucks are running.'

Mike blew on his coffee cautiously, then took a sip. 'I'm not sure they're wrong,' he admitted.

'Not sure – hmm?'

'Not sure they're right, either.' Mike shrugged. 'I just know we're not tackling this effectively. It's the old story: if the only tool you've got is a hammer, every problem looks like a nail. Matt's former associates are a problem, okay? Only we can't get at them, can we? Which leaves policing techniques to get them the hell out of our home turf. So why the emphasis on the military stuff? I half suspect some guys who know a lot more than us figure that this *is* a situation which merits military force. It sure doesn't look like something we can do more than a holding action against from here, at any rate.'

'I don't agree. We've got to track down those safe houses they're still using. What Matt said about them being short of couriers – it's got to start hurting them sooner or later! If we can capture enough of them, we can stop them.'

Mike shook his head. 'If we do that, it just starts up all over again a generation later,' he said slowly. 'Unless we can get at their home turf. Which is a military, not a policing, solution. It may look like magic, but there's got to be some kind of way to do whatever they do, hmm? Bet you that's what the Los Alamos guys are into us for. Although whether they get anywhere . . .'

'Could be.' Pete sat back and scanned the shop one more time. 'It's getting a bit crowded in here. How's the home life?'

'Oh, you know.' Mike got the message, put his plate down. 'The cat thinks I'm a stranger, there's a layer of dust thick enough to ski on in the rec room, and my neighbors phoned the cops last time I went home because they thought I was a burglar. How 'bout you?'

'Huh. You need to get a girlfriend.'

'Not really.' Mike stirred his coffee. 'The job tends to put the good ones off.'

'Like, what was she called? That journalist you were seeing last year, or whenever it was.'

'Drop it, Pete.'

Pete stared at him. 'Getting you down, huh?'

'I said, drop it.' Mike looked up. 'Do *you* have a life? Or is it just me?'

'Wherever I hang my hat, there's my home. That's what Nikki tells me, anyway. Mostly I use the hook on the back of the office door. If I was earning overtime . . .'

'I'm saving up my vacation days.' Mike finished his coffee. 'When we get this under control I'm going to – I don't know. Get a life, I guess. Nine years and I could do the early retirement thing, head south and get a boat and go fishing forever. Except at this rate there won't be enough of me left to do any of that.'

'You've got to stop putting everything into the job,' Pete advised. 'At least, take a couple of evenings a week to have a life. You about finished?'

'Nearly.' Pete drained his coffee and pulled a face. 'Let's take a hike. I could do with some fresh air before I go back.'

They were half a block away before Pete said it. 'Loose lips, Mike. I know' – he waved off Mike's answer before it began – 'it's just not office politics as usual, is it?'

'No, it is not.' Mike chose his next words with care. 'Your data-mining hunt. Do you think they're giving you the runaround deliberately?'

'No, I –' Pete paused. 'No, it's not deliberate. I think what it is, is they've got you riding herd on Greensleeves and they had to find something to keep me out of trouble as I was in on that first debrief. But they don't expect to tackle this as a civil law enforcement problem, so they're not giving me any backup. You, they can use. Intelligence, in a word.' He shrugged. 'It makes me mad,' he added offhand.

'If they're not looking at it as a civil law enforcement problem, how do you think they're going to deal with it?'

'I don't know. And that gives me a very bad feeling.'

*

If the altitude doesn't give you a nosebleed, the interagency catfights will do it every time, Mike reflected mordantly as he waited at the elevator bank in the Boston office. He sniffed, mildly annoyed with himself. He'd only just got back from his lunch and chat with Pete, and had just about made up his mind to do something in the evening – some propitiatory gesture in the direction of *having a life*, like phoning his sister Lois (in Boulder, safely distant) or renting a movie – when his insecure phone rang. 'Mike? Deirdre here. Can you come

116

up to the meeting room, please? Eric would like a word with you.'
'Eric' – Colonel Smith – was one rung above him on the embryonic
org chart, and the colonel was more likely to give him a headache
than offer him a Tylenol. Odds were high that the phone call meant
he'd be working as late as usual tonight. *Bad cop, no life.* It was like
being on a homicide case twenty-four/seven.

The twenty-first floor had once been mahogany row, back when
these offices had belonged to a dot-bomb. FTO had leased them
cheap, from the sixth floor up. Everything below ten was a red zone –
at risk of enemy incursion. Mike's destination was the office meeting
room. It bore a red security seal, but there was no combination lock –
it was a meeting room, not a High Security Portal leading to an NSA-
style Vault Type Room. FTO didn't have enough secrets yet to fill a
bucket of warm spit, much less a multimillion-dollar bank vault in
the penthouse of an office block. It was a sign, in Mike's opinion, of
how badly the whole business was going. Or of how starved they were
for intelligence.

Mike hit the buzzer outside the door, next to the small CCTV lens.
'Mike Fleming, as requested. You wanted to see me?'

'Come in, Mike.' Smith normally tried to be friendly but sounded
unusually reserved today. Taking his cue, Mike straightened up as the
door opened.

Despite not being a full VTR, the meeting room was about as
friendly as Dracula's crypt – no windows, air-conditioning ducts and
ceiling and floor tiles made out of transparent Lexan so you could
check them visually for bugs, white-noise generators glommed
against every flat resonant surface to confound any bugging devices.
It hummed and whistled like an asthmatic air conditioner, mumbling
to itself incessantly to drown out any secrets the conferees might let
slip. Meetings in the crypt always sounded like a conference of deaf
folks: *Eh, what? Would you repeat that?*

Mike waited for Smith to unlock the door. Smith was in shirt-
sleeves, his collar undone and his tie loose. *Air conditioner must be
acting up again*, Mike thought before he registered the other man
sitting at the transparent table.

'What can I do for you, sir?' He glanced at the stranger, apprais-
ingly. *Red badge, purple stripe.* In the arcane color-coded NSA

hierarchy Smith had imported, that meant a visitor, but the kind of visitor who was allowed to ask pointed questions. 'Good afternoon,' Mike added, cautiously.

'Have a seat.' Smith dropped back into his own chair so Mike took his cue, settled at the other side of the table. The visitor was thin-faced, in his thirties or forties, and had a receding hairline. *Like Hugo Weaving in The Matrix*, Mike realized. Right down to the tie clip. That *had* to be deliberate. *An asshole, but a high-clearance asshole*, he thought irritably.

'Mike, this is Dr. Andrew James, from Yale by way of the Agency and the Heritage Foundation. Andrew, this is Senior Agent Mike Fleming, DEA, on secondment to FTO. So you know where you stand, Mike, Dr. James is our new Deputy Director of Operational Intelligence, which is to say, he's going to be running our side of the show once we achieve some organizational focus.' His cheek twitched. 'Any questions?'

'I'm very pleased to meet you, sir,' Mike said politely, trying to keep his face impassive. *Another fucking spook*. 'Spook' spelled 'cowboy', as far as Mike was concerned. They tended to know nothing about law enforcement, and care less. Which said something unpleasant about the direction this meeting was going to go in.

'I'm sure you're pleased.' James had a dry, gravelly voice. 'I know what you're thinking.' He didn't smile. He didn't frown. *He looks like a robot*, Mike thought. He rubbed his palms on his trousers, abruptly uneasy.

'You're dead right,' James continued. 'I *am* a political appointee. I'm here because certain parties in the administration want to keep a tight lock on the operational cycle of the Family Trade Organization and ensure it doesn't run wild. You're currently stovepiped into NSA and DEA, but that's got to change. We're keeping the DOJ connection, but it's been decided that the operational emphasis in the organization is going to be moved toward the military side. So my public title is Deputy Director, Political-Military Affairs, reporting to NSC. In reality, I'm going to be moving into your turf here as your DD/OI, liaising with NSC and the White House to keep them apprised of whatever you HUMINT guys can get out of our assets, and also to keep Justice in the loop. Are we clear, yet?' He cracked a wintry smile.

Mike glanced at Smith, registering his close-faced expression. *This is not good.* 'Not entirely, sir,' he said slowly, trying to get his thoughts in order. 'I understand the oversight aspect. But am I right in saying that you see this as primarily a national security problem, rather than a domestic policing one?'

'Yes.' James laid his hands flat on the tabletop, fingers spread wide across it. 'We will be emphasizing national security approaches. These – this "Clan" – is an external threat. They've got nuclear material, and the narcoterrorism angle is, in our view – that is, the strategic view received from the top down – of subsidiary importance to the question of whether a hostile power is going to start blowing up our cities.'

'Am I still needed?' Mike asked bluntly, a disturbing sense of helpless anger stealing over him. 'Or did you call me up here to re-assign me?'

James smiled again, like a shark circling wounded prey in the water. 'Not exactly. Colonel Smith tells me that in the eighty-one days since this organization got off the ground, the organization has laid its hands on just one willing HUMINT asset, and he's of questionable worth. You've been tasked with interrogating him, because you were his first contact. I find that kind of hard to believe – can you sum-marize for me?'

Mike felt his pulse quicken. *Smith set me up.* He glanced at his boss, who narrowed his eyes and shook his head infinitesimally. *No?* Then it was James. Spook tactics. Double-check everyone against everyone else, trust nobody, grab the situation by the throat – *hang on.* 'Can you confirm your clearances for me? No offense, but so far all I've got to go on is your word.' He nodded at Smith. 'Standard pro-tocol.' Standard protocol was trust nobody, accept nothing, and it was supposed to apply at all levels – which was why Swann checked Mike's ID and clearances every morning before giving him the keys to his own office. He tensed: if James wanted to make an issue of it –

But instead he nodded agreeably. 'Very good, Mr. Fleming. Badge reader over there.' He stood up and walked over to the machine. 'Why don't you clear yourself to me, at the same time?'

'I think that would be a very good idea, sir,' Mike said carefully. They both ran their badges through the scanner, and Mike noted James's list of clearances. It was about a third longer than his own. 'Great, I'm allowed to tell you that you exist.' He smiled, experimentally, and James nodded as he returned to his seat.

Mike took a deep breath. *Okay, so he's not a total jerk. I can live with that.* 'We do indeed have a problem with intelligence assets,' he began. 'So far all we've got is one willing defector and two prisoners. The defector, as usual, is willing to tell us one hundred and fifty percent of whatever he thinks we want to hear. And the prisoners not only aren't talking, I don't think they *can* talk.'

James grunted as if he'd been punched in the gut. 'Explain.' He held up one hand: 'I've read the backgrounder and played the debrief tapes from Matt. Color me an interested ignoramus and give it to me straight, I don't have time for excuses. Pretend I'm Daddy Warbucks, if you like. That's where this buck stops.'

'Uh, okay.' Mike sat down again, head whirling. *The Office of the Vice President? He's in charge, now?* Notoriously strong-willed, the VP in this administration more than made up for any lack of experience in the Oval Office. But this was still news to Mike. *Later.*

He cleared his throat. 'We got a windfall in the form of Matt. Without him, FTO wouldn't exist. We'd still be looking at eight to ten gigabucks of H and C per annum transshipping into the east coast with no clue how it was getting past the Coast Guard. We're still probably looking at half that, but for now – ' He shrugged. 'First thing first, Matt is probably the most valuable informer any American police or security department has acquired, ever.'

He swallowed. 'But we hit a concrete wall in the follow-through stage.'

'Concrete.' James made a steeple of his fingers, elbows braced on the transparent tabletop. 'What do you mean, concrete?'

'Okay. In our first week, Pete and I holed up with Matt and milked him like crazy. Apart from the side trip to the black box down in Crypto City, of course.' He nodded at Smith. 'By day six on the timeline we were ready to move. Thanks to the courier snatch on day two, the other side already knew we were active, so it wasn't much of a surprise when we rolled eight empty nests in a row. The haul was pretty good but the assets had flown, money and bodies and drugs. If you've seen the details of what we found' – James nodded – 'you'll know it was a very substantial operation. Disturbingly well structured. These guys are like a major espionage agency in their approach, sort of like the old-time KGB: organized in teams with secure communications and safe houses and an org chart. This isn't some street gang. But we didn't catch anyone. There's another raid going down today, as it happens, but I expect that one to draw a blank too. These guys are way too professional.'

James nodded, his expression thoughtful. 'Tell me about the two prisoners.'

'Well. Pete and I went back to Matt, who filled us in on the other side's security architecture. We put our heads together and took a stab, with Matt in the loop, at second-guessing how the other side's head, the Duke, would rearrange things in the light of Matt's disappearance. Matt said he'd arranged a cover that would make it look like he'd died, so we tried a few fallbacks on the working assumption that they hadn't twigged that Matt was in our pocket. We also hit another nine that we knew would be evacuated, in case they put two and two together about Matt. The decoys got the same treatment as the first wave of raids, but for the special targets we pulled strings to get some special assets in for the party.'

Mike leaned back. *Special assets* – the sort of people the CIA had been forbidden to deploy since the Church commission, the wake of Operation Phoenix, and the other deadly secrets from the sixties and early seventies. Guys with plastic-surgery fingerprints and briefcases full of very expensive custom-built toys. 'We drew a blank on one site, but number two had about sixty kilos of uncut heroin, plus a bunch of documents in Code Gamma. The third site, we hit pay dirt and three couriers. One of them died in the extraction process' – killed by fentanyl fumes, brain-dead before the special assets could hook her up to a ventilator – 'but the other two we bagged and tagged and shipped off to Facility Echo. Turns out there's no record of these guys anywhere – they're ghosts, they don't exist. Didn't even have any fake ID on them. I liaised with Special Agent Herz and we arranged a section 412 detention order. Because they're of no known nationality there's no one to deport them to, and once INS punches their ticket as illegal aliens we get to keep them out of the court system. Better than Camp X-Ray. Shame we can't get anything useful out of them,' he added apologetically.

James frowned. 'Why won't they talk?'

'Well, near as we can tell, they don't speak English.' Mike waited to see how James would react.

When it came, it was a minute nod. 'What about Spanish?'

'Nope.' Mike watched him minutely. No grasping at straws, no accusations of leg-pulling. *He's not so bad*, he thought grudgingly. *Not bad for a REMF spook*. 'We know about the tattoos, so we took precautions. Courier Able had a mirror tattoo on his head, under the hairline, and Courier Bravo had one on the inside of his left wrist. We kept them hooded and blindfolded until we had time to get a security-cleared cosmetologist with a laser in to erase them. But we're pretty sure that these guys don't speak English or Spanish – or French, German, Dutch, Portuguese, Italian, Greek, Russian, Czech, Serbo-Croat, Japanese, Latin, Korean, Mandarin, or Cantonese.' *And don't ask how we know* – the old fire drill trick could look very bad, very close to psychological torture, if a defense attorney dragged it up in front of a hostile jury. 'They *do* speak something Germanic, we got that much, and Matt checks out as a translator. They call it "Hochsprache", and it sounds like it diverged from various proto-German dialects about sixteen hundred years ago – it's about as similar to German as modern Spanish is to classical Latin.' He took another deep breath. 'I'm trying to learn it, but there's not much to go with – I mean, neither of the detainees are willing to help, and Matthias isn't exactly a foreign-language teacher. We're working on a lexicon, and we've got a couple of research linguists coming in as soon as we get their security clearances through, but it's a big problem. I figure these guys were drafted in as mules, shuttling back and forth between buildings in the same place in both worlds – what they call doppelgänger houses. To do that, they don't need to pass as Americans. But getting information out of them is difficult.'

Which is an understatement and a half, Mike added mentally. Matt was becoming a headache – increasingly demanding and sus-

picious, paranoid about the terms of his confinement and the likeli-
hood of his eventual release under a false identity. Sooner or later
he'd stop cooperating, and then they'd be in big trouble.

'Well, we are going to have a pressing need for that expertise in
the near future.' James sat up abruptly, as if he'd come to some decision. 'Mr. Fleming, I have some news for you which might sound
negative at first, so I hope you'll listen carefully and take it positively.
We have no functioning human intelligence assets at all in the place
they come from. Just like the situation in Afghanistan back in 2001 –
and we can't afford to be flying blind. I've been reviewing your
personnel file and, bluntly, you're nothing exceptional – except that
you've got a three-month lead over everyone else in the field in this
one area of expertise. So, with immediate effect I'm directing Colonel
Smith here to reassign you from Investigations Branch to a new core
team – on-location HUMINT. And your prisoner is going to be re-
assigned to military custody, although for the time being he'll stay
where he is.'

'Military custody?' Mike raised an eyebrow. 'I'm not sure that's
legal.'

'It will be when the AG's office delivers their ruling,' James said
dismissively. 'As I was about to say, you will continue to work on language skills and continue debriefing Matthias, and liaise with
Investigations Branch as necessary – but you're also going to go back
to school. Field operations school, to be precise. You're going to ride
shotgun on a code word operation you haven't heard of before now,
code word CLEANSWEEP, and you have BLUESKY clearance. Your
primary job will be to learn who these people are and how they think,
and their language and customs, and anything else that lets us get a
handle on their minds. And you're going to learn them well enough to
learn how to move among them undetected. Do you understand me?'

'Yes, I think I do.' Mike's mouth was dry. *So they're taking this
military?* 'You're asking for a spy. Right?' *Can they do this? Legally?*
He had a feeling that any objections he raised would be steamrolled.
And expressing them in the first place might be rather dangerous.

'Not just a simple spy.' James nodded thoughtfully. 'You're going
to be recruiting, training, and running other officers, in a way that we

haven't really been good at since the Cold War. Over the past couple of decades we've come to rely too heavily on electronic intelligence sources – no offense,' he added in Smith's direction, 'and we just can't operate that way in fairyland. So you're going to go in and run our field operation. We're going in – we're going over *there*, carrying the war to the enemy. That is the mission we are tasked with, from the top down. Got that?'

'It's a lot to take in,' Mike said slowly. His head was spinning. *What the hell? It sounds like he's planning an invasion!* 'You mentioned some kind of special clearances, projects? Uh, CLEANSWEEP? BLUESKY?'

James nodded to Smith. 'You tell him.'

Smith sat up. 'The, uh, Clan pose a clear and present danger to the integrity of the United States of America,' he said quietly. 'In fact, it's not overdramatizing things too much to say that they're a rogue state. So word is that we're to prepare, if possible, for a situation in which we can go in to, ah, impose a change of regime. BLUESKY is the intelligence enabler and CLEANSWEEP is the project to conduct espionage operations in hostile territory.'

'All of this assumes we can reliably send spies into a parallel universe and bring them back again,' Mike said quietly. 'How would we do that?'

Dr. James glanced at Colonel Smith. 'You were right about him,' he murmured. To Mike: 'You aren't cleared for that yet. Let's just say that we've got some long-term ideas, research projects under way. But for the time being' – he smiled at Mike, a frighteningly intense expression that revealed more teeth than a human being ought by rights to have – 'we've got two enemy couriers, and they *will* work for us, whether they want to or not. We'll use them to capture more. And then we'll make those fuckers sorry they ever messed with the United States.'

REPRODUCTIVE POLITICS

It was a shaken, thoughtful Miriam who followed the coach attendant and the other passengers in her car up to the dining carriage. Some of them had dressed for dinner, but Miriam found she wasn't too out of place once she shed the jacket: a lucky break, for she hadn't been paying enough attention to maintaining her cover. As with the Gruinmarkt, issues of public etiquette frequently baffled her – it was easy to get things wrong, especially when she was worrying about other matters. *What on earth is going on with that report? What does it mean?* she wondered as the attendant ushered her into a seat between a ruddy-faced grandmother and her bouncing ten-year-old charge, evidently out of some misplaced concern for her solitary status. *I'm being trolled. That's the only explanation that makes sense. Someone* expected *me to look in the bag* –

'Marissa! Fold your hands and stop playing with your fork. I'm sorry, travel makes her unmanageable,' the grandmother blared at Miriam. 'Wouldn't you say so?'

Miriam smiled faintly, keeping a tight lid on her irritation at the interruption. 'I don't like to speak ill of people I hardly know.'

'That's all right, you know us now. Marissa, put that *down*! I'm Eleanor Crosby. You are . . . ?'

Trapped. 'I'm Gillian,' said Miriam, rolling out the cover identity Clan logistics had prepared for her. They'd warned her it should be used as little as possible: it wouldn't stand up to serious scrutiny. The steward was walking the length of the table with a tureen of soup balanced on one arm, ladling spoonfuls into bowls in time with the sway of the carriage. *I'm trying to think, so kindly shut up and stop bugging me.*

'Wonderful! You must be traveling to see your family? Where are you from, London or the south?'

'London,' said Miriam. As soon as the waiter was past her she picked up her spoon and started on her bowl. The onion soup might have tasted good if she hadn't burned her mouth on the first sip, but it was either tuck in now or deal with Mrs. Crosby's curiosity all the way to Dunedin. As it was, she had to remain alert for the entire meal, because little Marissa's every tic and twitch seemed to attract Eleanor's loud and very vocal ire. Her place setting was a battlefield, and Mrs. Crosby seemed unable to grasp the possibility that Miriam might not want to be induced to spill her life's story before a stranger. Which was doubly frustrating because right then Miriam would have been immensely grateful for someone to share her conundrum with – had it not been both a secret and a matter of life and death.

After the ordeal of dinner, Miriam returned to her compartment to discover that someone had been there while she'd been eating. One of the bench seats had been converted into a compact bunk bed. For a moment her pulse raced and she came close to panic, but the carpetbag was untouched, still innocently stuffed into the luggage rack above the door. She bolted the door and carefully lifted the bag down, intending to continue her search.

When she'd opened it before dinner, carefully checking the lock first, she'd discovered the bag didn't contain the cargo she'd expected: no neatly taped bags of white powder here. Instead, there was a layer of clothing – *her* clothing, a skirt and blouse and a change of underwear from her house in the Boston of this world. *Bastards!* She'd felt faint for a moment as she stared at it. *They set me up!* Then she calmed down slightly. What if the Constabulary pulled her in for questioning and looked in her bag? What would they find? Miriam puzzled for a while. *Surely they wouldn't waste a precious cargo run just to test a cover identity?* she asked herself. Which meant – ah. *This is meant to survive a search, isn't it?*

There were more items that smacked of misdirection in the bag: a small pouch of gold coin muffled inside the newssheet wrapping of an antique vase. That would buy her a hefty fine or a month in prison if they found it (*they* being the hypothetical police agents, searching everybody as they came off the train) and it would more than suffice to explain her nervousness. Then she'd come to the bottom of the bag and found the battered manila envelope with its puzzling contents, which she'd just had time to glance through before the cabin attendant knocked to tell her it was time for dinner.

Now she sat on the bunk, reopened the bag, and pulled out the envelope. It contained a manuscript, printed in blurry purplish ink on cheap paper in very small type, the pages torn and yellowed at the edges from too many fingers: *The Tyranny of Reason* by Jean-Paul Mavrides, whoever he was. It looked to her eyes like something smuggled out of the old Soviet Union – battered and beaten but blazingly angry, a condemnation of the divine right of kings and an assertion that only in a perfect democracy based on the common will of humanity could the common man free himself from his oppressors. 'Well, I wanted something to read,' she told herself mordantly, 'even if I wasn't looking at a seven-year stretch for possession of republican propaganda . . .'

She began to flick through it rapidly, pausing when she came to the real meat, which was embedded in it in neatly laser-printed sheets interleaved every ten pages or so. *Purloined letter.* She could see the setup now, in her mind's eye, and it was less obviously a set-up. They wouldn't be planning to shop her – not with a bunch of DESTROY BEFORE READING Clan security correspondence on her person. Even though it was likely that the arresting constables would simply log it as an item from the Banned List and pitch it straight into the station fireplace. So it *was* just a routine precaution, multiple layers of concealment for the letters. Which didn't help her much: with a few eye-catching exceptions they were mostly incomprehensible. She kept coming back to the letter from Dr. Darling to Angbard. *What the hell is a W* heterozygote?* she wondered. *This is significant. What is Angbard doing, messing around with a fertility clinic?* She could think of a number of explanations, none of them good –

There was a knock at the door.

Sudden panic gripped her. She shuddered and shoved the incriminating samizdat into the bag, her palms slippery with sweat. The train was moving. *If I have to try to get away –*

Another knock, this time quieter. Miriam paused, then let go of her left sleeve cuff with her right hand. The panic faded, but the adrenaline shock was still with her. She forced herself to take a deep breath and stand up, then shot the bolt back on the door. 'Yes?' she demanded.

'Are you a constabule?' asked the girl Marissa, staring up at her with wide eyes. 'Coz if so, I wants to know, when's you going to arrest my mam?'

'I am *not* –' Miriam stopped. 'Come in here.' The little girl moved as if to step back, but Miriam caught her wrist and tugged lightly. She didn't resist but came quietly, as if sleepwalking. She didn't seem to weigh anything. 'Sit down,' Miriam said, pointing at the bench seat opposite her bunk. She slid the door shut. 'Why do you think I'm going to arrest your mam?' *Her* mother? Miriam thought, aghast: she'd taken Mrs. Crosby for sixty, but she couldn't be much older than Miriam herself. She suddenly realized she was looming over the kid. *This can't be good.* She sat down on the bunk and tried to compose her features. 'I'm not going to arrest anyone, Marissa. Why, did you think I was a constable?'

Marissa nodded at her, looking slightly less frightened. 'You's look like the one as nicked my nuncle? You talk all posh-like, an' dress like a rozzer. An' you got that way of looking aroun' at people, like you's sizing them for a cage.'

Am I frightening the little children now? Miriam laughed nervously. 'I'm not a, a rozzer, girl.' *And what's her mother afraid of? Is that why she was grilling me over dinner?* 'But listen, it's not safe to go asking people if they're Polis. I mean, if they aren't it's rude, and if they are, you're telling them you're afraid. If you tell them you're frightened they'll ask *why* you're frightened, understand? So you don't do that, you just ignore them. Besides, if I was with the Polis, why would I tell you the truth?'

Miriam paused, aware she'd sawn off the logical branch her argument was sitting on: *Hope she doesn't spot it.* She stared at Marissa. Marissa had long, stringy hair lying heavy down her back and wore a smock that hadn't been laundered too recently. When she was older she'd probably have cheekbones to kill for, but right now she just looked starved and frightened. *She's about the age Rita would be – stop that.* Miriam hadn't seen Rita, her daughter, since she gave her up for adoption at the age of two days: Rita had been a minor personal disaster, an unplanned intrusion while Miriam was in med school, and the less remembered the better. 'Listen. I think you should go back to your mother – you didn't tell her you were coming here, did you?' A vigorously shaken head. 'Good. You don't tell her you came to see me because she'll worry. And she's got enough to worry about already, hasn't she?' *Traveling first-class, but her kid hasn't eaten much recently and her brother's been arrested?* Similarly vigorous nodding confirmed Miriam's suspicions. 'What did they arrest your uncle for?'

'Sedition,' Marissa said shyly.

For a moment Miriam felt light-headed with anger. 'Well.' She reached down into the bag and fumbled around, finding the vase and its decoy contents. She fumbled in it with clumsy fingers then brought out a small coin. 'Here, do you have somewhere to hide this?'

The kid looked baffled for a moment, made as if to push it away.

'What is it?'

'Mam said not to – '

'Ah.' Miriam paused for a moment. Take, and double-take: 'Marissa, what will your mam do if she finds out you've been to see me?'

The kid looked frightened. 'You wouldn't!'

'Take. This.' She pushed the coin into the girl's hand, folding the fingers around the buttery gleam of the royal groat – withdrawn from circulation a decade since to offset the liquidity crisis following the Persian war, now worth a hundred times its face value. 'Give it to your mam. Tell her the *truth*. You came to see me, to ask. I told you, you were silly and shouldn't ask those questions. Then I gave you this.' Marissa looked puzzled. 'Go on. Your mam won't thump you, not if you give her this. She'll sleep better, because a constable wouldn't do that.' *And maybe she'll be able to buy you some more meals,* Miriam added silently.

Marissa jerked, as if she'd suddenly awakened from a bad dream. 'Thank'y,' she gasped, then turned and scrabbled at the door. A moment later she was gone, darting off down the corridor.

Miriam shut and bolted the door again, then rubbed her

forehead. 'Bastards,' she muttered. There was an unhappy picture here: she could put any number of interpretations to it, a countless multitude of sad little just-so stories to explain the desperate women in the frame. A mother and her kid selling the house, selling the furniture, using their savings to get away by the first train available. The uncle on his way to a work camp – whether he was a real uncle or a live-in companion made no odds, such things were winked at but not admitted publicly – by way of a beating and interrogation in the cells. *Sedition.* It was a movable feast. It could mean reading the wrong books (like the one in her bag, Miriam realized uncomfortably), attending the wrong meetings, even being seen in the same bars as campaigners for a universal franchise. (They campaigned for the universal *male* franchise, mostly – votes for women or nonwhites were the province of wild-eyed dreamers.) *This is a police state, after all*, Miriam reminded herself. Back home in the United States, most people had an overly romantic view of what a monarchy – not the toothless, modern constitutional monarchies of Europe, but the original *l'état c'est moi* variety – was like. In reality, a monarchy was just a fancy name for a hereditary dictatorship, Miriam decided.

It was only later, lying awake in the stuffy darkness of her compartment, that Miriam's worries caught up with her. And by then it was too late to take back the coin (*What if the Clan counts the decoy cash?*) or to unopen the bag (*What if they're testing me again?*) or unread the peculiar memoranda (*What's a W* heterozygote?*) or even the samizdat tract by the executed French dissident Jean-Paul Mavrides.

*

The remainder of her outbound trip went uneventfully. Miriam turned out of bed at seven in the morning, forced down as much of a light breakfast as she could manage in the already oppressive heat, then alighted with her bag at Dunedin station. From there it was a brief cab ride to the safe house, an anonymous classical villa in the middle of a leafy suburb on the edge of the city center. She knocked on the door, and her contact ushered her into a basement room. Then he waited outside while she opened one of the two lockets she wore on a fine gold chain around her neck and focused on it.

The usual headache clamped around her head, making her feel breathless and sick. But she was back in the Gruinmarkt again – or rather, in an outpost in the middle of the Debatable Lands, the great interior void unclaimed by the eastern marcher states or the empire on the west coast. Three bored-looking men sat around a log table in the middle of the room, one dressed to play Davy Crockett and the other two in sharp suits and shades. It might have been a frontier cabin, except frontier cabins didn't come with kerosene heaters, shortwave radio sets, and a rack of Steyr assault rifles by the door.

'Courier route blue four, parcel sixteen,' Miriam said in her halting Hochsprache as she stepped off the taped transit area on the floor and planted her carpetbag on the table. Davy Crockett passed her a clipboard wordlessly, boredom clear on his face. Miriam signed off.

Sharp Suit Number One picked up her bag. 'Well, I'll be going,' he said, signing the board. Walking over to the far side of the room he pulled a gleaming metal suitcase off the top of a chest, then stuffed the entire carpetbag inside it. Back on the transit area he picked up the case, nodded at Davy Crockett, then at Miriam, and clicked his heels together. 'There's no place like home,' he intoned, staring into a niche in the wall that Miriam hadn't noticed before. Then he wasn't there anymore. *He didn't make a sound*, she realized, massaging her forehead: not that she'd ever paid much attention to other world-walkers in their comings and goings, but – *doesn't teleportation imply air displacement?*

'Would you like coffee? Or wine?' asked Sharp Suit Number Two.

'Uh, coffee is be good –' Miriam's Hochsprache broke down completely as she made it to the table. 'And ibuprofen.' She fanned herself with her hat. 'Is it always this hot here?'

'Stupid question.' At last Davy Crockett spoke. 'I've had a requisition for a portable air conditioner and solar power pack in for, oh, two years.'

Two years? Miriam quailed at the idea of being assigned to babysit a frontier safe house like this for any length of time.

'Still not enough hands for a game of poker,' Sharp Suit Number Two said regretfully. He blinked, slightly owlishly.

'The clock is ticking,' intoned Davy Crockett. 'Two hours.' He nodded at Miriam. 'When's your train?'

'Um. The return leaves just after four, so allow an hour to get to the station – '

'No problem.' He picked up his pack of cards, shuffled the deck, and began dealing some kind of a solitaire hand. 'We'll get you there.'

'Is there anything to do here?' Miriam asked.

'Play cards. Seriously, you don't go out that door unless the roof is on fire. Wouldn't like the company hereabouts, anyways, and you've got a train to catch in five hours.'

'Oh.' Miriam shifted uneasily on her chair.

'I'll tell them you've arrived,' said the stationmaster. He stood up heavily and shambled over to the shortwave set.

Sharp Suit Number Two fussed over the kerosene stove; presently he turned it down and returned to the table bearing a metal espresso pot. 'So,' he said, hunching his shoulders conspiratorially, 'what's it like, then?'

Miriam looked at him blankly. 'What's what like?'

'Over *there*. You know.' He waved at her, a gesture that took in everything she was wearing. 'Different, isn't it, to America? In Chicago you'd stand out like, oh, obvious.'

'Oh, *there*.' It was clearly going to be a long wait. 'Well, for starters, they don't have air-conditioning . . .'

*

The return journey went smoothly, with no troublesome signs of recognition. There were no unwelcome traveling companions, no desperate Marissa to spark Miriam's paranoia, and no delays. Miriam managed to keep her nimble fingers away from the courier bag, having remembered to pause in the railway station kiosk before departure and pick up a selection of newspapers and a cheap novel or two. The headlines, as always, perplexed and mystified her as she tried to make sense of them. *Comptroller-General Announces Four-Fifths per Gross Increase in Salt License Fee* – what on earth did that mean? Licensing *salt*? And there was more inside. *Sky Navy to Impress Packets* just about made sense, but when she got to the sports pages

(*Chicxulub Aztecs versus Eton Barbarians: Goal Scored!*) it turned baffling. Not only did they not play football or baseball, they didn't even play soccer or cricket: instead they had other esoteric team games – like the Aztecs versus Barbarians wall ball match, in which the Aztecs had apparently just scored the first goal in a major league match for fourteen years.

A day on a train gave Miriam a lot of time for thought. *I need bargaining power,* she concluded. *Otherwise they're going to keep me on a short leash forever. And sooner or later they'll get serious about marrying me off.* Serried ranks of W* heterozygote babies line-danced in her imagination when she closed her eyes and tried to sleep. *How did I get into this bind?*

Asking herself that question was pointless: if she pursued the answer far enough, she came to the uncomfortable conclusion that it was her own fault: her dogged tendency to dig for the truth had gotten her into the Clan's business. (And behind that story lay Iris's shady history, her mother's attempt to escape from an unhappy Clan-decreed dynastic marriage – but some subjects were best treated with kid gloves.) *If I want some personal space I'm going to have to manufacture it for myself.* But persuading her distant relatives to back off was not easy: privacy seemed to be in scant supply outside the United States. Especially if you harbored valuable genes or looked like your mere presence might upset the established order. And as to just *why* privacy was in short supply . . .

By the time she reached the safe house in the New London suburbs she was feeling tired, irritable, and increasingly itchy and dirty. She'd been in transit for three days, and the trains didn't have so much as a shower on board. *Next time I'll take an extra change of clothes,* she resolved – this kind of issue obviously didn't affect the Clan courier operations in the United States.

When she signed off the courier bag, Miriam got her first surprise: a coach was waiting for her in the courtyard of Lord Brunvig's town house, and Brill beside it, in an agony of impatience. 'Milady! It's almost two o'clock! Quick, we must get you back to your rooms immediately, there's barely time.'

'Time? For what?' Miriam asked, pausing on the bottom step of the boarding platform with a sense of exquisite dread. *Oh no –*

'The royal entertainment! It's tonight! Oh, Miriam, if I had *realized* it would take you three days I would have yelled at his lordship – '

'Well, none of us thought of it, did we?' Miriam said as she climbed into the carriage. 'Everything happens more slowly over there.' She gritted her teeth and settled down into a corner, her nose wrinkling. *It's unavoidable*, she thought to herself. *I really* am *going to have to answer him*. The question the king himself had asked her, nearly six months ago. Brill, sitting opposite her, looked anxious. 'Do I have time to clean up first?' Miriam asked. 'And a bite to eat?'

'I hope so – '

'Well, then it'll all work out.' Miriam managed a tired smile. 'So how about telling me what's been going on while I've been away?'

Three hours later she was still hungry, even more tired, and back in the carriage with Brill. This time they were on their way to the summer palace with an escort of mounted guards, clutching scented kerchiefs to their faces to keep the worst of the stench of the open sewers at bay. *A fortune in jewelry, the most expensive luxurious clothes they can afford to impress one another with, but the drains are medieval: typical Clan priorities*. Miriam shrugged, trying to get comfortable against the hard seat back. Her maids had squeezed her into the most excessive gown she'd ever set eyes on. It seemed to weigh half a ton even before they'd added a tiara and a few pounds of gold and pearls. It was uncomfortably tight, and the layered skirts had a train that dragged along the ground behind her in a foam of lace and got in the way when she walked. *Romantic and feminine be damned, I'm going to be lucky to make it as far as the front door without tripping*. Brill had been saying something. 'What was that?' she asked, distracted.

'I was saying, did you want the high points again?' Brill sniffed pointedly. 'I know you're tired, but it's important.'

'I know it's important,' Miriam said sharply. 'Forgive me. Not your fault.' *These formal events always seem to bring out the worst in me, don't they?* 'This gown needs adjusting. I'm uncomfortable – and a bit tired.'

'I'll arrange another session with Mistress Tanzig when we get back, milady. For tomorrow. I hope you won't hold it against her – it's hard to get the cut right when your ladyship's absent.' Brill leaned forward to peer at her. 'Hmm. You're being Miriam, Miriam. A word of commendation?'

'Uh, yes?'

'Try to be Helge. For tonight, just for tonight.'

'But I –' She bit her tongue as she saw Brilliana's expression.

'You don't like being Helge,' Brill said. 'It's not as if you go out of your way to conceal it. But just this once –' Her eyes narrowed, calculatingly, as she fanned herself. 'Milady, Miriam is too *American*. Prickly about the wrong things. But this isn't a crowded garden party, this is an intimate informal household entertainment, just us and fifty or sixty family members and courtiers and ministers. If Miriam offers offense . . .'

'I . . . I'll try.' Helge fanned herself weakly in the warm, clammy air and tried to relax. 'I'll try to be me. For the evening.'

'That's perfect!' Brilliana smiled. 'Now, the high points. You've met his royal highness, the princes Egon and Creon, and the Queen Mother. But this evening you're also likely to encounter his grace the Prince of Eijnmyrk and his wife, Princess Ikarie – his majesty's youngest sister – and the Duke du Tostvijk. Main thing to remember is that his grace the prince's marriage is what you would term morganatic. Then there are the high ministers and his holiness the Autonomé du Roma, high priest of Lightning Child . . .'

*

An intimate informal household entertainment – by the standards of the social world of the Niejwein aristocracy it was, indeed, uncomfortably small. Helge was introduced to one smiling face after another, assessed like a prize brood mare, forced to make small talk in her halting Hochsprache, and stared at in mild disbelief, like a counting pig. At the end of it all her head was spinning with the effort of trying to remember who everybody was and how she was meant to address them. And then the moment she'd been secretly dreading arrived: 'Ah, how charmed we are to see you again,' said the short, portly fellow with the rosy bloom of broken blood vessels around his nose and the dauntingly heavy gold chain draped around his shoulders. He swayed slightly as if tired or slightly drunk. Helge managed to curtsey before him without saying anything. 'Been what, half a year?'

Helge nodded, not trusting herself to speak. Last time they'd met he'd made her an offer which, in all probability, had been kindly meant.

'Walk with us,' said His Royal Highness Alexis Nicholau III, in a tone of such supreme self-confidence that refusal seemed inconceivable.

There was a state dining room beyond the doors at the end of the gallery, but Alexis drifted slowly toward a side door instead. Two lords or captains or bodyguards of rank followed discreetly, while a third slipped ahead to open the door. 'Haven't seen much of you at court, these past six months,' remarked the king. 'Pressure of *work*, we understand.' He rubbed the side of his nose morosely, then glanced at the nearest guard. 'Glass of sack for the lady, Hildt.' The guard vanished. 'We hear a bit about you from our man Henryk. Nothing too outrageous.' He looked amused about something – amused, and determined.

Helge quailed inside. King Alexis might be plump, short, and drunk, but he was the *king*. 'What can I do for your majesty?' she managed to ask.

'It's been six months.' The guard returned, extended a glass of amber fortified wine for the king – and, an afterthought, a smaller fluted glass for Helge. 'Just about any situation can change in six months, don't you know. Back then I said you were too old. Seems *everyone* is too old these days, or otherwise unsuitable, or married.' He raised an eyebrow at her. 'Wouldn't do to marry a young maid to the Idiot – come now, do you think I don't know what my own subjects call my youngest son?'

'I've never met the . . . uh, met Creon,' Helge said carefully. 'At least, not to talk to. Is he, really?' She'd seen him before, at court. Prince Creon took after his father in looks, except that his father didn't drool on his collar. 'My duties kept me away from court so much that I know too little – I mean to cause no offense – '

'Of course he's an idiot,' Alexis said grimly. 'And the worst is, he need not have been. A tragedy of birth gifted him with a condition called, by the Clan's doctors, PKU. We knew this, for our loyal subjects render their services to the crown without stint. One can live with it, we are told, without problems, if one restricts the diet carefully.'

Aspartame poisoning? For a moment Helge was fully Miriam. Miriam, who had completed pre-med before switching educational tracks. She knew enough about hereditary diseases – of which phenylketonuria was quite a common one – to guess the rest of the story. 'Someone in the kitchen added a sweetener to his diet while he was an infant?' she hazarded.

'Oh yes,' breathed the king, and for an instant Miriam caught a flicker of the rage bottled up behind his calm facade. She suppressed a flinch. 'By the time the plot was exposed he waś . . . as you see. Ruined. And the irony of it is, *he* is the one who inherited his grandmother's trait. My wife' – for a moment the closed look returned – 'never learned this. She died not long after, heartbroken. And now the doctors have discovered a way of knowing, and they say Creon is a carrier while my golden boy, my Egon – is not.'

'How can they tell?' Helge asked artlessly, then concealed her expression with her glass.

'In the past year, they have developed a new blood test.' Alexis was watching her expression, she realized, and felt her cheeks flush. 'They can tell which child born of a world-walker and an – a, another – inherit the trait, and which do not. Creon is, the duke your uncle tells me, a carrier. His children, by a wife from the Clan, would be world-walkers. And unless the doctors conspire to make it so, they would not inherit his condition.'

'I – understand,' Helge managed, almost stammering with embarrassment. *How do I talk my way out of this?* she asked herself, with growing horror. *I can't tell* the king *to fuck off – how much does he know about me? Does he know about Ben and Rita?* Ben, her exhusband, and Rita, her adopted-out daughter. Not to mention the other boyfriends she'd had since Ben, up to and including Roland. *Would that work? Don't royal brides have to be virgins or something, or is that only for the crown prince?* 'It must be a dilemma for you.'

'You have become a matter of some small interest to us,' Alexis said as he took her elbow and gently steered her, unresisting, back toward the door and the dinner party. 'Pray sit at my left side and delight me with inconsequentialities over supper. You need not worry about Mother, she won't trouble you tonight with her schemes. You have plenty of time to consider how to help us with our little headache. And think,' the king added quietly, as the door opened before them and everybody turned to bow or curtsey to him, 'of the leverage that being a princess would bring you.'

INTERNMENT

It had been twelve weeks, and Matt was already getting stir-crazy.

'I'm bored,' he announced from the sofa at the far side of the room. He looked moody, as well he might. 'You keep me down here for weeks, months – no news! I hear no things about how my case is progressing, just endless questions, "what is this" and "what is that". And now this dictionary! What is a man to do?'

'I feel your pain.' Mike frowned. *Has it only been twelve weeks?* That was how long they'd been holding Matt. For the first couple of weeks they'd kept him in a DEA safe house, but then they'd transferred him here – to a windowless apartment hastily assembled in the middle of an EMCON cell occupying the top floor of a rented office block. Matt's world had narrowed until it consisted of an efficiency filled with blandly corporate Sears-catalog furniture, home electronics from Costco, and soft furnishings and kitchenware from IKEA. A prison cell, but a comfortably furnished one.

Smith had been quite insistent on the prisoner's isolation; there wasn't even a television in the apartment, just a flat-screen DVD player and a library of disks. A team of decorators from spook central had wallpapered the rooms outside the apartment with fine copper mesh: there were guards on the elevator bank. The kitchenette had a microwave oven, a freezer with a dozen flavors of ready meal, and plastic cutlery in case the prisoner tried to kill himself. Nobody wanted to take any chances with Matthias.

Not that he was being treated like a prisoner – not like the two couriers in the deep sub-basement cell who lived like moles, seeing daylight only when Dr. James's BLUESKY spooks needed them for their experiments. But Matt wasn't a world-walker. Matt could tell Mike everything Mike wanted to know, but he couldn't take him *there*. As Pete Garfinkle had crudely put it, it was like the difference between a pre-op transsexual and a ten-buck crack whore: Matt just didn't have the equipment to give FTO what they wanted.

'Listen, I'd like to get you somewhere better to live, a bit more freedom. A chance to get out and move about. But we're really up in the air here. We don't have closure; we need to be able to question any Clan members we get our hands on ourselves. So my boss is on me to keep pumping you until we've got a basic grammar and lexicon so if anything happens to you – say you had a heart attack tomorrow – we wouldn't be up shit creek.'

'Stop bullshitting me.' Matthias had been staring at the fake window in the corner of the room. (Curtains covering a sheet of glass in front of a photograph of the cityscape outside.) Now he turned back to Mike, clearly annoyed. 'You do not trust me to act as interpreter, is all. Am I right?'

Mike took a deep breath, nodded. 'My boss,' he said, almost apologetically. And to some extent it was true; never mind Colonel Smith, the REMF – James – acted like he didn't trust his own wrist watch to give him the time of day. And *he* reported to Mr. Vice-President Cheney by way of the NSC – and Mike had heard all about that guy. 'Using you as an interpreter would risk exposing you to classified information. He's very security-conscious.'

'As he should be.' Matthias snorted exasperatedly. 'All right, I'll work on your stupid dictionary. When are we going to start creating my new identity?'

'New identity?' Mike did a double take.

'Yah, the Witness Protection Scheme *does* try to provide the new identity, doesn't it?'

'Oh.' Mike stared at him. 'The Witness Protection Program is administered by the Department of Justice. This isn't a DOJ operation anymore, it got taken off us – I was seconded because I was already involved. Didn't you know?'

Matthias frowned. 'Who owns it?' he demanded. 'The military?' Mike forced himself not to reply. After a moment Matt inclined his head fractionally. 'I see,' he murmured.

Mike licked his suddenly dry lips. *Did I just make a mistake?* 'You don't need to worry about that,' he said. 'Nothing has changed.'

'All right.' Matt sat down again. He sent Mike a look that clearly said, *I don't believe you.*

Mike rubbed his hands together and tried to change the subject. 'What would happen if – say – you were a world-walker, and you tried to cross over while you were up here?' he asked.

'I'd fall.' Matt glanced at the floor. 'How high . . . ?'

'Twenty-fourth floor.' The set of Matt's shoulders relaxed imperceptibly. Mike had no problem reading the gesture: *I'm safe from them, here.*

'Would you always fall?' Mike persisted.

'Well – not if there was a mountain on the other side.' Matt nodded thoughtfully. 'Might be doppelgängered with a tower, in which case he'd get a bad headache and go nowhere. Or the world-walker might be lying down, in contact with a solid object – go nowhere then, too.'

'Do you know if anyone has ever tried to world-walk from inside an aircraft?' Mike asked.

Matt laughed raucously.

'What's so funny?' Mike demanded.

'You Americans! You're so crazy!' Matthias rubbed his eyes. 'Listen. The Clan, they *know* if you world-walk from high up you fall down, yes? Planes are no different. Now, a parachute – you could live, true. But where would you land? In the Gruinmarkt or Nordmarkt or the Debatable Lands, hundreds of miles away! The world is a huge and dangerous place, when you have to walk everywhere.'

'Ah.' Mike nodded. 'Has anyone ever world-walked from inside a moving automobile?' he asked.

'That would be suicidal.'

'Even if the person were wearing chain mail? Metal armor?' Mike persisted.

'Well, maybe they'd survive . . .' Matt stared at him. 'So what?'

'Hmm.' Mike made a mental note. Okay, that was two more of the checklist items checked off. He had a long list of queries to raise with Matt, questions about field effects and conductive boundaries and just about anything else that might be useful to the geeks who were busting their brains to figure out how world-walking worked. *Now to change the subject before he figures out what I'm looking for.* 'What happens if someone world-walks while holding a handcart?'

'Everyone knows handcarts don't work,' Matt said dismissively.

'Okay. So it really is down to whatever a world-walker can carry, then? How many trips per day?'

'Well.' Matt paused. 'The standard corvée duty owed to the Clan by adult world-walkers requires ten trips in five days, then two days off, and is repeated for a whole month, then a month off. So that would be one hundred and twenty return trips per year, carrying perhaps fifty kilograms for a woman, eighty to a hundred for a man. More trips for professional couriers, time off for pregnant women, but it averages out.'

'There's an implicit "but" there,' Mike prodded.

'Yes. Women in late pregnancy with a child that will itself be a world-walker cannot world-walk at all. Or if they try, the consequences are not pretty. But anyway: the timing of the corvée is *negotiated*. To a Clan member, the act of world-walking is painful. Do it once, they suffer a headache; twice in rapid succession and a hangover with vomiting is not unusual. Thrice – they won't do it three times, unless in fear of life and limb. There are drugs they can take, to reduce the blood pressure and swaddle the pain, but they are of limited effectiveness. Four trips in eight hours, with drugs, is punishing. I have seen it myself, strong couriers reduced to cripples. If used to destruction, you might force as many as ten crossings in a period of twenty-four hours; but likely you would kill the world-walker, or put them in bed for a month.'

'So.' Mike doodled a note on his paper pad. 'It *might* be possible for a strong male courier, with meds, to move, say, five hundred kilograms in a day. But a more reasonable upper limit is two hundred kilograms. And the load must be divided evenly into sections that one person can carry.'

Matthias nodded. 'That's it.'

'Hmm.' *An SADM demolition nuke weighs about fifty kilos, but no way has the Clan got one of them*, Mike told himself, mentally crossing his fingers. They'd all been retired years ago. If the thin white duke was going to do anything with his nuclear stockpile, it would probably be a crude bomb, one that would weigh half a ton or more and require considerable assembly on site. There was no risk of a backpack nuclear raid on 1600 Pennsylvania Avenue, then. Good. *Still, if James's mules are limited like that, we won't be able to do much more than send a couple of spies over, will we?*

'Okay, so no pregnant couriers, eh? What do the Clan's women do when they're pregnant? I gather things are a bit basic over there; if they can't world-walk, does that mean you have doctors –' Mike's pager buzzed. 'Hang on a minute.' He stood up. There was an access point in the EMCON-insulated room. He read the pager's display, frowning. 'I've got to go. Back soon.'

'About the military –' Matthias was on his feet.

'I *said* I'll be back,' Mike snapped, hurrying toward the vestibule. 'Just got to take a call.' He paused in front of the camera as the inner door slid shut, so the guard could get a good look at him. 'Why don't you work on the dictionary for a bit? I'll be back soon as I can.'

*

One of the guards outside Matt's room had a Secure Field Voice Terminal. Mike took it, ducked into the Post-Debriefing Office, plugged it into one of the red-painted wall sockets, and signed on to his voice mail. *The joy of working for spooks*, he thought gloomily. Back at DEA Boston, he'd just have picked up the phone and asked Irene, the senior receptionist, to put him through. No pissing around with encrypted Internet telephony and firewalls and paranoid INFOSEC audits in case the freakazoid hackers had figured out a way to hack in. Sometimes he wondered what he'd done to deserve being forced to work with these guys. 'Mike here. What is it?'

'We got the thumbs-up.' No preamble: it was Colonel Smith. 'BLUESKY has emplaced the cache and on that basis our NSC cutout has approved CLEANSWEEP and you are go for action.'

'Whoops.' Mike swallowed, his heart giving a lurch. 'Okay, what happens now?'

'Where are you?'

'I'm on the twenty-fourth – sorry, I'm in Facility Lambda. Just been talking to Client Zero.' More time-wasting code words to remember for something that was really quite straightforward.

'Well, that's nice to hear. Listen, I want you in my office soonest. We've got a lot to discuss.'

'Okay, will comply. See you soon.'

Smith hung up, and Mike shut down the SFVT carefully, going through the post-call sanitary checklist for practice. (A radiation-hardened pocket PC running some NSA-written software, the SFVT could make secure voice calls anywhere with a broadband Internet connection – as long as you scrubbed its little brains clean afterward to make sure it didn't remember any classified gossip, a chore that made Mike wish for the days of carrier pigeons.) 'Got to go,' he told the guard. 'If Matt asks, I got called away by my boss and I'll be back as soon as I can.'

He signed out through the retina scanners by the door, then waited for the armed guard in front of the elevator bank. Mike gestured at one of the doors. 'Get me the twenty-second.' The guard nodded and pushed the call button. He'd already signed Mike in, knew his clearances, and knew what floors he was allowed to visit. A minute later the elevator car arrived and Mike went inside. It could have been the elevator in any other office block, except for the cameras in each corner, the call buttons covered by a crudely welded metal sheet, and the emergency hatch that was padlocked shut on the outside. *No escape*, that was the message it was meant to send. *No entry. High security. No alternative points of view.*

Mike found Smith in his office, a cramped cubbyhole dominated by an unfeasibly large safe. Smith looked tired and aggravated and energized all at once. 'Mike! Grab a seat.' He was busy with something on his Secure Data Terminal – a desktop computer in NSA-speak – and turned the screen so that Mike couldn't see it from the visitor's chair. 'Help yourself to a Diet Coke.' There was a pallet-load of two-liter plastic bottles of soda just inside the door – it was Smith's major personal vice, and he swore it helped him think more clearly. 'I'm just finishing . . . up . . . this!' He switched the monitor off and shoved the keyboard away from him, then grinned triumphantly. 'We've got the green light.'

Mike nodded, trying to look duly appreciative. 'That's a big deal.' *How big?* Sometimes it was hard to be sure. Green light, red light –

when the whole program was black, unaccountable, and off the books, who knew what anything meant? 'Where do I come into it?' *I'm a cop, dammit, not some kind of spook.*

Smith leaned back in his chair. With one hand he picked up an odd, knobby plastic gadget; with the other he pulled a string that seemed to vanish into its guts. It began to whirr as he rotated his wrist. 'You're going into fairyland.'

'Fairyland?'

'Where the bad guys come from. Official code name for Niejwein, as of now. Doc's little joke.' *Whirr, whirr.* 'How's the grammar?'

'I'm –' Mike licked his lips. 'I have no idea,' he admitted. 'I try to talk to Matt in Hochsprache, and I've got some grasp of the basics, but I have no idea how well I'll do over there until –' He shrugged. 'We need more people to talk to. When can I have access to the other prisoners?'

'Later.' *Whirr, whirr.* 'Thing is, right now they're our only transport system. Research has got some ideas, but there's a long way to go.'

'You're using them for transport? How?' Mike frowned.

'You're a cop. You wouldn't approve.'

I'm not going to like this. 'Why not?'

'The first army lawyers we tried had a nervous breakdown as soon as we got to the world-walking bit – does *posse comitatus* apply if it's geographically collocated with the continental USA? – but I figure the AG's office will get that straightened out soon enough. In the meantime, we got a temporary waiver via a signing order from the White House. If these guys want to act like a hostile foreign government, they can *be* one – it makes life easier all round. They're illegal combatants, and we can do what we like with them. There's even some question over whether they're *human* – being able to cross their eyes and think themselves into another universe is kind of unusual – but they're still working on that line of legal argumentation. Meanwhile, we've found a way to make them cooperate. *Battle Royale.*'

'What?'

Smith reached into one of his desk drawers and pulled something out. It looked like a giant padlock, big enough to go round a man's neck. 'Ever seen one of these?'

'Oh shit.' Mike stared, sick to his stomach. 'The Shining Path used them . . .'

'Yeah, well, it works for the good guys, too.' Smith put the collar-bomb down. 'We put one on a prisoner. Set it for three hours, give him a backpack and a camera, and tell him to bury the backpack in the other world, photograph the location, then come back so we can take the collar off. We're careful to use a location at least five miles from the nearest habitation in fairyland, to stop 'em finding a tool shop. So far they've both come back.'

'That's –' Mike shook his head, at a loss for words. *Ruthless* sprang to mind. *Abuse of prisoners* wasn't far behind. Something about it crossed the line that divided business as usual from savagery.

'Before we sent them the first time, we showed them what happened when one of these suckers counts down. Trust me, we've got no intention of killing them unless they try to escape.' *Whirr, whirr.* 'But we can't risk them getting loose and telling the Clan what we're doing, can we?'

'Crazy.' Mike shook his head again. 'So you've got two tame couriers.'

'For very limited values of tame.'

'So.' Mike licked his dry lips.

The thing in Smith's rapidly swiveling hand was now making a high-pitched whine. He caught Mike staring at it. 'Gyroball exerciser. You should try it, Mike. They're really good. I'm spending too much time with this damn computer mouse, if I don't exercise my wrist seizes up.'

Mike nodded jerkily. *What's going on?* Smith was serious-minded, committed, highly professional, and just a bit more paranoid than was good for anyone. The collar-bomb thing had to be a need-to-know secret. 'So why are you telling me this?'

'Because you're going to cross over piggyback on one of our mules before the end of the month, and once there you'll be staying for at least two weeks,' Smith said, so casually that Mike nearly choked.

'Jesus, Eric, don't you think you could give me some *warning* when you're going to spring something like that?' Mike paused. Since Dr. James's visit he'd known this was coming, sooner or later – but he'd been expecting more time. 'Look, the lexicon and dictionary aren't done yet, our linguists aren't through their in-processing, and Matt's not competent to work on it on his own. If something goes wrong while I'm on the other side and you lose Matt's cooperation as well, it'll seriously jeopardize my successor's ability to pick up the pieces. Anyway, don't I know too much? Last week I had a GS-12 telling me I'm not allowed to leave the country on vacation, I can't even go to fricken' *Tijuana*, and now you're talking about a hostile insertion and a theater assignment? I'm a cop, not James Bond!'

'Relax, Mike, it's all in hand. We've cut orders for some army linguists, they're already cleared. You don't need to know everything about the contingency planning that's going into this. More to the point, by the time you go out into the field you'll be far enough out of the core decision loop that even if the bad guys capture you, you won't be able to give them anything.'

'That's supposed to make me feel better? Listen, this is all ass-backward. We ought to be trying to arrest more couriers on this side before we even think about going over there. We can secure our own soil without engaging in some kind of insane adventure, surely?'

Smith shook his head slowly, clearly disappointed. 'You're still thinking like a cop. I'd be right with you, except we've got a big tactical security problem, son. We're not dealing with some Trashcan-istan where the State Department can make the local kleptocrats shit themselves just by sneezing: we're in the dark. We have zero assets, SIGINT is useless when the other guy's infrastructure is pony express . . . We're going to need to get intelligence on the ground, not to mention establishing a network of informers. We don't even know what local political tensions we can leverage. So we've got to put someone in charge on the ground with enough of an overview to know what's important – and the hat fits you.'

'You're talking about making me semi-autonomous,' Mike said, then licked his lips. 'What is this, back to the OSS?' He was referring to the almost legendary Second World War agency – the predecessor to the CIA – and the cowboy stunts that had led to its postwar shutdown.

'Not entirely.' Smith looked serious. 'And yes, you're right.

Normally we wouldn't let someone like you loose in the field, much less with the degree of autonomous authority this job implies. It's against doctrine. But you're on the inside, you're one of our local language and custom experts, and you can hand Matt over to someone else – '

'But I can't! Not if we want to preserve his cooperation and keep getting useful stuff out of him. He's a key witness – '

'He's not a witness,' Smith said quietly. 'You forget he's an unlawful combatant. He's just one who's chosen to cooperate with us, and we're giving him the kid-glove treatment because of that. For now.'

'He's enrolled in the Witness Protection Program,' Mike persisted. 'Meaning he's on the books, unlike your two mules. There's no need to treat this like Afghanistan; we can crack the Clan over here by handling it as an enforcement problem.'

'Wrong. If you go digging you'll find that Source Greensleeves has vanished from the DEA evidence trail and the WPP. Look, you're looking at this with your cop head on, not your national security head. The Clan are a geopolitical nightmare. All our conventional bases are insecure: they're designed on the assumption that security is about keeping bad guys at arm's length – except now we're facing a threat that can close the distance undetected. It's like a human stealth technology. Nor are our traditional allies going to be worth a warm bucket of spit. Firstly, they don't know what we're up against, and if they did, they'd be up against their own private insurgencies as well. Secondly, they're positioned badly – we can't use 'em for basing, they can't use us, the normal rules don't apply. And then it gets worse. Imagine what al-Qaeda could do to us if they could hire these freaks for transport. Or North Korea?'

'Oh.' Mike hunched his shoulders. *The spooks have legitimate fears*, he told himself. *But how do I know they're legitimate? How do I know they're not seeing things?* Then: *But what do we really know about the Clan? What makes them tick?*

'Some of those sneaky bastards we call allies would stab us in the back as soon as look at us,' said Smith, mistaking Mike's thoughtful silence for complicity. 'This isn't the Cold War anymore, and we're not up against godless communism, we're up against drug smugglers *sans frontières*. If you think the Dutch are going to be any use – '

Mike, who had been to Amsterdam on business a couple of times, and had a pretty good idea what the Dutch authorities would think about drug smugglers with a plutonium supply, held his silence. Smith's venting was just that – effusions born of the frustration of fighting an invisible foe with inadequate intelligence and insufficient reach. More to the point . . . *They've dragged me into their covert ops world*, he realized. *If I make a fuss, will they let me out again?*

'Phase one,' Mike said when Smith ran down. 'When does it kick off? What should I be doing?'

Smith scribbled a note on his yellow legal pad. 'I'll e-mail you the details, securely. First briefing is Tuesday, kickoff should be week after next. You'd better keep your overnight bag by your desk, and be prepared to relocate on my word.' He paused. 'In a couple of days you're going back to school, like Dr. James said. You'll be studying Spying 101. It'll be fun . . .'

*

Mike had been home for barely an hour when the entryphone rang.

Home wasn't somewhere he saw a lot of these days: since joining the magical mystery tour from spook central, his personal life had been patchy at best. From working the mostly regular hours of a cop – regular insofar as they varied wildly and he could be called out at odd times of day or night, but at least got shifts off to recover – he'd found himself putting in eighty- to hundred-hour weeks in one or another of the secure offices the Family Trade Organization had established. Helen the cleaner had taken Oscar in for a couple of weeks at one point, and the tomcat still hadn't forgiven him. That hurt; he and Oscar went back a long way together. Oscar had been with him before he'd been married to his ex-wife. Oscar had watched girlfriends come and go, then mostly had the place to himself since 9/11. But everyone had to make sacrifices during wartime – even elderly tomcats.

Mike had showered and unloaded the dishwasher and stuck a meal in the microwave, and he was working on a tin of pet food for Oscar (who was encouraging him by trying to trip him up) when the doorbell rang. 'Shit.' Mike put the can down. Oscar yowled reproachfully as he fumbled the handset of the entryphone. 'Yes?'

'Mike?' It was Pete Garfinkle. Pete had moved sideways into Monitoring and Surveillance lately. 'Mind if I come up?'

'Sure, be my guest.'

By the time Pete knocked on the apartment door, Oscar was head down in the chow and Mike was well into second thoughts. The microwave oven buzzed for attention just as the door rattled. 'Come on in. I was just about to eat – '

'S'okay.' Pete held up a plastic bag. 'I figured you wouldn't turn away a six-pack, and I hit Taco Bell on the way over.' The bag clinked as he planted it on the kitchen table.

Mike nodded. 'Grab a chair. Glasses in the top cupboard.'

'Glasses? We don't need no steenkin' glasses!'

Mike planted his dinner on a plate, still in the plastic container, and grabbed a fork and two glasses. 'Mm. Smells like . . . chicken.' He pulled a face. 'I've got a freezer-load of sweet 'n' sour chicken balls, can you believe it? The job lot was going cheap at Costco.'

'Lovely.' Pete eyed Mike's food warily, then twisted the cap off a bottle. 'Sam Adams good enough?'

'It'll go down nicely.' Mike started on his rice and chicken as Pete poured two bottles into their respective glasses. 'What's with the Taco Bell thing? I thought Nikki liked to cook.'

Pete shrugged sheepishly. 'Nikki likes to cook,' he said. '*Healthy* thing, y'know? Once in a while a man's got to do what a man's got to do, 'specially if it involves a barbecue and a slab of dead meat. And when it's not barbecue season, a dose of White Castle, or maybe Taco Bell . . .'

'I see.' Mike ate junk food out of necessity born of eighty-hour working weeks: Pete ate junk food because he needed a furtive vice and most of the ordinary ones would cost him his job. 'What's she doing?'

'It's her yoga class tonight.' Pete took a long mouthful of beer. 'Figured I'd come by and cheer you up. Chat about a little personal problem I've been having.'

Mike looked at him sharply. 'Beer first,' he suggested. 'Then let's take a hike.' Pete didn't *do* personal problems: he had what by Mike's envious standards looked like an ideal marriage. He especially didn't drop around co-workers' apartments to vent about things, which meant . . . 'Is it that thing we were talking about over lunch the other day?'

'Yeah. Yeah, I guess it is.' Pete managed to look furtive and scared over his beer glass, which put the wind up Mike even more. 'How's the beer?'

'Beer's fine.' Mike shunted his dinner aside and stood up. 'C'mon, let's go down the backyard and sit out. There's a couple of chairs down there.'

Outside, the air hit him like a freshly washed towel, heavy and hot and damp enough to make breathing hard for a moment. Mike waited until Pete cleared the doorway, bag of bottles in hand. 'Spill it.'

'Chairs first. You'd better be sitting down for this.'

Mike gestured at the tatty deck chairs on the rear stoop. 'How bad is it?'

'Bad enough.' Pete dropped into one of the chairs and handed Mike a bottle. 'Go on, sit down.'

Mike sat. 'I don't think anyone's listening here.'

'Indoors.' It was a statement, not a question.

'They lock everything down.' Mike popped the lid off the beer. 'Can't blame them for being suspicious of cops – we don't have that kind of home life.'

'Yeah, well.' Pete glanced up at the roof suspiciously, then shrugged. The rumble of traffic and the scritching of cicadas would make life hard for any eavesdroppers. 'I called Tony Vecchio up today.'

Mike sat bolt upright. 'Shit, man! Not from work – '

'Relax, I'm not that stupid.' Pete took another swig from his bottle.

Mike peered at him. He was obviously rattled. Maybe even as badly rattled as Mike was, in the wake of his little chat with Smith. *Explosive collars. What else is going on?* 'I'm not going to like this, am I?'

'I needed to ask some questions.' Pete looked uncomfortable. 'We've gone native, you know? Inside FTO, surrounded by the military and their national security obsession, we've stopped trying to do our jobs properly. I don't know about you, but I swore an oath to uphold the law – remember that? Anyway, I wanted to get some perspective. Tony knew about Matt because he was there when Matt came in, so I figured he'd help.'

'You wanted a priest to hear your confession.'

'Exactly.'

Mike sighed. 'Okay, so spill it.'

'Tony stonewalled!' Pete looked angry for a moment. 'First he said he didn't know anything. Then he told me that he'd never heard of Matt, that nobody of that name had come in, there were no WPP admissions this year. *Then* he told me I'd been suspended on full pay, medical disability in the line of work, for the past ten weeks, and he appreciated how I must feel! I mean, what the fuck?'

'Shit.' Mike tipped the last of his bottle down his throat, then leaned forward. 'You want to know what I think.'

'Yes?'

'Close call.' He wiped his forehead. 'Listen, what you did was *amazingly* stupid. If you'd asked me . . . shit. They've farmed us out to the military. We belong to Defense right now, we don't exist on personnel's books – I mean, I'll bet if you went digging you'd find that we've both been listed on medical leave ever since this thing started. And the paperwork on Matt will be a whitewash. He's a ghost, Pete, like the fuckers in Gitmo, bugs trapped in the machine. Have you met Dr. James yet?'

'James? Isn't he Smith's boss? The political one?'

'Yeah, him. I take it you haven't met . . . James is a Company man, all the way through. Works for the NSC, runs covert ops, the whole lot. That's who we're working for. And you know what happens to people who go outside official channels in CIA land? You just don't *do* that. I've been doing some reading in my copious spare time. You, me, we got sucked in because we were already on the edge of something very big and very classified and very black. Eric told me some, some stuff. About how the military perceive the national security implications of what we're up against. It made my hair stand on end. I think he's wrong about some – maybe most – of this, but I couldn't tell him that to his face. Now, I happen to think we ought to be treating this more like a policing problem, ought to be enforcing the law – but doesn't that sort of presuppose that we're dealing with criminals? What I'm hearing is that like Matt, they think we're dealing with another government, a rogue state, like North Korea or Cuba in the fifth dimension or something. And right now, they've won the argument. I don't see us getting any backup from Justice, Pete. If you start going behind their backs without evidence, they will stick it to you hard. But if we don't, who knows what kind of mess they're going to get us into?'

'Shit.' Pete stared at him.

'Drink.' Mike reached into the bag, thrust another bottle at Pete. 'Listen, we'll work on this together. Just keep an eye on what's going on, okay? Compare notes. Try to remember who we are and what kind of job we're supposed to be doing, so that if the spooks fuck up we'll be in the clear and able to carry on. Maybe talk to Judith, she's FBI, I think she'll see it our way. Form a, I guess, a Justice Department net-work.' He found he was waving his hands around helplessly. 'We're the underdogs right now. Defense grabbed the ball while our team's back was turned. But it's not going to last forever. And when we get an opportunity to make our case we need to be ready . . .'

TELEPHONY INTERCEPT TRANSCRIPT
LOGGED 18:47 04/06

'Hello, who's this?'

'Paulie?'

'Miriam – I mean, hi babe! Wow! It's been ages, I've been worrying
about you – '

'Yeah, well, there's been some heavy stuff going down. I take it you
heard – '

'How could I *not*? I'm, like, this side of things is completely firewalled
from, you know, your uncle's *other* business interests, but I've
been catching it from all sides. You were right about the shit
hitting the fan, then Brill turned up with her usual calm head on
and sorted most of it out, but they've been running me ragged

and I haven't heard *anything* from you, you could have written! So what's going on in fairyland?'

'Politics, I think. First they dragged me over there full time, then they wouldn't let me out of the gilded cage. I've been out of the loop so long: I mean, I'm frightened. Anyway, now I'm running some errands for them in New Britain they've eased up a bit. I get to cross over here and make phone calls, y'know, like prisoner's privileges? But that's all I can do right now, until they're sure nobody's made me. I'm officially in France, at least that's what the INS think. Anyway, I *am* going to get them to clear me so we can do lunch and start putting things back together, soon. Trust me on this, right? Tomorrow I've, well, I've managed to wangle a week in New London. I'm supposed to be moving carpetbags of confidential letters about, but I've figured out a better way. So I get to drop by the works and see who's holding it together, or not as the case may be, bang heads and kick ass, that kind of thing. Then let's do lunch, hey?'

'Sounds like a plan, babe.'

'Well, that's most of the plan, anyway. There *is* something else. Two somethings, actually. Tell me no if you don't want to get involved, okay?'

'Miriam, *would* I?'

'Just saying. Look, one of them's probably not an issue. I want you to round me up a prescription for a friend. Nothing illegal but he can't get to see a doctor – he's out of the country – so if you could order it from one of those dodgy Mexican websites and mail it to me I'd be ever so grateful.'

'Um, okay. If you say so. What's it you're wanting?'

'Um. Two packs of RIFINAH-300 antibiotic tablets, one hundred tabs per pack, not the small twenty-tablet bottles. They should only set you back a few bucks – it's dirt cheap, they use it all over the third world. As soon as you've got it, mail it to me via your, uh, contact. Family postal service should reach me soon enough.'

'Okay, I think I've got that, RIFINAH-300, a hundred tablets per pack, two packs. That it?'

'Well, there's the other thing. But that's the one I think you might want to punt on.'

'Hmm. Tell me, Miriam, okay? Let me make my own mind up?'

'Okay, it's this: I want all the information you can find – public stuff, company financials, profiles of directors, that sort of thing – on two companies. The first is the Gerstein Center for Reproductive Medicine, in Stony Brook. The second is an outfit called Applied Genomics Corporation. In particular I'm interested in any details you can find about financial transfers from Applied Genomics Corporation to the Gerstein Center – and especially about when they started.'

'Applied Genomics, eh? Is this – is this like our old friends at Proteome?'

'Yes, Paulie. That's why I said you could say no. Just walk away from it and pretend you never heard from me.'

'I couldn't do that.'

'Yeah, well, *couldn't* and *should* are – look, Paulie, I'm sticking my nose into something it's not supposed to be in again, and I don't want to get you burned. So the first order of the day is cover your ass. Don't do *anything* that might draw attention to yourself. Don't post the stuff to me or call me about it, that's why I'm using a pay phone. I'll come collect when we do lunch, and I don't mind if all you've got is their annual filings and disclosures.'

'What are they *doing*?'

'I – I'm not sure. But, uh, sometime in the past year my relatives have come up with a genetic test for, uh, the family headache. And I was wondering *how* they did that when this other thing, the connection with this fertility clinic, crawled out of the woodwork and bit me. Paulie, there's something – stuff about some kind of W-star genetic trait – that gives me an itchy feeling. The same itch I got when we were investigating that money-laundering scam that turned out to be – well. I think it might have something to do with why they're giving me the runaround, why I'm being pressured to . . .'

'Pressured to what?'

'Never mind. One thing at a time, huh? Look, I've got to go soon. And then I'm going to be on the other side for a week. Let's do lunch, okay?'

'Okay, kid! See you around. Take care and give my best to Brill and Olga.'

'Will do. You take care too. Especially around, uh, the second job. I mean that, I want you to be around so I can buy you lunch. It's been too long, okay?'

'Yeah. Nice to hear from you!'

'Bye.'

'Bye.'

TRANSCRIPT ENDS – DURATION 00:06:42

DIFFERENCES OF OPINION

'What the *hell* do you think you're doing in my office?' Miriam asked in a dangerous voice.

The man in the swivel chair turned round slowly and stared at her with expressionless eyes. 'Running it,' he said slowly.

'I see.'

The office was cramped, a row of high stools perched in front of the wooden angled desks that formed one wall; they were the only occupants. Miriam had just stepped through the front door, not even bothering to go check on the lab. She'd meant to hang her coat up first, then go find Roger or the rest of the lab team before chasing up the paperwork and calling on her solicitor and then on Sir Alfred Durant, her largest customer. Instead of which –

'Morgan, just who told you that you were running the show?'

Morgan leaned back in his swivel chair. 'The duke.' He smiled lazily. She'd met Morgan before: a strong right hand, but not the sharpest tool in the box when it came to general management. 'Angbard. He sent me over here after the takedown in Boston. Said I was too hot to stay over there, and he needed someone to keep an eye on things here. Anyway, it's on autopilot, just ticking over. Every week I get a set of instructions, and execute them.' He stared at her. 'I don't recall being notified that you had *permission* to be here.'

'I don't recall having given Angbard permission to manage *my* company,' Miriam replied. 'Never mind the fact that he knows as much about running a tech R&D bureau as I know about fly-fishing. Neither do you, is my guess. What have you been up to while I was in Niejwein?' It was a none-too-subtle jab, to tell Morgan that she had the ear of important people. Maybe it worked: he sat up.

'Expansion plans – the new works – are on hold. I had to let two of your workmen go, they were insubordinate – '

'Workmen?' She leaned across the desk toward him. '*Which* work-men?'

'I'd have to look their names up. Some dirty-fingered fellow from the furnace room, spent all his time playing with rubber – '

'Jesus. Christ.' Miriam stared at him with thinly concealed contempt. 'You fired Roger, you mean.'

'Roger? Hmm, that may have been him.'

'Well, well, well.' Miriam breathed deeply, flexing her fingertips, trying to retain control. *Give me strength!* 'You know what this company makes, don't you?'

'Brake pads?' Morgan sniffed dismissively. Like most of the Clan's sharp young security men, he didn't have much time for the plebian pursuits of industrial development.

'No.' Miriam took another deep breath. 'We're a design bureau. We *design* brakes – better brakes than anyone else in New Britain, because we've got a forty- to fifty-year lead in materials science thanks to our presence in the United States – and sell licenses to manufacture our *designs*. So. Did it occur to you that it might just be a *bad idea* to fire our senior materials scientist?'

Morgan's eyes narrowed. 'That was a *scientist*?'

I'm going to strangle him, Miriam thought faintly, *so help me I am*. 'Yes, Morgan, Roger is a real live scientist. They don't wear white coats here, you see, nor do they live in drafty castles in Bavaria and carry around racks of smoking test tubes. Nor do they wear placards round their necks that say SCIENTIST. They actually *work for a living*. I spent five months getting Roger up to speed on some of the new materials we were introducing – I was going to get him started on productizing cyanoacrylate adhesives, next! – and you went and, and *sacked* him – '

She stopped. She was, she realized, breathing too fast. Morgan was leaning backward again, trying to get away from her. 'I didn't know!' he protested. 'I was just doing what Angbard told me. Angbard said no, don't buy the new works, and this artisan told me I was a fool to my face! What was I meant to do?'

Miriam came back down to earth. 'You've got a point about Angbard,' she admitted. 'Leave him to me, I'll deal with him when I can get through to him.' Morgan nodded rapidly. 'Did he tell you to shut down the business? Or just put the expansion on hold?'

'The latter. I don't think he's paying much attention to what goes on here. He's fighting fires constantly at present.'

'Well, he could have avoided adding to them right here if he'd left me in charge; the one thing you can't afford to do with a business like this is ignore it. How many points are you on?'

Morgan hesitated for a moment. 'Five.' Five thousandths of the gross take, in mob-speak.

Ten, or I'm a monkey's aunt. 'Okay, it's like this. Angbard wants a quiet life. Angbard doesn't need to hear bad news. But if you let this company drift it will be an ex-company very fast – it's a start-up, do you know what that means? It's got just *one* major product and *one* major customer, and if Sir Alfred realizes we're drifting he'll cut us loose. He can afford to tie us up in court until we go bust or until Angbard has to bail us out, and he'll do that if we don't show signs of delivering new products he can use. I think you can see that going bust would be bad, wouldn't it? Especially for your points.'

Morgan was watching her with ill-concealed fear now. 'So what do you think I should do?'

'Well –' Miriam hesitated for a moment, then pressed on. *What the hell can he do? It's my way or the highway!* 'I suggest you listen to me and run things my way. No need to tell Angbard, not yet. When he sends you instructions you just say "yes sir," then forward them to me, and I'll tell you how to implement them, what else needs doing, and so on. If Angbard doesn't want me expanding fast, fine: I can work around that. In the short term, though, we've got to position the company so that it's less vulnerable – and so that when we're ready to expand we can just pump money in and do it. In the long term, I'll work on Angbard. I haven't been able to get in to see him for months, but the crisis won't last forever – you leave him to me. I can't be around as much as I want – I've got this week to myself, but they keep dragging me back to the capital and sooner or later I'm liable to be stuck there for a while – so you're going to have to be my general manager here. *If* you want the job, and if you follow orders until you've learned enough about the way things work not to sack our

159

most important employee because you've mistaken him for the janitor.'

He looked sour. 'What's in it for me?'

Miriam shrugged. 'You've got five points. Do you want that to be five points of nothing if it goes bust, or five points on an outfit that's going to be turning over the equivalent of a hundred million dollars a year?'

'Ah. Okay.' Morgan nodded, slowly this time. Miriam put on her best poker face. She wasn't happy; Morgan was barely up to the job and was a long way from her first choice for a general manager, but on the other hand he was here. And available to be bribed, which made everything possible. If there was one thing the Clan had taught Miriam, it was the importance of being able to hammer out a quick compromise when one was needed, to build coalitions on the fly – and to recognize when a palm crossed with gold would trump weeks of negotiations. Normally she was bad at it, as events in Niejwein had demonstrated, but here was an opportunity to do it right. 'I'll take it,' he said, with barely concealed ill grace. 'You didn't leave me a choice, did you?'

'Oh, you had a choice. You could have decided to wreck the company I created, screw yourself out of a fortune, and look like an idiot all at the same time. Not much of a choice, is it?'

'Okay, my lady capitalist. So what *do* you suggest I do? Now that I'm running this business under your advice?' He crossed his arms.

Miriam walked around the desk. 'You start by giving me back my chair,' she said. 'And then we go look round the shop and come up with an action plan. But I can tell you this much, the first item on it will be to track down Roger and offer him his old job back. Along with all the back pay he lost when you sacked him. Now' – she gestured at the door – 'shall we go and assess the damage?'

*

Five days of hard work, stressful and unpleasant, passed her by like a bad dream. At the end of the first day, Miriam went home to her house on the outskirts of Cambridgetown, to find it shuttered, dark, and cold, the servants nowhere to be found. On the second day, she met with her company lawyer, Bates; on the third day, Morgan reported finding the misplaced Roger; and on the fourth day, she actually began to feel as if she was getting somewhere. The agency Bates recommended had sent her a cook, a gardener, and a maid, and the house was actually inhabitable again. (In the meantime, she'd spent two nights in the Brighton Hotel, rather than repeat the first night's fitful shivering on a dust-sheeted sofa.) A visit to Roger, cap in hand, had begun to convince him that it was all an unfortunate mistake, but she was getting *very* tired of telling everybody that she'd been hospitalized with a fever during a business trip to Derry City and had taken a month to convalesce afterward. Whether they believed the story . . . well, why hadn't she written? Never mind. Her earlier reputation for mystery and eccentricity, formerly a social handicap of the worst kind, suddenly came in handy.

On the fifth day, while Morgan was away performing his corvée duty for the Clan, a parcel arrived.

Miriam was in the office that morning, going over the accounts carefully – Morgan had left that side of things almost completely to Bates's clerk, and Miriam wanted to double-check him – when the bell outside the window rang. She stood up and slid the window back. 'Yes?' she asked.

'Delivery.' An eyebrow rose. 'Hah! Fancy seeing you here. Sign, please.' It was Sharp Suit Number Two from the verminous hole of a post office near Chicago, wearing a fetching magenta tailcoat over the oddly flared breeches that seemed to be the coming fashion for gentlemen this year.

'Thanks.' Miriam signed off on his pad. 'Want to come in? Or . . . ?'

'No, no, must be going,' he said hastily. 'Just didn't realize this was a Clan operation.'

'It is.' Miriam nodded. *Isn't it?* she asked herself. 'Good day to you.'

'Adieu.' He tipped his bicorn hat at her, then turned away. She slid the window closed and carried the parcel over to the desk. Inside it were two large plastic bottles of RIFINAH-300 tablets and a handwritten note from Paulette: *Here's your first item, the other will be ready by tomorrow.* 'Good old Paulie,' Miriam muttered to herself. She tucked the bottles into her shoulder bag, went back to the accounts. They'd wait until after lunch. Then she had to go and visit a friend.

Lunch. Standing up stiffly, Miriam put the heavy ledger back in its place on the shelf, then walked through into the laboratory. John Probity was bent over a test apparatus, tightening something with a spanner. 'I shall be calling on a business contact after lunch,' Miriam announced to his back, 'so I may not be back this afternoon. If you could shut up shop in the evening I would be obliged. Either I, or Mr. Morgan, will be in the office tomorrow if anyone calls.'

'Aye, mam,' Probity grunted. A fellow of grim determination and few words, the only time she'd ever seen him look happy was when she'd announced that Roger would be rejoining the company on Monday next. So rather than waiting for any further response, Miriam turned on her heel and headed out to catch a cab back home. Not only was she hungry, she needed a change of clothes: it would hardly do for her to be seen in the vicinity of Burgeson the pawnbroker while dressed for the office – that is, as a respectable moneyed widow of some independent means. Lips might flap, and flapping lips had an alarming tendency to draw the attention of the Royal Constabulary.

The electric streetcar rattled its way across the trestle bridge over the river, swaying slightly as it went. The air was slightly hazy, a warm, damp summer afternoon that smelled slightly of smoke. Traffic was heavy, horse-drawn carts and steam trucks rumbling and rattling past the streetcar, drivers shouting at one another – Miriam peered out of the window, watching for her stop. She'd traded her dove-gray shalwar suit and cape for the pinafore of a domestic, worn with a slightly threadbare straw hat. With the 'Gillian' identity papers tucked in her shabby shoulder bag, there was nothing to mark her out as anything other than a scullery maid on a scarce day off, except the two jars of pills in her bag – and she'd decanted them into glass bottles rather than leaving them in their original plastic wrappers. *Nothing to it*, she thought dreamily, staring out at the paddlewheel steamers on the Charles River, letting a beam of sunlight warm her face. *I could be anyone I want.* Once you took the first step and got used to the idea of living under a false identity, it was easy . . .

It was a seductive fantasy, but it was hardly practical. Not with so many strange relatives wanting to get their claws into her skin, to graft a piece of her onto the family tree. A year ago she'd been an only child, adopted at that, with no relatives but an elderly mother and a daughter she hadn't seen in years. Now, she found she craved nothing quite as much as placid anonymity. *I want my freedom back*, she realized. *No amount of money or power can make up for losing it.* It was something that the Clan, with their sprawling extended families and their low-tech background, didn't seem to understand about her. A flash of anger: *I'm just going to have to take it back, aren't I?*

She'd grown up in a world where she'd been led to expect that she could create her own identity, her own success story, rather than vicariously acquiring her identity from her role in a hierarchy, the way the Clan seemed to expect her to. And it was at times like this – when independence seemed a streetcar ride away – that their expectations were at their most tiresome and her natural instinct to rebel came to the fore, an instinct bolstered by the self-confidence she'd acquired from starting up her own business in this strange, subtly alien city.

Highgate High Street, tall brick-fronted houses huddling against one another as if for comfort against the winter gales. Holmes Alley, piles of uncleared refuse lining the gutters. She stepped around the worst of the filth carefully. The shop front was shuttered and dark, and her heart gave a small downward lurch. *I thought they had let him go. Or have they arrested him again?* Miriam glanced over her shoulder, then walked past the shop to the battered door with the bellpull: E. BURGESON, ESQ. When she tugged, it took almost a second for the rattle of the doorbell upstairs to reach her. She waited for the chimes to die away, waited and waited, pulled the doorbell again, waited some more. *Damn, he's not home*, she thought. She began to turn away, just as there was a click from the latch.

'Please, no deliveries –' A hideous fit of coughing doubled the man in the doorway over, racking him painfully.

Miriam stared. Burgeson the pawnbroker, her first contact in New Britain, possibly the nearest thing to a friend she had here, was coughing his lungs bloody.

'Erasmus?' she asked. 'You're ill, aren't you?' *He looks awful*, she realized, abruptly worried. In the dusty sunlight filtering down between the houses he looked half dead already.

'Euh, euw –' He tried to straighten up, succeeded after another bout of rattling coughing. 'Miriam? How – hah – good to see you.' *Cough.* 'But not in. This state.'

'Let's go inside,' she suggested firmly. 'I want to take a look at you.'

Miriam followed Burgeson's halting progress up the steeply pitched spiral staircase, up to the front door of his apartment. She'd been here before, seen the cavernous twelve-foot ceiling walled on both sides by dusty, tottering shelves of books, the perfectly circular living room with its overstuffed sofa and scratched grand piano. The genteel bachelor-pad disarray of a cultured life going slowly downhill in the grip of chronic illness. Much of his life was a mystery to her, but she'd picked up some tantalizing hints. He'd once had a family, before he'd spent seven years in one of his majesty's prison camps out in the northwestern wilderness. And he wasn't as old as he looked. But his usual gauntness had now given way to the stooped, cadaverous, sunken-cheeked look of the terminally ill. 'Make yourself at home. Can I' – he paused for the coughing fit – 'make you a pot of tea?' He finished on a croak.

Miriam perched tensely on the edge of the sofa. 'Yes, please,' she said. Remembering the pain of a childhood vaccination, she added, 'It's the consumption, isn't it?' *Consumption. The white death, tuberculosis.* He'd picked it up in the camps, been in remission for a long time. *But this is as bad as I've ever seen him –*

'Yes.' He shuffled toward the kitchen. 'I've not so many months left in me.'

He's whistling past the graveyard, she realized, appalled. 'How old are you, Erasmus?' she called through the doorway.

'Thirty-nine.' The closing kitchen door cut the rest off. Miriam stared after him, horrified. She'd taken him for at least a decade older, well into middle age. This was a roomy apartment, top of the line for the working classes in this time and place. It had luxuries like indoor plumbing, piped town gas, batteries for electricity. But it was no place to live alone, with tuberculosis eating your lungs. She stood up and followed the sounds through to the kitchen.

'Erasmus –' She paused in the doorway. He had his back turned to her, washing his hands thoroughly under a stream of water piped from the coal-fired stove.

'Yes?' He half-turned, his face in shadow.

'Have you eaten in the past hour or two?' she asked.

Evidently she'd surprised him, for he shut the tap off and turned round, drying his hands on a towel. 'What kind of question is that to be asking?' He cocked his head on one side, and something of the old Erasmus flickered into light.

'I'm asking if you've eaten,' she said impatiently, tapping her toe.

'Not recently, no.' He put the towel down and reached back into his pocket for his handkerchief.

'Okay.' She dug around in her bag. 'I've got something for you. You're *certain* what you've got is consumption?'

'Ahem –' He coughed, hacking repeatedly, into the handkerchief. 'Yes, Miriam, it's the white death.' He looked grim. 'I've seen it take enough of my friends to know my number's come up.'

'Okay.' She tipped two tablets out into the palm of her hand, held them out toward him: 'I want you to take these right now. Wash them down with tea, and make sure you don't eat anything for half an hour afterwards.'

He looked at her in confusion, not taking the tablets. After a moment he smiled. 'More of your utopian nonsense and magic, Miriam? Think this'll cure me and make me whole again?'

Miriam rolled her eyes. 'Humor me. Please?'

'Ah, well. I suppose so.' He took the two tablets and swallowed them one at a time, looking slightly disgusted. 'What are they meant to do? I've got no time for quack nostrums as a rule . . .' The kettle began to whistle, and he turned back to the stove to pour water into a tarnished metal teapot.

'Remember the DVD player I showed you? The movie?' Miriam asked his turned back.

He froze.

'It's not magical,' she added. 'You need to take two of these tablets at the same hour, on an empty stomach, every day *without fail*, for six months. That should – I hope – stop the disease from progressing. It won't make your lungs heal from the damage already done, and there's a chance, about one in ten, that it won't work, or that it'll make you feel even more sick, in which case I'll have to find some different medicine for you. But you should lose the coughing in a couple of weeks and begin to feel better in a month. Don't stop taking them, though, until six months are up, or it will come back.' She paused. 'It's not a utopia I come from, and the drugs don't always work. But they're better than anything I've seen here.'

'Not a utopia.' He turned to face her, holding the teapot. 'You've got some very strange notions, young lady.'

'I'm thirty-three, *old man*. You want to put that teapot down before you spill it? And no, it's not a utopia. Thing is, the bac – germs – that cause consumption, they evolve over time to resist the drugs. If you stop taking the medicine before you're completely cured, there's a chance that you'll develop a resistant strain of infection and these drugs will stop working. Too many homeless people where I come from stopped taking them when they felt better – the result is, there are still people dying of tuberculosis in New York City.' He was halfway back to the living room as she followed him, lecturing his receding back. 'That stuff is the cheap first-line treatment. And you'll by god finish the bloody course, because I need you alive!'

He put the teapot down. When he turned round he was grinning. 'Hah! Now that's a surprise, ma'am.'

'What?' Miriam, stopped in midstream, was perplexed.

He exhaled through a gap between his teeth. 'You've shown no sign of needing anyone ever before, if I may be blunt. You're a veritable force of nature.'

Miriam sat down heavily. 'A force of nature with family problems. And a dilemma.'

'Ah. I see. And you want to tell me about it?'

'Well –' She paused. 'Later. What brought the tuberculosis back? How long did they hold you for?' *How have you been?* she wanted to ask, but that might imply an intimacy in their relationship that had never been explicit in the past.

'Oh, questions, questions.' He poured tea into two china cups, neither of them chipped. 'Always the questions.' He chuckled painfully. 'The kind of questions that turn worlds upside down. One lump or two?'

'None, thank you.' Miriam accepted a cup. 'Did they charge you?'

'No.' Burgeson looked unaccountably irritated, as if the Political Police's failure to charge him reflected negatively on his revolutionary credentials. 'They just banged me up and squatted in my shop.' He brightened: 'Some party or parties unknown – and not related to my friends – did them an extreme mischief on the premises.' He cracked his knuckles. 'And I was in custody! Clearly innocent! The best alibi!' He managed not to laugh. 'They still charged me with possession – went through the bookshelves, seems I'd missed a tract or two – but the beak only gave me a month in the cells. Unfortunately that's when the cough came back, so they kicked me out to die on the street.'

'Bastards,' Miriam said absently. Burgeson winced slightly at the unladylike language but held his tongue. 'I've been seeing a lot of that.' She told him about the train journey, about Marissa and her mother who was afraid Miriam was an informer or police agent. 'Is something happening?'

'Oh, you should know better than to ask me that.' He glanced at her speculatively. When she nodded slightly, he went on: 'The economy.' He raised a finger. 'It's in the midden. Spinning its wheels fit to blow a boiler. We have plenty out of work, queues for broth around the street corners – bodies sleeping in the streets, dying in the gutter of starvation. Go walk around Whitechapel or Ontario if you don't believe it. There's a shortage of money, debtors are unable to pay their rack, and I am having to be very careful who I choose to give the ticket to. Nobody likes a pawnbroker, you know. And that's just the top of it: I've heard rumors that in the camps they're going through convicts' teeth in search of gold, can you believe it? Claiming it as Crown property. *Secundus*.' He raised another finger. 'The harvest is piss-poor. It's been getting worse for a few years, this unseasonable strange weather and peculiar storms, but this year it hit the corn. And with a potato blight rotting the spuds in the field –' He shrugged. A third finger: 'Finally, there is the game of thrones. Which heats up apace, as the dauphin casts a greedy eye at our beloved royal father's dominions in the Persian Gulf. He's an ambitious little swine, the dauphin, looking to shore up his claim to the iron throne of Caesar in St. Petersburg, and a short victorious war that would leave French boots a-cooling in the Indian ocean would line his broadcloth handsomely. Would you like me to elaborate?'

'Um, no.' Miriam shook her head. 'Different players, but the game's the same.' She sipped her tea. *Global climate change? What is the world's population here, anyway?* Suddenly she had a strange vision, a billion coal-fired cooking stoves staining the sky with as bad a smog as a billion SUVs. *Convergence . . .*

'So times are bad and the constabulary are getting heavyhanded. The Evil Empire is rattling its sabers and threatening to invade, just to add to the fun. And the economy is stuck in a liquidity trap that's been getting worse for months, with deflation setting in . . . ?' She shook her head again. 'And I thought things were bad back home.'

'So where have *you* been?' Erasmus asked, cocking his head to one side. There was something birdlike about his movements, but now Miriam could see that it was a side effect of the disease eating him from the inside out, leaving him gaunt and huge-eyed. 'I thought you'd abandoned me.' He said it in such a self-consciously histrionic tone that she almost laughed.

'Nothing so spectacular! After you were arrested, the shit hit the fan' – she ignored the wince and continued – 'and – well. The people who were trying to kill me have been neutralized. But one of them defected to the police in my own . . . in the world I grew up in. He, his man, killed –' She stopped for a moment, unable to continue. 'Roland's dead. And, and.' *Nothing else matters in comparison.* It was true; she couldn't care less about everything. Roland's absence still felt like a gaping hole in her life, every time she woke up, every time she noticed it.

After a few seconds she forced herself to continue. 'The Clan's entire fortune there, in my world, is based on smuggling. They've been driven underground. Some of them seem to have blamed me for it; as a result, they've been keeping me on a very short leash. I'm not the family black sheep anymore, but I'm not exactly trusted, and it took me a lot of work just to be allowed out here on my own. Some of them have got a scheme to marry me off. They're big on arranged marriages,' she added bitterly. 'It's a good way of silencing inconveniently loud women.'

'You're not so easy to silence,' Erasmus noted after she'd stopped talking. He smiled. 'Which is a good thing: it is our willingness to allow ourselves to be silenced easily that allows scoundrels to get away with so much, as a friend of mine put it – you might like to drop in on her next time you're in New London, incidentally. She's another loud woman who doesn't believe in being silenced. She's called Margaret, Lady Bishop, and you can find her at Hogarth Villas: I think you've got a lot in common.' He cracked his knuckles again. 'But you haven't told me why you wanted to see me. Much less, why you wanted to save my life.'

'I didn't?' She shook herself. 'Damn, I'm stupid. It's – well. Look, I managed to steal a week over here, and it's nearly over, and I've wasted most of it repairing the damage Morgan inflicted on my company through neglect – '

'I thought you said he was stupid and lazy?'

'He is. But – '

'Well then, imagine how much damage he could have done if he was stupid and *energetic*.'

'I did: that's why I made him general manager. I think I've got him sufficiently house-trained to minimize the damage in future. Only time will tell.'

'Ah, nepotism,' Erasmus said, nodding sagaciously. 'But your week is up and you have nothing to show for it?'

'Well.' She looked at him speculatively. 'I've been doing some thinking. And it seems to me that I've been letting them take me for granted. They have their own set of assumptions about how I should behave, and if I let them apply those assumptions to me they'll back me into a corner. So I need to do something, acquire leverage. Make them let me alone.'

'That could be dangerous,' Erasmus said neutrally.

'You bet it's dangerous!' Miriam rolled her teacup between her hands, fidgeting. 'They've got my mother.' Tight-lipped: 'She's dependent on certain medicines. They think that's enough to get a handle on me. But if I can establish my autonomy, *I* can provide her meds. I just have to get them to leave me alone.'

'Hmm. As I understood it, when you first told me about your turbulent family, they wouldn't leave you alone because you signify an inheritance of enormous wealth, is that not the case?' He raised an eyebrow at her.

'Yes,' she said grudgingly. 'Not that it makes a lot of difference to me.'

'Hah. Perhaps not, but they might be reluctant to leave you alone not because they insist on controlling you for control's own sake but because they fear the disposition of such wealth in directions inimical to their own interests. In which case you will need a tool with which to express your urgency somewhat persuasively . . .'

'I was leaning toward blackmail, myself.' She frowned. 'Their pressure is relatively subtle, social expectations and so forth. There are lots of secrets in this kind of culture, embarrassing facts best not aired in public and so on. Given a handful of truths it's possible to suggest to people that they butt out' – her expression brightened – 'and if there's one thing I'm told I'm good at, it's digging up embarrassing truths.'

Erasmus tried again. 'But, that is to say – you are applying your not-inconsiderable reasoning skills to this as a social paradox. Your real problem is a temporal, political one. If you try to blackmail them – '

'They're aristocrats. The personal is political,' she said dismissively. 'Once you get a pig by the nose, its body will follow, right?'

'Right,' he agreed, reluctantly.

'I'd better hope so,' she added, 'because if I'm wrong about them, well, it doesn't bear thinking about. So I'm not going to worry about it. But everything I've seen *so far* tells me that it's going to work. Matthias blackmailed Roland . . .' She stared bleakly at the thin patina of dust on top of the lid of Erasmus's piano. 'Blackmail seems to be a way of life inside the Clan. So I'd better get with the program.'

*

'Hi, Paulie!'

Miriam waved from across the station concourse, smiling when Paulette spotted her and headed straight to where she was standing.

'Hey, Miriam, that's a great coat! You're looking good. Listen, there's this new brasserie just outside the center, you up to eating or do you just want to hang out? We could go back to the office – '

'Eating would be good.' Miriam rubbed her forehead. 'Made two crossings this morning; I need something in my stomach so I can take the ibuprofen.' She winced theatrically. 'I'd rather not go near the office,' she added quietly as Paulie led her toward one of the side doors of the station. 'Too much chance someone's bugged it.'

'Uh-huh.' Paulette didn't break stride: not that Miriam had expected her to. Back when Miriam had been a senior reporter for *The Industry Weatherman* Paulette had been her research assistant – right up until one of Miriam's investigations had gotten them both escorted off the premises with extreme prejudice. Then when Miriam had gotten mixed up with the Clan she'd hired Paulie to look after her interests back home in Boston, United States timeline. Paulette knew about the Clan, had grown up in a tough neighborhood where some of the residents had mob connections. Angbard knew about Paulette, which meant there was a very real risk the office was indeed bugged, and thus Miriam had arranged to meet up with her at Penn Station.

The brasserie was crowded but not totally logjammed yet, and Paulette managed to get them a table near the back. 'I need breakfast,' Miriam said. 'What's good?'

'The bruschetta's passable, and I was going to go for the spaghetti alle polpette. To drink, the usual hangover juice, right?'

'Yeah, a double OJ it is.' At which point the waitress caught up with them and Miriam held back until Paulette had ordered. 'Now, did you get me the stuff I asked for?'

'Sure.' Miriam felt something against her leg – the plastic shopping bag Paulie had been carrying. It was surprisingly heavy – lots of paper, a box file perhaps. 'It's in there.'

'Okay. *All* of that is for me?'

Paulette grinned. 'Give me credit.'

'Yeah, I know you're good – but *that* much?'

'I have my ways,' Paulie said. Quieter: 'Don't worry, I kept it low-key. First up are the public filings, SEC stuff, all hard copy. The downloads I did in an internet cafe, using an anonymous Hotmail account I never access from home. To pay for the searches, I got an account with a special online bank: they issue one-time credit card numbers you can use to pay for something over the Net. The idea is, you use the number once, the transaction is charged to your account at the bank, then the number goes away. Anyone wants to trace me, they're going to have to break the bank's security first, okay?'

'You've been getting very good at the anonymous stuff.'

'Knowing whose toes you might be treading on kind of incentivized me! I'm not planning on taking any risks. Look, at first sight it all looks kosher – I mean, the clinic is just a straightforward reproductive medicine outfit, specializing in fertility problems, and the company you fingered, Applied Genomics, is a respectable pharmaceutical outfit. They manufacture diagnostic instruments, specializing in lab tests for inborn errors of metabolism: simple test-tube stuff that's easy to use in the field. They've got a neat line in HIV testing kits for the developing world, that kind of thing. You were right about a connection, though. Next in the stack after the filings, well, I found this S.503(c) charity called the Humana Reproductive Assistance Foundation. Applied Genomics pays a big chunk of money to HRAF every year and none of the shareholders have ever queried it, even though it's in six or sometimes seven figures. HRAF in turn looks pretty kosher, but what I was able to tell is that for the past twenty years they've been feeding money to a whole bundle of fertility clinics. The money is earmarked for programs to help infertile couples have children – what *is* this, Miriam? If it's another of your money-laundering leads, it looks like a dead end.'

'It's not a money-laundering lead. I think it really *is* a fertility clinic.' The drinks arrived and Miriam paused to take a tablet and wash it down with freshly squeezed orange juice. 'It's something else I ran across, okay?'

Paulette glanced away.

'I'm sorry, I didn't mean to snap. Been having a shitty time lately.'

'You have?' Paulette shook her head, then looked back at Miriam. 'Things haven't been so rosy here, either.'

'Oh no. You go first, okay?'

'Nah, it's nothing. Man trouble, no real direction. You've heard it all before.' Paulie backed off and Miriam eyed her suspiciously.

'You're tap-dancing around on account of Roland, aren't you? Well, there's no need to do that. I've – I've gotten used to it.' Miriam glanced down as the waitress slid a platter of bruschetta onto the table in front of her. 'It doesn't get any better, but it gets easier to deal with the, with the . . .' She gave up and picked up a piece of the bread, nibbling on it to conceal her sudden spasm of depression.

'So call me an insensitive cow, but what else is eating you?' Paulette asked.

'It's' – Miriam waved a hand, her mouth full – 'reproductive politics. You'd think they'd figure I'm too old for it but no, you're *never* too old for the Clan to start looking for something to do with your ovaries. Fallout from the civil war they had a few decades ago: they don't have enough world-walkers, so the pressure is on those they *do* have to breed like a bunny. But I didn't have the story completely straight before. You know all the stuff about arranged marriages I told you? I should have asked who did the arranging. It turns out to be the old ladies, everyone's grandmother. There's a lot of status tied up in it, and it seems I got a whole bunch of great-aunts ticked off at me just because I exist. To make matters worse, Ma's turned strange on me – she's gone native, even seems to be playing along with the whole business. I think she's being blackmailed, crudely, over her medication. The king, *his* mother's part of the Clan, he's trying to set up the younger son, who is a basket case into the bargain – brain damage at an early age – and he's got me in his sights. And the elder son seems to have decided to hate me for some reason. Don't know if it's connected, but there's more.' Miriam took another mouthful of orange juice before she could continue.

'I ran across this secret memo, from the director of the Gerstein Center to Angbard, of all people, talking about the results of some project that Applied Genomics is funding. And I smell a rat. A great, big, dead-and-decomposing-under-the-front-stoop, reproductive politics rodent. Angbard is paying for in-vitro fertilization treatments. Meanwhile everybody keeps yammering about how few world-walkers there are and how it's every woman's duty to spawn like a rabbit, and then there's this stuff about looking for W-star heterozygotes.

Carriers for some kind of gene-linked trait, in other words. And I just learned of a genetic test that's become available in the past year, god knows from where, that can tell if someone's a carrier or an active world-walker. You fill in the dotted lines, Paulie – you tell me I'm not imagining things, okay?' Miriam realized her voice had risen, and she looked around hastily, but the restaurant was busy and the background racket was loud enough to cover her.

Paulette stared at her, clutching her bread knife in one fist as if it were the emergency inflation toggle on a life jacket. 'I've never heard such a . . . !' She put the knife down, very carefully. 'You're serious.'

'Oh yes.' Miriam took another bite of bruschetta. It tasted of cardboard, despite the olive oil and chopped tomato. 'What would be the point of being flippant?'

Paulette picked up her bruschetta and nibbled at it. 'That is so monumentally paranoid that I don't know where to begin. You think Angbard is paying for IVF for these families and using donors from the Clan.' She thought for a minute. 'It wouldn't work, would it? They wouldn't be world-walkers?'

'Not as I understand it, no.' Miriam finished her starter. The din and clatter of the restaurant was making her headache worse. 'But they'd have a huge pool of, in effect, outer family members. Half of them female. Thousands, adding many hundreds more every year. Suppose – how long has this been going on for? How long has HRAF been going?'

'I don't know.' Paulette looked uncomfortable. 'Sixteen years?'

'Okay. Suppose. Imagine HRAF is about creating a pool of outer family people living in the United States who don't know what they are. In, say, another five years they start hitting age twenty-one. Six hundred . . . call it three hundred women a year. HRAF have their details. They send them all letters asking if they're willing to accept money to be surrogate mothers. What does a surrogate cost – ten, twenty thousand bucks? Maybe nine out of ten will say no, but that leaves thirty women, each of whom can provide a new world-walker every year – or walkers, you're not going to tell me that the Gerstein Center isn't going to dose them to try for twins or triplets. Call it fifty new world-walkers per year. Say half of the surrogate mothers agree to continue for four years, and you've got, let's see, a hundred and twenty-five new world-walkers per annual cohort from Angbard's breeding program. Paulie, there are only about a thousand world-walkers in the Clan! In just eight years, half the world-walkers will come from this scheme – in twenty years, they'll outnumber the Clan's native-born world-walkers, even if the average Clan female produces four world-walking children.' She drank the rest of her orange juice.

'It's like that movie, *The Boys from Brazil*,' Paulie said. 'Cloning up an army of bad guys and making sure they're raised loyal to the cause.' She looked uncomfortable. 'Miriam, I met Angbard. He isn't the type to do that.'

'Um. No.' Miriam stared at her plate. All of a sudden she didn't feel hungry. 'Charming, ruthless, and manipulative, I'll grant you. Liable to back a conspiracy to create a test-tube master race? I'm – I'm not seeing it either. Except, I *saw* that memo! With my own eyes! If it's real, it looks like there's something really smelly going on at that clinic. And I need to get a handle on it.'

'Why?' Paulette stabbed at her bruschetta with a knife. 'What *is* getting into you, Miriam? What have they got on you?'

'They –' She stopped for a moment. 'Blackmail is business as usual. I figure I need to get an edge of my own, before they marry me off to the Idiot Prince. Simple as that.'

'Huh.' Paulette put her knife down with exaggerated care. 'Miriam. I told you about what things were like when I was growing up.'

'Yes.' Miriam nodded. 'Wiseguys. Well, I was born into the mob, I guess, so using their own tactics – blackmail seems to be the family sport – '

'Miriam!' Paulette reached across the table and took her hand. 'Listen. As your agent, and as your legal adviser, I would really be a lot happier if you would drop this. You're right, the clinic shit sounds dirty. But if your uncle is involved, it means there's money involved too, or security. The tough guys, they used to cut their wives and children a lot of slack – as long as they didn't try to nose in on the business. You see what I'm saying? This is family business and they're going to take it a whole lot differently if you go digging – '

'Nuh-uh, no way.' Miriam shook her head vehemently. 'I know them, Paulie. They're more medieval than that. Everything is on the outside, you know? Their politics is entirely personal. So's their business. If I get the goods on this scheme, then I've got a handle on whoever's running it –' Miriam stopped dead as the waitress sashayed in and scooped up her plate with a smile.

'I still don't like it. I *mean* that. I think you're misreading them. Just because you're little miss heiress, it doesn't make you invulnerable. They've got their code: item number two on it, after "Don't talk to the cops", is "Don't stick your nose where it doesn't belong". And this sounds like exactly the sort of business people wake up dead for sticking their nose in.'

Miriam shrugged. 'Paulie, I've got status among them. I couldn't just vanish. Too many people would ask questions.'

'Like they did when you appeared out of nowhere? Miriam. Seriously, one last time, I've got a bad feeling about this. *Please*, just for me, will you drop it?'

Miriam crossed her arms, irritated. 'Who's paying your wages?'

The main course appeared, savory meatballs in a hot, sweet tomato sauce. Paulie ignored it, her face frozen. 'Okay, if that's how you want to do it,' she said quietly. 'You're the boss, you know best. Okay?'

'Oh . . . okay.' *I went too far*, Miriam realized. *Shit. How do I apologize for* that? She glanced down at her plate. 'Yeah, that's how I want to play it,' she said. *Play it all the way*, then *apologize*. Paulie was a mensch, she'd come round.

'First I have to figure out if it really *is* what it seems to be. Although given that stuff about W-star heterozygotes, I can't see what else it might be. Then if I'm right, I have to figure out how to use it. At best' – she bit into a meatball – 'it could give me all the leverage I need. They couldn't touch me, not even my psycho grandmother could. Hmm, great meatballs. So yeah, I think I need to go pay the clinic an anonymous visit.' She flashed Paulette a fragile smile. 'Do you know where I can buy a stethoscope around here?'

ARRESTED

The auditor smiled as she walked in the door. 'I've come to see Dr. Darling,' she announced, parking her briefcase beside the desk. Her expression was disturbingly cheery as she raised an ID card: 'FDA, clinical audit division. I don't have an appointment.'

The receptionist visibly teetered on the edge of a panic attack for a few seconds. 'I'm afraid Dr. Darling isn't –' She lost her thread. The auditor didn't look particularly threatening: just another office worker in a conservative suit, shoulder-length black hair, severe spectacles. But she was from the FDA. And *unannounced*! 'I'll just see if I can get him? Wait right here . . .'

The auditor tapped her toe a trifle impatiently as the receptionist fielded two incoming calls and paged Dr. Darling. Glancing round, the auditor took in the waiting area, from the bleached pine curves of the desk to the powder-blue modular sofa for visitors to sit on. The walls were hung with anodyne still-life paintings of fruit baskets, alternating with certificates testifying that this HMO or that insurance company had voted the clinic an award for excellence in some obscure field. It was all very professional, nothing that could possibly offend anyone. A classic medical industry head office, all promises and no downside. Not a hint that it might be dabbling in eugenics. 'Excuse me?' She looked up. 'Dr. Darling will be right with you.'

The door opened. Dr. Andrew Darling was forty-something, excessively coiffed and sporting a ten-thousand-dollar smile. 'Good morning! You must be from the FDA, Dr., ah . . . ?'

'Anderson,' said Miriam, holding up the ID card and mentally crossing her fingers. *Get me a fake ID*, she'd told Brill. *Not police or DEA or anything like that, but I want to be able to walk into any restaurant or drugstore and scare the living daylights out of the manager.* And Brill had just narrowed her eyes and looked at Miriam thoughtfully and nodded, and all of a sudden Miriam was an FDA standards compliance officer called Julie Anderson.

It was, she reflected, a bit like magic. The Clan could – of necessity – do things with false ID that beggared the imagination, far better than anything she'd had to work with on undercover investigations for *The Industry Weatherman*. It was funny what a few million dollars a year in the right pockets could buy you. As long as you had the chutzpah – the sense of personal invulnerability – to make effective use of it. Miriam's wrist itched under the temporary tattoo. *Yes*, she thought.

'Ah, Dr. Anderson.' Darling barely examined her card. 'If you'd care to follow me?'

Darling turned and led her through a maze of cubicles and corridors lined with the usual water coolers, photocopiers, and wilting rubber plants, to an office that seemed too cluttered and compact to be that of an executive. There were files of hardcopy case notes on his desk and a subsiding heap of medical journals behind the glass front of a very used-looking bookcase. 'I wasn't expecting a compliance audit this month,' he said.

'I know. You should have received a preliminary e-mail by now, though. This isn't the start of a full investigation, I hope; more of a precautionary check, I didn't bring a full team with me. To be frank, I'm hoping you can just clarify a few points for me and we can leave it at that?'

'That's very irregular.' Darling looked slightly puzzled.

Another false note and he'll see through me, Miriam realized nervously. But it was too late for second thoughts now. She stared at him through the lenses of her false spectacles and concentrated on playing her role to perfection. 'We've been asked to investigate quietly. By another government agency.' She tapped her briefcase. 'You've been dealing with Applied Genomics via a cutout trust. All perfectly aboveboard. Don't tell me this is the first time anyone's asked you about it?'

She'd struck pay dirt: Darling's face turned gray. 'Who sent you here?'

'You know I can't tell you that.' Miriam did her best to look irritated but patient. 'It's the Reproductive Assistance Foundation children, the W-star heterozygotes. I've been asked some inconvenient questions by our sister agency. What are your postnatal follow-up protocols? What process did you subject your study guidelines to for ethical clearance, and what facilities do you have in place to recall patients in the event that it turns out that there are complications – if, just for the sake of argument, the W-star trait is associated with inborn errors of metabolism such as a hyperlipidemia or phenylketonuria? I am – surprised – Dr. Darling, to put it mildly, that there doesn't seem to be any mention of screening for this trait in the approvals filing for your clinic. And I was hoping you could offer me an explanation that doesn't necessitate further investigation.'

Darling blinked rapidly. 'I – the W-star trait, where did you *hear* about that? Nobody's supposed to –' He stood up hastily and walked over to the office door, pushed it shut.

'I can't disclose my sources.' Miriam stared at him coolly.

'Was it Homeland Security?'

'I can neither confirm nor deny that.'

'Why are you here on your own?' There was a nasty edge to his voice.

Here comes the hard sell. 'Because this is best dealt with quietly.' She concentrated on thinking herself into the skin of the person who was using Julie Anderson, compliance inspector, FDA, as a convenient cover identity. 'I repeat, I can't tell you who I am. I wasn't here, I don't exist. We know about your relationship with Applied Genomics. Mr. Angbard is the subject of an ongoing federal investigation. I'm here to follow up a loose end and make sure nothing unravels when I pull on it, if you follow me. This is all going to be swept under the rug so tightly that it didn't happen, it never existed, nobody's going to admit anything, and there won't be any prosecutions – at least not in public. Are you with me so far? We do not want any scandals. But we need to know several things. We need to know *how many*, and *when they were born*, and *where they live* and *who they are*. And then we're going to make sure that when Mr. Angbard and his interesting supply of money vanishes quietly – no, don't ask – your problem goes away too. Did you ever see the Indiana Jones movies, Dr. Darling? If you like, I'm from the Federal Warehouse. I'm one of the curators. And I want your address list, in hard copy, before I walk out of this building. Do you understand me?'

Darling swallowed. 'What you're asking for is unethical as hell, not to mention illegal,' he said. 'Doesn't medical confidentiality mean anything to you people?'

Miriam smiled humorlessly. She was really getting into this, she decided: being a spook was *fun*. 'I'm sure using substituted semen for in-vitro fertilization is also unethical and illegal. Now are we going to do this quietly, or am I going to have to go away and come back with a FEMA emergency court order and an arrest warrant?'

'Shit.' It was the sweet sound of surrender. 'Are you going to indemnify me? Or entertain a plea bargain? If you get this stuff, I want immunity from prosecution arising from it.'

'You are not the target of this investigation,' Miriam stonewalled. *If he expects paperwork . . .* 'And this isn't prosecution territory in any event, as I believe I already said. I was never here, you didn't give me any files, there's not going to be any fallout or any collateral damage. We don't want a paper trail. Do you follow?'

'I – oh hell.' Darling shuffled. 'Okay, I'll get you the files.' He glanced at the door. 'Will hard copy do? We don't keep this stuff on a networked server.'

'Paper will be fine. In the first instance, we're just after a contact sheet for the W-star subjects. I can come back for their full medical records later.' *Not that I'm going to, because they won't be worth a three-dollar bill.*

'Okay. Wait here.' Darling stood up and left the office, closing the door quietly.

Miriam shut her eyes and breathed a sigh of relief. *Okay, he's doing it*, she decided. *He's bought the story. Right?* This was always the hardest part of an investigation, getting the target's trust. But after about thirty seconds she opened her eyes again. *Am I missing something?* She rubbed her palms on her knees: they were damp. She hadn't been on this end of an investigation for more than a year, and it made her as nervous as a cat passing the back fence of a boarding kennel. She thought she'd laid the groundwork adequately, but . . . *Darling's been falsifying IVF donor records for Angbard by way of this nonprofit trust. I've just dropped the hammer on him. What could go wrong at this stage?*

Well, in the worst case scenario Darling could just pick up the phone and *call* Angbard, tell him someone from the FDA was sniffing around the operation. But that wasn't very likely, and in any case it would take time for Angbard to send Clan security round to deal with her, time in which she could simply vanish from the scene. (She resisted the urge to push back her left sleeve and glance at the temporary tattoo: if she bugged out now she'd probably end up somewhere in the wild woods, over on the other side, with a splitting headache.) Next worst scenario: Darling was going to phone the FDA, and would discover pretty quickly that there was no field inspector called Anderson. At which point she could either run away or pull the full black-helicopters tinfoil-hat spook thing. This being a deeply paranoid decade, the odds were that he'd believe her – and if not, she could still bug out. But the third worst case –

Miriam stood up as the door opened. It was Darling, and there was a security guard with him. 'That's her,' he said. The guard took a step forward and Miriam flicked her sleeve back to stare at the knot-work design in brown henna that writhed on the back of her wrist like a snake endlessly swallowing its own tail, inducing feelings of nausea. 'Arrest her.'

The guard reached out to grab Miriam as she brought the knot into focus, putting her mind into the state in which she could world-walk with the ease of long practice. Hands closed around her right arm as lightning stabbed at the base of her skull. 'Ow!' She winced, vision flickering, and tried again. *Nothing.* Her stomach twisted and she began to double over, head a throbbing wall of pain. *What the hell* –

'On the ground!' said the guard. 'Lie down!' Something hard shoved into the base of her skull. 'Okay, I don't think she's armed, sir. If you can help me with these – '

Handcuffs. Miriam tried to move her wrists but they didn't want to respond, flopping around behind her as the guard pinioned them. *The building must be doppelgängered*, she realized through the crippling headache. *Which means* the whole clinic *is a Clan front – that's impossible!*

Her stomach flip-flopped. Hands were lifting her: something sharp pressed against the side of her neck. 'Okay, that's ten mills of valium. Wait two minutes, then get the cuffs off her and take her down to recovery ward B, there's a spare room off the main bay. I'll meet you down there.'

'Going . . . be sick . . .' She'd spoken aloud, she thought. But there was a great empty hollow space inside her, and everything felt warm and wet, as if she were dissolving in a vast salty ocean of comfort and sleep. *Valium?* she thought. *What went wrong?* It was the last thing she thought for a long time.

*

It was dark, and her head hurt. Miriam tried to stretch and found she couldn't move. *That's odd*, she thought fuzzily, *I don't remember going to bed*. She tried to stretch again, but her head was spinning and her knees ached and she felt a sudden urge to urinate. She was lying on her back. *Why am I on my back?* The urge was irresistible and for some reason she couldn't fight it. But that was okay. If it wasn't for the headache and the knee thing she could fall asleep again; she felt warm and comfortable, as if a hot pillow was pressing down on her. *Drugs*, she thought vaguely, *I'm sedated*. It was so funny she felt like giggling, but laughter was too much like hard work.

' – sample bottle please, and get her a new catheter bag –' The words made no sense.

Miriam tried to ask, 'What's going on?' but nothing came out. There was an unpleasant pressure between her legs and a sensation of cold, uncomfortable and intimate. *Not due for a smear test*, she thought irrelevantly, and managed to make an indignant grunt.

'She's too light, give me another five mikes,' said the same voice. Then there was a prickling at her wrist and the world went away for a while.

The next time she woke up was both better and worse. She had a pounding headache and her mouth felt as if a family of small rodents had camped out on her tongue – but she was in a bed, and fully conscious, the soft valium blanket no longer pressing down on her. Instead, she was alert – and acutely conscious of just how stunningly stupid she'd been.

In her careful list of what might have gone wrong, she'd overlooked option three: the entire clinic was a front for Angbard's organization, in which case it was no surprise at all that it was doppelgängered. And Darling had known she was a hoaxer as soon as she opened her mouth, because none of the IVF scheme details had been registered with the relevant FDA supervisory committees. Nobody outside the Clan had ever *heard* of W* heterozygotes. So . . .

She groaned and tried to roll over, away from the too-bright sunlight that was hurting her eyelids, only to be brought up short by a metal bracelet locked around her left wrist. She opened her eyes to see a whitewashed concrete wall inches away from her nose. *I'm a prisoner.*

The realization was crushing, and with it came a sense of total despair at her own stupidity. *I told Paulie to take care and not go barging in, why couldn't I listen to my own advice?* She pushed herself upright and looked around, taking stock of her situation.

She was lying on a narrow cot in a room about five feet wide and maybe eight feet long. Next to the end of the bed, a stainless-steel sink was bolted to the wall. At the foot of the bed she could see a similarly grim-looking commode next to the door. The bed had a foam pillow and a sheet, and that was it. They'd dressed her in a hospital gown, taken her clothes, and handcuffed her to a ring in the wall by a length of chain. There was a window set high up in another wall, through which the morning – or afternoon – sunlight slid, and a naked bulb recessed in the ceiling, but she couldn't see a light switch. There was no mirror over the washbasin, no handle on the inside of the door, and absolutely no sign to betray where she was. But she already knew what this place had to be, and where. It was a doppelgänger cell in one of the Clan's surviving safe houses. An oubliette. People could vanish in here, never be seen again. For all she knew, maybe that was the idea – there'd be a sealed room on the other side, air full of carbon monoxide or some other silent killer so that if she somehow unchained herself and tried to world-walk . . .

Miriam shook her head, desperately trying to dispel the bubbling panic. *I do not need this now*, she told herself faintly. *I mustn't go to pieces*. But telling herself didn't help much. In fact, it seemed to make things worse. She'd stuck her nose into Angbard's business, and she'd have to be a blind fool to imagine that Angbard would just slap her lightly across the wrist and say 'Don't do it again' at this point. Angbard's authority was based on the simple, drastic fact that everybody knew that you didn't cross the duke. Roland had been terrified of him, Baron Oliver and her grandmother the dowager had given Angbard a wide berth, focusing instead on weaklings among his associates – the only person she'd known to openly cross Angbard was Matthias, and he'd just *vanished*. Quite possibly she was going to find out where he'd gone. If not – she cringed. It wasn't as if she could try to bluff that it was just a stupid, sophomoric prank, an attempt to get his attention. Angbard wasn't an idiot, and more important, he didn't think *she* was. Which meant that he was bound to take her seriously. And the last thing she wanted was for Angbard to get it into his head that she was looking for – not to use any euphemisms – blackmail material. She glanced at her wrist, halfway desperate enough to try and world-walk anyway, risking the doppelgänger room. Then she gave an involuntary moan of despair. Her temporary tattoo was gone.

There must have been a hidden camera or spy hole somewhere in the walls, because she didn't have to wait long. Maybe half an hour after she awakened, the door rattled and slammed open. Miriam flinched away but was brought up short by the chain. Two guys in business suits stared at her from the doorway like leashed hounds watching a rabbit. Behind them stood an older man with a dry, sallow face and an expression like a hungry ferret: 'We can do this two ways, easy or hard. Easy is, you sit in this wheelchair and don't say nothing. You don't want hard.'

'Do you know who I am?' asked Miriam.

One of the hounds glanced at the ferret for approval: receiving it, he stepped forward and punched her in the solar plexus. She writhed on the bed, trying to suck in enough air to scream, while the ferret watched her. 'We know who you are,' he said after a minute, so quietly that she nearly missed his words beneath the noise of her own racking gasps. 'Boys, get her into the chair. She'll be easy now – won't you?'

There was a wheelchair waiting in the corridor and they got her into it in short order, transferring the handcuff and discreetly tucking it under her robe. Miriam didn't pay much attention to the ride. Her chest was on fire, she'd lost bladder control when the guard punched her, and she felt too frightened and humiliated to risk meeting anyone's eyes.

They wheeled her to an elevator, then along another hallway, and she caught a brief glimpse of daylight before they pushed her up a ramp into the back of an ambulance, all stainless-steel fittings and emergency kits strapped to the walls. Ferret clambered in with her, and after they secured the chair to the floor both hounds climbed out. They shut the doors, and a short time later the ambulance moved off. Miriam stared at the ferret and licked her lips. 'Can I talk now?'

'No.' She flinched in anticipation but he didn't hit her. The ambulance turned a corner and accelerated, then the driver goosed the siren.

Ferret caught her looking at him. 'Always talking,' he said tiredly. 'Do you want anything?'

Miriam stared. 'Do I want anything?' She shook her head. 'Got a towel?'

He reached out and grabbed a handful of tissues from a box, dumping them in her lap with an expression of mild distaste. 'When we get where we're going I'm going to wheel you out in that chair and take you to a transfer station. You will use the sigil there to follow me across. You won't speak to anyone, under any circumstances. You will be given clothes, then you will follow me to a room where somebody important will give you orders. You will do exactly what they tell you to do. If you do not obey their orders I will hurt you or kill you as they direct me, because that's my job. Do you understand?'

The siren cut in again. Miriam stared at him some more: then she nodded, frightened into speechlessness. This quiet, middle-aged man terrified her. Something about him suggested that if he thought he should kill her he wouldn't hesitate for a second – and he'd sleep soundly in his bed afterward.

The ferret looked satisfied. He shook his head, then leaned back. His suit coat fell open far enough that Miriam could see his handgun.

She licked her lips: if she'd been a comic-book heroine, she supposed she would lean forward and make a grab for it. But she wasn't a superhero. Comic-book Miriam lived in the land of make-believe, and it was real-world Miriam who'd somehow have to get out of this mess intact. Comic-book Miriam wouldn't let herself get trapped, beaten, and cowed in the back of an ambulance with a fifty-something hit man, on her way to an appointment with someone who had the power to have her killed. She wouldn't have pissed herself the first time one of the hounds punched her, or ignored Paulie and Erasmus, or gone in to see Dr. Darling without backup, or tried to get to see Baron Henryk without preparation . . . *I'm a fuckup*, she thought miserably. *I'm not safe to be allowed out on my own.*

The ambulance braked hard, turned, and slowed to a stop. 'Remember what I said. And no yakking.' The doors opened, revealing an underground car park and both hounds – this time one of them cradled a short-barreled Steyr AUG. *Definitely Clan Security*, Miriam registered, her knees going weak with dread. *They've got me dead to rights*, except that as far as Security were concerned, nobody had any rights: the Clan had been in a state of perpetual warfare since long before she was born, and even before that they'd taken a very medieval approach to dealing with dissent.

The garage was pretty clearly part of a Clan transshipment station, just like the others she'd seen: carefully designed to look like corporate offices from the outside, but equipped as a trans-dimensional fortress/post office once you got past the discreetly armored doors. The Clan had an almost Roman approach to standardizing the design of their bases. As the ferret directed her toward the stairs at the back of the vehicle park Miriam looked around, sickly certain that she wouldn't be seeing its like again – not for a long, long time. They'd taken her locket, emphasizing the point by scrubbing her temporary tattoo. Escape was not an option they had in mind for her.

As it turned out, they weren't going to leave her any options at all. The ferret and his helpers rolled her out of the ambulance, still in the chair, and wheeled her over to an elevator at the back of the garage. She glanced over her shoulder: from the inside, the garage doors looked huge and intimidating, reinforced against the risk of a police raid. They rode in silence down to a sub-basement level, then the guards wheeled her down a short dusty passage to a room walled in pigeonholes. The room was dominated by an open area marked out with yellow tape on the floor, in front of what looked like a window bay covered by a green baize curtain. 'When the curtain opens, use the sigil,' said the ferret, wheeling her into position. 'I'll be right behind you.'

'But I'm in a chair –' Miriam began to rise, but a hand pushed down on her shoulder.

'You're electrically insulated. Rubber tires.'

Miriam sat down again. *Electrically insulated?* she wondered. Her office chair, the one she'd first world-walked in while sitting at home, had plastic castors for feet –

The curtain opened on stomach-churning disorder. Miriam glanced round. The hound was waiting. She looked back and let her mind go blank. A moment later she was facing a closed red curtain, her head pounding as if someone were hammering a railroad spike through it. Her already-sore guts knotted in pain. She glanced round again.

'Don't even think it,' the ferret murmured as he wheeled her out of the transfer zone. 'Remember what I told you.'

Another corridor rolled past, this time featuring a tiled floor and wooden panels on the walls. It was narrow and gloomy, illuminated by weak electric bulbs. *A great Clan house, but which one?* She shifted in the wheelchair, wincing against the headache that was clogging her thoughts. Whoever they were, just maintaining an electrical system was a sign of wealth and influence. And they were somewhere near New York, near the capital city Niejwein, in other words. Her guts were close to cramping with dread. Clan Security had its own infrastructure, separate from the Clan Trade Committee's postal service. Whoever she was being taken to see, they weren't low down the pecking order. Baron Henryk, perhaps – or possibly the duke himself. Or –

The ferret stopped beside a door and knocked twice. Someone unseen opened it from the inside. 'Consignment delivered,' the ferret told the worried-looking maidservant in the entrance, as he unlocked the handcuff securing her to the wheelchair with a flourish of a key ring she hadn't even noticed him holding. 'Stand up,' he told Miriam. To the servant: 'You've got ten minutes. Then I want her back, ready or not.'

Miriam pushed herself upright, wincing as she was assailed by various aches and pains. She took a stumbling step forward and the maid caught her arm. 'This way, please you,' she said haltingly, her accent thick enough to cut with a knife. Miriam nodded as the ferret disappeared and another servant closed the door behind her. 'We are, please you, to disrobe – '

They had clothing waiting for her, a bodice and shift. Day wear for Niejwein. Miriam let them lace her up without speaking. Her hair was a mess, but they had a plain linen cap to cover it up. *If they were just going to kill me out of hand they wouldn't bother with this*, Miriam told herself, and desperately tried to believe it.

*

Ten minutes later there was another rap on the door. One of the maids went to answer it. There was a whispered exchange of Hochsprache, then the ferret stepped inside and looked her up and down. 'She'll do,' he said tersely. 'You. This way.'

The ferret led her up the corridor to a narrow servants' staircase, then along a landing to a thick oak door. It opened without a knock. 'Go through,' said the ferret. 'He's waiting for you.' He gave her a light shove in the small of the back; unbalanced, Miriam lurched forward into the light.

The room was large, high-ceilinged, and cold in the way that only a room in a palace heated by open fires can be cold. High windows drizzled sunlight across about an acre of handwoven, richly embroidered carpet. There was no furniture except for a writing desk and a chair against one wall, situated directly beneath a dusty oil painting of a man in a leather coat standing beside a heavily laden pony.

Miriam took a couple of steps toward the middle of the room before she realized who was sitting behind the desk, poring over a note. She stopped dead, her heart flip-flopping in panic. 'Great-uncle, I – '

'Shut up.' It was Baron Henryk, the head of the royal secret police, not kindly, casual Uncle Henryk, who faced Miriam from behind the desk. Uncle Henryk was amusing and friendly. Baron Henryk looked anything but friendly. 'Do you know what this is?' He brandished the sheet of paper at her.

Miriam shook her head.

'It's an execution warrant,' said Henryk, pushing a pair of reading glasses up his nose. 'Stand over here, where I can see you.' He jotted something on the sheet of paper, then folded it once and moved it to an out-tray. 'Not the full-dress public variety, more what the Americans' CIA would call a termination expedient order. Your uncle runs them past me as partly a courtesy to the Crown – as a duke he has the right of high justice, should he choose to use it – but also as a measure of prudence.' Reflectively: 'It's a little hard to undo afterward if it turns out you switched someone off by mistake.'

'You, you approve execution warrants for the Clan?'

'Don't you tell me you didn't suspect something of the kind.' Henryk stared at her for a moment, then looked at the next note on his in-tray and frowned. 'Hmm.' He picked up a different pen and scrawled a red slash across the page, folded it, and put it in the out-tray. 'I don't think so.' He put the pen down as carefully as if it were a loaded gun, then looked back at Miriam. 'I'm not ready to give up on you yet.'

Miriam took a deep breath. 'What – who – was that?'

'It could have been you.' His lips quirked. 'We can't protect you forever, you know.' He carefully drew a black velvet cloth across the papers and turned round to face her. 'Especially if you keep putting your head through every snare you come across.'

'Why am I here?' She wanted to ask, *How much do you think I know?* But right now that might be a very bad idea indeed. Possibly she knew more than Henryk realized, and if that was the case, admitting it could be a fatal mistake.

'You're here because you stuck your nose where it didn't belong. *I'm* here because I'm trying to control the damage.' He took his reading glasses off and folded them carefully, then placed them on top of the black cloth. 'Let's get this straight. We know you learned about something you aren't supposed to know about. That's . . . not good. Then you compounded it by getting involved – and getting involved personally! You could have been identified. The next step might have been full public disclosure, with who knows what consequences. Helge, that is not acceptable. Before, before all this started, you came to me complaining that you were being treated as if you were under arrest. This time, make no mistake, you *are* under arrest.'

She tried to stay silent, but it was too hard. 'What are you going to do with me?'

Baron Henryk didn't reply at first. Instead, he looked up at the windows for a while, as if inspecting the quality of the plasterwork of the surrounds. 'Interfering with the Clan post is a capital offense,' he said, pushing back his chair. He stood up heavily and crossed the carpet to the far side of the room, limping slightly. Miriam stood as if rooted to the spot. 'Just so that you understand how serious the situation is, I was not exaggerating when I said that execution warrant might be yours.' Henryk turned and squinted at her across the room from between fingers held in a frame, like a cinematographer assessing a camera angle. 'Hmm.'

Miriam shivered involuntarily and took a step toward him. 'Then why – '

'Because you are still useful to us,' Henryk said calmly. 'Stop, stand still.' He walked across to the other corner of the room, looked at her from between crossed fingers. 'That's good. As I was saying, you made a habit of sticking your nose into affairs where it has no business. Luckily this time we found out before it became common knowledge – otherwise I would have had to approve a great deal more death warrants in order to cover up your misbehavior, and your mother would never forgive me.' He made the rectangle again.

'What are you doing?'

'I'm thinking of taking your portrait; be still.' He squinted and shifted a little. 'It's a hobby of mine, plate-glass daguerreotyping.' He lowered his hands and limped back toward his desk. 'The Queen Mother approves of you.'

Miriam took another deep breath, distressed. 'What's that got to do with things?'

'It suggests a way out of the dilemma.' Henryk stopped, just out of arm's reach, and watched her. 'Interfering with the post, Helge, isn't the only capital offense. Making the head of Clan Security look like an idiot – *that* is a capital offense, albeit a more subtle one for which the punishment is never made public. As for jeopardizing relations between the Clan and the Crown, that is *really* serious. Lèse-majesté, possibly treason. Not that you're guilty of the latter two, not yet, but I wouldn't put it past you, given how you've got the crown prince's nose out of joint already. We can't afford to give you any more rope to play with, Helge, or you will succeed in hanging yourself, and possibly a number of unfortunates alongside you. I'm afraid this is where the buck stops.' He walked back to his desk and unfolded the black cloth, swearing mildly as he spilled his spectacles. '"Deferred pending over-riding necessity", Helge, that's all the slack I can buy you.' He held up the folded paper. 'So here's what is going to happen:

'You will speak to nobody about reading the post, without my permission, or that of the duke your uncle. The, ah, loose ends who might have deduced your activity have been tied off neatly. If you do not speak of it, and we do not speak of it, it did not happen. This paper will remain on file for a few years, until we feel we can trust you. *But.*' He paced back toward the other side of the room. 'You will have nothing more to do with the Clan postal service ever again, Helge, ever again. This is the immediate consequence of your actions. You are to be permanently removed from the corvée, and temporarily deprived of the ability to walk between worlds.' He grimaced. 'Don't force us to make it permanent, there are ways and means short of execution that would achieve that end' – he picked up a pen-sized cylinder and held it for her to see, then put it down again – 'do you see?'

Miriam swallowed. *That's a laser! He's talking about blinding me!* The idea of spending the rest of her life unable to see horrified her. 'I understand,' she managed to croak.

'Good.' Baron Henryk nodded. 'I'm sure you appreciate that your position is somewhat fraught. But the Queen Mother approves of you.' Pace, pace, pace: he was off again, as if he didn't want to face her. 'She has requested your attendance upon her and her youngest surviving grandson at your convenience, Helge. I trust you know what this is about.'

Miriam felt the blood draining from her face. 'What?' she asked nervously.

'Face facts.' Henryk could sound as fussily pedantic as any schoolteacher when he was upset. 'You are a Clan lady of high birth, single, still of childbearing age. If you can't serve the commerce committee, how else may you serve us? There's not a lot else for you to do,' he said, almost apologetically. 'So you're going to go back to your residence and wait there, and work on your, what you think of as, your cover identity. Countess Helge voh Thorold d'Hjorth. You're not going to be allowed to be Miriam Beckstein again until we're sure we can trust you. We know about your dissociative tendencies, this unfortunate proclivity toward imposter syndrome. It's time we gave you some help in breaking the habit. Think of it as an enforced vacation from the pressures of modern life, *hein*? Practice your Hochsprache and persist with the gentle arts, and try not to overexert yourself too much. One way or the other, you're going to make yourself of use, even if only by way of giving us another generation of world-walkers or a royal heir. It will go easier for you if you cooperate of your own free choice.'

'You want to marry me off to the Idiot,' she heard herself saying. 'You want me to bear world-walking children who are in line for the throne. If Egon were to die – '

'That would be treason,' Henryk said sharply, staring at her. 'The Clan would never, *ever*, countenance treason.'

The blood was roaring in Miriam's ears: *You wouldn't dabble, but you might play at it in earnest*, she thought. *Get me out of here!* A monstrous sense of claustrophobia pressed down on her, and her stomach twisted. 'I feel sick,' she said.

'Oh, I hope not.' Henryk looked alarmed. 'It's much too soon for *that*.'

FORCED ACCULTURATION

The ferret was waiting outside with two men-at-arms. They hand-cuffed her wrists behind her back, then marched her down the narrow staircase and out to a walled courtyard at the rear of the building where a carriage was waiting. The windows were shuttered, screens secured with padlocks. Miriam didn't resist as they loaded her in and bolted the door. What would be the point? Henryk was right about one thing – she'd screwed up completely, and before she tried to dig her way out of this mess it would be a good idea to think the consequences of her actions through very carefully indeed.

The carriage was small and stuffy and wandered interminably along. The noise of a busy street market reached her, muffled by the shutters. Then there was shouting, the clangor of hammers on metal. *Smith Alley*, she thought. Every time the carriage swayed across a rut in the cobblestone road surface it lurched from side to side, throwing her against the walls. It stank of leather, and stale sweat, and fear.

After a brief eternity the carriage lurched to a halt, and someone unlocked the door. The light was harsh: blinking, Miriam tried to stretch the kinks out of her back and legs. 'This way,' said the ferret.

It was another mansion with closed courtyards and separate servants' quarters. Miriam panted as she tried to keep up, half-dazzled by the glare of daylight. The ferret's two minions seized her by the elbows and half-dragged her to a small door. They propelled her up four flights of stairs – passing two servants who stood rigidly still, their faces turned to the wall so that they might not see her disgrace – then paused in front of a door. *At least it's not the cellar,* Miriam thought bleakly. She'd already seen what the Clan's dungeons looked like. The ferret paused and stared at her.

'These will be your quarters.' He glanced at the door. 'You may consider yourself under house arrest. Your belongings will be moved here, once we have searched them. Your maidservants likewise, and you may continue your activities as before, with reservations. I will occupy the outer chamber. You will not leave your quarters without my approval, and I will accompany you wherever you go. Any messages you wish to send you will give to me for approval. You will not invite anyone to visit you without my prior approval. If you attempt to disobey these terms, then' – he shrugged – 'I stand ready to do my duty.'

Miriam swallowed. 'Where are we?' she asked.

'Doppelgängered.' The ferret's cheek twitched. Abruptly, he turned and pushed the door open. He stepped behind her and unlocked the cuffs. 'Go on in.'

Miriam shuffled through the door to her new home, staring at the floor. It was rough-cut stone, with an intricate handwoven carpet laid across it. Behind her, the door scraped shut: there was a rattle of bolts. She looked up, across a waiting room – perhaps a little smaller than her chambers in Thorold Palace had been – at a window casement overlooking the walled courtyard they'd brought her in through.

'It could have been worse,' she told herself quietly. The place was furnished – expensively, by local standards – although there was no electric lighting in evidence. Doors led off to other rooms. The fireplace was about the size of her living room back in Cambridge, but right now it was unlit. 'Where are the servants?' She was beginning to feel hungry: it was the stomach-stuck-to-ribs haven't-eaten-for-days kind of hunger that sometimes came on after extreme stress. She walked over to the nearest door, opened it. A housemaid jumped to her feet from a stool just inside the doorway and ducked a deep curtsey.

'Do you know who I am?' Miriam asked.

The woman looked confused. 'Myn'demme?'

Of course. 'I am Countess Helge,' Miriam began in her halting Hochsprache. 'Where – what – is food here?' The woman looked even more confused. 'I am – to eat –' she tried again, a sinking feeling in her heart. It was, she realized, going to be very hard to get anything done.

*

It took Miriam only an evening to appreciate how far her universe had shrunk. She had four rooms: a bedroom dominated by a huge curtained bed, the reception room, a waiting room that doubled as a dining area, and the outer vestibule. The ferret lived in the vestibule, so she avoided it. What lay beyond its external door, which was formidably barred, she had no idea. The only window with a view, in the reception room, overlooked the courtyard but was not high enough to see over the crenellated walls. This wasn't a show house in the style of Thorold Palace, but a converted castle from an older, grimmer age. A window with a scenic view would have been an invitation to a crossbow bolt. The sanitary facilities were, predictably, primitive.

Three maidservants came when she tugged the bellpulls in the bedroom or the reception room. None of them spoke English, and they all seemed terrified of her. Or perhaps they were afraid of being seen talking to her by the ferret. She was forced to communicate in her halting Hochsprache, but they weren't much use when it came to getting language practice.

On the evening of her first day, after she'd picked over a supper of cold cuts and boiled Jerusalem artichokes, the ferret came and ordered her into the vestibule. 'Wait here,' he said, and went back into the reception room, locking the door. Miriam worked her way into an anxious frenzy while he was gone, terrified that Baron Henryk had revisited his decision to leave her alive; a distant thumping on the other side of the door suggested structural changes in progress. When the ferret opened the door again and returned to his seat by the barred door, Miriam looked at him in disbelief. 'Go on,' he said impatiently; 'I told you your possessions would be moved in, didn't I?'

There was a huge wardrobe in her bedroom now, and a dresser. Relieved, Miriam hurried to look through them – but there was nothing in the drawers or on the chest but the garments Mistress Tanzig had laboriously assembled for her. No laptop, no books, no Advil, no CD Walkman, nothing remotely reminiscent of American life. 'Damn,' said Miriam. She sat on the embroidered backless bench that served for a chair. 'Now what?' Obviously Henryk's security people considered anything that hinted of her original home to be suspect, and after a moment's thought she couldn't fault them. The laptop – if she'd had a digital camera she might have loaded a picture of the Clan sigil into it, then made her escape. Or she might have slipped a Polaroid between the pages of a book. They'd made a clean sweep of her possessions, taking everything except that which a noblewoman of the Gruinmarkt might have owned – even her battered reporter's notebook and automatic pencil were gone. Which left her with a wardrobe full of native costumes and a jewel box with enough ropes of pearls to hang herself with, but nothing that might facilitate her flight. *Henryk really does expect me to revert to being Helge*, she thought. She looked around in mild desperation. There was a strange book on the dresser. She reached for it, opened the leather cover: *Notes towards a Hochsprache-Anglaische Grammarion* it said, printed in an old-fashioned type. Succumbing to the inevitable, Miriam started reading her homework.

The next morning she wore a local outfit. *Better get used to it*, she thought resignedly. *No jeans and tees here.* She was sitting on the bench by the window casement, staring out at the courtyard to relieve her eyes from studying the grammarian, when the door to the vestibule opened without warning. It was the ferret, with two unfamiliar maidservants standing behind him, and another man: avuncular-looking, with receding hair and spectacles and a beer gut. He was holding a large leather briefcase. 'Milady voh Thorold d'Hjorth?' he said in a slightly creepy way that made Miriam take an instant dislike to him.

'Yes?' She frowned at the ferret.

'If you will permit me to introduce myself? I am Dr. Robard ven Hjalmar. Your great-uncle the baron asked me to pay a house call.'

'What kind of doctor are you?'

'The medical kind.' He managed a smile that was halfway between a simper and a smirk.

'A medical –' Miriam paused. 'I don't need a doctor,' she said automatically. 'I'm fine.' Which wasn't strictly true – her ribs ached from the punch, and she was feeling unnaturally torpid and depressed – but something about ven Hjalmar made her mistrust him instinctively.

'You don't need a doctor *now*,' he said fussily, and planted his case on the floor. 'However, I have been asked to take you on as one of my patients.'

The ferret cleared his throat. 'Dr. ven Hjalmar ministers to the royal family.'

'Oh, I see.' Miriam put the book down, carefully positioning the bookmark. 'What does that entail?' *Why me?*

'I am required to testify to your health and fitness.' Ven Hjalmar's gaze slid around the room nervously, avoiding her. 'You are, I am sure you are aware, of a certain age – not too old for a first confinement, but certainly in need of care and attention. And I understand you may have other medical needs. If you would be so good as to retire to your bedchamber, your maids will relieve you of your outerwear so that I may prepare my report. You need not be afraid, you will be chaperoned and your guardian will be right outside the door.'

Miriam looked at the ferret. 'Do I get an opportunity to say no?'

The ferret stared right back. 'Remember your instructions.' The two unfamiliar maids stepped forward and took Miriam by the arms. She tensed, on the edge of panic: but the ferret was watching her.

What happened next was one of the most unintrusive but oddly unpleasant medical examinations Miriam had ever undergone. The servants led her into the bedroom; then, with the door closed, one of them (a beefy blond woman with rosy cheeks and the look of an amateur boxer to her) held Miriam's wrists together while the other unlaced her bodice. Neither of them spoke. 'Let me – go,' Miriam tried, but boxer-woman just stared at her dumbly.

'Stand still, please.' It was ven Hjalmar. Boxer-woman refused to let go, holding her pinioned. 'Open your mouth. Ah – hah. Very good.' He stepped around her and she felt a stethoscope through her chemise. 'Breathe in – and out. Ah, good.' He worked fast, giving her a basic examination. Then: 'I gather you were given a pap smear on the other side. I'll have the results of that back in a day or so. Meanwhile, I'd like to ask you some questions about your medical history.'

Pap smear? Miriam blinked. 'Make them let me go,' she said stubbornly, flexing her wrists.

'Not yet.' Ven Hjalmar looked down his nose at her, standing there in her underwear with her wrists immobilized by boxer-woman. 'When, exactly, did you lose your maidenhood?'

'None of your business.' She tried not to snarl. *If you do not obey your orders I will hurt you*, the ferret had said: she didn't dare forget.

'I assure you, it is very much my business.' Ven Hjalmar shrugged. 'And it will be the worse for you if you don't answer.'

'Why do you want to know?' she demanded. Boxer-woman tugged on her left wrist, hard enough to make her wince. 'What *is* this?'

'I am attempting to compile a report for the Crown,' Ven Hjalmar said primly. 'You are thirty-three years old, I understand? You are in good health and disease-free, and I am informed already that you are not a virgin, but this is old for a first pregnancy, such as you will be attempting within the next year. I need to know everything about your reproductive history. If you will not tell me, I will have to examine you intimately, and then guess as to the rest. Which would you prefer?'

'It won't be a first pregnancy,' Miriam admitted through gritted teeth. *Damn, why couldn't I have gotten my tubes tied?* She knew why: she'd never gotten around to it. She even knew why she'd never gotten around to it – the sneaking suspicion that one day there might be a right time and a right man to start a family with. The huge irony being that as a direct result she was now being lined up to start a family with absolutely the wrong man at the wrong time. 'I was twenty-one.' She tried to pull away again. 'Make her let go of me.'

'Keep talking,' said ven Hjalmar.

Miriam tensed, but boxer-woman was developing an evil Nurse Ratched glare. 'One child. Girl, the father was my ex-husband, I was still studying – a contraceptive accident. I didn't want an abortion but we couldn't afford to bring her up so Mom suggested we adopt out – '

Scribble scribble. Ven Hjalmar's pen was busy. Miriam kept talking, her mind blank; she managed one barefaced lie (that she didn't know anything about the adopters), but that was it. Abject surrender. She felt dirty. What business was it of this quack to pick over her sexual history? He wanted to know everything: had she suffered from morning sickness, what medicines had they prescribed, had she ever had bladder problems – *only when your hired thugs punch me in the gut* – and more. He went on for hours. Miriam made another stab at resistance when he started asking for names of every man she'd slept with, but at that point he dropped the matter and switched to asking about her hearing. But the interrogation left her feeling unaccountably dirty, like shop-soiled linen on display for all to see.

Finally, ven Hjalmar muttered something to Nurse Ratched, who let go of Miriam. Miriam took a step back, then sat down on the padded bench. 'Yes?' she asked wearily.

'You have something of an attitude problem, young lady.'

'No shit.' Miriam drew her knees up beneath her shift and crossed her arms defensively around them. 'You're the one giving me the third degree in front of an audience.'

'They won't say anything.' Ven Hjalmar smiled and said something to the other servant woman. She made a gabbling noise, incoherent and liquid, and turned to face Miriam. 'As you can see.'

Miriam looked away the moment she saw the tongueless ruin inside the woman's mouth. 'I see,' she said weakly, trying to recover what was left of her shredded dignity. 'What did she do to deserve that?'

'She discussed her mistress's intimate details.' Ven Hjalmar shook his head lugubriously. 'The royal family takes medical confidentiality very seriously.'

Unaccountably, Miriam felt slightly less disheartened. *So even* you *are afraid, huh? We'll see what we can do with that.* 'So what happens next?'

'I think we can skip the virginity test. It isn't as if you are being considered for the crown prince, after all.' Ven Hjalmar stood up. 'I believe you are a perfectly fit young woman, of sound body, perhaps a little disturbed by your circumstances but that will pass. If you would like something to help your mood, I am sure we can do something about that – have you considered Prozac? Guaranteed to cure all black humors, so I'm assured by the manufacturer. I shall take my leave now, and your own maidservants will help return you to your usual peak of feminine beauty.' He produced the odd, simpering smile once again. 'Incidentally,' he added sotto voce, 'I understand and commiserate with the difficult circumstances of your marriage. If it's any consolation, you may not have to lie with the, ah, afflicted one if you do not wish to. A sample can be obtained and a douche prepared, if you prefer.'

'What if I don't want to become pregnant?'

Ven Hjalmar paused with his hand on the door handle. 'I really don't think you ought to trouble yourself with such unrealistic fantasies,' he said.

'But, what if?' Miriam called to him. Her fingernails bit into her palms hard enough to draw blood.

'Prozac,' said ven Hjalmar, as he opened the door.

*

Three days after Dr. ven Hjalmar's humiliating interrogation, Miriam was beginning to wish she'd taken him up on the offer of antidepressants when the ferret knocked on the door.

'What is it?' she asked, looking up from her book.

'You have an invitation,' he said in Hochsprache. He'd taken to using it almost all the time, except when she was obviously floundering. As ever, her jailer's expression was unreadable. 'The baron says you may accept it if you wish.' He repeated himself in English, just in case she hadn't got the message.

'An invitation.' *Where to?* Her imagination whirled like a hamster on a wheel: *Not the royal court, obviously, or it would be compulsory . . .*

'From the honorable Duchess Patricia voh Hjorth d'Wu ab Thorold. Your mother. She begs your forgiveness for not writing and invites the Honorable Countess Helge voh Thorold d'Hjorth to visit with her for lunch tomorrow.'

'Tell her I'd, I'd –' Miriam licked her lips. 'Of course I'll go.'

'I shall tell her.' The ferret began to withdraw. 'I shall make arrangements. You will be ready to travel by eleven and you will be back here no later than five of the afternoon.'

'Wait!' Miriam stood up. 'Can I see Olga Thorold Arnesen?'

'No.' He began to close the door.

'Or Lady Brilliana d'Ost?'

The ferret stopped and stared at her. 'You are in no position to make demands. If you continue to do so I will punish you.' Then he shut the door.

Miriam paced back and forth across the reception room in a blind panic, stir-crazy from confinement but apprehensive about whatever Iris would say to her. *Of course Henryk will have told her*, she thought. But blood was thicker than water, and surely Iris wouldn't side with him against her – or would she? *She's been so distant and cold since she rejoined the Clan.* The change in her mood had been like a safety curtain dropping across the stage at the end of a play, locking in the warmth and the light. *Mom's got her own problems. She said so.* Like her own mother, the poisonous dowager Hildegarde. *The old women's plot.* She crossed her arms. *Henryk must have told her, or she wouldn't have known where to send the invitation*, she thought. *If I can persuade her to give me a locket I could make a clean break for it –*

But a cold, cynical thought still nagged at her. *What if Mom wants me to marry Prince Stupid? She wouldn't do that . . . would she?*

The ruthless reproductive realpolitik within the Clan had made an early victim of Patricia voh Hjorth: her own mother had forced her into marriage to a violent sociopath. The scars had taken a long time to scab over, even after Patricia had made her run to the other world and settled down to life as Iris Beckstein for nearly a third of a century. Iris wouldn't have dreamed of forcing her own daughter into a loveless marriage of convenience. But now she was back in the suffocating bosom of the Clan, which way would Patricia jump – especially if her own skin was at stake?

*

Back home in Cambridge, Miriam's mother had never made a big thing about wanting grandchildren. But that was then.

They took Miriam to visit her mother for lunch in a sealed sedan chair carried by two strapping porters. It was a hot day, but there were no windows, just a wooden grille behind her head. It was impossible to see out of. She protested when she saw it, but the ferret just stared at her. 'Do you want to attend the duchess, or not?' he asked. Miriam gave in, willing to accept one more indignity if it gave her a chance to talk to Iris. *Maybe she'll be able to get me out of this,* she told herself grimly.

The box swayed like a ship on choppy water. It seemed to take forever to make its way across town. By the time the porters planted it with a bone-jarring thump, Miriam had gone from being off her appetite to the first green-cheeked anticipation of full-blown nausea: she welcomed the rattle of chains and the opening of the door like a galley slave released from belowdecks, blinking and gasping. 'Are we there?'

'Momentarily.' The ferret was imperturbable. 'This way.' Another closed courtyard with barred windows. Miriam's spirit fell. *They're just shuffling me between prisons,* she realized. *I'm surprised he didn't handcuff me to the chair.*

Now the nerves took over. 'Where is – she isn't under arrest too, is she?'

Unexpectedly, the ferret chuckled. 'No, not exactly.'

'Oh.' Miriam followed him, two paces ahead of the guards he'd brought along. She glanced at the walls to either side, half-wishing she could make a break for freedom. A couple of gulls squawked raucous abuse from the roofline. She envied them their insolent disdain for terrestrial boundaries.

They came to a solid door in one wall, where a liveried servant exchanged words with the ferret, then produced a key. The door opened on a walled garden. There was a gazebo against the far wall, glass windows – expensively imported, a hallmark of a Clan property – propped open to allow the breeze in. 'Go right in,' said the ferret. 'I believe you are expected. I will collect you later.'

'What? Aren't you coming in with me? I thought you were supposed to be watching me at all times?'

The ferret snorted. 'Not here.' Then he stepped back through the gate and closed it with a solid click.

Wow. Miriam narrowed her eyes as she looked at the gazebo. *Mom's got clout, then?* She marched up to the door. 'Hello?' she asked.

'Come right in, dear.'

Her mother watched her from a nest of cushions piled on top of a broad-winged armchair. She looked more frail than ever, wearing a black velvet gown with more ruffles and bows than a lace factory. 'Has someone died?' Miriam asked, stepping into the shadow of the gazebo.

'Sit down, make yourself comfortable. No one's died yet, but I'm told it was a close-run thing.'

Miriam sat in the only other chair, next to the circular cast-iron table. Iris watched her: she returned her mother's gaze nervously. After a while she cleared her throat. 'How much has Henryk told you?'

'Enough.'

Another silence.

'I know I shouldn't have done it,' Miriam said, when she couldn't take it anymore. 'But I was being deliberately cut out of my own affairs. And they've been trying to set me up – '

'It's too late for excuses, kid.' Miriam stared. Her mother didn't look angry. She didn't look sad, but she didn't look pleased to see her, either. The silence stretched out until finally Iris sighed and shuffled against her cushions, sitting up. 'I wanted to look at you.'

'What?'

'I wanted to look at you again,' said Iris. 'One last time. You know they're going to break you?'

'I don't break easily.' Miriam knew it was false bravado even as the words left her mouth. The great hollow fear congealing inside her gave the lie away. But what else could she say?

Her mother glanced away evasively. 'We don't bend.' She shook her head. 'None of us does – not me, not you, not even your grandmother. But sooner or later we break. Thirty-three years is what it took, kid, but look at me now. One of the old bitches already.'

'What do you mean?' Miriam tensed.

'I mean I'm about to sell you down the river. At least, that's how it's going to seem at first. I'm not going to lie to you: I don't see any alternatives. We're stuck playing the long game, kid, and I'm still learning the rules.'

'Suppose you explain what you just said.' There was an acid taste in her mouth. Miriam forced herself to unclench her fingers from the arms of her chair. 'About selling me down the river.'

Iris coughed, wheezing. Miriam waited her out. Presently her mother regained control. 'I don't like this any more than you do. It's just the way things work around here. I don't have any alternatives, I'm locked up here and you managed to get caught breaking the unwritten rules.' She sighed. 'I thought you had more sense than to do that – to get caught, I mean. Anyway, we're both out of alternatives. If *I* don't play the game, neither of us is going to live very long.'

'I don't need this!' Miriam finally let go of her tightly controlled frustration. 'I have been locked up and policed and poked and pried at and subjected to humiliating medical examinations, and it's all just some game you're playing for status points? What did you do, promise the Queen Mother you'd marry me off to her grandson if she beat you at poker?'

Iris reached out and grabbed her wrist. Startled, Miriam froze. Her mother's hand felt hot, bony, as weak as a sparrow: 'No, never that! But if you knew what it was like to grow up here, fifty years ago . . .'

Miriam surprised herself: 'Suppose you tell me?' *Go on, justify yourself*, she willed. There were butterflies in her stomach. Whatever was coming, it was bound to be bad.

Her mother nodded thoughtfully. Then her lips quirked in the first sign of a smile Miriam had seen since she'd arrived.

'You know how the Clan braids its families, one arranged first-cousin marriage after another to keep the bloodline strong.' Miriam nodded. 'And you know what this means: the meddling old grannies.'

'But Mom, Henryk and Angbard – '

'Hush. I know about the breeding program. Angbard told me about it. He's not stupid enough to think he can push it through without . . . without allies. In another ten years the first of the babies will be coming up for adoption. He needs to convince the meddling old grannies to accept them, or we'll be finished as a trading network within another couple of generations. So he asked me for advice. I'm his consultant, I guess. I don't think most of the families realize just how close to the edge we are, how badly the civil war damaged us. Small gene pool, insufficient numbers – it's not looking good. I've seen the numbers. If we don't do something about it, the Clan will be extinct within two centuries.' Her voice hardened. 'But then you barged right in, doing what you do – investigating. Yes, I know it's what you did for a living for all those years, but you've got to understand, you can't do that right now. Not here, it's much too dangerous. People here who *really* want to keep secrets tend to react violently to intruders. And there's a flip side to the coin. I know you and the-bitch-my-mother don't get on well' – a twinkle in her eye as she said this; Miriam bit her tongue – 'but Hildegarde is just doing what she's always done, playing the long game, defending her status. Which is tenuous here because we are, let's face it, women. Here in the Gruinmarkt – hell, everywhere in the whole wide world – power comes with a big swinging dick. We, you and me, we're badly adjusted misfits: you've got the illusion that you're anybody's social equal and I, I've been outside . . .'

She fell silent. Miriam shook her head. 'This isn't like you, Mom.'

'This *place* isn't like me, kid. No, listen: what happens to the Clan if Angbard, or his successor, starts introducing farmed baby world-walkers in, oh, ten years' time? Without tying them in to the existing great families, without getting the old bitches to take them in and adopt them as their own? And what happens a generation down the line when they become adults?'

Miriam frowned. 'Um. We have lots more world-walkers?'

'Nuts. You're not thinking like a politician: it shifts the balance of power, kid, that's what happens. And it shifts it away from the braids, away from the meddling old grannies – away from *us*. It's ugly out there, Miriam, I don't think you've seen enough of the Gruinmarkt to realize just how nasty this world is if you're a woman. We're insulated by wealth and privilege, we have a role in the society of the Clan. But if you take that all away we are, well . . . it's not quite as bad as Afghanistan under those Taliban maniacs, but it's not far off. This is what I'm getting at when I talk about the long game. It's the game the old women of the Clan have been playing for a century and a half now, and the name of the game is preserving the status of their granddaughters. Do you want a measure of control over your own life? Because if so, you've got to beat the old bitches at their own game. And that's' – Iris's voice wavered – 'difficult. I've been trying to help you, but then you kicked the foundations out from underneath my position . . .'

'I –' Miriam paused. 'What *is* your position? Is it the medicines?'

'I take it you've met Dr. ven Hjalmar?'

'Yes.' Miriam tensed.

'Who do you think he works for? And who do you think I get my meds from? Copaxone and prednisone, by the grace of Hildegarde. If there's an accident in the supply chain, a courier gets caught out and I go short – well, that's all she wrote.' Iris made a sharp cutting gesture.

'Mom!' Miriam stared, aghast.

'Blackmail is just business as usual,' Iris said with heavy irony. 'I've been trying to tell you it's not pretty, but would you get the message?'

'But –' Miriam was half out of her chair with anger. 'Can't you get Angbard to help you out? Surely they can't stop you crossing over and visiting a doctor – '

'Shush, Miriam. Sit down, you're making me itch.' Miriam forced herself to untense: she sat down again on the edge of her chair, leaning forward. 'If I bring Angbard into this, I lose. Because then I owe him, and I've dragged him into the game, do you see? Look, the rules are really very simple. You grow up hating and fearing your grandmother. Then she marries you off to some near-stranger. You lie back and let him fuck you until you get pregnant a time or three. A generation later, you have your own grandchildren and you realize you've got to hurt them just the way your own great-aunts and grandmother hurt you, or you'll be doing them an even worse disservice; if you don't, then instead of a legacy of some degree of power all they'll inherit is the status of elderly has-been chattel. *That* is what the braid system means, Miriam. You're – you're old enough and mature enough to understand this. I wasn't, I was about sixteen when my great-aunt – my grandmother was dead by then – leaned on the-bitch-my-mother and twisted her arm and made her give me reason to hate her.'

'Um. It sounds like –' Miriam winced and rubbed her forehead. 'There's something about this in game theory, isn't there?'

'Yes.' Iris looked thoughtful. 'I told Morris about it, years ago. He called it an iterated cross-generational prisoner's dilemma. That haunted me, you know. Your father was a very smart man. And kind.'

Miriam nodded; she missed him. Not that he was her real father. Her real father had been killed in an ambush by assassins shortly after Miriam's birth, the incident that had prompted Iris to run away and go to ground in Boston, where she'd met and lived with Morris and brought Miriam up in ignorance of her background. But Morris had died years ago, and now . . .

'When I gave you the locket I didn't expect you to jump straight in and get caught up in the Clan so rapidly. I was going to warn you off. But once you got picked up, there wasn't much else I could do. So I called up Angbard and came back in. I figure I'm not good for many more years, even with the drugs, but while I'm around I can watch your back. Do you see?'

'That was a mistake, it would seem.'

'Oh yes.' Iris was silent for almost a minute. 'Because there are no grandchildren, and in the terms of the game that means I'm not a full player. I thought for a while your business plans on the other side would serve instead, but there's the glass ceiling again: you're a woman. You've set yourself up to do something that just isn't in the rules, so lots of people want to take you down. They want to make you play the game, to conform to expectations, because that re-inforces their own role. If you don't conform, you threaten them, so they'll use that as an excuse to destroy you. And now they've got me as a hostage to use against you.'

'Oh. Oh dear.'

'You can say that again.' Iris reached out and tugged a bellpull. There was a distant chime. 'Do you want some lunch while you're here? I wouldn't blame you if all this has put you off your appetite . . .'

*

Miriam succumbed to depression on the way back to her prison. The sedan chair felt like a microcosm for her life right now, boxed in and darkly claustrophobic, the walls pressing tighter on every side, forcing her into a coerced and unwilling conformity. When she was very young she'd sometimes played the *I'm really a Disney princess but I was swapped at birth for a commoner* make-believe game. Somehow it had never involved being locked inside a swaying leather-lined box that smelled of old sweat and potpourri, her freedom restricted and her independence denied. The idea that once people decided you were going to be a princess, or a countess, your life stopped being your own, your *body* stopped being private, had never occurred to her back when she was a kid. *I need to talk to someone*, Miriam realized. Someone other than Iris, who right now was in as much of a mess as she was. *Otherwise I am going to go crazy*.

It had not escaped her attention that there were no sharp-edged implements in any of the rooms she had access to.

When they let her out in the walled courtyard, Miriam looked up at the sky above the gatehouse. The air was close and humid, and the clouds had a distinct yellowish tinge: the threat of thunder hung like a blanket across the city. 'You'd better go in,' said the ferret, in a rare sign of solicitude. Or maybe he just wanted to get her under cover and call a guard so that he could catch some rest.

'Right.' Miriam climbed the staircase back to her rooms tiredly, drained of both energy and optimism.

'Milady!' Miriam looked up as the doors closed behind her with a thud. 'Oh! You look sad! Are you unwell? What's wrong?'

It was Kara, her young, naive lady-in-waiting. Miriam managed a tired smile. 'It's a long story,' she said. Gradually she realized there was something odd about Kara. 'Hey, what happened to your hair?' Kara had worn it long, down her back: now it was bundled up in an intricate coil atop her head. And she was wearing traditional dress. Kara loved to try imported American fashions.

'Do you like it? It's for a wedding.'

'Oh? Whose?'

'Mine. I'm to be married tomorrow.' Kara began to cry – not happily, but the quiet sobbing of desperation.

'What!' The next thing Miriam knew, she was hugging Kara while the younger woman shuddered, sniffling, her face pressed against Miriam's shoulder. 'Come on, relax, you can let it all out. Tell me about it.' She gently steered Kara toward the bench seat under the window. Glancing around, she realized that the servants had made themselves scarce. 'You're going to have to tell me how you convinced them to let you in here. Hell, you're going to have to tell me how you *found* me. But not right now. Calm down. What's this about a wedding?'

That set Kara off again. Miriam gritted her teeth. *Why me? Why now?* The first was easy: Miriam had unwittingly designated herself as adult role model when she first met Kara. The second question, though –

'My father – after you disappeared last week – he summoned me urgently. I know the match was not his idea, for last we spoke he said I should perhaps wait another summer, but now he said his mind was made up and that a week hence I should be married into a braid alliance. He seemed quite pleased until I protested, but he said you had written that you no longer wanted me and that I should best find a new home for myself! I, I could not believe that! Tell me, milady, it isn't true, is it?'

'It's not true,' Miriam confirmed, stroking her hair. 'Be still. I didn't write to your father.' *I'll bet someone else did, though.* 'Isn't this a bit sudden? I mean, don't these things take time to arrange? Who's the lucky man, anyway?' *You haven't been sneaking a boyfriend, have you?* she wanted to ask, but that seemed a little blunt given Kara's delicate state of mind.

'It's sudden.' Kara sniffled against her shoulder for a while. 'I've never *met* the man,' she wailed quietly.

'What, never?'

'Ouch! No, never!' Miriam forced herself to relax her grip as Kara continued. 'He's called Raph ven Wu, second son of Paulus ven Wu, and he's ten years older than me and I've never met him and what if I hate him? It's all about money. Granma says not to worry and it will all work out – '

'Your grandmother talked to you?'

'Yes, Granma Elise is really kind and she says he's a well-man-nered knight who she has known since he was a babe and who is honorable and will see to my welfare – but he's terribly old! He's almost thirty. And I'm afraid, I'm afraid –' Her lower lip was quivering again. 'Granma says it will be all right but I just don't know. And the wedding's to be tomorrow, in the Halle Temple of Our Lady of the

Dead, and I want you to come. Will you be there?' She held on to Miriam like a drowning woman clutching at a life raft.

'You didn't say how you found me,' Miriam prodded gently.

'Oh, I petitioned Baron Henryk! He said you were staying here and I could see you if I wanted. He even said I should invite you to witness at my wedding. Will you come? Please?'

Oh, so that's *what it's about.* To Miriam the message couldn't have been clearer. And she had no doubt at all that it *was* a message, and that she was the intended recipient. She looked out of the window, turning her head so that Kara wouldn't see her expression. 'I'll come if they let me,' she said, surprising herself with the mildness of her tone.

'Of course they'll let you!' Kara said fiercely. 'Why wouldn't they? Are you in trouble, milady?'

'You could say that.' Miriam thought about it for a moment. 'But probably no worse than yours.'

*

Afterward, Erasmus Burgeson always wondered why he hadn't seen it coming.

It was a humid evening, and he'd sat on the open top deck of the streetcar as it rattled toward the hotel downtown where he was to meet his contact. He breathed deeply, relishing the faint smoky tang of the air now that his sore old lungs had stopped troubling him: *I wonder where Miriam is?* he idly thought, opening and refolding his morning newssheet. She'd changed his life with that last visit and those jars of wonder pills. *Probably off somewhere engaging in strange new ventures in exotic worlds far more advanced than this one,* he told himself. Democracies, places ruled by the will of the people rather than the whim of a nearsighted tyrant. He sighed and focused on the foreign affairs pages.

Nader Demands Rights to Peshawar Province. The Persian situation was clearly deteriorating, with the Shah's greedy eyes fastened on the southern provinces of French Indoostan. Of course, the idiot in New London wouldn't be able to let something like that slip past him: *Government Offers to Intercede with Court of St. Peter.* As if the French would listen to British representations on behalf of a megalomaniac widely seen as one of John Frederick's cat's-paws . . . *Prussian Ambassador Wins Duel.* Well, yes – diplomatic immunity meant never having to back out of a fight if you could portray it as an affair of honor. Burgeson sniffed. *Bloody-handed aristocrats.* The streetcar bell dinged as it rattled across a set of points and turned a wide corner.

Erasmus folded the paper neatly and stood up. *Nothing to do with the price of bread*, he thought cynically as he descended the tight circular staircase at the rear of the car. The price of bread was up almost a third over its price at this time last year, and there had been food riots in Texico when the corn flour handed out by the poor boards had proven to be moldy. Fourteen dead, nearly sixty injured when the cavalry went in after the magistrates read the riot act. The streetcar stopped and Erasmus followed a couple of hopeful hedonists out onto the crowded pavement outside. The place was normally busy, but tonight it was positively fizzing. There was something unusual in the air. He took another deep breath. Not having his chest rattle painfully was like being young again: he felt lively and full of energy. And the night was also young.

The Cardiff Hotel – named for Lord Cardiff of Virginia, not the French provincial capital of Wales – was brightly lit with electricals, broad float-glass doors open to the world. A green-and-white-striped canopy overhung the pavement, and a pianist was busy banging both keyboards on his upright instrument for all he was worth, the brass-capped hammers setting up a pounding military beat. Burgeson stepped inside and made his way to the back of the bar, searching for the right booth. A hand waved, just visible above the crowd: he nodded and joined his fellow conspirator.

'Nice evening,' Farnsworth said nervously.

'Indeed.' Erasmus eyed the other man's mug: clearly he was in need of the Dutch courage. 'Can I get you something?'

'I'm sure – ah.' A table-runner appeared. 'Have you any of the hemp porter?' Farnsworth enquired. 'And a drop of laudanum.'

'I'll have the house ale,' said Erasmus, trying not to raise an eyebrow. *Surely it's a bit early for laudanum?* Unless Farnsworth really *was* upset about something.

When the table-runner had left, Farnsworth raised his tankard and drained it. 'That's better. I'm sorry, Rudolf.'

Burgeson leaned forward. 'What for?'

'The news –' Farnsworth waved his hand helplessly. 'I have no images, you understand.'

Burgeson tried to calm his racing heart. He felt light-headed, slightly breathless: 'Is that all? There's no reason to apologize for that, my friend.'

Farnsworth shook his head. 'Bad news,' he croaked.

The table-runner returned with their drinks. Farnsworth buried his snout in his mug. Erasmus, trying to rein in his impatience, scanned the throng. It was loud, too loud for even their neighbors in the next booth to overhear them, and there were no obvious signs of informers. 'What is it, then?'

'Prince James is – it's not good.'

'Ah.' Erasmus unwound a little. Not that he was pleased by news of the crown prince's suffering – no matter that the eight-year-old was destined to grow up to be tyrant of New Britain, he was still just a bairn and could not be held responsible for his parents' misdeeds – but if it was just more trivial court gossip it meant the sky hadn't fallen in yet. 'So how is he?'

'The announcement will be made in about two hours' time. I have to be back at the palace by midnight to plan his majesty's wardrobe for the funeral.'

'The –' Erasmus stopped. *'What?'*

'Oh yes.' Farnsworth nodded lugubriously. 'It will mean war, you mark my words.'

War? Erasmus blinked. 'What are you talking about?'

'Don't you know?' Farnsworth seemed startled.

'I've been on a train all afternoon,' said Erasmus. 'Has something happened?' *Something more than a sick little boy dying?*

'They caught one of the assassins,' Farnsworth explained. 'An Ottoman subject.' He peered blearily at Burgeson's uncomprehending face. 'Prince James was murdered just after lunchtime today; shot in the chest from a building overlooking the Franciscan palace. It was a conspiracy! Bomb-throwing foreigners on our soil, spreading terror

212

and fomenting fear. Naval intelligence says it's a message for his majesty. The crisis in the Persian Gulf. Sir Roderick is recommending a bill of attainder to his majesty that will seize all Ottoman assets held by institutions here unless they back down.'

Burgeson stared at him. 'You. Have got to be kidding.'

Farnsworth shook his head. 'All hell's broken loose, the seventh seal has sounded, and I very much fear that we are about to be bathed in the blood of ten million lambs – conscripted into a war started as a distraction from the empty larders of the provinces, a matter which has most exercised the prime minister these past weeks.' He grabbed Burgeson's hand. 'You've got to do something! Make your friends listen! It's the outside threat to distract and befuddle us, the oldest trick in the library. A brief successful war to wrap themselves in the glory of the flag and justify calls for austerity and belt-tightening, and to distract attention from the empty coffers and supply a pretext to issue war bonds. Only this time, we know the Frogs have got corpses. And so have we. So it's going to be an unusually violent war. And of course they'll clamp down on dissenters and Ranters. They'll implement French rule here, if you give them the chance.' French rule – summary justice, the martial law of the Duc du Muscovy. *The Stolypin necktie* as an answer to all arguments, as that strange otherworld history book Miriam had given him had put it. Erasmus felt cold sweat spring out at the back of his neck.

'I'll tell them immediately,' he said, rising.

'Your drink – '

'You finish it. You look as if you need it more than I do. I've got a job to do.'

'Good luck.'

Erasmus dived into the throng of agitated, wildly speculating men filling the bar and worked his way outside. A street hawker was selling the last of the evening edition: he snagged a copy and stared at the headlines. MUSSELMAN TERROR screamed the masthead in dripping red letters above an engravature of the boy prince lying on the ground, his eyes open. 'Damn.' Erasmus looked around, searching for a cab. *I'll have to notify Lady Bishop*, he thought, *and Iron John. Find out what the Central Committees want to do about the situation.*

Another thought struck him. *I must talk to Miriam; she knows of other worlds more advanced than this. They're ruled by republics, they must have corpuscular weapons – I wonder what she knows about them?* A cab pulled up and he climbed in. *Perhaps we could achieve a better negotiating position if the movement had some . . .*

BREAKOUT

Mike realized something was wrong the moment he passed the checkpoint on the fourteenth floor and found Pete Garfinkle and Colonel Smith waiting for him, with a blue-suiter behind them. The guard was carrying a gun and trying to look in six different directions simultaneously. This worried Mike. Armed guards were a normal fact of life in the FTO, but nervous ones were something new.

'What's up?' he asked.

'We have a problem,' said Smith.

'Matt went for a walk about two hours ago,' said Pete, nervously fingering his document folder.

'Went for a –'

'Down the express elevator from the twenty-third floor, or so it would appear judging from the elevator logs,' Smith added. 'Although there's no evidence he was actually in the elevator car except for the RFID tags concealed in his underwear. Which he is no longer wearing. And there's a missing window on the twenty-third floor. Shall we talk about it?'

They went up to the newly installed Vault Type Room on the nineteenth floor and Smith signed them in. Then they authenticated each other and locked the door. The blue-suiter waited outside, which was a relief to Mike – but only a temporary one. 'Do we know where he went?' he asked as soon as they were seated around the transparent conference table.

'Not a clue.' Smith inclined his head toward Pete. 'Dr. James is going to shit a brick the size of the Empire State Building as soon as he finds out, which is' – he glanced at his wristwatch – 'going to happen in about thirty minutes, so it is *important* that we are singing from the same hymn book before he drops in. Unless we can find our runaway first.' The colonel grimaced. 'So. From the top. How would you characterize Client Zero's state of mind last time you spoke to him?'

I'm not on the spot, Mike realized with an enormous sense of guilt-tinged relief – because it meant someone else was going to catch it in the neck. 'He seemed perfectly fine, to be honest. A bit stir-crazy, but that's not unexpected. He wasn't depressed or suicidal or excessively edgy, if that's what you're looking for. Why? What happened?'

Colonel Smith shook his head and shoved his voice recorder closer to Mike's side of the table. 'Summarize first. Then we'll go round the circle. Treat this as a legal deposition. Afterward I'll fill you in.'

'Okay.' Mike recounted his last meeting with Matthias. 'He was asking about his Witness Protection Program status, but –' Mike stopped dead. 'You said he took a lift down from the twenty-third-floor window. He was on the twenty-*fourth* floor. With no direct elevator between them. How'd he get downstairs?' *Through two security checkpoints and four locked doors and then downstairs in an elevator car with a webcam and a security guard?*

'Later,' Smith said firmly.

'Uh, I'd like to register a note of caution here. Did anyone *see* Client Zero move between floors twenty-four and twenty-three? And was there any evidence that he left the building by one of the ground-level doors?'

There was a pregnant pause.

'I'd have to say that we don't know that,' said Smith. His eyes tracked, almost imperceptibly, toward the door outside which the blue-suiter with the gun would be standing guard.

'Oh.' *Oh shit,* thought Mike.

'I'm betting he got riled up and broke out,' said Smith, his voice even. 'How he managed that is a troubling question, as is why he chose to do it right at this moment. But he's a smart cookie, is Client Zero. Just in case he had outside help, we're going to full Case Red lockdown. Nobody goes below the tenth floor without an armed escort until we've clarified the situation.'

'He can't have evaded our monitoring completely, even if he managed to bypass the guards.'

Smith's pager beeped for attention. He glanced at it, then stood up: 'I'm going to deposit this, then take a call. Back in ten minutes.' He disappeared through the door, taking the voice recorder and leaving Mike and Pete alone in the windowless room with the glass furniture and the vault fittings.

'He got stir-crazy,' said Mike.

Pete looked at him.

'What am I not hearing?' asked Mike.

Pete coughed. 'After your last meeting I dropped in on him. He was pissed – you said you'd been called away – '

'By Eric, he can confirm it – '

'Well sure, but Matt didn't see it that way, he thought you were bullshitting. He was worried. So to get him calmed down I tried to draw him out a bit about why he came over to us. I mean, you've been doing all those grammar sessions and he was getting bored, you know?'

'Okay.' Mike leaned back to listen.

Pete got into the flow of things. 'He had this crazy paranoid-sounding rant about how he was a second-class citizen as far as the bad guys are concerned, on account of how he can't do the magic disappearing trick – well, I'll buy that. And then something about a long-lost cousin turning up and destabilizing some plans of his. Seems she grew up on our side of the fence, worked in Cambridge as some kind of tech journalist. They rediscovered her by accident and she made the wheels fall off Matt's little red wagon by snooping around and stirring up shit. So Matt tried to persuade this Helga woman to get off his case and she – she's called Miriam something here, something Jewish-sounding – '

Can't be, thought Mike. *She can't be the same woman.* The idea was too preposterous for words.

Pete stopped. 'What is it?' he asked.

'Nothing. So what happened? What went wrong with Matt's plans?'

'She wouldn't blackmail – he said she wouldn't play ball, but that's my reading – and there's some stuff about her discovering a whole other world where the Clan guys have got a bunch of relatives who

217

don't like them and who were paying Matt to look after their interests – he's always been a bit of a moonlighter – and the upshot is, he had to cut and run. He's still pissed at her. He came to us because he figured we'd protect him from his former associates.'

'Uh-huh.' Mike nodded. *Miriam – what was her other name?* 'What's this got to do with the time of day?'

'Well.' Pete looked embarrassed. 'I asked him how he thought it had worked, and that was when he got agitated. Said you'd told him something about him being in military custody now? So I tried to get him calmed down, told him it wasn't what it sounded like. But he wasn't having it. And at about five in the morning he went missing. Do I have to draw you a diagram?'

'No,' said Mike. He sighed. 'I knew this military thing was a bad idea.'

'Yeah, well. Which of us is going to tell Smith?'

*

They found the colonel at the security checkpoint by elevator bank B, talking to one of the guards. He didn't look terribly happy. 'What are you doing here?' he demanded.

'I've got a hypothesis I'd like to test, sir. I think Matt may still be in the building. Did we catch him leaving?'

'That's what I was just ascertaining,' said Smith. He glanced around irritably. 'Get me . . .' He snapped his fingers, searching for a name. 'Sergeant Scoville, mister.'

'Sir.' The guard pulled out his walkie-talkie and began talking to someone.

'So.' Smith pointed a bony finger at Mike. 'Explain.'

'Client Zero is no dummy. He knows he's upstairs. He decided he wants to take a walk. We can be fairly sure he can move between floors but he's not on camera, so either he's been holding out on us – and I don't believe he's got what it takes to hack our sensors – or he's gone to ground. My bet is either under the false floor or over the suspended ceiling, probably on the twenty-third but possibly on the twenty-fourth or twenty-fifth floors. He probably ran into the security zone on the twenty-second and bounced. Now he'll be waiting for an opportunity to go elevator surfing or a chance to slip outside while we're distracted.'

'Okay. Now tell me why he's doing this. Where's he likely to go?'

Mike glanced at Pete. 'I think he's breaking out because he thought he was looking at a comfortable relax-a-thon in the Witness Protection Program, and a new identity afterward, with us to protect him from his former associates. Unfortunately, once Dr. James switched him to military custody we lost track of the WP program and his new identity, and he finally twigged that he was one step away from being given the whole unlawful-combatant treatment. As for where he's going – I bet he's got other spare identities stashed away, from before he decided to come in. They won't be as good as what we could have given him *if* we'd kept him in witness protection, but it beats being a ghost detainee.'

'Right.' The guard offered Smith his handset. 'Jack? Our current best guess is that the target's still in the building, above the security zone on ten. My top priority is, I want you to secure the entry zone and the lobby. Nobody leaves the building even if a Boeing flies into the top floor: our target may try to provoke an evacuation so he can escape in the crowd. I want a security detail to start on floor ten and work their way upstairs, one level at a time, until they get to the roof. They will need torches, floor-tile lifters, and ladders because they're going to check the crawlways and overheads, and they need to be armed because our target is dangerous. How soon can you get that started? How many bodies have we got up here anyway?' He listened for a few seconds. 'Damn, I'd hoped for more. Okay, assemble them. Smith out.' He glanced back at the two DEA agents. 'Right. Any other suggestions?'

Mike took a deep breath. 'Is he still valuable to us, if we can get him back?'

'Possibly.' Smith stared at him. 'Your call, son.'

Time stood still. 'I need to work on my grammar,' Mike said slowly. 'But of course, after CLEANSWEEP we'll have more subjects to work with.'

Smith held out his hand for the walkie-talkie, watching Mike's face as he spoke: 'Sergeant? Change of plan. Hold the floor sweep, I don't think we've got enough people to risk it, if the target manages to arm himself . . . Instead I want you to stand by to execute code BLUE-BEARD. That's BLUEBEARD. I'm going to make an announcement in a couple of minutes. If the fugitive doesn't give himself up, we'll exe-cute BLUEBEARD, then ventilate and search the place afterward.'

Pete looked shocked. Mike elbowed the younger agent in the ribs to get his attention. 'Go get us all respirators,' he said. Smith nodded at him. 'You really going to do it, sir?'

Smith nodded again. 'We need to test the security system, anyway.'

'Ri-ight.' The desk guard was watching nervously, as if the colonel had sprouted a second head. Mike grimaced. 'I love the smell of nerve gas in the morning.' Pete reappeared and handed over a sealed poly-thene pack containing a respirator mask and a preloaded antidote syringe.

'It's not nerve gas, it's fentanyl,' Smith corrected him. 'Where's the PA mike on this level?' he asked the desk guard.

'Fentanyl is a controlled substance,' said Pete, a conditioned reflex kicking in.

Mike looked round edgily. BLUEBEARD was a last-ditch antiter-rorist defense; on command, compressed gas cylinders plugged into the air-conditioning on each floor would pump a narcotic mist throughout the building. Sure, there was an antidote, and the ventila-tor masks ought to stop it dead, but the only time it had ever been used for this purpose – in Russia, when a bunch of Chechen terror-ists had taken a theater crowd hostage – more than a fifth of the bystanders had been killed. Gas and confined spaces did not mix well.

'Relax, boys.' Smith looked bored, if anything. 'If you're thinking about that Russian thing, forget it – they didn't have respirator masks there. You're perfectly safe.' He pulled the gooseneck PA mike toward his mouth and hit the red button. 'Is this thing – yes, it's live.' His voice rumbled through the corridors and floor, amplified through hidden speakers. 'Matt, I know you're in here. You've got five minutes to surrender. If you want to live, come out from wherever you're hiding, and go to the nearest elevator bank. Hit the button for the tenth floor, then lie down on the floor of the elevator car with your hands on your head. This is your only warning.'

He killed the PA and turned to the walkie-talkie: 'Okay, you heard me, Sergeant. Fifteen minutes from my mark, I want you to execute BLUEBEARD on all floors above ten. You've got ten minutes from right *now* to do a cross-check on all personnel and make sure they're ready. Antidote kits out, boys. Over.'

Smith unsealed his respirator kit. 'What are you waiting for?'

'The broken window on the twenty-third,' Mike said slowly. 'Has it been repaired? And has anyone secured the window-cleaning system?' He opened the packaging around his respirator as he spoke, peeling the polythene wrapper away and yanking the red seal tab to activate the filter cartridge.

'The –' Pete's eyes narrowed.

'We've agreed Matt's not stupid. He probably guessed we'd have something like BLUEBEARD. Maybe he broke the window because he wanted fresh air to breathe?' Mike pointed toward the nearest outside wall. 'That got me thinking. Someone's got to clean the windows, haven't they? That means a motorized basket, right? Maybe he figured he could ride it down past the security zone while we're busy trying not to choke ourselves?'

'Point.' Smith began to reach for the walkie-talkie again.

'How about Pete and I check out floor twenty-three?' Mike asked, pulling the mask over his head. 'We've got respirators, we're armed, we can take a walkie-talkie. More to the point, maybe we can talk him down. Is that okay by you?'

Smith thought for a moment. Finally he nodded. 'Okay, you have my approval. Stick together, don't take any risks, and remember – I'm not going to cancel BLUEBEARD if he gets the drop on you. Especially not if he takes one of you hostage. Understood?'

'Yes.' Mike glanced at Pete, who nodded.

Smith gestured at the charging station by the security desk: 'Take one of these, they're fully charged.' He picked up his own walkie-talkie. 'Sergeant, I want you to check out the janitorial facilities, find out how they clean the windows above the tenth floor. If there's an outside winch, I want it secured.'

Mike headed for the central service core, opening his holster. 'Come on,' he told Pete, his voice muffled by the mask.

'What's the plan?'

'I want to check out the floor tiles where he smashed the window. Where is it?'

'Twenty-third floor. You turn left at the checkpoint, then take the first transverse corridor past the service core. You want to follow me?'

'He's not armed, is he?'

'I don't think so.' Pete sounded uncertain.

'Well, then.' Mike held his gun at his side and gestured at the door onto the fire stairs with his free hand. 'Let's go.'

They took the steps fast. Mike rapidly discovered that breathing through a gas mask was hard work. He paused, gasping for air, on the twenty-second-floor landing, leaning against a brace of drab green pipes running up and down. Pete seemed to be doing fine: *There's no justice*, he thought. 'I can't run in this thing.' *I'm too old for this SWAT-team game. I'm not thirty-six yet, and I can't run up flights of stairs in a gas mask anymore. What's wrong with me?* He pulled his mask off and shoved it into the inside pocket of his jacket.

'You sure it's safe to do that?' asked Pete. Mike noticed that he wasn't wearing his mask, either.

'I'll hear when Smith trips the gas tanks,' he said with a confidence he didn't feel. 'Anyway, make sure you've got yours, right? Okay, here's how we'll do it when we come out of the stairwell. I'll go first, covering the floor. You follow me, covering the ceiling and my back. We head for the window, and if he's not there, we head for the security station and the PA mike for this floor and I try talking to him. What's wrong with this picture?'

Pete shook his head. 'Nothing obvious to me.'

'Okay, let's go.' Mike shoved himself back onto the stairs and took the last two flights, paused to catch his breath just inside the door, then pushed through.

*

The twenty-third floor was eerily deserted, a high-altitude *Mary Celeste*. Beige carpet tiles, slightly scuffed and in need of cleaning, floored corridors where doors stood open on unfurnished office suites. The black bubbles of surveillance cameras sprouted from ceiling tiles, some of them discolored by water seepage. One of the reasons floor twenty-three had been left vacant was that it had needed more refitting than the rest of the building, thanks to a burst pipe the previous winter. Some of the lighting panels flickered erratically. Mike headed up the corridor, cautiously checking side doors opening off it for any sign of human presence. *Just because we don't think he's armed doesn't mean he isn't,* he told himself, whenever he felt self-conscious.

He turned the corner onto the last stretch of passageway. There was no door at the end, just a wide open-plan office space, almost a thousand square feet of it, walled in windows. Abandoned desks and shelving units clustered in forlorn huddles around the floor. He could hear something now, the whistle of wind blowing past an empty gap in the glass side of the building. It was slightly chilly, even though it was a hot day down below. Mike paused just outside the door and glanced over his shoulder at Pete, who was staring tensely at the ceiling behind them. 'Going in.'

'Okay.'

Mike ducked through the entrance and spun round. Anticlimax: nobody was lurking in the corners behind him. *But what about the desks* – he crouched, casting his gaze around at ankle level. No, there were no giveaway legs visible under the furniture. Nothing, no sign that anybody had visited the place.

'He's not here?'

'Hush.' Mike backed toward the wall beside the door. 'Keep me covered from right there.' He slid along the wall, around the edge of the room. *Three minutes left,* he thought. *What if –*

There was nobody behind any of the furniture. None of the ceiling or floor tiles had been disturbed. The room looked abandoned, except for the missing window unit. Those double-glazed cells didn't break easily; they were toughened glass, held in place by plastic gaskets and screws. Someone had removed the thing, probably unscrewed it, and then shoved it right out of the frame. The breeze was rustling playfully around him, tugging at his jacket, pinching his trouser cuffs. Mike crouched down below the level of the windows and looked up, and out, letting his eyes grow accustomed to the bright daylight above him.

There. Outside the glass, barely visible – it ran behind one of the concrete pillars framing the stretch of glazing – a vertical wire. It was quite a thick wire, but it was almost invisible against the bright daylight. Only a slight vibration gave it away. Mike looked back at Pete, raised a finger to his lips, then beckoned urgently. He cast his gaze along the wall. Another wire stood out on the far side of the missing window pane. *Gotcha.*

Pete hunkered down next to him. 'What is it?' he whispered.

'There's a window-cleaning car somewhere below us, right outside the open cell. I figure he's waiting while we run BLUEBEARD. Then he's going to try to break back in while everyone's expecting him to be down and out.'

'You say that as if you think there are other options.'

'I can think of several, but Matt's not stupid – he knows the more elaborate the scheme, the more likely it is to go wrong. I mean, he might have just done this as a distraction, but then what if we didn't notice it at all? Whatever, I think he's down there, below us.'

'In which case, all we have to do is get him to come back in.'

'Yeah. But he obviously wants out, and – listen, these cars are self-propelled. He's probably as low as he can go, waiting for everyone to clear out before he breaks another window.'

'Right.' Pete straightened up, holding his pistol. 'I'll reel him in.' And before Mike could move to stop him he leaned out of the window, shoulders set, aiming straight down. 'Hey – '

A gray shadow dropped across the window, accompanied by a grating of metal on metal. Pete vanished beneath it, tumbling out of the window.

'Fuck!' Mike jumped up in time to register two more wires and the basketwork cage of a window-cleaning lift wobbling behind the glass with someone inside it: then Matt swung the improvised club he was holding at the window cell Mike was standing next to, and to Mike's enormous surprise it leapt out of its frame and fell on him. He stumbled backward, away from the wall, his arm going numb. *How did he get above us?* he thought, dazed and confused. Then he registered that he'd dropped his pistol. *That's bad*, he thought, his stomach heaving.

Someone kicked it away from him. *Not fair*. He felt dizzy and sick. Things grayed out for a moment. When they came back into focus he was sitting down, his back to a desk. There was something wrong with his face – it was hard to breathe. *The mask*. He looked up.

Matthias squatted on his heels opposite him, holding the gun, looking bored. 'Ah, you're with me again. I was beginning to worry.'

Those window cells had to weigh thirty or forty pounds each – thick slabs of double-glazed laminate clamped between aluminum frames. Matt must have unscrewed it first, then dropped decoy lines below the window-cleaning car before retreating up top to wait like a spider above his trap. The damn thing had hit his head when Matt shoved it at him. A flash of anger: 'Like you worried about Pete when you pulled that stunt? We could have worked something out – '

'I doubt it.' Something about Matt's tone sent a chill down Mike's spine.

'Why are you doing this?'

'Because your organization has failed to protect me. It was worth a try – if you'd gone after the Clan as a police operation, that would have given the thin white duke something more urgent to worry about than a missing secretary, no? But the military – that was a bad idea. I'm not going to Camp X-ray, Michael.'

'Nobody said you were.' Mike tried to push himself up against the desk, but a growing sensation of nausea stopped him.

'And now I will leave. Get up.'

Mike took a deep breath, trying to ignore his butterfly diaphragm. 'What do you want?'

'I want you to take me downstairs. And then we will get into a car and drive somewhere where I will contrive to make you lose me.'

'You know that's not possible.'

Matt shrugged. 'I don't care whether it is possible or not, it is what will happen. Seeking your government's help was a mistake. I'm going underground.'

Mike took another deep breath. His stomach clenched; he waited the spasm out, trying to will the blurring in his vision and the pounding at his temples away. 'No. I mean. Why? What do you hope to achieve?'

'Revenge. Against the bitch.'

'Who?'

Mike must have looked puzzled, because Matt threw back his head and laughed, a rich belly-chuckle that would have given Mike an opening if he'd been in any condition to move. 'The queen in shadow.' Matt stopped laughing. 'Anyway, we're leaving.'

'They won't let you,' Mike said tiredly.

'Want to bet? Remember the sample of metal I gave you, from the duke's private stockpile?'

The plutonium ingot. Mike could see it coming, like a driver stalled on a level crossing at night staring into the lights of an oncoming freight train. He blinked tiredly, trying to focus his double vision. 'What, the, the – '

'There are several of them,' Matthias explained. 'Bombs made with this magic metal of yours. The current duke's father arranged to take possession of several of them three decades ago . . . anyway. I have the keys to the stockpile. They are held in storage areas across the United States. It is the Clan's ultimate deterrent, if you like: they were much more paranoid during the, the seventies when the civil war was being fought. I arranged to deploy one before I defected. It is on a timer, a very long timer, but if the battery runs down, it will explode. The battery is good for a year. I thought, when I came to you months ago, you would let me out in time and I would reset it and that would be all, an insurance policy against your good intentions, nothing more. But now' – he looked irritated – 'you leave me no alternative.'

'Oh Jesus.' Mike stared at him. 'Tell me you didn't.'

'I did. Or at least, you cannot prove that I *didn't*. So, you see, as soon as you are ready to stand, we will go down and talk to your boss, yes? And you will explain that you have to drive me somewhere. And you and I, we will go and I will get lost. But before I go, I will take you to the lockup and you will wait with the device, of course, until it can be defused, and we will all be happy and nobody will be hurt. Yes?'

'You'll tell me where it is?' Mike demanded.

'Of course. I know where the others are, too. They aren't active yet – if you do not follow me, I will not need them, no?'

Three images of a smirking Matt hovered in front of Mike's nose; the back of his neck prickled in a cold sweat. *I'm going to be sick*, he realized. *I'm probably concussed.* The idea that the Clan had planted atomic bombs in storage lockers across the United States was like something out of a bad thriller – like the idea Islamic terrorists would crash hijacked airliners into the World Trade Center, before 9/11. *I've got to tell someone!* 'I feel sick.'

'I know.' Matt peered at him. 'Your eyes, the pupils are different sizes. Stand up now. It is very important you do not go to sleep.' Matt straightened up and took a step back. Mike pushed against the panel behind him and shoved himself upright, wobbling drunkenly. 'To the elevators,' said Matt, gesturing with Mike's own stolen gun.

What have I forgotten? Mike wondered dizzily. He stumbled and lurched toward the doorway. *Feel sick . . .*

'Elevator first. There is a telephone there, no?'

'Mmph.' His stomach heaved: he tried desperately not to throw up.

'Go on.'

Mike stumbled on down the corridor. He was certain he'd forgotten something, something important that had been on his mind before he got distracted, before the slab of window landed on him and Matt made his outrageous claim about the nuclear time bomb. Matt closed the door on the room with the damaged windows behind him, an unconscious slave to habit. Mike leaned against the wall, head down.

'What is it?' Matt demanded, pausing.

'I don't feel so well –' *What's going to happen?* Mike had a nagging sense that it was right on the tip of his tongue. Then his stomach gave a lurch. 'Ugh.'

Matt took a step back, standing between Mike and the elevator core. He blinked, disgustedly. 'Get it over with.'

'Going to be –' Mike never finished the sentence. A giant's fist grabbed him under the ribs and twisted, turning his throat into a fire hose. He doubled over, emptying his guts across the carpet and halfway up the wall opposite.

Matt's face twisted in disgust. 'You're no use to me like that. Wait here.' The next door along was a restroom. 'I'll get you some towels – '

There was a ringing in Mike's ears, and a hissing. His guts stopped heaving, but he felt unaccountably tired. *What have I forgotten?* he asked himself, as he sat down and leaned against the wall. He felt his eyes closing. Something hard-edged was digging into his ribs. *Oh, that. Must be time, then.* He could put the mask on again in a few minutes, couldn't he? *Just a quick nap* . . . Almost without willing it he felt his hand fumbling for the respirator, dragging it out of his inside pocket. His hands felt incredibly hot, but not in a painful way – it was like the best, most wonderful warm bath he'd ever had, all the heat concentrated in his extremities. He wanted it to never stop. But that was all right: he managed to raise the mask to his face, doubling over to get his head low enough to reach, and inhaled through the filter. *I wonder if Matt heard Eric's announcement?* he thought dizzily. *If he was outside the building, at the time* . . .

He was still breathing through the respirator when they found him twenty minutes later, put him on a stretcher, and hauled him off to hospital in an ambulance with blaring siren and flashing lights. But it took them another ten minutes to find Matthias – and by then it was five minutes too late to ask him whether he'd been bluffing.

ULTIMATUM

Miriam found it hard to believe that she'd never attended a wedding among the great families of the Gruinmarkt in the months she'd been living among them. After a sleepless night, she chivvied her maids into helping her into the outfit Kara had picked from her wardrobe, then waited while the ferret rousted out the sedan chair bearers.

Another tedious, uneven magical mystery tour: another bland mansion with walled grounds, somewhere else in the city. Miriam straightened her back as the ferret and his guards waited. 'This way,' he indicated, nodding toward a narrow passageway. 'You will wait at the back, behind the wooden screen. You will say nothing during the ceremony. Observe, do not interfere or it will be the worse for you. I will fetch you from the reception afterward.'

'Worse?' she asked – rhetorically, for she had a very good idea what he meant. 'All right.' She stuck her nose in the air and marched down the corridor as though her guards didn't exist, as if she were attending this function of her own accord, and the occasion were a happy one.

The passage led to a small chapel, located near the back of the building in the oldest construction. The walls were of undressed stone, woodwork blackened with age. Her first surprise was that it was tiny, barely larger than her reception room. Her second surprise was the altar, and the brightly painted statues behind it. She'd have taken them for saints, but the iconography was wrong – no trinity here, but a confusing family tree of bickering authorities, a heavenly bureaucracy with responsibility for everything from births, marriages, and deaths to law enforcement, tax returns, and the afterlife. The post-migration Norse-descended tribes who had eventually settled the eastern seaboard of North America in this world had adopted the Church of Rome, but the Church of Rome hadn't adopted Christianity, or Judaism, or anything remotely monotheistic. The Church here was a formalization and outgrowth of the older Roman pantheon, echoes of which had survived in the Catholic hierarchy of saints, the names and roles of the gods updated for more recent usage with a smattering of Norse add-ons. *But no blood eagles*, Miriam thought, as she walked past the pews of menfolk to take her place behind the wooden latticework screen at the back, behind the women of the two households.

There were only about ten women present, and about twice that number of men; they were mostly servants and bodyguards, as far as Miriam could tell. A couple of heads turned as she walked in, including one formidable-looking lady. 'Wer ind'she?'

'Excuse me, I am Helge. Kara asks me to, to come,' she managed in her halting Hochsprache.

'Ah.' The woman frowned. She wasn't much older than Miriam, but her attitude and the deference the others showed her suggested she was important. And there was a family resemblance. *Mother? Aunt?* Miriam dipped her head. The frown vanished. 'I am . . . please? You are here,' she said in heavily accented English. 'I am Countess Frea. My daughter . . .' She shrugged, reaching the limits of her linguistic ability, and muttered something apologetic-sounding in Hochsprache, too fast for Miriam to catch.

Miriam smiled and nodded. Some of the younger women were whispering, but then one of them moved aside and gestured to her. A seat at the back. *Yes, well.* Miriam accepted it silently, annoyed that her grasp of the language was insufficient to tell whether she was being snubbed or honored. *I've been depending on Kara too much. And Brill*, she told herself. *Wherever she's gotten to.* Brilliana's other duties made guessing at her whereabouts much less easy than dealing with Kara.

Another knot of women arrived, with much bowing and nodding and kissing of cheeks on both sides: an old lady with her daughters – both older than Kara's mother, Frea – and their attendants. A brief introduction: Miriam bobbed her head and was happy enough to be ignored. At the front a couple of priests in odd vestments had begun chanting something in what might have been a mutant dialect of

Latin, filtered through many generations of Hochsprache-speaking colonials. A young lad swung an incense censer, spilling fumes across the altar as they continued. To Miriam's uneducated eye (she'd been raised by her mother and her agnostic Jewish foster-father, and churchgoing hadn't been on the agenda) it looked vaguely Catholic – until a third priest emerged from the not-a-vestry at the back, clutching an indignant white chicken and a silver knife. At which point Miriam was grateful for her place at the rear, which meant nobody was in a position to notice the way she closed her eyes until the squawking and gurgling stopped. It wasn't that she was particularly squeamish herself, but she found the idea of killing an animal in cold blood as part of a religious ritual disturbing. *I got the impression from Olga that they didn't do that anymore. What else did I get wrong?*

Things speeded up after the sacrifice, which the priests dedicated to the Lady of the Hearth, the Lord of the Household, and sundry other parties who were contractually obliged to bless familial alliances, as far as Miriam could tell, or who at least had to be bought off in order for the whole enterprise not to end in a messy annulment some hours later. Two men walked up to the altar, neither of them particularly young: Frea's eyes lingered on the older one, making Miriam suspect he might be a relative. *Kara's father?* The priests asked him a whole bunch of questions, the answers to which seemed to boil down to 'Yes, she's my daughter to give away.' The other man waited patiently. Miriam couldn't see him clearly because of the screen, but she had an impression that he was in his thirties, balding, and stockily built. And there was a sword at his belt. *A sword? In church? I don't understand these people* . . . Now it was his turn to answer questions. They sounded a lot like 'How much are you willing to pay for this guy's daughter?' to Miriam, but she was barely catching one word in four. It could have been anything from 'Will you take her as your wife and love her and cherish her?' to 'That'll be three pounds of silver and sixteen goats, and make sure you keep her away from the wine.' The questioning went on and on, until Miriam's eyes began to glaze over with boredom.

Some sort of resolution seemed to be reached. One of the priests turned and marched into the back room. A few seconds later he reappeared, followed by a subdued-looking Kara. They didn't go in for frothy white wedding dresses and veils here: Kara was wearing a rich gown, but nothing significantly different from what she might have worn for any other public event. The bald guy with the sword asked her something, and she nodded; and a moment later the other priest offered them both a cup containing some kind of fluid. *I hope that's wine*, Miriam thought with a sinking feeling as they sipped from it. She couldn't see the chicken anymore. *Somehow I don't think these guys hold with abstractions like transubstantiation.*

Conversation started up on the bench ahead of her almost immediately. 'It's done,' or 'That's that,' if she understood it correctly. Two of the younger maids (daughters? nieces? servants?) stood up, and one of them giggled quietly. Up front, the men were already rising and filing out of the side door. 'You will with us, come?' asked the old woman in front of Miriam, and it took her a moment to realize she was being spoken to.

'Yes,' she said uncertainly.

'Good.' The old lady reached out and grabbed Miriam's wrist, leaning on it as she levered herself up off the wooden bench. 'You've got strong bones,' she said, and cackled quietly.

'I have?'

'Your babies will need that.' She let go of Miriam's arm, oblivious to her expression. 'Come.'

They filed upstairs, into a chilly ballroom where servants with trays circulated, keeping everyone sufficiently lubricated with wine to ensure a smooth occasion. Miriam ended up with her back to a wall, observing the knots of chattering women, the puff-chested clump of young men, the elders circulating and talking to one another. The menfolk mostly had swords. It wasn't something she'd seen in a social setting before – but many of her social encounters had been in the royal court, or with other senior members of the nobility present. Carrying ironwork in the presence of the monarch was a faux pas of the kind that got you executed. *I've been sheltered. Or I just had too small and too skewed a sample to see much of how things* really *work here.*

Kara and the bald guy had been installed on two stools on a

raised platform, and had much larger cups than anyone else. Miriam tried to establish eye contact, but the bride was so focused on the floorboards that it would probably take a two-by-four to get her attention. *A happy occasion indeed*, she thought, and drained her glass. *How long until I can get away from this?*

A hand clutching a bottle appeared in front of her and tilted it over her glass. 'A drop more, perhaps?'

'Um.' Startled, Miriam looked sideways. 'Yes, please.' He was in his late twenties, as far as she could tell, and he looked as if he had southeast Asian ancestry, which made him stand out in this crowd as effectively as if he'd had green skin and eyes on stalks. He was dressed like most of the men hereabouts, in loose-cut trousers and a tunic, but unlike the others he didn't have a sword, or even a dagger, on his belt. 'Do I know you?'

'I think not.' His English was oddly accented, but it wasn't a Hochsprache accent – there was something familiar about it. 'Allow me to introduce myself? I am James, second son of Ang, of family Lee.' He looked slightly amused at her reaction. 'I see you have heard of me.'

'I met your brother,' she said before she could stop herself. 'Do you know who *I* am?'

He nodded, and she tensed, scanning the room for the ferret, his guards, anyone – because the circumstances under which she'd met his brother were anything but friendly. *Damn, where are they? Why now?* Her pulse roared and she took a deep breath, ready to yell for help, but then he chuckled and slopped a bolus of wine into her glass. 'You convinced the thin white duke to send him back to us alive,' said Lee. He raised his own glass to her. 'I would thank you for that.'

Miriam felt her knees go weak with relief. 'It was the sensible thing to do,' she said. The roaring in her ears subsided. She took a sip of wine to cover her confusion, and after a moment she felt calm enough to ask, 'Why are you here?'

'Here? At this happy occasion in particular, or this primitive city in general?' He seemed amused by her question. 'I have the honor of being a hostage against my brother's safe return and the blood treaty between our families.' Was it really amusement, or was it ironic detachment? Miriam blinked: she was finding James Lee remarkably difficult to read, but at least now she could place his accent. Lee's family had struck out for the west coast two centuries ago. In the process they'd gotten lost, detached from the Clan, world-walking to the alien timeline of New Britain rather than the United States. His accent was New British – a form of American English, surely, but one that had evolved differently from the vernacular of her own home. 'I cannot travel far.' He nodded toward a couple of unexceptional fellows standing near the door. 'But they let me out to mingle with society. I know Leon.' Another nod at the balding middle-aged groom, now chatting animatedly to Kara's father from his throne at the far end of the room. 'We play cards regularly, whist and black knave and other games.' He raised his glass. 'And so, to your very good health!'

Miriam raised her own glass: 'And to yours.' She eyed him speculatively. He was, she began to realize, a bit of a hunk – and with brains, too. What that implied was interesting: he was a hostage, sure, but might he also be something more? A spy, perhaps?

'Are you here because of, of her?' asked Lee, glancing at the platform.

'Yes. She was my lady-in-waiting. Before this happened.'

'Hmph.' He studied her face closely. 'You say that as if it came as a surprise to you, milady.'

'It did.' *Damn, I shouldn't be giving this much away!* 'I wasn't asked for an opinion, shall we say.' It was probably the wine, on an empty stomach, she realized. She was feeling wobbly enough as it was, and the sense of isolation was creeping up on her again.

'I'd heard a rumor that you were out of favor.'

He was fishing, but he sounded almost sympathetic. Miriam looked at him sharply. *Handsome is as handsome does*, she reminded herself. 'A rumor?'

'There's a, a grapevine.' He shrugged. 'I'm not the only guest of the families who is gathered to their bosom with all the kind solicitude due a rattlesnake' – he snorted – 'and people will talk, after all! One rumor made play of a scandal between you and a youngblood of the duke's faction who, regrettably, died some months ago in an incident nobody will discuss: according to others, you kicked up a fuss suffi-cient to wake the dead, rattling skeletons in their closets until other parties felt the need to move you from the game board to the toy box, if you will pardon the mixed metaphor.' He raised an eyebrow. 'I'm sure the truth is both less scandalous and more sympathetic than any of the rumors would have it.'

'Really.' She smiled tightly and took a full mouthful of wine. 'As a matter of fact *both* the rumors are more or less true, in outline at least. I'm pleased you're polite enough not to raise the third one: it would be interesting to compare notes on the climate in New Britain some day, but right now I suspect we'd only upset our minders.'

Now it was Lee's turn to look unhappy. 'I want you to know that I did not approve of the attempts on your life,' he said rapidly. 'It was unnecessary and stupid and – '

'Purely traditional.' Miriam finished her wine and pushed her glass at him. 'Right. And you're young and sensible and know how your hidebound grandparents ought to be running the family if they weren't stuck in the past?'

He gave her an ironic smile as he refilled both their glasses. 'Exactly. Oh dear, this bottle appears to be empty, I wonder how that happened?' He made a minute gesture and a servant came sidling up to replace it: *How does he do that?* Miriam wondered.

'Let me guess.' Her nose was beginning to prickle, a sure sign that she'd had enough and that she needed to be watching her tongue, but right now she didn't care about discretion. Right now she felt like letting her hair down, and damn the consequences for another day. Besides, Lee was handsome and smart and a good listener, a rare combination in this benighted backwater. 'You'd been kicking shins a little too hard, so the honorable head of the family sent you here when he needed a hostage to exchange with Angbard. Right?'

James Lee sighed. 'You have such an interesting idiom – and so forthright. To the bone. Yes, that is exactly it. And yourself . . . ?'

Miriam frowned. 'I don't fit in. They want to shut me in a box. Y'know, where I come from, women don't take that. Not second-class citizens, not at all. I grew up in Boston, the Boston of the United States. Able to look after myself. It's different to the world you know:

women have the vote, can own property, have legal equality, run businesses –' She took a deep breath, feeling the bleak depression poised, ready to come crashing down on her again. 'You can guess how well that plays here.'

'Hmm.' His glass was empty. Miriam watched as he refilled it. 'It occurs to me that we shall both be drunk before this is over.'

'I can think of less appropriate company to get drunk in.' She shrugged, slightly unbalanced by everything. A discordance of strings sought their tune from a balcony set back above the doorway, musicians with acoustic instruments preparing to play something not unlike a baroque chamber piece. 'And in the morning we'll both be sober and Kara will still be married to some fellow she hadn't even met yesterday.' She glanced around, wishing there was somewhere she could spit to get the nasty taste out of her mouth.

'This is a problem for you?'

'It's not so much a problem as a warning.' She took a step backward and leaned against the wall. She felt tired. 'The bastards are going to marry me off,' she heard herself explaining. 'This is so embarrassing. Where I grew up you just don't *do* that to people. Especially not to your daughter. But Mom's got her – reasons – and I suppose the duke thinks he's got his, and I, I made a couple of mistakes.' *Fucking stupid ones*, she thought despairingly. *It could be worse; if I wasn't lucky enough to be a privileged rich bitch and the duke's niece to boot, they'd probably have killed me, but instead they're just going to nail me down and use me as a pawn in their political chess game. Oops.* She put a hand to her mouth. *Did I say any of that aloud?* Lee was watching her sympathetically.

'We could elope together,' he offered, his expression hinting that this suggestion was not intended to be taken entirely seriously.

'I don't think so.' She forced a grin. *You're cute but you're no Roland. Roland I'd have eloped with in a split second. Damn him for getting himself killed . . .* 'But thanks for the offer.'

'Oh, it was nothing. If there's anything I can do, all you need is to ask.'

'Oh, a copy of the family knotwork would do fine,' she said, and hiccuped.

'Is that all?' He shook his head. 'They'd chase you down if you went anywhere in the three known worlds.'

'Three *known* worlds?' Her glass was empty again. Couples were whirling in slow stately circles around the dance floor, and she had a vague idea that she might be able to join them if she was just a bit more sober: her lessons had covered this one –

'Vary the knotwork, vary the destination.' James shrugged. 'Once that much became clear, two of our youngsters tried it. The first couple of times, they got headaches and stayed where they were. On the second attempt one of them vanished, then came back a few hours later with a story about a desert of ice. On the third attempt, they both vanished, and stayed missing.'

Miriam's eyes widened. 'You're kidding!'

He took her glass and placed it on the floor, alongside his own, by the skirting board. Then he straightened up again. 'No.'

'What did they find?'

He offered her his hand. 'Will you dance? People will gossip less . . .'

'Sure.' She took it. He led her onto the floor. In deference to the oldsters the tempo was slow, and she managed to follow him without too much stumbling. 'I'm bad at this. Not enough practice when drunk.'

'I shouldn't worry.' The room spun around her. 'In answer to your question, we don't know. Nobody knows. The elders forbade further experiments when they failed to return.'

'Oh.' She leaned her weight against him, feeling deflated, the elephantine weight of depression returning to her shoulders. For a moment she'd been able to smell the fresh air drifting through the bars of her cell – and then it turned out to be prison air-conditioning. The music spiraled to an end, leaving her washed up on the floor by the doorway. The ferret was waiting, looking bored. 'I think this is my cue to say good-bye,' she told Lee.

'I'm sure we'll meet again,' he said, smiling a lazy grin of intrigue.

*

As several days turned into a week and the evenings grew long and humid, Miriam grew resigned to her confinement. As prisons went, it was luxurious – multiple rooms, anxious servants, no shortage of basic amenities, even a walled courtyard she could go and walk in by prior arrangement – but it lacked two essentials that she'd taken for granted her entire life: freedom and the social contact of her equals.

After Kara's marriage, she was left with only the carefully vetted maids and the ferret for company. The servants didn't have a word of English between them, and the ferret had a very low tolerance for chitchat. After a while Miriam gritted her teeth and tried to speak Hochsprache exclusively. While a couple of the servants regarded her as crack-brained, an imbecile to be humored, a couple of the younger maids responded, albeit cautiously. A noblewoman's wrath was subject to few constraints: they would clam up rather than risk provoking her. And it didn't take long for Miriam to discover another unwelcome truth: her servants had been chosen, it seemed, on the basis of their ignorance and tractability. They were all terrified of the ferret, frightened of her, and strangers to the city (or overgrown town) of Niejwein. They'd been brought in from villages and towns outside, knew nobody here outside the great house, and weren't even able to go outside on their own.

About a week into the confinement, the boredom reached an excruciating peak. 'I need something to read, or something to write,' she told the ferret. 'I'll go out of my head with boredom if I don't have something to do!'

'Go practice your tapestry stitch, then.'

Miriam put her foot down. 'I'm crap at sewing. I want a notepad and mechanical pencil. Why can't I have a notepad? Are you afraid I'll keep a diary, or something?'

The ferret looked at her. He'd been cleaning his fingernails with a wickedly sharp knife. 'You can't have a notepad,' he said calmly. 'Stop pestering me or I'll beat you.'

'Why not?'

Something in her expression gave him pause for thought: 'You might try to draw an escape knot from memory,' he said.

'Ri-ight.' She scowled furiously. 'And how likely do you think that is? Isn't this place doppelgängered in New York?'

'You might get the knot wrong,' he pointed out.

'And kill myself by accident.' She shook her head. 'Listen, do you really want me depressed to the point of suicide? Because this, this –' The phrase *sensory deprivation* sprung to mind, but that wasn't quite right. 'This *emptiness* is driving me crazy. I don't know whose idea keeping me here was, but I'm not used to inactivity. And I'm rubbish at tapestry or needlepoint. And the staff aren't exactly good for practicing conversational Hochsprache.'

He stood up. 'I will see what I can do,' he said. 'Now go away.' And she did.

*

Two days later a leather-bound notebook and a pen materialized on her dresser. There was a note in the book: *Remember you are thirty feet up*, it said. The ferret insisted on holding it whenever she went downstairs to walk in the garden. But at least it was progress. Miriam drew a viciously complicated three-loop Möbius strip on the first page, just to deter the ferret from snooping inside, then found herself blocked, unable to write anything. *I should have studied shorthand*, she thought bitterly. Privacy, it seemed, was a phenomenon dependent on trust – and if there was one thing she didn't have these days, it was the confidence of her relatives.

One foggy morning, almost two weeks after Kara's arranged wedding, there was a knock at the door to her reception room. Miriam looked up: this usually meant the ferret wanted to see her. Today, though, the ferret tiptoed in and stood to one side as two tough-looking men in business suits and dark glasses – Secret Service chic – entered and rapidly searched the apartment. 'What's going on?' she asked, but the ferret ignored her.

One of the guards stepped outside. A moment later, the door opened again. It was Henryk, leaning heavily on a walking stick. The ferret scurried to fetch a padded stool for the baron, positioning it in front of Miriam's seat in the window bay. Miriam stared at Henryk. Her heart pounded and she felt slightly sick, but she stayed seated. *I'm not going to beg*, she told herself uncertainly. *What does the old bastard want?*

'Good morning, my dear Helge. I hope you are keeping well?' He spoke in Hochsprache, but the phrases were stock.

'I am well. I thank you,' she said haltingly, frowning. *I'm not going to let him show me up –*

'Good.' He turned to the ferret: 'Clear the room. Now.'

Thirty seconds later they were alone. 'What require – do you *want*?' she asked.

'Hmm.' He tilted his head thoughtfully. 'Your accent is atrocious.' She must have looked blank: he repeated himself in English. 'We can continue in this tongue if you'd rather.'

'Okay.' She nodded reluctantly.

'Tonight there will be a private family reception at the summer palace,' Henryk said without preamble. 'A dinner, to be followed by dancing. Let me explain your role in it. Your mother will be there, as will her half-brother, the duke. His majesty, and the Queen Mother, and his youngest son, will also be there. There will be a number of other notables present as guests, but you are being given a signal honor as a personal guest of his majesty. You will be seated with them at the high table, and you will behave with the utmost circumspection. This means, basically, *think* before you open your mouth.' He paused. 'And don't talk out of turn.'

'Huh.' Miriam frowned. 'What about the crown prince? Is he going to be there?'

'Egon?' Henryk looked bemused. 'No, why should he be? He's off on a hunting trip somewhere, I think.'

'Oh.' *One less thing to worry about*, Miriam thought. 'Is that all?'

'Not quite.' Henryk paused again, as if uncertain how to continue. 'You know what our plans for you are,' he said slowly. 'There are some facts you need to understand. The younger prince – you have met him.' Miriam nodded, suppressing a shudder. The prince belonged in a hospital ward with nursing attendants and a special restricted diet. *Brain damage.* 'He's a little slow, but he is not a vegetable, Helge. You should respect him. If he had not been poisoned –' A shadow crossed his face.

'What do you expect me to do?'

'I expect you to marry him and bear his children.' Henryk looked pained at being made to spell it out. 'Nothing more and nothing less, and it is not just what *I* expect of you – the Clan proposes and the

240

Clan disposes. But you can do this the easy way, if you like. Go through the ceremony, then Dr. ven Hjalmar will sort you out. You don't need to worry about bedding the imbecile, if that thought upsets you: the doctor can arrange for artificial insemination. You'll be pregnant, but you'll have the best antenatal care we can provide, and a private maternity clinic on the other side for the delivery. The well-being of your child will be a matter of state security. Once you are mother to a male child in the line of succession, a certain piece of paper can be discreetly buried. Two or more children would be better, but I shall leave that as a matter for you and your doctor to decide upon – your age, after all, is an issue.'

'Um.' Miriam swallowed her distaste. *Spitting would send entirely the wrong message*, she thought, her head spinning. And besides, she'd been angry about this for weeks already, to the point where the indignation and fury had lost their immediate edge. It wasn't simply the thought of pregnancy – although she hadn't enjoyed her one and only experience of it more than ten years ago – but the idea of compulsion. The idea that you could be compelled to bear a child was deeply repugnant. She'd never been one for getting too exercised over the abortion debate, but Henryk's bald-faced orders brought it into tight focus. *You* will *be pregnant. Huh. And how would you like it if I told you that you were going to be anally probed by aliens, baron?* 'And what's your position on this?' she asked.

'My position?' Henryk seemed puzzled. 'I don't *have* a position, my dear. I just want you to have a happy and fruitful marriage to the second heir to the throne – and to keep out of trouble. Which, thankfully, won't be a problem for a while once you're pregnant, and afterwards . . .' He looked at her penetratingly. 'I think you'd make a very good mother, once you come to terms with your situation.'

Not if you and everybody blackmail me into it, she thought. 'Is that the only option you see for me?'

'Truthfully, yes. It's that or, well, we're not unreasonable. You'd just go to sleep one night in your bed and not wake up in the morning. Case completed.'

Miriam stared at him. Everything was gray for a while; finally some atavistic reflex buried deep in her spine remembered she needed to breathe, and she inhaled explosively. '*Well*,' she said. 'I just want to make sure that I've got it straight. I go through with this – marry the imbecile, get pregnant, bear at least one child. Or I tell you to fuck off, and you kill me. Is that the whole picture?'

'No.' Henryk regarded her thoughtfully for a while. 'I wish it were. Unfortunately, your history suggests that you don't take well to being coerced. So additional pressure is needed. If you refuse to go through with this, we will withdraw your mother's medication. I repeat: If you don't cooperate, you will be responsible for her death, as well as your own. Because we need an heir to the royal blood who is one of us much more badly than we need you, or her, or indeed anyone else. Do you understand?'

Miriam was halfway out of her chair before she knew it, and Henryk's hands were raised protectively across his face. She managed to regain her control a split second short of striking him. *That would be a mistake*, she realized coldly, through a haze of outrage. She wanted to hurt him, so badly that it was almost a physical need. 'You fucking *bastard*,' she spat in Hochsprache. Henryk turned white. Olga had taught her those words: *bastard* was worse than *cunt* in English, much worse.

'If you were a man I'd demand satisfaction for that.' Henryk backhanded her across the face. Miriam staggered backward until she fell across the window seat. Henryk leaned over her: 'You are an adult – it's time you behaved like one, not a spoiled brat,' he spat at her, quivering with rage. She licked her lips, tasting blood. 'You have a family. You have responsibilities! This foolish pursuit of independence will hurt them – worse, it may *kill* them – if you continue to indulge it. You disgust me!'

He was breathing deeply, his hands twisted around the head of his cane. Miriam felt sticky dampness on her lip: her nose was bleeding. After a moment Henryk took a step back, breathing heavily.

'I hate you,' she said quietly. 'I'm not going to forget this.'

'I don't expect you to.' He straightened up, adjusting his short cape. 'I'd be disappointed in you if you did. But I'm doing this for everyone's good. Once the Queen Mother placed her youngest grandson in play . . . well, one day you'll know enough to understand I was right, although I don't ever expect you to thank me for it, or even admit it.' He glanced at the window. 'You have enough time to get ready. A coach will be waiting for you at nine. It's up to you whether you go willingly, or in leg-irons.'

'Did Angbard approve this scheme?' *Would he really sacrifice Mom? His half-sister?*

Henryk nodded. His cheek twitched. 'It wasn't his idea, and he doesn't like it, but he believes it is essential to bring you to heel. And he agreed that this was the one threat that you would take seriously. Good day.' He turned and strode toward the door, leaving her to gape after him, slack-jawed with helpless fury.

TRANSLATED TRANSCRIPT BEGINS

CONSPIRATOR #1: 'I am most unhappy about this latest development, Sudtmann.'
CONSPIRATOR #2: 'As am I, your royal highness, as am I.' (*Metallic clink.*)
CONSPIRATOR #3: (*Unintelligible.*) '– deeply worrying?'
CONSPIRATOR #1: 'Not really. *More wine, now.*' (*Pause.*) 'That's better.'
(*Pause.*)
CONSPIRATOR #2: 'Your highness?'
CONSPIRATOR #1: (*Sighs.*) 'It may be better to be feared than to be loved, but there is a price attached to maintaining a bloody reputation. And it seems the bill must still be honored whether the debtor be prince or pauper.'
CONSPIRATOR #3: 'Sir? I don't, do not – '
CONSPIRATOR #1: 'He's *weak*. To be backed into the stocks like a goat! This is the plan of the tinkers, mark my word: the poison she-snake in our bosom intends to get an heir to the throne in her grasp soon enough. And he cannot gainsay her!'
CONSPIRATOR #2: 'Sir? Your brother, surely he is unsuitable – '
CONSPIRATOR #1: 'Yes, but any whelp of his would be another matter! And the libels continue apace.'

CONSPIRATOR #4: 'The libels play into our hands, sire. For the bloodier they be, the more feared you become. And fear is currency to the wise prince.'

CONSPIRATOR #1: 'Yes, but it wins me nothing should my accession not meet with the approval of the court of landholders. And the court of landholders is increasingly in the grip of the tinkers. A tithe of their rent would repay a quarter of the promissory notes my father and his father before him took from the west, but does he – '

(*Pause.*)

(*Noises.*)

(*Unintelligible.*) '– regularity of bowels.'

CONSPIRATOR #2: 'I'll see to it, sir.'

CONSPIRATOR #3: 'A pessary of rowan. There are other subtleties to consider.'

CONSPIRATOR #4: 'It will be suspicious. And remember, two may keep a secret – if one of them is dead.'

CONSPIRATOR #1: 'Enough skulking!'

CONSPIRATOR #2: 'Sir?'

CONSPIRATOR #1: 'It is clearly treasonable intent that we confront in this instance. They've addled whatever is left of my father's wits, turned him against me, and once they are sure of a succession I'll doubtless meet with a convenient hunting accident. I cannot – *will* not – permit this. But once it becomes clear that the witch-tinkers are not the force they once were, I'll be seen as the savior of the realm. *And* feared without scruple of libel: honestly, as a prince should be.'

CONSPIRATOR #4: 'There is a reinforced company of the Life Guards stationed across the river. We shall have to move fast.'

CONSPIRATOR #1: 'On the contrary, they will do as I tell them – whose life did you think they were supposed to guard? Hah! But I am concerned about your alchemists and their expensive mud pie. Have they succeeded in killing themselves yet?'

CONSPIRATOR #4: 'On the contrary. And they have enough fine powder stockpiled to blow down the wolf's lair. Not much use for the artillery, but . . .'

CONSPIRATOR #1: 'We have a use for it on the stage. Arrange to have a roundup of plotters, marked for execution afterward – I'm sure you can arrange some witnesses, Sudtmann, guards who will swear to our instructions at the question? More in sorrow than in anger, I shall dispatch the traitors in the name of the Crown. And the kingdom will be secure against the blasted witches for another generation, at least.'

CONSPIRATOR #3: 'But your father – '

CONSPIRATOR #1: 'He'll fall in with me of necessity.' (*Metallic noise.*) 'He may be weak, but he's not stupid. Once the witches realize the dice are cast, they will declare blood feud against the Crown. He'll have to do it. I stress, this is not a coup *against* the Crown, it is a coup *for* the Crown, to defend it from the enemies within.'

CONSPIRATOR #3: 'And none shall call it by any other name.'

CONSPIRATOR #2: 'And if the blast should fail to live up to expectations?'

CONSPIRATOR #1: 'Then I shall lead the guards in a heroic attempt to rescue the palace from the rebels who appear to have seized it. Long live the king!'

CONSPIRATOR #4: 'I should give the alchemists their final reward then, sir.'

CONSPIRATOR #1: 'Make it so, and may Sky Father have mercy on them in the afterlife, for their services to the Crown.'

TRANSCRIPT ENDS

GOING IN

Recovery from fentanyl poisoning was relatively rapid: the pain came later. They kept asking *questions*, even when he was on a drip and hallucinating. 'What happened? What did he say?' All Mike could do was shake his head and mutter incoherently. Later, he made a full statement. And another. A whole goddamn committee camped by his hospital bed for an afternoon, trying to come up with an agreed timeline for the fuckup. Mike was expecting to be suspended pending investigation, but from the noises they were making it sounded like they wanted to sweep everything under the rug, pretend Matt had never existed. Maybe that was how the DOD dealt with unwelcome problems; or maybe they just didn't want to admit that they'd destabilized a willing defector. Later another committee came by to grill him about Matt's nuclear threat, but when he asked what action they were taking on it they told him he had no need to know – from which he deduced that they were taking it very seriously indeed.

It didn't matter to Mike. He was out of the loop, officially injured in the line of duty. He lay in bed for two days, numb with apathy and guilt, mind constantly circling back to worry at the same unwelcome realization. *I fucked up*. On the second day a card arrived from Nikki, an invitation to Pete's funeral. And then, just as he was graduating from depression to self-loathing, Smith dropped in.

'How are you feeling?'

'Better.' Which was a lie. 'Not sleeping so good.'

'Yeah, well.' Smith mustered a sympathetic expression that looked horribly artificial to Mike. 'We need you back on duty.'

'Huh?'

The colonel dragged the nearest chair over and sat down next to Mike's bed. Mike peered at him, noticing the bags under his eyes for the first time, the two-day stubble. 'I'd like to be able to give you a month off, refer you for counseling, and let you recover at your own pace. Unfortunately, I can't. You were due for in-processing today and you're on the critical path for CLEANSWEEP. And your immediate backup was Pete.'

'Oh.' Mike was silent for a moment. 'I was expecting an enquiry, you know?'

'There's *been* a board of enquiry.' Smith leaned forward. 'We don't have time to piss around, Mike. We had a video camera on you when Source Greensleeves offed Pete and took you hostage, it turned up yesterday. Left hand didn't know what the right hand was doing, excessive compartmentalization in our security architecture, et cetera. Nobody's blaming you for what happened; if anyone gets blamed it's going to be me for sending you guys in in the first place. *But*. We're moving too fast to play the blame game right now – '

Mike gestured at the table on the other side of the bed: 'Pete's funeral is tomorrow. I was planning on being there.'

Smith looked worried. 'Shit, our schedule puts you on a ranch in Maryland – wait, hang on, it's not like that. I'll get you to the funeral, even if I have to bend a few rules. But I really *do* need you back on duty.'

Mike stared at him. 'Spill it.'

Smith stared right back. 'Spill what?'

'*It.*' Mike crossed his arms. 'This setup *stinks*. Whatever happened to your professional assets? I thought you guys majored in infiltrating hostile territory. You're the military, you go to exotic places and meet interesting people and kill them. I'm just a cop. Why do you need me so badly?'

'Hold onto that thought.' Smith paused for a moment. 'Look, I think you habitually overestimate what we can do. We're very good at blowing shit up, that's true. And NSA can tap every phone call on the planet, break almost any code,' he added, with a trace of pride. 'But . . . we're *not* good at human intelligence anymore. Not since the end of the Cold War, when most of the old HUMINT programs were shut down. You don't get promoted in Langley by learning Pashtun and freezing your butt off in a cave in central Asia for six years, among people who'll torture you to death in an eyeblink if they figure out

247

who you are. The best and the brightest go into administration or electronic intelligence; the people who volunteer for spying missions and get through the training are often, bluntly speaking, nutjobs. A couple of years ago we had to fire the CIA station chief in Bonn, did you know that? One of our top guys in Germany. He'd been invoicing for a ring of informers but it turned out he was a member of an evangelical church, and what he was really doing was bankrolling a church mission. Anyway, you've got a three-month lead on anyone we could train up to do the job, and whatever your own opinion of your abilities, you are not *bad*. You've done police undercover work and stakeouts and run informers – that's about ninety-five percent of the skill set of a field agent. So rather than pulling one of our few competent field agents out of whatever very important job they're already doing, and *trying* to teach them Hochsprache, we figured we'd take you and give you the additional five percent that you'll need.'

'Bullshit. What *else*?'

'What do you mean?'

'You know damn well I'm unreliable. I'm not acculturated, I still *think like a cop*, even if you're right and the job overlap is significant. I'm unreliable from a departmental point of view: I've got the wrong instincts. I stay within the law. And this isn't a Hollywood movie where delicate operations get handed to maverick outsiders. So. What aren't you telling me?'

Smith shrugged. 'I told them you'd see through it,' he said, glancing at the door. Then he reached into his vest pocket and pulled out a photograph. 'When did you last see this woman?'

'Who – oh. Her. What's she got to do with this?' Mike's mouth went dry.

Smith glared at him, clearly irritated. 'Now *you're* the one who's playing games. You've been through the clearance process, we know what color underpants you wear, we interviewed your ex-wife, we grabbed your home phone records.' He waved the photograph. 'Confession is good for the soul, Mike. Level with me and I'll level with you. How well do you know this woman?'

Shit. Should have guessed they'd figure it out. 'There's not much to tell.' Mike struggled to drag his scattered thoughts back together.

'I met her a few years ago. She's a journalist, she was doing a story about drug testing for the glossy she worked for. It worked out really well at first. Did a couple of dates, began to get serious.' *How much do they want to know?* It was still a sore point for him. 'Yes, we did sleep together.'

'Mike. Mike.' Smith shook his head. 'That's not what this is about, we're not the East German Stasi.'

'Well, what *did* you want to know?' Mike glared at him. 'She's a *journalist*, Colonel. She wasn't faking it. I picked her up at the office a couple of times. I didn't have a fucking clue she was anything else! Let me remind you that I didn't know the Clan existed, back then. None of us did. I don't think she did, either.'

'I'm not – I wasn't –' For a moment Smith looked embarrassed. 'Carry on. Tell me in your own words.'

'It didn't work out,' Mike said slowly. 'We were talking about taking a vacation together. Maybe even moving in. But then something spooked her. We had a couple of rows – she's a liberal, we got bickering over some stupid shit. And then –' He shook his head. 'It didn't work out.'

'How long have you known she was involved with the Clan?' asked Smith.

Mike shook his head. 'Not known. Wasn't remotely sure.' *But Pete was*, he realized. And what Matthias said – 'Listen, it's over between us. Two, three years ago. I didn't put two and two together about the woman who Source Greensleeves kept ranting about until he waved it in my face, and even then – how many journalists called Miriam are there?'

Smith put the photograph away. Then he nodded at Mike. 'How would you characterize your relationship with her?' he asked.

'Turbulent. And over.' Mike reached over to the bedside stand and picked up a glass of water. 'If you're thinking what I think you're thinking, it won't work.'

'And maybe I'm not thinking what you think I'm thinking.' Smith suddenly grinned. 'Honey traps were an old Stasi trick, and they didn't work consistently – in this situation, the collateral damage from blowback if it goes wrong is too high. But can you confirm that you do – *did* – know Miriam Beckstein, journalist, last employed by *The Industry Weatherman*? And that she knew you were employed by the DEA?'

Mike nodded.

'Well, there's your explanation! Now do you see why you're needed?'

Mike nodded warily. 'What do you want me to do?'

'Well, like Dr. James told you two weeks ago, we want you to set up a spy ring in Niejwein. That hasn't changed. What *has* changed is that we now have a list of starting points for you. It's a very short list, and she's right at the top of it. If we're right – if she's a recent recruit, dragged in by her long-lost family – she may be a potential asset. As long as she's inside the Clan, that is: she's not a lot of use to us over here, except as another mule.'

Mike shivered momentarily, visualizing a collar bomb around a throat he'd buried his face in. 'When?' he asked.

'We know roughly where the royal palace is, in Niejwein: it over-laps with Queens. Niejwein isn't a big city, it won't be hard for you to get there with the right disguise and cover story. Which, by the way, is that you're a Clan member from the west coast. It won't stand up to scrutiny, but from what we know about Niejwein it won't come in for much unless you try and play it for real. They're pretty primitive over there. And we've got an extra edge I haven't mentioned. We captured a courier last week.'

'You did?' Mike sat up.

'And his dispatches.' Smith frowned. 'You don't need to know the details. Anyway, it seems your girlfriend is going up in the world. She's due to be the guest of honor at a royal reception in two weeks' time, and the document taken from the courier includes what appears to be an invitation to a country cousin.' Smith looked smug for a moment. 'One of the things the Clan are good at is postal security – which works against them at times like this. As long as they don't know we've got couriers working for us, you're in the clear.'

'Hey, are you telling me . . .'

'Yes. You're going to crash a royal garden party and make her an offer she can't refuse.'

*

A week of twelve-hour days in a training camp on the edge of a sprawling army base couldn't prepare Mike Fleming for the experience of his first world-walk. On the contrary: he'd been led to expect a glossy high-tech send-off, and instead what he was getting looked very much like a ringside seat at a gangland execution.

It was nearly noon. His personal trainer, who he knew only as John, had woken him at six o'clock and rushed him through breakfast. John had a halting grasp of Hochsprache, but insisted Mike speak nothing else to him, playing dumb whenever Mike lapsed into English out of frustration or in search of some unmapped concept. Then he'd been taken on a tour of Facilities. A quiet woman who looked like she worked weekends in Macy's kitted him out in what they figured would pass for local costume – no cod-medieval 'men in tights' nonsense, but rough woolen fabric leggings, an overtunic and leather boots.

Next on his itinerary was the armory. A hatchet-faced warrant officer checked him out and told him what was what in English. 'This is your sword. Nearest we've got to it is a cutlass, note the curve in the blade – forget point work. If you ever did any fencing at school, forget that too. This is strictly for edge work, German-style. Oh, and if you have to use it you're probably dead. We don't have a couple of months to train you up to beginner-level competent. Luckily for you, you're also allowed one of these.' He held up a nylon holster, already laden with a black automatic pistol. 'Glock 20C, fifteen-round magazine, ten mill.' Just like the handguns 'James Morgan' had been buying and, presumptively, a standard Clan issue. 'You have two spare magazines. I take it you've checked out on one.' In answer to Mike's mute head shake, he swore and glared at John: 'What *is* it with you folks? Are you *trying* to get him killed?'

Half an hour on the range upstairs from the armory reassured Mike marginally and seemed to mollify the armorer. He could hit things with it, strip it down, and could reload and clean it. 'Next trip,' said John. 'We have a, a thing that flies – '

Thing that flies turned out to be John's best attempt at saying *helicopter* in Hochsprache. It gave Mike a splitting headache as it thudded along in the direction of Long Island. When it landed at the

Downtown Manhattan Heliport, John handed him a trenchcoat and a broad-brimmed hat. 'Very funny,' he snarled, still half-deafened by the rotor noise.

'Wear it.' A minivan with blacked-out windows was waiting in the parking lot; funnily enough, there were no other cars present.

'Huh.' Mike clambered down from the chopper and trudged across the barge to the minivan. The side door opened. Inside it, Colonel Smith was waiting for him.

'Sorry 'bout the cloak-and-dagger nonsense,' Smith said unapologetically as their driver pulled out into the approach road behind another minivan. Mike glanced over his shoulder as a third van discreetly joined the convoy. 'Can't take any chances.'

'What? Where are we going?'

'Nearest geographical cognate we could get.' Smith pulled back his sleeve. He was wearing something that looked like a pregnant digital watch – after a moment Mike recognized it as a GPS receiver. Smith frowned. 'Doesn't work too well – too many skyscrapers.'

The minivan slid through the New York traffic in fits and starts, bumper to bumper with a yellow cab that had somehow intercalated itself in the convoy. Mike lost track of where they were going after a couple of minutes and a baroque detour around some roadwork. 'What's the setup?'

Smith opened a folder with red and yellow stripes along its cover. 'Pay attention, you don't get to take this with you. A courier is ready to take you across to Zone Blue. You go over piggyback. In Zone Blue, we currently have a forward support team of three – Sergeant Hastert, PFC O'Neil, and PFC Icke. They'll look after you, and also give the courier a bunch of crap to bring back over to us. You do *exactly* what the sergeant tells you. After you leave Zone Blue, they'll exfiltrate. Let me emphasize, there won't be anybody there. What there *will* be is a buried radio transmitter, like this.' Smith pulled an egg-shaped device with a stubby aerial out of his pocket. 'You dig it up, push the button, and the backup team will be alerted to come check you out for shadows. If you've got unwelcome company, they will kill it or take it prisoner – at their discretion – or leave you the fuck alone. They will not be more than an hour away from you at any time, so if they don't show up within an hour, someone's in trouble. Procedure is to revisit the zone at daily intervals for one week, then back off to once a week for a month. You also need to memorize *this*. Directions to Zone Green, which is your fallback site. There's no equipment or personnel there, so if you're captured and tortured you can't give anyone away, but if you go there you'll be observed and contacted.'

Mike studied the sheet of typed directions, feeling a bead of sweat trickle down his forehead. *It's real*, he realized. *It's not some kind of elaborate joke. It's really going to happen.* Nervous dread made a hollow nest in his stomach. 'The palace –' He'd seen maps of that already, a big stone pile near a small town, at one end of a road lined with slightly smaller stone piles.

'Over the page.' A basic sketch map showed Zone Blue in relation to the palace. 'There are complications to do with the transport protocol for this run.'

'What do you mean?' Mike looked up.

'It's in the center of town. The courier may try to escape.' Smith stared at him. 'You're going piggyback. Hold out your hand.'

'What –'

Smith snapped a bracelet shut around Mike's wrist. 'Transmitter. *Very* short range. Here's the key.' He handed Mike a key. 'Turn clockwise to release the transmitter. Two twists counterclockwise and it will send the detonate command. If Three tries to attack you –'

'Okay.' Mike stared at the thing, repelled and fascinated. 'What do I do with it?'

Smith shrugged. 'If it goes according to plan and Team X-ray meets you in, they hold Courier Three while you take the bracelet off and hand it to him. Then you send him back over to us and we take the necklace off and put him back in his box. If he tries to run, or attacks you, kill him. I'm serious. If he does either of those things, he'll try to kill *you*. Wouldn't you, in his situation?'

In his situation – Mike tried to get a handle on it, but his mind kept slipping into unwelcome channels, looking into irrelevances. 'Courier Three – I thought you only had two?'

'Need to know.' Smith shook his head. 'Look, we're there.'

*

Manhattan wasn't just skyscrapers; old brownstones still thrived in the shadow of the tall towers. Smith waited for the other minivans to draw up, then opened the door and led Mike up the front steps of an ordinary-looking house while half a dozen men and a couple of women in the sort of business attire that yelled 'cop' stood discreet guard.

The house looked ordinary enough from inside – but Smith headed straight for an unobtrusive door and into what had probably been a living room before someone ripped out the furniture, boarded up the windows, installed antiblast paneling and floodlights, then spray-painted a big X in the middle of the floor. Now there was something sinister about it, a cramped, dark terminus that needed only a trapdoor and a dangling noose to turn it into a place of execution. 'Wait here.'

Mike waited while Smith and two of his underlings bustled back out again. A minute later they returned, half-supporting and half-dragging a third man between them. He was unshaven and looked tired, bent forward with his hands cuffed tightly behind his back; his scalp had been shaved and there was a big dressing taped to one temple. As he looked around and saw Mike his eyes widened with fear. Then another of the anonymous guards stepped forward and swiftly clamped a metal collar around his throat.

'Shizz . . .' His knees sagged.

'Wait,' Mike said, trying his Hochsprache. 'You – carry – me. Yes?' He saw the other man's eyes. The expression of terror began to fade. 'Come – go – back here.' Mike paused. 'Does he know what the collar is?' he asked Smith, lapsing into English.

Smith nodded.

'They take' – gesture at throat – 'undress, off. You run' – tap at wrist, at the bracelet Smith had put there, then finger across throat. 'Understand?'

'Yes,' said the prisoner. Then a gabble of words jumbled together too fast for Mike to parse.

'Slower.'

Courier Three fell silent. 'Not kill.'

'No. You carry me.'

'I carry, yes, I carry!'

The courier's head bobbed as if his neck had been replaced by loose springs. Mike tasted stomach acid, swallowed. *This isn't right. I'm supposed to capture more people, so we can use them like* this? Even a prison cell had to be better than being led to a death chamber and having a bomb clamped to your neck.

'Ready?' asked Smith.

'Yeah.' Mike pointed to the X on the floor. 'Stand here.' Courier Three crouched down on the spot, legs and arms braced. Mike looked at him, momentarily perplexed. 'What do I do now?' he asked.

'You sit on him,' said Smith. He was holding something. 'Go on.'

'Okay.' With some trepidation, Mike lowered himself onto Courier Three's back. The man grunted. Mike could feel his spine, the warmth of his ribs through the seat of his pants. *This is weird*, he began to think, just as Smith held something under Three's nose. Then the world changed.

*

Mike blinked at the darkness. Someone tapped him on the back of the head with something hard. 'Say your name.'

'Mike Fleming.' His seat groaned and began to collapse, and he fell over sideways. 'What the fuck – '

A thud was followed by a muffled groan. 'Okay, wiseass, cut that out!' Light appeared, and Mike rolled over onto his back and tried to sit up.

Someone else was groaning – *Courier Three?* he wondered. 'What's going on?'

'All under control, sir,' drawled the man with the gun. 'You just sort yourself out while we keep watch.'

Mike nodded, taking stock of the situation. He was in some kind of room with no windows, a door, a dirt floor, three armed strangers, and a captured Clan courier wearing a bomb around his neck. The good news was that the desperados were pointing their guns at the courier, the door, and the ground, respectively – which left none for him. Ergo, they were friendly. 'Which of you is Sergeant Hastert?' he asked.

'I am.' Hastert was the one covering the ground. He grinned at Mike, an expression he'd have found deeply alarming if it wasn't for the fact that any other expression would have been infinitely worse. Courier Three groaned again. Mike realized he was clutching his head. 'Dennis, keep laughing boy here covered. Mr. Fleming, you've got the remote control. If you'd care to pass it to me, we can take care of the mule until it's time for him to go home. Meanwhile, you'n I've got some talking to do.'

'Okay.' Mike unlocked his bracelet with a shudder of relief and passed it to the sergeant, who leaned over Courier Three while one of the others kept his AR-15 pointed at the prisoner the whole time.

'Listen, you,' said Hastert. 'This here won't go off now –' He was speaking English, loudly and slowly.

'He doesn't understand,' said Mike.

'Huh?'

'He doesn't speak English. He thought we were going to kill him, back in New York.'

'Hmm.' Hastert stared at him with pale blue eyes. 'You try, then.'

Mike stared at Courier Three. 'You go. Soon, now, back over. Not die. Shoot if run? Yes.'

The prisoner nodded slightly. Then went back to groaning quietly and clutching his head.

'Not much to look at, ain't he?' Hastert was genial.

'Let's get out of here.'

Hastert opened the door and led Mike through into another bare room with a dirt floor, leaving the two other soldiers with their precious courier. There was a window in here, with wooden shutters, and Hastert switched off his flashlight. As Mike's eyes adjusted he got a good look at what the sergeant was wearing: rough woolen trousers and jerkin over another layer that bulged like a bulletproof jacket. 'We stay indoors during the day,' Hastert said, acknowledging his curiosity. 'But this is a special occasion. Keep your voice low, by the way. It's a crowded neighborhood.'

'You know where the palace is?'

'Yeah. We'll get you there. Once laughing boy has gotten over his headache and gone home.'

'Huh.' Mike sank down into a crouch against one wall. It was whitewashed, he noticed, but the plaster or bricks underneath it were uneven. 'This the best hotel you could get?'

'You should see how they live hereabouts. This is the Sheraton. Let me fill you in . . .'

Mike tried to listen, but he was too tense. There were noises outside: occasional chatter, oddly slurred and almost comprehensible snatches of Hochsprache. The thud of horses' hooves passed the door from time to time, followed by the creak and rattle of carts. After about an hour, the inner door opened and one of the other soldiers came out. He nodded. 'All done.'

Mike shifted. 'What now?'

Hastert checked his watch. 'One hour to go, then we move out. Jack, go dig out a couple of MREs, and you and Dennis chow down. Sir, do you know what this is?' He held up a radio transmitter, like the one Colonel Smith had shown Mike earlier.

'Yes.' Mike nodded. 'Radio transmitter. Right?'

'Right.' Hastert looked at him thoughtfully, then reached into a shapeless-looking sack on the floor beside him and pulled out an entrenching tool. 'We're going to put it in right – *here*.' He buried the gadget under a thin layer of soil and tamped it down, then scattered the residue. 'Think you can find it?'

Mike mentally measured the distance from the door. 'Yes, I think so.'

'Good. Your life depends on it.' Hastert didn't smile. 'Because when you get back here, we won't be around.'

'I've been briefed.' Mike tried not to snap. It was warm and stifling in the dirt-floored shack, and the endless waiting was getting to him.

'Yes, sir, but I didn't see you being briefed, so if you'll excuse me we'll go over it again, shall we?'

'Okay . . .' Mike swallowed. 'Thanks.'

The next hour passed a bit faster, which made it all the more shocking when the inner door opened and the other two men came through. 'Ready when you are, boss.' It was the taller one, O'Neil. Mike blinked. *Hey, all three of them are white*, he realized: a statistical anomaly, or maybe something else. *No sugar trade here means no*

African slave trade. Just another personnel headache that Smith was dealing with behind his back, finding special forces troops who looked like locals.

'Let's go.' Hastert stood up. 'Far as the garden party, we're your bodyguard. Once you're inside, we'll split. Anything goes wrong, make for the garden gate opposite the ceremonial parade ground – I'll point it out to you.'

*

He opened the door. It was late afternoon outside, dusty and bright and hot, but with a breeze blowing off the sea that took the edge off the heat. The shack turned out to be one of a whole row fronting a narrow dirt track: a similar row faced them. Half the doors and windows were wide open, with chickens and geese wandering in and out freely to peck in the roadside dirt. There were *people*. Ragged, skinny children, stooped women and men in colorless robes or baggy trousers. People who looked away when Hastert stared at them, hastily finding somewhere else to go, something else to do. The road was filthy, an open gutter down the middle running with sewage. 'Come on,' said O'Neil, behind Mike. 'You're blocking the door.'

Mike stepped forward, trying to project confidence. *I'm a big man*, he told himself. *I'm armed, I've got bodyguards, my clothing's new, and I'm well-fed.* He glanced up the street. Nothing on this row was straight: whoever built it hadn't heard of zoning laws, or even a straight line. A cart pulled by a couple of bored oxen, piled high with sacks, was slowly rattling toward them. Behind it, a mass of sheep bleated plaintively, spilling into doorways in a slow woolly flood. 'Follow me, and try to look like you're leading,' Hastert muttered.

The walk through the town seemed to take forever, although it was probably more like twenty or thirty minutes. Mike tried not to gape like a fool; sometimes it was hard. Smells and sounds assailed him. Wood smoke was alarmingly common, given that most of the houses were timbered. It almost covered up the pervasive stench of shit rising from the hot, fetid gutters. In the distance some kind of street vendor was shouting over and over again – briefly they walked past one edge of a kind of open square, cobblestoned and lined with a dizzying mess of stalls like open-walled huts. Wicker baskets full of caged chickens, scrawny and sometimes half-bald. A table covered in muddy beetroot. Rats, glimpsed out of the corner of the eye, scurrying under cover. *Is this where she's been living?* he wondered, momentarily aghast. Remembering Miriam's attitude to food hygiene and her nearly aseptic kitchen worktop, he suddenly had a moment of doubt.

Who am I kidding? Mike wondered, tensed up as if he was about to go through the back door of some perp's meth lab. *This is crazy! I've got barely any grasp of the language, no way out, I'm in a hostile city in a foreign country and if they get their hands on me* – a sick certainty filled him as they reached a much wider road and turned onto it – *and I'm supposed to be making contact with an ex-girlfriend who dumped me the last time I called her!* He forced himself to straighten his back and move out into the clear middle of this road (no open sewers here), then took it in. Big stone walls to either side, imposing gatehouses with solid wooden doors. No windows at ground level. Multistory piles some way behind the walls, like pocket castles. *That's what they are*, he suddenly realized. *This place is* primitive. *No police, but heaven help you if the mob catches you stealing. The rich have their own small armies. Warlords, like Afghanistan.* A moment later his earlier thought overtook the latest one, colliding in a messy train-wreck: *And Miriam's rich. She's one of the people who own these castles. What does* that *mean?*

There were more people hanging around this street, and stalls mounted on brightly colored cart wheels were selling food and (by the smell) slightly rancid beer to them. The road ended ahead, not in a junction but in a huge gate with a park beyond it. Or something that looked like a park. In the distance, a huge palace loomed above tents and crowd. Mike took a deep breath. 'This it?' he asked Hastert.

'Yessir.' Hastert passed him a rolled-up piece of heavy paper. 'This will get you in. I'm told it's an invitation.'

'And you . . . ?'

'Got to stop at the gate, sir. Turns out there's a law against bringing guards. You're allowed to bear a gentleman's arms, you're supposed to be Sieur Vincensh d'Lofstrom, but we're . . . not. See that side gate? We'll run a rotating watch on it. Any trouble, hotfoot it there and we'll provide a distraction while we get you to Zone Green.'

'Check.' Mike glanced nervously at a passing bear, which watched him with ancient eyes until its owner jerked viciously on the chain riveted to its iron collar. 'If I'm not back in four hours, you'll know I'm in trouble.'

'Okay, four hours.' Hastert nodded. 'Good luck, sir.'

'Thanks.' Mike shivered. 'Hope I don't need it.' He took a deep breath and glanced at the guards by the gate, their bright red and yellow uniforms and eight-foot poleaxes. The other side of the gate was a confused whirl of people and sounds and smells, a Renaissance Faire with added stench and more alcohol. *Are you somewhere in there, Miriam?* he wondered. And: *What am I going to say when I find you?* Aloud: 'Here goes.'

INTERRUPTION

Miriam sat alone in her bedroom for a couple of hours, her mind spinning like a hamster in a wheel. *Should I stay or should I go?* The old Clash song held a certain resonance. *Give the bastards what they want and Iris doesn't get hurt.* The logic was sound, but the sick sense of humiliation she felt whenever she thought about it gave her a visceral urge to lash out. *Go through with it. One year, two at the most. And then what?*

They'd use artificial insemination. She'd have one or more small infants, be exhausted from the effort – it wasn't for nothing that it was called labor – and the babies would in turn be hostages to use against her. The idea of bringing up children didn't fill her with enthusiasm; she'd seen friends turned old before their days by the workload of diaper changes and late-night feedings. It was probably different for royalty: she'd have servants and wet nurses on call. But still, wasn't that a bit irresponsible? Miriam felt a twinge of conscience. She'd gotten into this mess of her own accord. It wouldn't be fair to take out her resentment on a baby who wasn't even around at the time. Or on the idiot prince. It wasn't *his* fault.

I wish I could just run away. She lay back on the bed and indulged her escape fantasies for a while, studiously not thinking about Iris. *I could go back to New Britain. I've got friends there.* But the Clan knew all about her company and her contacts. *I'd have to start from scratch. Talk to Erasmus about a new identity.* And without the Clan connection, she'd be a lot less useful to him and his friends. *What if he wanted to stay in their good books?* He could easily turn her over to Morgan. Worse, New Britain didn't look like a hot place to spend the rest of her days, especially starting out halfway broke in the middle of a recession while trying to hide from the Clan. Which obviously ruled out technology start-ups, businesses based on her existing know-how, anything that might draw their attention. *Iris found Morris. Who or what hope have I got?*

Her thoughts turned to Cambridge. Home. *I could go back to being a journalist*, she thought. *Yeah, right.* That would work precisely as long as it took for her to run into someone she'd interviewed at a trade conference. Or until she needed a bank account and a driving license. Post-9/11, disappearing and getting a new identity was becoming increasingly difficult –

Which leaves the feds, she thought. *I could go look up Mike. He worked for the DEA, didn't he?* Since Matthias went over the wall, something had clearly gone deeply wrong with the Clan courier networks. Matthias had blabbed to someone, and whatever he'd told them had caused the feds to start staking out safe houses. *Which means they know something about the Clan*, she told herself, with a dawning sense that she'd been far too slow on the uptake. She sat up. *I've been an idiot. If I defected, I could join the Witness Protection Program and then* –

She hit a brick wall. A series of unwelcome visions began playing themselves out in the theater of her imagination. There went Angbard – a scheming old bastard he might be, but still her uncle – shoved into a federal penitentiary at his age. *Lock him up for life and throw away the key.* And there went Iris – *The entire family, basically everybody, they could arrest us* all *for complicity, criminal conspiracy. Right?* There went Olga. And Brill – probably for murder, in her case, come to think of it. The government would play hardball. They'd find some way to come over here and mess things up. If necessary, they'd chop up a captured world-walker's brains to figure out what made them tick, grow it in a petri dish and mount it on a bomber. Before 9/11 she wouldn't have credited it, but this was a whole different world, these were dangerous times, and the administration might do *anything* if it thought there was a serious threat to the nation.

Forget law and order: it would be all-out war. Afghanistan was a source of hard drugs and terrorism before 9/11, and look what they'd done there when the rules changed. Everybody had cheered the collapse of the Taliban – and yes, those bastards had it coming – but what about the village goatherds on the receiving end of cluster

262

bombs, intended for sheep that looked like guerillas when viewed in infrared from thirty thousand feet? What about the women and children killed when some bastard up the road with a satellite phone decided to settle a local long-running blood feud using a B-52 bomber, by phoning the CIA and telling them that there were al-Qaeda gunmen in the next village?

I can't do that. She flopped back on the bed again. *I want out, sure. But do I want out badly enough to kill people?* If the only person to suffer was Baron Henryk, perhaps the answer was yes – and that asshole doctor, she wouldn't mind hurting him, or at least putting him through the same level of humiliation he'd inflicted on her. But the idea of turning everyone in the Clan over to the US government cut too close to the bone. *I* am *one of them,* she realized, turning the unwelcome idea over in her mind to examine it for feel. *I don't think like them and I hate the way they work, but I can't hand my family over to the government.* Leaving aside the fact that the Clan thought *they* were a government – and had a reasonable claim to being one – that thought clarified things somewhat.

And then there's Mom.

Miriam took a deep breath. Her mood crashed, giving way to bleak depression. *Henryk's got me. Iris is right, I'm out of options. Unless something unexpected happens, I am stuck with this. I'll have to go through with it.* She winced. *What did they say about pregnancy? You can't world-walk while you're expecting.* Another unwanted, hostile imposition on her freedom. *He won't need a prison cell while I'm pregnant,* she realized. *And afterward* . . . When Iris had made her escape she'd been young and healthy. By the time Miriam delivered, she'd be close to her mid-thirties.

There was a knock. Miriam pushed herself upright and stretched. The knock repeated, tentative, uncertain of itself. *Not the ferret,* she thought, walking over to the door. 'Yes?' she demanded.

'Milady, we're to –' She didn't understand the rest, but she knew the tone of voice. She opened the door.

'You are, me, to dress?' Miriam managed haltingly. The two servants bobbed. 'Good.' She shrugged. *This is going to happen,* she realized dismally, walking toward the wardrobe as if on autopilot. *Oh well. I guess I should leave this to Helge, then. Helge?* 'Now what am I to wear?' she asked aloud, surprising herself with her diction.

*

The Clan weren't big on subtle messages. Helge let the servants lace her into an underdress, then help her into a gown of black silk and deep blue velvet. It had long sleeves, full skirts, and a neckline that rose to a high collar. Current fashion favored a revealing décolletage, but she was in a funereal mood. She wrapped a thick rope of pearls around her waist as a belt, and looped another around her collar. Then she checked her appearance in the mirror. Her cheek was coming up in a fine bruise where Henryk had struck her, so she picked out a black lace veil, cloak, and matching gloves from her armoire. *Let 'em wonder what kind of damaged goods they're buying,* she thought bitterly. This outfit wouldn't give much away: truthfully, it looked like Victorian mourning drag. 'I'm ready to go now,' she announced, entering the reception room. 'Where is that, that idle – '

'Right here.' The front door was open, the ferret standing beside it. 'My, how mysterious.'

'Is the coach ready?'

'Yes. If you would care to follow me . . .'

She managed to descend the staircase without tripping, and she clambered into the coach that was waiting. A sealed coach, with shuttered windows, locked on the outside, she observed. *Still a prisoner, I see. Someone doesn't trust me.*

The air was close and the evening warm. Helge fanned herself as the coach clattered and swayed out of the courtyard and across the streets. Alone in the dark, she brooded listlessly. *Is this the right thing to do?* she wondered, then felt like kicking herself: *See any alternatives, stupid?* She felt stiff and defensive, her dress constricting and hot – more like a suit of armor than a display of glamour and wealth. *I'm going to look like an idiot,* she thought, *preposterously frumpy.* A moment later: *Why should I care what they think? Bah.*

After an interminable ride – which might have been five minutes or half an hour – the roadway smoothed, wheels crunching over gravel, and the carriage halted. Someone busied themselves with the padlock outside, then a glare of setting sunlight almost blinded Helge as she squeezed through the door.

'Milady.' It was – what was his name? *Some flunky of Henryk's*, she decided. He handed her down the steps to a small gaggle of guards and ladies-in-waiting and general rubberneckers. 'Please allow me to welcome you to the royal household. This is Sir Rybeck, master of the royal stables. And this is – '

It was a receiving line. For *her*. Helge offered her hand as she was gently moved along it, accepting bows and courtesies and strange lips on the back of her glove, smiling fixedly and trying not to bare her teeth. Two court ladies-in-waiting picked up the train of her cloak, and four guards in the red and gold of the royal troupe walked before her with long, viciously curved axes held aloft. *This is public*, she realized with a sinking feeling. *They're saying publicly that I rate the respect due a member of the royal household!* Which meant there'd have to be some kind of announcement soon. Which in turn meant that they were definitely going ahead with it.

She'd never paid too much attention to royal etiquette in the past, and anything she'd accidentally read about in her old life was inapplicable, but it was seriously intimidating. People were acting as if they were *afraid* of her. And if anyone thought her gown was unfashionable or noticed her bruised cheek under the veil, they were keeping quiet about it.

There was a huge banquet hall with several tables set up inside it, one of them on a raised platform at the back. People thronged the floor of the hall: as she entered the room there was a ripple of low-key conversation. Faces turned toward her. Butterflies flapped their wings in her stomach. 'What now?' she asked her guide quietly, gripping his arm, forcing her Hochsprache to perform.

'I escort you to the antechamber. You greet the king. You greet the prince. There will be drinks. Then there will be the meal.' He kept his diction clear and his phrases short, speaking slowly out of deference to her poor language skills. To her surprise, Helge understood most of what he said.

'Is the duke here? Angbard? Or Baron Henryk?' she asked.

His reply was a small shrug. 'Alas, matters of state keep both of them away.'

'Oh.' *Right*. Matters of state, it seemed, conspired to keep her from giving them a piece of her mind. She walked past the curious crowds – she smiled and nodded at enquiries, but kept her feet moving – then a door opened ahead of her. Guards grounded their axes. None of the nobles at *this* show were wearing swords. She went right ahead, then her escort stopped, a restraining hand on her arm. Miriam paused, then recognized the sad-faced man in front of her. Her mind went blank. *He's wearing a crown. You're supposed to be marrying his son. What am I supposed to do now?* Helge bent her knees in a deep curtsey. 'Your majesty. I am, it pleases, me to see you.'

'Countess Helge. Your presence brings light to an old man's eye. Please, take our arm.' He smiled hesitantly, his face wrinkling with the look of a man who'd born more cruel blows than anyone should face.

She bit her tongue and took the proffered arm gingerly. For an instant the urge to try a throw she'd learned in a self-defense class fifteen years ago taunted her. However, throwing the king over her shoulder might bring even less pleasant consequences than telling Baron Henryk to fuck off. 'Yes, your majesty,' she said meekly, falling back into the Helge role, and she allowed Alexis Nicholau III to lead her across the room toward the stooped figure of his mother the queen, and the equally stooped, but much huskier, figure of his son, Prince Creon.

'We understand you know why you are here?'

'I –' Helge tripped over her tongue. 'I am to marry, yes?'

'That is the idea.' The king frowned slightly. Then he reached up and lifted one corner of her veil. 'Ah. We understand now.' He let it fall. 'We apologize for our curiosity. Was it serious?'

'I –' *could break Henryk's career* right now, *for good*, she realized. *But that way it wouldn't be personal, would it?* 'I walk into bedpost,' she said slowly. She felt a sudden stab of rage. *Let him wonder when it's going to come.* 'Is nothing serious.'

'Good.' The frown lifted slightly. 'We trust you will willingly uphold your party's side of the bargain, then?'

Bargain? What bargain? She looked at him blankly, then realized what he must be talking about. 'I am the daughter of my mother.'

'That is more than sufficient.' He nodded. 'A glass of wine for the countess,' he casually dropped in the direction of a baron, who hustled away to find a waiter. 'Prince Creon is a troubling responsibility,' he said.

'Responsibility?' It was a new word to Helge.

'*Responsibility*,' he repeated in English. 'Hmm. Your tongue comes along wonderfully. Soon few will think you a half-wit like my son.'

Aha. 'That is the veil, the, uh, cover, for the marriage?'

'For now.' The king nodded. Miriam forced herself to unkink her fingers before she burst a seam in her gloves. They were curled into claws. *They think I'm an idiot?* 'It is a useful fiction.'

'But your son – '

'Can speak for himself.' The king smiled sadly. 'Can't you, Creon?'

'Muh-marriage?' Creon lurched toward Helge curiously, stopped when he was facing her.

Helge sighed. He *wasn't* ugly, that was the bad news. If you straightened his back, wiped away the string of drool, and unwound the genetic disorder that had left him wide-open to brain damage delivered by an assassin's dose of artificial sweetener in his food when he was a child, he'd be more than presentable: he'd be a catch, like his elder brother. The thought of the older one nearly made her shudder: she caught herself in time. *Remember what they call them, the Idiot and the Pervert*, she warned herself. 'Hello, Creon,' she said slowly.

'Muh-marriage?' he mumbled. 'I'm hungry – '

It was a miracle he was still walking. Or conscious. She pitied him. 'Do you know what that means?' she asked.

'Muh, muh –' He reached out a hand and she took it. He looked at her for a moment, puzzled as if by something far beyond his understanding, and squeezed. Helge yelped. Heads turned.

'We must apologize again,' said the prince's father, stepping in to detach his hand from her wrist. He did so gently, then raised an eyebrow. 'You are sure this is the prize you want?' he asked quietly.

Helge licked her lips. 'So my mother tells me.' *And the rest of my long-lost family. At gunpoint.*

'Ah well, on your head be it, just so long as you are gentle with him. He needs protecting. It is not his fault.'

'I –' *I'd like to find the assholes who did this to him and give them something in return.* 'I know that.' As unwilling arranged marriages went, Creon looked unlikely to be a demanding husband. *I just hope Doctor ven Hjalmar knows what he's doing,* she thought. *If he doesn't, if they expect me to* sleep *with Creon* . . . All of a sudden, test tubes and turkey basters held a remarkable allure. A glass of sparkling wine appeared in her hand and she drank it down in one mouthful, then held out her glass for a refill. 'I will look after him,' she promised, and was surprised to find that it came easily. *It's not his fault he's damaged goods,* she thought, then did a double take. *Is that what Henryk thinks I am?*

The king nodded. 'We must circulate,' he said. 'At dinner, you will be seated to our left.' Then he disappeared, leaving her with Creon and his discreet minders, and the Queen Mother. Which latter worthy grimaced at her horribly – or perhaps it was intended as an impish grin – and hobbled over.

'It will go well,' she insisted, gripping Helge's wrist. 'You are a modest young woman, I see. Good for you, Helge. You have good hips, too.' She winked. 'You will enjoy the fruits, if not the planting.'

'Uh. Thank you,' Helge said carefully, and detached herself as soon as she could, which turned out to be when Angelin's glass ran dry. She glanced around, wondering if she could find somewhere to hide. Her disguise wasn't exactly helping make her inconspicuous. Then she spotted a familiar face across the room. She slid along the wall toward his corner. His eyes slid past her at first: *What's wrong?* she wondered. Then she realized. *Oh, he doesn't recognize me.* She pushed back the veil and nodded at him, and James Lee started. 'Hi,' she said, reverting to English.

'Hi yourself.' He eyed her up and down. 'How – modest?'

'I'm supposed to be saving myself for my husband.' She pulled a face. 'Not that he'd notice.'

'Hah. I didn't know you were married.'

'I'm not. Yet. Are you?'

'Oh, absolutely not. So where's the lucky man?' He looked mildly irritated. *So, have I got your interest?* Miriam wondered idly.

'Over there.' She tilted her head, then spotted the Queen Mother looking round. ''Scuse me.' She dropped her veil.

'You're not –'He looked aghast. 'You're going to marry the Idiot?'

She sighed. 'I wish people wouldn't call him that.'

'But you –' He stopped. 'You *are*. You're going to do it.'

'Yes,' she said tightly. 'I have a shortage of alternative offers, in case you'd forgotten. A woman of my age and status needs to be grateful for what she can get' – and for her relatives refraining from poisoning her mother – 'and all that.'

'Ha. I'd marry you, if you asked,' said Lee. There was a dangerous gleam in his eye.

'If –' She took a deep breath, constrained by the armor of her role. 'I am *required* to produce royal offspring,' she said bitterly.

Lee glanced away. 'The traditional penalty for indiscretions with the wives of royalty is rather drastic,' he murmured.

She snorted quietly. 'I wasn't offering.' *Yet.* 'I'm not in the market.' *But get back to me after I've been married to Creon for a year or two. By then, even the goats will be looking attractive.* 'Listen, did you remember what I asked for?'

'Oh, this?' A twist of his hand, and a gleam of silver: a small locket on a chain slid into his palm.

Helge's breath caught. Freedom in a capsule. It was almost painful. If she took it she could desert all her responsibilities, her duty to Patricia, her impending marriage to the damaged cadet branch of the monarchy – 'What do you want for it?' she asked quietly.

'From you?' Lee stared at her for a long second. 'One kiss, my lady.'

The spell broke. She reached out and folded his fingers around the chain. 'Not now,' she said gently. 'You've no idea what it costs me to say that. But – '

He laid a finger on the back of her hand. 'Take it now.'

'Really?'

'Just say you will let me petition for my fee later, that's all I ask.'

She breathed out slowly. Her knees suddenly felt like jelly. *Wow, you're a sweet-talker.* 'You know you're asking for something dangerous.'

'For you, no risk is too great.' He smiled, challenging her to deny it.

She took another deep breath. 'Yes, then.'

He tilted his hand upside-down and she felt the locket and its chain pour into her gloved hand. She fumbled hastily with the buttons at her wrist, then slid the family treasure inside and refastened the sleeve. 'Have you any idea what this means to me?' she asked.

'It's the key to a prison cell.' He raised his wineglass. 'I've been in that cell too. If I wanted to leave badly enough – '

'Oh. Oh. I see.' The hell of it was, he was telling the truth: he could violate his status as a hostage anytime he felt like it – anytime he felt like restarting a war that his own family could only lose. She felt a sudden stab of empathy for him. *That's dangerous*, part of her realized. Another part of her remembered Roland, and felt betrayed. But Roland was dead, and she was still alive, and seemingly destined for a loveless marriage: why shouldn't she enjoy a discreet fling on the side? *But not now*, she rationalized. Not right under the eyes of the royal dynasty, not with half the Clan waiting outside for a grand dinner at which a betrothal would be announced. Not until after the royal wedding, and the pregnancy – her mind shied away from thinking of it as *her* pregnancy – and the birth of the heir. The heir to the throne who'd be a W* heterozygote and on whose behalf Henryk wouldn't, bless him, even *dream* of treason. After all, as the old epigram put it, *Treason doth never prosper: what's the reason? Why if it prosper, none dare call it treason.*

A bell rang, breaking through the quiet conversation. 'That means dinner,' said Lee, bowing slightly, then turning to slip away. 'I'll see you later.'

*

They filed out through the door, Helge on the king's arm, before an audience of hundreds of faces. She felt her knees knock. For a moment she half-panicked: then she realized nobody could see her face. 'Put back your veil, my dear,' the king murmured. 'Your seat.'

Hypnotized, she sat down on something extremely hard and unforgiving, like a slab of solid wood. *A throne*. A brassy cacophony of trumpetlike horns blatted from the sidelines as other notables stepped forward and sat down to either side of – then opposite – her.

She moved her veil out of the way, then recoiled. A wizened old woman – a crone in spirit as well as age – sat across the table from her. '*You,*' she said.

'Is that any way to address your grandmother?' The old dowager looked down her nose at her. 'I beg your pardon, your majesty, one needs must teach the young flower that those who stand tallest are the first to be cut down to size.'

'This is *your* doing,' Helge accused.

'Hardly. It's traditional.' Hildegarde snorted. 'Eat your sweetbreads. It's long past time you and I had a talk and cleared the air between us.'

'We'd listen to her, if we were you,' the king told Helge. Then he turned to speak to the elderly courtier on his right, effectively locking her out of his sphere of conversation.

'There's nothing to talk about,' Helge said sullenly. She toyed with her food, some sort of meat in a glazed sugar sauce.

'Your demeanor does you credit, my dear, but it doesn't deceive me. You're still looking for a way out. Let me tell you, there isn't one.'

'Uh-huh.' Helge took a mouthful of appetizer. It was disgustingly rich, implausible as an appetizer. Oily, too.

'Every woman in our lineage goes through this sooner or later,' said the dowager. She stabbed a piece of meat with her knife, held it to her mouth, and nibbled delicately at it with her yellowing teeth. 'You're nothing special, child.'

Helge stared at her, speechless with rage.

'Go on, hate me,' Hildegarde said indulgently. 'It goes with the territory.' She'd switched to English, in deference to her granddaughter's trouble with the vernacular, but now Miriam was having trouble staying in character as Helge. 'It'll go easier for you if you hate me. Go on.'

'I thought you didn't believe in me.' Miriam bit into the sweetbread. *Sheep's pancreas*, a part of her remembered. 'Last time we met you called me a fraud.'

'Allow me to concede that your mother vouched for you satisfactorily. And I will admit she is who she claims to be. Even after a third of a century of blessed peace and quiet she's hard to deny, the minx.'

271

'She's no – '

'Yes she *is*. Don't you see that? She even fooled you.'

'No she didn't.'

'Yes she did.' The dowager put her fork down. 'She's always been the devious viper in my bosom. She brought you up to be loyal to her and her only. When she decided to come in from the cold, she sent you on ahead to test the waters. Now she's making a play for the royal succession. And she's got you thinking she's a poor, harmless victim and you're doing this to protect her, hasn't she?'

Miriam stared at Hildegarde, aghast. 'That's not how it is,' she said.

Her grandmother looked at her disdainfully. 'As you grow older you'll see things more clearly. You won't feel yourself changing on the inside, but the outside – ah, that's different. You've got to learn to look beneath the skin, child. The war of mother against daughters continues, and you can't simply opt out of it by imagining there to be some special truce between your mother and yourself.' Servants were circulating with silver goblets of pale wine. 'Ah, it's time.'

'What?'

'Don't drink that yet,' the dowager snapped. 'It's mead,' she added, 'not that I'd expect you to know what that is, considering how Patricia neglected your upbringing.'

Miriam flushed.

There was another blast of trumpets. Everyone downed eating-knives and looked at the raised platform expectantly.

'A toast,' announced the king, raising his voice. 'This evening, we have the honor to announce that our son Creon offers his hand to this lady, the Countess Helge voh Thorold d'Hjorth, in alliance of marriage. Her guardian, the Dowager Duchess Hildegarde voh Hjorth d'Hjalmar, is present this evening. My lady, what say you?'

He's not talking to me, Miriam realized, as the dowager shuffled to her feet. 'Your majesty, my lord. On behalf of my family I thank you from the bottom of my heart for this offer, and I assure you that she would be delighted to accept.'

Miriam stared, rosy-cheeked with embarrassment and anger, at her ancient grandmother.

'Thank you,' the king said formally. 'May the alliance of our lines be peaceful and fruitful.' He raised his silver goblet. 'To the happy couple!'

Several hundred silver goblets flashed in the light from the huge chandelier that dominated the ceiling of the room. A rumble of approval echoed like thunder across the room. Miriam looked around, her head twitching like a trapped bird.

'You can drink now,' the dowager murmured, casting her voice over the racket. 'You look like you need it.'

'But I – do I get a chance to say anything?'

'No, for what would you say? In a decade you'll be glad you didn't speak. Just remember you owe me this opportunity to better yourself! I've worked hard for it, and if you let me down, girl – '

Incandescent with rage, Miriam glared across the table at her grandmother. 'You told Henryk to threaten Mom, didn't you?'

'What if I did?' The dowager stared at her. 'Your mother's misled you quite enough already. It's time you learned how the world works. You'll understand in your time, even if you don't like it now. And one day you'll be a player yourself.'

'I wouldn't cross the road to piss on you if you were on fire,' Miriam retorted half-heartedly. She took a deep mouthful of the mead. It tasted of honey and broken hearts. Her cheeks itched. Over-taken by an obscure emotion, she pulled her veil down again. Tears of sorrow, tears of rage – who could tell the difference? Not her. *I'll get you*, she thought. *I* will *be different! And nothing like this will ever happen to any daughter of mine!*

The thunder of applause didn't seem to be dying down. To her left, an elderly count was looking around in puzzlement. 'Eh, what-what?' The applause had a rhythmic note, almost thunderous, as if a huge crowd outside was stamping their feet in synchrony.

'That's enough,' called the king. 'You can stop now!' He sounded in good spirits.

People were looking around. *That's odd*, thought Miriam, puzzled. *That's not applause. If I didn't know better I'd say it was –*

There was an angry bang, with a harsh, flat note to it, then a sound, like a trillion angry bees. The windows overhead blew in,

273

scattering shards of glass across the diners. Amidst the screams Miriam heard a harsh banging sound from outside, the noise of wheel-lock guns firing. The king turned to her. 'Get under the table,' he said quietly: *'Now.'*

What? Miriam shuddered. Fragments of glass fell across the dining table. A jagged piece landed on the back of her hand, sticking into her glove. There was no pain at first. 'What – '

Abruptly the king wasn't there anymore. The dowager was gone, too. There was another deep thud that jarred her teeth and made her ears hurt. The main door to the hall was open, and smoke came billowing in through it.

Suddenly Miriam was very afraid. She tried to slide down under the table but her voluminous skirts got in the way, trapping her in a twisted mound of fabric. There was shouting, and more banging, gunfire. From off to one side she heard the flat crackle of an automatic weapon, firing in controlled bursts. People were running around the hall, trying to get out. She tugged and managed to get untangled. *What the hell is going on?* She ducked round the back of the throne, dropping to the floor behind the raised platform. Half a dozen servants and diners cowered there, including James Lee: he opened his mouth to ask her something.

A body fell from the platform in a spray of blood. Miriam crouched, arms covering her head. There was another bang from the room at the back where the royal party had assembled for dinner, an eternity ago. Men in black – black combat fatigues, torsos bulky with flak jackets, heads weirdly misshapen with gas masks – ran past the back of the dais, two of them staying to train guns behind. 'Get down!' screamed one of the men in black. Then he saw her. 'Milady? This way, *now.' Clan security, Angbard's men,* Miriam thought, dizzy with the need for oxygen. *What's happening?*

'This way.'

'Who's attacking us?'

'I don't *know,* milady – move!' She rose to a crouch, began to duckwalk along the back of the platform. 'You, sir! On your feet, have you a gun?'

There was a noise behind her, so loud that she didn't hear it so much as feel it in her abdomen. Someone thumped her hard in the small of her back and she went down, trying to curl up, her spine a red-hot column of agony. She was dimly aware of Clan guards rushing past. Blood on the floor, plaster and debris pattering down from the ceiling. There was more gunfire, some shouting.

As Miriam caught her breath she began to realize that the gunfire was continuing. And the Clan guards – *There's only a handful of them,* she realized. *They may have modern weapons, but that's a lot of muskets out there. And cannon, by the sound of it.* Fear gripped her. *What's going on?*

Miriam felt sick to her stomach. The pain in her back was easing. It was bad, but not crippling. She risked pushing herself to her knees and nothing happened. Then she looked round.

King Alexis Nicholau III sat with his legs sprawled apart, leaning against an ornamental pillar with an expression of ironic amusement on what was left of his face. About half of his brains were spread across the pillar, forming the body of an exclamation mark of which his face was the period.

'Surrender in the name of his majesty!' The hoarse voice sounded slightly desperate, as if he knew that if they didn't surrender his head was going to end up gracing the top of a pike. 'Yield in the name of his majesty, King Egon!'

Miriam kilted up her dress and began to crawl rapidly across the floor, past bodies and a howling, weeping old woman she didn't recognize. She passed a servant lying on his back with blood pooling around him: evidently he hadn't understood enough English. There was more smoke now, and it smelled of wood. *I've got to get out of here,* she realized. *Egon!* His accession to the throne depended on the support of the nobility, of course. *He'll have to kill everyone here,* she realized coldly. If he thought his father had decided to sideline him in favor of his younger brother, how better to assure himself of the support of the old nobility than to liquidate the one group of noble houses who were the greatest threat to him, and the greatest source of support for his rival?

She turned and crawled toward the door to the reception chamber. A bullet cracked off the tiled floor in front of her, spraying chips of marble, and she pulled back hastily.

*

It was twilight outside, and the chandelier was down. The soldiers outside seemed determined to bottle a couple of hundred people up inside a burning building with no fire extinguishers. People who'd come here to celebrate a betrothal. She felt a rising sense of nausea. Not that she'd wanted it herself, but this wasn't her idea of how to extract herself from the situation –

There was a side door, discreet and undecorated, behind one of the pillars. She eyed the bullet holes high up it warily, then glanced round at the dais. It was partly shielded. She crawled forward again, her shoulder blades twitching. People were screaming now, cries of alarm mingling with the awful panting gasps of the wounded.

The door opened onto darkness. Miriam stood up as she ducked inside. *Isn't this the passage they brought me through to see the queen, the first time?* she wondered. *If so, there should be another door here –*

She pushed the door carefully and it opened into another room, largely obscured by the pillar and drapes positioned to hide it from genteel attention. She froze in place, trying to look like another ornate swag of curtain. Half a dozen soldiers in what looked like stained leather overalls worn under chain-mesh surcoats were standing guard. Some held swords, but a couple were armed with modern-looking pistols. Two of them were covering a group of captives who lay facedown on the floor. 'You will guard these tinkers in the rear,' one of them told his companion. 'If there is any risk of escape, kill them.' He continued in rapid Hochsprache, too fast for Miriam's ear.

Two of the guards were yanking the captives to their feet. They seemed slow to move, disoriented. The guards were brutally efficient, dragging them forward toward the main door. The talkative one bent over a lump on the floor and did something. 'Hurry!' Then he followed the others out hastily.

That's got to be a bomb. As soon as he was out, Miriam scurried forward. It was green, it had shoulder straps, and there was some kind of timer on top of it. *One of Matthias's leftover toys. Why am I not surprised? If I move it –* She froze, indecisive. *What if there's a trembler switch?* She glanced at the door they'd left through. *I've got to get out of here!*

Miriam ducked into the next servants' passage, darting along it. She reached the outer receiving chamber with the floor-to-ceiling glass doors, worth a fortune in this place, just about the time the men in black were leaving it. Creeping forward, she looked out across a scene of devastation. Beyond the shattered windows lay what seemed to be half the palace guard. They had fallen in windrows, many of them still clutching their broken pikestaffs. Another gout of thunder and a lick of flame told her why: across the ha-ha at the end of the terrace, a group of figures moved urgently about their business, manhandling an archaic-looking cannon back into position to bear on the west wing of the palace. More isolated gunfire banged across the garden, the flat bursts of the black powder weapons sounding like a Fourth of July party.

Jesus, it's a full-scale coup, she thought, just as another distinctive figure stumbled around the front of the building.

'Creon!' she called out, forgetting that she was trying to hide. He was out in front, while she was at the back of the reception room, in near-darkness. He probably couldn't hear her anyway. Her heart lurched. *What's he doing? Who the hell knows what he thinks he's doing?* Right now he was silhouetted against the twilight outside, but in a moment –

Creon loped away from the front of the palace, toward the gun crew. He seemed to be waving his arms –

'Creon! No!' she yelled. Too late. One of the pikemen beside the cannon saw him, pointed: another soldier raised an ominously modern weapon, a rifle. *They're protecting their artillery*, she realized blankly. *Probably realize there'll be no more modern ammunition when* – Creon dropped like a stone.

Miriam shook herself, like a dog awakening from a deep sleep. Appalled, she took a step forward.

Someone grabbed at her from behind. He missed her, snagging her veil instead. She spun round and lashed out hard with her left fist, all the anger and frustration of the past days boiling up inside her. Then she doubled over in pain as her assailant punched her in the stomach.

'Aushlaant' bisch – '

She gasped for air, looking up. He had a dagger in his hand, and an expression on his face that made her elbows and knees turn to jelly. *He's going to –*

The back of the man's head vanished in a red spray, and he dropped like a stone.

'*Fuck!*' she screamed, finally getting her breath back.

'Miriam?' Hesitantly. *I know that voice*, she thought dizzily. 'Are you all right?'

'No,' she managed to choke. Putting one arm out she tried to lever herself up.

'Let me help – '

'No.' She managed to half sit up, then discovered tangled dress wouldn't let her. 'Yes.' *What the fuck are* you *doing here?* she wondered.

A hand under her left armpit gave her the support she needed. Her right hip hurt and her back and stomach felt bruised. She stood gasping for a minute, then turned and stared, too tired and bewildered to feel any surprise. He was wearing hiking gear and what looked like an army-surplus camo jacket under a merchant's robe, obviously picked up on his way here. It was the final surreal joke to cap a whole day of petty horrors. 'Tell me what you're doing here,' she said, trying to keep her tone level. *Think of the devil and he'll drop by to say hello . . .*

'I don't know,' he said shakily. 'It wasn't meant to go like this. I was just sent here to have a quiet chat with you, gunfights weren't on the agenda.' He stared at the body and swallowed.

'The agenda,' she said tartly, forcing herself to ignore it. 'Are you still working for the DEA? Would this happen to be their idea?'

He cleared his throat. 'I'm still a DEA agent, yes. In a manner of speaking. But there are chain-of-command issues. Any idea why that guy was trying to kill you?'

She felt an inane giggle trying to work its way up her throat, stifled it ruthlessly. *Three years older, three years wiser.* The last time she'd spoken to Mike she'd told him to scratch her name out of his address book. She'd been half-convinced he was a psychopath. Now she'd met some real psychopaths she wasn't so sure. 'People just sort of keep trying to kill me around here. It seems to be the national sport.'

'Poor Miriam.' His tone was mock-sympathetic, but when she looked at him sharply his expression was anything but light. 'I was sent here to have a little talk with you. Our intelligence was that this was a royal garden party: do they always blow the place up for kicks?'

'No. But the king was supposed to be announcing a royal wedding.' She glanced over her shoulder again. 'The groom's brother seems to have taken exception.'

'If this is their idea of a wedding party, I'd hate to see a divorce. Who're the happy couple?'

'That's the groom, over here.' She nodded at the window, at the darkness and flames beyond. 'This was meant to be my engagement.' *That's right, oversimplify the situation for him*, she mocked herself. 'Only it seems to have turned into the excuse for a coup. I reckon this bastard was one of Egon's thugs.'

'I'm sorry.'

'No, that's all right,' she said numbly. 'It was an arranged marriage. They like to deal with uppity women by marrying them off.' She stared at him fixedly. *I can't believe I'm standing in a burning palace talking to Mike Fleming!* 'So this is DEA business, right? I guess Matthias spilled his guts in return for protection?'

'DEA – Matthias –' He stared at her tensely. A thought struck Miriam: hoping he wouldn't notice, she clasped her hands together in front of her, trying to unobtrusively unfasten one cuff.

'How well did you know Matt?' Mike asked.

'He tried to kill me, and murdered my –' She bit her tongue. 'It's a long story.'

'I'll bet.'

The sleeve was coming loose. She looked him in the eye. 'Well?'

'Are you happy here?' he asked cautiously. 'Because you don't look it . . .'

'Am I –' The laugh from hell was back, trying to get out again. 'The fuck I am! If you can get me away from here –' Her voice broke. 'Please, Mike! Can you?' She hated the tremor of desperation but she couldn't stop it. 'I'm going mad!'

'I – I – oh shit.'

Her heart fell. 'What is it?'

'I.' His voice was small. 'I don't think I can.'

'Why not?'

'We're moving in over here,' he said, in a voice that sounded like he was trying to figure out how to give her some bad news. 'We need world-walkers.'

'You've come to the right place. Except the folks outside want them all dead; I think this could be a civil war breaking out, you know?'

'We need world-walkers.' He looked troubled. 'But what the organization is doing with them – I'm sorry, but I've got to ask – '

'Yes, I'm a goddamn world-walker!' Miriam vented. 'That's my mother you want to blame – she ran away decades ago, then they came and fetched her back and found me. Why do you want to know?'

He seemed to relax, as if coming to a decision. 'I've got to go now,' he said.

'Can you put me in the Witness Protection Program?' she asked.

'I'd love to – I'd like nothing better than to get you into a safe house and a debriefing program. But listen, I'd also say – and I'm not supposed to – you should wait a bit. They're using world-walkers as mules, Miriam. I mean, the folks I work for now, big-hat federal spooks. I was supposed to try and convince you to work as an informer for us, if that's possible, but I guess this shit means it's not . . .'

'It wouldn't have worked anyway,' she said heavily. 'They don't trust me.'

He paused. 'I can't say I'm surprised. But at least I can report that. Identify you as a sympathizer, I mean. That'll make things easier later on.' A longer pause. 'If you can get over to Boston, do you still have my home number?'

'Damn,' she said bleakly, staring at him. The old Mike would *never* have given a smuggler an even break. 'It's that bad, is it?'

'There's a turf war inside the bureaucracy. Cops like me are on the downside at present. Things are really bad. Matt created quite a mess.'

'I can imagine.' Miriam certainly could. She'd brainstormed a lot of things a determined world-walker could do; like reach the places other terrorists couldn't reach, and escape to do it over again. If the government thought they were dealing with more than just a ring of supernatural drug smugglers . . . 'Listen, this wasn't my idea.' She thought about the locket. 'Do you need a lift out of here?'

'No.' He turned, his back to the window. 'This was *supposed* to be a quick in and out, with maybe a friendly chat in the middle. I've got my own way out of this. Take my advice, Miriam: get the hell away from these people. They're pure poison. Go to ground, then phone me in a week or so and I'll see if there's a way to get you into the program without the spooks shutting you down.'

'Easier said than done,' she said bitterly, her shoulders shaking. *They've got me over a barrel, they've got Mom* – And this seemed to be her night for meeting unexorcised ghosts. 'They've got my mom.'

'Oh. That makes things difficult, doesn't it?' He took a deep breath. 'I've got to go now.' He glanced at the locket she was dangling openly. 'On foot, through the shit going down outside. Look, you get the hell out of here. Use your magic whatever. Call me. I won't be back for a week or so, but I'll see what I can do.'

'I'll remember that.'

'Right.' He began to back toward the window. 'Oh, and stay down until you world-walk. I don't want you getting shot by accident.'

'Okay.' She held her hands up.

Some impulse made her ask, 'Do you still have the hots for me, Mike?'

'In your dreams.'

Then he was gone. Miriam began to notice the screams and moans from the building, the pops and crackling and quiet roar of fire. And found she could smell smoke on the nighttime breeze.

I am in a burning building, she told herself. *The king's just been killed. The man I was supposed to marry is dead, there's a bomb behind me, the crown prince is holding a coup and shooting world-walkers.* She tittered in disbelief. *And not only did James Lee make a pass, but I just ran into an ex-boyfriend who's working for the DEA.*

She raised a fist to her mouth, the locket clenched tightly inside it.

If I run away, they'll think Egon's men got me, she thought slowly, trying to gather her scattered wits. *That means Mom's off the hook! And –*

If she could remember Mike's phone number, she could defect. There was something happening there, okay. It had already started, so it wouldn't be *her* fault if she sought sanctuary, the feds were already able to reach the Clan at home. 'I could do it,' she told herself. 'All I have to do is world-walk away from here. Then pick up the telephone.'

She glanced at the locket. 'Hang on. It was James's. Is it a Lee locket, or a Clan locket?' There was a big difference: a Lee locket would take her to New Britain, where a Clan locket would dump her somewhere in downtown New York. Which would be a pain, but if she could make it overnight, get some cash, she could phone Mike in the morning. Whereas if she ended up in New London . . . 'Only one way to find out.'

Miriam turned round and stared at the corpse. He wore a soldier's greatcoat. She'd need that: her current outfit wasn't exactly inconspicuous anywhere. Swallowing bile, she stooped and rolled the body over. It was surprisingly heavy, but the coat wasn't fastened and she managed to keep it out of the puddle. She pulled it over her shoulders: the pockets were heavy. Mentally she flipped a die, tensing. *New York or New London*. Please *let it be New York . . .*

She stared at the knotwork by the light of a blazing palace. It was hard to concentrate on world-walking, to find the right state of mind. The sky lit up behind her for a moment, as a pulse of sound slammed through her, then cut off suddenly. She stumbled, a dull ache digging into her temples, and her stomach flipped. The rich sweetbreads came up in a rush, leaving her bent over the stone gutter. The *stone* gutter. She straightened up slowly, taking in the narrow street, the loaf-shaped paving bricks, the shuttered houses leaning over her. The piles of stinking refuse and fish guts, the broken cartwheel at one corner.

'Fuck, I don't believe this,' she said, and kicked at the curbstone. It was New London, and her dream of easy defection shattered on the rock of reality. Frustrated, she looked around. 'I could go back,' she told herself. 'Or not . . .' She'd run into the Clan again, and she might not be able to get away. With Creon dead, and the US military able to invade the Gruinmarkt, Henryk might do anything: going back was far too dangerous to contemplate. *It'd be much harder to steal a Clan locket and run for New York, wouldn't it? Damn, I've got to find Erasmus . . .*

There was a chink of metal on stone, from about twenty yards up the alleyway.

A chuckle.

'Well, lookee here! And what's a fine girl like her doing in a place like this?'

Miriam's stomach lurched again. *Not only am I in New London instead of New York,* she realized, *I'm in the bad part of town.*

There was another chuckle. 'Let's ask her, why don't we?'

And the bad part of town had noticed her.

AFTER THE WEDDING PARTY

The wreckage still smoldered in the wan dawn light, sending a column of grayish-white smoke spiraling into the misty sky above Niejwein. Two mounted men surveyed it from a vantage point beside the palace gatehouse.

'What a mess.'

'Unavoidable, I think. The best laid plans . . . Have they found his majesty yet, your grace?'

The first speaker shrugged. His horse shuffled, blowing out noisily: the smell of smoke, or possibly the bodies, was making it nervous. 'If he was inside the great hall we might never find identifiable remains. That could be a problem: I believe the blast must have far exceeded the plotters' intent. The soldiers found the Idiot, though – what was left of him. Near chopped in half by the rebels' guns.'

It was not a cold morning, and the second speaker wore a heavy riding coat; nevertheless, he shivered. 'If these are the spells the witch families play with, then I think we may conclude that his presumptive majesty struck not a moment too soon. The tinkers have become too accustomed to having the Crown at their convenience. This could well be our best opportunity to break their grip before they bring damnation to us all.'

The first speaker stroked his beard. 'That is the direction of my thoughts.' He looked pensive. 'I think it behooves us to offer our condolences and our support in his hour of need to his majesty; a little bird tells me that he is of like mind. Then we should look to our own security. His lordship of Greifhalt has a most efficient levy which I think will prove sufficient to our immediate needs, and for the honor of his grandfather he has to come to our aid. We can count on Lyssa, too, and Sudtmann. For your part . . . ?'

'Count me among your party, your grace. I think I can contribute –' He paused, thinking. '– two hundred? Yes, two hundred of horse certainly, and perhaps more once I've seen to the borders.'

'That will be helpful, Otto. The more you can send, the better – as long as you do not neglect the essentials. We cannot afford to feed the scavengers, of whichever kind.' The first speaker shook his head again, looking at the smoking rubble. Stooped figures picked their way through it, inspecting the battlefield for identifiable bodies, their movements as jerky as carrion birds. ''But first, an appropriate demonstration of our loyalty is called for.'

The Duke of Innsford nudged his horse forward; his companion, Otto, Baron Neuhalle, followed, and behind him – at a discreet distance – the duke's personal company followed suit. The scale of destruction only became apparent as Innsford rode down the slope towards what had been the Summer Palace of Niejwein. 'It really does appear to have been visited by a dragon,' he commented, keeping Neuhalle in view. 'I can see why that story is spreading . . .'

'Oh yes. And it came to dinner with his late majesty and half the witch families' heads of household at his table for the feast,' Neuhalle agreed. 'They'll draw the right conclusion. But what a mess.' He gestured at the wreckage. 'Rebuilding the palace will take years, once the immediate task of ensuring that his majesty's reign is long and untroubled by tinkers and demon-traffickers is completed. And I do not believe that will be easy. The old fox will move fast – '

Neuhalle broke off, composing his face in an expression of attentive politeness as he reined in his horse. 'Otto Neuhalle, to pay his respects to his majesty,' he called.

'Advance and be recognized.' Neuhalle nudged his horse forward towards the guards officer supervising the salvage attempt. 'Ah, my lord. If you would care to dismount, I will escort you to the royal party at once.'

'Certainly.' Neuhalle bowed his head and climbed heavily down, handing the reins to his secretary. 'I have the honor of accompanying his grace, the Duke of Innsford. By your leave . . . ?'

The guards officer – a hetman, from his livery – looked past him, his eyes widening. 'Your grace! Please accept my most humble apologies for the poor state of our hospitality.' He bowed as elaborately as any courtier, his expression guarded as a merchant in the company of thieves: clearly he understood the political implications of a visit from the duke. 'I shall request an audience at once.'

'That will be satisfactory,' Innsford agreed, condescending to grace the earth with his boot heels. 'I trust the work proceeds apace?'

'Indeed.' A lance of Royal Life Guards came to attention behind the hetman, at the barked order of their sergeant: ''Tis a grim business, though. If you would care to follow me?'

'Yes,' said Innsford.

Neuhalle followed his patron and the hetman, ignoring the soldiers who walked to either side of him as if they were ghosts. 'His majesty – the former prince, I mean – I trust he is well?'

'Yes, indeed.' The hetman seemed disinclined to give much away.

'And is there any announcement of the blame for this outrage?' asked Innsford.

'Oh, yes.' The hetman glanced over his shoulder nervously, as if trying to judge how much he could disclose. 'His majesty is most certain of their identity.'

Neuhalle's pulse raced. 'We came to assure his majesty of our complete loyalty to his cause.' Innsford cast him a fishy glance, but did not contradict him. 'He can rely on our support in the face of this atrocious treason.' Although the question of whose treason had flattened the palace was an interesting one, it was nothing like as interesting to Neuhalle as the question of who the former crown prince was going to blame for it – for the explosion that had killed his father. After all, he couldn't admit to having done it himself, could he?

They rounded the walls of the west wing – still standing in the morning light, although the roof of the Queen's Ballroom had fallen in behind it – and passed a small huddle of Life Guards bearing imported repeating pistols at their belts. A white campaign pavilion squatted like a puffball on the lawn next to the wreckage of the west wing kitchens, and more soldiers marched around it in small groups or worked feverishly on a timber frame that was going up beside it. 'Please, I beg you, wait here a while.'

Innsford paused, leaning on his cane as if tired. Neuhalle moved closer to him, continuing the pretense that their escorts were as transparent as air while the hetman hurried towards the big tent, his progress punctuated interminably as he was passed from sentry to sentry. The guards were clearly taking no chances with their new monarch's life. 'A bad night for the kingdom,' he remarked quietly. 'Long live the king.'

'Indeed.' Innsford looked almost amused. 'And may his reign be long and peaceful.' It was the right thing to say under the circumstances, indeed the only thing to say – their escort looked remarkably twitchy, in the shadow of the ruined palace – but Neuhalle had to force himself not to wince. The chances that King Egon's reign would be peaceful were slim, at best.

They didn't have long to reflect on the new order in peace. The guards hetman came loping back across the turf: 'His grace the duke of Niejwein awaits you and bids me say that his majesty is in conference right now, but will see you presently,' he managed, a long speech by his standards. 'Come this way.'

The big pavilion was set up for the prince's guests: royal companions and master of hounds at one side, and smaller rooms for the royal functions at the other. The middle was given over to an open space. The duke of Niejwein sat on a plain camp stool in the middle of the open area, surrounded by an ever-changing swarm of attendants: a thin-faced man of early middle years, he was, as Innsford might have remarked, *one of us* – a scion of the old nobility, the first fifty families whose longships had cleaved the Atlantic waves four centuries ago to stake their claims to the wild forested hills of the western lands. He was no friend of the merchant princes, the tinker nobles with their vast wealth and strange fashions, who over the past century had spread across the social map of the Gruinmarkt like a fungal blight across the bark of an ancient beech tree. Neuhalle felt a surge of optimism as he set eyes on the duke. 'Your grace.' He bowed, while his patron nodded and clasped hands with his peer.

'Be welcome, sirs. I had hoped to see you here. Rise, Otto. You are both welcome in this time of sorrow. I trust you have been apprised of the situation?' Niejwein's left eyebrow levered itself painfully upwards.

'In outline,' Innsford conceded. 'Otto was entertaining me in

Oestgate when the courier reached us. We came at once.' They had ridden since an hour before dawn from thirty miles down the coast, nearly killing half a dozen mounts with their urgency. 'Gunpowder and treason.' His lips quirked. 'I scarcely credited it until I saw the wreckage.'

'His majesty blames the tinkers for bringing this down upon our heads,' Niejwein said bluntly.

'A falling out among thieves, perhaps?' Otto offered hopefully.

'Something like that.' Niejwein nodded, a secretive expression on his face. 'His Majesty is most keen to inquire of the surviving tinkers the reason why they slew his father using such vile tools. Indeed, he views it as a matter of overwhelming urgency to purge the body of the kingdom of their witchery.'

'How many of the tinkers survived?' asked Innsford.

'Oh, most of them. Details are still emerging. But beside the death of his majesty's father and his majesty's younger brother –' Otto started at that point '– it appears that his majesty is the only surviving heir for the time being.' Niejwein nodded to himself. 'The queen mother is missing. Of the tinkers, the heads of three of their families were present, some eighteen nobles in total, including the bitch they planned to marry to the Idiot –' Otto started again, then contained himself '– and sixty sundry gentles of other houses. The tinkers not being without allies.'

'But the main company of those families are untouched,' Innsford said.

'For the time being.' Niejwein's cheek twitched. *Has he the palsy?* Otto wondered. 'As I said, his majesty –' Niejwein stopped and rose to his feet, turning to face one of the side panels. A moment later he dropped to one knee; Otto scrambled to follow suit.

'Rise, gentlemen.' Otto allowed himself to look up at his new monarch. The Pervert – *no, forget you ever heard that name, on pain of your neck,* he told himself – was every inch a king: tall, hale of limb, fair of face, with a regal bearing and a knowing gleam in his eye. Otto, Baron Neuhalle, had known Egon since he was barely crawling. And he was absolutely terrified of him.

'Sire.' Innsford looked suitably grave. 'I came as soon as I heard the news, to pledge myself to you anew and offer whatever aid you desire in your time of need.' Not grief, Otto noted.

Prince Egon – now King Egon – smiled. 'We appreciate the thought, and we thank your grace for your thoughtfulness. Your inclination to avoid any little misunderstandings is most creditable.'

'Sire.' Innsford nodded, suppressing any sign of unease.

Egon turned to Niejwein. 'Is there any word of that jumped-up horse thief Lofstrom?' he asked offhandedly. Neuhalle kept his face still: to talk of Angbard, Duke Lofstrom, so crudely meant that the wind was blowing in exactly the direction Innsford had predicted. But then, it wasn't hard to guess that the new monarch – who had hated his grandmother and never seen eye-to-eye with his father – would react viciously towards the single biggest threat to his authority over the kingdom.

'No word as yet, sire.' Niejwein paused. 'I have sent out couriers,' he added. 'As soon as he is located he will be invited to present an explanation to you.'

'And of my somewhat-absent chief of intelligence?'

'Nor him, sire. He was leading the party of the tinkers at the past evening's reception, though. I believe he may still be around here.'

'Find proof of his death.' Egon's tone was uncompromising. 'Bring it to me, or bring *him*. And the same for the rest of the upstarts. I want them all rounded up and brought to the capital.'

'Sire. If they resist . . . ?'

Egon glanced at Innsford. 'Let us speak bluntly. The tinker vermin are as rich a target as they are a tough one, but they are not invulnerable and I *will* cut them down to size. Through magic and conspiracy, and by taking advantage of the good will of my forefathers, they've grown like a canker in my father's kingdom. But I intend to put a stop to them. One-tenth of theirs, your grace, will be yours if you serve me well. Another tenth for our good servant Niejwein here. The rest to be apportioned appropriately, between the Crown and its honest servants. Who will of course want to summon their families to attend the forthcoming coronation, and to take advantage of the security provided for them by the Royal Life Guards in this time of crisis.'

Neuhalle shrank inwardly, aghast. *He wants hostages of us?* He found himself nodding involuntarily. To do aught else would be to brand himself as a rebel, and it seemed that Egon had no intention of being the bluntest scythe in the royal barn; but to start a reign with such an unambiguous display of mistrust boded ill for the future.

'We are your obedient servants,' Innsford assured him.

'Good!' Egon smiled broadly. 'I look forward to seeing your lady wife in the next week or two, before the campaign begins.'

'Campaign –' Neuhalle bit his tongue, but the king's eyes had already turned to him. And the king was smiling prettily, as if all the fires of Hel didn't burn in the imagination concealed by that golden boy's face.

'Why, certainly there shall be a campaign,' Egon assured him, beaming widely. 'There will be no room for sedition in our reign! We shall raise the nobility to its traditional status again, reasserting those values that have run thin in the blood of recent years.' He winked. 'And to purge the kingdom of the proliferation of verminous witches that have corrupted it is but one part of that program.' He gestured idly at the wooden framework taking place on the lawn outside the pavilion. 'It'll make for a good show at the coronation, eh?'

Neuhalle stared. What he had thought to be the framework of a temporary palace was, when seen from this angle, the platform and scaffold of a gallows scaled to hang at least a dozen at a time. 'I'm sure your coronation will be a great day, sire,' he murmured. 'Absolutely, a day to remember.'

*

A damp alleyway at night. Refuse in the gutters, the sickly-sweet stench of rotting potatoes overlaying a much nastier aroma of festering sewage. Stone walls, encrusted in lichen. The chink of metal on cobblestones, and a woman's high, clear voice echoing over it: 'I don't believe this. Shit! *Ouch.*'

The woman had stumbled out of the shadows mere seconds ago, shaking her head and tucking away a small personal item. She wore a stained greatcoat over a black dress of rich fabric, intricate enough to belong in a stage play or in a royal court, but not here in a dank dead end: as she looked around, her forehead wrinkled in frustration, or pain, or both. 'I could go back,' she muttered to herself, then took a deep breath: 'or not.' She glanced up and down the alley apprehensively.

Another chink of metal on stone, and a cracked chuckle: 'Well, lookee here! And what's a fine girl like you doing in a place like this?'

The woman turned to stare into the darkness where the voice had spoken from, clutching her coat around her.

Another chuckle. 'Let's ask her, why don't we?'

The woman took a step backwards then stopped, brought up against the crumbling brick wall. Figures solidified out of the shadows beyond the flickering gaslight glow from the end of the alley-way. Her gaze darted across them as she fumbled with the pockets of her coat.

'Heya, pretty lady, what have you got for a growing boy?'

'Show us your tits!'

Miriam counted three of them as her eyes adapted to the darkness. It helped that she'd just stepped over, across a gap thinner than an atom – or greater than $10^{10^{28}}$ meters, depending how you measured it – from a lawn outside a burning palace, the night punctuated by the roar of cannon and the staccato cracking of the guards' pistols. *Three of them*, she realized, a sick tension in the pit of her stomach, *one of them's on the ground, crouching, or . . .* ?

The standing figure came closer and she saw that he was skinny and short, not much more than a boy, bow-legged, his clothing ragged. At five foot six Miriam didn't think of herself as tall, but she could almost look down on the top of his head. Unfortunately this also gave her a good view of the knife clutched in his right hand.

Desperation and a silvery edge of suppressed rage broke her paralysis. 'Fuck off!' She stepped forward, away from the wall, hands balling into fists in her black velvet gloves. 'That's it. I've had enough!'

The man with the knife looked surprised for a moment. Then he darted forward, as if to punch her. Miriam felt a light blow across her ribs as he danced back. 'Oof!' He was skinny, and short, and she outreached him, and his face was a frozen picture of surprise as she grabbed his arm, yanked him closer, stomped down on his foot, and then jerked her knee up inside his thigh. *Just like teacher said,* she thought, remembering the self-defense class she'd taken however many years ago. Her assailant made a short, whimpering gasp, then dropped like a log, rolling on the ground in pain. Miriam looked past him, hunting for his friends.

The one standing behind him took one look at her as if he'd seen a ghost, then turned tail and fled. 'Doan' leave me!' wailed the third in a thick accent, waving spidery arms at the ground: there was a rattling noise. Miriam stared. *He's got no legs,* she realized as he pawed at the ground with hands like oars, scooting away on a crude cart. *Why did the other one run?* She put a hand to her chest. There was a rip in her stolen coat. *That's funny.* She frowned, stuck a finger through the hole, and felt the matching rip in the outer fabric of her dress where the knife had slid across the boned front. 'Damn!' She looked down. The little guy with the knife lay at her feet, twitching and gasping for breath. The knife lay beside him in the gutter: the blade was about three inches long and wickedly sharp. 'You little shit!' She hauled up her skirts and kicked him in the ribs as hard as she could. Then she knelt down and took the knife.

The red haze of fury began to clear. She looked at the moaning figure on the cobblestones and shuddered, then stepped round him and quickly walked to the end of the alleyway. Cold sweat slicked her spine, and her heart pounded so hard it seemed about to burst. *I could have been killed,* she thought dizzily, tugging her coat into place with jerky motions, her hands shaking with the adrenaline aftershock. It wasn't the first time, but it never failed to horrify her afterwards. She moved unconsciously towards the street lights, panicky-tense and alert for any sign that knife-boy's friends had stopped running and were coming back for her. *He tried to stab me!* She felt sick to the pit of her stomach, and her usual post-world-walking headache had intensified unbearably, thumping in time with her pulse.

I've got to get help. Got to find Erasmus, she told herself, holding onto the thought as if it was a charm to ward off panic. The twisting road at the end of the alleyway was at least lit by rusting gas lamps. There was nobody in sight, so she put on a burst of speed, until she rounded a curve to see a main road ahead, more lights, closed shop fronts, a passing streetcar grinding its wheels on the corner with a shower of sparks from the overhead pickups. *Whoa.* She slowed, eyebrows furrowed, shoulders tensing as if there was a target pasted right above her spine at the base of her neck. *I can't go anywhere like this . . . !*

She stopped at the end of the side street, panting as she took stock. *I've got no money,* she realized. Which was not good, but there was worse: *I'm dressed like . . . like what?* Clothing wasn't cheap in New Britain; that had been a surprise for her the first time she came here. People didn't wear fancy dress or strange countercultural outfits, or rags – unless they could afford no better. If she'd had the right locket to reach New York, her own world, she might have passed for an opera buff or a refugee from a Goth nightclub; but here in New London she'd stick out like a sore thumb. And she did not want to stick out. *I need somewhere to blend in quick, or get a change. Contact Erasmus.* But Erasmus was what, two hundred miles away, in Boston? *What was that place he mentioned?* She racked her brains. *Woman called Bishop. Some place, satirist, Hogarth, that's it. Hogarth House, Hogarth –*

A cab was clattering along the nearly-empty high street. Miriam took a step forward and extended her right hand, trying to hold it steadily. The cabbie reined in his horse and peered down at her. 'Yuss?'

Miriam drew herself up. 'I want to go to Hogarth, Hogarth Villas,' she said. 'Immediately.'

The cabby's reaction wasn't what she expected: a low chuckle. 'Oh yuss indeedy, your ladyship. Hop right in and I'll take you right there in a jiffy, I will!' *Huh?* Miriam almost hesitated for a moment. But he obviously knew the place. *What's so funny about it?* She nodded, then grabbed hold of the rail and pulled herself up. The cabbie made no move to help her in, other than to look down at her incuriously. But if he had any opinion of her odd outfit he kept it to himself, for which she was grateful. As soon as she was on the foot plate, he twitched the reins.

I'm going to have to pay him, Miriam thought, furiously racking her brains for ideas as the cab rattled across the stone pavements. *What with?* She fumbled in her greatcoat's pockets. One of them disgorged a foul-smelling cheesecloth bag full of loose tobacco. The other contained nothing but a loose button. *Oh, great.* They were turning past Highgate now, down in what corresponded to the East Village in her world. Not an upmarket neighborhood in New London, but there were worse places to be – like inside a thief-taker's lockup for trying to cheat a cabbie of his fare. What was the woman's name, Bishop? Margaret Bishop? *I'm going to have to ask her to pay for me.* Miriam tensed up. *Or I could world-walk back to the other side, wait a couple of hours, and* – but her headache was already telling her no. If she crossed back to the Gruinmarkt she'd be good for nothing for at least three hours, and knowing her luck she'd come out somewhere much worse than an alley full of muggers. For the time being, returning to the other side was unthinkable. *Damn it, why did James have to give me the wrong locket?*

The journey seemed interminable, divided into a million segments by the plodding clatter of hooves. Probably a yellow cab in her own familiar New York would have gotten across town no faster – there was less traffic here – but her growing sense of unease was driving her frantic, and the lack of acceleration made her grind her teeth. *That's what's wrong with this world,* she realized, *there's no acceleration. You can go fast by train or airship, but you never get that surging sense of purpose –*

The traffic thickened, steam cars rattling and chuffing past the cab. The lights were brighter, some of the street lights running on electricity now: and then there was a wide curving boulevard and a big row of town houses with iron railings out front, and a busy rank of cabs outside it, and people bustling around. 'Hogarth Villas coming up, mam, Gin Lane on your left, Beer Alley to your right.' The cabbie bent down and leered at her between his legs. 'That'll be sixpence ha'penny.'

'The doorman will pay,' Miriam said tensely, mentally crossing her fingers.

'Is that so?' The leer vanished, replaced by an expression of contempt. 'Tell it to the rozzers!' He straightened up: 'I know your type.' A rattle of chain and a leather weather shield began to unroll over the front of the cab, blocking off escape. 'I'll get me fee out of you one way or the other, it's up to you how you pays.'

'Hey!' Miriam waved at a caped figure standing by the gate, pushing the side of the leather screen aside. 'You! I need to see Lady Bishop! Now!'

The caped figure turned towards her and stepped up towards the cab. The cabbie up top swore: 'Bugger off!'

'What did you say?' Miriam quailed. The man in the cape was about six feet six tall, built like a brick outhouse, and his eyes were warm as bullets.

'I need to see Lady Bishop,' Miriam repeated, trying to keep a deadly quaver out of her voice. 'I have no money and it's urgent,' she hissed. 'I was told she was here.'

'I see.' Bullet-eyes tracked upwards towards the cabbie. 'How much?'

'Sixpence, guv, that's all I need,' the cabbie whined.

Bullet-eyes considered for a moment. Then a hand with fingers as thick as a baby's forearm extended upwards. A flash of silver. 'You. Come with me.'

The weather screen was yanked upwards: Miriam lost no time clambering down hastily. Bullet-eyes gestured towards a set of steps leading down one side of the nearest town house. 'That way.'

'That –' Miriam was already halfway to the steps before several other details of the row of houses sank in. Lights on and laughter and music coming from the ground-floor windows: lights out and nothing audible coming from upstairs. The front doors gaped wide open. Men on the pavement outside, dressed for a good time by New London styles. Women visible through the open French doors in outfits that bared their knees – *Oh*, she thought, feeling herself flush. *So that's what's going on. Damn Erasmus for not telling me!* Halfway down the steps, which led to a cellar window and a narrower, grubbier, doorway, another thought struck her: a brothel would be a good place for Erasmus's friends to meet up. Lots of people could come and go at all hours and nobody would think it strange if they took measures to avoid being identified. Even her current fancy dress probably wasn't exceptional. Erasmus Burgeson, almost the first person she'd met on her arrival in New Britain, was connected to the Leveler underground, radical democrats in a country that had never had an American revolution, where the divine right of kings was still the unquestionable way the world was run. Which meant –

The door was snatched open in front of her. Miriam looked round. Bullet-eyes was right behind her, not threatening, but impossible to avoid. 'I need to see – '

'Shut it.' He was implacable. 'Go in.' It was a scullery, stone sinks full of dishwater and a couple of maids up to their elbows in it, a primitive clanking dishwasher hissing ominously and belching steam in the background. 'Through there, that way.' He steered her towards a door at the back that opened onto a narrow, gloomy servants' corridor and a spiral staircase. 'Upstairs.'

Another passage. Miriam registered the distant sound of creaking bedsprings and groaning, chatter and laughter and a piano banging away on the other side of a thin plasterboard wall. Her chest was tight: it felt hard to breathe in here. 'Is it much further?' she asked.

'Stop.' Bullet-eyes grabbed a door handle and shoved, glanced inside. 'You can wait here. Tell me again what you came for.'

Miriam tensed and looked at him. She'd seen dozens of men like this before, hard men, self-disciplined, capable of just about anything – her heart sagged. 'Erasmus Burgeson told me I should come here and talk to Lady Bishop next time I was in town,' she managed to explain. 'I wasn't planning on being here quite this early, without warning.' She sagged against the door-frame, abruptly exhausted. 'I'm in trouble.'

'Has it followed you?' His voice was even, quiet, and it made the hair on the back of her neck stand on end.

'No, not here. I lost it on the way.'

'Inside, then. I'll be back.' She stumbled into the room. He flicked a switch and a dim incandescent bulb glimmered into light. 'I may be some time.' The door closed behind her. The room was a servant's bedroom, barely longer than the narrow bed that occupied half of it. There was a window, but it opened onto a shaft of brickwork, another darkened window barely visible opposite. *Click.* Miriam spun round, a fraction of a second too late to see the lock mechanism latch home.

'Shit,' she moaned quietly, 'shit!' She sat down on the bed and rested her head in her hands, her energy and will to resist fading frighteningly fast. It had been a long and terrible day, and even standing up felt like a battle. *What have I done?* Erasmus was nuts, or playing a sick joke on her, sending her to a brothel to talk to the madam: although, on further thought, it didn't seem particularly strange compared to the rest of this eventful day. She'd been dragged out of her house arrest, shanghaied into a forced wedding, just missed being blown up by a bomb, seen the king and the prince she'd been engaged to gunned down (and who knew what the hell was going to happen in the Gruinmarkt now?) and run into an old heartthrob (and what the hell was he doing there, working for the DEA?). Then she'd fled for her life, been attacked by muggers, menaced by a cabbie who thought she was a prostitute, and finally locked up in another goddamned prison cell, this time in a brothel. *I'm going to go mad,* she thought dizzily, lying down on the lumpy mattress. *I can't take much more of this.* But instead, she fell asleep. And that was how they found her when they came for her, an hour after midnight.

*

It was shaping up to be a night to remember for all the wrong reasons, Mike decided. The flat metallic banging of musketry blended with the screams of wounded men and the sullen roar of the burning palace to form a hideous cacophony, punctuated by the occasional crack of modern smokeless-powder firearms and shouted orders. *This is worse than that mess down in Colombia, that mountain village.*

He inched carefully out from behind the broken wall. The stench of burnt gunpowder and charred wood lent an acrid taste to the nighttime air. About four meters from the wall, the indistinct shapes of a row of trees loomed out of the darkness. He turned his head, looking around cautiously.

That nameless village on a forested mountainside in Colombia: he'd been there as part of a DEA training team, working with the Colombian army to weed out cocaine plantations in the hilly back country. What he hadn't realized at first was that the cocaine plantations belonged to the other government – the Maoist guerrillas working to overthrow the authorities controlled vast swathes of territory, had battalions of expressionless men in green with machine guns and rifles. It wasn't a police raid, it was more like an army spearhead advancing into hostile territory. And then the shooting started . . .

He twitched back into focus, scanning the area for threats. The palace behind him was burning merrily, flames reaching through holes in the steeply pitched roof. Doors and windows had been blown out; some were half-blocked by improvised barricades where the defenders were trying to hold out. It was full dark, and they were trying to fight a battle against attackers who were shooting from outside the circle of light. The noises were getting louder. More banging of muskets, the hollow shotgun-like thump of a blunderbuss, then yells and a distant drumming of hooves, the sound of many horses running. He turned to face the darkness, closed his eyes for ten long seconds to let them adjust, then rose to a crouch and dashed towards the tree line, zigzagging madly and praying he'd make it without putting a foot in a rabbit hole or catching a tree root.

At least I got Miriam out of there. He dived past a tree, ducked under a low branch, and crouched down again to scan for watchers. *Wonder if she'll call.* It was just too weird: he'd known she'd be here, hell, that was the whole reason they'd inserted him, to see if he could make contact – but actually seeing her in the midst of all this weird medieval squalor, dolled up like an extra from a historical drama, brought it all home to him. She was part of the Clan: and she wanted out.

But he'd blown it. *You're going to make her an offer she can't refuse,* said the colonel, and instead he'd come out with the truth, limp-dicked and apologetic, and as good as told her to go to ground. *Phone me in a week or so,* he'd told her. And all because he'd seen it coming, like a slow-motion train wreck: Miriam was about as unlikely to co-operate with Smith as anyone he could imagine. And he couldn't stomach the idea of them turning her into a mule, like the guy in the cellar with the collar-bomb and the handcuffs, terrified that Mike was going to execute him.

Something moved in the brush behind him. Mike spun round, gun raised.

'Sir!' The hissed voice was familiar: Mike lowered his pistol immediately.

'That you, Hastert?'

The shadow in front of him nodded. 'O'Neil's twenty yards that way. Go to him now.' Bulky night-vision goggles half-covered Hastert's face, a surreal contrast to his baggy trousers and chain-mail vest. He held a machine pistol with a bulky silencer attached.

'Okay, I'm going, I'm going.' Mike scuttled away, his pulse hammering with the adrenaline aftershock. *I could have told her to come with me,* he told himself. *Could have lied, offered her witness protection. Hell, she asked for it! We could have gotten her out.*

But Miriam's potential value to Colonel Smith lay in her connection to the Clan hierarchy; and everything had gone to pieces. 'They've got my mom,' she'd said. What the hell was going on? 'O'Neil?' he whispered.

'Over here, sir. Keep down.'

O'Neil was crouched behind a deadfall. 'What's going on?'

'Looks like they're making whoopee.' His grin was a ghostly crescent in the darkness. 'Don't you worry, we'll get you out of here.'

A moment of rustling and crunching, and Sergeant Hastert appeared. 'Sitrep, Pete.'

'Sam's on point.' O'Neil gestured farther into the trees, where the ground fell away from the low hill on which the palace had stood. 'He's seen no sign of anybody in the woods. Bad news is, the aggressor faction have got sentries out and they're covering the approaches from the road. There's maybe thirty of them and they've got riders – we're cut off.'

'Get him back here, then.'

O'Neil vanished into the darkness. 'How bad is it?' asked Mike.

'Could be worse: nobody's shooting at us.' Hastert turned to look at him. 'But we'd better be out of here by dawn. Did you get what you wanted?'

'Yes and no.' Mike hunkered down. 'Everything we thought we knew about what was going on here is out of date. I got to talk to my contact, but she's in deep shit herself – didn't have much time, they were trying to kill her – '

A noise like a door the size of a mountain slamming shut a hundred meters away rocked Mike back on his heels.

'Down!' Hastert lurched against him, shoving Mike's face down on a matted bed of branches. Moments later, debris thudded off the branches above their heads, spattering down on the summer-dry soil. 'Get moving, we're too close.'

The next hour passed in a nightmarish crawl through the dark forest, heading always away from the boom and crash of gunfire and the shouts of the combatants. The royal palace, although nominally within the city of Niejwein, was surrounded by a walled garden the size of a large park – large enough that the palace itself was out of easy gunshot range of its neighbors. But in the chaos of the apparent coup, the shooters were inside the compound. Stray shots periodically came tearing through the treetops, so that Mike needed no urging to keep his head close to the dirt.

After an interminable crawl, Hastert tapped him on he shoulder. 'Stop here, wait till I get back.' He vanished into the darkness as silently as a ghost. Mike shivered violently. *Trouble?* he wondered. There was nothing he could do; on this part of the mission he was baggage, as much as Miriam would have been if he'd tried to extract her from whatever the hell that weird scene back at the palace had been about. *I can't believe I shot that guy without warning.*

Mike reran the scene in his mind's eye; the perp – even now, he couldn't drop the law enforcement outlook – with the knife, trying to stab the woman in black, the stink of burning wood, snarling fear, taking the time to aim carefully, waiting for a clear shot as the woman shoved back hard against her assailant . . . then the shock of recognition. *It's her!* It was like nothing had changed since that ambiguous last dinner at Wang's, just off Kendall Square. The shock of recognition was still with him: the realization that, all along, the world he moved in was smaller than he'd realized, that during the whole fruitless search for the east coast phantom network he'd been dating a woman who could have – if she herself had known what she was – put him right on top of it. *If.* Getting involved hadn't been good for her. *They've got Mom.* And an arranged marriage. The smell of raw sewage running through the gutters in the middle of the unpaved road –

'Wake up.' A hand touched his shoulder.

'I'm awake.' Mike looked round. Hastert crouched beside him.

'There's an open area about fifty yards wide before the wall, which is eight feet high. Just the other side of the wall there's a road. O'Neil's setting up a distraction. We have' – Hastert glanced at his watch – 'six minutes to get to the edge of the apron and wait. Then we have thirty seconds to get over the wall and across the road. Take the second alley on the left, proceed down it for twenty yards then take the right turn, fourth door on the left is transit house gamma. You ready?'

Mike nodded. 'Guess so.'

'Then let's get going.'

TRANSLATED TRANSCRIPT BEGINS

'Shit. He didn't.'

'I'm afraid so.'

(*Sigh.*) 'That means we're down by what, two, three seats on the council? And the king. This is an absolute disaster. Who else have we lost?'

(*Pause.*) 'Of our party, most of them. The dowager Hildegarde is yammering her head off, but she survived, as did her daughter. James Lee, we rescued. He's concussed but will live – '

'Small mercies. Damn her for – damn her!'

'It's not your fault, your grace, or hers, that this had to happen at the worst time.'

(*Sigh.*) 'Continue.'

'We lost Wilem, Maris, Erik, three juniors of Hjorth-Arnesen's cadet branch, and four others of middling rank. We lost her majesty the queen mother, and the cadet branch of the royal family in the person of Prince Creon. He's a confirmed kill, by the way. About thirty retainers and outer family members, but that's by the by. The main losses are the royal family – except for the crown prince – and Henryk, Wilem, Maris, Erik, and others.'

(*Long pause.*)

'Shit.'

'We've taken worse – '

'No, it's not that. It's the little shit. The Pervert. What's he up to?'

'Holed up with Niejwein on the back lawn, scheming about something. Everyone with half a clue is rushing over to offer their firstborn to him.'

'Has he sent up any smoke signals yet?'

'No.'

'Damn. That confirms it, he's got what he wants and we're going to get the blame. He's hated us all along, since he learned about Creon's latency, and if he's listening to that snake Niejwein . . .'

'Your grace?'

'I know, I'm rambling. What's your analysis?'

'I think we're in the shit, sir. I think –' (*Pause.*) ' – he's going to try to roll us up. All of us. Niejwein and Sudtmann and that crowd have been feeling their oats and they will take this opportunity once and for all to put us down. And the Pervert will use us as a lever to consolidate his power over them. He doesn't trust anyone, sir, and the rumors – '

'I don't care if he shags goats or rapes virgins, what I care about is *us*. Sky Father, this is a fifty-year setback!' (*Inaudible muttering.*) 'Yes, yes, I already thought of that. Oliver, I know we see eye to eye over very little – '

'Your grace is overstating matters – '

'Permit an old man his moment of humor in the chaos, if you please? Good. I do believe we see eye to eye on the fundamentals. This is a war to the knife. We have a rogue king on the throne, and even after we remove him from it we shall have civil war for the next decade – not family against family, but Clan against all. Do you agree?'

(*Pause.*) 'Yes, damn you.'

'Indeed: I am damned.'

(*Pause.*) 'What do you propose to do?'

'Whatever I can. First, we must take our own to safety – then we must prepare to defend our possessions. Identify our allies, I should add. But if we can no longer count on being able to run our caravans up the coast in safety we must look for alternatives.'

'That upstart bitch's plan.'

'Be careful what you call my late niece, sir.'

'I –' (*Pause.*) '– Please accept my apologies, your grace. You did not inform me of your bereavement. I had assumed she was rescued.'

'She was not. She's not among those confirmed to be dead, but after the palace burned . . .' (*Pause.*) 'I had high hopes for her.'

'But her plan! Come now. You can't really believe it will work?'

(*Sigh.*) 'No. I don't believe it will work. But I believe we should try it, with whatever energy we can divert from our defenses. Because if our ability to traffic in this realm is disrupted for any length of time, what other options do we have?'

TRANSCRIPT ENDS

FIRST LIGHT

A narrow spiral staircase wormed upwards through the guts of a building, its grimy windowpanes opening onto a space that might once have been an alleyway but was now enclosed on all four sides by building extensions, so that it formed a wholly enclosed shaft at the bottom of which a pile of noisome debris had accumulated over the years. Other windows also opened onto the tiny courtyard; windows that provided ventilation and light to rooms that could not be seen from any street, or reached other than by the twisting staircase, which was concealed at ground level by a false partition in the back of a scullery closet. Almost a quarter of the rooms in the building were concealed in this fashion from the outside world. And in a garret at the top of the secret stairwell, a middle-aged woman sat working at a desk.

Bent over her wooden writing box, she systematically worked her way through a thick stack of papers. Periodically she reached over to one side to pick up a pen and scrawl cryptic marginalia upon them. Less frequently, her brow furrowing, she would pick up a clean sheet of writing paper and dash off a sharp inquiry to one of her correspondents. Somewhat less frequently, she would consign a report – too hot to handle – to the glowing coals in the fireplace. The underground postal service that moved this mail was slow and expensive and prone to disruption: it might strike an ignorant observer as odd that Margaret, Lady Bishop, would treat its fruits so casually. But to be caught in possession of much of this material would guarantee the holder a date with the hangman. Every use of the Movement's post was a gamble with a postman's life: and so she took pains to file the most important matters only in her memory, where they would not – if she had any say on the matter – be exposed to the enemy.

The darkness outside the window was complete and the stack of files before her was visibly shrinking when there came a knock at the door. 'Come in,' she called sharply: there was no possibility of a surprise police raid here, not without gunshots and explosions to telegraph their arrival.

The door opened and the rough-looking fellow outside cleared his throat. 'Got a problem downstairs. Woman at the door, asking for you by name. Says *Burgeson* sent her.'

'Was she followed?' Lady Bishop asked sharply.

'She said not, and I had a couple of the lads go 'ave a word with the hack what brought her. Nothing to fear on that account.'

'Good. Who is she? What does she want?'

'Figured we'd best leave that for you. She's not one such as I'd recognize, and she's dressed odd, like: Mal took her for a madwoman at first, but when she used your name and mentioned Burgeson I figured she was too dangerous to let go. So we stashed her in a cell while we made arrangements.'

'Right, right.' Lady Bishop nodded to herself. 'Is the Miller prepared?'

'Oh, aye.'

'Then I suppose you'd better bring her up here and we can get to the bottom of this, Ed. I shall start with an interview – to give the poor woman a chance to excuse herself. But when you come, bring Mal. In case we have to switch her off.'

She spent the minutes before Ed's return with the prisoner methodically prioritizing her remaining correspondence. Then she carefully moved the manila paper folders to a desk drawer, closed and locked her writing case, and tried to compose herself. In truth, Lady Bishop hated interrogations. However necessary it might be for the pursuit of the declaration, the process always left her feeling soiled.

The rap at the door, when it came, was loud and confident. 'Enter,' she called. Edward opened the door; behind him waited a woman, and behind her, the shadow of Mal the doorman. 'Come in,' she added, and pointed to a rough stool on the opposite side of her desk: 'and sit down.'

The woman was indeed oddly dressed. *Is she an actress?* Margaret wondered. It seemed unlikely. And her outfit, while outlandish, was in any case both too well tailored and too dirty for a stage costume. Then Lady Bishop took a good look at the woman's face, and paused. The bruise on her cheek told a story: and so, when the woman opened her mouth, did the startling perfection of her dentistry.

'Are you Lady Bishop?'

Margaret, Lady Bishop, stared at the woman for a moment, then nodded. 'I am.' She had the most peculiar feeling that the woman on the stool opposite her was studying her right back, showing a degree of self-assurance she'd have expected from a judge, not a prisoner. *Titled? Or a lord's by-blow?*

'I'm Miriam Beckstein,' said the woman. 'I believe Erasmus has told you something about me.' She swallowed. 'I don't know how much he's told you, but there's been a change in the situation.'

Lady Bishop froze, surprise stabbing at her. *You're the* Beckstein *woman?* She turned to look at her assistants: 'Ed, Mal, wait outside.'

Ed looked perturbed. 'Are you sure, ma'am?'

'You don't need to hear this.' *Why in Christ's name didn't you say it was her in the first place?* She wanted to add, but not at risk of tipping off the prisoner about her place in the scheme of things.

Ed backed out of the room hastily and pulled the door shut. Margaret turned back to her unexpected visitor. 'I'm sorry; we weren't expecting you, so nobody told them to be on the lookout. Do you know who struck you?'

Beckstein looked startled for a moment, then raised a hand to her cheek. 'This? Oh, it's nothing to do with your men.' A distant expression crossed her face: 'The man who hit me died earlier this evening. Before I continue – did Erasmus tell you where I come from?'

Lady Bishop considered feigning ignorance for a moment. 'He said something about a different version of our world. Sounded like nonsense at first, but then the trinkets started showing up.' Her expression hardened. 'If you think we can be bought and sold for glass beads – '

'I wouldn't dream of it! But, uh, I needed to know. What he'd told you. The thing is, I ran into some trouble. I was able to escape, but I came here because it was all I could do – I got away with only the clothes on my back. I need to get back to Boston and contact some people to let them know I'm all right before they, before I can get everything back under control. I was hoping . . .' She ran out of words.

Lady Bishop watched her intently. *Do you really think I'm that naive?* she asked silently, permitting herself a moment's cold anger. *Did you really think you could simply march in and demand assistance?* Then a second thought struck her: *Or maybe you don't know who you're dealing with . . . ?*

'Did Erasmus tell you anything about me? Or who I am associated with?' she asked.

Beckstein blinked. 'He implied – oh.' Her eyes widened. 'Oh shit.'

Lady Bishop stifled a sigh of exasperation. Indelicacy on top of naivety? A very odd mixture indeed.

The Beckstein woman stared at her. 'Erasmus clearly didn't tell me enough . . .'

Margaret made up her mind. 'I can see that,' she said, which was true enough – just not the absolution it might be mistaken for. *Either you're really down on your luck and you thought I might be an easy touch, or perhaps you're truly ignorant and in trouble. Which is it?* 'Tell me who you think I am, and I'll tell you if you're right or wrong.'

'Okay,' said Beckstein. Margaret made a mental note – *What does that word mean?* – then nodded encouragement. 'I think you're a member of the Levelers' first circle. Probably involved in strategy and planning. And Erasmus was thinking about brokering a much higher-level arrangement between you and my, my, the people I represent. Represented.' She swallowed. 'Are you going to kill me?' she asked, only a faint quaver in her voice.

'If you were entirely right in every particular, then I would absolutely have to kill you.' Margaret smiled to take the sting out of her words before she continued. 'Luckily you're just wrong enough to be safe. But,' she paused, to give herself time to prepare her next words carefully: 'I don't think you're telling me the entire truth. And given your suspicions about my vocation, don't you think that might not be very clever? I want the truth, Miss Beckstein. And nothing but the truth.'

'I – ' Beckstein swallowed. Her eyes flickered from side to side, as if seeking a way out: Margaret realized that she was shaking. 'I'm not sure. Whether you'd believe me, and whether it would be a good thing if you did.'

This was getting harder to deal with by the minute, Margaret realized. The woman was clearly close to the end of her tether. She'd put a good face on things at first, but there was more to this than met the eye. 'I've seen Erasmus,' said Margaret. 'He told me about the medicine you procured for him.' She watched the Beckstein woman closely. 'And he showed me the disc-playing machine. The, ah, *DVD player*. One miracle might be an accident, but two suggest an interesting pattern. You needn't worry about me mistaking you for a madwoman. But you must tell me exactly what has happened to you. Right now, at once, with no dissembling. Otherwise I will not be able to save you . . .'

*

BAM.

Judith Herz tensed unconsciously, steeling herself for the explosion, and crossed her fingers as the four SWAT team officers swung the battering ram back for a second knock. Not that tensing would do any good if there was a bomb in the self-storage room . . .

'Are you sure this is safe?' asked Rich Wall, fingering his mobile phone like it was a lucky charm.

'No,' she snapped. *What do you expect me to say?* 'According to Mike Fleming, the asshole who sent us on this wild goose chase has a hard-on for claymore mines. That's why –' she gestured at the chalk marks on the cinder-block wall the officers were attacking, the heaps of dust from the drills, the fiber-optic camera on its dolly off to one side '– we're going in through the wall.'

BAM.

A cloud of dust billowed out. There was a rattle of debris falling from the impact site on the wall. They'd started by drilling a quarter-inch hole, then sent a fiber-optic scope through with the delicacy of doctors conducting keyhole cardiac bypass surgery. The black plastic-coated hose had snaked around, bringing grainy gray pictures to the monitor screen on the console like images from a long-sealed

Egyptian royal tomb. The dust lay heavy in the lockup room, as if it hadn't been visited for months or years. Something indistinct and bulky, probably a large oil tank, hulked a couple of feet beyond the hole, blocking the line of sight to the door to the lockup. The caretaker had kicked up a fuss when she'd told him they were going to punch through the wall from the other side – after unceremoniously ejecting the occupants' property – until she'd shown him her FBI card and the warrant the FEMA Sixth Circuit court had signed in their emergency *in camera* session. (Which the court had granted in a shot, the moment the bench saw the gamma ray spike the roving search truck had registered as it quartered the city, looking for a sleeping horror.) Then he'd clammed up and gone into his cubicle to phone the landlord.

'I think we're gonna need that jack,' called one of the cops with the ram. His colleagues laid the heavy metal shaft down while two more cops in orange high-visibility jackets and respirators moved to shovel the rubble aside. 'Should be through in a couple more minutes.'

Judith glanced at Rich. 'This is your last chance to take a hike,' she suggested.

'Naah.' Rich glanced down. He was fidgeting with his phone, as if it was a lucky charm. 'Let's face it, I wouldn't get far enough to clear the blast zone, would I?'

'That's true.' *Go on, whistle in the dark.* She shivered involuntarily. The guys with the battering ram didn't know what they were here for: all they knew was that the woman from the FBI headquarters staff wanted into the storage room, and wanted in bad. She'd done the old stony stare and dropped an elliptical hint about Mideast terrorists and fertilizer bombs, enough to keep them on their toes but not enough to make them phone their families and tell them to leave town *now*. But Rich knew what they were looking for, and so did Bob, who was suiting up in the NIRT truck in the back parking lot along with the rest of his team, and Eric Smith, back in Maryland in a meeting room in Crypto City. 'You could always step outside for a last cigarette.'

'I'm trying to give up. Last cigarettes, that is.' Rich shuffled from foot to foot as two of the cops grunted and manhandled a construction site jack into place beside the blue chalk X on the wall, where it was buckling ominously outwards.

'Okay, one more try,' called one of the cops – Sergeant McSweeny, Herz thought – as the ram team picked up their pole and began to work up their momentum.

BAM.

This time there was a clatter of rubble falling as overstressed bricks gave way. The dust cleared and she saw there was a hole in the wall where the ram had struck, an opening into the heart of darkness. The battering ram team shuffled backwards out of the way of the two guys with shovels, who now hefted sledgehammers and went to work on the edges of the hole, widening it. 'There's your new doorway,' said one of the ram crew, wincing and rubbing his upper arm: 'kinda short on brass fittings and hinges, but we can do you a deal on gravel for your yard.'

'Ri-ight,' drawled Rich. Judith glared at him, keeping her face frozen. *That's right, I'm a woman in black from a secret government agency,* she thought. *I've got no sense of humor and you better not get in my way.* Even if the black outfit was a wind cheater with a big FBI logo, and a pair of 501s.

The cop recoiled slightly. 'Hey, what's up with you guys?'

'You have no need to know.' Judith relented slightly. 'Seriously. You won't read about this in the newspapers, but you've done a good job here today.' She winced slightly as another sledgehammer blow spalled chips off the edge of the hole in the wall. Which was growing now, to the point where a greased anorexic supermodel might be able to wriggle through. A large slab of wall fell inward, doubling the size of the hole. 'Ah, showtime. If you guys could get the jack into position and then clear the area I think we will take it from here.'

Ten minutes later the big orange jack was screwed tight against the top of the opening, keeping the cinder blocks above the hole from collapsing. The SWAT team was outside in the parking lot, packing their kit up and shooting random wild-assed guesses about what the hell it was they'd been called in to do, and why: Judith glanced at the wristwatch-shaped gadget strapped to her left wrist and nodded.

It was still clean, showing a background count of about thirty becquerels per second. A tad high for suburban Boston, but nothing that couldn't be accounted for by the fly ash mixed into the cinder blocks. The idea of wearing a Geiger counter like a wristwatch still gave her the cold shudders when she thought about it, but that wasn't so often these days, not after three weeks of it – and besides, it was better than the alternative.

A big gray truck was backing in to the lot tail-first. Rich waved directions to the driver, as if he needed them: the truck halted with a chuff of air brakes, five feet short of the open door to the small ware-house unit. The tailgate rattled up to reveal a scene right out of *The X-Files* – half a dozen men and women in bright orange inflatable space suits with oxygen tanks and black rubber gloves, wheeling carts loaded with laboratory instruments. They queued up in front of the tail lift. 'Is the area clear?' Judith's earpieces crackled.

She glanced around. 'Witnesses out.' The SWAT team was already rolling up the highway half a mile away. They were far enough away that if things went really badly they might even survive.

'Okay, we're coming in.' That was Dr. Lucius Rand, tall and thin, graying at the temples, seconded to the Family Trade Organization from his parent organization. Just like Judith, like Mike Fleming, like everyone else in FTO – only in his case, the parent organization was Pantex. He was in his late fifties. Rumor had it he'd studied at Ted Taylor's knee; Edward Teller had supervised his Ph.D. The tailgate lift ground into operation, space-suited figures descending to planet Earth.

'We haven't checked for booby traps yet,' she warned.

'Well, what are you waiting for?' Rand sounded impatient.

Judith nodded to Rich as she pulled on a pair of disposable plastic shoe protectors: 'Let's go inside.'

The hole in the wall was about two feet wide and three feet high, a jagged gash. She switched on her flashlight – a tiny pocket LED lantern, more powerful than a big cop-style Maglite – and swept the floor. There were no wires. *Good.* She ducked through the hole, coughing slightly. Her Geiger watch still ticked over normally. *Better.* She stood up and looked around.

The room was maybe twenty feet long and eight feet wide, with a ten-foot ceiling. Naked unpainted cinder-block walls, a galvanized tin roof, and a concrete floor completed the scene. There was a big rolling door at one end and dust everywhere. But what caught her attention was the sheer size of the cylinder that, standing on concrete blocks, dominated the room. 'Sweet baby Jesus,' she whispered. It was at least ten feet long, and had to be a good four feet in diameter. There was barely room to walk around the behemoth. She shone her torch along the cylinder, expecting to see – 'What the hell?'

'Herz, report! What have you seen?'

'It's a cylinder,' she said slowly. 'About ten, twelve feet long, four, five feet in diameter. Supported on concrete blocks. One end is rounded; there's some kind of collar about three feet from the other end and four vanes sticking out, sort of like the fins on a bomb . . .' She trailed off. *Like the fins on a bomb,* she thought, dazed. *Jesus, this can't be here!* She shook herself and continued, 'There's some kind of equipment trolley near the back end, and some wires going into the, the back of the bomb.' She glanced down at her watch. The second hand was spinning round. It was a logarithmic counter, and it had jumped from tens of becquerels per second to tens of thousands as she crossed the threshold. Gamma emission from secondary activation isotopes created by neutron absorption, she heard the lecture replay in her mind's eye; Geiger counters can't detect neutrons until the flux is way too high for safety, but over time a neutron source will tend to activate surrounding materials, causing them to emit gamma radiation. 'I'm reading secondaries. I think we've got a hot one. I'm coming out now.' A quick sweep across the screen door in front of the gadget's nose revealed no telltale trip wires. 'No sign of booby traps.'

'Acknowledged. Judith, I want you and Rich to go back into the van and wait while I do a preliminary site survey. Don't touch anything on your way out. I want you to know, you've done good.' She realized she was shaking. *Don't touch anything. Right.* She clambered out through the hole in the wall, blinking against the daylight, and stood aside as two figures in bright orange isolation suits duckwalked past her. The cylinders hanging from their shoulders bounced under their rubber covers like hugely obese buttocks as they bent down to crawl through the hole. Two more suits waved her down with radiation detectors and stripped off her shoe protectors before pronouncing her clean and waving her into the truck.

The back of the NIRT truck was crowded with consoles and flashing panels of blinkenlights, battered laptops plastered with security inventory stickers, and coat rails for the bulky orange suits. This was a NIRT survey wagon, not the defuse-and-disarm trailer – those guys would be along in a while, as soon as Dr. Rand confirmed he needed them. Too many NIRT vehicles in one parking lot might attract the wrong kind of attention, especially in these days of Total Information Awareness and paranoia about security, not to mention closed-circuit cameras everywhere and journalists with web access spreading rumors. Rumors that NIRT were breaking into a lockup in Boston would be just the icing on a fifty-ton cake of shit if Homeland Security had to take the fall for a botched Family Trade operation. Rumors of any kind about NIRT would likely trigger a public panic, a run on the Dow, and a plague of boils inside the Beltway.

'Coffee?' asked Rich, picking up a vacuum flask.

'Yes, please.' Judith yawned, suddenly becoming aware that she felt tired. 'I don't believe what I just saw. This had better turn out to be some kind of sick prank.' Low-level lab samples of something radioactive stashed in an aluminum cylinder knocked together in an auto body shop, that would do it. *But it can't be,* she realized. *Nobody would be that crazy, just for a joke.* Charges of wasting police time didn't even begin to cover it. And it wasn't as if some prankster had tried to draw attention to the lockup: quite the opposite, in fact.

'Like hell. That thing had fins like a fifty-six Caddy. I swear I was expecting to see Slim Pickens riding it down . . .' Rich poured a dose of evil-looking coffee into a cup and passed it to her. 'Think it'll go off?'

'Not now,' Judith said with a confidence she didn't feel. 'Dr. Strangelove and his merry men are going over it with their stethoscopes.' There was a chair in front of one of the panels of blinkenlights and she sat down on it. 'But something about this whole setup feels wrong.'

Her earphone bleeped, breaking her out of the introspective haze. 'Yes?' she asked, keying the throat pickup.

'Judith, I think you'd better come back in. Don't bother suiting up, it's safe for now, but there's bad news along with the good.'

'On my way.' She put her coffee down. 'Wait here,' she told Rich, who nodded gratefully and took her place in the swivel chair.

When she straightened up inside the warehouse she found it bright and claustrophobic, the air heavy with masonry dirt and the dust of years of neglect. It reminded her of a raid on a house in Queens she'd been in on, years ago: one the mob had been using to store counterfeit memory chips. Someone here had found the long-dead light fitting and replaced the bulb. Seen in proper light, the finned cylinder looked more like a badly made movie prop than a bomb. Two figures in orange inflatable suits hunched over the open tail of the gadget, while another was busy taking a screwdriver to the fascia of an instrument cart that was wired into it. Dr. Rand stepped around the rounded front of the cylinder: 'Ah, Agent Herz. As I said, I've got good news and bad news.' There was an unhealthy note of relish in his voice.

Judith gestured towards the far end of the lockup from the NIRT team operatives working on the ass-end of the bomb. 'Tell me everything I need to know.'

Rand followed her then surprised Judith by unzipping his hood and throwing it back across his shoulders. He reached down to his waist and turned off the hissing air supply. His face was flushed and what there was of his hair hung in damp locks alongside his face. 'Hate these things,' he said conversationally. 'It's not going to go off,' he added.

'Well, that's a relief. So, is this the one?'

'That would be the bad news.' Rand frowned. 'Let me give it to you from the top.'

'Be my guest.' Sarcasm was inappropriate, she realized, but the relief –

'I've met this puppy before,' said Rand. 'It's a B53-Y2. We built a bunch of them in the sixties. It's a free-fall bomb, designed to be hauled around by strategic bombers, and it's not small – the physics package weighs about six thousand pounds. It's an oralloy core, high-purity weapons-grade uranium rather than plutonium, uses lithium deuteride to supply the big bang. We made a few hundred, but all but twenty-five were dismantled decades ago. It's basically the same as the warhead on the old Titan II, designed to level Leningrad in one go. The good news is, it won't go off. The tritium booster looks to be well past its sell-by date and the RDX is thoroughly poisoned by neutron bombardment, so the best you'd get would be a fizzle.' He looked pensive. 'Of course, what I mean by a fizzle is relative. A B53 that's been properly maintained is good for about nine megatons – this one would probably top off at no more than a quarter megaton or so, maybe half a megaton.'

'Half a –' Her knees went weak. She stumbled, caught herself leaning against the nose of the hydrogen bomb, and recoiled violently. *A quarter of a megaton?* The flash would be visible in New York City: the blast would blow out windows in Providence. 'But – '

'Calm down, it's not going to happen. We've already made sure of that.'

'Oh. Okay.' *Jesus. If that's the good news –*

'Funny thing about the timer, though,' Rand said meditatively. 'Sloppy wiring, dry joints where they soldered it to . . . well, the battery ran down a long time ago. Judging by the dust it's been there for years.'

'Timer?'

'Yes.' Rand shook himself. 'It was on a timer. Should have gone off ages ago, taking Boston and most of Cambridge with it. Probably back during the Bush I or Reagan administrations, at a guess. Maybe even earlier.'

'Holy, uh, wow.'

'Yes, I can see why you might say that. And we are going to have *real* fun combing the inventory to find out how this puppy managed to wander off the reservation. That's not supposed to happen, although I can hazard some guesses . . .'

'Huh. Six – did you say it weighs six thousand pounds?'

'Well, of course it does; did you think air-dropped multimegaton hydrogen bombs were small enough to fit in a back pocket? Why do you think we ship them around in B-52s?'

'Uh. And it's a, like, a single unit? You couldn't dismantle it easily?'

315

'No, I don't think so. We'll need to truck it away intact and examine it for – '

'Then we've messed up.'

'What makes you say that?'

'Because it's *too big*. A world-walker can't haul something any larger than they can lift. So it doesn't belong to the Clan.'

'Oh,' said Rand.

'You can say that again.' Judith turned to head back to the hole in the wall. 'Listen, I've got to go, this isn't Family Trade business anymore, okay? Run it through the normal NIRT channels, I've got to go report to the colonel now. See you around.' And with that, she ducked through the hole in the lockup wall, and headed back to the car park. Rich was waiting next to the truck. 'Come on,' he said, waving at her car.

'What's the story?'

'It's a nuke, but it's not our nuke,' Herz said as she started the car.

'Really?'

'Yes. Come on, I've got to get back to the office and report to Eric.'

'Shit.'

'Language, please.' Judith put the car in gear and crept out of the parking lot, leaving the gray NIRT van and the orange rubber-suited atomic bomb disposal specialists behind like a bad memory. 'What a way to start the week.' Somewhere out there in the city there was another bomb. Matt knew where: but Matt was dead, and Mike Fleming had failed to wheedle the location of the bomb out of him before he died – all they knew was, it was on a one-year countdown, and they had maybe two hundred days left to find it before they had to evacuate three or four million folks from Boston and Cambridge to avoid a disaster that would make 9/11 look like a parking violation.

*

Miriam had run through the emotional gamut in the past six hours, oscillating wildly between hope and terror, despair and optimism. Being taken out of the servant's room and escorted up to the top of this rickety pile of brick and lath by a pair of thugs, and ushered into a garret where a middle-aged woman with a kindly face and eyes like a hanging judge sat at a writing desk, and then being expected to give an account of herself, was more than Miriam was ready for. All she had to vouch for this woman was Erasmus Burgeson's word, and there was a lot more to the tubercular pawnbroker than met the eye. He had some very odd friends, and if he'd misread her when he suggested she visit this 'Lady Bishop', then it was possible she'd just stuck her head in a noose. But on the other hand, Miriam was here right now, and there were precious few alternatives on offer.

'I'd quite understand if you thought I was mad,' Miriam said, shivering slightly – it was not particularly warm in this drafty attic room. 'I don't really understand everything that's going on myself. I mean, I thought I did, but obviously not.' She felt her cheek twitch involuntarily.

Margaret Bishop leaned forward, her expression concerned. 'Are you all right?' she asked.

Miriam twitched again. 'No, I'm –' She took a deep breath. 'A few bruises, that's all. And I'm lucky to be alive, people have been trying to kill me all evening.' She took another deep breath. 'Sorry . . .'

'Don't be.' Lady Bishop rose to her feet and opened the door a crack. 'Bring a pot of coffee, please. And biscotti. For two.' She closed it again. 'Would you like to tell me about it? Start from the beginning, if you please. Take your time.' She sat down again. 'I must apologize for the pressure, but I really need to know everything if I am to help you.'

'You'd help me?'

'You've been very useful to us in the past. We tend to be suspicious, for good reasons – but we look after our friends. But I need to know more about you before I make any promises. Do you understand?'

Miriam's vision blurred: for a moment she felt vertiginous, as if the stool she sat upon was half a mile high, balanced in a high wind. Relief combined with apprehension washed over her. *Not alone* – It was like waking suddenly from a nightmare. The world had been narrowing around her like a prison corridor for so long that the idea that there might be a way out, or even people who would help her willingly, seemed quite alien for a moment. Then the dizziness passed. 'I'll tell you everything,' she heard herself saying, in a voice hoarse with gratitude. 'Just don't expect too much.'

'Take your time.' Lady Bishop sat back on her chair and waited while Miriam composed herself. 'We've got all night.'

'There are at least three worlds.' Miriam squeezed her tired eyes shut as she tried to fumble her way towards an explanation. 'I'm told there may be more, but nobody knows how to reach them. The people who *can* reach them . . . they're my relatives, apparently. It's a hereditary talent. It's what geneticists call a recessive trait, meaning you can't inherit it unless it was present in both sides of your family tree. It's difficult to do – painful if you do it too often, and you need a focus, a kind of knotwork design to look at to make it work – but it's made the families, the people who have the ability, rich. The world they live in is very backward, almost medieval: something went wrong, some blind alley in history a couple of thousand years ago, but they've risen into the nobility of the small feudal kingdoms that exist up and down the New England coastline.

'I'm . . . I'm an outsider. About fifty years ago the families started killing one another, there was a huge blood feud – what they called a civil war. My mother, who was pregnant at the time, was on the losing side of an ambush: she fled to the, the other of the three worlds we know about. Uh, I should have explained that the Clan families didn't know about this one at the time. There's a lost offshoot family of the Clan who ended up here more than a hundred years ago, who can travel from here to the Clan's world: they were the ones who kept the civil war going by periodically assassinating Clan leaders and pointing the evidence at the other families. The other world, the one I grew up in, is very different from either this one or the one the Clan comes from.'

There was a knock on the door. Miriam paused while one of the guards came in and deposited a tray on the table where Lady Bishop had been working on her papers. The coffee pot was silver, and the smell drifting from it was delicious. 'May I . . . ?'

'Certainly.' Margaret Bishop poured coffee into two china mugs. 'Help yourself to the biscotti.' The guard departed quietly. 'Tell me about your world.'

'It's –' Miriam frowned. 'It's a lot less different from yours than the Clan's world is, but it's still very different. As far as I can tell, they were the same until, um, 1745. There was an uprising in Scotland? A Prince Charles Stuart? In my world he marched on London and his uprising was defeated. Savagely. A few years later a smoldering war between Britain and France started – and while France eventually won a paper victory, there was no invasion of England. The wars between France and Britain continued for nearly eighty years, ending with the complete defeat of France and the British dominating the oceans.'

Lady Bishop shook her head. 'What is the state of the Americas in this world of yours?' she asked.

'There was a revolution . . . Why, is it important?'

'No, just fascinating. So, continue. Your world is very different, it seems, but from a more recent point of change?'

'Yes.' Miriam took a mouthful of coffee. 'Something went wrong here. I think it was something to do with the French administration of England after the invasion, in the eighteenth century. In my world, a lot of the industrialization you've had here in the past hundred years happened in the late eighteenth and nineteenth centuries, in England. Over in this world it started late and it's still happening here, in New Britain. Things are further ahead in the United States, the nation on this continent where I come from. And in other countries in the other world. That doesn't mean things are necessarily better – they've got big problems, too. But no kings, at least not many: most countries got rid of them over the past century. And better science and technology. Cures for tuberculosis.'

'How do your relatives, this Clan, account for their power? I'd have thought that if they live in a backward society it would be difficult to rise.'

Miriam put her mug down. 'They're smugglers,' she said bluntly. 'In their own world, they are the only people who can get messages across the continent in anything less than weeks. They use the U.S. postal service to accomplish miracles, in the terms of their own world. And they've got modern firearms and lots of toys, because in my world they smuggle illegal drugs: they can guarantee to get them past the Coast Guard and police and border patrols. They're immensely rich merchant princes. But they're trapped by the society they live in. The old nobility don't accept them, the peasants resent them, and the crown –' She shook her head, unable to continue.

'You said someone tried to kill you today. Which world did this happen in?'

'The Clan's,' Miriam said automatically. She picked her mug up, took a sip, rolled it nervously between her palms. 'I, when they discovered me, I needed to figure out a way to make some space for myself. I'm not used to having a big extended family who expect me to fit in. And there aren't enough of them. They wanted me to marry for political reasons. I tried to – well, I made a big mistake. Tried to get political leverage, to make them leave me alone. Instead I nearly got myself killed. They left the, the political marriage as a compromise, a way out. Tonight was meant to be the official betrothal. Instead . . .'

She put the mug down. 'The groom is dead. No, no need for condolences – I barely knew him. There was an attack on the betrothal party, and I only just managed to escape. And the United States government has found out about the Clan and discovered a way to get at the Clan's world.'

Her eyes widened. 'Hey, I wonder if Angbard knows?'

*

Mike's first hint that something had gone badly wrong was the scent of burning gunpowder on the night air.

He hunkered down behind a large, gnarled oak tree at the edge of the tree line and squinted into the darkness. Hastert and his men had night-vision goggles, but they hadn't brought a spare pair for Mike and the moon wasn't an adequate substitute. The stone wall across the clear-cut lawn was a looming black silhouette against a slightly lighter darkness. The sounds drifting over the wall told their own story of pain and confusion and anger: it sounded like there was a riot going on in the distance, still punctuated with the flat bangs of black powder weapons and the bellowing of men like cattle funneled into the killing floor of an abattoir.

A shadowy figure moved across the empty space. Someone tapped Mike lightly on the shoulder, and he jerked half-upright. 'Let's move,' whispered Hastert. 'After me.' He rose lightly, and before Mike could say anything he faded into the gloom.

Mike forced himself to stand up. He'd been crouching for so long that his knees ached – and the nervous apprehension wasn't helping, either. *What have I gotten myself into?* It seemed to be the story of his life, these days. He shifted his weight from side to side, restoring the circulation in his legs, then took a step through the undergrowth around the big oak tree.

There was a sharp cracking noise, a moment's vibration as if a bowstring the size of a suspension bridge had just been released, and an excruciating pain lanced through his left leg, halfway between ankle and knee. He gasped with agony, too shocked to scream, and began to topple sideways. The serrated steel jaws buried in his leg were brought up sharply by the chain anchoring them to the oak tree, and dug their teeth into his shattered leg. Everything went black.

An indeterminate time later, Mike felt an urgent need to spit. His mouth hurt; he'd bitten his tongue and the sharp taste of blood filled his mouth. *Why am I lying down?* he wondered vaguely. Then every nerve in his leg lit up like a flashlight, broken and burning. He drew breath to scream, and a hand covered his mouth.

'O'Neil, get me a splint. Lower leg fracture, looks like tibia and fibula both. Fleming, I'm going to stick a morphine syrette in you. Don't worry, we'll get you out of here. Fuck me, that's a nasty piece of work.' The hand moved away from his mouth. 'Here, bite this if it helps.' Something leathery pushed at his lips. Mike gritted his teeth and tried not to scream as the bones grated. 'I'm going to have to get this fucker off you before we can splint your leg and get you out of here.' A tiny sharpness bit into his leg near the searing agony. 'How does it . . . eh. Got it. This is going to hurt – '

A sudden flare of pain arrived, worse than anything that had come before. Mike blacked out again.

The next time he woke up, the pain had subsided. *That's better,* he thought drowsily. It was comfortable, lying down on the ground: *Must be the morphine.* Someone was tugging at his leg, lifting and moving it and tying stuff tightly around it. That was uncomfortable. Something told him he ought to be screaming his head off, but it was too much effort right now. 'What is it?' he tried to ask aloud, but what came out was a drunken-sounding mumble.

'You stuck your foot in some kind of mantrap. Spring-loaded, chained to the tree, scary piece of shit. It broke your leg and chewed up your calf muscles like a hungry great white. Fuck, why did nobody tell us these medievals had anti-personnel mines?' Hastert sounded distinctly peevish, in a someone's-going-to-get-hurt way. 'Now we're going to have to carry you.'

'Don't –' Mike tried to say. His mouth was dry, but he felt okay. *Just let me lie here for a couple of hours, I'll be fine,* he heard himself thinking, and tried to laugh at his own joke. The darkness was florid and full of patterns, retinal rod cells firing in aimless and fascinating fractals to distract him from the pain. *Medieval minefield, medieval minefield,* he repeated over and over to himself. Someone grunted and dragged his arm over their shoulder, then heaved him upright. His left leg touched ground and he felt light-headed, but then he was dangling in midair. *Shark bite. Hey, I'm shark bait.* He tried not to giggle. *Be serious. I'm in enemy territory. If they hear us . . .*

There was a wall. It was inconveniently high and rough, random stones crudely mortared together in a pile eight feet tall. He was floating beside it and someone was grunting, and then there was a rope sling around him. That was rough as it dragged him up the side of the wall, but Hastert and O'Neil were there to keep his leg from bumping into the masonry. And then he was lying on top of the wall, which was bumpy but wide enough to be secure, and on the other side of it he could see a dirt road and more walls in the darkness, and a couple of shadowy buildings.

His mangled leg ached distantly.

Consciousness came in fits and starts. He was lying on the muddy grass at the base of the wall, staring up at the sky. The stars were very bright, although wisps of cloud scudding in from the north were blotting them out. Someone nearby was swearing quietly. He could hear other noises, a rattling stomping and yelling like a demonstration he'd once seen, and a hollow clapping noise that was oddly familiar, pop-pop, pop-pop – hooves, he realized. *What do horses mean?*

'Fuck.' The figure bending over him sounded angry and confused. 'O'Neil, I'm going to have to call four-oh-four on Fleming. Cover – '

What's he doing with the knife? Mike wondered dizzily. The hoof-beats were getting louder and there was a roar; then a rattling bang of gunfire, very loud and curiously flat, not the crack of supersonic bullets but more like high-caliber pistol shots, doors slamming in his ears. There was a scream, cut off: something heavy fell across him as an answering stutter of automatic fire cut loose, O'Neil with his AR-15. *Who's trying to kill whom, now?* A moment of ironic amusement threatened to swallow Mike, just as a second booming volley of musket fire crackled overhead. Then there was more shouting, and more automatic fire, stuttering in short bursts from concealment at the other end of the exposed stretch of wall: *We climbed the wall right into a crossfire!*

He tried to focus, but overhead the stars were graying out, one by one: shock, blood loss, and morphine conspired to put him under. But unlike the others, he was still alive when the Clan soldiers covering the escape of their leaders from the Thorold Palace reached the killing zone and paused to check the identities of the victims.

SECURITY BREACHES

Angbard's bad day started out deceptively, with a phone call that he had taken for a positive development at first. It was not until later, when events began to spin out of control, that he recognized it for what it was – the very worst disaster to befall the Clan during his tenure as chief of external security.

This week his grace was staying on the other side, in a secluded mansion in upstate New York that he had acquired from the estate of a deceased record producer who had invested most of the money his bands had earned in building his own unobtrusive shrine to Brother Eater. (Not that they used the Hungry God's true name in this benighted land, but the principle was the same.) The heavily wooded hundred-acre lot, discreet surveillance and security fittings, and the soundproofed basement rooms that had once served as a recording studio, all met with the duke's approval. So did the building's other-side location, a hilly bluff in the wilds of the Nordmarkt that had been effectively doppelgängered by a landslide until his men had tunneled into it to install the concealed exits, supply dumps, and booby-trapped passages that safety demanded.

Of course the location wasn't perfect in all respects – in Nord-markt it was a good ten miles from the nearest highway, itself little more than an unpaved track, and in its own world it was a good fifty-minute drive outside Rochester – but it met with most of his requirements, including the most important one of all: that nobody outside his immediate circle of retainers knew where it was.

These were desperate times. The defection of the duke's former secretary, Matthias, had been a catastrophe for his personal security. He had been forced to immediately quarantine all his former posses-sions in the United States, the private jet along with the limousines and the houses: all out of reach for now, all contaminated by

Matthias's insidiously helpful management. He had holdouts, of course, the personal accounts held with offshore institutions that not even his secretary had known about – Duke Lofstrom had grown up during a time of bloody-handed paranoia, and never completely trusted anyone – but by his best estimate, it had cost him at least one hundred and twenty-six million dollars. And that was just how much it had cost *him*, as an individual. To the Clan as a whole, this disaster had cost upwards of two billion dollars. It was not beyond the realm of possibility that some of the more angry or desperate cousins might try to take their share out of his hide.

Events started with a phone call shortly after 11 p.m. Or rather, they started with what passed for a phone call where the duke was concerned: although he received it on an old-fashioned handset, it arrived at the safe house by a circuitous route involving a very off-the-books patch into the local phone company exchange, dark fiber connections between anonymous Internet hosts, and finally an encrypted data call to a stolen mobile phone handset. Angbard, Duke Lofstrom, might write his personal correspondence with a fountain pen and leave the carrying of mobile phones to his subordinates, but his communications security was the best that the Clan's money could buy.

When the phone rang, the duke had just finished dining with the lords-comptrollers of the Post Office: the two silver-haired eminences who were responsible for the smooth running of the Clan's money-making affairs to the same degree that he was responsible for their collective security. The brandy had been poured, the last plates removed, and he had been looking forward to a convivial exploration of the possibilities for expansion in the new territories when there was a knock on the dining room side door.

'Excuse me,' he nodded to his lordship, Baron Griben ven Hjalmar, causing him to pause in mid-flow: 'Enter!'

It was Carlos, one of his security detail, looking apologetic. 'The red telephone, my lord. It's ringing in your office.'

'Ah.' The duke glanced at his dining companions: 'I must apologize, perforce, but this requires my immediate attention. I shall return presently.'

'Surely, sir.' Baron ven Hjalmar raised his glass: 'Your health!' He smiled indulgently.

The duke rose and left the table without further ado. On his way out, Carlos took up the rear. 'Who is it?' he asked as soon as the dining room door had closed behind them.

'The officer of the day in the Thorold Palace has just declared an emergency. The signal is Tango Mike. He crossed over to report in person. He's on the phone now.'

'Who is he? On the duty roster?' The officer of the day was the Clan member entrusted with ensuring the security of Clan members in their area, and he would not cross over to the other world to make a report – effectively abandoning his post, if only for a few minutes – without a very good reason.

'I believe it's Oliver, Baron Hjorth.'

The duke swore. Then they were at his office door. He picked up the telephone before he sat down. 'Put him through.' His face fell unconsciously into an odd, pained expression: Oliver was a member of his half-sister's mother's coterie, an intermittent thorn in his side – but not one that he could remove without unpleasant consequences. What made it even worse was that Oliver was competent and energetic. If it wasn't for Hildegarde's malign influences, he might be quite useful . . . 'Good evening, Baron. I gather you have some news for me.'

A quarter of an hour later, when he put the phone down, the duke's expression was, if anything, even more stony. He turned to stare at Carlos, who stood at parade rest by the door. 'Please inform their lordships ven Hjalmar and Ijsselmeer that I deeply regret to inform them that there has been a development that requires –' He paused, allowing his head to droop. 'Let me rephrase. Please inform them that an *emergency* has developed and I would appreciate their assistance, in their capacity as representatives of the Post Office board, in conducting a preliminary assessment of the necessary logistic support for execution of the crisis plan in the affected areas. Then bring them here.' He sighed deeply, then looked up. 'Go on.'

'Sir.' Carlos swerved through the door and was gone.

The duke half-smiled at the closing door. The fellow was probably scared out of his wits by what he'd overheard of the duke's conversation with Baron Hjorth. Who should, by now, be back in Niejwein, and organizing his end of the crisis plan. The duke shook his head again. 'Why *now*?' He muttered to himself. Then he picked up the phone and dialed the digit 9. 'Get me Mors. Yes, Mors Hjalmar. And Ivan ven Thorold. Teleconference, right now, I don't care if they're in bed or unavailable, tell them it's an emergency.' He thought for a moment. 'I want every member of the council who is in this world on the line within no more than one hour. Tell them it's an emergency meeting of the Clan council, on my word, by telephone.' This was unprecedented; emergency meetings were themselves a real rarity, the last having been one he'd called at the behest of his niece barely six months ago. 'And if they don't want to make time, tell them I'll be *very annoyed* with them.'

Angbard hung up the phone and settled down to wait. A knock at the door: one of his men opened it. 'Sir, their lordships – '

'Send them in. Then fetch a speakerphone.' Angbard rose, and half-bowed to Hjalmar and Ijsselmeer. 'I must apologize for the informality, but there has been an unfortunate development in the capital. If you would both please be seated, I will arrange for coffee in a minute.'

Hjalmar found his voice first; diffidently – incongruously, too, for he was a big bear of a man – he asked: 'Is something the matter?'

'It's the crown prince.' Angbard grinned. Someone unfamiliar with him might have mistaken his expression for a smile: neither of his guests did so.

'What? Has Egon had an accident – '

'In a manner of speaking.' Angbard sat down again, leaning back in his chair. 'Egon has just murdered his own father and brother, not to mention Henryk and my niece Helge and a number of our cousins, at the occasion of his brother's betrothal. He's sent troops to lay siege to the Thorold Palace and he's issuing letters of attainder against us, promising our land to anyone who comes to his aid.' Angbard's grin turned shark-like. 'He's made his bid at last, gentlemen. The old high families have decided to cast their lot in with him, and we can't be having that. An example will have to be made. King Egon the Third is going to have one of the shortest reigns on record – and I'm calling this meeting because we need to establish who we're going to put on the throne once Egon is out of the way.'

Hjalmar blanched. 'You're talking about high treason!'

The old scar on Angbard's cheek twitched. 'It's never treason if you win.' His smile faded into a frown and he made a steeple of his fingers. 'And I don't know about you gentlemen, but I see no alternative. Unless we are to hang – and I mean that entirely literally – we must grasp the reins of power directly. The very first thing we must do is remove the usurper from the throne he's claimed.'

*

Morning in Boston: a thick fog, stinking of coal dust and burned memories, swirled down the streets between the brown brick houses, blanketing the pavement and forming eddies in the wake of the streetcars. Behind a grimy window in a tenement flat on Holmes Alley a man coughed in his sleep, snorted, then twitched convulsively. Distant factory bells tolled dolorously as he rolled over, clutching the battered pillow around his head. It was an hour past dawn when a bell of a different kind broke through his torpor, tinkling in the hallway outside the kitchen.

The gaunt, half-bald man sat up and rubbed his eyes, then fastened his gaze on a cheap tin alarm clock that had stopped, its hands mockingly pointed at the three and the five on the dial. He focused on it blearily and swore, just as the doorbell tinkled again.

For someone so tall and thin, Erasmus Burgeson could move rapidly. In two spidery strides he was at the bedroom door, nightgown flapping around his ankles; three more strides and his feet were on the chilly stone slabs of the staircase down to the front door. Upon reaching which he rattled the chain and drew back the bolts, finally letting the door slide an inch ajar. 'Who is it?' he demanded hoarsely as an incipient wheeze caught his ribs in its iron fist.

'Post Office electrograph for a Mister Burgeson?' piped a youthful voice. Erasmus looked down. It was, indeed, a Post Office messenger urchin, barefoot in the cold but wearing the official cap and gloves of that institution, and carrying a wax-sealed envelope. 'Thruppence-ha'penny to pay?'

'Wait one.' He turned and fumbled behind the door for his overcoat, in one pocket of which he always kept some change. Three and a half pence was highway robbery for an electrograph: the fee had gone up two whole pennies in the past year, a sure sign that the Crown was desperate for revenue. 'Here you are.'

The urchin shoved the envelope through the door and dashed off with his money, obviously eager to make his next delivery. Burgeson shut and bolted the door, then made his way back upstairs, this time plodding laboriously, a little wince crossing his face with each cold stone step. His feet were still warm and oversensitive from bed: with the fire embargo in effect on account of the smog, the chill of the stairs bit deep into his middle-aged bones.

At the top step he paused, finally giving in to the retching cough that had been building up. He inspected his handkerchief anxiously: there was no blood. *Good.* It was nearly two months, now, and the cough was just the normal wheezing of a mild asthmatic caught out by one of Boston's notorious yellow-gray smogs. Erasmus placed the electrograph envelope on the stand at the top of the staircase and shuffled into the kitchen. The cooking range was cold, but the new, gas-fired samovar was legal: he lit it off, then poured water into the chamber and, while it was heating, took the bottle of miracle medicine from the back of the cupboard and took two more of the strange cylindrical pills.

He'd barely dared believe Miriam's promises when she gave him the pills, but they seemed to be working. It was almost enough to shake his belief in the innate hostility of the universe. People caught the white death and they died coughing up their lungs in a bloody foam, and that was it. It happened less often these days, but it was still a terror that stalked the camps north of the Great Lakes – and there was no easy cure. Certainly nothing as simple as taking two tablets every morning for six months! And yet . . . *I wonder where she is?* Erasmus pondered, not for the first time: *Probably busying herself trying to make another world a better place.*

The water was close to boiling. He spooned loose tea into the brewing chamber then wandered over to the window, squinting against the smog-diffused daylight in hope of glimpsing one of the neighborhood clock towers. He'd have to wind and reset the alarm once he'd worked out by how long it had betrayed him. Still, nobody had jangled the bell-pull tied to the shop door handle while he was sleeping like a log. Business had boomed over the springtime and early summer, but things had fallen ominously quiet lately – nobody seemed to have the money to buy their possessions back out of hock, and indeed, nobody seemed to be buying much of anything. Even the local 'takers were slacking off on enforcing the vagrancy laws. Things seemed all right in the capital whenever his other business took him there to visit – *the rich man's cup spilleth over; the poor man gets to suck greedily on the hem of the tablecloth* – and the munitions factories were humming murderously along, but wages were being cut left, right and center as the fiscal crisis deepened and the banks called in their loans and the military buildup continued.

Finally the water began hissing and burbling up into the brewing chamber. Erasmus gave up on staring out the window and went in search of his favorite mug. A vague memory of having left it in the lounge drew him into the passage, between the bookcases stacked above head-height with tracts and treatises and rants, and as he passed the staircase he picked up the letter and carried it along. The mug he found sitting empty on top of a pyramid of antinomianist-utilitarian propaganda tracts and a tottering pile of sheet music.

Back in the kitchen, he spooned rough sugar into the mug. The samovar was still hissing like a bad-natured old cat, so he slit open the electrograph's seal while he was waiting for it to finish brewing. The letter within had been cast off a Post Office embosser, but the words had been composed elsewhere. YOUR SISTER IN GOOD HANDS DURING CONFINEMENT STOP MIDWIFE OPTIMISTIC STOP WHY NOT VISIT STOP BISHOP ENDS.

His eyebrows furrowed as he stared at the slip of paper, his morning tea quite forgotten. Nobody in the movement would entrust overtly coded messages to the government's postal service; the trick was to use electrographs for signaling and the movement's own machinery for substantive communications. But this wasn't a prearranged signal, which made it odd. He'd had a sister once, but she'd died when he was six years old: what this was telling him was that Lady Bishop wanted him to visit her in New London. He stared at it some more. It didn't contain her double-cross marker – if she'd signed her first name to a signal it would mean *I've been captured* – and it did contain her negative marker – if a message contained an odd number of words that meant *I am at liberty*. But it wasn't a scheduled meeting: however he racked his brains he couldn't think of anything that might warrant such an urgent summons, or the disruption to his other duties.

Does this mean we have a breach? He put the treacherous message down on the kitchen table and turned off the gas, then poured boiling hot tea into his mug. *If Margaret's been taken, it's a catastrophe. And if she hasn't* – Gears spun inside his mind, grinding through the long list of possibilities. Whatever the message meant, he needed to be on a train to the capital as soon as possible.

An hour later, Erasmus was dressed and ready to travel, disguised as himself (electrograph in wallet, along with ID papers). He carefully shut off the gas supply and, going downstairs, hung up the CLOSED DUE TO ILLNESS sign in the shop window. It needed no explanation to such folk as knew him, and in any case the Polis had been giving him a wide berth of late, ever since his relapse in their cells. *They probably think I'm out of the class struggle for good,* he told himself, offering it as a faint prayer. If he could ever shed the attention he'd attracted, what use he could make of anonymity with his age and guile!

It took him some time to get to the new station beside the Charles River, but once there he discovered that the mid-morning express had not yet departed, and seats in second class were still available. And that wasn't his only good fortune. As he walked along the pier past the streamlined engine he noticed that it had none of the normal driving wheels and pistons, but multiple millipede-like undercarriages and a royal coat of arms. Then he spotted the string of outrageously streamlined carriages strung out along the track behind it, and the way the gleaming tractor emitted a constant gassy whistling sound, like a promise from the far future. It was one of the new turbine-powered trains that had been all the talk of the traveling classes this summer. Erasmus shook his head. This was unexpected: he'd hoped to reach New London for dinner, but if what he'd heard about these machines were true he might arrive in time for late lunch.

His prognostications were correct. The train began to move as he settled down behind a newspaper, accelerating more like an electric streetcar than any locomotive he'd been on, and minutes later it was racing through the Massachusetts countryside as fast as an air packet.

Burgeson found the news depressing but compelling. **Continental Assembly Dismissed!** screamed the front page headline: **Budget Deadlock Unresolved**. The king had, it seemed, taken a right royal dislike to his Conservative enemies in the house, and their dastardly attempts to save their scrawny necks by raising tariffs to pay for the Poor Law rations at the expense of the Navy. Meanwhile, the rocketing price of Persian crude had triggered a run on oil futures and threatened to deepen the impending liquidity crisis further. Given a choice between a rock and a hard place – between the need to mobilize the cumbersome and expensive apparatus of continental defense in the face of French aggression, and the demands of an exhausted Treasury and the worries of bondholders – the king had gone for neither, but had instead dismissed the quarrelsome political mosquitoes who kept insisting that he make a choice between guns and butter. It would have struck Erasmus as funny if he wasn't fully aware that it meant thousands were going to starve to death in the streets come winter, in Boston alone – and that was ignoring the thousands who would die at sea and on foreign soil, because of the thrice-damned stupid assassination of the young prince.

There were some benefits to rule by royal edict, Erasmus decided. The movement was lying low, and the number of skulls being crushed by truncheons was consequently small right now, but with the dismissal of the congress, everyone now knew exactly who to blame whenever anything bad happened. There was no more room for false optimism, no more room for wishful thinking that the kindly Crown might take the side of the put-upon People against his wicked servants. The movement's cautious testing of the waters of public opinion (cautious because you never knew which affable drinking companion might be an agent provocateur sent to consign you to the timber camps, and in these days of gathering wartime hysteria any number of ordinarily reasonable folks had been caught up in the most bizarre excesses of anti-French and anti-Turkish hysteria) suggested that, while the king's popularity rose whenever he took decisive action, he could easily hemorrhage support by taking responsibility for the actions usually carried out by the home secretary in his name. No more lying democracy: no more hope that if you could just raise your thousand-pound landholder's bond you could take your place on the electoral register, adding your voice to the elite.

The journey went fast, and he'd only just started reading the small-print section near the back (proceedings of divorce and blasphemy trials; obituaries of public officials and nobility; church appointments; stock prices) when the train began to slow for the final haul into Queen Josephina Station. Erasmus shook his head, relieved that he hadn't finished the paper, and disembarked. He pushed through the turbulent bazaar of the station concourse as fast as he could, hailed a cab, and directed it straight to a perfectly decent hotel just around the corner from Hogarth Villas.

Half an hour later, after a tense walk-past to check for signs that all was in order, he was relaxing in a parlor at the back of the licensed brothel with a cup of tea and a plate of deep-fried whitebait, and reflecting that whatever else could be said about Lady Bishop's establishment, the kitchen was up to scratch. As he put the teacup down, the side door opened. He rose: 'Margaret?'

'Sit down.' There were bags under her eyes and her back was stooped, as if from too many hours spent cramped over a writing desk. She lowered herself into an overpadded armchair gratefully and pulled a wry smile from some hidden reservoir of affect: 'How was your journey?'

'Mixed. I made good time.' His eyes traveled around the pelmet rail taking in the decorative knick-knacks: cheap framed prints of music hall divas and dolly-mops, bone china pipe-stands, a pair of antique pistols. 'The news is – well, you'd know better than I.' He turned his head to look at her. 'Is it urgent?'

'I don't know.' Lady Bishop frowned. There was a discreet knock at the door, and a break in the conversation while one of the girls came in with a tea tray for her. When she left, Lady Bishop resumed: 'Did you know Adam is coming back?'

Erasmus jolted upright. 'He's *what*? That's insane! If they catch him –' That didn't bear thinking about. *He's coming back?* The very idea of it filled his mind with the distant roar of remembered crowds. *Inconceivable –*

'He seems to think the risk is worth running, given the nature of the current crisis, and you know what he's like. He said he doesn't want to be away from the capital when the engine of history puts on steam. He's landing late next week, on a freighter from New Shetland that's putting into Fort Petrograd, and I want you to meet him and make sure he has a safe journey back here. Willie's putting together the paperwork, but I want someone whom he knows to meet him, and you're the only one I could think of who isn't holding a ring or breaking rocks.'

He nodded, thoughtfully. 'I can see that. It's been a long time,' he said, with a vertiginous sense of lost decades. *It must be close on twenty years since I last heard him speak.* For a disturbing moment he felt those years fall away. 'He really thinks it's time?' he asked, still not sure that it could be real.

'I'm not sure I agree with him . . . but, yes. Will you do it?'

'Try and stop me!' He meant it, he realized. Despite most of a decade in the camps, and everything that had gone with that . . . and he still meant it. *Adam's coming back, at last.* And the nations of men would tremble.

'We're setting up a safe house for him. And a meeting of the Central Executive Committee, a month from now. There will be presses to turn,' she warned. 'He'll need a staff. Are you going to be fit for it?'

'My health – it's miraculous. I can't say as how I'll ever have the energy of a sixteen-year-old again, but I'm not an invalid any more, Margaret.' He thumped his chest lightly. 'And I've got lost time to make up for.'

Lady Bishop nodded, then took a sip of her tea.

'There's another matter, I needed to speak with you about,' She said. 'It's about your friend Miss Beckstein.'

'Yes?' Erasmus leaned forward. 'I haven't heard anything from her for nearly two months – '

'A woman claiming to be her turned up on my doorstep three nights ago: we've spent the time since then questioning her. I have no way of identifying her positively, and if her story is correct she's in serious trouble.'

'I can tell you –' Erasmus paused. 'What kind of trouble?'

Margaret's frown deepened. 'First, I want you to look at this portrait.' She pulled a small photograph from the pocket of her shalwar suit. 'Is this her?'

Erasmus stared at it for a moment. 'Yes.' It was slightly blurred but even though she was looking away from the camera, as if captured through the eye of a spy hole, he recognized her as Miriam. He looked more closely. Her costume was even more outlandish than when she'd first shown up on his doorstep, and either the lighting was poor or there was a bruise below one eye, but it was definitely her. 'That's her, all right.'

'Good.'

He glanced up. 'You were expecting a Polis agent?'

'No.' She reached for the picture and he let her take it. 'I was expecting a Clan agent.'

'A –' Erasmus stopped. He picked up his teacup again to disguise his nervousness. 'Please explain,' he said carefully. 'Whatever I am permitted to know.'

'Don't worry, you're not under restriction. Unfortunately, if Miss Beckstein is telling the truth, it's very bad news indeed. It appears she fell into disfavor with her family of the first estate – to the point where they imprisoned her, and then attempted to marry her off. But the arranged marriage provoked a violent backlash from the swain's elder brother, and it seems she is now destitute and in search of a safe harbor. Her family doesn't even know she's still alive, and she believes many of them are dead. Which leaves me with a very pressing dilemma, Erasmus. If this was subterfuge or skullduggery, some kind of plot to pressure us by her relatives, it would be easy enough to address. But under the circumstances, what should I do with her?'

Burgeson opened his mouth to speak, then froze. *Think very carefully, because your next words might condemn her.* 'I, ah, that is to say –' He paused, feeling the chilly fingers of mortal responsibility grasp the scruff of his neck like a hangman's noose. 'You invited me here to be her advocate.'

Lady Bishop nodded. 'Somebody has to do it.'

The situation was clear enough. The movement existed from day to day in mortal peril, and had no room for deadweight. Prisons were a luxury that only governments could afford. *At least Margaret invited me here to speak.* It was a generous gesture, taken at no small risk given the exigencies of communication discipline and the omni-present threat of the royal security Polis. Despite the organization's long-standing policies, Lady Bishop was evidently looking for an excuse *not* to have Miriam liquidated. Heartened by this realization, Erasmus relaxed a little. 'You said she turned up on your doorstep. Did she come here voluntarily?'

'Yes.' Lady Bishop nodded again.

'Ah. Then that would imply that she views us as allies, or at least as possible saviors. Assuming she isn't working for the Polis and this isn't an ambush – but after three days I think that unlikely, don't you? If she is then, well, the ball is up for us both. But she's got a story and she's been sticking to it for three days . . . ? Under extraordinary pressure?'

'No pressure. At least, nothing but her own isolation.'

Erasmus came to a decision. 'She's been a major asset in the past, and I am sure that she isn't a government sympathizer. If we take her in, I'm certain we can make use of her special talents.' He put his teacup down. 'Killing her would be a –' *tragic* '– waste.'

Lady Bishop stared at him for a few seconds, her expression still. Then she nodded again. 'I concur,' she said briskly.

'Well, I confess I am relieved.' He scratched his head, staring at the picture she still held.

'I value your opinions, Erasmus, you must know that. I needed a second on this matter; my first leaning was to find a use for her, but you know her best and if you had turned your thumb down –' She paused. 'Is there a personal interest I should know about?'

He looked up. 'Not really. I consider her a friend, and I find her company refreshing, but there's nothing more.' *Nothing more*, he echoed ironically in the safety of his own head. 'I incline towards leniency for all those who are not agents of the state – I think it unchristian and indecent to mete out such punishment as I have been on the receiving end of – but if I thought for an instant that she was a threat to the movement I'd do the deed myself.' And that was the bald unvarnished truth – a successful spy would condemn dozens, even hundreds, to the gallows and labor camps. But it was not the entire truth, for it would be a harsh act to live with afterwards: conceivably an impossible one.

Lady Bishop sipped her tea again. 'Then I think you'll be the best man for the job.'

'What job?'

'Finding a use for her, of course. In your copious spare time, while you're off being Sir Adam's errand boy.'

Erasmus blinked. 'Excuse me?'

'I'd have thought it obvious.' She put her teacup down. 'We can't keep her here. Her inexperience would render her dangerous, her strange ideas and ways would be hazardous and hard to conceal in the front of the house, and, bluntly, I think she'd draw unwelcome attention to herself. If we're not to send her to the Miller, it's essential to put her somewhere safe. You're the only person she knows or trusts here, so you drew the short straw. Moreover, I suspect you know more about how to make use of her unique ability than I do. So, unless you object, I'm going to assign her to you as an additional responsibility, after you see to Adam's travel arrangements. Take her in and establish how we can use her. What do you say?'

'I say – um.' His head was spinning: Erasmus blinked again. 'That is to say, that makes sense, but – '

Lady Bishop clapped her hands together before he could muster a coherent objection. 'Excellent!' She smiled. 'I'll have Edward sort out documents and some suitable clothing for her, and you can take her back to Boston as soon as possible. What do you say?'

'But –' *The servant's room is full of furniture in hock, the second bedroom doesn't have room to swing a cat for all the old clothing and books I've got stored in it, and the old biddies up the street will wag their tongues so hard their jaws explode* – 'I think the word Miss Beckstein would use is "okay".' He cleared his throat. 'This is going to be interesting.'

*

His Majesty King Egon the Third had convened his special assizes in the grand hall of the Thorold Palace – still smoking, and somewhat battered by his soldiers in their enthusiasm to drive out the enemy – precisely thirty-six hours after the explosion and subsequent attack on his father. 'By parties of great treachery in league with the tinker tribe,' as the gebanes dispatched by royal messenger to all his vassal lords put it: 'Let all know that by decree of this court in accordance with the doctrine of outlawry the afore-named families are declared outwith the law, and their chattels and holdings hereby escheat to the Crown.' The writs were flying by courier to all quarters of the kingdom; now his majesty was dictating a codicil.

'This ague at the heart of our kingdom pains us grievously, but we are young and healthy enough that it shall soon be overcome and the canker cut out,' his majesty said. 'To this end, a half of all real properties and chattels recovered from the outlaw band is hereby granted to whosoever shall yield those properties to the Crown.' He frowned: 'Is that clear enough do you suppose, Innsford?'

'Absolutely clear, my lord.' His excellency the duke of Innsford bobbed his head like a hungry duck plowing a mill pond. 'As clear as temple glass!' *Whether it is wise is another matter,* he thought, but held his counsel. Egon might be eager to rid himself of the tinker clan, and declaring them outlaw and promising half their estates to whoever killed them was a good way to go about the job, but in the long run it might come back to haunt him: other kings had been overthrown by ambitious dukes, with coffers filled and estates bloated by the spoils of a civil war fought by proxy. Innsford harbored no such ambitions – his old man's plans did not call for a desperate all-or-nothing gamble to take the throne – but others might think differently. Meanwhile, the scribe seated at the table behind him scratched on, his pen bobbing between ink pot and manuscript as he committed the King's speech to paper.

His majesty glanced up at the huge, clear windows overhead, frames occupied by flawless sheets of plate imported from the shadowlands by the tinkers. 'May Sky Father adorn his tree with them.' In the wan morning light his expression was almost hungry. Innsford nodded again. The king – a golden youth only a handful of years ago, now come into his full power as a young man, handsome as an eagle and strong as an ox – was not someone anyone would disagree with openly. He was fast to laugh, but his cruel streak was rarely far below the surface and his mind was both deceptively sharp and coldly untrusting. He kept his openness for a small coterie of friends, their loyalty honed beyond question by bleak years of complicity during the decade when his father had held him at arm's reach, suspicious of the brain rot inflicted on his younger brother Creon during a sly assassination attempt. The other courtiers (of whom there were no small number, Duke Innsford among them) would have a long wait until they earned his confidence.

And as Egon had demonstrated already, losing the royal confidence could be a fatal blunder.

Egon glanced at the scribe: 'That's enough for now.' He stood up, shifting his weight from foot to foot to restore the circulation that the hard wooden chair had slowed. 'My lord Innsford, attend us, please. And you, my lord Carlsen, and you, Sir Markus.'

The middle-aged duke rose to his feet and half-bowed, then followed as the young monarch walked towards the inner doors. Four bodyguards paced ahead of him, and two to the rear – the latter spending more time looking over their shoulders than observing their royal charge – with the courtiers Carlsen and Markus, and their attendant bodyguards, and Innsford's own retainers and guards taking up the tail end of the party. His majesty affected a scandalous disregard for propriety, dressing in exactly the same livery and chain-mail jerkin as his escorts, distinguishable only by his chain of office – and even that was draped around his neck, almost completely hidden by his tunic. It was almost as if, the duke mused, his majesty was afraid of demonic assassins who might spring out of the thin air at any moment. *As if.* And now that the duke noticed it, even Egon's courtiers wore some variation on the royal livery . . .

'Markus, Carl, we go outside. I believe there is an orangery?'

'Certainly, sire.' Carlsen – another overmuscled blond hopeful – looked slightly alarmed. 'But snipers – '

'That's what our guards are for,' Egon said dismissively. 'The ones you don't see are more important than the ones you do. We are at greater risk in this ghastly haunted pile – from tinker witches sneaking back in from the shadowlands to slip a knife in my ribs – than in any garden. The less they know of our royal whereabouts, the happier I'll be.'

'The land of shadows?' Innsford bit his tongue immediately, but surprise had caught him unawares: *does he really believe they come from the domain of the damned? How much does he know?*

The king glanced round and grinned at him lopsidedly, catching him unawares. It was an intimate expression, rendered frightening by the power of the crown. 'Where did *you* think they came from? They're the spawn of air and darkness. I've seen it myself: one moment they're there, the next . . .' He snapped his fingers. 'They walk between worlds and return to this one loaded with eldritch treasure, weapons beyond the ken of our royal artificers and alchemists: they buy influence and insidiously but instinctively pollute the purity of our noble bloodlines with their changeling get!' His grin turned to a glare. 'I learned of this from my grandmother, the old witch – luckily I did not inherit her bloodline, but my brother was another matter. Had Creon not been poisoned in his infancy there is no doubt that once he reached his majority I should shortly have met with an accident.'

He paused for a minute while his guards opened the thick oak side door and checked the garden for threats. Then he turned and strode through into the light summer rain, his face upturned towards the sky.

The formal gardens in the grounds of the Thorold Palace had been a byword for splendor among the aristocracy of the Gruinmarkt for decades. The hugely rich clan of tinker families had spared no expense in building and furnishing their residence in the capital: individuals might dress to impress, but stone and rampart were the gowns of dynasties. Some might even think that Egon had brought his court to the captured palace because it was (in the aftermath of the fighting that had damaged the Summer Palace) the most fitting royal residence in the city of Niejwein. Rows of carefully cultivated trees marched alongside the high walls around the garden; rose beds, fantastically sculpted, blossomed before the windowed balconies fronting the noble house. A pool, surmounted by a grotesque fountain, squatted in the midst of a compass rose of gravel paths: beyond it, a low curved building glinted oddly through the falling rain. The walls were made of glass, huge slabs of it, unbelievably regular in thickness and clear of hue, held in a framework of cast iron. Green vegetation shimmered beyond the windows, whole trees clearly visible like a glimpse into some fantastic tropical world. Egon strode towards it, not once glancing to either side, while his guards nervously paced alongside, eyes swiveling in every direction.

Innsford hurried to keep up with the royal personage. He cleared his throat: 'Your Majesty, if the tinkers suspect you are making free with their former estate –'

Egon rounded on him. 'It's not their estate,' he snapped. 'It's mine. And don't you forget it.' He continued, moderating his tone, 'Why do you think everyone around me dresses alike?' His ill-humor slipped away. 'Yes, they can send their assassins, but how will the assassin identify his target? And besides, I will not stay here long.'

They were at the orangery doors. 'Where does your majesty wish his court to reside?' the duke inquired.

'Right here. While I play the King of Night and Mist.' Egon glanced over his shoulder at Sir Markus. 'I need a beater for the royal hunt. Would you fancy the title of general?'

Markus, a strapping fellow with an implausibly bushy mustache, thrust his chest out, beaming with pride: 'Absolutely, sire! I am dizzy with delight at the prospect!'

'Good. Kindly make yourself scarce for a few minutes. You too, Carlsen, I'll have words with you both shortly but first I must speak in confidence with his grace.'

The orangery doors were open and the guards completed their study; Egon stepped over the threshold, and the small gaggle of courtiers followed him. Innsford studied Markus sidelong. Some backwoods peer's eldest son, beholden to Egon for his drinking space at a royal table, ancestral holdings down at heel over the past five decades: more interested in breaking heads and carousing than the boring business of politicking that his father before him was so bad at. And Egon had just casually offered him a post from which he could reap the drippings from the royal trencher? Innsford blinked slowly, watching the two young bloods bounce away into the glazed pavilion, marveling loudly and crudely about its trappings. 'A beater for the hunt should hold the title of general?' he asked.

'When you're hunting for armies, why yes, I believe that is customary.' His majesty's lips quirked slightly, in what might have been intended to be a smile. 'If I am in the field at the head of an army, I am clearly looking to the defense of my realm, am I not? Such a grand undertaking will have, I hope, a salutary effect on any secret ambitions the father of my betrothed might hold towards our lands. Leading an army against the tinkers will permit me to burnish my honor, strive for glory, and ensure that those who rally to my banner do so under my eyes so that their claims to the spoils of victory may be adjudicated immediately.' *Oh, so you don't trust your vassals to handle sharp implements out of your sight?* Innsford nodded gravely, while Sir Markus beamed like an idiot. *A useful idiot, come to think of it.* 'And the tinker assassins will have little success in striking from the shadows if they do not know, from one day to the next, where I make my bed.'

The duke nodded again. 'I am pleased by your majesty's perspicacity and foresight,' he said carefully. *Sky Father! He's sharp.* If Egon was going to go into the field at the head of an army, he was going to slay about six birds with one stone. Hunting down the tinker Clan's holdings in the wild would compel them to confront him on his own terms, while making it difficult for their assassins to stick a knife in his ribs. An army in being would prevent the neighbors from getting any ideas about picking off a province here or a holding there. Meanwhile, Egon had rung a bell to make his backwoods vassal dogs salivate at the thought of loot: now he would go into the field to gather the leashes of the men they had released for service. He could simultaneously claim the lion's share of the spoils he'd promised, while maintaining the appearance of generously disbursing treasure to his followers. Handled carefully it would raise him to the stature of a true warrior king – somebody only fools or the truly desperate would scheme against – without the attendant risks of declaring war on one of the neighboring kingdoms. *If it worked* – 'I see much in your plan to commend it.' Egon came to a halt in front of a bench at the center of a circle of low, dark green trees. Small orange fruits glimmered among their shadowy branches. 'But you did not summon me here to tell me this, your majesty.'

'Indeed not.' Egon inhaled deeply, closing his eyes for a moment. Innsford sniffed, but his sinuses – chronically congested, the aftermath of a broken nose in his youth – stubbornly refused to disclose the cause of Egon's blissful expression. The king opened his eyes: 'I have some – problems. I believe you might be able to assist me in their resolution.'

Ah. Here it comes. Innsford had lived through the reign of two kings before this young upstart; nevertheless, his stomach tingled and he felt a shiver of fear, as if a black cat walked across his future grave. 'I am yours to command, your majesty.'

'While I am on campaign, I must look to the good cultivation of my earthly field.' *Niejwein and territories,* Innsford translated. 'I must also look to the good administration of my army. Who am I to trust, in the halls of power while I am elsewhere?' For a moment the royal gaze fell on Innsford, unblinking and cold as a snake. 'His grace of Niejwein is under threat from the tinker knives if he stays in the capital whose name he bears: perhaps he would be safer were he to undertake a pilgrimage to the southern estates? His eldest son will be all too pleased to look to the household's duties in his father's absence, while his grace could earn my gratitude by looking to the good management of those provinces.'

Innsford stiffened. *But Niejwein's* your *man!* he thought indignantly. Then he unpacked Egon's plan further. *Niejwein's too powerful, here. Send him away from his power base while keeping his son – inexperienced – as a hostage, and he can serve your ends safely. Is that what you plan?* 'You have a task in mind for me.' It was an admission, but denying any awareness of the deeper political realities would merely suggest to Egon that he was too stupid to be of any use. And Innsford had a nasty feeling that being pigeonholed as useless by King Egon was unlikely to be conducive to a peaceful and prosperous old age. Especially if one was of high enough birth to be a potential threat.

'Indeed.' Egon smiled again, that disturbing smirk with a telltale narrowing of the eyes. 'Laurens – the next Duke of Niejwein, I should say – is none too bright himself. He'll need his hand holding and his back watching.' The smirk faded. 'The defense of Niejwein is no minor task, your grace, because I am certain the tinkers will attempt to retake the city. Their holdings are not well adapted to support a war of maneuver, and they are by instinct and upbringing cosmopolitans. Furthermore, Niejwein is the key to their necromantic trade with the land of shades. There are locations in this city that they need. I must assign an army to the defense of the capital, but I would be a thrice-damned fool to leave it in his grace of Niejwein's own hands. Will you take it?'

'I –' Innsford swallowed. 'You surprise me.'

'Not really!' Egon said lightly. 'You know as well as I the value of a certain – reputation.' His own reputation for bloody-handed fits of rage had served well enough at court to keep his enemies fearful. 'Should you accept this task, then this palace will be yours – and your son Franz? He is well, I trust? I will be needing a page. Franz will accompany me and win glory on the battlefield, and in due course he will inherit the second finest palace in the land from his father's prudence in this matter.'

'I wo-would be delighted to accept your gracious offer,' Innsford forced out. *You're going to leave me in charge of this death trap while you take my son as your page?* The audacity was offensive, but as an act of positioning it was a masterstroke: rebel against the king and Egon would already hold his firstborn hostage. *But meanwhile . . .* thoughts whirled in his head. 'You expect the tinkers to try to retake the city, my liege?' he asked: 'Is there sound intelligence to this effect?'

'Oh, indeed.' Egon's reply was equally casual in tone, and just as false. 'I have my ways. Well, truth be told, I have my spies.' He chuckled dryly. 'You understand more than you can politely say, my lord, so I shall say it for you: I trust no one. *No one.* But don't let that fool you. The rewards for being true and constant to my service will be great and in time you'll come round to my way of thinking, I'm sure. It is no blind ambition that desires my impression of your son: I have a nation to rid of witchcraft and nightmares, to make fit for men such as your son to live in. He will eventually play a privileged role at court; I would like to meet him sooner rather than later. But now –' He gestured at the orange grove around them. '– I have arrangements to make. There is a war to conduct, and once I have seen to my defense I must look to my arms.' He took another deep breath. 'If success smells half so sweet as this, I shall count myself a lucky man.'

*

The bench seat stank of leather, old sweat, gunpowder, and a cloying reek of fear. It rattled and bounced beneath Mike, to the accompaniment of a metallic squeaking like damaged car shock absorbers. His leg ached abominably below the knee, and whenever he tried to move it into a less painful position it felt as if a pack of rabid weasels were chewing on it. His face pressed up against the rear cushion of the seat as the contraption swayed from side to side, bouncing over the deep ruts in the cobblestone surface of the road.

Despite the discomfort, he was calm: everything was distant, walled off from him by a barrier of placid equanimity, as if he was wrapped in cotton wool. *They'll kill me when they find out,* he told himself, but the thought held no fear. *Wow, whatever Hastert stuck me with is* really *smooth.*

Not that life was entirely a bed of roses. He winced at a particularly loud burst of gunfire rattling past the carriage window. One of the women on the other bench seat rattled off something in Hochsprache: he couldn't follow it but she sounded scared. The old one tut-tutted. 'Sit down, you'll only get your head blown off if you give them a target,' she said in English.

More Hochsprache: something about duty, Mike thought vaguely.

'No, you shouldn't . . .'

The distinctive sound of a charging handle being worked, followed by a gust of cold air.

Crack. The sound of a rifle firing less than a meter from his ear penetrated Mike's haze. He pushed back against the seat back, rolling onto his back just as a particularly violent pothole tried to swallow one of the carriage's rear wheels, and the shooter fired again: a hot brass cartridge case pinged off the back of the seat and landed on his hand. Curiously, it hurt.

'*Ow –*' He twitched, shaking the thing off, wincing repeatedly as the woman in the fur coat leaning out of the carriage window methodically squeezed off another three shots. *What's the word for . . .* ? 'My leg, it hurts,' he tried.

'Speak English, your accent's atrocious,' said the old woman. 'It won't fool anyone.'

Mike stared at her. In the semidarkness of the carriage her face seemed to hover in the darkness, disembodied. Outside the window, men shouted at each other. The carriage lurched sideways, then bounced forward, accelerating. The shooter withdrew her head and shoulders from the window. 'That is all of them for now, I believe,' she announced, with an accent of her own that could have passed for German. She glanced at Mike, mistrustfully, and adjusted her grip on the gun. The full moon, outside, scattered platinum highlights off her hair: for a moment he saw her face side-lit, young and striking, like a Russian princess in a story, pursued by wolves.

'Close the window, you don't want to make a target of yourself,' said the babushka huddling beneath the pile of rugs. 'And I don't want to catch my death of cold.' A cane appeared from somewhere under the heap, ascending until it battered against the carriage roof. 'Shtoppan nicht, gehen'su halt!' She was old, but her lungs were good. She glanced at Mike. 'So you're awake, are you?'

Answering seemed like too much of an effort, so Mike ignored her: it was much easier to simply close his eyes and try to keep his leg still. That way the weasels didn't seem to bite as hard.

A moment later, the cane poked him rudely in the ribs. 'Answer when you're spoken to!' snapped the Russian princess. He opened his eyes again. The thing prodding his side wasn't a cane, and she might be pretty, but she was also clearly angry. *Is it something I did?* he wondered hazily. 'Where am I?'

'In a carriage,' said the old woman. 'I'd have thought that was obvious.' She snorted. 'The question you meant to ask is, how did I end up in this carriage in particular?'

'Jah: and, how am I, it, to leave, alive?' The Russian princess gave his ribs a final warning poke, then withdrew into the opposite corner of the cramped cabin, next to the old woman. Mike tried to focus: as his eyes adjusted he saw that under her fur coat she was wearing a camouflage jacket. The rifle – he focused some more – was exotic, some sort of foreign bullpup design with a huge night-vision scope bolted above its barrel. *Blonde bombshell with fur coat and assault rifle.* His gaze slid sideways to take in the older one, searching for reassurance: she smiled crookedly, one eyebrow raised, and he shuddered, déjà vu spiking through his guts as sharply as the pain from his damaged leg.

'That's enough, Olga,' the old lady said sharply, never taking her eyes off Mike. 'We've met, in case you'd forgotten.'

Oh fuck. The penny dropped: *That's the entire mission blown!* He stared at her in mortified disbelief, at a complete loss for words. His mind flashed back to events earlier in the evening, to a hurried snatch of conversation with Miriam, the way she'd stared at him in perplexity as if she couldn't quite fathom the meaning of his reappearance in her life: now he felt the same scene repeating, horribly skewed. 'You were –' He paused. 'Mrs. Beckstein. Well . . .' His lips were as dry as the day when Miriam had casually suggested they stop off on their way to the restaurant to say hello. *Just for ten minutes, so you've met my mother –* 'I'm surprised. I thought you'd adopted Miriam? What are you doing here?'

Olga, the Russian princess as he'd started thinking of her, glared at him malevolently: her rifle pointed at the floor, but he had no doubt she could bring it to bear on his head in an eyeblink. But Mrs. Beckstein surprised him. She began to smile, and then her smile widened, and she began to chuckle, louder and louder until she began to wheeze and subsided into a fit of coughing. 'You really believed that?

And you saw us together? What kind of cop are you?' Something else must have tweaked her funny bone because a moment later she was off again, lost in a paroxysm of thigh-slappingly disproportionate mirth. Or maybe it was just relief at being out of the firefight.

'I do not see the thing that is so funny,' Olga said, almost plaintively.

'Ah, well, but he was such a nice young –' Mrs. Beckstein began coughing again. Olga looked concerned, but given a choice between keeping Mike under observation and trying to help the older woman – 'Sorry, dear,' she told Olga, when she got her voice back. 'That's how Miriam described you.' She nodded at Mike. 'Before she changed her mind.'

Mike closed his eyes again. *Jesus, Mary, and Joseph, this is a fuckup!* He winced: obviously demons were feeding his leg-weasels crystal meth. 'He's called Mike,' Mrs. Beckstein continued remorselessly, 'Mike something-beginning-with-F, I've got it in my diary. And he works for the Drug Enforcement Agency. Or he used to work for the DEA. Do you still work for the DEA, Mike?'

He opened his eyes, unsure what to do: the painkillers were subsiding but he still felt unfocused, blurry about the edges. 'I'm not supposed to talk –'

'You *will* talk, boy.' Mrs. Beckstein glared at him, and he recoiled at the anger in her expression. 'You can take your chances with me, or you can make your excuses to my half-brother's men, but you are going to talk sooner or later.' She glanced at Olga. 'Sometimes I can't believe my luck,' she said dryly. She turned back to Mike, her expression harsh: 'What have you done with my daughter?'

'I –' Mike stopped. Time seemed to slow. *My brother's men. Jesus, she's been one of them all along! How deep does this go*? He shuddered, his guts churning. Until now he'd known, understood in the abstract, that Miriam was involved with these alien gangsters, narcoterrorists from Middle Earth: even meeting Miriam, dressed up for a medieval wedding in the middle of an exploding castle, hadn't really shaken what he'd thought he knew. But Miriam's mother was a different matter entirely, a disabled middle-aged woman living quietly in a small house in New England suburbia – *They're everywhere!* He swallowed, choking back hysterical laughter. 'I don't know where she went. She said she had a, one of the lockets, got it from a friend. Said she'd be in touch later. There was a perp in black, tried to stab her so I shot him – '

'Why?'

'Orders.' He cleared his throat. 'They told me, talk to her. Offer her whatever she . . . well, anything.'

Mrs. Beckstein glanced at the Russian princess: evidently her expression meant something because a moment later she turned back to him. 'You're colluding with Egon.'

'Who?' His bewilderment must have been obvious, because a moment later she nodded.

'All right. So how did you get over here?'

Mike stared at her.

Mrs. Beckstein took a deep breath. 'Olga, if Mr. Fleming here doesn't answer my questions, you have my permission to shoot him in the kneecap. At will.'

'Which one?' asked the Russian princess.

'Whichever you want.' Mrs. Beckstein sniffed. 'Mike, I want you to understand one thing, and one thing only – I'm concerned for my daughter's well-being. I'm especially concerned when an ex-boyfriend of hers with a highly dubious employment record appears out of nowhere at a –' she coughed '– joyous occasion, and all hell breaks loose. And I am more concerned than you can possibly begin to imagine that she has vanished in the middle of the sound and the fury, because there is an official decree in force that says if she world-walks without the permission of the Clan committee, her life is forfeit. She is my daughter, and blood is thicker than water, and I am going to *save her ass*. Call it atonement for earlier mistakes, if you like: I've not always been a terribly good mother.' She leaned closer. 'Now, you may be able to help me *save her ass*. If I think you might be useful to me, I can protect you up to a point. Or.' She nodded at Olga. 'Lady Olga is a friend of Miriam's. She's concerned for her welfare, too. Miriam has more friends than she realizes, you see. So the question is: are we all agreed that we are friends of Miriam, and that we intend to *save her ass*? Or –' she fixed Mike with a vulture stare '– were you stringing her along?'

'No!' he exclaimed. 'Whoa. *Ow.*' The weasels had graduated from carnivore school and were working on their diplomas in coyote impersonation. 'What do you want to know?'

'Let's start with, how you got over here.'

'Same way Matthias got over to our – my – world.' He could almost see the lightbulbs going on over Olga's and Mrs. Beckstein's heads. 'Family Trade captured a couple of world-walkers. Forced them to carry.' He tried to shrug himself into a more comfortable position, half-upright.

'Forced? How?' Olga stared at him. 'And what is Family Trade?'

'Collar . . . bombs. They carry a cargo and come back, Family Trade resets the timer. They don't come back, it blows their head off. When they're not world-walking, FTO keeps them in a high-rise jail.'

Mrs. Beckstein interrupted. 'Family Trade – this is some spook agency, isn't it?'

'Yes. I'm – seconded – to it. Not my idea. Matt walked into the Boston downtown office while Pete – my partner – and I were on the desk. That's all.'

'Ah.' Mrs. Beckstein nodded to herself. 'And they sent you here because they worked out that Miriam was . . . okay. I think I get it. Am I right?' She raised an eyebrow.

'Yes, mostly,' he said hastily: Olga was still glaring at him from her corner. 'We don't have much intel on the ground. Colonel Smith figured she'd be able to develop a spy ring for us, in return for an exit opportunity. He wants informants. I told him it was half-assed and premature, but he ordered the insertion.'

'He wants informants, does he?' Mrs. Beckstein grinned. 'What do you make of that, Olga?'

Olga's expression of alarm surprised Mike in its intensity, cutting through the fog of drugs: 'You can't be serious! That would be treason!'

'It's not treason if it's known to ClanSec in advance.' Mrs. Beckstein waved a hand in dismissal. 'One man's spy is another man's diplomatic back channel to the other side; it just depends who's playing the game and for what stakes.' Her eyes narrowed as she looked at Mike. 'Your colonel wants information? Well, he shall have it, and you shall take it to him. But in return, you're going to find my daughter.' A brief sideways nod: 'You and Lady Olga, that is.'

RUNNING DOG

The next day came too early for Erasmus. It was barely a quarter to eight when he checked out of the cheap traveler's hotel he'd stayed in overnight, and walked around to the rear entrance to Hogarth Villas. Lady Bishop's taciturn manservant Edward answered the door, then led him down a servants' passage and a staircase that led to a gloomy basement, illuminated by the dim light that filtered down to the bottom of an air shaft.

'Wait here,' said Edward, disappearing round a corner. A moment later, he heard a rattle of keys, and low voices. Then:

'Erasmus!'

He smiled stiffly, embarrassed by his own reaction. 'Miriam, it's good to see you again.'

'I'd been hoping –' She took two steps towards him, and he found himself suddenly at arm's length; he'd advanced without noticing. 'I'm not imagining things?'

'Everything will be all right.' His voice sounded shaky in his own ears. 'Come on, I'll explain as we go.' He forced himself to look past her face, to make eye contact with Edward (who grimaced and shrugged, as if to say *you're welcome to her*): 'Do you have any luggage?'

'It's here.' Edward hefted a leather valise. Erasmus took it. 'I'll be going now,' said the servant, 'you know the way out.'

A moment later they were alone. He found himself staring at Miriam: she looked back at him with a strange expression, as if she'd never seen him before. *Is this all a terrible mistake?* he wondered: *Is she going to be angry with me for sending her here?* 'You came. For me?'

'As soon as I heard.' He found it difficult to talk.

'Well, thank you. I was beginning to worry –' She shivered violently.

'My dear, this isn't the sort of establishment one drops in on unannounced.' He noticed her clothing for the first time; someone had found her a more suitable outfit than the gown she'd worn in Lady Bishop's spy-hole picture, but it would never do – probably a castoff from one of the girls upstairs, threadbare and patched. 'Hmm. When I asked them to find you something to wear I was expecting something a little less likely to attract attention.'

Her cheeks colored slightly. 'I'm getting sick of hand-me-downs. You've got a plan?'

'Follow me.' It was easier than confronting his emotions – predominantly relief, at the moment, a huge and fragile sense that something precious hadn't been shattered, the toppling vase caught at the last moment – and it was nonsense, of course, a distraction from the serious business at hand. He climbed the stairs easily, with none of the agonizing tightness in his chest and the crackling in his lungs that would have plagued him two months ago. The parlor was empty, the fireplace unlit. He placed the valise on the table. 'Let's see what we've got.'

Her shadow fell across the bag as he opened it. 'Ah, papers.' He opened the leather-bound passport and held the first page up to the light. 'That's a good forgery.' He felt a flash of admiration for Margaret's facilities; if he hadn't known better he'd have been certain it was genuine. Below it was a bundle of other documents: birth certificate, residence permit for the eastern provinces, even a – his cheeks colored. 'We appear to be married,' he murmured.

'Let me see.' She reached over and took the certificate. 'Damn, I knew something had slipped my mind. Must have been all the champagne at the reception. Dated two days ago, too – what a way to spend a honeymoon.' She sighed. 'What is it about this month? Everyone seems to want to see me married.'

'Lady Bishop probably thought it would be an excellent explanation for travel,' he said, heart pounding and vision blurred. The sense of relief had gone, shattered: blown away by a sense of disquiet, the old ache like a pulled tooth that he'd lived with for far too long. Remembering the last time he'd seen Annie, alive or dead. 'Or perhaps Ed wanted a little joke at our expense. If so, it's in very bad taste.' He made to take it from her hand, but Miriam had other ideas.

'Wait up. She's right, if we're traveling together it's a good cover identity.' She looked at him curiously. 'We're supposed to travel together?'

Erasmus pulled himself together, with an effort. 'I'm supposed to take you back to Boston and look after you. Find a way to make her – you – useful, Margaret told me. Personally, I don't know if that's possible or appropriate, but it gives her a respectable excuse to get you off her plate without sticking a knife in you first. What we do afterwards – '

'Okay, I get the idea.' Miriam picked up the passport and stared at it, frowning. 'Susan Burgeson. Right.' She glanced at him. 'I could be your long-lost sister or something if you've got trouble with the married couple idea.'

He shrugged. *Compartmentalize.* 'It's a cover identity. Nothing more.'

She looked thoughtful. 'Is Erasmus Burgeson a cover identity, too?'

God's wounds but she's sharp! 'If it was, do you think I'd tell you?'

'You'd tell your wife,' she said, teasingly – then did a double-take at his expression and looked stricken. 'Shit! I'm sorry, Erasmus! I'd – I didn't realize. I'm sorry . . .'

'Don't be,' he said tightly. 'Not your fault.'

'No, me and my –' She took his hand impulsively. 'I tend to dig, by instinct. Listen, if you catch me doing it again and it's sensitive, just tell me to back off, all right?'

He took a deep breath. *It's not your fault.* 'Certainly. I think I owe you that much.'

'You owe –' She shook her head. 'Enough of that. What else have we got?'

'Let's see.' The bag turned out to contain a suit of clothes, not new but more respectable than those they'd already given Miriam. 'If we're traveling together, you'd probably better change into these first. We'll look less conspicuous together.'

'Okay.' She paused. 'Right here?'

'I'll wait outside.'

He stood with his back to the parlor door for a few scant minutes that felt like hours. He spent some of those hours fantasizing about wringing Ed's neck – a necessary proxy, for the thought of challenging Lady Bishop over the matter was insupportable, but damn them! Why did they have to do that, of all things?

Miriam was a sharp knife, too sharp for her own good – sharp enough to cut both ways. Dealing with her as a contact and a supplier of contraband had been dicey, but not impossible. Living with her was an entirely different matter, but it wasn't exactly feasible to stick her in a tenement apartment and leave her to her own devices. *She'll figure everything out, sooner rather than later. And then what?* The precious vase was back teetering on the edge of the precipice, with no hand in place to catch it this time. And it was full of ashes.

There was a knock at the door. A moment later it opened, as he turned round. 'How do I look?' She took a step back.

'You look –' he paused to collect himself, 'fine.' The black walking suit was a little severe, but it suited her. However . . . 'Before we travel, I think we'd better find you a hairdresser.'

'Really?' She frowned. 'It's not particularly long – '

'Or a wig maker,' he explained. 'You're probably on the Polis watch list. But if you've got long blond or brown hair, a different name, and a husband, and the informants are all looking for a single woman with short black hair, that's a start. Details are cumulative: you can't just change one thing and expect to go unnoticed, you've got to change lots of different things about yourself simultaneously.'

'Right. It'll have to be blond. Damn it, I always get split ends.' She ran one hand through her hair. It was longer than he remembered. 'There's other stuff I need to do. When I can figure out what . . .'

A moment he'd been dreading: at least, a small one. She didn't seem to be committed to killing herself just yet. 'That will be a problem.'

'Ah.' She froze. 'Yes, somehow I didn't think it was going to be easy.'

'The – situation – you drew our attention to is troublesome. For the time being, I think it would be a very bad idea indeed for you to try to make contact with your Clan. Or with the other, ah, local faction. I can make inquiries on your behalf, discreet inquiries, if your relatives are still trying to run your company. But until we know how they will react to your reappearance, it would be best not to reappear. Do you agree?'

Miriam looked baffled for a moment: an achingly familiar bewilderment, the first bright moment of incomprehension that everyone felt the first time, as the doors to the logging camp swung open to offer a glimpse into a colder, harsher world. 'All I want is to go home.'

He reached out and rested a hand on her shoulder, surprising himself: 'Home is wherever you are. You've got to learn to accept that, to let go, or sooner or later you're going to kill yourself. Are you listening? Margaret told me your story. Do you want to go back to the situation you just escaped from? Or do you want the Polis to find you instead? I nearly killed myself once, trying to go back. I don't want you to make the same mistake. I think the best way forward would be for you to come with me. It's not forever: it'll last as long as, as long as it needs to. Eventually, I'm sure, you'll be able to go back. But don't . . . don't try to take on too much, Miriam. Not until you're ready.'

'I –' She reached up and removed his hand from her shoulder, but she didn't let go of it. 'You're too kind!' Without warning she stepped right up to him and put her arms around him, and hugged him. Too surprised to move, he stood rooted to the spot, at a loss for words: after a while she stepped away. 'I'm ready now,' she said quietly. 'Let's get out of here.'

*

Everyone gets a run of bad news sooner or later, thought Eric Smith, *but this is ridiculous.*

'This is not making my day any easier,' murmured Dr. James, leaning back in his chair as the door closed behind Agent Herz. He glanced sidelong at Eric. 'Got any bright ideas, Colonel?'

Eric stared at the hard copy of Herz's report, sitting on the blotter in its low-contrast anti-photocopying print and SECRET codewords, and resisted the impulse to pound his head on his desk. It would look unprofessional – there were few stronger terms of opprobrium in Dr. Andrew James's buttoned-down vocabulary – and more important, it wouldn't achieve anything. But on the other hand, banging his head on the desk would probably be less painful than trying to deal with the self-compounding clusterfuck-in-progress that was, of late, what passed for the Family Trade Organization's infant steps towards dealing with the transdimensionally mobile narcoterrorists they were hunting.

(And their goddamn stolen nukes.)

'Come on. What am I going to tell the vice president tonight?'

Eric took a deep breath. 'From the top?'

'Whatever order you choose.'

'Well, shall we get the small stuff out of the way first?'

'Start.'

Eric shrugged. 'I don't like to admit this, but the current operations we've got in train are all hosed. CLEANSWEEP has driven into a ditch and we're lucky we got anybody back at all – going by Agent MacDonald's observations, they got caught in the crossfire during some kind of red-on-red incident. We're lucky Rich was able to exfiltrate in good order, else we wouldn't even know that much. I think we can write off the alpha team and Agent Fleming, they're two days overdue and they've overrun their provisioning.

'On the plus side, Rich got out. We've continued to monitor the CLEANSWEEP team's dead letter drops from the OLIGARCH positions, and they look clean. The fact that nobody's visited or tried to stake them out suggests that the bad guys didn't take any of our men alive. So CLEANSWEEP isn't blown, and once we get more field-qualified linguists prepped we should be able to reactivate it – possibly in as little as three weeks. The real problem we've got is that we're multiply bottlenecked: bottlenecked on linguists, bottlenecked on logistics, bottlenecked on general intelligence. If we could find one of their safe houses we'd be in place to run COLDPLAY against them, but the trail's gone cold and there's a limit to how long I can hold on to an AFSOCOM team with no mission – they're needed in the Middle East.'

'Hmm.' James rolled his pen between the finger and thumb of his left hand. His lips whitened, forming a tight, disapproving line. Agent Smith, with a small lapel-pin crucifix and a Ph.D. from Harvard: 'I might be able to shake something loose on one of those fronts presently. But Mr. Cheney isn't going to be happy about the lack of progress.'

'Well, I'm not happy either!' Eric dug his fingers into the arms of his chair. His damaged carpal tunnels sent twinges of protest running up his arms. 'If you think I enjoy losing agents and trained special forces teams . . . hell.' He raised a hand and ran numb, tingling fingertips through his thinning hair. 'I'm sorry. But this failure mode wasn't anticipated. Nobody expected them to blow up the fucking palace and start a civil war in the garden. Maybe we should have anticipated it, if we'd been better informed about their internal political situation, but they don't exactly have newspapers over there and even if they did, we'd have trouble reading them. We'd have to have been fucking mind readers to spot a bunch of plotters running a coup!'

'Language, Colonel, please.'

'Shi – sorry.' Eric shook his head, angry at his own loss of control. 'I'm upset. We've now lost two high-clearance, high-value agents and an AFSOCOM specops team and we've only really been up and running for fourteen weeks.'

'I feel your pain,' James said dryly. Eric stared at him, taken aback. 'But I'm going to have to brief the vice president tonight on all the progress we haven't been making, and believe me, chewing on ground glass would be less painful,' he added. 'Now. I've heard from Herz. How's CLANCY going?'

'Badly.' CLANCY was the ongoing investigation into the nuclear device that Source GREENSLEEVES claimed he'd planted somewhere in the Boston/Cambridge area, before he'd so inconveniently managed to get himself killed. 'We hadn't found anything really noteworthy – a couple of meth labs, a walled-up cellar full of moonshine left over from the nineteen twenties, that sort of thing – until Judith turned up her anomaly yesterday. I was half-convinced GREENSLEEVES was lying to us, but now – well, I don't think we can afford to take that risk.' He shivered. 'Just who the he-heck stuck a B53 bomb on blocks in a warehouse and set it to go off on a ten-year timer?'

'Is that a question?' Dr. James leaned back in his chair,

steepling his fingertips again, and the piranha-like set of his lips quirked slightly. *Is he trying to smile?* wondered Eric.

'Only if I'm not treading on any classified toes,' Smith said warily.

'It's not a healthy question to ask. So I suggest you don't ask me about it. Then I won't have to tell you any lies.'

'Ah.' Smith dry-swallowed.

'Even if I did know anything about it. Which I don't,' James said, with a twitch of one eyebrow that spoke volumes.

'Right. Right.' *Change the subject, quick.* The fact that they were sitting in a secure conference cell that was regularly swept for bugs didn't mean that nobody was listening in, or at least recording the session for posterity: all it meant was that nobody outside the charmed circle of the national security infrastructure was eavesdropping. *But what kind of black operation would involve us nuking one of our own cities?* Smith filed the question away for later.

'Well, we're looking for a needle in a haystack. The original idea of taking the county planner's database and data mining it for suspicious activities is sound in principle, but it yields too many false positives in a city the size of this one. I mean, there are tens of thousands of business premises, many tens of thousands of homes with garages or large basements, and if only one percent of them flag as positives for things like lack of visible tenants or occupants, zero phone use but basic utility draw for heating, and so on, we're swamped. It might be a bomb installation, or it could equally well be Uncle Alfred's old house and he died six months ago and the estate's still in probate or something. Or it could be an overenthusiastic horticulturist trying to breed a better pot plant. On the other hand, hopefully the neutron scattering spectroscopes our NIRT liaisons are getting next week will allow us to make an exhaustive roving search. And we can cover for it easily, by telling the truth – we're testing a bomb detector for terrorist nukes. Everyone will assume we're worried about al-Qaeda, and if we actually do find GREENSLEEVES's gadget . . . well, do you suppose the VP would like to make hay with that?'

The raised eyebrow was back. 'I suppose you have a point.' James nodded slowly. 'Yes, that would kill two terrorist threats with one stone. What else do you have for me?'

'Well, I'm not saying we're not going to get another break – I think it's only a matter of time – but I can't give you a time scale for quantum leaps. I think if we can reactivate CLEANSWEEP, or figure out some way around the bottleneck in our logistics chain, we might be able to progress on CLANCY through other avenues. I mean, if we can get our hands on some useful intelligence about the Clan's nuclear capability, that might open up some avenues of inquiry about where GREENSLEEVES got his hands on a gadget, and where it might be now. But for the time being, we're not really pursuing a specifically intelligence-led investigation. Getting back into the Gruinmarkt is, in my opinion, vital – and the more force we can project there, the better.'

'I see.' James made a brief note on his pad. 'Well, I'm hoping we'll have a solution to the logistics issues shortly.'

'More couriers? A target for COLDPLAY?'

'Something better.' He looked smug.

Eric leaned forward. 'Tell me. Whatever you can. Is this more of that harebrained physics stuff from Livermore?'

'Of course.' Then something terrifying happened: Dr. James actually smiled. 'I think it's time to bring you in the loop on the, as you put it, logistics side of things. There's a cross-disciplinary team under Professor Armstrong from UCSD who've been working on a subject under, um, closed conditions. They haven't worked out everything that's going on yet, but they've made some fascinating progress that points to a physical explanation for their anomalous capability. I'm going to be flying out there tomorrow morning, and I was hoping you could join me.'

Eric glanced at his desk. It'd mean another couple of nights away from Gillian and the boys, and more apologies and tense silences at home, but it needed to be done. 'As long as I can be back here by Friday – if nothing new comes up in the meantime – I should be able to fit it in.' Briefly, he let his bitterness show: 'It's not as if I'm needed for the post-CLEANSWEEP debrief, or to report CLANCY as closed out.'

'Then you'll accompany me.' Dr. James rose abruptly, his expression as warm as a killer robot's. 'Now if you'll excuse me, I have an appointment it wouldn't do to be late to . . .'

'You called for me, sir.'

'Indeed I did, indeed I did. I trust you've been keeping well. Any trouble getting here?'

'Only the – not really. Not given the prevailing afflictions. I was most surprised to be summoned, though. Under the circumstances.'

'Well, you're here now. Have a seat. Make yourself comfortable, this may take some time – I must apologize in advance for any interruptions, I am somewhat busy at present.'

'There is nothing to apologize for, sir.'

'Ah, but there will be. I'm afraid I've got another delicate task for you. One that will require you to visit the new world and spend some considerable length of time working there on your own initiative.'

'But, the fighting! Surely I'm of use there?'

(*Clink of glassware.*) 'Glass of wine?'

'Ah – yes, thank you, sir.'

(*More clinking of glassware.*) 'Your health, my lady.'

'And yours, your grace. Sir, I don't understand. Is this more urgent than dealing with the pretender? As a need of immediacy?'

'Yes.'

'Oh.' (*Pause.*) 'Then I'll do it, of course. Whatever mysterious task you have in mind.'

'I wouldn't be so fast to accept. You may hear me out and deem it a conflict of loyalty.'

'Conflict of –' (*Pause.*) 'Oh.'

'Yes. I am afraid you're not going to like this.'

'It's about her grace, isn't it?'

'Partly. No, let me be honest: mostly. But, hmm, let me think . . . how clear are you on her current circumstances?'

(*Tensely.*) 'She didn't tell me anything. Before – whatever.'

'Indeed not, and I did not summon you to accuse you of any misdeeds. But. What is your understanding of what she did?'

(*Pause.*) 'Lady Helge has many bad habits, but her incurable curiosity is by far the worst of them. I was led to believe that she stuck her nose into some business or other of Henryk's, and he slapped her down for it. Confinement to a supervised apartment under house arrest, no contact with anyone who might conspire with her, living on bread and water, that kind of thing. Is there more to it?'

'Yes, you could say that.' (*Sigh.*) 'You could hold me responsible, as well. I – placed certain evidence where I *expected* her to encounter it. It was in the context of a larger operation which you are not privy to. I hoped she would rattle some cages and shake loose some useful fruit that was previously hanging out of reach. She has a tendency to stir things up, you will agree?'

'I'm afraid so . . .'

'The trouble is, she – well, she used unacceptable methods of inquiry: and worse, she allowed herself to be caught. Which indeed drew out certain conspirators at court, but not the ones I was looking for and not in the manner I had hoped. I trust this will go no further than your ears, but . . . she tampered with the Post.'

'You're kidding!'

'I wish I was.'

(*Pause.*) (*Muttered expletive.*)

'I didn't hear that, my lady.'

'I'm sorry sir, my tongue must have stumbled . . . that's terrible! I can see why she didn't talk to me first, if that is what she was thinking of doing, but how *could* she?'

'I'm afraid that's not the important question right now. Whyever and however, she did it – and was caught. Henryk had no option but to act fast to secure her obedience, even though that cost us any use we could hope to have made of her in the original plan: as it is, he has been accused of undue leniency by certain elderly parties, and I have had to call in many favors to placate the postal commission – or in some cases, to buy their silence. She has not been charged with the offense, and will not be: instead, Henryk offered her a way out – if she would bring us a child in the direct line of succession. She was as reluctant as you can imagine, but agreed to his proposal in the end.'

'I had no idea!'

'You weren't meant to: the groundwork was prepared in the deepest secrecy, and her marriage to Prince Creon announced – '

'Creon? The Idiot?'

'Please – sit down! Sit down at once, I say! . . . I'm not going to repeat myself!'

(*Pause.*) 'I'm sorry, sir.'

'No you're not. You're outraged, aren't you? It offends you because like all young women who've spent overmuch time in the other world you have absorbed some of their expectations, and the idea of an arranged marriage – no, let me be blunt, a forced marriage – is a personal affront to you. Am I right?'

(*Sullen.*) 'Yes.'

'Well, so it may be. And the idea of tampering with the Post does not also offend you?'

(*Pause.*) 'But that's – that's – '

'Need I remind you of the normal punishment for tampering with the Post?'

'No. I understand.'

'Are you sure? Let me be blunt: the countess Helge committed a serious crime, for which she might have been executed. She could not be trusted with the corvée anymore. Baron Henryk managed to make an alternative arrangement, by which the countess might be of sufficient use to us to justify sparing her, and might in time redeem the stain from her honor. As a punishment, I will concede that it was severe. But she was given the choice: and she accepted it of her own free will, albeit without grace.'

'Huh! I can't imagine she'd have taken such an imposition lightly. But Creon of all people – '

'Creon's grandmother, the queen mother, was one of us. Creon, unlike his brother the pretender, was outer family. The progeny of Creon and Helge would have been outer family beyond doubt, and half likely world-walkers as well.'

'But he's defective! How do we know they wouldn't have inherited the – '

'We know. We know why he was defective, too. He was poisoned as a child, not born that way. But it's irrelevant now. Creon – and the queen mother – died when the pretender made his move.

I believe they, and Helge, were in fact the real targets of the attack.'

'Surely, he's the legitimate heir in any case? He didn't need to do that!'

'You are too well meaning to make a politician, my lady. If Helge had borne children to Creon, Egon would have good reason to fear for his life. If Egon's reading of our consensus was that we wanted to place one of our own upon the throne, then his action was ruthless but entirely rational.'

'So Creon is dead? And the queen mother? What about Helge?'

'Ah. Well, you see, that's why I wanted to talk to you. There are more important tasks for you to be about than preparing a doppelgängered ambush for the pretender to the throne.'

(*Pause.*) 'You've lost her. Haven't you?'

'I very much fear that you are right.'

'Shit.'

'I do not know that she is still alive. But she has not been confirmed dead; her body was not found in the wreckage. And there are other reasons to hope she survived. She was reported to be speaking to James Lee, the hostage, shortly before the attack: he passed her something small.'

'Oh. You think she's in New Britain somewhere?'

'That would be the logical deduction. And were circumstances different I would expect her to report in within a day or two. But right now – well. She was told, in regrettably unequivocal terms, that if she world-walked without permission she would be killed. And we have systematically alienated her affections.'

'Why, damn it, sir? I mean, what purpose did it serve?'

(*Pause.*) 'As I indicated, I hoped she would – suitably motivated – lead me to something I wanted. But she is a dangerous weapon to wield, and in this case, she misfired. Then circumstances spun out of my independent control, and . . . you see how things are?'

(*Long pause.*) 'What do you want me to do?' (*Pause.*) 'I assume you want me to find her, wherever she's gone to ground, and bring her back?'

'You are one of the few people she is likely to trust. So that would be a logical deduction, would it not?'

(*Suspiciously*.) 'What else?'

(*Pause*.) 'I trust that you will do everything within your ability to find her and bring her back into the fold. To convince her, you may convey to her my assurances that she will face no retribution for having fled on this occasion – given the circumstances, it was entirely understandable. You may also remind her that Creon is dead, and the arrangement made on his behalf is therefore terminated. The events of the past week are swept away as if they never transpired.' (*Pause*.) 'You may also want to tell her that Baron Henryk was killed in the fighting. If she promises to cooperate fully, she has my personal guarantee of her safety.'

'That's not all, is it?'

(*Long pause*.) 'No.'

'Then . . . ?'

'I very much fear that Helge will *not* return willingly. She may want to go to ground on her own – or she might make overtures to the lost cousins. Worse, she might go back to her compulsive digging. She stumbled across a project that is not yet politically admissible: if she exposes it before the council, it could do immense damage. And worst of all, she might seek to obtain a copy of the primary knot and use it to return to her own Boston, then contact the authorities. They will believe her if she goes to them, and she is in a position to do even more damage than Matthias if she wants.'

'You're saying you want me to kill her if she's turned traitor.'

'I *don't* want you to kill her. However, it is absolutely vital that she be prevented from defecting to the new agency the Americans have set up. She could do us immense – immeasurable – damage if she did, and I would rather see her dead than turned into a weapon against us. Do you see now why I warned that you might see this as a conflict of loyalty?'

(*Long pause*.) 'Oh yes, indeed, sir.' (*Pause*.) 'If I say no, what happens?'

'Then I will have to send someone else. I don't know who, yet – we are grievously shorthanded in this task, are we not? Likely it will be someone who doesn't know her well, and doesn't care whether she can be salvaged.' (*Pause.*) 'I am not sending you to kill her, I am sending you to salvage her if at all possible. But I will not send you unless you are prepared to do your duty to the Clan, should it be necessary. Do you swear to me that you will do so?'

'I – yes, your grace. My liege. I so swear: I will do everything in my power to return Lady Helge voh Thorold d'Hjorth to your custody, alive. And I will take any measure necessary to prevent her adding her number to our enemies. Any –' (*Pause.*) '– measure.'

'Good. Your starting point is inconveniently located – she will have crossed over near the palace, from Niejwein – but I am sure you are equal to the task of hunting her down. You may draw any necessary resources from second security directorate funds; talk to the desk officer. Harald is running things today. You'll want a support team for the insertion, and a disguise.'

'I have a working cover identity on the other side already, sir. Was there anything else I should know?'

'Oh yes, as a matter of fact there is. It nearly slipped my mind. Hmm.'

'Sir?' (*Pause.*) 'Your grace?'

'Ah. Definitely a problem.' (*Pause.*) 'The arrangement with Creon . . . before the betrothal, she was visited more than once by Dr. ven Hjalmar. At the behest of Baron Henryk, I thought, but when I made inquiries I discovered it had been suggested by none other than Patricia.'

'Patricia? What's she doing suggesting – hey, isn't Ven Hjalmar the fertility specialist?'

'Yes, Brilliana, and the treatment he subjected the countess Helge to is absolutely unconscionable; but I believe it was intended as insurance against the Idiot being unable to . . . you know. Be that as it may, he *did* it. Consequently, you have about twelve weeks to find Helge and bring her back. After that time . . . well, you know what happens to women who world-walk while they're pregnant, don't you?'

END TRANSCRIPT

TRAVELERS

It was a warm day in New London, beneath the overcast. A slow onshore breeze was blowing, but the air remained humid and close beneath a stifling inversion layer that trapped the sooty, smelly effusions of a hundred thousand oil-burning engines too close to the ground for the comfort of tired lungs.

Two figures walked up the street that led away from Hogarth Villas, arm in arm: a tall, stooped man, his hair prematurely graying, and a woman, her shoulder-length black hair bundled up beneath a wide-brimmed sun hat. The man carried a valise in his free hand. They were dressed respectably but boringly, his suit clean but slightly shiny at elbows and seat, her outfit clearly well worn.

'Where now?' Miriam asked as they reached the end of the row of brick villas and paused at the curb, waiting for a streetcar to jangle and buzz past with a whine of hot electric motors. 'Are we going straight back to Boston, or do you have business to attend to first?'

'Come on.' He stepped out into the street and crossed hastily.

She followed: 'Well?'

'We need to take the Northside 'car, three miles or so downtown.' He was staring at a wooden post with a streetcar timetable pasted to a board hanging from it. 'Then a New Line 'car to St. Peter's Cross. I think there's a salon there.' He glanced sidelong at her hair. 'By the time we've got that out of the way – well, unless we find a mail express, I don't think we'll get back to Boston tonight, so I suggest we take a room in one of the station hotels and entrain at first light tomorrow.'

'Right.' She shrugged, uncomfortable. 'Erasmus, when I crossed over, I, um, I didn't bring any money . . .'

He glanced up and down the street, then reached into an inner pocket and withdrew a battered wallet. 'One, two – all right. Five pounds.' He curled the large banknotes between bony fingertips and slipped them into her hand. 'Try not to spend it all at once.'

Miriam swallowed. One pound – the larger unit of currency here – had what felt like the purchasing power of a couple of hundred dollars back home. 'You're very generous.'

'I owe you.'

'No, you –' She paused, trying to get a grip on the sense of embarrassed gratitude. 'Are you still taking the tablets?'

'Yes. It's amazing. But that's not what I meant. I still owe you for the last consignment you sold me.' A shadow crossed his face. 'You needn't worry about money for the time being. There are lockouts and beggars defying the poor laws on every other street corner. Nobody has money to spend. If I was truly dependent on my business for a living I would be as thin as a sheet of paper by now.'

'There's no money?' She took his arm again. 'What's the economy doing?'

'Nothing good. We're effectively at war, which means there's a blockade of our Atlantic trade and shipping raiders in the Pacific, so it's hit overseas trade badly. His majesty dismissed parliament and congress last month, you know. He's trying to run things directly, and the treasury's near empty: we'll likely as not be stopped at the Excise bench as we arrive in Boston, you know, just to see if there's a silver teapot hiding in this valise that could be better used to buy armor plate for the fleet.'

'That's not good.' Miriam blinked, feeling stupid. *How not good?* she wondered uneasily. 'Is the currency deflating?'

'I'd have said yes, but prices are going up too. And unemployment. This war crisis is simply too damned soon after the last one, and the harvest last year was a disaster, and the army is overstretched dealing with civil disorder – that means local rebellions against the tax inspectorate – on the great plains and down south.' It took Miriam a moment to remember that *down south* didn't mean the southern United States – it meant the former Portuguese and Spanish colonies that the New British crown had taken by force in the early nineteenth century, annexing to the empire around the time they'd been rebelling against their colonial masters across the ocean in the world she'd grown up in. 'And the price of oil is going up. It's doubled since this time last year.'

Miriam blinked again. The dust and the smelly urban air were getting to her eyes. That, and something about Burgeson's complaint sounded familiar . . . 'How's the government coping?' she asked.

He chuckled. 'It isn't: as I said, the king dismissed it. We're back into the days of *fiat reale*, like the way King Frederick the Second ran things during the slaveowners' rebellion.' He noticed her expression and did a double-take of his own. 'Seventeen ninety-seven to eighteen hundred and four,' he explained. 'I can find you a book on it if it interests you. Long and the short is, there was a war across the Atlantic and the states of Carolina, Virginia, and Columbia tried to rebel against the Crown, in collusion with the French. They nearly mustered a parliamentary majority for secession, too: invited in a French pretender to take their crown. So Frederick dissolved the traitor parliament and went through the plantation states with fire and the sword. He wasn't merciful, like your, ah, Mr. Lincoln. Frederick was not stupid, though: he recognized the snares of unencumbered absolute power, and he reconvened the estates and allowed them to elect a new parliament – once he'd gibbeted the traitors every twenty feet along the road from Georgetown to New London.'

'You're saying we're under martial law here, aren't you?'

'No, it's worse: it's the feudal skull showing through the mummified skin of our constitutional settlement.' Erasmus stared into the near distance, then stuck his arm out in the direction of the street. A moment later a streetcar lumbered into view round the curve of the road, wheels grinding against the rails as it trundled to a halt next to the stop. 'After you, ma'am.'

Miriam climbed onto the streetcar's platform, waited while Erasmus paid, then climbed the stairs to the upper deck, her mind whirling. Things have been going downhill fast, she realized: war, a liquidity crisis, and martial law? Despite the muggy warmth of the day, she shivered. Looking around, she realized the streetcar was almost empty. The conductor's bell dinged and the 'car moved off slowly as Erasmus came up the stairs, his hair blowing in the breeze that came over the open top of the vehicle. Sparks crackled from the pickup on top of the chimney-like tower behind her. 'I didn't realize things were so bad,' she remarked.

'Oh, they're bad all right,' he replied a little too loudly: 'I'll be lucky to make my rent this month.'

She gave him an old-fashioned look as he sat down beside her. 'Afraid of eavesdroppers?' she muttered.

'Yes,' he whispered, almost too quietly to hear.

Whoops. Miriam shut up and stared out the window as the city unrolled to either side. The layout was bewildering; from the citadel and palaces of Manhattan Island – here called New London – to the suburbs sprawling across the mainland around it, everything was different. There was no orderly grid, but an insane mishmash of looping and forking curlicues, as if village paths laid out by drunkards had grown together, merging at the edges: high streets and traffic circles and weird viaducts with houses built on top of them. Tenement blocks made of soot-stained brick, with not a single fire escape in sight. In the distance, blocky skyscrapers on the edge of the administrative district around the palace loomed on the skyline, but they weren't a patch on her New York, the New York of the Chrysler and the Empire State buildings and, not long ago, the Twin Towers. High above them a propeller aircraft droned slowly across the underside of the clouds, trailing a thin brown smear of exhaust. For a moment she felt very alone: a tourist in the third world who'd been told her ticket home was invalid. *I wanted to escape, didn't I? To cut loose and go where the Clan can't find me.* She pondered the irony of the change in her circumstances: it all seemed so long ago, now.

'Nearly there,' said Burgeson, and she noticed his hand tightening on the back of the chair in front of them.

'Nearly where?'

'New Line Crossing. Come on.' He unfolded from the seat and rolled towards the staircase, pulling the bell chain on his way. Miriam scrambled to follow him.

There were more people here, and the buildings were higher, and the air smelled of coal smoke and damp even in the summer heat. Miriam followed Burgeson across the street, dodging a horse-drawn cart piled high with garbage and a chuffing steam taxi. A lot of the people hereabouts were badly dressed, their clothing worn and threadbare and their cheeks gaunt: a wheeled stall at one corner was doing a brisk trade, doling out cupfuls of stew or soup to a long queue of shuffling men and women. She hurried to keep up with Erasmus as he walked past the soup kitchen. *Stagflation, that's it,* she remembered. *The treasury's rolling the presses to print their way out of the fiscal crisis triggered by the war and the crop failure, but the real dynamic is deflationary, so wages and jobs are being squeezed even as prices are going up because the currency is devaluing . . .* She remembered the alleyway three nights before, the beggar threatening her with a knife, and abruptly felt sick at the implications. *They were starving,* she realized. *This is the capital. What's going on, out in the boonies?*

Erasmus stopped so suddenly that she nearly ran into his back. 'Follow me,' he muttered, then lurched into the road and stuck an arm out. 'Cab!' he called, then stepped back sharply to avoid being run over by a steamer. 'Get in,' he told her, then climbed in behind. 'St. Peter's Cross,' he called forward to the driver: 'An extra shilling if you can get us there fast!'

'Aye, well.'

The driver nodded at him and kicked the throttle open. The cab lurched forward with a loud chuffing noise and a trail of steam as it accelerated, throwing Miriam backwards into the padded seat. Erasmus landed at the other side from her, facing. She grinned at him experimentally. 'What's the hurry?'

'Company.' Burgeson jerked his chin sideways. A strip of cobbled street rattled beneath the cab's wheels. 'We're best off without them.'

'We were followed?' A sudden sense of dread twisted her stomach. 'Who by?'

'Can't tell.' He reached out and slid the window behind the driver's head closed. 'Probably just a double-cross boy or a thugster, but you can't be too sure. Worst case, a freelance thief-taker trying to make his quota. Nobody you'd want to be nabbed by, that's for sure.'

'In broad daylight?'

He shrugged. 'Times are hard.'

She stared at him. His closed expression spoke volumes. 'What am I going to do?' she asked. 'My business. My house. They'll be under surveillance.'

He raised an eyebrow. 'I'm sure they will be.'

'But what can I – '

'You can start by relaxing,' he said. 'And letting the salon dye your hair. Then, once we have checked into the hotel, if you'd honor me with your presence at dinner, you can tell me all about your recent travails. How does that sound?'

'That sounds –' *This is going to be tougher than I realized,* she thought, as the cab lurched around a corner and pulled in opposite an imposing row of store windows near the base of a large stone building. '– acceptable.'

*

Late afternoon in NYC, midmorning in San Francisco. Colonel Smith had brought a laptop and a briefcase full of work with him on the Air Force Gulfstream, holing up at the back of the cabin while Dr. James worked the phones continuously up front. Dr. James had brought along a small coterie of administrative gofers from NSC, and two Secret Service bodyguards: the latter had sized Smith up immediately and, after confirming he was on their watch list, politely asked him to stay where they could keep their eyes on him. Which was fine by Eric. Every time he ventured down from one of the FTO aeries he got a sensation between his shoulder blades as if a sniper's crosshairs were crawling around there. Even Gillian had noticed him getting jumpy, staring at passing cars when they went places together – in the few snatched hours of domesticity that were all this job was leaving him. *Bastards,* he thought absently as he paged through the daily briefing roundup, looking for any sign that things weren't going as badly as he feared. *I hope this isn't a waste of time . . .*

Dr. James had been as infuriatingly unreadable as usual, saying nothing beyond the cryptic hints about some project at UC Berkeley. Lawrence Livermore Labs weren't exactly on campus in Berkeley – it wasn't even a daily commute – but that seemed to be where they were going. The gray Gulfstream executive jet touched down at San Francisco International and taxied towards a fenced-in compound where a couple of limos and two SUVs full of security contractors were waiting for them. 'Take the second car,' James had told Eric: 'The driver will take you to Westgate badge office to check you in before bringing you to JAUNT BLUE.' He nodded. 'I've got prior clearance and an appointment before I join you.'

'Okay.' Eric swung his briefcase into the back of the Lincoln. 'See you there,' he added, but James had already turned on his heel and was heading for the other car.

It took more than an hour to drive out to the laboratory complex, during which time Eric ran and reran his best scenarios for the coming meeting, absent-mindedly working his gyroball exerciser. *James wouldn't be visiting in person if he didn't think it was important, which means he'll be reporting to the vice president. Progress. But what are they doing here?* He'd pulled the files on the only professor called Armstrong who was currently on faculty at UCSD: some kind of expert on quantum computing. Then he'd had Agent Delaney do a quick academic literature search. A year ago, Armstrong had co-authored a paper with a neurobiologist, conclusively demolishing the Penrose microtubule hypothesis, coming up with a proof that quantum noise would cause decoherence in any circuit relying on tubulin-bound GTP, whatever the hell that was. Then he'd written another paper, about quantum states in large protein molecules, before falling mysteriously silent – along with his research assistants and postdocs. The previous year they'd put their names on eighteen papers: this year, the total was just three, and those were merely citations as co-authors with other research groups.

Quantum computing. Neurobiology. Quantum states in large protein molecules. Eric shook his head over the densely written papers Delaney had copied for him. *Then Armstrong dropped off the map, and now James is taking me to see him. I wonder if this means what I think it means.* The gyroball whirred down as he shifted it to his left hand, twisting his wrist continually, trying to drive out the stiffness and shooting pains by constant exercise.

Security at the sprawling laboratory complex – more like a huge university campus than anything else – was pervasive but not heavy-handed at first. His driver, Agent Simms, smoothed the way as he

373

checked in his mobile phone, laptop, and the hand exerciser with the security guards. 'You ready to visit JAUNT BLUE now, sir?'

'Take me there.'

Back in the car, it was another five-minute drive past endless rows of windowless buildings. Eric sat back, watching the chain-link fence and the site road unfold around him. One DoD site looked much like any other, but there were signs here for those who knew what to look for. Inner fences. Curious long berms humped up beneath a carpet of sunburned grass, like state secrets casually swept out of the view of passing spy satellites by a giant security-obsessed housekeeper. Driving past some clearly disused buildings, Simms turned into a side road then pulled over in front of a gate. 'Okay, sir, we walk from here. Building forty-seven.'

'Right.' Eric opened the door and got out, feeling the heat start to suck him dry. Late morning and it was already set to be a burning hot summer day. 'Which way?'

'Over here.' Simms walked over to one of the disused warehouse units. The walls were simple metal sidings and the doors and windows were missing, the building itself just a hollow shell.

'Here? But it's abandoned – '

'It's meant to look that way. Building forty-seven. If you'd follow me? Sir?'

The secret service agent was clearly sure of himself. *Someone's spent a lot on camouflage,* Eric told himself, clutching his briefcase and following behind. *What's going on?* The inside of the warehouse was no more promising than the exterior. Huge ceiling panels were missing, evidently the holes where air conditioning units had been stripped out. The concrete loading bay at the rear of the building was dusty and decrepit, the doors missing. Simms walked over to the near side, where a rusty trailer was propped up on blocks. Eric glanced past him, and for the first time noticed something out of place – a black dome, about the size of his fist, fastened to the wall somewhere above head height. Closed circuit cameras? In an abandoned shed?

Simms climbed a ramshackle flight of steps and opened the door of the trailer. 'This way, sir.'

Eric relaxed, everything clicking into place. The camera, the abandoned trailer, the shadows thick and black under the trailer – it was all intended to deal with visitors from the Clan. 'Okay, I'm coming.' He climbed the steps and found himself in a small lobby behind Simms, who was waiting in front of an inner door with a peephole set in it. The door was made of steel and opened from the inside.

'Agent Simms, Colonel Smith of FTO, visiting JAUNT BLUE,' Simms announced.

A speaker crackled. 'Close the outer door now.'

Eric reached back and pulled the door shut. The inner door buzzed for a moment, then whined open sideways to reveal the bare metal walls of a freight elevator. 'Neat,' he said admiringly as they descended towards the tunnels under the laboratory complex. 'If you can't go up without being obvious, go down.'

'This all used to be part of the high-energy physics group, back in the sixties,' Simms said laconically. 'They repurposed it this year. There are several entrances. Dr. James told me to show you in through the back door.' A back door disguised as a derelict building, complete with spy cameras and probably some kind of remotely controlled defense system: whatever James had going on down here, he didn't welcome unexpected visitors.

The freight elevator ground to a halt and Eric did a double-take. *Jesus, I've just fallen into* The Man from U.N.C.L.E.! He glanced around at the rough-finished concrete walls, fluorescent lights, innumerable pipes and conduits bolted overhead – and at the end of the passage, a vast, brightly lit space.

'Badges, please.' The Marine guards waiting in an alcove off one side of the corridor were armed, and not for show. Smith extended the badge he'd been issued and waited while one of the guards checked him off a list. 'You may proceed, sir.'

'Where's Dr. James's group?' he asked Simms's receding back.

'Follow me, sir.'

Smith followed, trying not to gape too obviously. He was used to security procedures on Air Force bases and some other types of sensitive installations, but he'd never seen anything quite like this. The main tunnel was domed overhead, rising to a peak about fifty feet up; it stretched to infinity ahead and behind. There were no windows, but more conduits and the boxy, roaring ducts of a huge air conditioning system overhead. The concrete piles that had once supported a mile-long linear accelerator were still visible on the floor, but the linac itself had long since been removed and replaced by beige office partitions surrounding a forlorn-looking clump of cubicles, and a line of mobile office trailers that stretched along one wall like a subterranean passenger train. The train didn't go on forever, though, and after they'd walked a couple of hundred feet from the 'back door' they reached the end of the column. Beyond it, the concrete tunnel stretched dizzyingly towards a blank wall in the distance, empty but for a grid of colored lines painted on the floor. *Lots of room for expansion,* he realized.

Simms gestured at the trailer on the edge of the empty floor space. 'Dr. James uses Room 65 as his site office when he's visiting. I believe he's in a meeting until fifteen hundred, but he told me to tell you that Dr. Hu will be along to give you the dog and pony tour at eleven thirty. If you make yourself at home, I'll find Dr. Hu and get things started.'

Eric paused at the door to the trailer. 'Dr. James didn't exactly tell me what it is you people do out here,' he said slowly. 'Can you fill me in on what to expect?'

Simms frowned. 'I think I ought to leave that to Dr. Hu,' he said.

'Is Dr. Hu one of Professor Armstrong's team?'

Simms nodded. 'I'll go get him.'

'Okay.' Eric climbed the step up to the site office trailer and went inside to wait.

BEGIN TRANSCRIPT

'You wanted to s-see me, sir?'

'Yes, yes I did. Have a seat, lad. Your parents: doing well, I hope?'

'. . .'

'Calm down, there's a good fellow. Try to relax, I'm not going to bite your head off. I'm sure they'll be perfectly fine, current

emergency notwithstanding. No, the pretender isn't about to go
haring off into the Sennheur marches, and if he does, they'll
have plenty of warning to evacuate. Now, where was I . . . ? Ah,
yes. I wanted to ask you about your studies.'

(*Mumble.*)

'Yes, I know. In the current situation, it's difficult. But I think it may
be possible for you to go back there in the fall, if things work out
well.'

'But I'll be behind. I should be working right now, with my
roommates – it's not like a regular school. They'll want to know
where I was while they were working on our project.'

(*Snorts.*) 'Well, you'll just have to tell them you were called away by
urgent family business. A dying relative, or something. Don't look
at me like that: worse things happen in wartime. If you go back
to your laboratory at all you will be luckier than many of our
less-talented children, Huw. But as it happens, I have a little
research project for you that I think will smooth your way. One
that you and your talking-shop friends will be able to get your
teeth into, and that will be much more profitable in the long
term.'

'A research project? But you don't need someone like me – I mean,
the kind of research your staff do, begging your pardons in
advance, your grace, aren't exactly where my aptitude lies – '

'Correct. Which is why I want you for a different kind of research.'

'I don't understand.'

'On the contrary, I think you'll understand all too well.' (*Pause.*) 'Red
or white?'

'Red, please.' (*Sound of glass being filled.*) 'Thank you very much.'

'Show me your locket.'

'My – ' (*Coughing.*) ' – locket? Uh, sure. Here – '

'Put it there. Yes, open. Don't focus on it. Now, this one. You can see
the difference if you look at them – not too close, now! What do
you think?'

'I'm – excuse me, it's easier to study them if you cover part of the
design and compare sections. Less distracting.'

'You sound as if you've done that before.'

(*Hurriedly.*) 'No sir! But it's only logical. We've been using the Clan
 sigil for generations. Surely – ' (*Pause.*) ' – Hey, I think the upper
 right arc of this one is different!'
'It is.' (*Sound of small items being cleared away.*) 'It came from our
 long-lost, lamentably living, cousins. The Lees. Who, it would
 appear, discovered the hard way that redesigning the knotwork
 can have catastrophic consequences.'
(*Pause.*) 'I'd heard they used a different design. But . . .' (*Pause.*)
 'Nobody thought to experiment? Ever?'
'Some of the Lee family did. Either they failed to world-walk, or they
 didn't come back. After they lost a couple, their elders banned
 further experimentation. For our part, with no indication that
 other realms than the two we know of might exist, who would
 bother even trying? Especially as most of the simple variations
 don't work. Look at yourself, Sir Huw! The finest education we
 can buy you, a graduate student at MIT, and you, too, took the
 family talent for granted.'
'I, I think – hell, I assumed that if it was possible to do something, it
 would already have been done, surely?'
'That's the assumption everyone who has given the subject a
 moment's thought comes up with. It tends to deter
 experimentation, doesn't it, if you believe an alley of inquiry
 has already been tried and found wanting? Even if the
 assumption is wrong.'
'I – I feel dumb.'
(*Pause.*) 'You're not the only one of us who's kicking himself. There
 have been a number of unexplained disappearances over the
 centuries, and simple murder surely doesn't explain all of them
 – but the point is, nobody who succeeded came back to tell the
 tale. Which brings me to the matter at hand. When Helge
 reappeared with the family Lee in unwilling thrall, I had reason
 to send for the archivists. And to have my staff conduct certain
 preliminary tests. It appears that the Lee family design has
 never been tested in the United States of America. And our
 Clan symbol doesn't work in New Britain. That is, it doesn't in
 the areas that correspond to the Gruinmarkt. The east coast.

But that's all we know, Huw, and it worries me. In the United States, the authorities have made their most effective attack on our postal service for a hundred years. This would be a crisis in its own right, but on top of that we have the pretender to the throne raising the old aristocracy against us in Niejwein. He can be contained eventually – we have means of communication and transport that will permit us to meet his army with crushing force whenever he moves – but that, too, would be crisis enough on its own. And I cannot afford to deal with any new surprises. So I want you – I have discussed this with members of the council – to set your very expensively acquired skills to work and do what our none-too-inquisitive ancestors failed to do.'

'You want me to, to find out how the sigil works? Or . . . what?'

(*Clink of glassware.*) 'When there was just one knot, life was simple. But we've got two, now, and three worlds. I want to know if there are more worlds out there. And more knots. I want to know why sometimes trying a design gives the world-walker a headache, and why sometimes the experimenter vanishes. I want to know, Sir Huw, so that I can map out the terrain of the battlefield we find ourselves on.'

'Is it really that bad?'

'I don't know, boy. None of us know. That's the whole point. Can you do it? More importantly, what would you do?'

'Hmm.' (*Pause.*) 'Well, I'd start by documenting what we already know. Maps and times. Then there are a couple of avenues I would pursue. On the one hand, we have two knots. I can see if the Clan knot is failing to work in New Britain because of a terrain anomaly. If, say, it leads to a world where the world-walker would emerge in the middle of a tree, or underwater, that would explain why nobody's been able to use it. And I'd do the same for the Lee family knotwork in the United States, of course. That's going to take a couple of world-walkers, some maps and surveying tools, and someone to report back if everything goes wrong. Next, well . . . once we've exhausted the possibilities, we've got two knots. I need to talk to a mathematician, see if we can work out the parameters of the knots and come up with a way of generating a family of relatives. Then we need to invent a protocol for testing new designs: not so much what to do if they don't work, but how to survive if they take us somewhere new. If this works, if there are more than two viable knots, we're going to lose world-walkers sooner or later. Aren't we?'

'I expect so.'

'That's awfully cold-blooded, isn't it, sir?'

'Yes, boy, it is. In case it has slipped your attention, it is my job to be cold-blooded about such things. I would not authorize – I suspect my predecessors *did not* authorize – such research, if the situation was not so dangerous. The risk of losing world-walkers is too high and our numbers too few for gambling with lives. Already there have been losses, couriers taken in transit by American government agents. You met the Countess Helge. Your opinion . . . ?'

'Helge? She's, she's – what happened to her? Shouldn't she be here, given her experience?'

'I am asking the questions, Sir Huw. What was your opinion of her?'

'Bright . . . inquisitive . . . fun, I think, in a scary way. Where is she?'

'"Fun, in a scary way" . . . yes, that's true enough. But she scared too many cousins, Huw, cousins who lack your sense of *fun*. I did what I could to protect her. If she surfaces again, well, circumstances have changed, and it may be possible to distract her pursuers, as long as she is not involved in the regrettable business unfolding in New York. But for the time being, she is not available, and so I am turning to you.'

'I'm, um, I'm at your disposal, sir. How would you like to proceed?'

'Write me a report. No more than three pages. Tell me what you're going to do, what resources you need, what people you need, and what you expect to learn from it. I want your report no later than the day after tomorrow, and I want you to be ready to begin work the day after that.'

'Sir! That's rather – '

'What, you're going to tell me you've never written a grant proposal in a hurry? Please don't insult my intelligence.'

'I wouldn't dream of it, sir! But it's going to cost, people and
        money – '
'Let me worry about that. You just tell me what you need, and I'll
        make sure you get it.'
'*Wow!* Thank you – '
'*Don't* thank me, boy. Not until it's over, and we're still alive.'

END TRANSCRIPT

*

Dr. Hu was alarmingly young and bouncy, a Vietnamese-American
postdoc with a ponytail, cargo pants, sandals, and a flippant attitude
that would have annoyed the hell out of Eric if Hu had been working
for him. Luckily Hu was someone else's problem, and despite everything, he'd been cleared by security to work on JAUNT BLUE. *Which
probably means the Republic is doomed,* Eric thought mordantly.
Ah well, we work with what we've got.

'Hey man, the professor told me to give you the special tour.
Where you wanna start? You been briefed or they dropping you in it
cold?'

'I'll take it cold.'

'Suits me! Let's start with . . . hell. What do you know about
parallel universes?'

Eric shrugged. 'Not a lot. Seen some episodes of *Sliders.* Been
catching up on some sci-fi books in my copious free time.' The
writers they'd sounded out hadn't been good for much more than
random guesses, and without priming them with classified information that was all they could be expected to deliver. It had been a waste
of time, in his opinion, but – 'And then there's the day job.'

'Heh. You bet, boss!' Hu laughed, a curious chittering noise. 'Okay,
we got parallel universes. There's some theoretical basis for it in string
theory, I can give you some references if you like, but I can only tell
you one thing for sure right now: we're not dealing with a Tegmark
Level I multiverse – that's an infinite ergodic universe, one where the
initial inflationary period gave rise to disjoint Hubble volumes realizing all possible initial conditions.'

Eric crossed his arms. 'So you've ruled that out.' *Asshole? Or show-off?*

'Yup!' Hu seemed unaccountably pleased with himself. 'We *can* get *there* from *here*, which rules out Level I, because in a Level I multiverse the parallel universes exist in the same space time, just a mind-bogglingly huge distance apart. Which means we're dealing with either a Level II, Level III, or Level IV multiverse. I'm in the cosmology pool – we've got an informal bet running – that it'll turn out to be a Level IV theory. Level II depends on a Linde chaotic inflationary cosmology, in which you get multiple branching universes connected by wormholes, but travel between universes in that kind of scheme involves singularities, and the phenomenon we're studying doesn't come with black holes attached.'

Bumptious enthusiast, no social skills, Eric decided. He forced himself to nod, drawing the guy out. 'So you're saying this isn't a large scale cosmological phenomenon – then what is it?' Some of this stuff sounded half-familiar from his physics minor, but the rest was just weird.

'We're trying to work out what it is by a process of elimination.' Hu thrust his hands in his pockets, looking distant. 'The thing is, we have no theoretical framework. We've got a lot of beautiful hypotheses but they don't account for what we're seeing: we're looking at an amazingly complex artifact and we don't understand how it works. It's like handing a nuclear reactor to a steam engineer in the nineteenth century. If you don't understand the physics behind it you might as well say it works by magic pixie dust as slow neutron-induced fission. Without a theoretical understanding all we can do is poke it and see if it twitches. And coming up with the theory is, uh, proving difficult.' He slowed down as he spoke, finishing on a thoughtful note.

Now's as good a time as any . . . 'What's the black box you think you're trying to reverse-engineer?' Eric asked, hoping to draw Hu back on track.

'Ah!' Hu jerked as if a dozing puppeteer had just realized he'd slackened off on the strings: 'That would be the cytology samples Dr. James provided two months ago. That's how we got started,' he added. 'Want to see them? Come down to the lab and see what's on the slab?'

Eric nodded, and followed Hu out through the door. *If this is The* Rocky Horror Picture Show, *all we're missing is the mad scientist.* Hu made a beeline towards the maze of brown cubicle-farm partitions at the edge of the floor, and dived into a niche. When Eric caught up, he found him sitting at a desk with a gigantic tube monitor on it, messing with something that looked like the bastard offspring of a computer mouse and a joystick. 'Here!' he called excitedly.

Eric glanced round. The neighboring cubicles were empty: 'Where is everybody?'

'Team meeting,' Hu said dismissively. 'Look. Let me show you the slides first, then we'll go see the real thing.'

'Okay.' Eric stood behind him. 'Take it from the top.'

Hu pulled up a picture and Eric blinked, taken aback for a moment. It was in shades of gray, somehow messy and biological looking. After a moment he nodded. 'It's a cellular structure, isn't it?'

'Yeah! This slide was taken at 2,500 magnification on our scanning electron microscope. It's a slice from the lateral geniculate nucleus of our first test sample. See the layering here? Top two layers, the magnocellular levels? They do fast positional sensing in the visual system. Now let's zoom in a bit.'

The image vanished, to be replaced by a much larger, slightly grainier picture in which individual cells were visible, blobs with tangled fibers converging on them like the branches of a dead umbrella, stripped of fabric.

'Here's an M-type gangliocyte. It's kind of big, isn't it? There are lots of dendrites going in, too. It takes signals from a whole bunch of rod and cone cells in the retina and processes them, subtracting noise. You with me so far?'

'Just about,' Eric said dryly. Image convolution had been another component of his second degree, the classified one he'd sweated for back when he'd been attached to NRO. 'So far this is normal, is it?'

'Normal for any dead dried human brain on a microscope slide.' Hu giggled. It was beginning to grate on Eric's nerves.

'Next.'

'Okay. This is where it gets interesting, when we look inside the gangliocyte.'

'What –' It took Eric longer, this time, to orient himself: the picture was very grainy, a mess of weird loops and whorls, and something else. ' – the heck is that? Some kind of contamination – '

'Nope.' Hu giggled again. This time he sounded slightly scared. 'Ain't nothing like this in the textbooks.'

'It's your black box, isn't it?'

'Hey, quick on the uptake! Yes, that's it. We went through three samples and twelve microscopy preparations before we figured out it wasn't an artifact. What do you think?'

Eric stared at the screen.

'What is it?'

A different voice said, 'It's a Nobel Prize – or a nuclear war. Maybe both.'

Eric glanced round in a hurry, to see Dr. James standing behind him. For a bureaucrat, he moved eerily quietly. 'You think?'

'Cytology.' James sounded bored. 'These structures are in every central nervous system tissue sample retrieved so far from targeted individuals. Also in their peripheral tissues, albeit in smaller quantities. At first the pathology screener thought he was looking at some kind of weird mitochondrial malfunction – the inner membrane isn't reticulated properly – but then further screening isolated some extremely disturbing DNA sequences, and very large fullerene macromolecules doped with traces of heavy elements, iron and vanadium.'

'I'm not a biologist,' said Eric. 'You'll have to dumb it down.'

'Continue the presentation, Dr. Hu,' said James, turning away. *Show-off,* thought Eric.

Hu leaned back in his chair and swiveled round to face Eric. 'Cells, every cell in your body, they aren't just blobs full of enzymes and DNA, they've got structures inside them, like organs, that do different things.' He waved at the screen. 'We can't live without them. Some of them started out as free-living bacteria, went symbiotic a long time ago. A very long time ago.' Hu was staring at Dr. James's back. 'Mitochondria, like this little puppy here –' he pointed at a lozenge-shaped blob on the screen '– they're the power stations that keep your cells running. This thing, the thing these JAUNT BLUE guys have, they look like they're repurposed mitochondria. Someone started with mitochondria but edited the mitochondrial DNA, added about two hundred enzymes we've never seen before. They look artificial, like it's a tinker-toy construction kit for goop-phase nano-technology – well, to cut a long story short, they make buckeyballs. Carbon-sixty molecules, shaped like a soccer ball. And then they use them as a substrate to hold quantum dots – small molecules able to handle quantized charge units. Then they stick them on the inner lipid wall of the, what do you call them, the mechanosomes. Re-engineered mitochondria.'

Eric shook his head. 'You're telling me they're artificial. It's nanotechnology. Right?'

'No.' Dr. James turned round again. 'It's more complicated than that. Actually, they're not mitochondria: if they were, they wouldn't be transferred during spermatogenesis. What we're looking at is a hereditable artificial subcellular endoparasite engineered to do something we don't really understand yet that involves quantum states. Dr. Hu, would you mind demonstrating preparation fourteen for the colonel?'

Hu stared at Eric. 'Prep fourteen is down for some fixes. Can I show him a sample in cell twelve, instead?'

'Whatever. I'll be in the office.' James walked away.

Hu stood up: 'If you follow me?'

He darted off past the row of cubicles, and Eric found himself hurrying to keep up. The underground tunnel looked mostly empty, but the sense of emptiness was an illusion: there was a lot of stuff down here. Hu led him past a bunch of stainless steel pipework con-necting something that looked like a chrome-plated microbrewery to a bunch of liquid gas cylinders surrounded by warning barriers, then up a short flight of steps into another of the ubiquitous trailer offices. This one had been kitted out as a laboratory, with worktops stretch-ing along the wall opposite the windows. Extractor hoods and laminar-flow workbenches hunched over assemblages of tubes and pumps that resembled a bonsai chemical plant. Someone had crudely sliced the end off the trailer and built a tunnel to connect it to the next one along, which seemed to be mostly full of industrial-size dishwashing machines to Smith's uneducated eye. A technician in a white bunny suit and mask was doing something in a cabinet at the far end of the room. The air-conditioning was running at full blast, blowing a low-grade tropical storm out through the door: 'Viola, the lab.'

Eric winced: the horrible itch to correct Hu's behavior was unbearable. 'It's *voilà*,' he snapped waspishly. 'I see no medium-sized stringed instruments here. And you'll have to tell me what everything is. I know that's a laminar-flow workbench, but the rest of this stuff isn't my field.'

'Hey, stay cool, man! Um, where do you want me to start? This is where we work on the tissue cultures. Over there, that's the incubation lab. You see the far end behind the glass wall? We've got a full filtered air flow and a Class Two environment; we're trying to get access to a Class Four, but so far AMRIID isn't playing ball, so there's some stuff we don't dare try yet. But anyway, what we've got next door is a bunch of cell tissue cultures harvested from JAUNT BLUE carriers. We keep them alive and work on them through here. We're using a 2D field-effect transistor array from Infineon Technologies. They're developing it primarily as an artificial retina, but we're using it to send signals into the cell cultures. If we had some stem cells it'd be easier to work with, but, well, we have to work with what we've got.'

'Right.' The president's opinion on embryonic stem-cell research was well known; it had never struck Eric as being a strategic liability before now. He leaned towards the contraption behind the glass shield of the laminar-flow cabinet. 'So inside that box, you've got some live nerve cells, and you've, you've what? You've got them to talk to a chip? Is that it?'

'Yup.' Hu looked smug. 'It'd be better if we had a live volunteer to work with – if we could insert microelectrodes into their optic nerve or geniculate nucleus – but as the action's happening at the intracellular level this at least lets us get a handle on what we're seeing.'

Live volunteers? Eric stifled a twitch. The 'unlawful combatant' designation James had managed to stick on Matthias and the other captured Clan members was one thing: performing medical experiments involving brain surgery on them was something else again. Somehow he didn't see any of them volunteering of their own free will: was Hu really that stupid? Or just naive? Or had he not figured out how the JAUNT BLUE tissue cultures came to be in his hands in the first place? 'What have you been able to do with the materials available to you?'

'It's amazing! Look, let me show you preparation twelve in action, okay? I need to get a fresh slide from Janet. Wait here.'

Hu bustled off to the far end of the lab and waved at the person working behind the glass wall. While he was preoccupied, Eric took inventory. *Okay, so James wants me to figure it out for myself. He wants a sanity check?* So far, so obvious. But the next bit was a little more challenging. *So there's evidence of extremely advanced biological engineering, inside the Clan members' heads. Quantum dots, fullerene stuff, nanotechnology, genetic engineering as well. Artificial organelles.* He shivered. *Are they still human? Or something else? And what can we do with this stuff?*

Hu was on his way back, clutching something about the size of a humane rat trap that gleamed with the dull finish of aluminum. 'What's that?' asked Eric.

'Let me hook it up first. I've got to do this quickly.' Hu flipped up part of the laminar-flow cabinet's hood and slid the device inside, then began plugging tubes into it. 'It dies after about half an hour, and she's spent the whole morning getting it ready for you.'

Hu fussed over his gadgets for a while, then plugged a couple of old-fashioned-looking coaxial cables into the aluminum box. 'The test cell in here needs to be bathed in oxygenated Ringer's solution at body temperature. This here's a peristaltic pump and heater combination –' He launched into an intricate explanation that went right over Eric's head. 'We should be able to see it on video here – '

He backed away from the cabinet and grabbed hold of the mouse hanging off of the computer next to it. The screen unblanked: a window in the middle of it showed a grainy gray grid, the rough-edged tracks of a silicon chip at high magnification. Odd, messy blobs dotted its surface, as if a microscopic vandal had sneezed on it. 'Here's an NV51 test unit. One thousand twenty-four field effect transistors, individually addressable. The camera's calibrated so we can bring up any transistor by its coordinates. These cells are all live JAUNT BLUE cultures – at least they were alive half an hour ago.'

'So what does it do?'

Hu shrugged. 'This is preparation twelve, the first that actually did anything. Most of the later ones are still – we're still debugging them, they're still under development. This one, at least, it's the demo. We got it to work reliably. Proof of concept: watch.'

He leaned close to the screen, muttering to himself, then punched some numbers into the computer. The camera slewed sideways and zoomed slightly, centering on one of the snot-like blobs. '*Vio* – sorry. Here we go.'

Hu hit a key. A moment later, Eric blinked. 'Where did it go? Did you just evaporate it?'

'No, we only carry about fifty millivolts and a handful of microamps for a fiftieth of a second. Look, let me do it again. Over . . . yeah, this one.'

Hu punched more figures into the keyboard. Hit the return key again. Another blob of snot vanished from the gray surface.

'What's this meant to show me?' Eric asked impatiently.

'Huh?' Hu gaped at him. 'Uh, JAUNT BLUE? Hello, remember that code phrase? The, the folks who do that world-walking thing? This is how it works.'

'Hang on. Wait.' Eric scratched his head. 'You didn't just vaporize that, that –' *Neuron*, he realized, understanding dawning. 'Wow.'

'We figured out that the mechanosomes respond to the intracellular cyclic-AMP signaling pathway,' Hu offered timidly. 'That's what preparation fourteen is about. They're also sensitive to dopamine. We're looking for modulators, now, but it's on track. If we could get the nerve cells to grow dendrites and connect, we hope eventually to be able to build a system that works – that can move stuff about. If we can get a neural stem-cell line going, we may even be able to mass-produce them – but that's years away. It's early days right now: all we can do is make an infected cell go bye-bye and sneak away into some other universe – explaining how that part of it works is what the quant group are working on. What do you think?'

Eric shook his head, suddenly struck by a weird sense of historical significance: it was like standing in that baseball court at the University of Chicago in 1942, when they finished adding graphite blocks to the heap in the middle of the court and Professor Fermi told his assistant to start twisting the control rod. *A Nobel Prize or a nuclear war? James isn't wrong about that.* 'I'd give my left nut to know where this is all going to end,' he said slowly. 'You're doing good work. I just hope we don't all live to regret the consequences.'

MANEUVERS

As forms of transport went, horse-drawn carriages lacked modern amenities – from cup holders and seat-back TV screens to shock absorbers and ventilation nozzles. On the other hand, they came with some fittings that took Mike by surprise. He gestured feebly at the raised seat cushion as he glanced at the geriatric Gruppenführer in the mound of rugs on the other side of the compartment: 'If you think I'm going to use *that* – '

'You'll use it when you need to, boy.' She chuckled for a moment. The younger woman, Olga, rolled her eyes and sent him a look that seemed to say, *Humor her.* 'We'll not be stopping for bed and bath for at least a day.'

'What are you going to do?' he asked.

Iris said nothing for a moment, while one wheel crunched across a rut in the path with a bone-shaking crash that sent a wave of pain through his leg. She seemed to be considering the question. 'We'll be pausing to change teams in another hour or so. Don't want to flog the horses; you never know when you'll need a fresh team. Anyway, you can't stick your nose outside: you wouldn't fool anyone. So the story is, you're unconscious and injured and we need to get you across to a hospital in upstate New York as soon as possible. If they're still using the old emergency routes –' she looked at Olga, who nodded '– there should be a postal station we can divert to tomorrow evening. If it's running, we'll ship you across and you can be home in forty-eight hours. If it's not running . . . well, we'll play it by ear; you've been hit on the head and you're having trouble with language, or something. Until we can get you out of here.'

Mike tried to gather his thoughts. 'I don't understand. What do you expect me to do . . . ?'

Miriam's mother leaned forward, her expression intent. 'I expect you to tell me your home address and zip code.' A small notepad and pencil appeared from somewhere under her blankets. 'Yes?'

'But – '

'You're working with spies, boy. Modern spies with lots of gizmos for bugging phone conversations and tapping e-mail. First rule when going up against the NSA: use no communications technology invented in the last half-century. I want to be able to send you mail. If you want to contact me, write a letter, stick it in an envelope, and put it in your trash can on top of the refuse sacks.'

'Aren't you scared I'll just pass everything to my superiors? Or they'll mount a watch on the trash?'

'No.' Eyes twinkled in the darkness. 'Because first, you didn't make a move on my daughter when you had the chance. And second, have you any idea how many warm bodies it takes to mount a twenty-four/seven watch on a trash can? One that's capable of grabbing a dumpster-diving world-walker without killing them?'

'I've got to admit, I hadn't thought about it.'

Olga cleared her throat. 'It takes two watchers per team, minimum. Five teams, each working just under thirty hours a week, in rotation, because they need to stay alert: two world-walkers can be in and out in under ten seconds. They'll need a blind, plus perimeter alarms, plus coordination with the refuse companies so they know when to expect a legitimate collection, and that's just the watchers. You need at least three spare bodies, too, in case of sickness or accidents. To be able to make a snatch, you need at least four per team. Do you have thirty agents ready to watch your back stoop, mister? Just in case her grace wishes to receive a letter from you, rather than sending a messenger to pay a local wino to pick it up?'

'Jeez, you sound like you've done this a lot.'

Mrs. Beckstein rapped a knuckle on the wooden window frame of the carriage: 'Fifty years ago there were three times as many world-walkers as there are now, and they didn't all die out because they forgot how to make babies.'

'Huh?'

Olga glanced down. 'Civil war,' she said. 'And now, your government.'

'Civil –' Mike paused. *Didn't Matthias say something about internal feuds?* 'Hold on. It killed *two-thirds* of you?'

'You can't imagine how lethal a war between world-walkers can be, boy.' Mrs. Beckstein frowned. 'You should hope the Clan Council never decides they're at war with the United States.'

'We'd wipe you out. Eventually.' He realized he was gritting his teeth, from anger as much as from the pain in his leg: he tried to force himself to relax.

She nodded thoughtfully. 'Yes, very probably. But right now you think you have a problem with terrorism, and I'm saying you have seen *nothing*, boy. We are not religious fanatics, no. We just want to live our lives. But the logic of power –' She paused.

'What do you want me to do?'

'I want my daughter out of this mess and home safe, Mr. Fleming. She had a sheltered upbringing: she's in danger, and her own ignorance is her worst enemy. Second . . . when she came over she raised a shit storm among our relatives. In particular, she aired some very dirty family linens in public half a year ago. Called for a complete rethink of the Clan's business model, in fact: she pointed out that the emperor has no clothes, and that basing one's income on an enemy's weakness – in this case, the continuing illegality of certain substances, combined with the continuing difficulty your own organization and others face in stopping the trade – is foolish. This made her a lot of enemies at the time, but it set minds a-thinking. The current upheavals are largely a consequence of her upsetting that apple cart. The Clan will change in due course, and switch to a line of work more profitable than smuggling, but as long as she remains among them, her presence will act as a reminder of the source of the change to the conservative faction, and will provoke them, and that will make her a target. So I want her out of the game.'

'Uh, I think I see where you're leading.' Mike shook his head. 'But she's missing . . . ?'

'She won't stay missing for long – not unless she's gotten herself killed.'

'Oh.' He thought for a moment. 'That's not all, is it?'

'No, Mr. Fleming, that is *not* all, not by a long way. I mentioned a conservative faction. You won't be surprised to know that there exists a progressive faction, too, and current circumstances – the fighting you may have noticed – are about to tip the scales decisively in their favor. Your interests would be served by promoting the progressives to the detriment of the conservatives, believe me.'

'And you're a progressive. Right?'

'I prefer to think of myself as a radical.' She leaned against the seat back as the coach hit another rough patch on the dirt track. 'Must be all the sixties influences. A real flower child, me.'

'Ah.' Verbal punctuation was easier than trying to hold his own against this intimidating old woman. 'Okay, what do the progressives want?'

'You'd best start by trying to understand the conservatives if you want to get a handle on our affairs. The Clan started out as the descendants of an itinerant tinker. They learned to world-walk, learned how to intermarry to preserve the family ability, and got rich. *Insanely* rich. Think of the Medicis, or the Saudi royal family. That's what the Clan represents here, except that "here" is dirt-poor, mired in the sixteenth or seventeenth century – near enough. It's not the same, never is, but there are enough points of similarity to make the model work. The most important point is, they got rich by trade in light merchandise, by running a postal service. The postal service ships high-value goods, whatever they are, either reliably – for destinations in your world, without fear of interception – or fast – for destinations in this world, by FedEx across a continent ruled by horseback.'

She pushed herself upright with her walking stick. 'Put yourself in their shoes. They want nothing to change, because they feel threatened by change – their status is tenuous. A postal network is a packet-switched network, like your internet. World-walkers carry packets. If world-walkers drift away from it, the bandwidth drops, and thus, its profitability. New ventures divert vital human capital. So they're in favor of producing more world-walkers, and locking them into the family trade. And they're against exploration, because they're scrambling to stay on top of the dung heap.'

'Sounds like –' Mike could think of a number of people it

sounded like, uncomfortably close to home – *Change the subject.* 'What about the progressives?'

'We want change, simple as that. Miriam observed that we are mired in a business that scales in direct proportion to the number of world-walkers, like a service business. She suggested – and her uncovering another world provided the opportunity – that we switch to what she called a technology-transfer model, trading information between universes.'

'How many are there?' he asked.

'At least three. We thought two, until a year ago. Now we know there are three, and we suspect there are many more. Yours is the most advanced we know of, but what might be lurking out there? We can trade, Mr. Fleming. We could be *very useful* to the United States of America. But first we need a . . . change of management? Yes, a change of management. We originated in a feudal realm, and our ability is hereditary: don't underestimate the effects of reproductive politics on the Clan's governance. Before we can change the way we do things, before we can end our unfortunate reliance on illegal traf-ficking, we need to break the grip of the conservative factions on the council, and to do that we need to entirely overturn our family and tribal foundations.'

'Your family structures?'

'Yes.' Olga pulled a face: Iris either ignored it, or pretended to do so. 'You must be aware of the implications of artificial insemination. There's been a quiet argument going on within the Clan's council for a generation now, over whether it is our destiny to continue existing as braided matrilineal families in a patriarchal society, or to become . . . well, not a family organization any more, but one open to anyone born with the ability, whatever their parentage.'

Mike shut his eyes. *I think my brain just melted,* he thought. 'Who are the progressives?'

'Myself for one, to your very great good fortune. My half-brother for another, although he is as circumspect in public as befits the head of the Clan's external security organization – a seat of significant power on the council. There are others. You do not need to know who they are. If you're captured or tortured, what you don't know you can't give away.'

'And the conservatives?'

'Miriam's Great-Uncle Henryk, if he's still alive. He was the late king's spymaster in chief. My mother, Hildegarde, who is also Miriam's grandmother. Baron Oliver Hjorth, about two-thirds of the council . . . too many to enumerate.'

'Okay. So you want me to set up a covert channel between you – your faction – and my agency? Or just me?'

'Just you, at first. You're injured. When you are back on your feet I will contact you. You will excuse me, but I am afraid I will require certain actions from you in order to demonstrate that you are trustworthy. Tokens of trust, if you like.'

I don't like the sound of this. 'Such as . . . ?'

'That's for me to know and you to find out.' She relented slightly: 'I can't do business with you if I can't trust you. But I won't ask you to do anything illegal – unlike your superiors.'

Mike shivered. *She's got my number.* 'What makes you think they'd issue illegal orders?'

'Come now, Mr. Fleming, how stupid do I look? How did you get here? If your superiors could move more than one or two people at a time they'd have sent the 82nd Airborne Division. They sent you because their transport capacity is tiny; they're using captured world-walkers.' Her expression shifted into one of outright distaste. 'Honor is a luxury when you reach the top of the dung heap. Everybody wants it, but it's in short supply. That's even more true in Washington, D.C. than over on this side, because aristocrats have at least to keep up the appearance of nobility. Let me give you a tip to pass on to your bosses: if you mistreat your Clan prisoners, their relatives will avenge them. The political is taken *very* personally, here.'

'That's –' he swallowed '– it may be true, but that's not how things work right now. Not since 9/11.'

'Then they're going to learn to regret it bitterly.' Her gaze was level. 'You *must* warn your superiors of this – the political is personal. If the conservatives think your government is mistreating their prisoners, they'll take revenge, horrible revenge. Timothy McVeigh and Mohamed Atta were rank amateurs compared to these people, and Clan security probably can't prevent an atrocity from happening if you provoke them. You need to warn your bosses, Mr. Fleming. They're playing with fire: or would you like to see a suicide bomber invite himself to the next White House reception?'

Whoops. Mike cringed at the images that sprang to mind. 'They're that crazy?'

'They're not crazy!' Her vehemence startled him. 'They just don't think about things the same way as you people. Your organization is trying to wage war on the Clan: all right, we understand that. But it is a point of honor to avenge blood debts, and that suicide bomber – that's the *least* of your worries.' She paused for breath. When she continued, she was much less strident: 'That's one of the things Miriam thought she could change, with her reform program. I tend to agree with her. That's one of the things we *need* to change – it's one of the reasons I reintroduced her to her relatives in the first place. I knew she'd react that way.'

'But she's your daughter!' It was out before he could stop himself.

'Hah. I told you, but you didn't listen, did you? We don't work the way you think we do – and it's not just all about blood debts and honor. There's also a perpetual intergenerational conflict going on, mother against daughter, grandmother for grandchild. *My* mother is a pillar of the conservative faction: by raising Miriam where Hilde-garde couldn't get her claws into her, I temporarily gained the upper hand. And –' she leaned forward again '– I would do anything to keep my granddaughter out of this mess.'

'You don't have a granddaughter,' Olga commented from the side-lines, 'do you?'

Iris glanced sideways. 'Miriam has not married a world-walker, so I do not have a granddaughter,' she said coldly. 'Is that understood?'

Olga swallowed. 'Yes, my lady.'

What was that about? The carriage bounced again, throwing Mike against the side of the seat and jarring his leg painfully. When he could focus again, he realized Iris had been talking for some time.

' – stopping soon, and we will have to lock you in the carriage overnight. I hope you understand. When we get to the waypoint Olga will carry you across, put you somewhere safe, call for an ambulance, then leave. I hope you understand the need for this? Olga, if you would be so good . . .'

The Russian princess was holding a syringe. 'No!' Mike tried to protest, but in his current state he was too weak to fight her off. And whatever was in the needle was strong enough that it stopped mattering very shortly afterwards.

*

Miriam had just been through two months under house arrest, preceded by three months in carefully cosseted isolation. Then she'd managed a fraught escape and then been imprisoned yet again, albeit for a matter of days. Walking the streets of New York again – even a strangely low-rise New York wrapped around the imperial palace and inner city of New London – felt like freedom. The sight of aircraft and streetcars and steam-powered automobiles and primitive flickering neon signs left her gaping at the sheer urban beauty of it all. As they moved closer to the center of the city the bustle of the crowds and the bright synthetic colors of the women's clothing caught her attention more than the gray-faced beggars in the suburbs. *I'm in civilization again,* she realized, half-dazed. *Even if I'm not part of it.* Erasmus paused, looking at a news vendor's stand displaying the stamp of the censor's office. 'Buy me a newspaper, dear?' she asked, touching his arm.

Erasmus jerked slightly, then recovered. 'Certainly. A copy of the *Register*, please.'

'Aye, sorr. An' here you is.'

He passed her the rolled-up newssheet as they moved up the high street. 'What bit you?' he asked quietly.

'I've been out of touch for a long time. I just need to –' *I need to connect,* she thought, but before she could articulate it he nodded, grinning ironically.

'You were out of touch? Did your family have you on a tight leash?'

'I had nothing to read but a grammar book for two months. And that wasn't the worst of it.' Now that she had company to talk to she

397

could feel a mass of words bubbling up, ideas seeking torrential release.

'You'll have to tell me about it later. I was told there was a public salon here – ah, that's it. Your hair, Miriam. You can see to it yourself?'

He'd stopped again, opposite a diamond-paned window. Through it she could just about make out the seats and basins of a hairdresser: some things seemed to evolve towards convergence, however distinct they'd been at the start. 'I think I can just about manage that.' She tried to smile, but the knot of tension had gotten a toehold back and wouldn't let go. 'This will probably take a couple of hours. Then I need to buy clothes. Why don't you just tell me where the hotel is, and I'll meet you there at six o'clock? How does that sound?'

'That sounds fine.' He nodded, then pulled out a pocket book and scribbled an address in it. 'Here. Take care.'

She smiled at him, and he ducked his head briefly, then turned his back. Miriam took a deep breath. A bell rattled on a chain as she pushed the door open; at the desk behind the window, a young woman looked up in surprise from the hardcover she'd been reading. 'Can I help you?'

'I hope so.' Miriam managed a smile. 'I need a new hairstyle, and I need it now.'

*

Six hours later, footsore and exhausted from the constant bombardment of strangeness that the city kept hurling at her, Miriam clambered down from the back of a cab outside the Great Northern Hotel, clutching her parcels in both hands. The new shoes pinched at toe and heel, and she was sweating from the summer weather; but she was more presentable than she'd have been in the shabby outfit they'd passed off on her at Hogarth Villas, and the footman leapt to open the doors for her. 'Thank you!' She nodded at him. 'The front desk, I'm meeting my husband – '

'This way, ma'am.'

Miriam was halfway to the desk when a newspaper rattled behind her. She glanced round to see Burgeson unfolding himself from a heavily padded chair. 'Susan! My dear. Let me help you with those parcels.' He deftly extricated her from the footman, guided her past the front desk towards an elevator, and relieved her of the most troublesome parcel. 'I almost didn't recognize you,' he murmured. 'You've done a good job.'

'It feels really strange, being a blonde. People look at you differently. And it's so heavily lacquered it feels like my head's embedded in a wicker basket. It'll probably crack and fall off when I go to bed.'

'Come on inside.' He held the door for her, then dialed the sixth floor. As the door closed, he added: 'That's a nice outfit. Almost too smart to be seen with the likes of me.'

She pursed her lips. 'Looking like a million dollars tends to get you treated better by the kind of people those million dollars hire.' She'd ended up in something not unlike a department store, buying a conservatively cut black two-piece outfit. It was a lot less strange than some of the stuff she'd seen in the shops: New London's fashion, at least for those who still had money to spend, was more experimental than Boston's. The lift bell chimed. 'Where are we staying?'

'This way.' He led her along a corridor like any other hotel corridor back home (except for the flickering tungsten bulbs), then used an old-fashioned key to unlock a bedroom door.

'There's, uh, only one bed, Erasmus.'

'We're supposed to be married, Miriam. I'll take the chaise.'

'I didn't mean it like that.'

'I'm sorry.' He rubbed his forehead. 'Blame Margaret's sense of humor.' He looked at her again: 'With hair that color, and curly, and – you've been using paints, haven't you? Yes, looking like that, I don't think anyone'll recognize you at first sight.'

'I think it's ugly. But Mrs. Christobell – she ran the salon – seemed to think it was the height of fashion.' She carefully hung her hat and jacket on the coat-rail then touched her hair gingerly. 'That feels really odd. Better keep me away from candle flames for a while.'

'I think I can manage that.' He laid his hat and newspaper on the occasional table. 'You did very well at making yourself look completely unlike yourself – it's going to take some getting used to.'

'That goes for me, too. I'm not sure I like it.' She headed for the table, but before she could reach it he ducked in and pulled a chair out for her. 'Thanks, I think.' She sat down, bent forward to get closer to her shoes, and sighed. 'I need to get these off for a bit – my feet are killing me.'

'Did you spend everything, or do you have some money left?'

'Not much.' She focused on his expression. 'Did you think I can keep up appearances by looting your shop?'

'No, but I –' He rubbed his forehead wearily. 'Forget it.'

'I had to do something about my appearance, make myself less recognizable. And I had to get hold of a respectable outfit, if I want to pass for your . . . spouse. And I had to buy shoes that fit, and a couple of changes of underwear, and some other stuff. It costs money, and takes time, but it's necessary. Are you still taking your medicine?'

He frowned at her effusion: 'Yes, every day, as you said.'

'Good. One less problem to solve.' She crossed her legs. 'Now, what have you been up to?'

'Getting the job done.' He looked in her direction, not focusing, and she shivered. *Who is he seeing?* 'I'm not planning on staying in Boston for long – I'm needed in Fort Petrograd, out west.' He looked her in the eye. 'You don't have to come with me – you can stay in my apartment if you prefer.'

'And do what, precisely? Sit down, pacing like that is making me itch.'

'I don't know.' He pulled out the chair opposite and sat down. 'I've got a job to do, and you turned up right in the middle of it.'

'I could keep the shop open.' She sounded doubtful, even to herself. *Do I want to be on my own in Boston? What if Angbard sends someone to look for me?* It would be the first place they checked. *Best not to wait until they start looking, then.*

'That's not practical.' He frowned. 'I trust you to do it – that's not in question – but there are too many problems. Business is very poor, and I'm already under observation. If I take a wife that's one thing, but employing a shop assistant while I take off to the wilds of California is something else: the local thief-takers aren't *completely* stupid. I'm supposed to be a pawnbroker, not a well-off storeholder. Unless you've got any better ideas?'

'I think . . . well, there's some stuff I need to pick up in Boston.

And then I need to get back in touch with my relatives, but carefully. How about if I went with you? How long will you be gone?'

'At least a week; it's three days each way by train, and flying would attract the wrong kind of attention. Frankly, I'd be grateful if you'd accompany me. It'd strengthen my cover on the way out – we could be traveling on our honeymoon – and if we arrived back together I could introduce you to the neighbors as someone from out west. Wife, sister, brother's widow, whatever. And, to be truthful, the three days out – one gets tired of traveling alone.'

'Oh yes,' she said fervently. 'Don't I know it.' *It was traveling alone that got me into this mess* – 'Before we skip town, though. There are some things I left in my office, at the works. I really need to get my hands on them. Do you think there's any way I could retrieve them?'

'You left your relatives running the business, didn't you? Do you know if it's still going? Or if you'd be welcome there if it is?'

'No.' She was shaking slightly. 'No to both questions. I don't know anything. I might not be welcome. But it's important.' She'd left a small notebook PC locked in a drawer in her office, and a portable printer, and a bunch of CD-ROMs with a complete archive of U.S. Patent Office filings going up to the 1960s. In this world, that was worth more than diamonds. But there was something on the computer that was even more valuable to her. In a moment of spare time, she'd scanned her locket using the computer's web cam, meaning to mess around with it later. If it was still there, if she could get her hands on it, and if it worked – *I'm free.* She could go any-where and do anything, and she'd had a lot of time to think about Mike's offer of help, back in the basement of Hogarth Villas. It wasn't the only option, but just being able to get back to her own world would be a vast improvement on her current situation. 'I need to get my stuff.'

'Would it be –' He licked his lips nervously. 'It's not safe, Miriam. If they're looking for you, they'll look there.'

'I know, I just need –' She stopped, balling her hands into fists from frustration. 'Sorry. It's not your fault. You're right, it's risky. But it's also important. If I can get my things, I can also world-walk home. To the United States, that is. I can – '

'Miriam.' He waited almost a minute before continuing, his voice gentle. 'Your relatives know where you'd go. They might have established a trap there. Can you think of another way to get what you need?'

'Huh?' She took a deep breath. 'Yes. Roger!'

'Roger?'

She leaned across the table and took Burgeson's hand: 'I need to write him a letter. If the business is still running, he'll be working there. He's reliable – he's the one I used to send you messages – I can ask him to take the items whenever it's safe for him, and have a cousin deliver them to your shop when we get back.' Erasmus pulled back slightly: she realized she was gripping his hand too hard. 'Can I do that?'

He smiled ruefully as he shook some life back into his fingers. 'Are they small and concealable?'

'About so big –' she indicated ' – and about ten pounds in weight. They're delicate instruments, they need to be kept dry and handled carefully.'

'Then we'll get you some writing paper and a pen before we board the train.' He nodded thoughtfully. 'And you'll tell him not to take the items for at least a week, and to have his cousin deliver them to somewhere else, a different address I can give you. A sympathizer. In the very worst possible circumstances they will know that you've visited Boston, my Boston, in the past week.'

'Thank you.' The knot of anxiety in her chest relaxed.

He stood up, pushing his chair back. 'It's getting on. Would you care to accompany me to dinner? No need to change – the carvery downstairs has no code.'

'Food would be good, once I get my shoes back on. If we've got that much travel ahead of us I'm going to have to break them in – what are you going to Fort Petrograd for?'

'I have to see a man about a rare book,' he said flippantly, offering Miriam her jacket. 'And then I think I should like to take a stroll along a beach and dip my toes in the Pacific Ocean . . .'

*

More wrecked buildings, another foggy morning.

Otto, Baron Neuhalle, had seen these sights twice already in the past week. His majesty had been most explicit: 'We desire you to employ no more than a single battalion in any location. The witches have uncanny means of communication, as well as better guns than anything our artificers can make, and if the entire army is concentrated to take a single keep, it will be ambushed. To defeat this pestilence, it will first be necessary to force them to defend their lands. So you will avoid the castles and strong places, and instead fall upon their weaker houses and holdings. You will grant no quarter and take no prisoners of the witches, save that you put out their eyes as soon as you take them into captivity, that they may work no magic. Some of the witches make their peasants grow weeds and herbs in their fields, instead of food. You will fire these fields and slay the witches, but you will not kill their peasants – it is our wish that they be fed from the stores of their former lords and masters. The witches seem to value these crops, so they are as much a target as their owners.'

His horse snorted, pawing the ground nervously at the smells and shouts from the house ahead. Neuhalle glanced at the two hand-men waiting behind him, their heavy horse-pistols resting across their saddles. 'Follow,' he ordered, then nudged his mount forward.

Before the first and fourth platoons had arrived, this had been a large village, dominated by the dome of a temple and the steeply pitched roof of a landholder's house – one of the Hjorth family, a poor rural hanger-on of the tinker clan. Upper Innmarch hadn't been much by the standards of the aristocracy, but it was still a substantial two-story building, wings extending behind it to form a horseshoe around a cobbled yard, with stables and outbuildings. Now, half of the house lay in ruins and smoke and flames belched from the roof of the other half. Bodies lay in the dirt track that passed for a high street, soldiers moving among them. Shouts and screams from up the lane, and a rhythmic thudding noise: one of his lances was battering on the door of a suspiciously well-maintained cottage, while others moved in and out of the dark openings of round-roofed hovels, like killer hornets buzzing around the entrances of a defeated beehive. More moans and screams split the air.

'Sir! Beg permission to report!'

Neuhalle reined his horse in as he approached the sergeant – distinguished by the red scarf he wore – and leaned towards the man. 'Go ahead,' he rasped.

'As ordered, I deployed around the house at dawn and waited for Morgan's artillery. There was no sign of a guard on duty. The occupants noticed around the time the cannon arrived: we had hot grapeshot waiting, and Morgan put it through the windows yonder. The place caught readily – too readily, like they was waiting for us. Fired a few shots, then nothing. A group of six attempted to flee from the stables on horseback as we approached, but were brought down by Heidlor's team. The villagers either ran for the forest or barricaded themselves in, Joachim is seeing to them now.' He looked almost disappointed; compared to the first tinker's nest they'd fired, this one had been a pushover.

'I think you're right: the important cuckoos had already fled the nest.' Neuhalle scratched at his scrubby beard. 'What's in the fields?'

'Rye and wheat, sir.'

'Right.' Neuhalle straightened his back: 'Let the men have their way with the villagers.' These peasants had been given no cause to resent the witches: so let them fear the king instead. 'Any prisoners from the house?'

'A couple of serving maids tried to run, sir. And an older woman, possibly a tinker though she didn't have a witch sign on her.'

'Then give them the special treatment. No, wait. Maids? An older woman? Let the soldiers use them first, *then* the special treatment.'

His sergeant looked doubtful. 'Haven't found the smithy yet, sir. Might be a while before we have hot irons.'

Neuhalle waved dismissively. 'Then hang them instead. Just make sure they're dead before we move on, that will be sufficient. If you find any unburned bodies in the house, hang them up as well: we have a reputation to build.'

'The peasants, sir?'

'I don't care, as long as there are survivors to bear witness.'

'Very good, sir.'

'That will be all, Sergeant Shutz.'

Neuhalle nudged his horse forward, around the burning country house. He had a list of a dozen to visit, strung out through the countryside in a broad loop around Niejwein. The four companies under his command were operating semi-independently, his two captains each tackling different targets: it would probably take another week to complete the scourging of the near countryside, even though at the outset his majesty had barely three battalions ready for service. *It won't be a long war,* he hoped. *It mustn't be. Just a series of terror raids on the Clan's properties, to force them to focus on the royal army – and then what? Whatever Egon is planning,* Neuhalle supposed. Nobody could accuse the young monarch of being indecisive – he was as sharp as his father, but untempered by self-doubt and deeply committed to this purge. Neuhalle's hand-men rode past him, guns at the ready. *It had better work,* he hoped. *If Egon loses, Niejwein will belong to the witches forever.*

The courtyard at the back of the house stank of manure and blood, and burning timber. A carriage leaned drunkenly outside the empty stable doors, one wheel shattered.

'Sir, if it please you, we should –' The hand-man gestured.

'Go ahead.' Neuhalle unholstered the oddly small black pistol he carried on his belt: a present from one of the witch-lords, in better times. He racked the slide, chambering a cartridge. 'I don't think they'll be interested in fighting. Promise them quarter, then hang them as usual once you've disarmed them.' *Just as his majesty desires.* His eyes turned towards the wreckage. 'Let's look this over.'

'Aye, sir.'

They'd cut the horses free and abandoned the carriage, but there was still a strong-box lashed to the roof, and an open door gaping wide. Otto dismounted carefully, keeping his horse between himself and the upper floor windows dribbling smoke – no point not being careful – and walked over to the vehicle. There was nobody inside, of course. Then the roof. The box wasn't large, but it looked heavy. Neuhalle's grin widened. 'You, fetch four troopers and have them take this down. Place a guard on it.'

'Aye sir!' His hand-man nodded enthusiastically: Neuhalle had promised his retainers a tithe of his spoils.

'There'll be more just like it tomorrow.' There was a loud crack, and Neuhalle looked round just in time to see the roofline of the west wing collapse with a shower of sparks and a gout of flames. 'And tomorrow . . .'

OIL TALK

Just as the guard handed Eric back his mobile phone, it rang.

'Hey, good timing!' The guard chuckled.

Eric flipped it open, ignoring the man. It had been a long day: back home it was about six in the evening, and he still had to fly back. 'Smith here.'

'Boss?' It was Deirdre, his secretary: 'I'm aware this is an insecure line, but I thought you might like to know that Mike is back from his sales trip, and he says he's got a buyer.'

'Wow!' Eric stood bolt-upright. 'Are you sure? That's amazing!' The sense of gloom that had been hanging over him for days lifted. He checked his watch: 'Listen, I'll be back in town late tonight – can you get him into the office for an early morning debrief? Around six hundred hours?' *I'll have to tell Gillian something, he realized. Not just an apology. Take her somewhere nice?*

'I, I don't think that will be possible,' Deirdre said, sounding distracted.

'Why not?' It came out too sharply: 'Sorry, I didn't mean to snap at you. What's the problem?'

'He's, um, he had a traffic accident. He's taken a beating, but he'll be all right once he's out of hospital. Judith Herz is with him.'

'Right.' Eric blinked furiously. He glanced round the guardroom, noticing the cop sitting patiently behind the counter, the polite SS agent with the car keys. 'Listen, I'll call you back from a secure terminal once I'm under way. Should be about an hour. I'll be expecting the best report you can pull together. If possible get Judith on the line for me, if she's spoken to him in person.'

He could just about see Deirdre's eye-rolling: 'That's about what I expected, boss. I'll be ready for you.'

'Okay, bye.'

He closed the phone with a snap and turned to Agent Simms: 'Come on, we've got a plane to catch!'

*

There was a secure terminal aboard the Gulfstream, and Eric wasted no time in getting to it as soon as they were airborne. But what Judith Herz had for him wasn't encouraging.

'He got chewed up – one leg is badly broken with surface lacerations, he's got bruising and soft tissue injuries consistent with being in a fight, and he's got a nasty infected wound. I got him checked in to the nearest trauma unit and it looks like he'll pull through and probably keep the leg, but he's not going to be up and about any time soon. Someone stuck a syringe full of morphine in him and dumped him at a roadside in upstate New York. They called an ambulance using a stolen mobile phone, and no, we didn't get a trace on it – they turned it on just before they called and switched off immediately after. He was still wearing his cover gear, but they'd disarmed him.'

'Shit. Excuse me.' Eric took a few moments to gather his scattered thoughts. Too many things were going on at once. His head was still spinning from the stuff in the buried laboratory under Building Forty-seven. He'd just about gotten used to the idea that Mike had made it home alive – and that was *really* good news – but this latest tidbit was a little hard to take. 'Okay. So someone sent him back to us? Any sign of Sergeant Hastert and his team?'

'Mike was awake when I saw him, sir.' He stiffened at her tone of voice, anticipating the bad news to come: 'He wasn't very lucid, but he said Hastert and O'Neil were killed. They walked in on some kind of war and they got caught in the crossfire. I'm sorry, sir: he wasn't very clear, but he wanted you to know they died trying to get him out.'

'Damn.' Eric rubbed his eyes tiredly. 'Any good news? Or was *that* the good news?'

'He says he made contact with the target briefly, but there were problems. And something about her mother.'

'What's her mother got to do with things?'

'We didn't get that far, sir. Like I said, he's been chewed up badly.

408

I mean, it looks like someone took a whack at his left leg with a chain saw then left it to fester for a couple of days. That's on top of the bruising and a cracked rib. The medics shoved me out of the room just as he was getting to the good stuff – he's out of the operating theater now but he won't be talking for a while. But I'm pretty sure he was trying to say something about the target's mother saving him. I don't know what he meant by that, he was medicated and being prepped for surgery at the time, but I figure you'll want to follow it up.'

'Dead right I will.' Eric took a deep breath. 'All right. So he's out of the operating theater now. As soon as he's safe to move, I want him in a military hospital with an armed guard *in* the room with him at all times – for his own protection. If they can find an underground room to put him in, so much the better. If possible, move him tonight – I want him safe, right now his brains are our crown jewels. Tell Deirdre to get John from OPFAC Four to coordinate with Milton and Sarah on setting it up. Page them if they've gone home, this is important. Got that?'

'I'm on it. Anything else? Will you be coming in tonight?'

'I'm touching down around half past midnight. If you get any pushback between now and then, call me and I'll come in. If it goes smoothly, I might as well get some sleep before I debrief him.' A thought struck him. 'Another thing. I want the guard with him at all times to have a voice recorder to hand in case he says anything. And I don't want random doctors or nurses eavesdropping.'

'Already taken care of.' Herz's laconic response made him want to kick himself. Of course it was taken care of: Herz was terrifyingly efficient when it came to police work like handling witnesses.

'Good. Good work, I mean, really good. Well, I won't keep you any longer. If you need backup, call me. Bye.'

The seatbelt light was off, the plane boring a hole in the sky towards the darkening eastern horizon. Eric unfastened his belt and stood up, then went forward to the desk where Dr. James was poring over a pile of printouts.

'What is it?' No polite small talk from James: he was almost robotic in his focus.

'It's CLEANSWEEP. I just got confirmation that we've had a positive outcome.'

It was Dr. James's turn to do a double take – or punch the air, if so inclined – and Eric was curious to see how he'd jump. Dr. James was not, it seemed, one for demonstrative gestures: he simply put his papers down, removed his spectacles, and said, mildly, 'Explain.'

'Agent Fleming is back. He's alive, but has serious injuries. His condition is stable and I've ordered him transferred to a secure facility pending debriefing. The preliminary report is that the specops team walked into a red-on-red crossfire of some sort, but Fleming was returned to us by someone who presumably wants to talk. There appears to be a factional split in fairyland. I'll know more tomorrow, when I've begun his debriefing: for now, I gather his injuries required operating theater time so we won't get much out of him just yet.'

James began to polish his bifocals with a scrap of tissue. '*Good.*' His fingertips moved in tiny circles, pinching the lens like a crab worrying at a fragment of decaying flesh. 'You'll debrief him without witnesses. Record onto a sealed medium and type up the report yourself. Use a typewriter, not a word processor.' He looked up at Eric with dead-fish eyes: 'The fewer witnesses the better.'

Eric cleared his throat. 'You know that's in direct contravention of our operational doctrine?'

James nodded. 'Sit down.' Eric sat opposite him. James glanced round, to make sure there were no open ears nearby, then carefully balanced the bifocals on the bridge of his nose. 'Off the record.'

'Yes?' Eric did his best to conceal the sinking feeling those words gave him.

'You're a professional, and you're used to playing by the rules. That's well and good. The reason that rule book exists is to prevent loose cannons from rolling around the deck, knocking things over and making a mess. We designed the policy on debriefing to ensure that no asshole can piss in the coffeepot and embarrass the owners. However, right now, you're working directly *for* the owners. Standard policy wasn't designed for this type of war and therefore we have to make a new rule book up as we go along – as and where it's necessary. Your job is to build up a HUMINT resource, taking us back into a kind of operational model we haven't ever been really good at, and that we gave up on almost completely in the seventies. But the flip side of HUMINT is COINTEL, and if we can spy on them, they can spy on us. So the zeroth rule of this operation is, minimize the eyeballs – minimize the risk of leaks. Clear?'

Eric nodded. Then a late-acting bureaucratic reflex prompted him to protest: 'I agree with your reasoning, but it doesn't help me out if they come after me with an audit.'

James stared at him coldly. 'Where's your loyalty, boy?'

'You're asking me to commit a federal felony, on your word. If you want to run HUMINT assets on the ground, *their* rule number one is that they've got to be able to trust their controllers. You're *my* controller.' He crossed his arms, hoping his anger wasn't immediately obvious to the other man.

James stared at him a moment longer, then nodded minutely. 'So that's the way it is.'

'It's the way it's got to be. It's not just me who's got to trust you, it's the whole chain of command, all the way down.' *Which right now consists of one guy in a hospital bed, but let's not remind him of that.* 'History says that the smart money is on this coming out, if not now, then in twenty years' time. This administration will be fodder for the history books by then – hell, with his heart condition, VPOTUS will probably be sleeping with the fishes – but I'm a career officer, and so are the folks in my outfit. If you don't give us a fig leaf, you're asking us to suck up time in Leavenworth. And we don't get to go on to a juicy research contract with the Heritage Institute, or a part-time boardroom post with some defense contractor when this is over.'

'What do you want?' James's intonation was precise and his voice even, but Eric didn't let it fool him.

'Something vague, but in writing. The vaguer the better. Something like, "In the interests of operational security and in view of the threat of enemy intelligence-gathering attempts aimed at compromising our integrity, all investigations are to be restricted to those with a need to know, and normal committee oversight will be suspended until such time as the immediate threat recedes." Just keep it vague. Then if I have to take the stand, I've simply misunderstood your intent. I'm obeying an order by a superior, you didn't intend your orders to breach the law. Nobody needs to get burned.'

James snorted abruptly, startling Eric. 'Is that all?'

Eric shrugged. 'That's how it's done. That's what kept the shit in check during Iran–Contra. Or did you expect me to fall on my sword when all I need is a note signed by teacher to say I'm an over-achiever?'

'Bah.' James glanced away, but not before Eric noticed a twinkle of crocodilian amusement in his eye. 'I thought you were an Air Force officer, not a politician.'

'You don't get above captain if you're politically blind, sir. With all due respect, it makes life easier for me if I can advise you – where appropriate – of steps I can take to do my job better. That's one of them. Off the record, of course.'

'I'll get you your fig leaf, then. Signed on the Oval Office blotter, if that makes you feel better. Now, talk to me.' James leaned back, making a steeple of his fingertips.

Eric relaxed infinitesimally. 'Someone sent Mike back to us. He didn't come by himself; his leg's busted up. That tells us something about what sort of operation we're fighting.'

'Go on . . .'

'I haven't debriefed him yet. But at a guess, what we've already done has hurt their operations on the east coast, and sending agents through after them is going to scare the shit out of them. They're going to have to negotiate or escalate. Leaving aside the business with GREENSLEEVES and the nuke, we're going to have to negotiate or escalate, too. Now, it's not for me to advise on policy, but I suspect we're going to find that Mike was sent back by someone who stands to gain from negotiating with us. Call them faction "A". The red-on-red action suggests there's a rival faction, call them "B". So we *really* need to keep a lid on this, because if the "B" faction figures that the "A" faction want to negotiate, they may try to torpedo things by pre-emptively escalating. And if GREENSLEEVES wasn't bluffing about the nuke, we could be in a world of hurt.'

Dr. James nodded minutely. 'What would your advice be?'

'We have to find that nuke, or rule it out. And we have to keep them talking while JAUNT BLUE get their shit together. Right now, we're fumbling around in the dark – but so are they. All they know is, we've whacked a bunch of their operations and figured out how to get an agent across. And if they're in trouble internally, presumably they'd love to get us off their backs while they clean up their own mess. They probably think we don't know about the nukes, and we can be pretty sure that they don't know about JAUNT BLUE. Everything we know about them suggests they just don't think in those terms, otherwise they'd be crawling all over us.'

'So. You propose that we debrief Agent Fleming, then use him to establish a back channel to the leadership of Group "A", with the goal of stalling them with the promise of negotiations while we clean up the missing nuke and get some results from JAUNT BLUE. Is that a fair summary?'

Eric blinked, then rubbed his forehead. 'You put it better than I did,' he said ruefully. 'It's been a long day.'

'Going to be longer,' James said laconically. He leaned back and stared at the ceiling air vents for a while, until Eric began to think he was planning on taking a nap; but just as he was about to stand up and leave, James sat up abruptly and looked at him. 'Your analysis is valid, but incomplete because there are some facts you are unaware of.'

Uh? 'Obviously,' Eric said cautiously. 'Should I be?'

'I think so.' James stared at him, his expression deceptively mild. 'Same rules as the Fleming debriefing. This goes nowhere near a computer or a telephone. You follow?'

Eric nodded.

'Number one. Obviously, I do not want – nobody wants – to see a terrorist nuke detonated in an American city. Even if it's in the People's Republic of Massachusetts, that would be very bad. But you need to understand this: if the worst happens, if that bomb goes off, a use will be found for it. The bloody shirt will be waved. Do you understand?'

Eric tensed. 'Who's the fall guy?'

'The President's got a hard-on for Mr. Hussein, and PNAC will fall in line, but –' Dr. James shook his head. 'I'm not sure who, Colonel.

All I can tell you is, it will be someone who we can hammer for it. The hammer is ready, and if the United States doesn't wield it from time to time the other players may begin to wonder if we're still willing. So if JAUNT BLUE is ready, the target might be the Clan. And if JAUNT BLUE isn't ready, we'll hit someone else, someone we can reach and need to nail flat. North Korea, Iraq, Iran, whoever. But. Whatever else happens, if there's a hard outcome, it will be used to strengthen our hand. We'll have carte blanche.' He stared at Eric. 'The code name for this plan – and I stress, it's a contingency plan, a political spin to put on a disaster – is MARINUS BERLIN.'

'Jesus.' Eric looked away. 'That's disgusting.'

'Yes. I know. But what else can we do?'

'Find the bomb.'

'Exactly!' James's frustration boiled over in Eric's face: 'If you've got some kind of magic superpowers that let you stare through concrete walls and pinpoint missing nukes, then I'd like to hear about them, Colonel. Failing that, if you have any better ideas, I'm sure this administration would like to know what else to fricking do if terrorists nuke one of our cities?'

'I'm sorry. Like I said, we're looking. I'll see if I can scare up some backup when we get back.'

'You'd better. Because falling on our swords is not on the agenda for this administration, son. We're not going to hand the country to the liberal surrender monkeys on the other team just because some assholes from another dimension fuck with us, any more than we did when bin Laden got uppity and bit the feeding hand.' James paused. 'I shouldn't have blown up then. Forget I said anything, I'm not mad at you. There's a lot at stake here that you aren't in on: the big picture is really scary. All the oil in fairyland, for starters.'

'All the *what*?'

Dr. James looked as if he'd bitten a lemon while expecting an orange. 'Oil, son. Makes the world go round. You know what the business with al-Qaeda is about? Oil. We're in Saudi Arabia because of the oil: bin Laden wants us out of Saudi because of the oil. We're going to go into Iraq because of the oil. Oil is leverage. Oil lets us put the Chinese and Europeans in their place. And we're running short of it, in case you hadn't noticed, there's this thing called peak oil coming and we've got analysts scratching their heads to figure out how we're going to field it. We're not going to run out, but demand is going to exceed supply and the price is going to start climbing in a few years. Our planetary preeminence relies on us having cheap oil for our industries, while everyone else pays through the nose for it. But we can't guarantee low prices if we're having to send our boys out to sit in the desert and keep the wells pumping. So it was looking bad until six months ago, but now there's a new factor in the equation . . .'

He took a deep breath. 'The Clan. A bunch of medieval jerks, squatting on our territory – or a good cognate of it. What's going down in Texas, Colonel Smith? Their version of Texas, not our Texas: what are they *doing* there? I'll tell you what they're doing: they're sitting on twice as much oil as Saddam Hussein, and that's what's got Mr Cheney's attention. Because, you see, if JAUNT BLUE delivers, eventually all that good black stuff is going to be ours . . .'

*

'Are we nearly there yet?'

Huw glanced in the driver's mirror, taking his eyes off the interstate for a couple of seconds. Elena sprawled across one half of the back seat of the Hummer H2 truck, managing to look louche and bored simultaneously. Petulant, that was the word. A twenty-one-year-old Clan princess – no, merely a contessa in waiting, should she inherit – fresh from her Swiss finishing school and her first semester at college: out in the big bad world for the first time, with two brave knights to look after her. File off the serial numbers and you could mistake her for a spoiled preppy kitten. Of course, the jocks who'd be clustering around the latter type didn't usually carry swords. Nor did normal preppies know how to handle the FN P90 in the gun case in the trunk. Still, Huw let his eyes linger on her tight jeans and embroidered babydoll tee for a second longer than was strictly necessary, before he glanced back at the road and the GPS navigation screen.

'About twenty miles to go. Eighteen minutes. We turn off in ten.'

'Boring.' She faked a yawn at him, slim hand covering pink lip gloss.

'I'm bored too,' snarked Hulius, from his nest in the front passenger seat. He took an orange from the glove box and began to peel it with his dagger. Citrus droplets swirled in the air-con breeze.

'We're all bored,' Huw said affably. 'Are you suggesting I should break the speed limit?'

Hulius paled. 'No – '

'Good.' The white duke took a dim view of traffic infractions, and supplemented the official fines with additional punishments of his own choice: ten strokes of the lash for a first offense. *Don't ever, ever draw attention to yourselves* was the first rule they drilled into everyone before letting them out the door. Which was why couriers on Post duty dressed like lawyers, and why the three of them were driving down the interstate at a sober two miles under the speed limit, in a shiny new Hummer, with every *i* dotted and *t* crossed on the paperwork that proved them to be a trio of MIT graduate students with rich parents, off on a field trip.

The green dot on the map inched south along Route 95, slowly converging on Baltimore and the afternoon traffic. The air-con fans hissed steadily, but Huw could still feel the heat beating down on the back of his hand through the tinted glass. Concrete rumbled under the magically smooth suspension of the truck. The scrubby grass outside was parched, burned almost brown by the summer heat. He'd made a journey part of the distance down this way once before on horseback, in a place with no air-conditioning or cars: it had been a fair approximation of hell. Doing the journey in a luxury SUV was heaven – albeit a particularly boring corner of it. 'Have you checked the charge on the goggles yet?'

'They're in the trunk. They'll be fine.' Hulius pulled off a slice of orange and offered it to Huw. 'You worry too much.'

'It's your neck I'm worrying over. Would you rather I didn't worry, bro?'

'If you put it that way . . .'

The last half hour of any journey was always the longest, but Huw caught the exit for Bel Air and parts east in time: then a couple more turns took them onto dusty roads linking faceless tracts of suburb with open countryside. The distance on the GPS counted down steadily. Finally he reached a stretch of trees and a driveway led up to an unprepossessing house. He brought the truck to a halt in front of the dayroom windows and killed the engine.

'You're sure this is the place?' Elena pushed herself upright then stretched, yawning.

'Got to be.' Huw rooted around in the dash for the bunch of house keys and the letter from the realtor. Then he opened the door and jumped out, taking a deep breath as the oppressive summer humidity washed over him. 'Number 344. Yup, that's right.'

Sneakers crunched on gravel as he walked towards the front door. Behind him, a clattering: Elena unloading the flat Pelican case from the trunk. Huw glanced up at the peeling white paint under the guttering, the patina of dust. Then he rang the doorbell and waited for a long minute, until Elena, holding the case behind him as if it was a guitar, began tapping her toes and whistling a tuneless melody of impatience. 'It pays to be cautious,' he finally explained, before he stuck the key in the lock. 'People hereabouts take a dim view of unexpected visitors.'

The key turned. Inside, the hallway was hot and close, smelling of dust and old regrets. Huw breathed in deeply, sniffing, secretly relieved. He'd set this up by remote control, one of ten test sites running down the coastline and across the continent all the way to the west coast, spaced five hundred kilometers apart. The realtor had been only too glad to rent it to him for a year, money paid up front: it had been unsalable ever since its former owner, a retired widower, had died of a heart attack in the living room one bleak winter evening. You could remove the carpet and the furniture, and even do something about the smell, but you couldn't remove the reputation.

Huw hunted around for the fuseboard for a while, then flipped the circuit breaker. A distant whir spoke of long-dormant air-conditioning. He checked that the hall lights worked, then nodded to himself. 'Okay, let's get moved in.'

It took the three of them half an hour to unload the Hummer. Besides backpacks full of clothing, they brought in a number of wheeled equipment cases, a laptop computer, and a couple of expensive digital camcorders. Finally, the air mattresses. 'Elena? You take the back bedroom. Yul, you and I are roughing it up front in the master room.'

Huw dragged his mattress into the front room and plugged the electric pump in. Some of the houses were still furnished, but not this one. *Be prepared* wasn't just for scouts. Her Grace Helge had done pretty much this same job, on a smaller, much less organized scale – but Huw had been thinking about it for the week since the white duke had called him in, and he thought he had some new twists on it. He mopped at his forehead. 'Listen, we're about done here and it's half past lunchtime, so why don't we head into town and grab a pizza while the air-conditioning makes this place habitable?'

'Works for me.' Hulius grimaced. 'Where's Lady Elena?'

'Here.' Elena leaned against the banister rail outside the door. 'Food would be good.' Her grin was impish: 'How about a couple of bottles of wine?' Like all Clan members, her attitude to wine was very un-American – tempered only by the duke's iron rule about attracting unwanted attention in public.

Huw nodded – slowly, for he was still getting used to playing the role of responsible adult around the other two. 'We'll pick something up if we pass a liquor store. But no drinking in public, okay?'

'Sure, dude.'

'Let's go, then.'

An hour later they were back in the under-furnished living room with pizza boxes, a stack of six-packs of Pepsi, and a discreet brown paper bag. 'Okay,' said Huw, licking his fingers. 'Taken your pills yet?'

'Um, 'scuse me.' Elena darted upstairs, returning with a toilet bag. 'Hate these things,' she mumbled resentfully. 'Make me feel woozy.' She threw back her head when she swallowed. *What fine bones she has*, thought Huw, watching her with unprofessional enthusiasm. That was one of the reasons she was along on this trip: because she weighed only sixty kilograms, the stocky Hulius could carry her piggyback with ease.

'Where were we?' asked Hulius, pausing with a slice of Hawaiian halfway to his mouth.

Huw checked his wristwatch. 'About an hour and a half short of time zero. You guys eat, I'll repeat the plan, interrupt if you want me to explain anything.'

'Okay,' said Hulius. Elena nodded, rolling her eyes as she chewed.

'First, we assemble the stage one kit. Clothing, boots, cameras, guns, telemetry belts. We triple-test the belt batteries and set them running at five minutes to zero hour. There's no post on this trip, even if we get some results. Elena piggybacks on Yul, on the first attempt. If you fail, we call it a wash today, switch off the telemetry, and break open the wine. If you succeed, you evaluate your surroundings and proceed to Plan Alpha or Plan Bravo, depending. Now.' He tore off a wedge of cooling pizza: 'It's your turn to tell me what you're supposed to do as soon as you find yourself wherever the hell you're going. Hoping to go. Plan Alpha first. Elena, if you could take me through your checklist . . . ?'

*

The carvery in the hotel wasn't anything Miriam would have described as a classy restaurant, but after being locked in a brothel for most of a week it felt like the Ritz. She was ravenous from a day pounding the sidewalks; but Erasmus, she noticed over the soup, ate slowly but methodically, clearing his plate with grim determination. 'Hungry?' she asked, lowering her spoon.

'I try never to leave my food.' He nodded, then tore off another piece of bread to mop his soup bowl clean. 'Old habit. Bad manners, I'm afraid: I apologize.'

'No offense taken. You need to put on weight, anyway. I haven't heard you coughing today, but you're so thin!'

'Really?' He made as if to raise his napkin to cover his mouth. 'When you start you know about it, but when something goes away . . . it's an unnoticed miracle.' A waiter arrived, silently, and removed their bowls. 'I don't feel ancient and drained anymore. But you're right, I need to eat. I wasn't always a sack of bones.' He shook his head ruefully.

'It was your time in the north, wasn't it?' The statement slipped out before Miriam could stop it.

Erasmus stared at her. 'Yes, it was,' he said quietly.

'Sorry. Didn't mean to say that.'

'Yes you did.' He glanced sidelong at the other occupants of the room: no one was paying them any obvious attention. 'But it's all right, I don't mind.'

'I don't mean to pry.' The waiter was returning, bearing two plates. She leaned back while he deftly slid her entrée in front of her. When he'd gone, she looked back at Burgeson. 'But I'd be crazy not to be curious. Months ago, when I said I didn't care what your connections were . . . I didn't expect things to go this way.'

He shrugged, then picked up his knife and fork. 'Neither did I,' he said. 'You are curious as to the nature of what you've gotten yourself into?'

She took a sip of wine, then began to methodically slice into the overcooked lamb chops on her plate. 'This probably isn't the right place for this conversation.'

'I'm glad you agree.'

He wasn't making this easy. 'So. Tomorrow . . . train back home? Then what?'

'It'll be a flying visit. Overnight, perhaps.' He shoveled a potato onto his fork, holding it in place with a fatty piece of mutton: 'I need to pick up my post, make arrangements for the shop, and notify the Polis.' His cheek twitched. 'I've reserved a suite on the night mail express, leaving tomorrow evening. It joins up with the Northern Continental at Dunedin, we won't have to change carriages.'

'A suite? Isn't that expensive?'

Erasmus paused, another forkful of food halfway to his mouth: 'Of course it is. But the extra expense, on top of a transcontinental ticket, is minor. You seem to expect travel to be cheaper than it is. It can be – if you don't mind sleeping on a blanket roll with the steerage for a week.'

'Yes, but . . .' Miriam paused for long enough to eat some more food: 'I'm sorry. So we're going straight through Dunedin and stopping in Fort Petrograd? How many days away?'

'We'll stop halfway for a few hours. The Northern Continental runs from Florida up to New London, cuts northwest to Dunedin, stops to take on extra carriages, nonstop to New Glasgow where it stops to split up, then down the coast to Fort Petrograd. We should arrive in just under four days. If we were really going the long way, we could change onto the Southern Continental at Western Station, keep going south to Mexico City, then cross the Isthmus of Panama and keep going all the way to Land's End on the Cape. But that's a horrendous journey, seven thousand miles or more, and the lines aren't fast – it takes nearly three weeks.'

'Hang on. The Cape – you mean, you have trains that run all the way to the bottom of South America?'

'Of course. Don't your people, where you come from?'

They ate in silence for a few minutes. 'I'd better write that letter to Roger right now and mail it this evening.'

'That would be prudent.' Burgeson lowered his knife and fork, having polished his plate. 'You'll probably want to go through my bookcases before we embark, too – it's going to be a long ride.'

After the final cup of coffee, Burgeson sighed. 'Let us go upstairs,' he suggested.

'Okay – yes.' Miriam managed to stand up. She was, she realized, exhausted, even though the night was still young. 'I'm tired.'

'Really?' Erasmus led the way to the elevator. 'Maybe you should avail yourself of the bathroom, then catch an early night. I have some business to attend to in town. I promise to let myself in quietly.'

He slid the elevator gate open and as she stepped inside she noticed the heavily built doorman just inside the entrance. 'If it's safe, that works for me.'

'Why would it be unsafe? To a hotel like this, any whiff of insecurity for the guests is pure poison.'

'Good.'

Back in the room, Miriam jotted down a quick note to her sometime chief research assistant, using hotel stationery. 'Can you mail this tonight?' she asked Erasmus. 'I'm going to have that bath now . . .'

The bathroom turned out to be down the corridor from the bedroom, the bath a contraption of cold porcelain fed by gleaming copper pipework. There was, however, hot water in unlimited quantities – something that Miriam had missed for so long that its availability came as an almost incomprehensible luxury.

The things we take for granted, she thought, relaxing into the tub: the comforts of a middle-class existence in New Britain seemed exotic and advanced after months of detention in a Clan holding in Niejwein. *I could fit in here.* She tried the thought on for size. *Okay, so domestic radios are the size of a photocopier, and there's no Internet, and they use trains where we'd use airliners. So what? They've got hot and cold running water, and gas and electricity. Indoor plumbing.* The jail Baron Henryk had confined her to had a closet with a drafty hole in a wooden seat. *I could live here.* The thought was tempting for a moment – until she remembered the thin, pinched faces in the soup queue, the outstretched upturned hats. Erasmus's hacking cough, now banished by medicines that she'd brought over from Boston – her own Boston. No antibiotics: back before they'd been discovered, a quarter to a third of the population had died of bacterial diseases. She lay back carefully to avoid soaking her brittle-bleached hair. *It's better than the Clan, but still . . .*

She tried to gather her scattered thoughts. New Britain wasn't some kind of nostalgic throwback to a gaslight age: it was dirty, smelly, polluted, and dangerous. Clothing was expensive and conservative because foreign sweatshops weren't readily available: the cost of transporting their produce was too high even in peacetime – and with a wartime blockade in force, things were even worse. Politics was dangerous, in ways she'd barely begun to understand: there was participatory democracy for a price, for a very limited franchise of rich land-owning white males who thought themselves the guardians of the people and the rulers of the populace, shepherding the masses they did not consider to be responsible enough for self-determination.

It wasn't only women's rights that were a problem here – and *that* was bad enough, as she'd discovered: women here had fewer civil rights than they had in Iran, in her own world; at least in Iran women could vote – here, anyone who wasn't a member of the first thousand families was second-class, unable to move to a new city without a permit from the Polis, a subject rather than a citizen. 'Fomenting democratic agitation' was an actual on-the-books felony that could get you sent to a labor camp in the far north. Outright chattel slavery might have fizzled away in the late nineteenth century, but casual racism was pervasive.

I just want to go home. If only I knew where home is!

The water was growing cold. Miriam finished her ablutions, then returned to the hotel room. It was close and humid in the summer heat, so she raised the sash window, dropping the gauze insect screen behind it. *Erasmus can let himself in,* she thought, crawling between the sheets. *How late will he –* She dozed off.

She awakened to daylight, and Erasmus's voice, sounding heartlessly cheerful as he opened the shutters: 'Rise and shine! And good morning to you, Miriam! I hope you slept well. You'll be pleased to know that your letter made the final collection: it'll have been delivered already. I'll be about my business up the corridor while you make yourself decent. How about some breakfast before we travel?'

'Ow, you cruel, heartless man!' She struggled to sit up, covering her eyes. 'What time is it?'

'It's half-past six, and we need to be on the train at ten to eight.'

'Okay, I'm awake already!' She squinted into the light. Burgeson was fully dressed, if a bit rumpled-looking. 'The chaise was a bit cramped?'

'I've slept on worse.' He picked up a leather toilet bag. 'If you'll excuse me? I'll knock before I come in.'

He disappeared into the corridor, leaving Miriam feeling unaccountably disappointed. *Damn it, it's unnatural to be that cheerful in the morning!* Still, she was thoroughly awake. Kicking the covers back, she sat up and stretched. Her clothing lay where she'd left it the evening before. By the time Erasmus knocked again she was prodding her hair back into shape in front of the dressing-table mirror. 'Come in,' she called.

'Oh good.' Erasmus nodded approvingly. 'I've changed my mind about breakfast: I think we ought to catch the morning express. How does that sound to you? I'm sure we can eat perfectly well in the dining car.'

She turned to stare. 'I'd rather not hurry,' she began, then thought better of it. 'Is there a problem?' Her pulse accelerated.

'Possibly.' He didn't look unduly worried, but Miriam was not reassured. 'I'd rather not stay around to find out.'

'In that case,' Miriam picked up the valise and began stuffing sundries into it: 'Let's get moving.' The skin in the small of her back itched. 'Are we being watched?'

'Possibly. And then again, it might just be routine. Let me help you.' Erasmus passed her hat down from the coat rack, then gathered up her two shopping bags. 'The sooner we're out of town the better. There's a train at ten to seven, and we can catch it if we make haste.'

Downstairs, the hotel was already moving. 'Room ninety-two,' Erasmus muttered to the clerk on the desk, sliding a banknote across: 'I'm in a hurry.'

The clerk peered at the note then nodded. 'That will be fine, sir.' Without waiting, Erasmus made for the front door, forcing Miriam to take quick steps to keep up with him. 'Quickly,' he muttered from the side of his mouth. 'Keep your eyes open.'

The sidewalk in front of the hotel was merely warm, this early in the morning. A newspaper boy loitered opposite, by the Post Office: early-morning commuters were about. Miriam glanced in the hotel windows as she followed Erasmus along the dusty pavement. A flicker of a newspaper caught her eye, and she looked ahead in time to see a man in a peak-brimmed hat crossing the road, looking back towards them. She tensed. She'd seen this pattern before – a front and back tail, boxing in a surveillance subject. 'Are we likely to be robbed in the street?' she asked Erasmus's retreating back.

He stopped dead, and she nearly ran into him: 'No, of course not.' He didn't meet her eyes, looking past her. 'I see what you see,' he added in a low, conversational tone. 'So. Change of plan – again.' He offered her his arm. 'Let's take this nice and easy.'

Miriam took his arm, holding him close to her side. 'What are we going to do?' she muttered.

'We're going to deliberately get on the wrong train.' He steered her around a pillar box, then into the entrance to the station concourse, and simultaneously passed her a stubby cardboard ticket. 'We want to be on the ten to seven for Boston, on platform six. But we're going to get on the eight o'clock to Newport, on platform eight, opposite platform six, and we're going to get on right at the front.'

'Then what?'

'It's sixteen minutes to seven.' He smiled and waved his ticket at the uniformed fellow at the end of the platform: Miriam followed his example. 'At twelve minutes to the hour, we cross over to the correct train. If we're stopped or if you miss it, remember your cover, we just got on the wrong train by mistake. All right? Let's go . . .'

Miriam took a deep breath. *This doesn't sound good,* she realized, her pulse pounding in her ears as an irrational fear made her guts clench. She resisted the urge to look over her shoulder, instead keeping hold of Burgeson's arm until he steered her towards a railway carriage that seemed to consist of a row of small compartments, each with its own doors and a running board to allow access to the platform. As she reached the train, she glanced sideways along the platform. The same two men she'd seen on the street were walking towards her: as she watched, one of them peeled off toward the carriage behind. *It's a box tail all right.* She forced herself to unfreeze and climbed into the empty eight-seat compartment, and Erasmus's arms.

'Hey!'

'This is the hard bit.' He steered her behind him, then pulled the door to and swiftly dropped the heavy leather shutters across the windows of the small compartment. Then he walked to the door on the other side of the carriage and opened it. 'I'll lower you.'

'I can climb down myself, thanks.' Miriam looked over the edge. It was a good five feet down to the track bed. 'Damn.' She lowered herself over the dusty footplate. 'Got the bags?'

'Right behind you.'

The track bed was covered in cinders and damp, unpleasant patches. She patted her clothes down and reached up to take the luggage Erasmus passed her. A second later he stood beside her, breathing hard. 'Are you all right?'

'A touch of – of – you know.' He wheezed twice, then coughed, horribly. 'All right now. *Move.*' He pointed her across the empty tracks, towards a flight of crumbling brick steps leading up the side of the platform. 'Go on.'

She hurried across the tracks then up the steps. She glanced back at Erasmus: he seemed to be in no hurry, but at least he was moving. *Damn, why now?* This was about the worst possible moment for his chest to start causing trouble. She looked round, taking stock of the situation. The crowd on the platform was thinning, people bustling towards open doors as if in a hurry to avoid a rain storm. A plump man in a tricorn hat was marching up the platform, brandishing a red flag. Nobody was watching her climb the steps from the empty track bed. *Come on, Erasmus!* She took a step towards the train, then another, and picked up her pace. A few seconds later, an open door loomed before her. She pulled herself up and over the threshold. 'Is this compartment reserved?' she asked, flustered: 'My husband – '

A whistle shrilled. She looked round, and down. Erasmus stood on the platform below her, panting, clearly out of breath. 'No reservations,' grumbled a fat man in a violently clashing check jacket. He shook his newspaper ostentatiously and made a great show of shifting over a couple of inches.

Miriam reached down and took Erasmus's hand. It felt like twigs bound in leather, light enough that her heave carried him halfway up the steps in one fluid movement. She stepped backwards and sat down, and he smiled at her briefly then tugged the door closed. The whistle shrilled again as the train lurched and began to pull away. 'I didn't think we were going to make it,' she said.

Burgeson took a deep breath and held it for a few seconds. 'Neither did I,' he admitted wheezily, glancing back along the platform towards the two running figures that had just lurched into view. 'Neither did I . . .'

BREAKTHROUGHS

It's all very simple, Huw tried to reassure himself. *It'll take us some-where new, or it won't.* True, the Lee family knotwork worked fine, as a key for travel between the worlds of the Gruinmarkt and New Britain. But the limited, haphazard attempts to use it in the United States had all failed so far. Huw had a simple theory to explain that: Miriam was in the wrong place when she'd tried to world-walk.

You couldn't world-walk if there was a solid object in your pos-ition in the destination world. That was why doppelgängering worked, why if you wanted protection against assassins for your castle in the Gruinmarkt you needed to secure the equivalent territory in the United States – or in any other world where the same geographical location was up for grabs. That explained why the Lee family had been able to successfully murder a handful of Clan heads over the years, triggering and fueling the vicious civil war that had decimated the Clan between the nineteen-forties and the late nineteen-seventies. And their lack of the pattern required to world-walk to the United States explained why, in the long run, the Lee family had fallen so far behind their Clan cousins.

'There are a bunch of ways the knotwork might work,' he'd tried to explain to the duke. 'The fact that two different knots let us travel between two different worlds is interesting. And they're similar, which implies they're variations on a common theme. But does the knotwork specify two endpoints, in which case all a given knot can do is let you shuttle between two worlds, A and B – or does it define a vector relationship in a higher space? One that's quantized, and commutative, so if you start in universe A you always shuttle from A to B and back again, but if you transport it to C you can then use it to go between C and a new world, call it D?'

The duke had just blinked at him thoughtfully. 'I'm not sure I understand. How will I explain this to the committee?'

Huw had to give it some thought. 'Imagine an infinite chessboard. Each square on the board is a world. Now pick a piece – a knight, for example. You can move to another square, or reverse your move and go back to where you started from. That's what I mean by a quantized commutative transformation – you can only move in multiples of a single knight's move, your knight can't simply slide one square to the left or right, it's constrained. Now imagine our Clan knotwork is a knight – and the Lee family's design is, um, a special kind of rook that can move exactly three squares in a straight line. You use the knight, then the rook: to get back to where you started you have to reverse your rook's move, then reverse the knight's move. But because they're different types of move, they don't go to the same places – and if you combine them, you can discover new places to go. An infinite number of new places.'

'That is a very interesting theory. Test it. Find out if it's true. Then report to me.' He raised a warning finger: 'Try not to get anyone killed in the process.'

The pizza crusts were cold and half the soda was drunk. It was midafternoon, and the house was cooling down now that the air-conditioning had been on for a while. Huw sat in the front room, staring at the laptop screen. According to the geographical database, the ground underfoot was about as stable as it came. There were no nearby rivers, no obvious escarpments with debris to slide down and block the approaches. He closed his eyes, trying to visualize what the area around the house might look like in a land bare of human habitation. 'You guys ready yet?' he called.

'Nearly there.' There was a clicking, rattling noise from the kitchen. Elena was tweaking her vicious little toy again. ('You're exploring: your job is to take measurements, look around, avoid being seen, and come right back. But if the worst happens, you aren't going to let anyone stop you coming back. Or leave any witnesses.')

'Ready.' Hulius came in the door, combat boots thudding.

Huw glanced up. In his field camouflage, body armor, and helmet Hulius looked like a rich survivalist who'd been turned loose in an army surplus store. 'Where's your telemetry pack?'

'In the kitchen. Where's your medical kit?'

Huw gestured at the side of the room. 'Back porch.' He slid the laptop aside carefully and stood up. 'How's your blood pressure?'

'No problems with it, I'm not dizzy or anything.'

'Good. Okay, so let's go . . .'

Huw found Elena in the kitchen at the back of the rental house. She had her telemetry belt on, and the headset, and had rigged the P90 in a tactical sling across her chest. 'Ready?' he asked.

'I can't wait!' She bounced excitedly on her toes.

'Let me check your equipment first.' She surrendered with ill grace to Huw's examination. 'Okay, I'm switching it on now.' He poked at the ruggedized PDA, then waited until the screen showed an off-kilter view of the back of his head. 'Good, camera's working.' He turned to Hulius. Gruffly: 'Your turn now.'

'Sure, dude.' Hulius stood patiently while Huw hung the telemetry pack off his belt, under the rucksack full of ration packs, drink cans, and survival tools. Hulius's was heavier, and included a Toughbook PC and a short-wave radio – unlike Elena he might be sticking around for a while.

'Got signal.'

'Cool. I'm ready whenever you are.'

'Okay, I'll meet you out back.'

Huw headed for the front room to collect the big first aid kit and the artist's portfolio, his head spinning. *Demo time, right?* Nobody had done this before; not this well-organized, anyway. He felt a momentary stab of anxiety. *If we'd done this right, we'd have two evenly matched world-walkers, able to lift each other, not a linebacker and a princess.* The failure modes scared him shitless if he stopped to think about them. Still, Yul and 'Lena were eager volunteers. That counted for something, didn't it?

The back door, opening off the kitchen, stood open, letting in a wave of humidity. Hulius and Elena stood in the overgrown yard, Elena facing Yul's back as he crouched down. 'Ready?' called Huw.

'Yo!'

Huw placed the first-aid kit carefully on the deck beside him, then unzipped the art portfolio. 'Elena, you ready?'

'Whenever big boy here gets down on his knees.'

'I didn't know you cared, babe – '

Huw stifled a tense grin. 'You heard her. Piggyback up, I'm going to uncover in ten. Good luck, guys.'

Hulius crouched down and Elena wrapped her arms around his chest from behind. He held his hands out and she carefully placed her feet in them. With a grunt of strain, he rose to his feet as Huw dropped the front cover of the folio, revealing the print within – carefully keeping it facing away from himself. 'Go!'

He tripped the stopwatch, then put the folio down, closing it. Heart hammering, he watched the yard, stopwatch in hand. *Five seconds*. Elena would be down and looking around, a long, slow, scan, her headset capturing the view. *Ten seconds*. The weather station on her belt should be stabilizing, reading out the ambient temperature, pressure, and humidity. *Fifteen seconds*. Her first scan ought to be complete, and the smart radio scanner ought to be logging megabits of data per second, searching for signs of technology. If there were no immediate threats she should be taking stock of Yul, making sure his blood pressure was stable from the 'walk. *Thirty seconds*. Huw began to feel a chilly sweat in the small of his back. By now, Hulius should have planted a marker and be on his way to the nearest cover, or would be digging in to wait out the one-hour minimum period before he could return. He'd have a bad headache right now – if he used the one-hour waypoint he'd be in bed for twenty-four hours afterwards, if not puking his guts up. Otherwise he'd stay a while longer . . .

Fifty-five. Fifty-eight. Fifty-nine. Sixty. *Oh shit*. Sixty-one. Sixty-two.

The scenery changed. Huw's heart was in his mouth for a moment: then he managed to focus on Elena. She was holding her hands out, thumbs-up in jubilation. 'Case green! Case green!'

Huw sat down heavily. *I think I'm going to be sick*. It had been the longest minute of his life. 'What happened?' he asked, dizzy with tension: 'Which schedule is Yul running to?'

She climbed the steps to the rear stoop. Her submachine gun was missing. 'Let's go inside, I need to take some of this stuff off before I melt.'

Huw held the door open for her with barely controlled impatience. 'What did you find?'

'Relax, it's all right, really.' She began to unfasten her helmet and Huw moved in hastily to unplug the camera. It was beaded with moisture and he swore quietly when he saw that the lens was fogged over.

'You need to remove the telemetry pack first, I need to get this downloaded.'

'Oh all right then! Here's your blasted toy.' For a moment she worked on her equipment belt fastenings, then held it up at arm's length with an expression of distaste. Huw grabbed it before she let it drop. 'It's perfectly safe over there. A lot cooler than it is here, and there are trees everywhere – '

'What kind of trees?'

She shrugged vaguely. 'Trees. Like in the Alps. Dark green, spiny things. Christmas-tree trees. You want to know about trees? Send a tree professor.'

'Okay. So it's cold and there are coniferous trees. Anything else?'

Elena laid her helmet on the kitchen worktop and began to unfasten her body armor. 'It was raining and the rain was cold. We couldn't see very far, but it was quiet – not like over here.'

Huw shook his head: *City girl.*

'Anyway, I checked over Yul and he said he felt fine and there was no sign of anybody, so I gave him the P90 and tripped back over. Whee!'

Huw managed to confine his response to a nod. 'When is he coming back?'

'Uh, we agreed on case green. That means four hours, right?'

'Four hours.' Elena laid her armor out on the kitchen table then began to unlace her combat boots. 'Then we can break out the wine, yay!'

'I'll be in the front room,' Huw muttered, cradling the telemetry belt. 'Would you mind staying here and watching the back window for a few minutes? If you see anything at all, call me.'

In the front room, Huw poked at the ruggedized PDA, switching off the logging program. He plugged it into the laptop to recharge and hotsync, then sighed. The video take would be a while downloading, but the portable weather station had its own display. He unplugged it from the PDA, flicked it on, and looked at the last reading. Temperature: 16 Celsius. Pressure: 1026 millibars. Relative humidity: 65%. 'What the fuck?' He muttered to himself. Sixteen Celsius – sixty Fahrenheit – in Maryland, in August? With high pressure? That was the bit that didn't make sense. It was over ninety outside, with 1020 millibars. 'It's twenty Celsius degrees colder over there? And the trees are conifers?'

The penny dropped. 'No wonder nobody could use the Lee family knotwork up in Massachusetts – it's probably under a half-mile-thick ice sheet!'

'Hey, you talking to me?' Elena called from the kitchen.

Huw glanced at the laptop. 'Be right back, buddy,' he told it, then carefully put it down on the battered cargo case, picked up the brown paper bag with the wine, and walked back towards Elena to wait for Hulius's return.

*

It was afternoon, according to the baleful red lights on the small TV opposite Mike's bed. He blinked at it sleepily, feeling no particular inclination to reach out for the remote control that sat on the trolley beside his bed. The curtains were drawn across what he took for a window niche, and he was alone in the small hospital room with nothing for company but the TV, the usual clutter of spotlights and strange valves and switches on the wall behind his bed, and the plastic cocoon they'd wrapped his leg in. The cocoon – *it's like something out of* Alien, he thought dreamily. Drainage tubes ran from it to the side of the bed, and there was a trolley with some kind of gadget next to him, and a hose leading to his left wrist. A drip. That was it. *I'm on a drip. Therefore, I must be home. I drip, therefore I am.* The thought was preposterously funny in a distant, swirly kind of way. Come to think of it, all his thoughts seemed to be leaving vapor trails, bouncing off the inside of his skull in slow motion. His leg ached, distantly, but it was nothing important. *I'm home. Phone home. Maybe I should phone Mom and Pop? Let them know I'm all right.* No, that wouldn't work – Mom and Pop died years ago, in the car crash with Sue. *Forget it.* He managed to roll his eyes towards

432

the table the TV stood on. There was no telephone. *Some hospital bedroom this is . . .*

He was too hot. Much too hot. He was wearing pajamas: that was it. Fumbling for the buttons with his right hand, he realized he was fatigued. It felt as if his arm was weak, a long way away. He managed to get a couple of buttons undone, just as the door opened.

'As you can see he's, oh my – '

'Mike? Can he hear me?'

'I'm too hot.' It came out funny.

'I'm real sorry, Mr. Smith, but he's running a fever. We've got him on IV penicillin for the infection, and morphine – '

'Penicillin? Isn't that old-fashioned; I mean, aren't most bacteria resistant to it these days?'

'That's not what the path lab report says about this one, praise Jesus; you're right, most infections are resistant, but he's had the good fortune to pick up an old-fashioned one. So, like I was saying, he's on morphine, his leg's an almighty mess, and they used a whole lot of Valium on him last night so he wouldn't pull out his tubes.'

'Mike?'

The voice was familiar, conjuring up images of a whirring hand exerciser, a tense expression. 'Boss?'

'Mike? Did you try to say something?'

Lips are dry. He tried to nod.

'Ah, h – heck. Is it the Valium? Or the morphine?'

'He ought to be better in a couple of hours, Mr. Smith.'

'Okay. You hang in there, Mike. I'll be right back.'

The door closed on discussion, and the sound of footsteps walking away. Mike closed his eyes and tried to gather his thoughts. *In the hospital. Doped up. Leg hurts a little. Morphine? Colonel Smith. Got to talk to the colonel . . .*

An indefinite time later, Mike was awakened by the rattle of the door opening.

'Huh – hi, boss.' The cotton wool wrapping seemed to have gone away: he was still tired and a little fuzzy, but thinking didn't feel like wading through warm mud anymore. He struggled, trying to sit up. 'Huh. Water.'

There was a jug of water sitting on the bedside trolley, and a couple of disposable cups. Eric sat down on the side of the bed and filled a cup, then passed it to him carefully. 'Can you manage that? Good.'

''S better.' *What's the colonel wanting? Must be really anxious for news to be here himself* . . . He cleared his throat experimentally. 'How . . . how long?'

'It's Sunday afternoon. You were dumped on our doorstep on Friday evening, two and a half days past your due date. Do you feel like talking, or do you need a bit more time?'

'More water. I'll talk. Is . . . is official debrief?'

'Yes, Mike. Fill me in and I promise to leave you alone to recover. If you need anything, I'll see what I can sort out. Guess you're not going to be in the office for a while.' He passed the refilled cup over and Mike drained it, then struggled to sit up.

'Here, let me – gotcha.' The motorized bed whined. Colonel Smith placed a small voice recorder on the bedside table, the tape spool visibly rotating inside it. 'That comfortable?'

'Y-yeah. You want to know what happened? Everything was on track until I got into the palace grounds. Then everything went to hell . . .'

For the next hour Mike described the events of the past week in minute detail, racking his brains for anything remotely relevant. Eric stopped him periodically to flip tape cassettes, then began to supply questions as Mike ran down. Mike held nothing back, his own ambiguous responses to Miriam notwithstanding. Finally, Eric switched the recorder off. 'Off the record. Why did you tell her we'd play hardball? Did you think we were going to burn her? How did you think it's going to sound if we have to go to bat with an oversight committee to keep your ass out of jail?'

Mike reached towards the water again. He swallowed, his throat sore. 'You should know: if you want to run HUMINT assets, you can't treat them like machines. They have to trust you – they *absolutely* have to trust you. So I gave her the unvarnished truth. If I'd spun her a line of bullshit, do you really think she'd have believed me? She knows me well enough to know when I'm lying.'

Smith nodded. 'Go on.'

'Her situation is shitty enough that – hell, her mom said she's on the run – she's short on options. If I'd told her we'd welcome her with open arms she'd have smelled a rat, but this way she's going to carry on thinking about it, and then eventually start sniffing the bait. At which point, we can afford to play her straight, and she's starting with low expectations. Offer her a deal – she cooperates with us fully, we look after her – and you'll get her on board willingly. You'll also get leverage over her mother, who is still in place and in a position to tell us what the leadership is up to. But I think the most important thing is, you'll have a willing world-walker who will do what we want, and – I figure this is important – try to be helpful. I can't quantify that, but I figure there's probably stuff we don't know that a willing collaborator can call out for us, stuff a coerced subject or a non-world-walker would be useless for. If Doc James gets some crazy idea about turning her into a ghost detainee, we're not going to be able to do that, so I figured I'd start by lowering her expectations, then raise the temperature at the next contact.'

'Plausible.' Eric nodded again. 'It's a plausible excuse.'

Mike put the cup down. His throat felt sore. 'Is this going to go to oversight?'

Eric was watching him guardedly. 'Not unless we fuck up.'

'Thought so.' *Get your cynical head on, Mike.* 'How do you mean to handle her, then?'

'We go on as planned.' Eric looked thoughtful. 'For what it's worth I agree with you. I had a run-in with James over how we deal with contacts, and while he's a whole lot more political than I thought, he's also a realist. Beckstein isn't a career criminal, you're right about that side of things. Not that it'd be a problem to nail her on conspiracy charges, or even treason – the DOJ has a hard-on for anyone it can label as a terrorist, especially if they're collaborating with enemy governments to make war on the United States – but there's no need to bring out the big stick if we don't need it. If you can coax her into coming in willingly, I'll do my best to persuade James to reactivate one of the old Cold War defector programs. You can tell her that, next time you see her.'

'Cold War defector program?'

'How do you think we used to handle KGB agents who wanted to come over? They'd worked for an enemy power, maybe did us serious damage, but you don't see many of them doing time in Club Fed, do you? You don't burn willing defectors, not if you want there to be more defectors in future. There were a couple of Eisenhower-era presidential directives to handle this kind of shit, and I think they're still in force. It's just a matter of working on James and figuring out what the correct protocol is.'

'Okay, I think I see what you're getting at.' Mike eased back against the pillows. 'It fits with the timetable. The only problem is, she hasn't gotten back in touch this week, has she? Are you tapping my home telephone?'

'You know I can't tell you that. I'm not aware of any contact attempts, but I'll make inquiries. I'd be surprised if nobody was watching your apartment – or mine, for that matter – but that's not my call to make.'

'Okay. Then can you tell me where I am? Or when I'm going to be let out of this place, or what the hell is happening to my leg in there?' Mike gestured loosely at the bulky plastic brace and the cocoon of dressings. 'It's kind of disturbing . . .'

'Damn.' Eric glanced away. 'I don't know,' he admitted. 'I'll ask one of the medics to tell you. They told me your leg was broken, got chewed up pretty badly – who the hell expected them to be using mantraps in this day and age?'

'It's not this day and age over there,' Mike said dryly.

Eric laughed, a brief bark: 'Okay, you got me! Listen, I figure the medics should give you the full rundown. What they told me is that you'll be off your legs for a few weeks and you won't be running any marathons for the rest of this year, but you should make a full recovery. They were more worried about the infection you brought home, except it responds well to penicillin, of all things. Something about there being no antibiotic resistance in the sample they cultured . . . anyway. You're in a private wing of Northern Westchester. We've closed it off to make it look like it's under maintenance, the folks who're seeing you are all cleared, there are guards on the front desk, and as soon as you're ready to move we're going to send you home. Officially you're on medical leave for the next month, renewed as long as the doctors think necessary. Unofficially, once I confirm this with Dr. James, you're going to be on station waiting for Iris Beckstein to get in touch. You can call in backup if you see fit – even a full surveillance team and SWAT backup – but from what you're telling me, she's got tradecraft, which would make that a high-risk strategy. Think you're up to it?'

'I'll have to be.' Mike reached for the water again. 'What a mess.'

'That's what you get when you go back to running agents.' Eric stood up. 'Enough of that, I've got to go type all this up.' He frowned. 'Be seeing you . . .'

BEGIN TRANSCRIPT

(*Coldly.*) 'You realize that if anyone else had done this, I'd have had them shot.'

'Yes, dear: I was counting on it. This way, hopefully the auld bitches won't be expecting it.'

'Sky Father, give me patience! What did you think you were playing at? We've got a war on, in case you hadn't noticed – '

'Oh, really? And I suppose the sky is a funny non-red color, too? I'm not playing, I'm deadly serious: this is more important than your little war.'

'Damn it, woman! Can't you leave your mother's embroidery circle alone just this once?'

(*Exasperated sigh.*) 'Who exactly do you think it was that started the war, brother?'

'What – excuse me. You can't be serious. Do you really expect me to believe that she's in cahoots with Egon?'

'Absolutely not! It would be beneath her dignity to be in cahoots with anyone below the rank of the Romish Pope-Emperor. But you know, she's always been opposed to the idea of marrying into the royal family, hasn't she? 'Marrying beneath our station,' indeed. She set up this stupid business with Creon by way of

Henryk, in order to provoke Egon. And really, do you believe for a moment that Egon was a real threat to us, absent her maneuvering? She set Helge up as a target while she had me under her proxy's thumb in Niejwein. If she hadn't overreached herself I'd still be stuck there.'

'That's . . . curiously plausible. Hmm. You said she overreached herself. Do you mean Hildegarde didn't expect Egon to mount the putsch then and there?'

'I doubt it.' (*Pause.*) 'She wouldn't have shown her precious nose at the betrothal if she thought it was going to be cut off by the hussars, would she? But her intent was there. I know her schemes, the way her mind works. I think she meant to provoke Egon into doing something stupid, like the way he poisoned his younger brother all those years ago. She doesn't like Helge, as you might have noticed. Thinks I poisoned her mind against her. Which in turn makes Helge disposable, from my mother's perspective. After what she did to her sister, do you question her ruthlessness?'

'All right.' (*Pause.*) 'Your mother's embroidery circle dabbles in dangerous waters, and it is a bad idea to cross them. They've stirred up a third of the nobility against us and Egon's raiders are harrowing the countryside with fire and the sword – at least until we force him to group his army so that we can crush it beneath our boot heel. As we shall, when the time comes, and make no mistake – they have carronades and musketry, but we have machine guns and radios. But, still. You have not yet explained why you did that thing. You'd best try to explain it to me, and get your story straight – the council will be a much less receptive audience, sister.'

'All right. You're not going to like it, though. Between your incredibly foolish machinations and mother-dearest's scheming, I've nearly lost my only child. That's not all I've lost, I'll concede, but unlike some of our relatives, I hold her dear. If I can get her back, I will move heavens and underworld to do so. That's the first thing I'd like to remind you of. The second point is – and this had better not be advanced before the council, or we are all lost beyond

redemption – your niece knows about the insurance policy,
but thanks to Henryk's stupidity and mother-dearest's venality,
she's on the outside. If you'd told me what bait you'd used on
her, I could have settled things, but oh no – '

'Henryk's men got to her first. He knows – knew – too, you
understand that?'

'I've never understood why any of the old assholes should be
allowed near the breeding program – '

'Stop and think about it. If we didn't at least let them observe, they'd
have assumed it's a conspiracy against them. (As indeed it is, but
not in such crude terms.) Henryk's participation was vital, to
prevent a new civil war.'

'Still. It's a delicate matter, you used it as a carrot for Helge to get
her teeth into, then you complain when the other donkey in the
stable bites her?'

'Enough. We can discuss might-have-beens some other time. But
what of the American spy?'

'If you must. When I found out who he was – at first he was an
"injured Clansman", you should remember – my first thought
was to hang him from the nearest available tree: but it turned
out he'd already spoken to her. It was too late.'

'Sky Father, you mean – '

'He was sent here to "talk to Miriam". He didn't know where she'd
gone after the battle – my guess is, with a Lee family locket,
she's somewhere in New Britain right now – but that's not the
point. She spoke to him. Let me assure you that hanging her
ex-boyfriend would be exactly the most effective way to make
her turn traitor. She grew up in America, remember. In my
opinion, the least damaging option was to spin him a line of
disinformation, let his leg fester a bit, then send him back.
If we're really lucky, we've got ourselves a back channel all the
way to the White House. And if not – well, let's just say, whoever
debriefs him is going to get a usefully skewed view of our
politics.'

(*Pause.*) 'That will probably keep the council from demanding your
head.'

'I know. Now let me draw you a diagram. The Americans have
captured world-walkers and worked out how to make them
serve. That means they know what they're dealing with. Helge –
being Miriam – is on the run, she knows about the breeding
program, and one of their agents has already tried to seduce her.
Why haven't you tried to kill her?'

'She's my niece. You are not the only one who feels some residual
loyalty, Patricia.'

'Rubbish. There's another reason, isn't there? Is it something she
knows? No? Oh. Something she did, no – the betrothal?'

'Henryk wanted to ensure a fruitful marriage. He was in a hurry. He
sent Dr. ven Hjalmar to see to her.'

'Tell me you didn't . . .'

'*I* didn't. *Henryk* did. With the queen mother's connivance, of course.
That's the point, you see. It's going to be a world-walker.'

'Oh no!'

'Oh yes. It was always going to be a very short betrothal, just long
enough for the pregnancy test to be confirmed. And, do you
know something? Once we've put down the pretender, all the
surviving witnesses who were present at the palace will swear
that it was, in fact, a lawful marriage ceremony, not just a
betrothal.'

'Holy mother of snakes! You're telling me that with Egon out of the
picture, she's carrying the lawful heir to the throne?'

'Yes. You did ask why I hadn't issued a death warrant, didn't you?'

(*Pause.*) 'Angbard, I've really got to hand it to you: that is the most
crazy, fucked-up, Machiavellian conspiracy I've heard of since
Watergate.' (*Pause.*) 'Does Hildegarde know?'

(*Pause.*) 'You know, I really hadn't thought about that.'

'Because as soon as she finds out, she's going to hit the roof. Who
did you send after Helge?'

'I sent Lady Brilliana after her. She's to stop Helge if she shows signs
of turning traitor – beyond that, she's to try to bring her home.
Ideally before the pregnancy goes too far.'

'Brilliana? That's a good choice. Might even be enough, if we're
lucky.'

'Enough? I hardly think Helge will be able to prevent her – '

'I meant, enough to stop the auld bitches' assassins. If you'll excuse me, Angbard, I have urgent arrangements to make. Is the prescription I asked for ready yet?'

'It's in the outer office.'

(*Chuckle.*) 'So you weren't planning to kill me after all! Admit it!'

'Don't tempt me. You believe Hildegarde will try to kill Helge?'

'Who said anything about Hildegarde? She'll be pissed about me having a granddaughter to call my own, especially one who's an heir and a world-walker, but it's still her lineage. No, what you've really got to worry about are the other members of the old ladies' embroidery circle and poisoning society. Hmm. Then again, Helge thinking she's Miriam – thinking she's an American woman – could really spoil all your plans.'

'I hardly think that changes anything – '

'Really? You're telling me you've never heard of *Roe v. Wade?*'

(*Pause.*) 'Who?'

END TRANSCRIPT

Miriam found the journey uncomfortable. It wasn't the compartment, for the seats were padded and the facilities adequate, but the lack of privacy. Of the eight places – there were two bench seats that faced each other across the compartment – she and Erasmus occupied one side. The other was taken by the plump man in the loud coat, sitting beside the window, and a pinch-faced woman of uncertain years who clutched her valise to her lap, her long fingers as double-jointed as the legs of a crane fly. When she wasn't flickering suspicious glances at the fellow in the check jacket, she parked her watery gaze on a spot fifteen centimeters behind Miriam's head. Whenever the discomfort of being stared at got the better of her, Miriam tried to stare right back – but the sight of the woman's stringy gray hair sticking out from under the rim of her bonnet made her feel queasy.

It was also hot. Air-conditioning was an exotic, ammonia-powered rarity, as likely to poison you as to quell the heat. A vent on the ceiling channeled fresh air down through the compartment while the train was moving, but it was a muggy, humid day and before long she felt sticky and uncomfortable. 'We should have waited for the express,' she murmured to Erasmus, provoking a glare from Crane Fly Woman.

'It arrives a few minutes later.' He sighed. 'Can't be late for work, can I?' He put a slight edge on his voice, a grating whine, and caught her eye with a sidelong glance. The fat man rattled his newspaper again. He seemed to be concentrating on a word puzzle distantly related to a crossword, making notes in the margin with a pencil.

'Never late for work, you.' She tried to sound disapproving, to provide the shrewish counterpart to his henpecked act. *What's going on?* She sniffed, and glanced out of the window at the passing countryside. *Where did Erasmus go last night? Why were those guys tailing us? Was it him or me they were after?* The urge to ask him about the incident was a near-irresistible itch, but one glance at the fellow travelers told her that any words they exchanged would be eavesdropped on and analyzed with vindictive relish.

Things improved after an hour. The train stopped at Bridgeport for ten minutes – a necessity, for only the first-class carriages had toilets – and as she stretched her legs on the platform, Erasmus murmured: 'The next compartment along is unoccupied. Shall we move?'

As the train moved off, Miriam kicked back at last, leaning against the wooden paneling beside the window. 'What was that about? At the station.' She prodded idly at an abandoned newspaper on the bench seat opposite.

Erasmus looked at her from across the compartment. 'I had to see a man last night. It seems somebody wanted to know who he was talking to, badly enough to set up a watch on the hotel and tail all his contacts. They got slack: I spotted a watcher when I opened the curtains.'

'Why didn't they just move in and arrest you?'

'You ask excellent questions.' Erasmus looked worried. 'It might be that if they were Polis, they didn't want to risk a poison pill. You can interrogate people, but they won't always tell you what you want to know, and if they do, it may come too late. If you take six hours out to break a man, by the time you get him to spill his guts his own people will have worked out that he's been taken, and they won't be home when you go looking for them.'

'Oh.' Her voice was very small. *Shouldn't you have been expecting this?* She asked herself. Then she looked back at his eyes. 'There's more, isn't there?'

He nodded, reluctantly. 'They didn't smell like Polis.' His expression was troubled. 'There was something wrong about them. They looked like street thugs, backstairs men, the kind your, ah, business rivals employed.' The Lee family's street fixers, in other words. 'The Polis aren't afraid to raise a hue and cry when their quarry breaks cover. And the way they covered us was odd.'

She glanced down at the floor. 'It's possible it's not you they're looking for,' she said. *I should have thought of this earlier: they know Erasmus is my friend, why wouldn't they be watching him? They're probably watching Paulette, too – I'm a trouble magnet.* 'Hair dye and a cover identity may not be enough.'

'Explain.' He leaned forward.

'Suppose someone in Boston spotted you leaving in a hurry, a day or two after I'd disappeared. They handed off to associates in New London. Either they followed you to your hotel, or they figured you'd pay for a room under your own name. They missed a trick; they probably thought you were visiting a brothel for the usual reason –' Were his ears turning red? ' – but when you reappeared with a woman they knew they'd found the trail. We threw them with the streetcar, and then I turned up at the hotel separately and in disguise, but they picked us up again on the way into the station and if we hadn't done the track side scramble they'd be –' Her eyes widened.

'What is it?'

'We'll have to be really careful if we go back to Boston.'

'You think they're looking for you, yes?'

'Well –' Miriam paused. 'I'm not sure. It could be the Polis tailing you. But if they were doing that, why wouldn't they turn over Lady Bishop's operation? I think it's more likely someone who decided you might lead them to me. In which case it could be nearly anyone. The cousins in this world, maybe. Or it could be the Polis looking for *me*, although I figure that's unlikely. Or it could be the Clan, in which case the question is, which faction is it? It's not as if – '

'The Clan factions would be a problem?'

'Yes.' She nodded. 'I've been thinking about it. Even if, *if*, I wanted to go back, I'd have to approach it really carefully. A random pickup could be disastrous. I need to get in touch with them or they'll think I've gone over the wall, and that's – I don't want to spend the rest of my life hiding from assassins. But I've got to get in touch with the right people there, see if I can cut some kind of deal. I've got information they need, so I might be able to work something out – but I don't trust that slimy shit Morgan who they put in charge of the Boston office.'

'But they've lost us, haven't they? They can't possibly overtake us before – '

'You're wrong. They've got two-way wireless communications better than anything the Royal Post can build. If it *is* Clan security, they'll have us in the Gruinmarkt before we get off the platform.'

Erasmus nodded thoughtfully. 'Then we won't be on this train when it arrives, will we?' He reached into his valise and pulled out a dog-eared gazetteer. 'Let's see. If we get off at Hartford, the next stopping train is forty-two minutes behind us. If we catch that one, we can get off at Framingham and take the milk train into Cambridge, then hail a cab. We'll be a couple of hours later getting home, but if we do our business fast we can make the express, and we won't be going through the city station. You know about the back route into the cellar. Do you think your stalkers know about it?'

Miriam blotted at her forehead. 'Olga would. But she's not who I'm worried about. She I can talk to. You're right, if we do it your way, we can probably get around them.' She managed a strained smile. 'I really don't need this. I don't like being chased.'

'It won't be for long. Once we're on the transcontinental, there's no way they'll be able to trace us.'

*

The shadows were lengthening and deepening, and the omnipresent creaking of cicadas provided an alien chorus as Huw sat in the folding chair on the back stoop, waiting for Hulius. Elena had installed her boom box in the kitchen, and it was pumping out plastic girl-band pop from the window ledge. But she'd gone upstairs to powder her nose, leaving Huw alone with the anxiety gnawing at his guts like a family of hungry rats. For the first hour or so he'd tried working on the laptop, chewing away at the report on research methodologies he was writing for his grace, but it was hard to concentrate when he couldn't stop imagining Yul out there in the chilly twilit pine forest, alone and in every imaginable permutation of jeopardy. *You put him there,* Huw's conscience kept reminding him: *You ought to be there instead.*

Well yes, he'd tell his conscience – which he liked to imagine was a loosely knit sock puppet in grime-stained violet yarn, with web-cams for eyes – *but you know what would happen. I don't have Yul's training. And Yul doesn't have the background to run this project if anything happened to me.* It sounded weak to his ears, even though it was true. He'd known Yul back when he'd been a tow-headed blond streak of mischief, running wild through the forest back of Östhalle keep with a child's bow and a belt of rabbit scalps to show for it – and Huw had been a skinny, sickly, bookish boy, looked down on pityingly by his father and his hale, hunting-obsessed armsmen. The duke's visit changed all that, even though the intensive English tuition and the bewildering shift to a boarding school in the United States hadn't felt like much of an improvement at the time. It wasn't until years later, when he returned to his father's keep and went riding with Yul again, that he understood. Yul was a woodland creature, not in an elfin or fey sense, but like a wild boar: strong, dangerous, and shrewd within the limits of his vision. But not a dreamer or a thinker.

Yul had gone to school, too, and there'd even been talk of his enlisting in the U.S. Marine Corps for a while – the duke's security apparatus had uses for graduates of that particular finishing school – but in the end it came to naught. While Huw had been sweating over books or a hot soldering iron, Hulius had enlisted in Clan security, with time off to serve his corvée duty with the postal service. And now, by a strange turnaround of fate that Huw still didn't quite under-stand, he was sitting with a first-aid kit on the back stoop of a rented house at twilight, worrying his guts out about his kid brother, the tow-headed streak who'd grown up to be a bear of a man.

Huw checked his wristwatch for about the ten-thousandth time. It was coming up on eight fifteen, and the sun was already below the horizon. Another half hour and it would be nighttime proper. *I could go over and look for him,* he told himself. *If he misses this return window, I could go over tomorrow.* Elena's video footage had been rubbish, the condensation on her helmet camera lens blurring everything into a madcap smear of dark green shade and glaring sunlight, but Hulius was wearing a radio beacon. If anything had happened –

Something moved. Huw's head jerked round, his heart in his mouth for an instant: then he recognized Yul's tired stance, and the tension erupted up from his guts and out of his mouth in a deafening whoop.

'Hey, bro!' Yul reached up and unfastened his helmet. 'You look like you thought I wasn't coming back!' He grimaced and rubbed his forehead as he shambled heavily towards the steps. 'Give me medicine. Strong medicine.'

Huw grabbed him for a moment of back-slapping relief. 'It's not easy, waiting for you. Are you all right? Did anything try to eat you? Let's get you inside and get the telemetry pack off you, then I'll crack open the wine.'

'Okay.' Hulius stood swaying on the stoop for a moment, then took a heavy step towards the doorway. Huw picked up the first-aid kit and laptop and hurried after him.

'Make your weapons safe, then hand me the telemetry pack first – okay. Now your backpack. Stick it there, in the corner.' He squinted at his brother. Yul looked much more wobbly than he ought to be. 'Hmm.' Huw cracked the first-aid kit and pulled out the blood pressure cuff. 'Get your armor off and let's check you out. How's the headache?'

'Splitting.' Hulius pawed at the Velcro fastenings on his armor vest, then dumped it on the kitchen floor. He fumbled at the buttons on his jacket. 'I can't seem to get this open.'

'Let me.' Huw freed the buttons then helped Hulius get one arm free of its sleeve. 'Blood pressure, *right now.*'

'Aw, nuts. You don't think – '

'I don't know what to think. Chill out and try to relax your arm.' The control unit buzzed and chugged, pumping air into the pressure cuff around Yul's arm. Huw stared at it as it vented, until the digits came up. 'One seventy-four over one ten.' *Shit.* 'You remember to take your second-stage shots on time, two hours ago?'

'Uh, I, uh, only remembered half an hour ago.' Hulius closed his eyes. 'Dumb, huh?'

Huw relaxed a little. 'Real dumb. You're not used to doing back-to-back jumps, are you?' *Lightning Child, he could have sprung a cerebral hemorrhage!* 'The really bad headache, that's a symptom. You need those pills. They take about an hour to have any effect, though, and if you walk too soon after you take them you can make yourself very ill.'

'It's just a headache – '

'Headache, balls.' Huw began to pack up the blood pressure monitor. 'All you can feel is the headache, but if your blood pressure goes too high the arteries and veins inside your brain can burst from it. You don't want that to happen, bro, not at your age!' Relief was making him angry. *Change the subject.* 'So how was it?'

'Oh, it was quiet, bro. I didn't see any animals. Funny thing, I didn't hear any birds either; it was just me and the trees and stuff. Quite relaxing, after a while.'

'Okay, so you had a nice relaxing stroll in the woods.' *Why needle him? It's not his fault you were chewing your guts out.* 'Sorry.' He glanced away from Hulius just as the door opened and Elena bounced in.

'Hulius! You're back! *Squeee!*'

Huw winced as Elena pounced on his brother. Judging from the noises he made, the headache couldn't be too serious. Huw cleared his throat: 'I'll be in the front room, downloading the take. You guys, you've got ten minutes to wash up. We're going out for dinner, and I'm buying.' He picked up the telemetry pack and slunk towards the living room, trying to ignore the giggling and smooching behind him. *Young love* – He winced again. He might be out from under the matrons' collective thumb, but being expected to chaperon Hulius

447

and Elena was one of the more unpleasant side effects of the man-power shortage. *If the worst happened . . . At least they're both inner family, and eligible.* A rapid wedding was a far more likely outcome than an honor killing if their parents found out.

Back in the front room, he set the tablet PC down and plugged it in. Yul's camera had worked out okay, although there wasn't a hell of a lot to see. He'd come out in a forested area, with nothing but trees in all directions, and spent the next hours stooging around semi-aimlessly without ever coming across open ground. The weather station telemetry told its own story, though. Sixty degrees Fahrenheit had been the daytime peak temperature, and towards nightfall it dipped towards freezing. *I bet there's going to be a frost over there tonight.*

Huw poked at the other instrument readings. The scanner drew a blank; nobody was transmitting, at least on any wavelength known to the sophisticated software-directed radio he'd acquired from a friend who was still working at the Media Lab. The compact air sampler wouldn't tell him much until he could send it for analysis – much as he might want one, nobody was selling a backpack-sized mass spec-troscope. He poked at the video, tripping it into fast-forward.

Trees. More trees. Elena hadn't been wrong about the tree surplus. *If we could figure out a way to get them back, we could corner the world market in cheap pine logs . . .* Yul had followed the plan at first, zipping around in a quick search then planting a spike and a radio beacon. Then he'd hunkered down for a while, probably listening. After about half an hour, he'd gotten up and begun walking around the forest, frequently pausing to scrape a marker on a trunk. *Good boy.* Then –

'Oh you have *got* to be kidding me.'

Huw hit the pause button, backed up a few frames, and zoomed in. Yul had been looking at the ground, which lay on a gentle slope. There were trees everywhere, but for once there was a view of the ground the trees were growing in. For the most part it was a brownish carpet of dead pine needles and ferns, interspersed with the few hardy plants that could grow in the shadow of the coniferous forest – but the gray-black chunks of rocky material off to one side told a different story. Huw blinked in surprise, then glanced away, his mind churning with possibilities. Then he bounced forward through the next half hour of Hulius's perambulations, looking for other signs. Finally, he put the laptop down, stood up, and went back into the hall.

'Yul?' he called.

'Hello?' A door opened, somewhere upstairs.

'Why didn't you tell me about the ruins, Yul?'

Hulius appeared at the top of the staircase, wearing a towel around his waist, long blond hair hanging damply: 'What ruins?'

'The black stones in the forest. Those ruins.'

'What stones –' Yul looked blank for a moment, then his expression cleared. 'Oh, *those*. Are they important?'

'Are they –' Huw tugged at his hair distractedly. 'Lightning Child! Do I have to explain everything in words of one syllable? Where's Elena?'

'She's in the – hey, what's up?'

I'm hyperventilating again. Stop it, Huw told himself. Not that it seemed to help much. 'There's no radio, it's really cold, and you stumbled across a fucking road! Or what's left of one. Not a dirt track or cobblestones, but asphalt! Do I have to do all the thinking around here?'

'What's so special about asphalt?' Hulius asked, hitching up his towel as he came downstairs.

'What's so special? Well, maybe it means there was a civilization there not so long ago!' Nervous energy had Huw bouncing up and down on the balls of his feet. 'Think, bro. If there was a civilization there, what else does it mean?'

'There were people there?' Hulius perked up. 'Hey, I think that rates at least a bottle of wine . . .'

'We're going back over, tomorrow,' Huw announced. 'I'll e-mail a report to the duke tonight. Then we're going to double-check on that road and see where it leads.'

PURSUIT

The small house hunkered a short way back from the sidewalk, one of a row of houses in an area that wasn't exactly cheap – nowhere in Boston was cheap – but that had once been affordable for ordinary working people. Brilliana knew it quite well. She'd been watching it discreetly for over an hour, and she was pretty sure that nobody was home and, more important, nobody else was watching it. Which suited her just fine, because if it was under surveillance what she was about to do would quite possibly get her killed.

Swallowing to clear her over-dry mouth, Brill opened the car door and stepped out into the hot summer sunlight. She slung the over-sized leather handbag on her left shoulder, cautiously checking that she could get a hand into it in a hurry, then let the door of the rental car swing shut. The key was in the ignition: the risk of someone stealing the car was, in her view, minor compared to the risk of not being able to get away fast if things went wrong.

The road was clear. She glanced both ways before crossing it, a final check for concealed watchers. *I hope Paulie's all right,* she fretted. The ominous turn of recent events was bad enough for those who could look after themselves. Paulette wasn't a player, and didn't have the wherewithal to escape if things spun out of control. And Brill owed her. Not that she'd had much time to demonstrate it, lately – the past week had run her ragged, and this was the first free day she'd had to spend in the United States for weeks.

She paused for a moment at the front door, straining for any sign of wrongness, then shrugged. The key slid into the lock and turned smoothly: Brill let herself inside, then closed the door behind her. 'Paulie?' She called softly.

No reply. The house felt empty. Brill began to relax. *She's shopping, or at work.* Whatever 'work' meant these days – Brill couldn't be sure, but the huge mess that Miriam had landed in had probably cut Paulie loose from her sinecure. She glanced around the living room. The flat-screen TV was new, but the furniture was the same. *Yo, big spender!* Paulette wasn't stupid about money. She kept a low profile. Hopefully she'd avoided being caught up in the dragnet so far.

Brill put her bag down on the kitchen counter and pulled out a black box. Switching it on, she paced out the ground floor rooms, front to back, checking corners and walls and especially light fittings. The bug detector stayed stubbornly green-lit. 'Good,' she said aloud as she stashed it back in the bag. Next, she pulled out another box equipped with a telephone socket and extension cable, and plugged each of the phone handsets into it in order. A twitter of dialing tones, but the speaker on the box stayed silent: nobody had sneaked an infinity bug onto her landline. That left the Internet link, and Brill didn't know enough about that to be sure she could sweep Paulie's computer for spyware; but she was pretty sure that unplugged PCs didn't snoop on conversations.

'Okay . . .' Brill picked up her bag and scouted the top floor briefly, then returned to the kitchen. The carton of half-and-half in the fridge was fresh, and there was a neat pile of unopened mail on the tabletop, the most recent postmarked the day before. And there was no dust. She checked her watch: ten past four. *Might as well wait,* she thought, and began to set up the coffee machine.

An hour later, Brill heard footsteps on the front path, and a rattle of keys. She dropped her magazine and stood up silently, standing just inside the living room door as the front door opened. One person, alone. She tensed for a moment, then recognized Paulette. 'Hey, Paulie,' she called.

'What!' A clatter of dropped bags. Brill stepped into the passageway. 'Brill! How did you – '

Brill raised a finger to her lips. Paulette glared at her, then bent down to pick up the spilled grocery bags. 'Let me,' Brill murmured. 'Shut the door.' She gathered the bags: Paulette didn't need prompting twice, and locked the front door before turning back to stare at her, hands on hips.

'What do you want?'

Brilliana shrugged apologetically. 'To talk to you. Do you have a cellular telephone?'

'Yes.' Paulie's hand tightened on her handbag.

'Please switch it off and remove the battery.'

'But –' Paulie looked round once, then shook her head. 'Like that, is it?' she asked, then reached into her bag and pulled out a phone. 'What happens next?' Brilliana waited. After a moment Paulette slid the battery out of the phone. 'Is that what you wanted?'

Brill nodded. 'Thank you. I'd already swept your house for bugs. Would you like a coffee? I'm afraid I've been here a while, it's proba-bly stale, but I could make some more – '

Paulette managed a brief chuckle of laughter. 'You slay me, kid.'

'No, never.' Brill managed a wan smile. 'I apologize for breaking in. But I had to check that you weren't under observation.'

'Observation –' Paulette frowned '– why do I get the feeling I'm not going to like this?'

'Because you're not going to like it. Before I say any more – when did you last see Miriam?'

'Shit.' For a moment Paulette's face twisted in pain. 'She's in trouble, isn't she?'

'When did you last see her?' Brilliana repeated.

'Must be, let me see . . . about three months ago. We did lunch. Why?' Her expression was guarded.

'You're right, she's in trouble. The good news is, I've been ordered to get her out of it. The duke thinks it can be papered over, if she cooperates. I can't promise you anything, but if you happen to see her, if you could make sure that's the first thing you tell her . . . ?'

Paulie frowned. 'I'm telling you the truth.'

'I know that. Not everybody would choose to believe you, though. They'd want to believe you're protecting her. She's missing, Paulie. Nobody's seen her for a week, and we're pretty sure she's on the run. I'm talking to you because I figure if she makes it over here you're one of the first people she'll turn to for help – '

'What do you mean, if?'

'It is a long story.' Brill pulled out one of the kitchen chairs and sat down. 'I know part of it. I think you know another part of it?' She raised an eyebrow, but Paulette stared at her mulishly and refused to answer. 'All right. Three months ago, Miriam did something really foolish. She stole some information about a project she was not supposed to know of, and then she tried to bluff her way into it. It's a Clan operation on this side, that's all I'm allowed to say, and she tampered with the Clan's postal service – that alone is a high crime. To make matters worse, she was caught by the wrong person, a conservative member of the council's security oversight board. What Miriam did, that sort of thing –' she shrugged uncomfortably '– carries the death penalty. I'm not exaggerating. Sneaking into that particular operation –' She stopped. 'You know the one I'm talking about?'

Paulie nodded once, sharply. 'She told me what she was going to do. I tried to talk her out of it, but she wasn't listening.'

Brilliana rolled her eyes. 'I am going to pretend I didn't hear what you just said, because if I had heard you say it, certain superiors of mine would want to know why I didn't kill you on the spot.'

'Ah –' Paulette's face paled. 'Thanks, I think.'

'No problem. Just remember, those are the stakes. Don't let *anyone* else know that you know.' Brill gestured at the coffee machine. 'Shall I refill it? This may take some time.'

'Be my guest.' There was no trace of irony in Paulette's voice. 'You meant that. About the Clan's involvement in a fertility clinic being so secret people can be killed out of hand for knowing about it?'

Brill stood up and walked over to the coffee machine. 'Yes, Paulie, I am absolutely serious. The project the center is working on is either going to change the structure of the Clan completely, and for the better – or it will trigger a civil war. What's more, the authorities here are now aware of the Clan's existence. There have been disturbing signs of covert operations . . . If they discover what has been happening at the clinic, we can't be certain how they will respond, but the worst case is that several thousand innocent teenagers and their parents will find themselves on a one-way trip down the rabbit hole.' She finished with the coffeemaker and switched it on.

'I find that hard – '

'What do you think the clinic's doing?' Brill demanded.

'What? It's a fertility clinic, isn't it? It helps people have babies. Artificial insemination, that kind of . . .' She trailed off.

'Yup,' Brill said lightly. 'And they've been helping couples have children for nearly twenty years now. The fact that the children just happen to be de facto outer family members, carriers of the world-walking trait, is an extra. The clinic is still helping couples who're desperate to have children.' She looked down at the table. 'Half of the children are female. In due course, some of them will be getting letters from a surrogacy agency, offering them good money for the use of their wombs. And they'll be helping other couples have children, too. Children who will be world-walkers. And when they grow up, they'll get a very special job offer.'

Paulette nodded slowly. 'I see. I think.'

'About twenty years from now, the Clan's going to have to absorb a thousand Miriams and their male counterparts. They'll all arrive at once, over about a decade. A torrent of world-walkers. At the peak of our power, before the civil war, there were less than ten thousand of us; now, I'm not sure, but I think only a couple of thousand, at most. Think what that change means. One of the reasons everyone has been bearing down on Miriam is that she's, she's a *prototype*, if you like. Raised outside the Clan. Not uncivilized, but she thinks like an American. They all want to see how – if – she can be integrated. If she's going to fit in. If Miriam can learn to be part of the Clan, then so can the children. But if not . . . in fifty years' time they could be a majority of our members. And the established elders will not willingly give up their power, or that of their children, in favor of uncivilized upstarts. Think what Miriam is going to do to their lives, if she makes a mess of things now!' Brill stopped abruptly. Her shoulders were shaking.

'What's it to you?' Paulie demanded. She stared at Brilliana for a few seconds, then jammed her fist across her mouth. 'Oh. Oh shit. I'm sorry. I didn't realize.'

'Not your fault. My mother had . . . difficulties. Around the time the clinic was being set up. Angbard proposed to my father that he and my mother . . .'

'Oh. Oh dear.'

'My father has *issues*,' Brill said bitterly. 'I believe that is the accepted euphemism. Over here, it's easy enough to say "test tube

454

baby".' Over there . . .' She lapsed into silence as the coffee machine began to burble and spit. 'In any case. To the matter in hand: Miriam stuck her nose into sensitive business – making life much harsher for people she has never met – and was imprisoned, under house arrest. Baron Henryk decided to see if he could domesticate her, using the stick alongside the carrot.'

'What kind of carrot? And stick?'

'He promised not to execute her, if she married the King's younger son, the Idiot. She agreed – reluctantly. And to ensure the succession, he arranged for artificial insem – are you all right, my lady?'

Paulette finished coughing. 'Bastards.' She stared at Brill blearily. 'The bastard. He did *that*?'

Brill shrugged. 'Evidently. He didn't tell Angbard: this all came to light later, by which time it was too late. There was a betrothal ceremony, to be followed by a wedding at the palace. Egon – the Idiot's elder brother – got wind of it, and realized he would be a liability once the younger brother's wife bore a child, so he – '

'Hang on, this is the crown prince we're talking about? Why would his younger brother's offspring be a threat?'

'Creon might be damaged, but he's outer family. There's a test. The clinic only developed it in the past two years. Egon is not even outer family, he is merely royalty. Obviously, he was afraid that once a royal Clan member was to hand, he might suffer an unfortunate hunting accident. So he contrived an explosion in the great hall and proceeded to kill his father, usurp the throne, and start a civil war in the Gruinmarkt. In the middle of all this, Miriam disappeared. She is either here, or in New Britain. I have agents searching for her over there, and over here – I thought she'd come to you if she was in trouble.'

'Oh sweet Mary, mother of God . . .' The coffeemaker spluttered and hissed as Paulette stood up and shuffled over to it. She pulled two mugs down from the cupboard: 'How do you take yours? White, no sugar, isn't it?'

'Yes, please.' Brill waited while Paulette filled the mugs and carried them over to the table. Finally she said, in a small voice, 'Her plight is perilous.'

Paulette froze for a few seconds. 'I seem to recall you said this was good news. Is there anything worse?'

'Oh, plenty.' Brill picked up her mug. 'Your government knows about us now. We have reason to believe they know Miriam is connected to us, too. They obviously don't know about you yet, because they haven't dragged you off to a secret underground detention facility. Hopefully they won't notice you – they are tracing the Clan courier routes, which you have never been connected with – but if she shows up on your doorstep, there is a chance they will follow her and find you.' She reached into her handbag and pulled out a business card case. 'Here's my cell number. If Miriam shows up, ring me at once. If I'm not there, the phone will be answered by a trusted associate. Tell them the word *bolt-hole*. You will remember that?'

'Bolt-hole.' Paulette licked her lips.

'They'll tell you where to go and what to do. From that moment on, we will ensure your security. Once we've got Miriam back, if you want to go home we'll make sure it's safe to do so.' She paused. Paulette was staring at something on the table. Following her gaze, Brill noticed her handbag was gaping. 'Oh. I am sorry.' She reached across and flipped it shut.

'You're carrying. Concealed.'

'Yes.' Brill met her gaze evenly. 'It's not meant for you.'

'Why –' Paulette stopped for a moment. 'Why don't you shoot me? If there's such a security risk? Surely I know too much?'

'I don't believe you know anything that could jeopardize our security. The breeding program is being moved: the patient records are already in a safe location while a new clinic is set up. So, strictly speaking, you can't actually harm us. Besides.' She pulled up a wan grin: 'I try not to kill my friends.'

Paulette chuckled weakly. After a moment, Brill joined in. *Especially when the friend in question is one of the two people who Miriam is most likely to go to for help*, she added silently, and resolved to check back on what progress her employees had made with the other one as soon as possible.

*

Things in New Britain had clearly gone to hell in a handbasket while she'd been away, but Miriam's first intimation that they might have more personal consequences for her came from the set of Erasmus's shoulders as the streetcar rumbled and clanked past the end of the street.

'What is it?' she asked, as he raised his newspaper to shield his face from the window.

'We're getting off at the next stop,' he said, standing up to ring the bell. The streetcar turned a corner, wheels screeching on their track, and began to slow. 'Come on.'

Miriam followed him out onto the high street's sidewalk. 'Something's wrong, isn't it?'

'The shop's under surveillance.'

'I see.' They walked past a postbox.

'I'm going back there, by the back alley.' He reached into an inner pocket and passed her a small envelope. 'You might want to wait in the tearoom up New Bridge Way. If I don't reappear within half an hour – '

'I've got a better idea,' she interrupted. 'I'm going first. If there's someone inside – '

'It's too – '

'No, Erasmus, going in on your own is the dumbest thing you can do. Come on, let's go.'

He paused by the entrance to an alleyway. 'You don't want to make my life easy, woman.'

'I don't want to see you get yourself arrested or mugged, no.'

'Hah. Remember last time?'

'Come on.' She entered the alley.

Piles of rubbish subsided against damp-rotted brickwork: galvanized steel trash cans composting week-dead bones and fireplace ashes. Miriam stifled a gag reflex as Burgeson fumbled with a rusting latchkey set in a wooden gate. The gate creaked open on an overgrown yard piled with coal and metalwork. Erasmus headed for a flight of cellar steps opening opposite. Miriam swallowed, and squeezed past him. 'What exactly are we picking up?' she asked.

He glanced over his shoulder: 'Clothing, cash, and an antiquarian book.'

'Must be some book.' He nodded jerkily. 'Who was watching the shop?'

'Two coves. Ah, you mean why? I'm not sure. They didn't look like Polis to me, as I said. I think they may be your friends.'

'In which case –' She briefly considered a direct approach, but rejected it as too risky: if they *weren't* Clan Security, or if ClanSec had gotten the wrong idea about her, she could be sticking her head in a noose. '– we can just nip in and out without them seeing us. But what if there's someone in your apartment, waiting?'

'There'd better not be.' They were at the foot of the steps now.

'I'm getting sick of this.' She pushed the door open. 'Follow me.'

She duckwalked into a cellar, past a damp-stained mattress, then through a tangle of old and decrepit wooden furniture that blocked off the back wall. Erasmus followed her. There was a hole in the brick-work, and he bent down to retrieve a small electric lantern from the floor just inside it. As he stood up, he began to cough.

'You can't go in like that, they'll hear you.' Miriam stared at him in the gloom. 'Give me the lamp. I'll check out the shop.'

'But if you –'

She rested a hand lightly on his shoulder. 'I'll be right back. Remember, I'm not the one with the cough.' *And besides, I'm sick of just waiting for stuff to happen to me.* At least this made it feel as if she was back in control of her destiny.

Erasmus nodded. He handed over the lantern without a word. She took it carefully and shone it along the tunnel. She'd been this way before, six months ago. *Is this entirely sensible?* She asked herself, and nearly burst into hysterical laughter: nothing in her life had been entirely sensible for about a year, now, since her mother had sug-gested she retrieve a shoebox full of memories from the attic of the old family house.

The smuggler's corridor zigzagged underground, new brick and plasterwork on one side showing where neighboring tenement cellars had been encroached on to create the rat run. A sweet-sick stink of black water told its own story of burst sewer pipes. Miriam paused at a T-junction, then tiptoed to her left, where the corridor narrowed before coming to an end behind a ceiling-high rack of pigeonholes full of dusty bundles of rags. She reached out and grabbed one side of the rack. It slid sideways silently, on well-greased metal runners. The cellar of Erasmus's store was dusty and hot, the air undisturbed for days. Flicking the lamp off, Miriam tiptoed towards the central passage that led to the stairs up to the shop. Something rustled in the darkness and she froze, heart in mouth; but it was only a rat, and after a minute's breathless wait she pressed on.

At the top of the stairs, she paused and listened. *It's empty,* she told herself. *Isn't it? It's empty and all I have to do is take two more steps and I can prove it.* Visions paraded through her mind's eye, the last time she'd ventured into a seemingly unoccupied residence, a horror-filled flashback that nailed her to the spot. She swallowed convulsively, her hand tightening on the rough handrail nailed to the wall. She'd gone into Fort Lofstrom, ahead of the others, and Roland had died – *This is crazy. Nothing's going to happen, is it?*

She took a step forward, across inches that felt like miles: then another step, easier this time. The short passage at the top of the stairs ended in the back room. She crept round the door: everything was as empty as it should be. The archway leading to the main room – there was an observation mirror, tarnished and flyspecked. Relaxing, she stepped up to the archway and peered sidelong into the shop itself.

It was a bright day, and sunbeams slanted diagonally across the dusty window display shelves and the wooden floorboards. The shop was empty, but for a few letters and circulars piling up under the mail slot in the door. If it had been dark, she wouldn't have noticed anything out of the ordinary, and if she'd been coming in through the front door she wouldn't have seen it until it was too late. But coming out of the dimness of the shop . . . her breath caught as she saw the coppery gleam of the wire fastened to the door handle. The sense of déjà vu was a choking imposition on her fragile self-confidence. She'd seen too many trip wires in the past year: Matt had made a bad habit of them, damn him, wherever he was. She turned and retraced her steps, gripping the banister rail tightly to keep her hands from shaking.

'The shop is empty, but someone's been inside it. There's a wire on the door handle.' She shuddered, but Erasmus just looked curious.

'This I must see for myself.'

'It's too dangerous!'

'Obviously not,' he replied mildly. 'You're still alive, aren't you?'

'But I –' she stopped, unable to explain the dread that gripped her.

'You saw it in time. It won't be a petard, Miriam, not if it's the Polis, probably not if it's your relatives. Your bête noir, the mad bomber, is unlikely, isn't he? We'll take care not to trip over any other wires. I'll wager you it turns out to be a bell, wired to wake up a watcher next door. Someone wants to know when I return, that's all.'

'That's *all*?' She wanted to stamp her feet in frustration. 'They broke into your shop and installed a trip wire and you say that's all? Come on, let's go – you can buy new clothes – '

'I need the book.' He was adamant.

She took a deep breath. 'I don't like it.'

'Neither do I, but . . .' He shrugged.

Paradoxically, Miriam felt herself begin to relax once they returned to the back room. Trip wires and claymore mines were Matthias's stock in trade, a nasty trick from the days of the Clan-on-Clan civil war. But Matthias wasn't a world-walker, and he couldn't be over here, could he? He'd gone missing in the United States six months earlier, a week before the first series of targeted raids had shut down the Clan's postal service. While she waited patiently, Erasmus sniffed around his shelves, the writing desk and dusty ledgers, the battered sink with the tin teapot and oil burner beside it, the cracked frosted-glass windowpane with the bars on the outside. 'Nobody's touched these,' he said after a few minutes. 'I'm going to look in the shop.'

'But it's under observation! And there's the wire – '

'I don't think anyone outside will be able to see in, not while the sun's out. And I want to fetch some stuff. Come help me?'

Miriam tensed, then nodded.

Erasmus slowly walked into the front of the shop, staying well back from the windows. He paused between two rails of secondhand clothing. 'That's interesting,' he said.

'What is it?'

He pointed at the door handle. 'Look.' The copper wire ran to the doorframe, then round a nail and down to the floor where it disappeared into a small gray box, unobtrusively fastened to the skirting board. 'What's that?'

Miriam peered at the box. It was in shadow, and it took her a few seconds to make sense of what she was seeing. 'That's not a claymore –' She swallowed again.

'What is it?' he asked.

It was gray, with rounded edges – as alien to this world as a wooden automobile would be in her own. And the stubby antenna poking out of its top told another story. 'I think it's a rad – a, uh, an electrograph.' And it sure as hell wasn't manufactured over here. 'It might be something else.'

'How very interesting,' Erasmus murmured, stooping further to retrieve the letters. 'You were right, earlier,' he added, glancing her way: 'if this was planted by the men who followed us in New London, they're not looking for me. They're looking for you.'

And they're not the same as the men staking out the front door, damn it. She nodded. 'Let's get your stuff and hit the road. I don't like this one little bit.'

*

They hanged the servants beneath the warmth of the early afternoon sun, as Neuhalle's minstrel played a sprightly air on the hurdy-gurdy. It was hard work, and the men were drinking heavily during their frequent breaks. 'It takes half the fun out of it, having to do all the heavy lifting yourself,' Heidlor grumbled quietly as he filled his looted silver tankard from the cask of ale sitting on the cart.

Neuhalle nodded absently as another half-naked maid swung among the branches, bug-eyed and kicking. The bough groaned and swayed beneath its unprecedented crop, much of which was still twitching. 'You don't have to,' he pointed out. 'Your men seem to be enjoying themselves.'

'Maybe, but it's best to set a good example. Besides, they'll change their minds when they run out of beer.'

The tree emitted another ominous creak, like the half-strangled belch of a one-eyed god. 'Start another tree,' Neuhalle ordered. 'This one is satisfied. That one over there looks like he's willing to serve.'

'Aye, sir.'

'Sky Father will be grateful for your work today,' Neuhalle added, and his sergeant's face split in a broad grin.

'Oh, aye, sir!'

It paid to put a pious face on such affairs, Otto reflected, to remind the men that the sobbing women and shivering, whey-faced lads they were dispatching were a necessary sacrifice to the health of the realm, a palliative for the ailment that had afflicted the royal dynasty for the past three generations. The servants of the tinker families – *no, the clan of witches,* Neuhalle reminded himself – weren't the problem: the real problem was the weakness of the dynasty and the debauched compliance of the nobility. Egon might be unable to sacrifice himself or another of the royal bloodline for the strength of the kingdom, but at least he could satisfy Sky Father by proxy. The old ways were bloody, sure enough, but sometimes they provided a salutary lesson, strengthening the will of the state. And so these unfortunates' souls would be dedicated to Sky Father, the strength of their lives would escheat to the Crown, and their gold would pay for the royal army's progress.

Neuhalle was sitting on his camp chair with an empty cup, watching his soldiers manhandle a hog-tied and squalling matron towards the waiting tree, when a horseman rode up to the ale cart and dismounted. He cast about for a moment, then looped his reins around the wagon's shaft and walked towards Otto. Otto glanced at the fellow, and his eyes narrowed. He stood up: as he did so, his hand-men appeared, clearly taking an interest in the stranger with his royalist sash and polished breastplate.

'Sir, do I have the honor of addressing Otto, Baron Neuhalle?'

Second impressions were an improvement: the fellow was young, perhaps only twenty, and easily impressed – or maybe just stupid. 'That would be me.' Otto inclined his head. 'And who are you?' He kept his right hand away from his sword. A glance behind the fellow took in Jorg, ready to draw at a moment's notice, and he nodded slightly.

'I have the honor to be Eorl Geraunt voh Marlburg, second son of

462

Baron voh Marlburg, my lord. I am here at the word of my liege his majesty –' He broke off, nonplussed, at a particularly loud outbreak of wailing and prayers from the corral. '– I'm sorry, my lord, I bear dispatches.'

Otto relaxed slightly. 'I would be happy to receive them.' He snapped his fingers. 'Jorg, fetch a tankard of ale for Eorl Geraunt, if you please.' Jorg nodded and headed for the ale cart, his hand leaving his sword hilt as he turned, and the other hand-man, Hein, took a step back. 'Have you had a difficult time finding us?'

'Not too difficult, sir.' Geraunt bobbed his head: 'I had but to follow the trail of wise trees.' Behind Otto, the wailing prayers were choked off abruptly as his men raised further tribute to Sky Father, 'His majesty is less than a day's hard ride away.'

Otto glanced at Geraunt's horse. He could take a hint. 'Henryk, if you could find someone to see to the eorl's horse . . .' He turned back to Geraunt as his other hand-man strode off. 'How fares his majesty?'

Sir Geraunt grinned excitedly. 'He does great deeds!' A nod at the tree: 'Not to belittle your own, my lord, but he sweeps through the countryside like the scythe of his grandsire, reaping the fields of disorder and uprooting weeds!' He reached into the leather purse dangling from his belt and pulled out a parchment envelope, sealed with wax along its edges. 'His word, as I stand before you, my lord.'

'Thank you.' Otto accepted the letter, glanced at the seal, then slit it open with his small knife. Within, he found the crabbed handwriting of one of Egon's scribes. 'Hmm.' The message was short and to the point. He glanced round, as Jorg returned with Geraunt's beer and Heidlor walked over.

'Sergeant, how long until you are finished with the prisoners?'

Heidlor shrugged. 'Before sundown, I would say, sir. Perhaps in as little as one bell.'

Otto frowned. This was taking too long. 'We have orders to march. Much as it pains me to deprive Sky Father of his own, I think we'd better speed things up. So once the men have finished decorating that branch –' he pointed: there was barely room for another three hanging bodies '– hmm, how many are we left with? Two score?' This particular house had been full of refugees, and the village with collaborators. 'Strip them naked, whip them into the woods, and fire the buildings with their clothes and chattels inside. We'll have to rely on winter to do the rest of our work here.'

Sir Geraunt blanched. 'Isn't that a bit harsh?' he asked.

'His majesty was most specific.' Otto tapped his finger on the letter. 'I don't have time to gently send them to their one-eyed father – you say his majesty is a day's ride away? We have to meet with him by this time tomorrow. With my men.'

'Oh, I see. If I may be permitted to ask, did he issue orders for my disposition, my lord? I am anxious to return – '

'You may ride with us.' He turned and walked away, towards his tent. 'I'm sure there'll be enough wise trees for everyone if he's right about this,' he muttered to himself, for the summons was unequivocal: *It is time to seek a concentration of fluxes,* his majesty had ordained. To draw the tinker-witches into a real battle, by threatening a target they couldn't afford to lose with force they couldn't ignore. It would mean attacking a real target, not just another of these tedious manor estates. It would probably be either Fort Lofstrom or Castle Hjorth, and Otto would be willing to bet good money on the latter.

BEGIN TRANSCRIPT

'Good evening, your grace!'

'Indeed it is, indeed it is, Eorl Riordan. A lovely evening. And how are you?'

'I am well, sir. As well as can be expected.'

'For a fellow who is well, your face is uncommonly glum. Here, sit down. A glass of the Cabernet, perhaps?'

'Thank you, sir. What can I do for you?'

'Hmm, direct and to the point. Let me ask you a leading question, then. You may answer as indiscreetly as you care – it will go no farther than this room. How do you rate our performance?'

'Tactical or strategic? Or logistic and economic?'

'Whichever you deem most important. I want to know, in

confidence, what you think we're doing wrong and what you think we're doing right.'

'Doing *right*?' (*Brief laughter*.) 'Nothing.'

'That's –' (*Pause*.) '– a provocative statement. Would you elaborate?'

'Yes, your grace. May I start with a summary?'

'Be my guest.'

'We are engaged in a war on two fronts. I shall ignore the first hostility for now, and concentrate on the second, because that's the one you assigned me to deal with. Hostilities started when the former crown prince usurped the throne. It is evident from the speed and nature of his actions that he had been planning to do so for some time, and that he had already assured himself of the support of a sufficiently broad base of the nobility, before he moved, to have some hope of success. However, his move may well have been reactive – a response to the imminent marriage of his younger brother. So to start with, we are fighting an opponent who has studied his enemies and who has prepared extensively for this conflict, but whose execution was rushed.'

'Hmm. How do you evaluate his preparations?'

'They were confoundedly good, your grace. His control over the Royal Life Guards, for one thing – that was a nasty surprise. His ability to install explosives in the palace – his possession of them – speaks of a level of planning that has given me sleepless nights. The Pervert may be many things but he isn't stupid. Despite his well-known antipathy for our number, he has studied us closely. It is impossible to now ask his grand-dame how much lore she may have passed on to him, but we should take it as read that when he refers to us as 'witches' he knows exactly what we are capable of. For example, rather than holding Niejwein and the castles surrounding it, he immediately departed for the field, where I am told he sleeps among his troops, never in the same tent twice. Sir, he clearly knows how the civil war was fought: he knows exactly what tactics we would first think to use against an enemy noble, and his defenses are as good as anything we could muster for one of our own.'

'You've considered the usual routes, I take it? An assassination team from the other side?'

'Yes, your grace. It would be suicidal. For one thing, as I said, he
   sleeps among his men, in the field, always moving – for another,
   he has body doubles. We have identified at least two of them
   on different occasions, and they're good actors: there is a good
   chance we would be striking at a puppet rather than their
   master. Finally, he has bodyguards. And I fear we have been too
   liberal with our gifts over the past decades: either that, or they've
   captured some hedge-lord's private cabinet of arms, because
   I have confirmation that his majesty's hand-men carry MP5s.'
(*Pause.*) 'All right, so the Pervert's a hard target. Now. The strategic
   picture?'
'Certainly, your grace. The enemy has divided his forces into
   battalion-strength raiding units. They're in the field and they're
   hurting us. It's a – this is embarrassing – a classic insurgency.
   The royal battalions fall on our outlying villages, hit them hard,
   massacre and destroy everything they can get their hands on,
   then disappear into the forest again. It's absolutely not how
   you'd expect an eastern monarch to fight, it's downright
   dishonorable – but it's how the Pervert is fighting. He's serious,
   sir, he's trying to force us to divide our strength. And he's
   succeeded. We've had to move as many dependents as possible
   over to the other side, and keep couriers on standby everywhere.
   And even that's not enough. We've used helicopters to rush
   armed detachments into position on the other side a couple
   of times, and it worked on that bastard Lemke – he won't be
   burning any more villages – but the more we do it, the greater
   the risk that the Americans will notice. He's got us on the
   defensive, and each time he hits us we either lose a village or we
   lose men we can't afford to – and he gains honor. This week I've
   lost eleven dead and fourteen injured badly enough they won't
   be fighting again for months. That's not including the outer
   family members, dependents, servants, peasants and the like. I
   think we've accounted for a good couple of hundred of the foe,
   but they're not stupid: usually the first warning of an attack we
   have is when a cannonball comes through a manor house door.
   There's a limit to what a lance with M16s and a SAW can do

against a battalion of dragoons and a cavalry squadron – some of whom have Glocks.'

'Ah, yes. I thought you'd bring that up. Be glad you don't have to explain it to the council, Eorl Riordan. They know it's wrong, but they still can't help but petition for protection, which is why three-quarters of our number are guarding strategic hamlets or sitting in helicopter hangars on the other side. It's what we exist for, and we're being nibbled to death by mice. What would you do, were you in charge?'

'I'd set up a mousetrap, your grace. We can't afford to suffer the death of a thousand cuts – Clan Security has, what? Two hundred inner family? Nearly a thousand armed and trained retainers? And up to six hundred world-walkers to call in for the corvée, if we need logistic support. The usurper outnumbers us five to one, but we've got SAWs and two-way radio while they're limited to roundshot, grapeshot, and horseback couriers. We should be able to massacre those raiding parties, if we can just once anticipate not only their next target, but their path of advance.'

'Hmm. Suppose I were to tell you exactly where the enemy is planning to mass for a major strike, next Tuesday. Not just one of their battalions, but three of them, a goodly chunk of the royal army. Would that enable you to prepare a suitable reception for him?'

'Would – your grace! Please say it's true!'

(*Pause.*) 'The source is . . . troubling. I would not completely discount all risk of it being a deliberate leak, intended to lure us into a trap. Still. Be that as it may, I am informed – by one who stands to profit from that information – that there is a high probability of an attack on Castle Hjorth within the next two weeks. Which strikes me as suicidal, given the location and defenses of the castle, so I advise you to bear in mind the possibility that even if my source is telling the truth, they are not telling us everything. But, having said that, I want you to work out what we're going to do about it. Because if it is true, my informer tells me that the Pervert himself will lead the attack. And this might be our best opportunity to kill him and end the war.'

END TRANSCRIPT

INTERACTION

As it happened, Mike didn't get to go home that day – or the next. 'You live on your own in a second-floor apartment, and you've got a lovely spiral fracture plus soft-tissue injuries and a damaged Achilles tendon, Mr. Fleming. Listen, I'll happily sign you out – if you fill in a criminal negligence waiver for me, first. But I really think it's a bad idea right now. Maybe tomorrow, when we've got you a nice fiberglass box and a set of crutches, after we set you up with an appointment with physio. But if you check out today, you'll wish you hadn't.'

The time passed slowly, with the inane babble of daytime TV as a laugh track, interrupted occasionally by nursing orderlies and interns checking up on him. Smith hadn't left him any reading matter, classified or otherwise, and he was close to climbing the walls by the morning of the second day after Smith's visit, when he had a surprise visitor: Judith Herz, the FBI agent who'd been sucked into Family Trade at the same time at Mike.

'Smith sent me. You're checking out,' she said crisply, and dropped an overnight bag on the chair. 'Here's your stuff, I'll be back in ten.'

She shut the door briskly, leaving Mike shaking his head. *What got her so pissed?* He opened the bag and pulled out the clothing. It was the stuff he'd been wearing over a week ago, before the CLEANSWEEP mission ran off the rails. He shook it out and managed to get the trouser leg over his cast without too much trouble. By the time Herz opened the door again, he was buttoning his jacket. 'Yes?' he asked.

'I'm your lift.' She waved a key fob at him. 'You going to be okay walking, or do you need a wheelchair?'

'I'll walk. Give me time, I'm not used to these things.' He eased his weight onto the crutches and took an experimental step forward. 'Let's go.'

She said nothing more all the way to the parking lot. As they neared a black sedan Mike's impatience got the better of him. 'You're not in the taxi business. What's the big problem?'

'I wanted to talk to you without eavesdroppers.' She squeezed the key fob: lights flashed and doors unlocked.

'Okay, talk.' Mike's stomach twisted. *Last time someone said that to me, he ended up dead.*

She opened the passenger door. 'Here, give me those, I'll put them in the trunk.' A minute later she slid behind the wheel and moved off. 'Your house is under surveillance.'

'Yeah, I know.'

She gave him a look. 'Like that, is it? Care to explain why?'

'Because –' he stopped in mid-sentence '– what business of yours is it?'

She braked to a stop, near the end of the exit ramp, looking for a gap in the traffic. 'It'd be kind of nice to know that I've been taken off hunting for a ticking bomb and told to stake out a colleague's house for a good reason.' Her voice crackled with quiet anger.

Mike swallowed. *Good cop,* he realized. *What to say . . . ?* 'It's not me you're staking out. I'm expecting a visitor.'

'Okay.' She hit the gas hard, pushing out into a too-small gap in the traffic: a horn blared behind them for a moment, then they were clear. 'But they'd better be worth it.'

'Listen. You know the spooks are calling the shots. I got dragged off into fairyland, but you don't have to follow me down the rabbit hole.'

'Too late. I'm in charge of the team that's watching you. I just found out about it yesterday. If it's not you, who am I meant to be keeping an eye open for?'

'Someone who may be able to tell us whether he was bluffing or if there really *is* a bomb – and if so, where he might have planted it.'

Herz swung left into the passing lane. 'Good answer.' Her fingers tightened on the wheel. 'That's what I wanted to hear. Is it true?'

Mike took a deep breath. 'The NIRT guys are still working their butts off, right?'

'Yes . . .'

'Then in the absence of a forensics lead or an informant you're not delivering much value-added, are you? They're the guys with the neutron-scattering spectrometers and the Geiger counters. You're the detective. What did the colonel tell you to do?'

Herz took an on-ramp, then accelerated onto the interstate: 'Stake you out like a goat. Watch and wait, twenty-four by seven. You're supposed to tell me what to do, when to wrap up the case.'

'Hmm.' *What have I gotten myself into here?* 'I really ought to get the colonel to tell me whether I can fill you in on a couple of code words.'

Herz set the cruise control and glanced at him, sidelong. 'He told me you'd been on something called CLEANSWEEP, and this is the follow-up.'

Mike felt the tension ease out of his shoulders. 'I hate the fucking spook bullshit,' he complained. 'Okay, let me fill you in on CLEAN-SWEEP and how I got my leg busted up. Then maybe I can help you figure out a surveillance plan . . .'

*

Miriam watched from the back room while Erasmus systematically looted his own shop. 'Go through the clothing and take anything you think you'll need,' he told her. 'There's a traveling case downstairs that you can use. We're going to be away for two weeks, and we'll not be able to purchase any necessities until we reach Fort Kinnaird.'

'But I can't just –' Miriam shook her head. 'Are you sure?'

'Whose shop is it?' He flashed her a cadaverous grin. 'I'll be upstairs. Got to fetch a book.'

The traveling case in the cellar turned out to be a battered leather suitcase. Miriam hauled it up into the back room and opened it, wrinkling her nose. It looked clean enough, although the stained silk lining, bunched at one side, made her wonder at its previous owner's habits. She stuffed the contents of her valise into it, then scoured the rails in the back for anything else appropriate. There wasn't much there: Erasmus had run down the stock of clothes since she'd last seen the inside of his shop. A search of the pigeonholes behind the counter yielded a fine leather manicure case and a good pen. She was tucking them into the case when Erasmus reappeared, carrying a couple of books and a leather jewelry case.

'What's that?' she asked.

'Stock I'm not leaving in an empty shop for two weeks.' He pulled another suitcase out from a cubby behind his desk and opened it: 'I'm also taking the books to prove I'm their rightful owner, just in case.' It all went in. Then he opened the partition at the back of the counter and rummaged around inside. 'You might want to take this . . .' He held a small leather box out to Miriam.

'What –' She flicked the catch open. The pistol was tiny, machined with the precision of a watch or a camera or a very expensive piece of jewelry. 'Hey, I can't take – '

'You must,' Burgeson said calmly. 'Whether you ever need to use it is another matter, but I believe I can trust you not to shoot me by mistake, yes?'

She nodded.

'Then put it away. I suggest in a pocket. The case and spare rounds can go – here.' He picked out the pistol then slipped the case through a slit in the lining of the suitcase that Miriam hadn't even noticed. 'It's loaded with three rounds in the cylinder, the hammer is on the empty fourth chamber. It's a self-arming rotary, when you pull the trigger it will cock the hammer – double-action – do you see?' He offered it to her.

She took the pistol. 'You really think I'll need it?'

'I hope not.' He glanced away, avoiding her gaze. 'But these are dangerous times.'

He bustled off again, into the front of the shop, leaving Miriam to contemplate the pistol. *He's right*, she realized with a sinking heart. She double-checked that the hammer was, indeed, on the empty chamber, then slipped it into her coat pocket just as Erasmus returned, clutching a wad of envelopes.

'You have mail.' He passed her a flimsy brown wrapper.

'I have –' 'She did a double take. 'Right.' There was no postage stamp; it had been hand-delivered. She opened it hastily. The neat copperplate handwriting she recognized as Roger's. The message was much less welcome:

Polis raided yr house, watching yr factory. Am being watched, can't help. Think yr stuff is still where it was, locked in the office.

'Shit!'

She sat down hard on the wooden stool Erasmus kept in the back office.

'What troubles you?'

She waved the note at him. 'I need to collect this stuff,' she said.

'Yes, but –' He read the note rapidly, his face expressionless. 'I see.' He paused. 'How badly do you need it?'

The moment she'd been half-dreading had arrived. How would Burgeson respond if she told him the unvarnished truth?

'Very.' She meshed her fingers together to avoid fidgeting. 'The machine I need to collect has . . . well, it's more than just useful to me. It stores pictures, and among them there's a copy of the original knotwork design I need if I'm going to get back to my own world by myself. If I've got it, I'm not stuck with a choice between permanent exile here and a, a feudal backwater. Or going back to the Clan. If I *do* decide to make contact with them and ask to be taken in, it's a bargaining lever that demonstrates my bona fides because I had a choice. And if I don't, it gives me access to my own, my original, world. Where it's possible to get hold of things like the medicine I got you.'

He waited for several seconds after she finished speaking. 'That's not all, is it?' he said.

'Are you planning on keeping me a prisoner here?' she asked. 'Because that's what denying me the ability to go back to the United States amounts to.'

'I'm not! I apologize. I did not mean to imply that I thought you were going to cut and run. But there's more to this device of yours than a mere pictographic representation, isn't there?'

'Well, yes,' she admitted. 'For one thing, it contains a copy of every patent filed in my home country over more than a century.' Erasmus gaped. 'Why do you think I started out by setting up a research company?'

'But that must be – that's preposterous!' He struggled visibly to grapple with the idea. 'Such a library would occupy many shelf-feet, surely?'

'It used to. But you saw the DVD player. Every second, that machine has to project thirty images on screen, to maintain the illusion of motion. How much storage do you think they take up? In my world, we have ways of storing huge amounts of data in very small spaces.'

'And such a library would be expensive,' he added speculatively.

'Not if it was old. And the cost of the storage medium was equivalent to, say, a reporter's notebook.' Her patent database might not include anything filed in the past fifty years, but a full third of its contents were still novelties in New Britain.

'We must seem very primitive to you.' He was scrutinizing her, Miriam realized, with a guarded expression that was new and unwelcome.

'In some ways, yes.' She relaxed her hands. 'In other ways – no, I don't think so. And anyway, there are probably any number of other worlds out there that are as far beyond this one, or the one I came from, as this is beyond the Gruinmarkt. Where the Clan come from,' she clarified. 'Bunch of medieval throwbacks.' *Throwbacks who are your family,* she reminded herself. 'Look, from my point of view, I need to make sure I've got something, anything, that'll stop them coming after me if they realize I survived the massacre.' *Assuming they survived.* 'If I've got the laptop I can threaten to throw myself on the mercy of the security agencies in the U.S., whoever Mike is working for. Or I can claim loyalty and demonstrate that I didn't do that, even though I could have. And if I don't have anything to do with them I can use it to set up in business again, over here.'

'Do you plan to throw yourself on the mercy of your friend's agency?' Erasmus asked, raising an eyebrow.

Miriam shuddered. 'It's a last resort. If the Clan come after me and try to kill me, they might be able to keep me alive.' *But then again –* Mike's words came back to haunt her: *They're using world-walkers as mules, there's a turf war inside the bureaucracy.* Things might go really well. And then again, she might end up vanishing into some underground equivalent of Camp X-ray, into a nightmarish gulag that would make house arrest in Niejwein seem like paradise. 'I don't want to risk it unless I have to.'

'So what are you going to do?' he asked gently. She blinked, and realized he was watching her hands. A double take: *He gave me a pistol*, she realized.

'I'm going to take back what's mine,' she said calmly, 'and I'm going to get clean away with it. Then we're going to go on a long rail trip while the fuss dies down.' She stood up. 'Do you mind if I go through your stock again? There's some stuff I need to borrow . . .'

*

Two hours later, a mousy-looking woman in black trudged slowly past a row of warehouses and business premises, pushing a handcart. Her back hunched beneath an invisible load of despair, she looked neither left nor right as she trailed past an ominously quiet light metal works and a boarded-up fabric warehouse. The handcart, loaded with a battered suitcase and a bulging sack, told its own story: another of the victims of the blockade and the fiscal crisis, out on her uppers and looking for work, or shelter, or a crust before nightfall.

The streets weren't deserted, but there was a lack of purposeful activity; no wagons loading and unloading bales of cloth or billets of mild steel, and a surfeit of skinny, down-at-heel men slouching, hands in pockets, from one works to another – or optimistically holding up crude signboards saying WILL WORK FOR FOOD. Some messages were universal, it seemed.

The woman with the handcart paused in the shadow of the textile mill, as if out of breath or out of energy on whatever meager rations she'd managed to obtain that morning. Her dull gaze drifted past a couple of idlers near the gates to a closed and barricaded glass factory: idlers a trifle better fed than the run of the mill, idlers wearing boots that – if she'd stopped to look – she might have noticed were suspiciously well-repaired.

A little further up the road, a shabby vendor with a baked potato stand was watching another boarded-up building. The woman's gaze slid past him, too. After a minute or so she began to put one weary

474

foot in front of another, and pushed her cart along the sidewalk towards the boarded-up works.

As she hunched over the handles of her cart, Miriam rubbed her wrist and squinted at the small pocket watch she'd wound around it. *Any minute now*, she told herself, half-sick with worry. The last time she'd tried something like this she'd ended up in Baron Henryk's custody, guarded by cold-faced killers and under sentence of death. If she was wrong about the watchers, if there were more of them, this could end up just as badly.

From the alleyway running alongside the boarded-up workshop there was a crash and a tinkle of broken glass. Miriam shuffled slowly along, overtly oblivious as the potato-vendor left his stand and strolled towards the side of the building. Behind him the two idlers she'd tagged began to walk briskly in the opposite direction, setting up a pincer at the other end of the alley. She felt a flash of triumph. Now all it would take was for the street kids Erasmus had paid to do their job . . .

The watchers were out of sight. Miriam dropped the handles of her cart, grabbed her suitcase, and darted towards the workshop's office doorway. A heavy seal and a length of rope held the splintered main door closed with the full majesty of the law, and not a lot besides: she tugged hard at the seal, ducking inside as the door groaned and threatened to collapse on her. *One minute only*, she told herself. It might take them longer to work out that the urchins were a distraction, but she wasn't betting on it.

Inside the entrance the building was dark and still, and cold – at least, as cold as anything got at this time of year. Moving fast, with an assurance born of having worked here for months, Miriam darted round the side of the walled-off office and felt for the door handle. It had always been loose, and her personal bet – that the Polis wouldn't lock up inside a building they were keeping under surveillance – paid off. The door handle flexed as she stepped inside her former office, raising her suitcase as a barrier.

She needn't have bothered. There was nobody waiting for her: nothing but the dusty damp smell of an unoccupied building. The high wooden stools lay adrift on the floor under a humus of scattered papers and overturned drawers. A flash of anger: *The bastards didn't need to do this, did they?* But in a way it made things easier for her. Dealing with a stakeout by the secret police was trivially easy compared to sneaking her laptop out past Morgan and making a clean getaway.

Thirty seconds. The nape of her neck was itching. Miriam stumbled across the overturned furniture, then bent down, fumbling in the leg well below one scribe's position. The hidden compartment under the desk was still there: her hands closed on the wooden handle and pulled down and forward to open it. It slid out reluctantly, scraping loudly. She tugged hard, almost stumbling as it came out and the full weight of its contents landed on her arms.

The suitcase was on the floor. *Forty-five seconds.* She fumbled with the buckles for a heart-stopping moment, but finally the lid opened. Scooping the contents out of the hidden drawer – the feel of cold plastic slick against her fingertips – she swept them into the pile of bundled clothing within, then grabbed the bag by its handles. There was no time to buckle it closed: she picked it up in one hand and scurried back into the body of the empty works.

One minute. Was that a shout from outside? Miriam glanced briefly at the front door. *Doesn't matter,* she thought: *they'll work it out soon enough.* Moving by dead reckoning, her free hand stretched out to touch the wall beside her, she headed deeper into the building, following the deepening shadows. Another turn and the shadows began to lighten. At the end of the corridor she turned left and the grimy daylight lifted, showing her the dust and damage that had been brought to bear on her business, in the name of the law and by the neglect of her peers. It was heartbreaking, and she stopped, briefly unable to go on. *I'll rebuild it,* she told herself. *Somehow.* The most important tools were in her suitcase, after all.

Then she heard them. A bang from the front door, low-pitched male voices, hunters casting around for the scent. Burgeson's distraction had worked its purpose, but if she didn't hurry, it would be all for nothing. Grimly determined, Miriam stepped into the abandoned workshop and gripped her suitcase. Standing beneath the skylight, she pulled the locket out of her pocket and narrowed her eyes, focusing on it and clearing her mind of everything else as the police agents stumbled towards her through the darkness.

This is it, she told herself. *No more nice-guy Miriam. Next time someone tries to do this to me, I'm not going to let them live long enough to regret it.*

And then the world changed.

*

Huw slept badly after he finished drafting the e-mail report to the duke. It wasn't simply the noises Yul and Elena were making, although that was bad enough – young love, he reflected, was at its worst when there wasn't enough to go round – but the prospects of what he was going to have to face on the morrow kept him awake long after the others had fallen asleep.

A new world. There couldn't be any other explanation for the meteorological readings. Temperatures that low, that kind of subarctic coniferous forest, hadn't been found in this part of the world since the last of the ice ages. The implications were enormous. For starters, this was the second new world that the Lee family's knotwork could take a world-walker to. *What happens if I use the original knot, from somewhere in this fourth world? Probably it takes me to yet another . . .* Even without discovering new topologies, ownership of both knotwork designs implied access to a lot more than three, or even four, worlds. *The knots define a positional transformation in a higher-order space. Like the moves of different pieces on a chessboard – able to go forward or backward, but if you used your bishop to make a move in one direction, then swapped your bishop for a rook, you could go somewhere else.* It meant everything was up for grabs.

For over a century the Clan's grandees had doppelgängered their houses – building defenses in the other world they knew of, to protect their residences from stealthy attack – without realizing that the Lee family could attack them from a third world. Now there was a fourth, and probably a fifth, a sixth . . . where would it end? *Our core defensive strategy has just been made obsolete, overnight.* And that wasn't the worst of it. The Lee family knot was a simple mistake, the lower central whorl superimposed over the front of the ascending spiral, rather than hidden behind it. There would be other topologies, encoding different positional transformations. That much seemed clear to Huw, although he'd had to limit his forays into Mathematica to half an hour per day – trying to work out the knot structure was a guaranteed fast-track route to a migraine. *There will be other worlds.*

He lay awake long after Yul and Elena had dozed off, staring at the ceiling, daydreaming about exploration and all the disasters that could befall an unwary world-walker. *We'll need oxygen masks.* (What if some of the worlds had never evolved photosynthesis, so that life was a thin scum of sulfur-reducing bacteria clustered around volcanic vents, at the bottom of a thick blanket of nitrogen and ammonia?) *Trickster-wife, we may need space suits.* (What if the planet itself had never formed?) *Need to map the coastlines and relief, see if plate tectonics evolves deterministically in all worlds* . . .

He blinked at the sunlight streaming in through the front window. How had it gotten to be morning? His mouth tasted of cobwebs and dust, but his head was clear. 'Gaah.' There was no point pretending to sleep.

Someone was singing as he wandered through into the kitchen, rubbing his eyes. It was Elena: she'd found the stash of kitchenware and was filling the coffeemaker, warbling one of the more salacious passages of a famous saga to herself with – to Huw – a deeply annoying air of smug satisfaction.

'Humph.' He rummaged in the cupboard for a glass but came up with a chipped coffee mug instead. Rinsing it under the cold water tap, he asked, 'Ready to face the day?'

'Oh yes!' She trilled, closing up the machine. She turned and grinned at him impishly. 'It's a wonderful day to explore a new world, don't you think?'

'Just as long as we don't leave our bones there.' Huw took a gulp of the slightly brackish tap water. 'Yuck.' *Ease up, she's just being exuberant,* he told himself. 'Where's Yul?'

'He's still getting dressed –' She remembered herself and flushed. 'He'll be down in a minute.'

'Good.' Huw pressed his lips together to keep from laughing.

Memo to self: do not taunt little brother's girlfriend, little brother will be tetchy. 'Coffee would be good, too, thanks,' he added.

'What are we going to do today?' she asked, eyes widening slightly.

'Hmm. Depends.'

'I was thinking about doing breakfast,' rumbled Hulius, from the doorway.

'That –' Huw brightened '– sounds like a great idea. Got to wait for the duke's say-so before we continue, anyway. Breakfast first, then we can get ready for a camping trip.'

Huw drove into town carefully, hunting for a diner he'd spotted the day before. He steered the youngsters to a booth at the back before ordering a huge breakfast – fried eggs, bacon, half a ton of hash browns, fried tomatoes, and a large mug of coffee. 'Go on, pig out,' he told Elena and Hulius, 'you're going to be sorry you didn't later.'

'Why should I?' asked Elena, as the waitress ambled off towards the kitchen. 'I'll be sorry if I'm fat and ugly before my wedding night!'

Huw glanced at his brother: Yul was studiously silent, but Huw could just about read his mind. *Not the sharpest knife in the box . . .* 'We're going back to the forest,' Huw explained, 'and we're staying there for at least one night, maybe two, in a tent. It's going to be very cold. Your body burns more calories when you're cold.'

'Oh!' She glared at him. 'Men!' Yul winked at him, then froze as the waitress reappeared with a jug of coffee. 'No sense of humor,' she humphed.

'Okay, so we're humor-impaired' Huw started on his hash browns. 'Listen, we –' he paused until the waitress was out of earshot '– it depends what orders we receive, all right? It's possible his grace will tell me to sit tight until he can send a support team . . . but I don't think it's likely. From what I can gather, we're shorthanded everywhere and anyone who isn't essential is being pulled in for the corvée, supporting security operations, or running interference. So my best bet is, he'll read my report and say "carry on." But until I get confirmation of that, we're not going across.'

Elena stabbed viciously at her solitary fried egg. 'To what end are we going?'

'To see if that stuff Yul found really is the remains of a roadbed. To look around and get some idea of the vegetation, so I can brief a real tree doctor when we've got time to talk to one. To plant a weather station and seismograph. To very quietly see if there's any sign of inhabitation. To boldly go where no Clan explorer has gone before. Is that enough to start with?'

'Eh.' Yul paused with his coffee mug raised. 'That's a lot to bite off.'

'That's why all three of us are going this time.' Huw took another mouthful. 'And we're all taking full packs instead of piggybacking. That ties us down for an hour, minimum, if we run into trouble, but going by your first trip, there didn't seem to be anybody home. We might have wildlife trouble, bears or wolves, but that shouldn't be enough to require an immediate withdrawal. So unless the duke says "no," we're going camping.'

They managed to finish their breakfast without discussing any other matters of import. Unfortunately for Huw, this created a zone of silence that Elena felt compelled to fill with enthusiastic chirping about Christina Aguilera and friends, which Hulius punctuated with nods and grunts of such transparently self-serving attentiveness that Huw began to darkly consider purchasing a dog collar and leash to present to his brother's new keeper.

Back at the rented house, Huw got down to the serious job of redistributing their packs and making sure everything they'd need had a niche in one rucksack or another. It didn't take long to put everything together: what took time was double-checking, asking, *What have I forgotten about that could kill me?* When finally they were all ready it was nearly noon.

'Okay, wait in the yard,' said Huw. He walked back inside and reset the burglar alarm. 'Got your lockets?' This time there was no need for the flash card, no need to keep all their hands free for emergencies. 'On my mark: three, two, one . . .'

The world shifted color, from harsh sunlight on brown-parched grass to overcast pine-needle green. Huw glanced round. A moment earlier he'd been sweating into his open three-layer North Face jacket: the chill hit him like a punch in the ribs and a slap in the face. There were trees everywhere. Elena stepped out from behind a waist-high tangle of brush and dead branches and looked at him. A moment later Hulius popped into place, his heavy pack looming over his head like an astronaut's oxygen supply. 'All clear?' Huw asked, ignoring the pounding in his temples.

'Yup.' Yul hefted the meter-long spike with the black box of the radio beacon on top, and rammed it into the ground.

'It looks like it's going to rain,' Elena complained, looking up at the overcast just visible between the treetops. 'And it's cold.'

Huw zipped his jacket up, then slid his pack onto the ground carefully. 'Yul, you have the watch. Elena, if you could start unpacking the tent?' He unhooked the scanner from his telemetry belt and set it running, hunting through megahertz for the proverbial needle in a thunderstorm, then began to unpack the weather station.

'I have the watch, bro.' Yul's backpack thudded heavily as it landed in a mat of ferns, followed by the metallic clack as he chambered a round in his hunting rifle. 'No bear's going to sneak up on you without my permission.'

'I'm so glad.' Huw squinted at the scanner. 'Okay, nothing on the air. Radio check. Elena?'

'Oh, what? You want – the radio?'

'Go ahead.'

Elena reached into her jacket pocket and produced a walkie-talkie. 'Can you hear me?'

Huw winced and turned down the volume. 'I hear you. Your turn, Yul –' 'Another minute of cross-checks and he was happy. 'Okay. Got radio, got weather station, acquired the beacon. Let's get the tent up.'

The tent was a tunnel model, with two domed compartments separated by a central awning, for which Huw had a feeling he was going to be grateful. Elena had already unrolled it: between them they managed to nail the spikes in and pull it erect without too much swearing, although the tunnel ended up bulging in at one side where it wrapped around an inconveniently placed trunk.

Huw crossed the clearing then, stretching as high as he could, slashed a strip of bark away from the trunk of the tree nearest the spike. Then he turned to Yul. 'Where was that chunk of asphalt?'

'That way, bro.' Hulius gestured down the gentle slope. The trees blocked the line of sight within a hundred meters. 'Want to go check it out?'

'You know it.' Huw's stomach rumbled. *Going to have to find a stream soon,* he realized, *or send Elena back over to fill up the water bag.* 'Lead off. Stay close and stop at twenty so I can mark the route.'

It was quiet in the forest, much too quiet. After a minute, Huw realized what he was missing: the omnipresent creaking of the insect chorus, cicadas and hopping things of one kind or another. Occasionally a bird would cry out, a harsh cawing of crows or the *tu-whit tu-whit* of something he couldn't identify marking out its territory. From time to time the branches would rustle and whisper in the grip of a breeze impossible to detect at ground level. But there was no enthusiastic orchestra of insects, no rumble of traffic, nor the drone of engines crawling across the upturned bowl of the empty sky. *We're alone,* he realized. And: *it feels like it's going to snow.*

Yul stopped and turned round. He grinned broadly and pointed at the nearest tree. 'See? I've been here before.'

Huw nodded. 'Good going. How much farther is it?'

'About six markers, maybe a couple of hundred meters.'

'Right.' Huw glanced round at Elena. 'You hear that?'

'Sure.' She chewed rhythmically as she reached up with her left hand to flick a stray hair away from her eyes. She didn't move her right hand away from the grip on the P90, but kept scanning from side to side with an ease that came from long practice – she'd done her share of summer training camps for the duke.

'Lead on, Yul.' Huw suppressed a shiver. Elena – was she really as brainless as she'd seemed over breakfast? Or was she another of those differently socialized Clan girls, who escaped from their claustrophobic family connections by moonlighting as manhunters for ClanSec? He hadn't asked enough questions when the duke's clerk had gone down his list of names and suggested he talk to her. But the way she moved silently in his footsteps, scanning for threats, suggested that he ought to have paid more attention.

Ten, fifteen minutes passed. Yul stopped. 'Here it is,' he said quietly.

'I have the watch.' Elena turned in a circle, looking for threats.

'Let me see.' Huw knelt down near the tree Hulius had pointed to. The undergrowth was thin here, barely more than a mat of pine needles and dead branches, and the slope almost undetectable. Odd lumpy protuberances humped out of the ground near the roots of the tree, and when he glanced sideways Huw realized he could see a lot farther in one direction before his vision was blocked by more trees. He unhooked the folding trench shovel from his small pack and chopped away at the muck and weedy vegetation covering one of the lumps. 'Whoa!'

Huw knew his limits: what he knew about archeology could be written on the sleeve notes of an Indiana Jones DVD. But he also knew asphalt when he saw it, a solid black tarry aggregate with particles of even size – and he knew it was old asphalt too, weathered and overgrown with lichen and moss.

'Looks like a road to me,' Yul offered.

'I think you're right.' Huw cast around for more chunks of half-buried roadstone. Now that he knew what he was looking for it wasn't difficult to find. 'It ran that way, north-northeast, I think.' Turning to look in the opposite direction he saw a shadowy tunnel, just about as wide as a two-lane road. Some trees had erupted through the surface over the years, but for the most part it had held the forest at bay. 'Okay, this way is downhill. Let's plant a waypoint and –' he looked up at the heavy overcast '– follow it for an hour, or until it starts to rain, before we head back.' He checked his watch. It was just past two in the afternoon. 'I don't want to get too far from base camp today.'

Hulius rammed another transponder spike into the earth by the road and Huw scraped an arrow on the nearest tree, pointing back along their path. The LED on top of the transponder blinked infrequently, reassuring them that the radio beacon was ready and waiting to guide them home. For the next half hour they plodded along the shallow downhill path, Hulius leading the way with his hunting rifle, Elena bringing up the rear. Once they were on the roadbed, it was easy to follow, although patches of asphalt had been heaved up into odd mounds and shoved aside by trees over the years – or centuries – for which it had been abandoned. Something about the way the road snaked along the contours of the shallow hillside tickled Huw's imagination. 'It was built to take cars,' he finally said aloud.

'Huh? How can you tell?' asked Yul.

'The radius of curvature. Look at it, if you're on foot it's as straight as an arrow. But imagine you're driving along it at forty, fifty miles per hour. See how it's slightly banked around that ridge ahead?' He pointed towards a rise in the ground, just visible through the trees.

They continued in silence for a couple of minutes. 'You're assuming –' Yul began to say, then stopped, freezing in his tracks right in front of a tree that had thrust through the asphalt. '*Shit.*'

'What?' Huw almost walked into his back.

'Cover,' Yul whispered, gesturing towards the side of the track. 'It's probably empty, but . . .'

'What?' Huw ducked to the side of the road – followed by Elena – then crept forward to peer past Yul's shoulder.

'There,' said Hulius, raising one hand to point. It took a moment for Huw to recognize the curving flank of a mushroom-pale dome, lightly streaked with green debris. 'You were looking for company, weren't you? Looks like we've found it . . .'

*

It wasn't the first time Miriam had hidden in the woods, nursing a splitting headache and a festering sense of injustice, but familiarity didn't make it easier: and this time she'd had an added source of anxiety as she crossed over, hoping like hell that the Clan hadn't seen fit to doppelgänger her business by building a defensive site in the same location in their own world. But she needn't have worried. The trees grew thick and undisturbed, and she'd made sure that the site was well inland from the line the coast had followed before landfill in both her Boston and the strangely different New British version had extended it.

She'd taken a risk, of course. Boston and Cambridge occupied much the same sites in New Britain as in her own Massachusetts, but in the Gruinmarkt that area was largely untamed, covered by deciduous forest and the isolated tracts and clearings of scattered village estates. She'd never thought to check the lay of the land collocated with her workshop, despite having staked out her house: for all she knew, she might world-walk right into the great hall of some hedge-lord. But it seemed unlikely – Angbard hadn't chosen the site of his fortified retreat for accessibility – so the worst risk she expected was a twisted ankle or a drop into a gully.

Instead Miriam stumbled and nearly walked face-first into a beech tree, then stopped and looked around. 'Ow.' She massaged her forehead. This was bad: she suddenly felt hot and queasy, and her vision threatened to play tricks on her. *Damn, I don't need a migraine right now.* She sat down against the tree trunk, her heart hammering. A flash of triumph: *I got away with it!* Well, not quite. She'd still have to cross back over and meet up with Erasmus. But there were hours to go, yet . . .

The nausea got worse abruptly, peaking in a rush that cramped her stomach. She doubled over to her right and vomited, whimpering with pain. The spasms seemed to go on for hours, leaving her gasping for breath as she retched herself dry. Eventually, by the time she was too exhausted to stand up, the cramps began to ease. She sat up and leaned back against the tree, pulled her suitcase close, and shivered uncontrollably. 'What brought that on?' She asked herself. Then in an attempt at self-distraction, she opened the case.

The contents of the hidden drawer were mostly plastic and base metal, but in her eyes they gleamed with more promise than a safe full of rubies and diamonds: a small Sony notebook PC and its accessories, a power supply and a CD drive. With shaking hands she opened the computer's lid and pushed the power button. The screen flickered, and LEDs flashed, then it shut down again. 'Oh, of course.' The battery had run down in the months of enforced inactivity. Well, no need to worry: New Britain had alternating current electricity, and the little transformer was designed for international use, rugged enough to eat their bizarre mixture of frequency and voltage without melting. (Even though she'd had a devil of a time at first, establishing how the local units of measurement translated into terms she was vaguely familiar with.)

Closing the suitcase, she felt the tension drain from her shoulders. *I can go home*, she told herself. *Any time I want to.* All she had to do was walk twenty-five paces north, cross over again at the prearranged time, and then find an electric light socket to plug the computer into. She glanced at her watch, surprised to discover that fifty minutes had passed. She'd arranged to reappear in three hours, the fastest crossing she felt confident she could manage without medication. But that was before the cramps and the migraine had hit her. She stood up clumsily, brushed down her clothes, and oriented herself using the small compass she'd found among Burgeson's stock. 'Okay, here goes nothing.'

Another tree, another two hours: this time in the right place for the return trip to the side alley behind the workshop. Miriam settled down to wait. *What do I really want to do next?* she asked herself. It was a hard question to answer. Before the massacre at the betrothal ceremony – already nearly a week ago – she'd had the grim luxury of certainty. But now . . . *I could buy my way back into the game,* she realized. *The Idiot's dead so the betrothal makes no sense anymore. Henryk's probably dead, too. And I've got valuable information, if I can get Angbard's ear.* Mike's presence changed everything. Hitherto, all the Clan's strategic planning and internecine plotting had been based on the assumption that they were inviolable in their own estates, masters of their own world. But if the U.S. government could send spies, then the implications were going to shake the Clan to its foundations. *They've been looking for the Clan for years,* she realized. But now they'd found the narcoterrorists – *One world's feudal baron is another world's drug lord* – the whole elaborate game of charades that Clan security played was over. The other player could kick over the card table any time they wanted. *You can doppelgänger a castle against world-walkers, but you can't stop them crossing over outside your walls and planting a backpack nuke.* In an endgame between the Clan and the CIA's world-walking equivalent, there could be only one winner.

'So they can't win a confrontation. But if they lose . . .' They had her mother. *Could I let her go*? The thought was painful. And then there were others, the ones she could count as friends. Olga, Brill, poor innocent kids like Kara. Even James Lee. If she cut and run, she'd be leaving them to – *No, that's not right.* She shook her head. Where did this unwelcome sense of responsibility come from? *I haven't gone native!* But it was too late to protest: they'd tied her into their lives, and if she just walked out on them, much less walked willingly into the arms of enemies who'd happily see them all dead or buried so deep in jail they'd never see daylight, she'd be personally responsible for the betrayal.

'They'll have to go.' Somewhere beyond the reach of a government agency that relied on coerced and imprisoned world-walkers. 'But where?' New Britain was a possibility. Her experiment in technology transfer had worked, after all. *What if we went overt?* She wondered. *If we told them who we were and what we could do. Could we cut a deal?* Build a military-industrial complex to defend against a military-industrial complex. *The Empire's under siege. The French have the resources to . . .* She blanked. *I don't know enough.* A tantalizing vision clung to the edges of her imagination, a new business idea so monumentally vast and arrogant she could barely contemplate it. Thousands of world-walkers, working with the support and resources of a continental superpower, smuggling information and ideas and sharing lessons leeched from a more advanced world. *I was thinking small. How fast could we drag New Britain into the twenty-first century?* Even without the cohorts of new world-walkers in the making that she'd stumbled across, the product of Angbard's secretive manipulation of a fertility lab's output, it seemed feasible. More than that: it seemed desirable. *Mike's organization will assume that any world-walker is a drug mule until proven otherwise. It won't be healthy to be a world-walker in the USA after the shit hits the fan. But things are different in New Britain. We'll* need *that world.*

Miriam checked her watch. The hours had drifted by: the shadows were lengthening and her headache was down to a dull throb. She stood up and dusted herself down again, picked up her suitcase, and focused queasily on the locket. 'Once more, with spirit . . .'

Bang.

Red-hot needles thrust into her eyes as her stomach heaved again: a giant gripped her head between his hands and squeezed.

Cobblestones beneath her boots, and a stink of fresh horseshit. Miriam bent forward, gagging, realized *I'm standing in the road* – and a narrow road ‚it was, walled on both sides with weathered, greasy brickwork – as the waves of nausea hit.

Bang.

Someone shouted something, at her it seemed. The racket was familiar, and here was a car (or what passed for one in New Britain) with engine running. Hands grabbed at her suitcase: she tightened her grip instinctively.

'Into the car! *Now!*' It was Erasmus.

''M going to be *sick* – '

'Well you can be sick in the car!' He clutched her arm and tugged.

Bang.

Gunshots?

She tottered forward, stomach lurching, and half-fell, half-slid through the open passenger compartment leg well, collapsing on the wooden floor. The car shuddered and began to roll smoothly on a flare of steam.

BANG. Someone else, not Erasmus, leaned over her and pulled the trigger of a revolver, driving sharp spikes of pain into her ear drums. With a screech of protesting rubber the car picked up speed. *BANG.* Erasmus collapsed on top of her, holding her down. 'Stay on the floor,' he shouted.

The steam car hit a pothole and bounced, violently. It was too much: Miriam began to retch again, bringing up clear bile.

'Shit.' It was the shooter on the back seat, wrinkling his face in disgust. 'I think that's –' he paused ' – no, they're trying to follow us on foot.' The driver piled on the steam, then flung their carriage into a wide turn onto a public boulevard. The shooter sat down hard, holding his pistol below seat level, pointing at the floor. 'Can you sit up?' he asked Miriam and Erasmus. 'Look respectable fast, we're hitting Ketch Street in a minute.'

Erasmus picked himself up. 'I'm sorry,' he said, his voice shaky. Miriam waited for a moment as her stomach tried to lurch again. 'Are you all right?'

'Head hurts,' she managed. Arms around her shoulders lifted her to her knees. 'My suitcase . . .'

'On the parcel shelf.'

More hands from the other side. Together they lifted her into position on the bench seat. The car was rattling and rocking from side to side, making a heady pace – almost forty miles per hour, if she was any judge of speed, but it felt more like ninety in this ragtop steamer. She gasped for air, chest heaving as she tried to get back the wind she'd lost while she was throwing up. 'Are you all right?' Burgeson asked again. He'd found a perch on the jump seat opposite, and was clutching a grab-strap behind the chauffeur's station on the right of the cockpit.

'I, it never hit me like that before,' she said. Amidst the cacophony in her skull she found a moment to be terrified: world-walking usually caused a blood pressure spike and migraine-like symptoms, but nothing like this hellish nausea and pile-driver headache. 'Something's wrong with me.'

'Did you get what you wanted?' he pressed her. 'Was it worth it?'

'Yes, yes.' She glanced sideways. 'We haven't been introduced.'

'Indeed.' Erasmus sent her a narrow-eyed look. 'This is Albert. Albert, meet Anne.'

Gotcha. 'Nice to meet you,' she said politely.

'Albert' nodded affably, and palmed his revolver, sliding it into a pocket of his cutaway jacket. 'Always nice to meet a fellow traveler,' he said.

'Indeed.' *Fellow traveler, is it?* She fell silent. Burgeson's political connections came with dangerous strings attached. 'What's with the car? And the rush?'

'You didn't hear them shooting at us?'

'I was busy throwing up. What happened?'

'Stakeout,' he said. 'About ten minutes after your break-in they surrounded the place. If you'd come out the front door –' The brisk two-fingered gesture across his throat made the message all too clear. 'I don't know what you've stirred up, but the Polis are *very* upset about something. So I decided to call in some favors and arrange a rescue chariot.'

'Albert' nodded. 'A good thing too,' he added darkly. 'You'll excuse me, ma'am.' He doffed his cap and began to knead it with his fingers, turning it inside out to reveal a differently patterned lining. 'I'll be off at the next crossroads.' Erasmus turned and knocked sharply on the wooden partition behind the chauffeur: the car began to slow from its headlong rush.

'Where are we –' Miriam swallowed, then paused to avoid gagging on the taste of bile '– where are we going?'

The car slowed to a near halt, just short of a streetcar stop. 'Wait,' said Erasmus. To 'Albert' he added: 'The movement thanks you for your assistance today. Good luck.' 'Albert' nodded, then stepped onto the sidewalk and marched briskly away without a backward glance. The car picked up speed again, then wheeled in a fast turn onto a twisting side street. 'We're going to make the train,' said Erasmus. 'The driver doesn't know which one. Or even which station. I hope you can walk.'

'My head's sore. But my feet . . .' She tried to shrug, then winced. Only minutes had passed, but she was having difficulty focussing. 'They were trying to kill me. No warnings.'

'Yes.' He raised an eyebrow. 'Maybe your friend was under closer surveillance than he realized.'

Miriam shuddered. 'Let's get out of here.'

It took them a while to make their connection. The car dropped them off near a suburban railway platform, from which they made their way to a streetcar stop and then via a circuitous route Erasmus had evidently planned to throw off any curious followers. But an hour later they were waiting on a railway platform in downtown Boston, not too far from the site of Back Bay Station in Miriam's home world. *Geography dictates railroads,* she told herself as another smoky locomotive wheezed and puffed through the station, belching steam towards the arched cast-iron ceiling trusses. *I wonder what else it dictates?* The answer wasn't hard to guess: she'd seen the beggars waiting outside the ticket hall, hoping for a ride out west. Erasmus nodded to himself beside her, then tensed. 'Look,' he said, 'I do believe that's ours.'

Miriam glanced towards the end of the long, curving platform, through the thin haze of steam. 'Really?' The ant column of carriages approaching the platform seemed to vanish into the infinite distance. It was certainly long enough to be a transcontinental express train.

'Carriage eleven, upper deck.' He squinted towards it. 'We've got a bit of a walk . . .'

The Northern Continental was a city on wheels – wheels six French feet apart, the track gauge nearly half as wide again as the ordinary trains. The huge double-deck carriages loomed overhead, brass handrails gleaming around the doors at either end. Burgeson's expensive passes did more than open doors: uniformed porters took their suitcases and carried them upstairs, holding the second- and third-class passengers at bay while they boarded. Miriam looked around in astonishment. 'This is ridiculous!'

'You don't like it?'

'It's not that –' Miriam walked across to the sofa facing the wall of windows and sat down. The walls of the compartment were paneled in polished oak as good as anything Duke Angbard had in his aerie at Fort Lofstrom, and if the floor wasn't carpeted in hand-woven Persian rugs, she was no judge of weaving. It reminded her of the expensive hotels she'd stayed at in Boston, when she'd been trying to set up a successful technology transfer business and impress the local captains of industry. 'Does this convert into a bed, or . . . ?'

'The bedrooms are through there.' Erasmus pointed at the other end of the lounge. 'The bathroom is just past the servants' quarters – '

'Servants' quarters?'

Erasmus looked at her oddly. 'Yes, I keep forgetting. Labor is expensive where you come from, isn't it?'

Miriam looked around again. 'Wow. We're here for the next three or four days?'

A distant whistle cut through the window glass, and with a nearly undetectable jerk the carriage began to move.

'Yes.' He nodded. 'Plenty of time to take your shoes off.'

'Okay.' She bent down automatically, then blinked stupidly. 'This doesn't come cheap, does it?'

'No.' She heard a scrape of chair legs across carpet and looked up, catching Erasmus in the process of sitting down in a spindly Queen

Anne reproduction. He watched her with wide, dark eyes, his bearing curiously bird-like. Behind him, Empire Station slid past in ranks of cast-iron pillars. 'But one tends to be interfered with less if one is seen to be able to support expensive tastes.'

'Right . . . so you're doing this, spending however much, just to go and see a man about a book?'

A brief pause. 'Yes.'

Miriam stared. *And you gave me a gun to carry? Either you're mad, or you trust me, or . . .* She couldn't complete the sentence: it was too preposterous. 'That must be some book.'

'Yes, it is. It has already shaken empires and slain princes.' His cheek twitched at some unspoken unpleasantness. 'I have a copy of it in my luggage, if you'd like to read it.'

'Huh?' She blinked, feeling stupid. 'I thought you said you were going to see a man about a book? As in, you were going to buy or sell one?'

'Not exactly: perhaps I should have said, I'm going to see a man about *his* book. And if all goes well, he's going to come back east with us.' He glanced down at his feet. 'Does Sir Adam Burroughs mean anything to you?'

Miriam shook her head.

'Probably just as well. I think you ought to at least look at the book, after dinner. Just so you understand what you're getting into.'

'All right.' She stood up. 'Is there an electrical light in the bed-room? I need to plug my machine in to charge . . .'

*

The fridge was half empty, the half-and-half was half past yogurt, and Oscar clearly thought he was a burglar. That was the downside of coming home. On the upside: Mike could finally look forward to sleeping in his own bed without fear of disturbances, he had a crate of antibiotics to munch on, and Oscar hadn't thrown up on the carpet again. *Home. Funny place, where are the coworkers and security guards? Out on the street, obviously.* Mike stood on the porch and watched as Herz drove off, then closed the door and went inside.

The crutches got in the way, and the light bulb in the hallway had blown, but at least Oscar wasn't trying to wrap his furry body around the fiberglass cast in a friendly feline attempt to trip up the food ape. *Yet.* Mike shuffled through into the living room and lowered himself into the sofa, struggled inconclusively with his shoe, and flicked on the TV. The comforting babble of CNN washed over him. *I need some time out,* he decided. *This hospitalization shit is hard work.* Spending half an hour as a couch potato was a seductive prospect: a few minutes later, his eyelids were drooping shut.

Perhaps it was the lack of hospital-supplied Valium, but Mike – who didn't normally remember his dreams – found himself in a memorable but chaotic confabulatory realm. One moment he was running a three-legged race through a minefield, a sense of dread choking him as Sergeant Hastert's corpse flopped drunkenly against him, one limp arm around his shoulders; the next, he was lying on a leather bench seat, unable to move, opposite Dr. James, the spook from head office. 'It's important that you find the bomb,' James was saying, but the cranky old lady on the limousine's parcel shelf was pointing a pistol at the back of his head. 'Matthias is a traitor; I want to know who he was working for.'

He tried to open his mouth to warn the colonel about the madwoman with the gun, but it was Miriam crouching on the shelf now, holding a dictaphone and making notes. 'It's all about manipulating the interdimensional currency exchange rates,' she explained: then she launched into an enthusiastic description of an esoteric trading scam she was investigating, one that involved taking greenbacks into a parallel universe, swapping them for pieces of eight, and melting them down into Swiss watches. Mike tried to sit up and pull Pete out of the line of fire, but someone was holding him down. Then he woke up, and Oscar, who'd been sitting on his chest, head-butted him on the underside of his chin.

'Thanks, buddy.' Oscar head-butted him again, then made a noise like a dying electric shaver. Mike figured his bowl was empty. He took stock: his head ached, he had pins and needles in one arm, the exposed toes of his left foot were cold to the point of numbness, and the daylight outside his window was in short supply. 'Come here, you.' He reached up to stroke the tomcat, who was clearly intent on exercising his feline right to bear a grudge against his human whenever it suited him. For a moment he felt a bleak wave of depression. The TV was still on, quietly babbling inanities from the corner of the room. *How long is this going to take?* Mrs. Beckstein had said it could be weeks, and with Colonel Smith tasking him with being her contact, that could leave him stuck indoors here for the duration.

He pushed himself upright and hobbled dizzily over to the kitchen phone – the cordless handset had succumbed to a flat battery – and dialed the local pizza delivery shop from memory. Working out what the hell to do with this surfeit of time (which he couldn't even use for a fishing trip or a visit to his cousins) could wait 'til tomorrow.

The next morning, the long habit of keeping office hours – despite a week of disrupted sleep patterns – dragged Mike into unwilling consciousness. He took his antibiotics, then spent a fruitless half-hour trying to figure out how to shower without getting water in his cast, which made his leg itch abominably. *This is hopeless,* he told himself, when the effort of trying to lift an old wooden stool into the shower left him so tired he had to sit down: *I really am ill.* The infection – thankfully under control – had taken out of him what little energy the torn-up and broken leg had left behind. The difficulty of accomplishing even minor tasks was galling, and sitting at home on full pay, knowing that serious, diligent people like Agent Herz were out there busting their guts to get the job done made it even worse. But there was just about nothing he could do that would contribute to the mission, beyond what he was already doing: sitting at ground zero of a stakeout.

Mike had never been a loafer, and while he was used to taking vacations, enforced home rest was an unaccustomed and unwelcome imposition. For a while he thought about going out and picking up some groceries, but the prospect of getting into the wagon and driving with his left leg embedded in a mass of blue fiberglass was just too daunting. *Better wait for Helen,* he decided. His regular cleaner would be in like clockwork tomorrow – he could work on a shopping list in the meantime. *There's got to be a better way.* Then he shook his head. *You're sick, son. Take five.*

Just after lunchtime (a cardboard-tasting microwave lasagna that had spent too long at the bottom of the chest freezer), the front door-bell rang. Cursing, Mike stumbled into the hall, pushing off the walls in a hurry, hoping whoever it was wouldn't get impatient and leave before he made it. He paused just inside the vestibule and checked the spy hole, then opened the door. 'Come in!' He tried to take a step back and ended up leaning against the wall.

'No need to put on a song and dance, Mike, I know you feel like shit.' Smith nodded stiffly. 'Go on, take your time. I'll shut the door. We need to talk about stuff.' He was carrying a pair of brown paper grocery bags.

'Uh, okay.' Mike pushed himself off from the wall and half-hopped back towards the living room. The crutch would have come in handy, but he knew his way around well enough to use the furniture and door frames for support. 'What brings you here?' he called over his shoulder. 'I thought I was meant to be taking it easy.'

'You . . . are.' Smith glanced around as he came into the main room. *Not used to visiting employees at home*, Mike realized. 'But there's some stuff we need to talk about.'

I do not need this. Mike lowered himself onto the sofa. 'You could-n't tell me in the hospital?' he asked.

'You were still kind of crinkle-cut, son. And there were medics about.'

'Gotcha.' Mike waved at the door to the kitchen. 'I'd offer you a coffee or something but I'm having a hard time getting about . . .'

'That's all right.' Smith put one of the grocery bags down on the side table, then walked over to the kitchen door and put the other on the worktop inside. Then he made a circuit of the living room. He held his hands tightly behind his back, as if forcibly restraining him-self from checking for dust on top of the picture rail. 'I won't be long.'

'Are we being monitored?'

Smith glanced at him. 'I sure hope so.' He gestured at the walls. 'Not on audio, but there's a real expensive infrared camera out there, and a couple of guys in a van just to keep an eye on you.'

'There are?' Mike knew better than to get angry. 'What are they expecting to see?'

'Visitors who don't arrive through the front door.' Smith slung one leg over the arm of the recliner and leaned on it, inspecting Mike pensively.

'Oh, right.' For a second, Mike felt the urge to kick his earlier self for passing on absolutely everything he'd learned. The impulse faded: he'd been fever-ridden, and anyway it was what he was supposed to do. But still, if he hadn't done so, he wouldn't be stuck out here under virtual house arrest. He might be back in hospital, with no worries about groceries. And besides, Smith had a point. 'You might want to warn them I'm expecting a housekeeper to show tomorrow – she drops by a couple of times a week.'

'I'll tell them.' Smith paused. 'As it happens, I know you're not being listened in on, unless you lift the receiver on that phone – I signed the wiretap request myself. There's stuff we need to talk about, and this place is more private than my office, if you follow my drift.'

'I'm not being listened in on right now? Suits me.' Mike leaned back in the sofa. 'Talk away. Sorry if I don't, uh, if I'm not too focused: I feel like shit.'

'That's why you're on sick leave. You may be interested to know that your story checks out: Beckstein's mother disappeared six months ago. Her house is still there, the bills are being paid on time, but there's nobody home. We haven't gotten a trace on her income stream so far; her credit cards and bank account are ordinary enough, but the deposits are coming in from an offshore bank account in Liechtenstein and that's turning out to be hard to trace. Anyway, we confirmed that she's one of them.' He stood up again and paced over to the kitchen door then back, as if his legs were incapable of standing still. 'This is a, a tactical mess. We'd hoped to get at least a few successful contacts in place before our ability to operate in fairyland was blown. What this means is that they, uh, Beckstein senior's faction, are going to be alert for informants from now on. On the other hand, if they're willing to talk we've got an – admittedly biased – HUMINT source to develop. Contacts, in other words.'

Mike stared at him. Smith was just about sweating bullets. 'Who do we talk to in the Middle East?' he asked. 'I mean, when we want to know what al-Qaeda is planning?'

'That's a lot more accessible, believe it or not. This, these guys, it's like China in the fifties or sixties.' Smith looked as if he was sucking on a lemon. 'Look.' He picked up the second grocery bag and handed it to Mike. 'This stuff is strictly off the books because, unfortunately, we're off the map here, right outside the reservation.'

'What –' Mike upended the bag and boxes fell out. A cell phone, ammunition, a pistol. 'The fuck?'

'Glock 18, like their own people use. The phone was bought anonymously for cash. Listen.' Smith hunkered down in front of him, still radiating extreme discomfort. 'The phone's preprogrammed with Dr. James's private number. This is running right from the top. If you have to negotiate with them, James can escalate you all the way to Mr. Cheney himself.'

Mike was impressed, despite himself. *They're briefing the vice president?* 'What's the gun for?'

'In case the other faction come calling for you.'

'Hadn't thought of that,' Mike admitted. 'What do you want me to do?'

'Find out if GREENSLEEVES was blowing smoke. If all he had was a couple of slugs of hot metal, that's still bad – but right now it would be really good if we could call off the NIRT investigation. On the other hand, you might want to tell the Beckstein faction what will happen if one of our cities goes up.'

'Huh. What would happen? What could we do, realistically?'

Smith paused for a few seconds. 'I'm just guessing here, you understand. I'm not privy to that information. But my guess is that we would be very, very angry – for all of about thirty minutes. And then we'd retaliate in kind, Mike. The SSADM backpack nukes have been out of inventory since the early seventies, and the W54 cores were retired by eighty-nine, but they don't have to stay that way. The schematics are still on file and if I were a betting man I'd place a C-note on Pantex being able to run one up in a few weeks, if they haven't done so already. Mr. Cheney and Dr. Wolfowitz are both gung ho about developing a new generation of nukes. It could get really ugly really fast, Mike. A smuggler's war, tit for tat. But we'd win, because we've got a choke hold on the weapons supply. And if it comes to it, I don't think we'd hold back from making it a war of extermination. It's not hard to stick a cobalt jacket on a bomb when there's zero risk of the fallout coming home.'

'Wow, that's ugly all right.' 9/11 had been bad enough: the nightmare Smith was dangling before him was far worse. 'Anything else?'

'Yep.' The colonel stood up. 'From now on, until you're through with this thing or we call it off, you're in a box. We don't want you in day-to-day contact with the organization. The less you know, the less you can give away.'

'But I – oh. You're thinking, if they kidnap me – '

'Yes, that's what we're afraid of.'

'Right.' Mike swallowed. 'So. I'm to tell Mrs. Beckstein about Matt's bomb threat, and we either want it handed over right now, or convincing evidence that he was bluffing. Otherwise, they're looking at retaliation in kind. What else?'

'You give her the mobile phone and tell her who it connects to. There's a deal on the table that she might find interesting.' Smith nodded to himself. 'And there's one other thing you can pass on at the same time.'

'Yes?'

'Tell her we're working on the world-walking mechanism. Her window of opportunity for negotiation is open for now – but if she waits too long, it's going to slam shut.' He stood up. 'Once we aren't forced to rely on captured couriers, as soon as we can send the 82nd Airborne across, we aren't going to need the Clan any more. And we want her to know that.'

*

In Otto's opinion one armed camp was much like another: the only difference was how far the stink stretched. His majesty's camp was better organized than most, but with three times as many men it paid to pay attention to details like the latrines. King Egon might not like the tinkers, but he was certainly willing to copy their obsession with hygiene if it kept his men from succumbing to the pestilence. And so Otto rode with his retinue, tired and dusty from the road, past surprisingly tidy rows of tents and the larger pavilions of their eorls and lords, towards the big pavilion at the heart of the camp – in order to ask the true whereabouts of his majesty.

The big pavilion wasn't hard to find – the royal banner flying from the tall mast anchored outside it would have been a giveaway, if nothing else – but Otto's eyes narrowed at the size of the guard detachment waiting there. *Either he mistrusts one of his own, or the bluff is doubled,* he thought. Handing his horse's reins to one of his hand-men he swung himself down from the saddle, wincing slightly as he turned towards the three guards in household surcoats approaching from the side of the pavilion. 'Who's in charge here?' he demanded.

'I am.' The tallest of them tilted his helmet back.

Otto stiffened in shock, then immediately knelt, heart in mouth with fear: 'My liege, I did not recognize you – '

'Good: you weren't meant to.' Egon smiled thinly. 'No shame attaches. Rise, Otto, and walk with me. You brought your company?'

'Yes – all who are fit to ride. And your messenger, Sir Geraunt.'

'Excellent.' The king carefully shifted the strap on his exotic and lethal weapon, pointing the muzzle at the ground as he walked around the side of the tent. Otto noticed the two other household guards following, barely out of earshot. They, too, carried black, strangely proportioned witch weapons. 'I've got something to show you.'

'Sire?' Behind him, Heidlor was keeping his immediate body-guard together. *Good man.* The king's behavior was disturbingly unconventional –

'The witches can walk through another world, the world of shadows,' remarked Egon. 'They can ambush you if you keep still and they know where you are. Armies are large, they attract spies. Constant movement is the best defense. That, and not making a target of one's royal self by wearing gilded armor and sleeping in the largest tent.'

Ah. Otto nodded. So there was a reason for all this strangeness, after all. 'What would you have me do, sire?'

Behind the royal pavilion there was a hummock of mounded-up earth. Someone – many someones – had labored to build it up from the ground nearby, and then cut a narrow trench into it. 'Pay atten-tion.' His majesty marched along the trench, which curved as it cut into the mound. Otto followed him, curious as to what his majesty might find so interesting in a heap of soil. 'Ah, here we are.' The trench descended until the edges were almost out of reach above him, then came to an abrupt end in an open, circular space almost as large as the royal pavilion. The muddy floor was lined with rough-cut planks: four crates were spaced around the walls, as far apart as possible. The king placed a proprietorial hand on one of the crates. 'What do you make of it?'

Otto blanked for a moment. He'd been expecting something, but this . . . 'Spoils?' he asked, slowly.

'Very good!' Egon grinned boyishly. 'Yes, I took these from the witches. Hopefully they don't realize they're missing. Tonight, another one should arrive.'

'But they're –' Otto stared. 'Treasure?' His eyes narrowed. 'Their demon blasting powder?'

'Something even better.' A low metal box, drab green in color, lay on the planking next to the crate. Egon bent down and flicked open the latches that held the lid down. 'Behold.' He flipped the lid over, to reveal the contents – a gun.

'One of the tinkers',' Otto noted, forgetting to hold his tongue. 'An arms dump?'

'Yes.' Egon straightened up. 'My sources told me about them, so I had my – helpers – go looking.' He looked at Otto. 'Twenty years ago, thirty years ago, the witch families handed their collective security to the white duke. He standardized them. Their guns, your pistol –' he gestured at Otto's holster – 'when you run out of their cartridges, what will you do?'

Otto shrugged. 'It's a problem, sire. We can't make anything like these.'

Egon nodded. 'They have tried hard to conceal a dirty little secret: the truth is, neither can they. So they stockpile cartridges of a common size and type, purchased from the demons in the shadow world. Your pistol uses the same kind as my carbine. But they kept something better for themselves. This is a, an M60, a *machine gun.*' He pronounced the unfamiliar, alien syllables carefully. 'It fires bigger bullets, faster and farther. It outranges my six-pounder carronades, in fact. But it is useless without cartridges, big ones that come on a metal belt. And they are profligate with ammunition. So the duke stockpiled cartridges for the M60s, all over the place.'

Otto looked at the gun. It was much bigger than the king's MP5, almost as long as a musket. Then he looked at the crate. 'How much do you have, sire?'

'Not enough.' Egon frowned. 'Four crates, almost eighty thousand rounds, six guns. And some very fine blasting powder.'

'Only six –' Otto stopped. 'They haven't noticed?'

The king lowered the lid back on top of the gun. 'Ten years ago, the witches began to re-equip with a better weapon.' He patted the MP5: 'These are deadly, are they not? But it is a sidearm. They held the M60s to defend their castles and keeps. But they're heavy and take a lot of ammunition. They have a new gun now, the M249. And it takes different ammunition, lighter, with a shorter range – still far greater than anything we have, though, near as far as a twelve-pounder can throw shot, and why not? A soldier with one of the new demon-guns can carry twice as much ammunition, and war among the witches is always about mobility. So they gradually forgot about the M60s, leaving the crates of ammunition in the cellars of their houses, and they forgot about the guns, too.' The royal smile re-appeared. 'Their servants remembered.'

'Sire! How would you have me use these guns?'

The royal smile broadened.

'The foe has been informed, by hitherto unimpeachable sources, that I will be attacking Castle Hjorth in the next week. They will con-centrate in defense of the castle, which as the gateway to the Eagle Hills would indeed be a prize worth capturing. Baron Drakel, who is already on his way there at the head of a battalion of pike and musketry, has the honor of ensuring that the witches have targets to aim their fire at. Meanwhile, the majority of the forces camped here will leave on the morrow for the real target. Your task is to spend a day with your best hand-men, and with my armorers, who will remain behind, instructing you in the use of the machine guns, and the explosives. Then you will follow the main force, who will not be aware of your task.'

'Sire! This is a great honor, I am sure, but am I to understand that you do not want to bring these guns to bear in the initial battle?'

'Yes.' Egon stared at the baron, his expression disturbingly mild. 'There are traitors in the midst of my army, Otto. I know for a fact that you are not one of them –' Otto shuddered as if a spider had crawled across his grave '– but this imposes certain difficulties upon my planning.'

Otto glanced round. The two royal bodyguards stood with their backs to him. 'Sire?'

'The witches cannot be defeated by conventional means, Otto. If we besiege them, they can simply vanish into their shadow world. There they can move faster than we can, obtain weapons of dire power from their demonic masters, and continue their war against us. So to rid my kingdom of their immediate influence, I must render their castles and palaces useless as strong points.'

Egon paced around the nearest ammunition crate. 'At the outset, I determined to pin them down, forcing them to defend their holdings, to prove to my more reluctant sworn men that the witches are vulnerable. Your raids were a great success. For every village you put to the sword, another ten landholders swore to my flag, and for that you will be rewarded most handsomely, Otto.' His eyes gleamed. 'But to allow you to live to a ripe old age in your duchy –' he continued, ignoring Otto's sharp intake of breath '– we must force the witches to concentrate on ground of our choice, and then massacre them, while denying them the ability to regroup in a strong place. To that end, it occurs to me that a castle can be as difficult to break *out* of as it is to break *in* to – especially if it is surrounded by machine guns. This is a difficult trick, Otto, and it would be impossible without the treachery of their servitors and hangers-on, but I am going to take the Hjalmar Palace – and use it as an anvil, and you the hammer, to smash the witches.'

*

Traveling across New Britain by train in a first-class suite was a whole lot less painful than anything Amtrak or the airlines had to offer, and Miriam almost found herself enjoying it – except for the constant nagging fear of discovery. Discovery of what, and by whom, wasn't a question she could answer – it wasn't an entirely rational fear. *I still feel like an impostor everywhere I go,* she realized. Erasmus's attempts to engage in friendly conversation over dinner didn't help, either: she'd been unable to make small talk comfortably and had lapsed into a strained, embarrassed silence. The tables in the wide-gauge dining car were sufficiently far apart, and the noise of the wheels loud enough, that she wasn't worried about being overheard; but just being on display in public made her itch as if there was a target pinned to her back. The thing she most wanted to ask Erasmus about was off-limits, anyway – the nature of the errand that was taking a lowly shopkeeper haring out to the west coast in the lap of luxury. *I'm going to see a man about his book?* That must be some book – this journey was costing the local equivalent of a couple of around-the-world airline tickets in first class, at a time when there were soup kitchens on the street corners and muggers in the New London alley-ways who were so malnourished they couldn't tackle a stressed-out woman.

That was more than enough reason to itch. Things had gone bad in New Britain even faster than they had in her own personal life, on a scale that was frightening to think about. But the real cause of her restlessness was closer to home. *Sooner or later I'm going to have to stop drifting and* do *something,* she told herself. Relying on the comfort of near-strangers – or friends with secret agendas of their own – rankled. *If only the laptop was working!* Or: *I could go home and call Mike. Set things moving. And then* – Her imagination ran into a brick wall.

After dinner they returned to the private lounge, and Miriam managed to unwind slightly. There was a wet bar beside the window, and Erasmus opened it: 'Would you care for a brandy before bed?'

'That would be good.' She sat down on the chaise. 'They really overdid the dessert.'

'You think so?' He shook his head. 'We're traveling in style. The chef would be offended if we didn't eat.'

'Really?' She accepted the glass he offered. 'Hmm.' She sniffed. 'Interesting.' A sip of brandy and her stomach had something else to worry about: 'I'd get fat fast if we ate like that regularly.'

'Fat?' He looked at her oddly. 'You've got a long way to go before you're fat.'

Oops. It was another of those momentary dislocations that reminded Miriam she wasn't at home here. New British culture held to a different standard of beauty from Hollywood and the New York catwalks: in a world where agriculture was barely mechanized and shipping was slow, plumpness implied wealth, or at least immunity from starvation. 'You think so?' She found herself unable to suppress a lopsided smile of embarrassment, and dealt with it by hiding her face behind the brandy glass.

'I think you're just right. You've got a lovely face, Miriam, when you're not hiding it. Your new hairstyle complements it beautifully.'

He looked at her so seriously that she felt her ears flush. 'Hey! Not fair.' A sudden sinking feeling, *Is that what this is about? He gets me alone and then –*

'I'm –' He did a double-take. 'Oh dear! You – Did I say something wrong?'

Miriam shook her head. He seemed sincere: *Am I misunderstanding?* 'I think we just ran into an etiquette black hole.' He nodded, politely uncomprehending. 'Sorry. Where I come from what you said would be something between flattery and an expression of interest, and I'm just not up to handling subtlety right now.'

'Expression of . . . ?' It was his turn to look embarrassed. 'My mistake.'

She put the glass down. 'Have a seat.' She patted the chaise. Erasmus looked at it, looked back at her, then perched bird-like on the far end. *Better change the subject*, she told herself. 'You were married, weren't you?' she asked.

He stared at her as if she'd slapped him. 'Yes. What of it?'

Whoops. 'I, uh, was wondering. That is. What happened?'

'She died,' he said. He glanced at the floor, then raised his brandy glass.

Miriam's vision blurred. 'I'm sorry.'

'Why? It's not your fault.' After a long moment, he shrugged. 'You had your fellow Roland. It's not so different.'

'What –' she swallowed '– happened to her?' *How long ago was it?* she wondered. Sometimes she thought she'd come to terms with Roland's death, but at other times it still felt like yesterday.

'It was twenty years ago. Back then I had prospects.' He considered his next words. 'Some would say, I threw them away. The movement – well.'

'The movement?'

'I was sent to college, by my uncle – my father was dead, you know how it goes – to study for the bar. They'd relaxed the requirements, so dissenters, freethinkers, even atheists, all were allowed to affirm and practice. His majesty's father was rather less narrow than John Frederick, I don't know whether that means anything to you. But anyway . . . I had some free time, as young students with a modest stipend do, and I had some free thoughts, and I became involved with the league. We had handbills to write and print and distribute, and a clear grievance to bring before their lordships in hope of redress, and we were overly optimistic, I think. We thought we might have a future.'

'The league? You had some kind of political demands?' Miriam racked her brains. She'd run across mention of the league – *league of what* had never been clear – in the samizdat history books he'd loaned her, but only briefly, right at the end, as some sort of hopeful coda to the authorial present.

'Yes. Little things like a universal franchise, regardless of property qualifications and religion and marital status. Some of the committee wanted women to vote, too – but that was thought too extreme for a first step. And we wanted a free press, public decency and the laws of libel permitting.'

'Uh.' She closed her mouth. 'But you were . . .'

The frown turned into a wry smile. 'I was a young hothead. Or easily led. I met Annie first at a public meeting, and then renewed her acquaintance at *The People's Voice* where she was laying type. She was the printer's daughter, and neither he nor my uncle approved of our liaison. But once I received my letters and acquired a clerk's post, I could afford to support her, which made her father come round, and my uncle just muttered darkly about writing me out of his will for a while, and stopped doing even that after the wedding. So we had a good four years together, and she insisted on laying type even when the two boys came along, and I wrote for the sheets – anonymously, I must add – and we were very happy. Until it all ended.'

Miriam raised her glass for another sip. Somehow the contents had evaporated. 'Here, let me refill that,' she said, taking Erasmus's glass. She stood up and walked past him to get to the bar, wobbling slightly as the carriage jolted across a set of points. 'What went wrong?'

'In nineteen eighty-six, on November the fourteenth, six fine fellows from the northeast provinces traveled to the royal palace in Savannah. There had been a huge march the week before in New London, and it had gone off smoothly, the petition of a million names being presented to the black rod – but the king himself was not in residence, being emphysemic. That winter came harsh and early, so he'd decamped south to Georgia. It was his habit to go for long drives in the country, to take the air. Well, the level of expectation surrounding the petition was high, and rumors were swirling like smoke: that the king had read the petition and would agree to the introduction of a bill, that the king had read the petition and threatened to bring home the army, that the king had this and the king had that. All nonsense, of course. The king was on vacation and he refused to deal with matters of state that were anything less than an emergency. Or so I learned later. Back then, I was looking for a progressive practice that was willing to take on a junior partner, and Annie was expecting again.'

Miriam finished pouring and put the stopper back in the decanter. She passed a glass back to him: 'So what happened?'

'Those six fine gentlemen were a little impatient. They'd formed a ring, and they'd convinced themselves that the king was a vicious tyrant who would like nothing more than to dream up new ways to torment the workers. You know, I think – judging by your own history books – how it goes. The mainstream movement spawns tributaries, some of which harbor currents that flow fast and deep. The Black Fist Freedom Guard, as they called themselves, followed the king in a pair of fast motor carriages until they learned his habitual routes. Then they assassinated him, along with the queen, and one of his two daughters, by means of a petard.'

'They what? That's crazy!'

'Yes, it was.' Erasmus nodded, outwardly calm. 'John Frederick himself pulled his dying father from the wreckage. He was already something of a reactionary, but not, I think, an irrational one – until the Black Fist murdered his parents.'

'But weren't there guards, or something?' Miriam shook her head. *What about the secret service?* she wondered. If someone tried a stunt like that on a U.S. president it just wouldn't work. It wouldn't be *allowed* to work. Numerous whack-jobs had tried to kill Clinton when he was in office: a number had threatened or actually tried to off the current president. Nobody had gotten close to a president of the United States since nineteen eighty-six. 'Didn't he have any security?'

'Oh yes, he had security. He was secure in the knowledge that he was the king-emperor, much beloved by the majority of his subjects. Does that surprise you? Today John Frederick goes nowhere without a battalion of guards and a swarm of Polis agents, but his father relied on two loyal constables with pistols. They were injured in the attack, incidentally: one of them died later.'

He took a deep, shuddering breath, then another sip of the brandy. 'The day after the assassination, a state of emergency was declared. Demonstrations ensued. On Black Monday, the seventeenth, a column of demonstrators marching towards the royal complex on Manhattan Island were met by dragoons armed with heavy repeaters. More than three hundred were killed, mostly in the stampede. We were . . . there, but on the outskirts, Annie and I. We had the boys to think of. We obviously didn't think hard enough. The next day, they arrested me. My trial before the tribunal lasted eighteen minutes, by the clock on the courtroom wall. The man before me they sentenced to hang for distributing our newssheet, but I was lucky. All they knew was that I'd been away from my workplace during the massacre, and I'd been limping when I got back. The evidence was circumstantial, unlike the sentence they gave me: twelve years in the camps.'

He took a gulp of the brandy and swallowed, spluttering for a moment. 'Annie wasn't so lucky,' he added.

'What? They hanged her?' Miriam leaned toward him, aghast.

'No.' He smiled sadly. 'They only gave her two years in a women's camp. I don't know if you know what that was like . . . no? All right. It was hard enough for the men. Annie died – 'he stared into his glass '– in childbed.'

'I don't understand – '

'Use your imagination,' Erasmus snapped. 'What do you think the guards were like?'

'Oh god. I'm so sorry.'

'The boys went to a state orphanage,' Erasmus added. 'In Australia.'

'Enough.' She held up a hand: 'I'm sorry I asked!'

The fragile silence stretched out. 'I'm not,' Erasmus said quietly. 'It was just a little bit odd to talk about it. After so long.'

'You got out . . . four years ago?'

'Nine.' He drained his glass and replaced it on the occasional table. 'The camps were overfull. They got sloppy. I was moved to internal exile, and there was a – what your history book called an underground railway. "Erasmus Burgeson" isn't the name I was known by back then.'

'You've been living under an assumed identity all this time?'

He nodded, watching her expression. 'The movement provides. They needed a dodgy pawnbroker in Boston, you see, and I fitted the bill. A dodgy pawnbroker with a history of a couple of years in the camps, nothing serious, nothing *excessively* political. The real me they'd hang for sure if they caught him, these days. I hope you don't mind notorious company?'

'I'm –' She shook her head. 'It's crazy.' *You were writing for a newspaper, for crying out loud! Asking for voting rights and freedom of the press! And those are hanging offenses?* 'And if what you were campaigning for back then is crazy, so am I. What's the movement's platform now? Is it still just about the franchise, and freedom of speech? Or have things changed?'

'Oh yes.' He was still studying her, she realized. 'Eighty-six was a

wake-up cry. The very next central council meeting that was held –
two years later, in exile – announced that the existence of a hereditary
crown was a flaw in the body politic. The council decreed that nothing less than the overthrow of the king-emperor and the replacement
of their Lordships and Commons by a republic of free men and
women, equal before the law, would suffice. The next day, the Commons passed a bill of attainder against everyone in the movement.
A month after *that* the pope excommunicated us – he declared
democracy to be a mortal sin. But by then we already knew we were
damned.'

HOT PURSUIT

Another day, another Boston. Brill walked up the staircase to the front office and glanced around. 'Where's Morgan?' she demanded.

'He's in the back room.' The courier folded his newssheet and laid it carefully on the desk.

'Don't call ahead.' She frowned, then headed straight back to the other office, overlooking the backyard collocated with Miriam's house's garden in the other Boston, in New Britain.

The house – Miriam's house, according to the deeds of ownership, not that it mattered much once she'd allowed her start-up submarine to surface in the harbor of the Clan's Council deliberations – was a stately lump of shingle-fronted stonework with a view out over the harbor. But over here the building was distinctly utilitarian, overshadowed by a row of office towers. The architecture in New Britain was stunted by relatively high material and transport costs: planting fifty-thousand-ton lumps of concrete and steel on top of landfill was a relatively recent innovation in New Britain, and hadn't corrupted their skyline yet. But this one was different.

Oskar was waiting outside the door to the rear office. He looked bored. The cut of his jacket failed to conceal his shoulder holster. 'How long are you here for?'

'I came to see Morgan.' She stared at him. 'Then I need to cross over, get changed into native garb, and draw funds. I may be some time. It depends.'

'Cross over. Right.' Oskar twitched. 'You know there's a problem.'

'Problem?'

'You'd better ask the boss.' Oskar backed up, rapped on the door twice, then opened it for her.

'Who –' Morgan looked up. He had his feet up on the mahogany desk, a half-eaten burger at his right hand, and judging by his expression her appearance was deeply unwelcome.

'Hello there. Don't let me keep you from your food.'

'Lady Brilliana!' He swung his feet down hastily, almost knocking his chair over in his hurry to stand up.

'Sit down.' She walked around the desk and pulled out the chair on his right, then sat beside him. 'Oskar tells me there's a *problem*. On the other side.'

Morgan twitched even more violently than Oskar had. 'You're telling me. Have you come to fix it?'

'Tell me about it first.'

'You don't know –' He swallowed his words, but the look of dismay was genuine enough in her estimate.

'I need to cross over and run a search in New Britain,' she said evenly. 'If there's a problem with our main safe house in Boston, I need to know it.'

'The Polis – the security cops? They raided the house. We barely pulled everybody out in time.'

Brilliana swallowed a curse. 'When was this?'

'Three days ago. I thought everyone knew – '

'Was it coordinated action?' she demanded.

Morgan shook himself, visibly trying to pull himself together. 'I don't think so,' he admitted. 'The situation over there's been going to the midden, frankly, and the Polis are running around looking for saboteurs and spies under every table. Six weeks ago they turned over the workshop and shut it down: some of the staff were arrested for sedition. We were already lying low – '

'What about Burgeson?' Brill demanded.

'Oh,' he said. 'That.'

'Yes, *that*.' She nodded. 'I came as soon as I heard. How long has the watch been running?'

'All week, since before the raid. I can't be sure, my lady, but I think our activities might be what attracted the interest of the Polis. We were using the house as a staging post, and when he went down to New York . . .' His shrug was eloquent.

'I see.' Brilliana paused for a moment. *It would fit the picture*, she considered. If the Polis were already watching the house, and strangers based there keeping watch on a suspect would get their attention. *And if Burgeson headed for the capital and the strangers followed him* . . . That would be when they'd bring down the hammer, right enough. 'But you lost the trail in Man – New London.'

'He started evading,' Morgan protested. 'Like a seasoned agent!'

'He was last seen with a female companion,' Brilliana pointed out coldly. 'Which was the whole point of the watch on him.'

'It's not her,' Morgan dismissed her concern. 'Some bint he picked up from a brothel in New London – '

'You sound awfully sure of that. Would you like to place a wager on it? Either way? The last joint on your left little finger, against mine?'

He turned white. 'No, no, it'd be just my luck if – look, he was deliberately trying to throw his tail, that's what Joseph said! And the business with them changing trains? I had Oskar and Georg waiting at the station but Burgeson and his companion weren't on it when it pulled in.'

'Morgan. *Morgan.*' Brill smiled again, baring her teeth. The way it made Morgan wince was truly wonderful. He probably thought she was reporting direct to the thin white duke. 'I already know that you're undermanned and don't have enough pairs of boots on the ground. And you've lost your forward base, due to enemy action, not negligence.' At least, not *active* negligence. Nobody could accuse Morgan of spontaneous activity – he might be stupid, but at least he was lazy. His sins were seldom those of commission. 'So why are you trying so hard to convince me it's not your fault? Anyone would think you were trying to hide something! Whereas if it's just Burgeson giving you the slip . . .' She shrugged.

'It's embarrassing, that's what it is.' He squinted at her suspiciously. 'And I know what you think of me.'

You do? Really? The temptation to tell him what she *really* thought of him was hard to resist, but she managed to restrain herself. *Later.* 'The shop. You've checked the door alarm, haven't you?'

'I've had it staked out since the train departed.' Morgan looked pleased with himself.

512

'Right. Team in the street? A wire and transmitter on the door?' He nodded. 'You know there's a secret back way in? And you know about Helge's experience with trip wires?' His smile slipped. 'Here's what's going to happen. Oskar and I are going to disguise ourselves then cross over via the backup transfer site. While we are checking the shop out – and I expect our birds have already flown the coop – you'll finish your lunch then send a messenger across to cable the railway ticket office asking if they have any reservations in the name of, let's see, a Mr. and Mrs. Burgeson would spring to mind? That *is* the alias they were using at the hotel? And if so, I want to know where they're going, and where the train stops en route, so I can meet them before they get to the final destination.' Brill had allowed her voice to grow quieter, so that Morgan was unconsciously leaning towards her as she finished the sentence.

'But if they're on a train – they could be on their way to Buenos Aires, or anywhere!'

'So what? The Clan bizjet is on standby for me at Logan.' She stood up. 'I'll be back in two hours, and I expect a detailed report on the surveillance operation and Burgeson's current location, so I can set up the intercept and work out who to draft in. We'd better be in time. And you'd better find out where they're going, because if we lose her again, the duke will be *really* pissed.'

*

The council of war took place in a conference room in the Boston Sheraton, just off the Hyatt Center, with air-conditioning and full audiovisual support. All but two of the eighteen attendees were male, and all wore dark, conservatively cut business suits: they were polite but distant in their dealings with the hotel staff. The facilities manager who oversaw their refreshments and lunch buffet got the distinct impression that they were foreign bankers, perhaps a delegation from a very starchy Swiss institution. Or maybe they were a committee of cemetery managers. It hardly mattered, though. They were clearly the best kind of customer – quiet, undemanding, dignified, and utterly unlikely to make a mess or start any fights.

'Helmut. An update on the opposition's current disposition, if you please,' said the graying, distinguished-looking fellow seated at the head of the table. 'Are there any indications of a change in their operational deployments?'

'Yes, your grace.' Helmut – a stocky fellow in his mid-thirties with an odd pudding-bowl haircut – stood up and opened his laptop. His suit jacket flexed around well-muscled shoulders: he obviously worked out between meetings. 'I have prepared a brief presentation to show the geographical distribution of targets . . .'

The video projector flickered on, showing a map of the eastern seaboard as far inland as the Appalachians, gridded out in uneven regions that bore little resemblance to state boundaries. Odd names dotted the map, vaguely Germanic, as one might expect from a Swiss lending institution. Helmut recited a list of targets and names, clicking the laptop's track pad periodically to advance through a time series of transactions. It was curiously bloodless, especially once he began discussing the losses.

'At Erkelsfjord, resistance was offered: the enemy burned the house, hanged all those of the outer family and retainers who surrendered – twenty-eight in all – then stripped the peasants and drove them into the woods, firing the village. We lost but one dead and two injured of the inner families. At Isjlmeer, quarter was offered and accepted. The lentgrave accepted and, with his family, left the keep, whereupon he and all but two sons and one daughter were struck down by crossbow fire. The servants were flogged, stripped, and taken into slavery, but the villagers were left unharmed. The next day, a different company of light cavalry struck Nordtsman's Keep. The baron was present and had raised his levies and, forewarned, had established a defensible perimeter: he took the enemy with enfilading fire from their left flank, forcing a retreat. Total enemy casualties numbered sixty-seven bodies, plus an unknown number who escaped.

'At Giraunt Dire, the eorl emplaced his two light machine guns to either side of the bridge across the river Klee, beating off an attack by two companies of horse led by Baron Escrivain . . .'

The map flickered with red dots, like smallpox burning up the side of a victim's face. As the conflict progressed, dotted red arrows appeared, tracking the course of the pestilence. The litany of sharp engagements began to change, as more of the defenders – fore-warned and prepared – put up an effective defense. Helmut's presentation kept a running tally in the bottom right corner of the screen, a profit and loss balance sheet denominated in gallons of blood. Finally he came to an end.

'That's the total so far. Thirty-one attacks, twenty-two successful and nine beaten off with casualties. In general, we have lost an average of two inner members per successful attack and one per successful defense; our losses of retainers and outer family members are substantially higher. The enemy has lost at least three hundred dead and probably twice that number wounded, although we cannot confirm the latter figure. The four columns appear to be converging near Neuhalle, and it is noteworthy that this one has at no time ventured further than a fifteen-mile march from one of the pretender's sworn vassals' keeps.'

The projector switched off: Helmut directed a brief half-bow towards the other end of the table, then sat down.

The silence lay heavy for nearly a minute after he finished speaking, the only sounds in the room the white noise of the air-conditioning and the faint scribble of pens on the note pads of a couple of the attendees. Finally, the chairman directed his gaze towards a bluff, ruddy-faced fellow in early middle age, whose luxuriant handlebar mustache was twitching so violently that it threatened to take wing. 'Carl. You appear to have something on your mind. Would you care to share it with us?'

Carl glanced around the table. 'It's a calculated outrage,' he rumbled. 'We've got to nail it fast, too, before the decree of outlawry convinces everyone that we're easy pickings. While we're pinned down in our houses and keeps, the pretender can run around at will, taking whichever target is cheapest. It sends entirely the wrong message. Why hasn't he been assassinated yet?'

'We've tried.' The chairman stared at him. 'It's difficult to assassinate a target when the target is taking pains to avoid mapped killing grounds and is sleeping and working surrounded by his troops. Do you have any constructive suggestions, or shall we move on?'

There was a crunching sound. Eyes swiveled towards Carl's hand, and the wreckage of what had been a Pelikan Epoch mechanical pencil. Carl grunted. 'A conventional infiltrator could get close to him . . .'

The chairman nodded, very slightly, and a certain tension left the room. 'That might work, but as you already observed, if it takes too long it doesn't buy us anything. He's already in the field, and levies are being recruited to his vassals' forces. I've had no reports of the pretender adding to his own body of men. To all intents and purposes he is surrounded by a thousand bodyguards at all times. Moreover, if we just kill him, it'll trigger a race for the succession among his vassals – and the only outcome that is guaranteed is that every last one of them will consider us a mortal threat. To resolve this problem, we're going to have to defeat his forces in detail as well as producing an heir to the throne.'

'But he's refusing to concentrate where we can hit him!' Carl opened his meaty hand above his blotter: two hundred dollars' worth of pencil scattered across the pad in fragments. 'We must do something to bring him to battle! Otherwise he will continue to make us look like fools!'

'You're quite right.'

Carl looked up at the chairman, perplexed by his agreement. 'Your grace?'

'I'd like to call Eorl Riordan next, Carl. Eorl Riordan, would you care to explain next week's operation to the baron?'

'Certainly, your grace.' The new speaker, square-jawed and short-haired, had something of a wardroom air about himself. 'On the basis of intelligence indicating that the pretender is preparing a major offensive against one of our most prominent fortifications, his grace asked me to prepare a plan for the defense of Castle Hjorth – which we have reason to believe is the most likely target – with fallback plans to ensure that our other high-value fortifications remain defensible. The resulting plan requires us to stockpile supplies at the likely targets in preparation for the arrival of a mobile reinforcement group. The reinforcement group will be based in this world, while courier elements in our Gruinmarkt assets will rotate regularly and

516

report on their status. As soon as one of our sites goes dark, or as soon as we receive confirmation of contact from one of our scouts in the field, the reinforcement group will redeploy to the target. The primary target, Castle Hjorth, is already locked down and defended by a platoon of outer family guards, backed up by a team of eighteen couriers on logistic support. When the enemy attacks, here's how we will defend ourselves . . .'

*

The dome was big.

Huw hadn't been able to grasp the scale of it at first: it was buried in the forest, and apart from the segment looming over the clear roadway, the trees had obscured its curvature. But as he studied it, moving quietly from tree trunk to deadfall as Elena and Hulius stood watch, he came to realize that it was huge. It was also very old, and looked – although he wasn't about to jump to any conclusions – abandoned.

There was a convenient fallen tree trunk about twenty meters out from the rough white dome. Huw settled down behind it, waved to the kids, and pulled out his compact binoculars and the walkie-talkie. 'Yul, do you read?'

'Yes, bro.' Yul was so laid-back he sounded bored. 'Got you covered.'

'Copy,' Elena added tersely.

'No features visible on the outside.' Huw scanned laterally with the binoculars, looking for anything that would give him traction on the thing. 'Going by the trees . . . I make it fifty to eighty meters in radius. Very approximate. There's green stuff on the surface. Looks rough, like concrete. I'm going to approach it when I finish talking. If anything happens I'll head toward the road. Over.'

Nothing was moving. Huw took a deep breath. He was nervously aware of his heartbeat, thudding away like a bass drum: *What is this doing here?* All too acutely, he felt a gut-deep conviction that historic consequences might hinge on his next actions. *Helge didn't feel anything like this when she stumbled on the Lee family's world, did she?* Well, probably not – but that world was inhabited, and by people who spoke a recognizable language, too. No evidence of weird climato-logical conditions, no strange concrete domes in ancient subarctic forests. He checked his web cam briefly, then stood up in full view of the dome.

Anticlimax: nothing happened. *Well, that's a relief.* The small of his back itched. He walked around the deadfall, pacing towards the dome. Close up, he realized it was bigger than he'd thought: the curve of its flank was nearly vertical at ground level, stretching away above and to either side of him like a wall. *Hmm, let's see.* He looked down at the base, which erupted smoothly from a tumble of ferns and decaying branches. Then he looked up. From this close, he could see the treetops diverge from the curve of the convex hull. 'Scratch the size estimate, it's at least a hundred meters in radius.'

A gust of wind rattled the branches above him. The top of the dome was hard to make out against the background of gray clouds. Huw shivered, then reached out and touched the dome. It was cold, with the grittiness of concrete or sandstone. He leaned close and peered at it. The surface was very smooth, but occasional pockmarks showed where it had been scarred by the surface cracking away under the chisel-like blows of ice forming in tiny fissures on its surface. Finally, he leaned against it and listened.

'I don't hear anything, and it's cold – probably at ambient temper-ature. I think it's empty, possibly abandoned. I'm going to proceed around it, clockwise.'

The direction he'd chosen took him downslope, away from the road. He walked very slowly, pausing frequently, taking care not to look back. If someone was observing him, he didn't want to tip them off to Yul and Elena's presence. The dome extended, intact, curving gradually away from the road. In places, trees had grown up against it, roots scrabbling for purchase in the poor soil. Some of them were very large. It took Huw a quarter of an hour to realize that none of them had actually levered their way into the concrete or stone or whatever the dome was made of. 'It's not quite a flawless finish,' he reported, 'but I've got a hunch it's been here a very long time.' He rubbed his gloved hands together to warm them: there was a dis-tinct bite in the air, and the gusts were growing more frequent.

In the end, the hole in the dome came as a surprise to Huw. He'd been expecting some sort of opening, low down on the slope: or perhaps a gatehouse of some sort. But one moment he was walking around the huge, curving flank of the thing, and the next moment the curved edge of the dome disappeared, as if a giant the size of the Goodyear Blimp had taken a huge bite out of it. Huw stopped for a minute, inspecting the edge of the hole with his binoculars. 'The opening starts at ground level and extends two-thirds of the way to the top of the dome. Must be at least fifty meters wide. I'm going closer . . . the edge looks almost melted.' He looked down. The trees were thinner on the ground, shorter, and the ground itself fell away in front of the opening, forming a shallow bowl. *Like a crater*, he realized. A trickle of water emerged from the shadowy interior of the dome, feeding down a muddy, overgrown channel into a pond in the depression. The pond was almost circular. *Something cracked the dome open. Something from* – he walked away from the opening, trying to get a perspective on it – *something firing downwards, from above.*

He shook his head, and suddenly the whole scene dropped into perspective. The dark shadows inside the dome, looming: *piles of debris.* The melted edges: *either the dome is self-healing, or it's made of something a whole lot more resilient than concrete.* It hadn't shattered like masonry – it had melted like wax. He keyed his walkie-talkie again: 'The dome's split open here. Something energetic, punching down out of the sky. A long time ago.' *The way the crater had filled with water, the way the trees were so much shorter than their neighbors, almost as if –*

Huw fumbled with his telemetry belt, then slipped one hand free of its glove in order to pull out the Geiger tube. 'Got you,' he muttered, holding it out in front of him. 'Let's see.' He flicked the switch on the counter pack, then advanced on the depression. The counter clicked a few times, then gave a warning crackle, like a loose connection. Huw paused, swinging around. It popped and crackled, then as he took a step forward it buzzed angrily. 'Hmm.' He turned around and walked back towards the dome. The buzzing subsided, back down to a low crackle. He moved towards the edge of the dome. As he approached the melted-looking edges the counter began to buzz – then rose to an angry whine as he brought the tube to within a couple of centimeters of the edge. 'Shit!' He jumped back. 'Yul, Elena, listen up – the edge of the hole is radioactive. Lots of beta and maybe alpha activity, not much gamma. I don't think –' he swallowed ' – I don't think we're going to find anyone alive in here. And I don't want you touching the edge of the dome, or walking through the stream running out of it.'

He swallowed again. *What am I going to tell the duke this time?* He wondered.

A hypothesis took root and refused to shake free: *Imagine a nuclear installation or a missile command site or a magic wand factory. Or something.* There'd been a war. It all happened a long time ago of course – hundreds of years ago. Everyone was dead, nobody lived here anymore. During the war, someone took a shot at the dome with a high-energy weapon. Not an ordinary H-bomb, but something exotic – a shaped nuclear charge, designed to punch almost all of its energy out into a beam of radiation going straight down. Or a gamma-ray laser powered by a couple of grams of isomeric hafnium. Maybe they used an intercontinental ballistic magic wand. Whatever it was, not much blast energy reached the ground – but the dome had been zapped by a stabbing knife of plasma like Lightning Child's fiercest punch, setting up a cascade of neutrons from shattered nuclei, leaving the edges of the wound seeded with secondary isotopes.

Huw looked up at the underside of the dome. A gust of wind set up a sonorous droning whistle, ululating like the ghost of a dead whale. The dome was thick. He froze for a moment, staring, then raised his binoculars one-handed. With his other hand he raised his dictaphone, and began speaking. 'The installation is covered by a dome, and back in the day it was probably guarded by active defenses. You'd need a nuke to crack it open because the stuff it's made of is harder and more resilient than reinforced concrete, and it's at least three, maybe four meters thick. Coming down from the zenith, perhaps eighty meters off-center, the shotgun-blast of lightning-hot plasma has sheared through almost fifteen meters of this –

call it supercrete? Carbon-fiber reinforced concrete? – and dug an elliptical trench in the shallow hillside. It must have vaporized the segment of the dome it struck. How in Hell the rest of the dome held – must have a tensile strength like buckminsterfullerene nanotubes. That's probably what killed the occupants, the shockwave would rattle around inside the dome . . .'

The tree branches rustled overhead as the drone of the dead whale rose. Huw glanced up at the clouds, scudding past fast in the gray light. He sniffed. *Smells like snow.* Then he glanced over his shoulder, and turned, very deliberately, to raise a hand and wave.

Elena was the first to catch up with him. 'Crone's teeth, Huw, what have you found?'

'Stand away from there!' he snapped as she glanced curiously at the edge of the gaping hole in the dome. 'It's radioactive,' he added, as she looked round and frowned at him. 'I think whatever happened a long time ago was . . . well, I don't think the owners are home.'

'Right.' She shook her head, looking up at the huge arch that opened the dome above them. 'What are we going to do?'

'Yo.' Yul trotted up, rifle cradled carefully in his arms. 'What now – '

Huw checked his watch. 'We've got half an hour left until it's time to head back to base camp. I don't know about you guys, but I want to do some sightseeing before I go home. But first, I think we'd better make sure it doesn't kill us in the process.' He held up his Geiger counter: 'Get your tubes out.' A minute later he'd reset both their counters to click, rather than silently logging the radiation flux. 'If this begins to crackle, stop moving. If it buzzes, back away from wherever the buzzing is highest-pitched. If it howls at you, run for your life. The higher the pitch, the more dangerous it is. And don't touch *anything* without checking it out first. Never touch your counter to a surface, but hold it as close as you can – some types of radiation are stopped by an inch of air, but can kill you if you get close enough to actually touch the source. Got that? If in doubt, don't touch.'

'What are we looking for again, exactly?' Yul asked.

'Magic wands.' Any sufficiently advanced technology was indistinguishable from magic. 'C'mon, let's see what we've got.'

*

The trouble with trains, in Miriam's opinion, was that they weren't airliners: you actually went *through* the landscape, instead of soaring over it, and you tended to get bogged down in those vast spaces. About the best thing that could be said about it was that in first class you could get a decent cooked meal in the dining car then retire to your bedroom for a night's sleep, and wake up seven or eight hundred miles from where you put your head on your pillow. On the other hand, the gentle swaying, occasional front-to-back lurching of the coaches, and the perpetual clatter of wheels across track welds combined to give her a queasy feeling the like of which she hadn't felt since many years ago, when she'd let her then-husband argue her into a boating holiday.

I seem to be spending all my time throwing up these days. Miriam sat on the edge of her bed, the chamber pot clutched between her hands and knees in the pre-dawn light. A sense of despondency washed over her. *All I need right now is a stomach bug . . .* She yawned experimentally, held her breath, and let her back relax infinitesimally as she realized that her stomach was played out. *Damn.* She put the pot back in its under-bunk drawer and swung her legs back under the sheets. She yawned again, exhausted, then glanced at the window in mild disgust. *Might as well get started now*, she told herself. There was no way she'd manage another hour's sleep before it was time to get up anyway: the train was due to pause in Dunedin around ten o'clock, and she needed to get her letter written first. The only question was what to put in it . . .

She glanced at the door to the lounge room. Erasmus insisted on sleeping in there – not that it was any great hardship, for the padded bench concealed a pullout bed – which would make it just about impossible for her to get the letter out without him noticing. *Well, there's no alternative*, she decided. She was fresh out of cover stories: who else could she be writing to, when she was on the run? *Sooner or later you've got to choose your allies and stick by them.* So far, Erasmus had shown no sign of trying to bar her from pursuing her own objectives. *I'll just have to risk it.*

Sighing, she rummaged in the bedside cabinet for the writing-box. People here were big on writing letters – no computers or e-mail, and typewriters the size of a big old laser printer meant that everyone got lots of practice at their cursive handwriting. There was an inkwell, of course, and even a cheap pen – not a fountain pen, but a dipping pen with a nib – and a blotter, and fine paper with the railway corporation crest of arms, and envelopes. *Envelopes.* What she was about to attempt was the oldest trick in the book – but this was a world that had not been blessed by the presence of an Edgar Allan Poe.

Biting her lip, Miriam hunched over the paper. Best to keep it brief: she scribbled six sentences in haste, then pulled out a clean sheet of paper and condensed them into four, as neatly as she could manage aboard a moving train.

Dear Brill, I survived the massacre at the palace by fleeing into New Britain. I have vital information about a threat to us all. Can you arrange an interview with my uncle? If so, I will make contact on my return to Boston (not less than seven days from now).

Folding it neatly, she slid the note into an envelope and addressed it, painstakingly carefully, in a language she was far from easy with.

Next, she took another sheet of paper and jotted down instructions upon it. This she placed, along with a folded six-shilling note, inside another envelope with a different name and address upon it.

Finally, she took the locket from under her pillow, and copied the design onto the envelope, making a neat sketch of it in place of a postage stamp – taking pains to cover each side of the knotwork as she drew the other half, so that she couldn't accidentally focus on the whole.

And then she waited.

Dunedin was the best part of a thousand miles from New London, a good nine hundred from Boston – the nearest city in her own world to it was Joliet. In this world, with no Chicago, Dunedin had grown into a huge metropolis, the continental hub where railroad and canal freight met on the southern coast of the great lakes. There was a Clan post office in Joliet, and a small fort in the unmapped forests of the world the Clan came from – a no-man's-land six hundred miles west of the territory claimed by the eastern marcher kingdoms – and now a post office in Dunedin too, a small house in the suburbs where respectable-looking men came and went erratically. Miriam had been there before, had even committed the address to memory for her courier runs: an anonymous villa in a leafy suburb. But the train would only pause for half an hour to change locomotives; she wouldn't have time to deliver it herself.

Eventually she heard shuffling and muttering from the other side of the door – and then a tentative knock. 'Who is it?' she called.

'Breakfast time.' It was Erasmus. 'Are you decent?'

'Sure.' She pulled on her shoes and stood up, opening the through door. The folding bunk was stowed: Erasmus looked to have been up for some time. He smiled, tentatively. 'The steward will bring us our breakfast here, if you like. Did you sleep well?'

'About as well as can be expected.' She steeled herself: 'I need to post a letter when we get to Dunedin.'

'You do?'

She nodded. The chair opposite the bench seat was empty, so she sat in it. 'It's to, to one of my relatives who I have reason to trust, asking if it's safe for me to make contact.'

'Ah.' Erasmus nodded slowly. 'You didn't mention where you are or where you're going?'

'Do I look stupid? I told Brill to be somewhere in a week's time, and I'd make contact. She wasn't at the royal reception so she's probably still alive, and if she gets the letter at all she's in a position to act on it. In any event, I don't expect the letter to reach her immediately; it'll take at least a couple of days.'

'That would be – ah.' He nodded. 'Yes, I remember her. A very formidable young woman.'

'Right. If she shows up in Boston in a week's time, you'll know what it means. If she tells me it's safe to come in from the cold, then and *only* then I'll be able to talk to my relatives. So. What do you think?'

'I think you ought to send that letter.' Erasmus paused. 'What will you do if a different relative shows up looking for you?'

'That would be bad.' She twitched: 'I've got to try. Otherwise I'll end up spending the rest of my life looking over my shoulder, always keeping an eye open for assassins.'

'Who doesn't?' he said ironically, then reached up and pulled the bell rope. 'The steward will post the letter for you. Now let's get some breakfast . . .'

SURPRISE PARTY

Despite the summer heat, the grand dining hall in the castle harbored something of a damp chill. Perhaps it was the memory of all the spilled blood that had run like water down the years: despite the eighty-degree afternoon outside, the atmosphere in the hall made Eorl Riordan shiver.

'Erik, Carl, Rudi. Your thoughts?'

Carl cleared his throat. Unlike the other two, he was attired in local style, although his chain shirt would have won few plaudits at a Renaissance Faire on the other side. Machine-woven titanium links backing a Kevlar breastplate and U.S. Army-pattern helmet – the whole ensemble painted in something not unlike urban camo – would send entirely the wrong, functional message. Even without the P90 submachine gun strapped to his chest, and the sword at his hip.

'I think he'd be stupid to invest us. The fort's built well, nobody's taken it in the past three hundred years, and it has a commanding view of the river and land approaches. Even with cannon, it'll take him a while to breach the outer curtains. I've inspected the outer works and Villem was right – we've got a clear field of beaten fire over the six hundred yards around the apron. If he had American artillery, maybe, or if we give him time to emplace bombards behind the ridge line – but a frontal assault would be a fruitless waste of lives. The pretender may be many things, but I will not insult his victims by calling him stupid.'

'What about treachery?' asked Erik. A younger ClanSec courtier of the goatee-and-dreadlocks variety, his dress was GAP-casual except for the Glock, the saber, and the bulky walkie-talkie hanging from his belt.

Eorl Riordan looked disapproving. 'That's only one of the possibilities.' He held up a hand and began counting off fingers. 'One, the pretender really is stupid, or has taken leave of his senses. Two, it's a tactical diversion, planned to tie us up defending a strategic necessity while he does something else. Three, treachery. Four, weapons or tactics we haven't anticipated. Five . . . two or more of the above. My assessment of the pretender is the same as yours, Sieur Carl: He's crazy like a rat. I forgot to bring a sixth finger, so kindly use your imaginations – but I think he is playing a game with the duke's intelligence, and he wants us here for some reason that will not redound to our benefit. So. Let's set up a surprise, shall we? Rudi, how are the scouts doing?'

'Nothing to report.' Rudi was another of the younger generation, wiry and gangling in hoodie and cutoffs. 'They're checking in regularly but we've only got twelve of them between here and Isjlemeer: he could march an army between them and we might never know. I can't give you what you want unless you let me use Butterfly, whatever the duke thinks of it.'

Riordan snorted. 'You and your kite. You know about the duke's . . . feelings?'

'Yep.' Rudi just stood there, hands in pockets. Riordan, about to take him to task, noticed the oversized watch on Rudi's skinny left arm and paused. 'It's too late to get started today but, weather permitting, I could give you what you want tomorrow.'

It was a tempting offer. Riordan considered it. Normally he'd have jumped on any junior officer who suggested such a thing, but he'd been given a very specific job to get done, and Rudi wasn't wrong. He made a quick executive decision. 'You can do your thing tomorrow on *my* authority, if we haven't made contact first. The duke will forget to be angry if you get results. But.' He shook a finger at Rudi: 'There *will* be consequences if you make an exhibition of your craft. Do you understand?'

'Uh, yes, sir. There won't be any problems. Apart from the weather, and, worst case, we've still got the scouts.'

'Go get it ready,' Riordan said tersely. Rudi nodded, almost bowing, and scurried out of the room in the direction of the stables. Riordan didn't need telepathy to know what was going through his mind: the duke had almost hit the roof back when Rudi had first admitted to smuggling his obsession across, one component at a time, and it had been all Riordan and Roland had been able to do to talk Angbard out of burning the machine and giving the lad a severe flogging. It wasn't Rudi's fault that forty years ago a premature attempt to introduce aviation to the Gruinmarkt had triggered a witchcraft panic – superstitious peasants and 'dragons' were a volatile combination – but his pigheaded persistence in trying to get his ultralight off the ground flew in the face of established security doctrine. Riordan glanced at Carl, acknowledging his disapproval. 'Yes, I know. But I don't think it can make the situation any worse at this point, and it might do some good. Now, the defensive works. We've got a couple of hours to go until sunset. Think your men will be expecting a surprise inspection . . . ?'

*

Brill realized she was being watched as soon as she turned to lock the front door of the shop behind her.

She'd spent a frustrating hour in Burgeson's establishment. The monitor on the door was working exactly as intended – she couldn't fault Morgan for that – but the fact remained, it hadn't been triggered. And it didn't take her long to figure out that somebody had been in the shop recently. The drawers in the desk in the back office were open, someone had been rummaging through the stock, and the dust at the top of the cellar stairs was disturbed. She'd looked down the steps into the darkness and swore, realizing exactly what had happened. Morgan had secured the front door, and even the back door onto the yard behind the shop, but it hadn't occurred to him that a slippery customer like Burgeson would have a rat run out through the cellar. *Better check it out,* she thought grimly, extracting a pocket flashlight from her handbag.

The cellar showed more signs of recent visitors: disturbed dust, a suspicious freshness to the air. She glanced around tensely, aiming the flashlight left-handed at the nooks and crannies of the cellar. *The floor* . . . She focused the beam, following a scuffed trail in the dust. It led through a side door into another cellar full of furniture, and dead-ended against a wooden cabinet full of labeled cloth bundles. Brill walked towards it. The back of the cabinet was dark, too dark. 'Clever,' she muttered, peering past a bundle: there was a gap between the cabinet and the side wall, and behind it, she saw another wall – two feet farther in. The smell of dust, and damp, and something else – something oily and aromatic, naggingly familiar – tugged at her nostrils. She took a sharp breath, then slipped behind the cabinet and edged along it, through the hole in the bricks at the other end of the cellar, into the tunnel. There was a side door into another, hidden back room: the smell was stronger here. Tarpaulins covered wooden barrels, a thin layer of dust caking them. She raised a cover, glanced inside, and nodded to herself. If someone – Burgeson? Miriam? – hadn't left the back door open, the smell wouldn't have given it away, but down here the stink of oiled metal was almost overpowering. She let the tarp fall, then slid back out of the concealed storeroom. *Miriam keeps dangerous company,* she reminded herself, her lips quirking. *Maybe that's no bad thing right now.*

But it certainly wasn't a *good* thing, and as she turned to lock the front door she paid careful attention to the reflections in the window panes in front of her. Maybe it was pure coincidence that a fellow in a threadbare suit was lounging at the corner of the alley, and maybe it wasn't, but with at least twenty rifles stashed in that one barrel alone, Brill wasn't about to place any bets. She walked away briskly, whistling quietly to herself – let any watchers hurry to keep up – and turned left into the high street. There were more people here, mostly threadbare men hanging around the street corners in dispirited knots, some of them holding out hats or crudely lettered signs. She paused a couple of doors down the street to glance in a shop window, checking for movement behind her. Alley Rat was trying to look inconspicuous about fifty feet behind her, standing face-to-cheek with one of the beggars who wore a shapeless cloth hat and frayed fingerless gloves as gray as his face.

I've acquired a tail. Brill tensed, glancing up the street. 'How annoying,' she murmured aloud. There were no streetcars in sight, but plenty of alleyways. *Worse than annoying,* she added to herself as she thrust her right hand into her bag. *Try to shed him,* first . . .

She started moving again, hurrying, letting her stride lengthen.

She glanced over her shoulder – there was no advantage in hiding her awareness now, if she needed cover from civilians she could just say she was being chased – and spotted Mr. Threadbare and Mr. Hat blundering towards her, splitting in a classic pincer. Most of the bystanders had evaporated or were feigning inattention – nobody wanted to be an audience for this kind of street theater. Brill took a deep breath, stepped backwards until she came up against the brick wall of a shop, then held her handbag out towards Mr. Hat, who was now less than twenty feet away. 'Stop right there,' she said pleasantly, and when he didn't, she shot him twice. The handbag jerked, but the suppressor and the padding kept the noise down to the level of an enthusiastic handclap. She winced slightly and shook her wrist to dislodge a hot cartridge as Mr. Hat went to one knee, a look of utter surprise on his face, and she spun sideways to bear on Mr. Thread-bare. 'Stop, I said.'

Mr. Threadbare stopped. He began to draw breath. She focused on him, noting absently that Mr. Hat was whimpering quietly and slumping sideways against a shopfront, moving one hand to his right thigh. 'Who do you think – '

Brill jerked her hand sideways and shot Mr. Hat again. He jerked and dropped the stubby pistol he'd been drawing, and she had her bag back on Mr. Threadbare before he could reach inside his jacket. 'If you want to live, you will walk ten feet ahead of me,' she said, fight-ing for calm, nerves screaming: *Where's their backup? Clear the zone!* 'Move.'

Mr. Threadbare twitched at Mr. Hat: 'But he's – '

An amateur. Brill tensed up even more: amateurs were unpre-dictable. 'Move!'

Mr. Threadbare moved jerkily, like a puppet in the hands of a trainee. He couldn't take his eyes off Mr. Hat, who was bleeding quite copiously. Brill circled round the target and toed the gun away from him, in the direction of the gutter. Then she gestured Mr. Threadbare ahead of her, along the sidewalk. For a miracle, nobody seemed to have noticed the noise. Mr. Threadbare shuffled slowly: Brill glanced round quickly, then nodded to herself. 'Turn left into the next alley-way.'

'But you – '

She closed the gap between them and pushed the gun up against the small of his back. 'Don't look round. Keep walking.' He was shaking, she noticed, and his voice was weak. 'Left here. Stop. Face the wall. Closer. That's right. Raise your right hand above your head. Now raise your left.' Nobody in the alley, no immediate witnesses if she had to world-walk. 'Who do you work for?'

'But I –' He flinched as brick dust showered his face.

'That's your last warning. Tell me who you work for.'

'Red Hand thief-taker's company. You're in big trouble, miss, Andrew was a good man and if you've killed – '

'Be quiet.' He shut up. 'You tailed me. Why?'

'You burgled the pawnbroker's – '

'You were watching it. Why?'

'We got orders. The Polis – '

Thief-takers – civilian crime prevention, mostly private enterprise – working for the polis – government security? 'What were you watching for?' she asked.

'Cove called Burgeson, and some dolly he's traveling with. He's wanted, under the Sedition Act. Fifty pounds on his head and the old firm's taking an interest, isn't it?'

'Is it now?' Brill found herself grinning, teeth bared. In the distance, a streetcar bell clanged. 'Kneel.'

'But I told you – '

'I said, kneel. Keep your hands above your head. Look away, dammit, that way, yes, over there. I want you to close your eyes and count to a hundred, slowly. One, two, like that, I'll be counting too. If you leave this alley before I reach a hundred, I may shoot you. If you open your eyes before I reach a hundred, I may shoot you. Do you understand?'

'Yes, but – '

'Start counting. Aloud and slowly if you value your life.'

On the count of ten, Brill backed away towards the high street. Seeing Mr. Threadbare still counting as fervently as a priest telling his rosary, she turned, lowered her handbag, and darted out into the open. The streetcar was approaching: Mr. Hat lolled against a wall like an early drunk. She held her arm out for the car, forcing her cheeks into an aching smile. *Miriam, what have you gotten yourself into this time?*

*

The Hjalmar Palace fell, as was so often the case, to a combination of obsolescent design, treachery, and the incompetence of its defenders. And, Otto ven Neuhalle congratulated himself, only a little bit of torture.

About three hundred years ago, the first lord of Olthalle had built a stone tower on this site, a bluff overlooking the meeting of two rivers – known in another world as the Assabet and Sudbury – that combined to feed the Wergat, gateway to the western mountains. Over the course of the subsequent decades he and his sons had fought a bitter grudge war, eventually driving the Musketaquid wanderers west, deeper into the hills and forests of the new lands where they'd not trouble the ostvolk. But then there'd been a falling out among the coastal settlements in the east. An army had marched up the river and burned out the keep and its defenders, leaving smoking ruins and a new lentgrave to raise the walls afresh. He learned from his predecessor's mistake, and built his walls thick and high.

More years passed. The Olthalle tower sprouted a curtain wall with five fine round bastion towers and a gatehouse larger than the original keep. Within the grounds, airy palace wings afforded the baron's family a measure more comfort than the heavily fortified castle. The barons of Olthalle fell on hard times, and seventy years earlier the Hjalmars had married into the castle, turning it into a gathering place for the clan of recently ennobled tinker families. They'd bridged the Wergat, levying tolls, then they'd driven a road into the hills to the west and wrestled another fortune from the forests. The town of Wergatfurt had grown up a couple of miles downstream, a thriving regional market center known for its timber yards and smithies. His majesty had been unable to leave such a vital asset in the hands of the witches – the Hjalmar estates were a geopolitical dagger aimed at the heart of his kingdom. And so, it had come to this . . .

The festivities had started at dawn, when Sir Markus, beater for the royal hunt, had led his levies up to the gates of Wergatfurt and laid his demands before the burghers of the town. Open the gates to the royal army, accept the Thorold Palace edicts, surrender any witches and their get, and be at peace – or defy the king, and suffer the consequences. He had put on a brave show, but (at Otto's urging) had carefully not placed troops on the town's southwestern, upstream, side. And he'd given them until noon to answer his demands.

Of course, Otto's men were already in position in the woods, half a kilometer short of the palace itself. And when they brought the first of the captives to him in early afternoon, bound so tight that the fellow could barely move, he had found Otto in an uncharacteristically good humor. 'You're Griben's other boy, aren't you? What a surprising coincidence.'

'You –' The lad swallowed his words. Barely old enough to be sprouting his first whiskers, barely old enough to know enough to be afraid: 'What do you want?'

Otto smiled. 'An excuse not to hang you.'

'I don't know –' The boy's brow furrowed, then the meaning of Otto's words sank in. 'Lightning's blood, you're just going to burn me anyway, aren't you?' He glared at Otto with all the hollow bravado he could muster. 'I'm no traitor!'

'Perhaps.' Otto glanced towards the stand of trees that concealed his position from the castle's outermost watch-towers. 'But you're not one of them, either. You don't have their blood-spell, you'd never have inherited their wealth, all you are to them is a servant. A dead, loyal servant – the moment my men find another straggler who's willing to listen to reason.' He turned back to the prisoner. 'It's quite simple. Show me the way in and I'll have Magar here turn you loose in the woods, a mile downstream of here. We never met, and nobody saw you. Or.' He shrugged: 'We hold you for the king. I hear he's a traditionalist; takes a personal interest in the old folkways. And he doesn't approve of people who put his arms-men to the trouble of laying siege to a castle. If you're lucky he'll hang you.' Otto paused for effect. 'I gather he holds with the Blood Eagle for traitors.' His nose wrinkled: the kid had pissed himself. And fainted.

'Do you mean to scare him to death, sir?' asked Magar, toeing the prone prisoner with professional disdain: 'Because if so, I can fetch a burial detail . . .'

'I don't think that'll be necessary.' Otto peered at the unconscious boy. The Pervert's carefully cultivated reputation for perpetrating unspeakable horrors on people who crossed him had certainly come in useful on this campaign, he reflected: *All I have to do is hint about his majesty and they fall apart on me like overcooked pullets.* It was an interesting lesson. 'You understand that when I said you'd turn him loose in the woods, I didn't promise that *you* wouldn't kill him?'

'Aye, I got that much, sir.' The boy was twitching. Magar kicked him lightly in the ribs. 'You, wake up.'

Otto bent over the prisoner, so that when the lad opened his eyes there'd be no escape. 'What's it to be?' Otto asked, not unkindly. 'Do you want to –' He straightened up and looked over the boy's head. '– time's up, looks like we've got another prisoner coming in – '

'I'll show you! I'll show you!' The boy was almost hysterical, tears of terror flowing down his cheeks.

'Really?' Otto smiled. 'Thank you. That wasn't so hard now, was it?'

*

The problem with castles was not that they were hard to get into, but that they tended to be equally hard to get out of. And people take shortcuts.

To enter the Hjalmar Palace by road, a polite visitor would ride across the well-manicured apron in front of the walls, itself a killing zone two hundred meters across, then up the path to the gatehouse. There was a moat, of course, a ten-meter-wide ditch full of water diverted from the river (that, during particularly hot moments of a siege, could be layered in burning oil). A stone bridge spanned half the width of the moat. The gatehouse was a small castle in its own right, four round towers connected by stone walls a meter thick, and its wooden drawbridge was a welcome mat that could be withdrawn back to the castle side of the moat if the occupants weren't keen on entertaining guests. In case that wasn't a sufficiently pointed deterrent to intruders, the bridge towers were topped by steel shields and the ominous muzzles of belt-fed machine guns, and the drawbridge itself opened into a zigzagging stony tunnel blocked at several choke points by metal grilles, and covered from above by a killing platform from which the defenders could rain molten lead.

And that was before the visitors reached the outer walls, which in addition to the usual glacis and arrow slits, had acquired (under the custody of the Hjalmar branch of the Clan) such luxuries as imported razor wire, claymore mines, and defenders with automatic weapons.

But such defenses were inconvenient. To leave the central keep by the front door required a descent down a steep flight of steps, a march around half the circumference of the tower, then the traversal of a murder tunnel through the foundations of one of the inner bastions, then a ride halfway along the circular road that lined the inner wall, then another murder tunnel, then the gatehouse, four portcullises, and the drawbridge – it could take half an hour on foot. And so the defenders had come up with shortcuts. They'd installed sally ports in the bases of bastions to allow raiding parties to enter and leave. Toilet outfalls venting over the moat could, at a pinch (and with nose held tight) serve for a hasty exit. A peacetime road battered through the wall, straight into the stable yard, ready to be blocked by a deadfall of boulders at the first alarm. And then there were the usual over-the-wall quick routes out for soldiers and servants in search of an evening of drinking and fucking in the beer cellars of Wergatfurt.

In the case of the Hjalmar Palace, the weak point in its defenses was the water supply. The water supply had to feed the moat, if attackers tried to dam it off from the river: it also had to keep the defenders in drinking water. Some tactical genius a century or two earlier had dug a trench nearly two hundred meters long, under the curtain wall to the river. He'd lined it with stone, floored it with fired clay pipe, then roofed it over and buried it. The aquaduct wasn't just a backup water supply: it was a tactical back door for raiding parties and scouts, a fire escape for the terminally paranoid. The stone blockhouse on the upstream slope of the hill was overgrown with bushes and trees, nearly invisible unless you knew what you were looking for, and when properly maintained – as it was, now – it was guarded by sentries and booby traps. An intruder who didn't know the word of the day, or the positioning of the trip wires for the mines embedded in the walls of the tunnel, or the different code word for the guards in the waterhouse attached to the walls of the inner keep, would almost certainly die.

Unfortunately for the roughly one hundred guards, stable hands, cooks, smiths, carpenters, dog handlers, lamplighters, servants, and outer family members sheltering behind those walls, thanks to his prisoner Baron Otto ven Neuhalle knew all of these things, and more.

Even more unfortunately for the defenders, one of the unpalatable facts of life is that in close quarters – at ranges of less than three meters – firearms are generally less useful than swords, of which Neuhalle's troops had many. Nor were they expecting an attacking force armed with machine guns of their own to appear on the walls of the keep itself.

By the time night fell, his troops were still winkling the last few stubborn holdouts out of their stony shells, but the Hjalmar Palace was in his hands.

And now to start building the trap, Otto told himself, as he summoned his hand-men to him and told them exactly what was needed.

*

The first day at home was the worst. Mike was still getting used to the plastic cocoon on his leg, not to mention being short on clean clothes, tired, and gobbling antibiotics and painkillers by the double handful. But a second night in his own bed put a different complexion on things. He awakened luxuriously late, to find Oscar curled up on the pillow beside him, purring.

The fridge was no more full than it had been the day before, but the grocery bag Smith had dumped in the kitchen turned out to be full of honest-to-god groceries, a considerate touch that startled Mike when he discovered it. *He might be a hyperactive hard-ass, but at least he cares about his people,* Mike decided. He fixed himself a breakfast of bagels and cream cheese and black coffee, then tried to catch up on the lighter housework, running some clothes through the washing machine and doing battle with the shower again – this time more successfully. *I must be getting better,* he told himself optimistically.

Around noon, he got out of the house for a couple of hours, driven stir-crazy by the daytime TV. It took him nearly ten minutes to get the car seat adjusted, and an hour of hobbling around Barnes and Noble and a couple of grocery stores left him feeling like he'd run a marathon, but he made it home uneventfully. Then he discovered that he hadn't figured on carrying the grocery sacks and bag of books and magazines up the front steps. He ended up so exhausted that by the time he got the last bag in and closed the door he was about ready to drop. He hobbled into the lounge clutching the bookbag, and lowered the bag onto the coffee table before he realized the lounger was already occupied.

'So, Mr. Fleming! We meet again.' She giggled, ruining the effect. It was unnecessary, in any case: the pistol in her lap more than made up for her lack of personal menace.

'Jesus!' He staggered, nearly losing his balance.

'Relax, I'm not planning to shoot you. Are you well?'

'I'm –' He bit back his first angry response. *What are you doing in my house?* That question was the elephant in the living room: but it wasn't one he felt like asking the Russian princess directly, not while she was holding a gun on him. 'No, not very.' He shuffled towards the sofa and lowered himself down into it. 'I'm tired. Been shopping,' he added, redundantly. *And how did you get past Judith's watch team?* 'What brings you here?'

'Patricia sent me to see how you were,' she explained, as if it was the most natural thing in the world for killer grannies from another dimension to send their ice-blonde hit-woman bodyguards to check up on him. 'She was concerned that you might be unwell – your leg was hard to keep clean in the carriage.'

'Yeah, right.' Mike snorted. 'She's got nothing but my best interests at heart.'

Olga leaned forward, her eyes wide: 'It is the truth, you know! You will be of little use to us if you die of battle fever. Are you well?'

'I'm as well as –' he bit back the words, *any man facing an armed home intruder* – 'can be expected. Spent a couple of days in hospital.

537

Off work for the next several weeks.' He paused. 'Getting about. A bit.'

'Good.' Olga sat back, then made the pistol disappear: 'Excuse me.' She looked apologetic. 'Until I was sure it was you . . .'

'That's all right,' Mike assured her sarcastically. 'I quite under-stand. We're all paranoids together here.' A thought struck him. 'How did you get in?'

She smiled. 'Your housekeeper is taking the day off.'

'Ah.' *Shit.* Mike had a sharp urge to bang his head on the wall. *Who's staking out who?* Of course she'd had time to set everything up while he was in hospital; possibly even before they'd dropped him back in the right universe. The Russian princess and her world-walking friends could have been watching his apartment for days before Herz and her team moved in to set up their own surveillance op. *They don't work like the Mafia, they work like a government,* he remembered. *A feudal government.* 'So Pat – what did you call her? Sent you to check up on me. I thought she was going to mail me instead?'

'Your mail is being intercepted,' Olga pointed out. 'Consequently, we felt it best to talk to you in person. There is mail, too, and you can respond to it if you wish. Have you reported to your liege yet?'

'Have I?' The sense of grinding gears was back: Mike forced him-self to translate. 'Uh, yes.' He nodded, stupidly. 'I have a cellular phone for you. It's off the official record. There's a preprogrammed number in it that goes direct to my boss's boss. He's authorized to negotiate, and if necessary he can talk to the top. To the office of the Vice President. But it's all deniable, as I understand things.' He pointed at the paper bag on the side table. 'It's in there.'

Olga didn't move. 'What guarantee have we that as soon as we dial the number, your assassins won't locate the caller? Or that there isn't a bomb in the earpiece?'

'That's –' Mike swallowed. 'Don't be silly.'

'I'm not being silly. Just prudent.' She reached out and took the bag, removed the phone, and started to fiddle with the case. 'We'll be in touch. Probably not with this telephone, however.'

'There are certain requirements,' Mike added.

'What?' She froze, holding the battery cover in one hand.

'The sample that Matthias provided.' He watched her minutely. 'I'm told they're willing to negotiate with you. But there's an absolute precondition. Matt told us he'd planted a bomb, on a timer. We want it disarmed, and we want the pit. If it goes off, there's no deal – not now, not ever.'

Olga's expression shifted slightly. *She's not a poker player,* Mike realized. 'A time bomb? I understand that is not good, but what do your lords think we can do about such a thing? Surely it's no more than a minor . . .' She trailed off. 'What kind of bomb?'

Mike said nothing, but raised an eyebrow.

'Why would he plant a bomb?' she persisted. 'I don't see what he could possibly hope to achieve.'

Too much subtlety, maybe. 'He brought a sample of plutonium with him when he wanted to get our attention. It worked.'

'A sample of ploo-what?' Her expression of polite incomprehension would have been hilarious in any other context.

'Oh, come on! What world did you –' Mike stopped dead. *Whoops.* 'You're serious, aren't you?'

'I don't understand what you're talking about,' she said.

He boggled for a moment, as understanding sank in. *She's not from around these parts, is she?* 'Do you know what an atom bomb is?'

'An atom bomb?' She looked interested. 'I've seen them in films. An ingenious fiction, I thought.' Pause. 'Are you telling me they're real?'

'Um.' *You're* really *not from around here, are you?* On the other hand, if you stopped a random person in a random third-world country and asked them about atom bombs and how they worked, what kind of answer would you get? 'They're real, all right. Matthias had a sample of plutonium.' She gave no sign of recognition. 'That's the, the explosive they run on. It's very tightly controlled. Even though the amount he had is nothing like enough to make a bomb, it caused a major panic. Then he claimed to actually have a bomb. We want it. Or we want the rest of your plutonium, and we want to know exactly how and where you got it so that we can verify there's no more missing. That's a nonnegotiable precondition for any further talks.'

'Huh.' She frowned. 'You are serious about this. How bad could such a bomb really be? I saw *The Sum of All Fears* but that bomb was so magically powerful – '

'The real thing is worse than that.' He'd spent the past couple of weeks deliberately not thinking about Matt's threat, trying to convince himself it was a bluff: but Judith had told him about the broken nightmare they'd found in the abandoned warehouse, and it wasn't helping him get to sleep.

'Assuming Matthias wasn't bluffing, and planted a real atom bomb near Faneuil Hall. Make it a small one. Imagine it goes off right now.' He gestured at the window. 'It's miles away, but it'd still blow the glass in, and if you were looking at it directly, it would burn your eyes out. You'd feel the heat on your skin, like sticking your head into an open oven door. And that's all the way out here.' If it was the size of the one Judith found, Boston and Cambridge would be a smoking hole in the coastline – but multimegaton H-bombs weren't likely to go world-walking and were in any case unlikely to explode if they weren't maintained properly. 'We don't want to lose Boston. More importantly, *you* don't want us to lose Boston. Because if we *do* –' he noticed that she was looking pale ' – you saw the reaction to 9/11, didn't you? I guarantee you that if someone nukes one of our cities, the response will be a thousand times worse.'

'I – I don't know.' Olga was clearly rattled: 'I was not aware of this. This bomb that Matthias claimed to – I don't know about it.' She shook her head. 'I will have to tell Patricia. We'll have to investigate.'

'You will? No shit. This other faction in your clan – if it's theirs, they're playing with fire. Maybe they don't understand that.'

She finished extracting the battery from the mobile phone. 'You said that this, it goes to the vice president?'

'To one of his staff,' Mike corrected her.

'We'll be in touch.' She slid it into a pocket gingerly, as if it might explode. 'I will see you later.' She stood up briskly and walked into the front hall, and between one footstep and the next she vanished.

Mike stared at the empty passage for a moment, then shook his head. The shakes would cut in soon, but for now all he could feel was a monstrous sense of irony. 'What a mess,' he muttered. Then he reached for the phone and dialed Colonel Smith's number.

*

The dome was huge, arching overhead like the wall of a sports stadium or the hull of a grounded Zeppelin. Small, stunted trees grew in the gap in its wall, their trunks narrow and tilted towards the thin light. Mud and rubble had drifted into the opening over the years, and the dripping trickle of water suggested more damage deep inside. Huw shuffled forward with arthritic caution, poking his Geiger counter at the ground, the rocks, the etiolated trees – treating everything as if it might be explosive, or poisonous, or both. The results were reassuring, a menacing crackle that rarely reached the level of a sixty-cycle hum, much less the whining squeal of real danger.

As he neared the dribble of water, Huw knelt and held the counter just above its surface. The snap and pop of stray radiation events stayed low. 'The pool outside the dome is hot, and the edges of the dome are nasty, but the stream inside isn't too bad,' be explained to his microphone. 'If the dome's leaky, the stream probably washed most of the hot stuff out of it ages ago.' He looked up. 'This place feels *old*.'

Old, but still radioactive? He felt like scratching his head. Really dangerous radioisotopes were mostly dangerous precisely because they decayed very rapidly. If what had happened here was as old as it felt, then most of the stuff should have decayed long ago. The activity in the dome's edge was perplexing.

'You want a light, bro?'

Huw glanced over his shoulder. Yul was holding out the end of a huge, club-like Maglite. 'Thanks,' he said, shuffling the Geiger counter around so that he could heft the flashlight in his right hand. He pressed the button just as a cold flake of snow drifted onto his left cheek. 'We don't have long.'

'It's creepy in here,' Elena commented as he swung the light around. For once, Huw found nothing to disagree with in her opinion. The structures the dome had protected were in ruins. A flat apron of magic concrete peeped through the dirt in places, but the buildings – rectangular or cylindrical structures, rarely more than two or three stories high – were mostly shattered, roofs torn off, walls punched down. Their builders hadn't been big on windows (although several of them sported gaping doorways). The skeletal wreckage of metal gantries and complex machinery lay around the buildings. Some of them had been connected by overhead pipes, and long runs of rust-colored ductwork wrapped around some of the buildings like giant snakes. 'It looks like a chemical works that's been bombed.'

Huw blinked. 'You know, you might be right,' he admitted. He walked towards the nearest semi-intact building, a three-story high cylindrical structure that was sheltered from the crack in the dome by a mass of twisted rubble and a collapsed walkway. 'Let's see, shall we?'

The Geiger counter calmed down the farther from the entrance they progressed, to Huw's relief. He picked his way carefully over a low berm of crumbled concrete-like stuff, then reached the nearest gantry. It looked familiar enough – a metal grid for flooring, the wreckage of handrails sprouting from it on a triangular truss of tubes – but something about its proportions was subtly wrong. The counter was content to make the odd click. Huw whacked the handrail with his flashlight: it rang like metal. Then he took hold of it and tried to move it, lifting and shoving. 'That's odd.' He squinted in the twilight. A thin crust of flaky ash covered the metal core. Paint, or something like it. That was comfortingly familiar – but the metal was too light. Yet it hadn't melted. 'Got your hammer?' He asked Yul, who was look-ing around, gaping like a tourist.

'Here.'

He took the hammer and whacked the rail, hard. 'It's not soft like aluminum. Doesn't melt easily.' He tugged it, and it creaked slightly as it shifted. 'You have *got* to be kidding me.'

'What's wrong?' Hulius asked quickly.

'This railing. It's too light to be steel, it's not aluminum, but who the fuck would make a handrail out of titanium?'

'I don't know. Someone with a lot of titanium? Are you sure it's titanium? Whatever that is.'

'Fairly sure,' Huw said absently. 'I don't have any way to test it, but it's light enough, and hard, and whatever flash-fried the shit in here didn't touch it. But titanium's expensive! You'd have to know how to make lots of it really cheap before you got anywhere near to making walkways with it . . .' He trailed off, glancing up at the twilight recesses of the dome overhead. 'Let's get on with this.'

The black rectangle, set in the cylindrical structure at ground level, looked like a doorway to Huw. It was high enough, for sure, but there were no windows and no sign of an actual door. He waited for Yul and Elena to close up behind him, then walked towards it. The counter was quiet. There was a pile of debris just inside the opening, and he approached it cautiously, sniffing at the air: there was no telling what might have made its lair in here. Thinking about the chill outside reminded him of wolves, of saber-toothed tigers and worse things. He shivered, and pointed the torch into the gloom.

'Over there.' Elena scuttled sideways, her gun at her shoulder, pointing inside.

'Where –' Huw blinked as she flicked on the torch bolted beneath her barrel. 'Oh.' The thing she was pointing at might have been a door once, but now it lay tumbled on the floor across a heap of junk: crumbled boxes, bits of plastic, pieces of scaffolding. And some more identifiable human remains, although wild animals had scattered the bones around. 'Good, that's helpful.' He stepped across the threshold, noting in the process that the wall was about ten centimeters thick – too thin for brick or concrete – and the inner wall was flat, with another sealed door set in it.

A skull leered at him from the far corner of the room, and as the shadows flickered across the pile of crap inside the doorway he saw what looked like a stained, collapsed one-piece overall. The overall glowed orange in the light, slightly iridescent, then darkened to black where ancient blood had saturated the abdominal area. Huw held his breath, twisting the flashlight to focus on the shoulder, where some kind of patch was embossed on the fabric. He squinted. 'Yul, can you get a photograph of that?' he said, pointing.

'What's it say –' Yul closed in. 'That's not Anglische sprach. Or . . . Huh, I don't recognize it, whatever it is.'

'Dead right.' Huw held the light on the remains while Yul pulled out his camera and flashgunned it into solid state memory. 'What do you think it means?'

'Why would you expect Anglische here?' Elena asked archly.

'No reason, I guess,' Huw said, trying to conceal how shaken he was. He pointed the flashlight back at the skull sitting on the floor. 'Hang on.' He peered closer. 'The teeth. Shit, *the teeth!*'

'What?' Elena's flashlight swung around wildly for a moment.

'Point that away from me if you're going to be twitchy – '

'It's okay, little brother. I've got it.' Yul hooked a finger into each eye socket and spun the skull upside down for Huw to examine. It had been picked clean long ago and had aged to a sallow dark yellow-brown, but the teeth were all there.

'Look.' Huw pointed at the upper jaw. 'Bony here has *all his dentition*. And.' He peered at them. 'There are no fillings. It's like a plastic model of what a jawbone ought to be. Except for this chipped one here, this incisor.'

'Whoa!' Hulius lowered the skull reverently. 'That's some orthodontist.'

'Don't you get it?' Huw asked impatiently.

'Get what?' Yull asked flippantly.

'That's not dentistry,' Huw said, gritting his teeth. 'You know what it's like back home! The Americans, they're good at faking it, but they're not *this* good.' He glanced at the door on the inner wall. *No obvious hinges,* he realized. *Fits beautifully.* 'Domes the size of a sports stadium that try to heal themselves even when you crack them open with a nuke. Metal walkways made out of titanium. Perfect dentistry.' He snapped his fingers. 'Have you got the ax?'

'Sure.' Yul nodded. 'What do you want me to hit?'

'Let's see what's inside that door,' Huw decided. 'But then we leave. Magic wands? Dentistry.'

'They're more advanced than the Americans,' Elena commented. 'Is that what you're saying?'

'Yes. I'm not quite sure what it means, though . . .'

'What about their burglar alarms?'

'After all this time?' Huw snorted. 'Let's see what else is in here. Yul?'

'I'm with you, bro.' He winked at Elena. 'This is a real gas!'

And with that, he swung the fire ax at the edge of the door.

*

The Boeing Business Jet had reached cruising altitude and was somewhere over the Midwest, and Brill had just about managed to doze off, when her satellite phone rang.

'Who's speaking?' She cleared her throat, trying to shake cobwebs free. The delay and the echo on the line made it sound like she was yelling down a drainpipe.

'It's me, Brill. Update time.'

'*Scheiss* – one minute. I'll take it in the office.' She hit the button to raise her chair then stood up and walked back towards the door at the rear of the first-class cabin. Rather than a cramped galley or a toilet, it opened onto a compact boardroom. As the only passenger on the luxury jet – a refitted Boeing 737 airliner – she had it all to herself except for the cabin attendants, but she still preferred to have a locked door between herself and any flapping ears. 'Okay, Olga. What ails you?'

'Are you secure?'

Brill yawned, then sat down. Beyond the windows, twilight had settled over the plains. It was stubbornly refusing to lift, despite the jet's westward dash. 'I'm on the BBJ, arriving at SFO in about three hours. I was trying to get some sleep. Yes, I'm secure.'

'I've got to report to Angbard, so I'd better keep this brief. I went to see Fleming today. You know what that little shit Matthias did? He convinced the DEA, this new FTO outfit, everybody who matters, that he'd planted a gadget in downtown Boston. Then he managed to get himself killed before he could tell them where it was. So now they're blaming us, and they want it handed over.'

'He *what?*' Brill blinked and tried to rub her eyes, one-handed.

'I'm not kidding. Fleming wasn't kidding either – at least, he believed what he'd been told. I played dumb with him, pretending not to know what he was talking about, but afterwards I went and told Manfred and he ran an audit. The little shit was telling the truth. One of our nukes is missing.'

'*God on a stick!* If the Council finds out – '

'It gets worse. Turns out it's one of our FADMs. Long-term storable, in other words, and there's a long-life detonation controller that's *also* turned up missing. The implosion charges were remanu-factured eighteen months ago, so it's probably nearing a service interval, but those charges were modified to survive storage under adverse conditions for up to a decade. If we don't find it, we're in a world of hurt – what do you think they'll do if Boston or Cambridge goes up? – and if we *do* find it and hand it over as a sign of our commitment to negotiate, it'll take them all of about ten seconds to figure out where it came from.'

Brilliana closed her eyes and swore, silently for a few seconds. She'd known about the Clan's nuclear capability; she and Olga were among the handful of agents whose job would be to emplace the weapons, if and when the shit ever truly hit the fan. But the nukes weren't supposed to go walkies. They were supposed to sit on their shelves in the anonymous warehouse, maintained regularly by the engineers from Pantex while U.S. Marine Corps guards patrolled the site overhead.

Based on a modified W54 warhead pattern, the FADMs were a highly classified derivative of the MADM atomic demolition device. They'd been built during the mid-1970s as backup for the CIA's Operation Gladio, to equip NATO's 'stay behind' forces in Europe, after a Soviet invasion, with a storable, compact, tactical nuclear weapon. Most nukes required regular servicing to replace their neutron-emitting initiators and the plastic explosive implosion charges. The FADM had been tweaked to have a reasonable chance of detonation even after several years of unmaintained storage; the designers had replaced the usual initiator with an electrically powered neutron source, and added shielding to protect the explosive lenses from radiation-induced degradation. The wisdom of supplying underground cells with what was basically a U.S. inventory-derived terrorist nuke had been revisited during the Reagan administration, and the weapons returned to the continental USA for storage – but they'd been retained long after the other man-portable demolition nukes had been destroyed, because the advantages they offered had been too good for certain spook agencies to ignore. More recently, the current administration – pathologically secretive and dealing with the aftermath of 9/11 – had wanted to pack every available arrow in their quiver, even if some of them were broken by design.

And they *were*. Because the Clan, with their ability to get into places that were flat-out impossible for home-grown intruders, had been treating them as their own personal nuclear stockpile for the past two decades.

'Listen, why are you telling me this? Why haven't you briefed Uncle A? It's his headache – '

'Uncle A is fielding another problem right now: the pretender's just rolled over the Hjalmar Palace and there's a three-ring, full-dress panic going down in Concord. He's pulling me in – I'm supposed to be looking for a thrice-damned mole, who everybody tells me is probably a disgruntled outer family climber, and in case you'd missed it, we've got a civil war on. The bomb's been missing for months, it'll wait a couple of hours more. But I think when you get back from the west coast you're going to find that locating it is suddenly everyone's highest priority. And I've got a feeling that the spy who's feeding Egon and the nuclear blackmail thing are connected. Matt wasn't working alone, and I smell a world-walker in the picture. So I figure you and I, we should do some snooping together.' She paused. 'Just what are you doing out in California, anyway? Is it something to do with the Wu clan?'

Brill sighed. 'No, it's Helge. We've located her. While I was flailing around in Boston doing the breaking and entering bit, she mailed me a letter via the New Britain office at Dunedin. The duty clerk caught it in time, opened it, and faxed the contents on: meanwhile we identified her aboard a westbound train that's en route for Northern California. I need to find her before the New Britain secret police arrest her. So I'm taking a shortcut.'

'Huh. Much as I like her, isn't finding Matt's plaything a slightly higher priority?'

'Not when she's carrying an heir to the throne, Olga.' She waited for the explosion of spluttering to die down. 'Yes, I agree completely. You and I can have a little talk about professional ethics with Dr. ven Hjalmar later, perhaps? Assuming he survives the current unpleasantness, I'd like to make sure that he needs a new pair of kneecaps. But you've got to admit that we'll need a king – or queen – after we nail Egon, won't we? And if he really *did* artificially inseminate her with Creon's seed, and if we have witnesses to the handfasting, then it seems to me that . . . well, which would you rather deal with? Egon trying to have us all hanged as witches, or Miriam as queen regent with Uncle A pulling the strings?'

'I'm not sure,' Olga said grimly. 'She'll be furious. Gods, that's why he sent you, isn't it? She trusts you. If anyone can get her calmed down and convince her to play along, it'd be you. But if not . . .'

'Uncle A wants her back in play,' Brill said, mustering up what calm she could. 'But if she's left loose, she's as dangerous as that time bomb you're hunting. Isn't she?'

'Yes.'

'She was getting too close to James Lee, the hostage,' Brill added.

Olga's voice went flat. 'She was?'

'We don't need another faction on the board,' Brill said.

'No. I can see that.' Olga paused. 'You'll just have to charm her, won't you?'

'Yes,' Brill agreed. 'Now, if you don't mind, I'm going back to sleep. Give my regards to Uncle.'

'I'll tell him. Bye . . .'

Quietly closing the boardroom door behind her, Brill padded back to her first-class chair. She paused at the storage locker next to it, and opened it briefly: the specialized equipment was undisturbed, and she nodded, satisfied. It was the biggest single advantage of flying on the Clan's own executive jet, in her opinion – in the course of her business she often required access to certain specialized items, and commercial airlines tended to take a dim view of her carrying her sniper kit in hand luggage. She sat down and strapped herself in, then tilted her chair back and dimmed the overhead lights. Tomorrow was going to be a long day, starting with arranging a reception for a train at a station she didn't even know the precise location of, and trying to make contact with Miriam one jump ahead of the Homeland Security Directorate goon squad who'd surely be waiting for her when the train arrived.

BOMBARDIERS

It was a good morning for flying, thought Rudi, as he checked the weather station on the north tower wall. *No, make that a* great *morning.* After all, he'd never flown over his homeland before. It would be a personal first, not to mention one in the eye for the stick-in-the-muds. Visibility was clear, with a breeze from the southwest and low pressure, rising slowly. He bent over the anemometer, jotting down readings in the logbook by the dawn light. 'Hans? I'll be needing the contents of both crates. Get them moved into the outer courtyard. I'll need two pairs of hands to help with the trike – make sure they're not clumsy. I'll be down in ten minutes.'

'Aye, sir.' His footman, Hans, gave him an odd look, but hurried down off the battlements all the same. He clearly thought his master was somewhat cracked. *Well, he'll change his mind before the day is out,* Rudi told himself. *Along with everyone else. Just as long as nothing goes wrong.* He was acutely aware that he hadn't kept his flying hours up since the emergency began, and there were no luxuries (or necessities) like air traffic control or meteorology services over here.

In fact, he didn't even have as much fuel as he'd have liked: he'd managed to squirrel away nearly twenty gallons of gas before some killjoy or other – he harbored dark suspicions about Erik – had ratted out his scheme to Riordan, who'd had no option but to shout at him and notify the duke. Who in turn had threatened to have him flogged, and lectured him coldly for almost half an hour about the idiocy of not complying with long-standing orders . . .

Rudi had bitten his tongue while the duke threatened to burn the trike, but in the end the old man had relented just a little. 'You will maintain it in working order, and continue to practice your skills in America, but you will *not* fly that thing over our lands without my explicit orders, delivered in person.' Eorl Riordan wasn't the duke, but on the other hand, he was in the chain of command: and that was enough for Rudi. *Flying today.*

It took him closer to half an hour to make his way down to the courtyard, by way of his room – his flying jacket and helmet were buried deeper than he'd remembered, and he took his time assembling a small survival kit. Then he had to divert via the guardhouse to check out a two-way radio and a spare battery. 'Where do you think you're going, cuz?' asked Vincenze, looking up from the girlie magazine he was reading: 'A fancy dress party?'

Rudi grinned. 'Got a date with an angel,' he said. 'See you later.'

'Heh. I'll believe it when I see it –' But he was talking to Rudi's back.

Down in the courtyard next to the stables, he found that Hans had enlisted a couple of guards to move the crates, but hadn't thought to bring the long tubular sack or the trike itself. 'Come on, do I have to do everything myself?' he demanded.

'I didn't know what you wanted, sir,' Hans said apologetically. 'You said it was delicate . . .'

'Huh. Okay. Come here. Take this end of the bag. I'll take the other. It's heavy. Now! The courtyard!'

Half an hour later, performing in front of an audience of mostly useless gawpers (occasionally he'd need one of them to hold a spar in position while he tightened a guy-wire), Rudi had the wing unpacked and tensioned. At eight meters long and weighing fifty kilos the Sabre 16 had been murder to world-walk across – it was too long to fit in the Post Office room – but it was about the smallest high-performance trike wing he'd been able to find. At least he'd been able to unbolt the engine from the trike body. 'Go get the trike,' he told Hans and the guards. 'Push it gently, it'll roll easily enough once you get it off the straw.'

Another half hour passed by in what felt like seconds. By then he'd gotten the wing mounted on top of the trike's mast and bolted together. The odd machine – a tricycle with a petrol engine with a propeller mounted on the back and a pair of bucket seats – was beginning to resemble a real, flyable ultralight. He was double-checking his work, making sure there was no sign of wear on any of the cables and that everything was secure, when someone cleared his throat behind him. He glanced round: it was Eorl Riordan, along with a couple of sergeants he didn't recognize. 'How's it going?' asked Riordan, his tone deceptively casual.

'It's going all right, for now.' Rudi glanced up at the sky. *Partial cloud cover, at least five thousand feet up* – no problem for the time being. 'Thing is, I'm about to trust my neck to this machine. There's no backup and no air traffic control and no help if something goes wrong. So I want to make sure everything is perfect before I take her up.'

'Good.' Riordan paused. 'You've got a radio.'

'Yeah. And binoculars.' He gestured to the small pile sitting beside the fuel drum. 'If you need it, I can take a camera. But right now, this is going to be pretty crude, visual flying only in good weather, staying below two thousand feet, and if I see anything I'll probably only be able to pinpoint it to within a mile or so. I max out at about fifty-five miles per hour, so that's not going to take me far from here, and I've got enough fuel for a couple of three-hour-long flights, but I'd prefer not to go up twice in one day. It's pretty physical.'

'Three hours and a hundred and fifty miles ought to be enough.' Riordan nodded to himself. 'What I wanted to say – I'd like you to do a circuit of the immediate area. If there's any sign of troops on the ground within thirty miles, I'd like to know about it. We're expecting a move from the southeast, and I know it's well forested down there so I don't expect miracles, but if you do see anything, it's important. Also, I'd like you to take a look at Wergatfurt. We got an odd call half an hour ago, there's something going on down there. Can you do that?'

'Probably, yes.' Rudi patted his pocket. 'I'm using relief maps from the other side for navigation, it's close enough to mostly work, and the Wergat's pretty hard to miss. The only thing I will say is, if the weather starts closing in I need to get down on the ground fast. The Hjalmar Palace is about an hour, hour and ten minutes away from here, as the trike flies – it'll cut into my ability to do a sweep around to the north. Are you sure you want that?'

Riordan rubbed the side of his nose thoughtfully. 'I think . . . if you don't see signs of soldiers southeast of here within thirty miles, then I definitely want to know what's going on down along the Wergat. If you see those soldiers, call me up and we'll discuss it.' He nodded to himself. Then he pointed at Rudi's survival kit. 'Why the gun? Can you shoot from a moving aircraft?'

'It's not for when the trike's flying: but if anything goes wrong while I'm forty miles out, over open forest . . .'

Riordan nodded. 'Good luck.'

'Thank you, sir. I'll try not to need it.'

*

In the end, what saved them was Huw's nose hair.

It was, Huw sometimes reflected, one of those fine ironies of life that despite being unable to grow a proper beard, he suffered inordinately from the fine hairs that clogged his nostrils. Nostril hair was neither sexy nor obviously problematic to people who didn't have to put up with it: it was just . . . *icky*. That was the word Elena had used when she caught him in the bathroom with an open jar of Vaseline and one finger up a nostril. It played seven shades of hell with his sense of smell, and had driven his teenage self into an orgy of nose-picking that resulted in a series of nosebleeds before he'd figured out what to do about it. And now . . .

In the flashlight-lit wreckage of a building inside a shattered dome, standing before a wall with a tightly sealed doorway in it, his kid brother raised a fire ax and swung it down hard towards the left side of the door.

As the ax struck the door, Huw, who was standing a good two meters behind and to the left of him, sneezed. The sneeze had been building up for some time, aggravated by the cold, damp air in this new world and the low priority Huw had attached to his manicure in the face of the mission of exploration. Nevertheless, the eruption took Huw by surprise, forcing him to screw his eyes shut and hunch his shoulders, turning his face towards the floor. The noise startled Yul, who began to turn to his right, towards Huw. The movement took him out of the direct line of the door. And it also surprised Elena, who was standing off to the right near the entrance to the building with her vicious little machine pistol at the ready. She ducked, and this took her out of the direct line of sight on the portal.

Which was why they survived.

As the ax blade bit into the edge of the door, there was a brilliant flash of violet-tinted light. Huw registered it as a flicker of red behind his closed eyelids and might have ignored it – but the rising noise that followed it was impossible to write off.

'Ouch! What's that –' Yul began.

Huw, opening his eyes and straightening up, grabbed his brother's arm, and yanked. 'Run!'

The hissing sound from the edge of the door grew louder; the center of the door bowed inward slightly, as if under the pressure of a giant fist from their side. Yul barely spared it a glance before he dropped the ax and took to his heels. Huw was a stride behind him. Two seconds brought them to the twilit entrance to the room. 'Hit the ground!' yelled Huw, catching one glimpse of Elena's uncomprehending face as he threw himself forward and rolled sideways, away from the open doorway.

Behind them, the creaking door – far thinner than Huw had realized – creaked once more, and gave way. And all hell broke loose.

The hissing and whistling gave way to a deep roaring, and the breeze in Huw's face began to strengthen. Huw glanced over his shoulder once, straining to look over the length of his body towards the inner chamber. A strange mist curdled out of the air, obscuring whatever process was at work there. The wind was still strengthening. 'Take cover!' he called out. 'There's hard vacuum on the other side of that – thing – watch out for flying debris!' *It'll blow itself out soon*, he told himself. *Won't it?* A sudden frisson of fear raised the hair on the back of his neck: *That skeleton was* old, *the door can't have held in a vacuum that long. So something's pumping the air on the other side out, something that's still working . . .*

But that didn't make sense. *Come on, Huw, think!* The wind wasn't slackening. Dust and leaves blew past, vanishing towards the gulping maw behind the doorway. Huw pushed himself up on hands and knees and began to crawl sideways, away from the damaged front of the building. He waved to Yul and Elena, beckoning them after. The seconds stretched out endlessly. The wind was refusing to die. 'Meet me behind the building!' he yelled, jabbing his hands to indicate the direction. Yul raised a thumb and began to crawl away, tracking round the building.

Once Huw was away from the frontage, he risked standing up. Out of the direct line of the door, the wind was a barely noticeable breeze. 'Huh.' He slapped the knees of his fatigues, then hurried round to meet Yul and Elena. *It's still running,* he realized. *Can't be a pump; it'd take a jet engine to shift that much mass flow.* He glanced around. A nasty idea was inching its way into his mind: *Utterly preposterous, but . . .*

'Well, bro, what do you reckon?'

Yul was characteristically unfazed by his near-miss. Elena, however, was anything but pleased: 'What were you playing at? Hitting that thing with an ax, we could all have been killed!'

'It looked like a door to me,' Yul shrugged.

'Did you see the flash – '

'Flash?' Huw glanced at her. 'There was a flash?'

'Yes, a bright flash of light as the big oaf here hit it!' Elena swatted Yul on the arm. 'You could have been killed!' she chided him. Then she glared at Huw. 'What were you playing at?'

'I'm not sure yet.' Huw licked his left index finger and held it up to feel the breeze. 'Yes, it's still going. Hmm.'

'What *is* it?'

'I'm not sure,' Huw said slowly, 'but I'll tell you what I think. It was behind the door, sealed in until Yul broke something. It's got hard vacuum on the other side, like a – a hole in space. Not a black hole, there's no gravitational weirdness, but like – imagine a door leading into yet another world? Like the thing we do when we world-walk, only static rather than dynamic? And the universe it leads to is one where there's no planet Earth. You'd come out in interplanetary space.'

'But why – '

Huw rolled his eyes. 'Why would anyone want such a thing? How would I know? Maybe they used to keep a space station there, as some kind of giant pantry? You put one of those doors in your closet, build airtight rooms on the other side of it, and you'll never have to worry about where to keep your clothes again – it gives a whole new meaning to wardrobe space. But you keep an airtight door in front of the – call it a portal – just in case.'

He gestured around the dome. 'Something bad happened here, a long time ago. Centuries, probably. The guy with the perfect teeth was trying to hide in the closet, but didn't make it. Over time, something went wrong on the other side – the space station or whatever you call it drifted off-site – leaving the portal pointing into interplanetary space. And then we came along and fucked with the protective door.'

Elena's eyes widened. 'But won't it suck all the air out?'

Huw shrugged. 'Not our problem. Anyway, it'll take thousands of years, at a minimum. There's plenty of time for us to come back and drop a concrete hatch over it.' He brightened: 'Or an airlock! Get some pressure suits and we can go take a look at it! A portal like that, if we can figure out how it works –' he stopped, almost incoherent with the sudden shock of enlightenment. 'Holy Sky Father, Lightning Child, and Crone,' he whispered.

'What is it, bro?' Yul looked concerned. 'Are you feeling all right?'

'I've got to get back to base and report to the duke *right now.*' Huw took a deep breath. 'This changes everything.'

*

After two days aboard the Northern Continental, Miriam was forced to reevaluate her opinion of railroad travel – even in luxury class. Back when she was newly married she and Ben had taken a week to go on a road trip, driving down into North Carolina and then turning west and north. They'd spent endless hours crawling across Illinois, the landscape barely changing, marking the distance they'd covered by the way they had to tune the radio to another station every couple of hours, the only marker of time the shifting patterns of the clouds overhead.

This was, in a way, worse: and in another way, much better. Travel via the Northern Continental was like being sentenced to an enforced vacation in a skinny luxury hotel room on wheels. Unfortunately,

New British hotels didn't sport many of the necessities a motel back home would provide, such as air-conditioning and TV, much less luxuries like a health suite and privacy. Everything was kept running by a small army of liveried stewards, bustling in and out – and Miriam hated it. 'I feel like I can't relax,' she complained to Burgeson at one point: 'I've got no space to myself!' And no space to plug her notebook computer in, for that matter.

He shrugged. 'Hot and cold running service is half of what first-class travel is all about,' he pointed out. 'If the rich didn't surround themselves with armies of impoverished unfortunates, how would they know they were well off?'

'Yes, but that's not the point . . .' Back in Baron Henryk's medieval birdcage she'd at least been able to shunt the servants out of her rooms. Over here, such behavior would draw entirely the wrong kind of attention. She waved a hand in wide circles, spinning an imaginary hamster wheel. 'I feel like I'm acting in a play with no script, on a stage in front of an audience I can't see. And if I step out of character – the character they want me to play – the reviewers will start snarking behind my back.'

'Welcome to my world. It doesn't get any better after a decade, let me assure you.'

'Yes, but –' Miriam stopped dead, a sarcastic response on the tip of her tongue, as the door at the carriage end opened and a bellboy came in, pushing a cart laden with clean towels for the airliner-toilet-sized bathroom. 'You see what I mean?' she asked plaintively when he'd gone.

The train inched across the interior at a laborious sixty miles per hour, occasionally slowing as it rattled across cast-iron bridges, hauling its way up the long slope of the mountains. Three or four times a day it wheezed to a temporary halt while oil and water hoses dropped their loads into the locomotive's bunkers, and passengers stretched their legs on the promenade platform. Once or twice a day it paused in a major station for half an hour. Often Miriam recognized the names, but as provincial capitals or historic towns, not as the grand cities they had become in this strange new world. But sometimes they were just new to her.

On the first full day of the voyage (it was hard to think of anything so protracted as a train journey) she left the train for long enough to buy a stack of newspapers and a couple of travel books from the stand at the end of the platform at Fort Kinnaird. The news was next to impenetrable without enlisting Erasmus as an interpreter, and some of the stuff she came across in the travel books made her skin crawl. Slavery was, it seemed, illegal throughout the empire largely because hereditary indentured servitude was so much more convenient; one particular account of the suppression of an uprising in South America by the Royal Nipponese Ronin Brigade left her staring out of the window in a bleak, reflective trance for almost an hour. She was not surprised by the brutality of the transplanted Japanese soldiers, raised in the samurai tradition and farmed out as mercenaries to the imperial dynasty by their daimyo; but the complacent attitude to their practices exhibited by the travel writer, a middle-aged Anglican parson's wife from Hanoveria, shocked her rigid. Crucifying serfs every twenty feet along the railway line from Manaus to São Paulo was simply a necessary reestablishment of the natural order, the correction of an intolerable upset by the ferocious but civilized and kindly police troops of the Brazilian Directorate. (All of whose souls were in any case bound for hell: the serfs because they were misguided papists and the samurai because they were animists and Buddhists, the author felt obliged to note.)

And then there was the *other* book, and the description of the French occupation of Mesopotamia, which made the New British Empire look like a bastion of liberal enlightenment . . .

What am I doing here? she asked herself. *I can't live in this world! And is there any point even trying to make it a better place? I could be over in New York getting myself into the Witness Protection Program . . .*

On the second day, she gave in to the inevitable. 'What's this book you keep trying to get me to read?' she asked, after breakfast.

Erasmus gave her a long look. 'Are you sure?' he asked. 'If you're concerned about your privacy – '

'Give.' She held out a hand. 'You want me to read it, right?'

He looked at her for a while, then nodded and passed her a book that had been sitting on the writing desk in full view, all along. 'I think you'll find it stimulating.'

'Let's see.' She turned to the flyleaf. 'Animal husbandry? You're having me on!'

'Why don't you turn to page forty-six?' he asked mildly.

'Huh?' She swallowed acid: breakfast seemed to have disagreed with her. 'But that's –' she opened it at the right page '– oh, I see.' She shook her head. 'What do I do if someone steals it?'

'Never use a bookmark.' He was serious. 'And if someone *does* steal it, pray to the devil that they're a fellow traveler.'

'Oh.' She stared at the real title page, her brow furrowed: *The Ethical Foundations of Equality*, by Sir Adam Burroughs. 'It's a philosophy textbook?'

'A bit more than that.' Burgeson's cheek twitched. 'More like four to ten years' hard labor for possession.'

'Really . . .' She licked her lips. It was a hot day, the track was uneven, and between her clammy skin and her delicate stomach she was feeling mildly ill. 'Can you give me a synopsis?'

'No. But I should like it very much if you would give *me* one.'

'Whoa.' She felt her ears flush. 'And I thought you were being a perfect gentleman!'

He looked at her anxiously. 'Did I say something offensive?'

'No,' she said, as her guts twisted, 'I'm just in a funny mood.' Her hand went to her mouth. 'And if you'll excuse me now, I'm feeling sick – '

*

Days turned into hours, and the minor nuisances of keeping a round-the-clock watch on a suburban house sank into the background. So when the call she'd been half-dreading finally came through, Judith Herz was sitting in the back of her team's control van, catching up on her nonclassified e-mail on a company-issue BlackBerry and trying not to think about lunch.

'Ma'am?' Agent Metcalf leaned over the back of the seat in front, offering her a handset tethered to the van's secure voice terminal: 'It's for you.'

She managed to muster a smile as she put down the BlackBerry and accepted the other phone: 'Who is it?'

Metcalf didn't say anything, but his expression told her what she needed to know. 'Okay. Give me some privacy.' Metcalf ducked back into the front. A moment later, the door opened and he climbed out. She waited for it to close before she answered. 'Herz here.'

'Smith speaking. Authenticate.' They exchanged passwords, then: 'I've got an errand for you, Judith. Can you leave the watch team with Sam and Ian for a couple of hours?'

'A couple of –' She bit back her first response. 'This had better be worth it. You're aware my watch team's shorthanded right now?'

'I think it's worth it,' he said, and although the fuzz the secure channel imposed on the already-poor phone line made it hard to be sure, she got the impression that he meant it. 'How far from the nearest MBTA station are you?'

Herz blinked, surprised. 'About a ten-minute ride, I figure,' she said. 'I could get one of the guys to drop me off, if you're willing to cut the front cover team to one man for a few minutes. Why, what's come up?'

'We've got a lead on your last job, and I thought you'd want to be in on the close-out. I'm out of town right now and I need a pair of eyes and ears I can trust on the ground. What do you say?'

'The last –' That was the search for the elusive nuke source GREENSLEEVES had claimed he'd planted. 'You found it?'

'It's not definite yet but it looks like it's at least a level two.' They'd defined a ladder of threat levels at the beginning of the search, putting them into a proper framework suitable for reporting on performance indicators and success metrics. A level five was a rogue smoke detector or some other radiation source that tripped the NIRT crews' detectors – all the way up to a level one, a terrorist nuke in situ. The nightmare in the lockup in Cambridge was still unclassified – Judith had pegged it for a level one, and still didn't quite want to believe it – but a level two was serious enough; gamma radiation at the right wavelength to suggest weapons-grade material, location confirmed.

'Okay. Where do you want me to go?'

'Blue Line, Government Center. It's the station itself. Go there and head for the Scollay Square exit. Rich will meet you there. He and Rand are organizing the site search. The cover story we're going with is that it's an exercise, training our guys for how to deal with a terrorist dirty bomb – so you can anticipate some press presence. You'll be wearing your old organization hat and you can tell them the truth, you're an agent liaising with the anti-terror guys.'

Herz winced. Wheels within wheels – how better to disguise a bunch of guys in orange isolation suits trampling around a metro station in search of a terrorist nuke than by announcing to the public that a bunch of guys in isolation suits would be tramping around the station in search of a pretend-terrorist nuke? 'What if they don't find Matt's gadget?' she asked.

'That's okay, they've got a mock-up in the van. You'll just have to run in with it and tell any reporters who get in your way that we forgot to install it earlier.'

A dummy nuke, in case we don't find a real one? 'When does it kick off?'

'Rich is shooting for fourteen hundred hours.'

'Okay, I'm on my way.' She hung up the phone and cracked the window. Metcalf was smoking a cigarette. 'Hey, Ian.'

He turned, surprised. 'Yes, ma'am?'

'We've got a call. Time to roll.'

Metcalf carefully stubbed the cigarette out on the underside of his shoe then climbed back into the driver's seat. 'What's come up?'

'I need a lift to Alewife. Got a T to catch.'

'You're being pulled off the site?'

'It's urgent.' She put an edge in her voice.

'I'm on it.' He slid the van into gear and pulled away. 'How long are you going to be?'

'A couple of hours.' She picked up her briefcase and zipped it shut to stop her hands trembling with nervous anticipation. 'I'll make my own way back.'

The train ride to Downtown Crossing went fast, as did her connection to Government Center. Early afternoon meant that there was plenty of space in the subway trains, but the offices in the center of town would be packed. Herz tried not to think about it. She'd had months to come to terms with the idea that there might be a ticking bomb in the heart of her city – or not, that it might simply be a vicious hoax perpetrated by a psychopath – and now was not the time to have second thoughts about it. Still. 'Our man has a thing about trip wires and claymore mines,' Mike Fleming had told her. *Right. Booby traps.* She resolved to keep it in mind. Not that it wasn't in the orchestral score everyone was fiddling along to, but if it slipped some other player's mind at the wrong moment . . .

On her way out of the station Herz had time to reflect on the location. The JFK Federal Building loomed on one side, a hulking great lump of concrete: around the corner in the opposite direction was the tourist district, Faneuil Hall and Quincy Market and a bunch of other attractions. The whole area was densely populated – not quite as bad as downtown Manhattan, but getting there. A small backpack nuke would cause far more devastation and more loss of life than a ten-megaton H-bomb out in the suburbs. But the search teams had already combed this district – it was one of the first places they'd looked. *So what's come up now?*

Rich was waiting just inside the station exit, tapping his toes impatiently. 'Glad you could make it,' he said, leading her out onto the plaza. 'We're ready to go.'

Judith froze for a moment. There was an entire three ring circus drawn up on the concrete: police cars with lights flashing, two huge trucks with an inflatable tent between them, Lucius Rand and his team wandering around in bright orange suits, hoods thrown back, chatting to each other, the police. There was even a mobile burger van – someone's idea of lunch, it seemed. 'What's this?' she asked quietly.

'This is Operation Defend Our Rails,' Rich announced portentously. 'In which we simulate a terrorist attack on a T station with weapons of mass destruction, and how we'd respond to it. Except,' his voice dropped a dozen decibels, 'it's not a simulation. But don't tell *them.*' He nodded in the direction of a couple of bored-looking reporters with a TV camera who were filming the orange-suited team.

'What do the cops know?'

'They know nothing.'

'Okay.' Judith steered him towards what looked to be the control vehicle. 'Tell me why we're here, then.'

'Team Green rescanned the area with the new gamma spectroscope they just got hold of from Lockheed. The idea was to calibrate it against our old readings, but what they found – they thought it was an instrument error at first. Turns out that MBTA's civil engineers recently removed the false walls at the ends of the Blue Line platforms so they could run longer trains. That's when we began getting the emission spectra. More sensitive detectors, less concrete and junk in the way – that's how it works. There's an older platform behind the false walls, and it looks like there's something down there.'

Down? 'How far down?' she asked.

'Below the surface? Not far. This lot is all built up on reclaimed land – if that's what you're thinking.'

She nodded. 'Suppose it's not deep at all, in fairyland. Suppose it's on the surface. They could just waltz in and plant a bomb. Nobody would notice?'

'It's not that simple,' said Dr. Rand, taking her by surprise. 'Let's get you a hard hat and jacket and head down to the site.'

'You've already opened it up?' she demanded.

'Not yet, we were waiting for you. Step this way.'

All railway stations – like all public buildings – have two faces. One face, the one Herz was familiar with, was the one that welcomed commuters every day: down the stairs into the MBTA station, through the ticket hall and the steps or ramps down to the platforms where the Blue Line trains and Green Line streetcars thundered and squealed. The other face was the one familiar to the MBTA workers who kept the system running. Narrow corridors and cramped offices up top, anonymous doors leading into dusty, ill-lit engineering spaces down below, and then the trackside access, past warning signs and notices informing the public that they endangered both their lives and their wallets if they ventured past them. 'Follow me, sir, ma'am,' said the MBTA transit cop Rand was using as an escort. 'It's this way.'

From one end of a deserted Blue Line platform – its entrance sealed off by police tape, the passengers diverted to a different part of the station – he led them down a short ramp onto the trackside. Herz glanced up. The roof of the tunnel was concrete, but it was also flat, a giveaway sign of cut and cover construction: there couldn't be much soil up there. Then she focused on following the officer as he led them alongside the tracks and then through an archway to the side.

'Crazy.' Judith glanced around in the gloom. 'This is it?' Someone had strung a bunch of outdoor inspection lamps along the sixty-foot stretch of platform that started at shoulder height beside her. It was almost ankle-deep in dirt, the walls filthy.

'No, it's down here,' said Lucius, pointing.

She followed his finger down, and realized with a start that the platform wasn't solid – it was built up on piles. The darkness below seemed almost palpable. She bent down, pulling her own flashlight out. 'Where am I supposed to be looking?' she asked. 'And has anyone been under here yet?'

'One moment,' said Rand. 'Officer, would you mind going back up for the rest of my team? Tell Mary Wang that I want her to bring the spectroscope with her.'

Herz half-expected the cop to object to leaving two civilians down here on their own, but evidently someone had got to him: he mumbled an acknowledgment and set off immediately, leaving them alone.

'No, nobody's been under there yet,' said Rand. 'That's why you're here. You mentioned that the person behind this incident had some disturbing habits involving trip wires, didn't you? We're going to take this very slowly.'

'Good,' said Herz, suppressing an involuntary shudder.

The next half hour passed slowly, as half a dozen members of Rand's team made their way down to the platform with boxes of equipment in hand. Wang arrived first, wheeling a metal flight case trailing a length of electrical cable behind. She was petite, so short that the case nearly reached her shoulders. 'Let's see where it is,' she said encouragingly, then proceeded to shepherd the case along the platform at a snail's pace, pausing every meter or so to take readings, which she marked on the platform using a spray can.

'Where do you make it?' Rand asked her.

'I think it's under there.' She pointed to a spot about two-thirds of the way down the platform, near the rear wall. 'I just want to double-check the emission strength and recalibrate against the reference sample.'

Rand pulled a face then glanced at Herz. 'Granite,' he said. 'Plays hell with our instruments because it's naturally radioactive.'

'But Boston isn't built on – '

'No, but where did the gravel in the aggregate under the platform come from? Or the dye on those tiles?' His gesture took in the soot-smudged rear wall. 'Or the stones in the track ballast?'

'But granite – '

'It's not the only problem we've got,' Rand continued, in tones that suggested he was missing the classroom: 'Would you believe, bananas? Lots of potassium in bananas. You put a bunch of bananas next to a gamma source and a scattering spectrometer on the other side and they can fool you into thinking you're staring at a shipping container full of yellowcake. So we've got to go carefully.' Wang and a couple of assistants were hauling her bulky boxful of sensors over the platform again, peering at the instrument panel on top with the aid of a head-mounted flashlight.

'It's here!' she called, pointing straight down. 'Whatever it is,' she added conversationally, 'but it sure looks like a pit to me. Lots of HEU in there. Could have come right out of one of our own storage facilities, it's so sharp.'

'Nice work.' Rand eased himself down at the side of the platform and lowered himself to the track bed. He looked up at Herz. 'Want to come and see for yourself? Hey, Jack, get yourself over here!'

Judith jumped down to the track bed beside him. Her hands felt clammy. *Is this it?* she asked herself. The sense of momentous events, of living through history, ran damp fingertips up and down her spine. 'Watch out,' she warned.

'No problem, ma'am.' Rand's associate, Jack, had an indefinite air about him that made her think, Marine Corps: but not the dumb stereotype kind. 'Let's start by looking for lights.'

Another half hour crept by as Jack – and another three specialists, experts in bomb disposal and booby traps – checked from a distance to ensure there were no surprises. 'There are no wires, sir,' Jack finally reported to Dr. Rand. 'No IR beams either, far as I can tell. Just a large trunk over against the wall, right where Mary said.'

The hair on Judith's neck rose. *It's real,* she admitted to herself. 'Okay, let's take a closer look,' said Rand. And without further ado, he dropped down onto hands and knees and shuffled under the platform. Herz blinked for a moment, then followed his example. *At least I won't have to worry about the dry-cleaning bill if Jack's wrong,* part of her mind whispered.

Jack had set up a couple of lanterns around the trunk. Close up, down between the pillars supporting the platform, it didn't look like much. But Rand seemed entranced. 'That's our puppy all right!' He sounded as enthusiastic as a plane spotter who'd managed to photograph the latest black silhouette out at Groom Lake.

'What exactly is it?' Herz asked.

'Looks like an FADM to me. An enhanced storage version of the old SSADM, based on the W54 pit. Don't know what it's doing here, but someone is going to catch it in the neck over this. See that combination lock there?' He pointed. 'It's closed. And, wait . . .' He fell silent for a few seconds. 'Got it. Did you see that red flash? That's the arming indicator. It blinks once a minute while the device is live. There's a trembler mechanism and a tamper alarm inside the casing. Try to move it or crack it open and the detonation master controller will dump the core safety ballast and go to detonate immediately.' He fell silent again.

'Does "detonate immediately" mean what I think it means?' asked Herz. *It's been here for months, it's not going to go off right away,* she told herself, trying to keep a lid on her fear.

'Yes, it probably does.' Dr. Rand sounded distracted. 'Hmm, this is an interesting one. I need to think about it for a while.'

You need to – Herz wrenched herself back on track. 'What happens now?' she asked.

'Let's go up top,' suggested Rand.

'Okay.' They scrambled backwards until they reached the track bed, and could stand up. 'Well?' she asked.

'I got its serial number,' Rand said happily. 'Now we can cross-check against the inventory and see where it came from. If it's on the books, and if we can trust the books, then we can just requisition the PAL combination and open it up, at which point there's a big red OFF switch, sort of.' A shadow crossed his face: 'Of course, if it's a ghost device, like the big lump of instant sunshine you stumbled across in Cambridge, we might be in trouble.'

'What kind of trouble? Tell me everything. I've got to tell the colonel.'

'Well . . .' Rand glanced from side to side, ensuring nobody else was within earshot. 'If it's just a pony nuke that's been stolen from our own inventory, then we can switch it off, no problem. *Then* we get medieval on whoever let it go walkabout. But you remember the big one? That wasn't in our inventory, although it came off the same production line. If this is the same, well, I *hope* it isn't, because that would mean hostiles have penetrated our current warhead production line, and that's not supposed to be possible. And we won't have the permissive action lock keys to deactivate it. So the best we can hope for is a controlled explosion.'

'A controlled –' Herz couldn't help herself: her voice rose to a squeak ' – *explosion*?'

'Please, calm down! It's not as bad as it sounds. We know the geometry of the device, where the components sit in the casing. These small nukes are actually very delicate – if the explosive lens array around the pit goes off even a microsecond or two out of sequence, it won't implode properly. No implosion, no nuclear reaction. So what happens is, we position an array of high-speed shaped charges around it and blow holes in the implosion assembly. Worst case, we get a fizzle – it squirts out white-hot molten uranium shrapnel from each end, and a burst of neutrons. But no supercriticality, no mushroom cloud in downtown Boston. We've got time to plan how to deal with it, so before we do *that* we pour about a hundred tons of barium-enriched concrete around it and hollow out a blast pit under the gadget to contain the fragments.' He grinned. 'But these bombs don't grow on trees. I'm betting that your mysterious extradimensional freaks stole it from our inventory. In which case, all

I need to do is make a phone call to the right people, and they give me a number, and –' he snapped his fingers '– it's a wrap.'

'But you forgot one thing,' Judith said slowly.

'Oh, yes?' Rand looked interested.

'Before you do anything, I want you to dust for fingerprints around the lock,' she said, barely believing her own words. 'And you'd better hope we find prints from source GREENSLEEVES. Because if not . . .'

'I don't under – '

She raised a hand. 'If these people have stolen one nuke, who's to say they haven't stolen others?' She looked him in the eye and saw the fear beginning to take hold. 'We might have found Matt's blackmail weapon. But this isn't over until we know that there aren't any others missing.'

*

Rudi hung above the forest with the wind in his teeth, a shit-eating grin plastered across his face (what little of it wasn't numb with cold) and the engine of the ultralight sawing along behind his left ear like the world's largest hornet. The airframe buzzed and shuddered, wires humming, but the vibration was acceptable and everything was holding together about as well as he'd hoped for. Unlike a larger or more sophisticated airplane, the trike was light enough for one world-walker to shift in a week of spare time, and simple enough for one aviator to assemble and fly: and now Rudi was reaping his reward for all the headaches, upsets, reprimands, and other cold-sweat moments he'd put into it. 'On top of the world!' he yelled at the tree-tops a thousand feet below him. *'Yes!'*

The sky was as empty as a dead man's skull; the sun beat down, casting sharp shadows over his right shoulder. Hanging below the tri-angular wing, with nothing below his feet but a thin fiberglass shell, Rudi could almost imagine that he was flying in his own body, not dangling from a contraption of aluminum and nylon powered by a jumped-up lawn mower engine. Of course, letting his imagination get away from him was not a survival-enhancing move up here, a thousand feet above the forests that skirted the foothills of the

Appalachians in this world – but he could indulge his senses for a few seconds between instrument checks and map readings, saving the precious memories for later.

'Is that the Wergat or the Ostwer?' he asked himself, seeing the glint of open water off to the northwest. He checked his compass, then glanced at the folded map. One advantage of using an ultralight: with an airspeed of fifty-five, tops, you didn't wander off the page too fast. A few minutes later he got it pinned down. 'It's the Ostwer all right,' he told himself, penciling a loose ellipse on the map – his best estimate of his position, accurate to within a couple of miles. 'Hmm.' He pushed gently on the control bar, keeping one eye on the air speed indicator as he began to climb.

The hills and rivers of the western reaches of the Gruinmarkt spread out below Rudi like a map. Over the next half hour he crawled towards the winding tributary river – it felt like a crawl, even though he was traveling twice as fast as any race-bred steed could gallop – periodically scanning the landscape with his binoculars. Roads hereabout were little more than dirt tracks, seldom visible from above the trees, but a large body of men left signs of their own.

That's odd. He was nearly two thousand feet up, and a couple of miles short of the Ostwer – glancing over his left shoulder at a thin haze of high cloud that looked to be moving in – when a bright flash on the ground caught his eye. He stared for a moment, then picked up his binoculars.

Out towards the bend in the river – after the merger that produced the Wergat, where the trees thinned out and the buildings and walls and fields of Wergatfurt sprouted – something flashed. And there was smoke over the town, a thin smudge of dirty brown that darkened the sky, like a latrine dug too close to a river. 'Hmm.' Rudi leaned sideways, banking gently to bring the trike round onto a course towards the smoke, still climbing (there was no sense in overflying trouble at low altitude on one engine), and took a closer look with his binoculars.

He was still several miles out, but he was close enough to recognize trouble when he saw it. The city gates were open, and one guardhouse was on fire – the source of the smoke.

'Rudi here, Pappa One, do you read?'

The reply took a few seconds to crackle in his earpiece: 'Pappa One, we read.'

'Overflying Wergatfurt, got smoke on the ground, repeat, smoke. Guardhouse is on fire. Over.'

'Pappa One to Rudi, please repeat, over.'

'Stand by . . .'

Minutes passed, as Rudi checked his position against the river, and buzzed ever closer to the town and the palace three miles beyond it. The smoke was still rising as Rudi closed on the town, now at three thousand feet, safely out of range of arrows. He looked down, peering through binoculars, at a scene of chaos.

'Rudi here, Pappa One. Confirm trouble in Wergatfurt, cavalry force, battalion level or stronger. Cannon emplaced in town square, northeast guard tower on fire, tents outside city walls. Now heading towards Hjalmar Palace, over.'

'Pappa One, Rudi, please confirm number of troops, over.'

Rudi looked down. A flash caught his eye, then another one.

'Rudi here, am under fire from Wergatfurt, departing in haste, over.' His hands were clammy. Even though none of the musketry could possibly reach him, it was unnerving to be so exposed. He pulled back on the bar to nose gently down, gathering speed: the sooner he checked out the palace and got the hell away from this area, the happier he'd be.

Tracking up the shining length of the river, Rudi headed towards the concentric walls of the castle overlooking the Wergat. The Hjalmar Palace was an enormous complex, sprawling across a hillside, surrounded on three sides by water. It stood in plain sight, proud of the trees that clothed the land around it. Rudi raised his glasses and stared at the walls. From a mile out, it looked perfectly normal. Certainly the cannon stationed in Wergatsfurt hadn't bitten any chunks out of those walls yet.

'Pappa One, Rudi, update please, over.'

'Rudi here. Approaching Hjalmar Palace at two five hundred feet. Looks quiet. Over.'

'Pappa One, Rudi, be advised palace has missed two watch rotations, over. Be alert for – '

Rudi missed the rest. Down below, sparks were flashing from the gatehouse. Startled, he let go of the binoculars and threw himself to the left, side-slipping away from the tower. A faint crackling sound reached his ears, audible over the buzz of the engine. 'Rudi, Pappa One, am under fire from the palace, over.' He leaned back to the right, feeling a bullet pluck at the fabric of his wing. *This shouldn't be happening*, he told himself, disbelieving: the altimeter was still showing two thousand feet. *How are they reaching me?* A horrible suspicion took hold. 'Pappa One, Rudi, they've got – shit!'

For a moment he glanced down at the shattered casing of the radio, blinking stupidly. Then he leaned forward, trying to squeeze every shuddering mile per hour that was available out of the air-frame, fuming and swearing at himself for not bringing a spare transceiver.

His unwelcome news – that whoever had taken the Hjalmar Palace had taken its heavy machine guns and knew how to use them – would now be delayed until he returned to Castle Hjorth.

*

It took them two hours to stagger back up the track to the waypoints blazed on the trees, and another half hour to reach the marked tran-sit point. Walking in near-darkness with early flakes of snow whirling around them wasn't Huw's idea of a happy fun vacation: but his sense of urgency pushed him on, even though he was halfway to exhaustion. *We've got to tell someone about this,* he kept telling himself. *Important* didn't begin to describe the significance of the door into nowhere. *We might not be the only people who can world-walk – or even the most effective at it.*

Eventually he staggered into the clearing where they'd pitched the tent – now a dark hump against a darker backdrop of trees, lonely and small in the nighttime forest. 'You ready?' he asked Yul.

'I think you should go first, bro,' his brother said. 'You're the one who understands that stuff.'

'Yes but –' He made a snap decision: '– follow me at once, both of you. We can recover the camp later if we need to. I may need witnesses to back me up.'

'I'd kill for a bath!' Elena ended on a squeak. 'Let's go!'

'Count of three,' said Huw. He bared his wrist to the chilly air and squinted. 'One, two – '

He lurched as the accustomed headache kicked in, then gasped as the humid evening air of home hit him in the face like a wet flannel. The noise of insects was almost deafening after the melancholy silence of the forest. To his left, Elena blinked into view and winced theatrically. 'I'm going to the bathroom,' she announced, unslinging her P90. 'I may be some time.'

'Whatever.' Huw waited a few seconds before he turned to his brother, who was grinning like an idiot. 'Is she always like this?'

'What? Oh, you should see her in polite society, bro.' He stared after her longingly.

Huw punched him on the arm. 'Come on inside, I've got to report this immediately.'

He headed for the front room, shedding his pack and boots and finally his jacket and outer waterproof trousers as he went. The cell phone was where he'd left it, plugged in and fully charged. He picked it up and unlocked it, then dialed by hand a number he'd committed to memory. It took almost thirty seconds to connect, but rang only once before it was answered. 'This is Huw. The word today is "interstitial". Yes, I'm well, thank you, and yourself, sir. I want to speak to the duke immediately, if you can arrange it.'

Hulius watched him from the doorway, a faintly amused expression on his face. From upstairs, the sound of running water was barely audible.

Huw frowned. 'Please hold,' Carlos had said. He was the duke's man; he would have been told that Huw was working on a project for him, surely?

'Trouble?' asked Yul.

'Too early to say.' Huw sat down on the bedroll, cradling the phone. 'I'm on hold – oh. Yes, sir, I am. We're all there. I have an urgent report – what? Yes. Um. Um. Can you repeat that, please? Yes. Okay, I guess. Transfer me.'

He clamped his free hand over the mouthpiece and grimaced horribly at Yul. 'Shit. We've been nobbled.'

'What –' Yul began, but Huw's face turned to an attentive mask before he could continue.

'Yes? My lady? Yes, I remember. What's going on? It's about – *oh*, yes, indeed. You want – you want us to meet you *where*? – When? – Tomorrow? But that's more than a thousand miles! We could fly – oh. Are you sure?' He rolled his eyes. 'Yes, my lady. Um. We'll have to get moving right away. Okay. You have my number? We'll be there.'

He hung up then put the phone down deceptively gently, as if he'd rather have thrown it out the window.

'What was *that* about?'

Huw looked up at his brother. 'We'd better roust Elena out of her bath.' He shook his head.

'Bro?'

'That was my lady d'Ost – one of his grace's agents. I got through to the duke's office but he's busy right now. Carlos passed on orders to submit a written report: meanwhile we're to get moving *at once*. We've got to drive all the way to the west coast and back on some fucking stupid errand. We're to take our guns, and we've got to be in Las Vegas by noon tomorrow, so we're going to be moving out *right now*. There's a private plane waiting for us near Richmond but we've got to get there first and it's going to take eight hours to get where we're going once we're airborne. Some kind of shit has hit the fan and they've got *my* name down as one of the trustees to deal with it!' He trailed off plaintively. 'What's going on?'

Hulius grunted. 'Two and a half thousand miles, bro. They must really want you there badly.'

'Yeah. That's what I'm afraid of. Hmm, Lady d'Ost. I wonder what she does for the duke?'

*

Otto stared at the buzzing gnat in the distance, and swore.

'Gregor, my compliments to Sir Geraunt and I request the pleasure of his company in the grand hall as a matter of urgency.'

The hand-man dashed off without saluting, catching the edge in his voice. The faint hum of the dot in the sky, receding like a bad dream of witchcraft, put Otto in mind of an angry yellowjacket. He could barely hear it over the ringing in his ears; the morning smelled of brimstone and gunsmoke. *Too early*, he thought. He'd barely taken the inner keep an hour ago: he'd counted on having at least a day to arrange things to his advantage. 'Heidlor,' he called.

'Sir?' Heidlor had been saying something to one of the gunners, who was now hastily swabbing out the barrel of his weapon.

'Get the fishermen into the grand hall and have them set their nets up between ankle and knee level, leaving areas free as I discussed. Once they've done the hall they're to do the barracks room, the duke's chambers, the kitchen, and the residences, in that order. The carpenters are to start on the runways in the grand hall as soon as the fishermen are finished, and to move on in the same order. This is of the utmost urgency, we can expect visitors at any time. Should any of the craftsmen perform poorly, make an example of them – nail their tools to their hands or something.'

'Yes, sir.' Heidlor paused. 'Anything else?'

Otto swallowed his first impulse to snap at the man for hanging around: he had a point. 'Find Anders and Zornhau. Their lances are to go on duty as soon as they are able. Station the men with the fishers and carpenters, one guard for each craftsman, with drawn steel. In the grand hall, place one man every ten feet, and a pistoleer in each corner. For the cleared spaces, position two guards atop a chair or table or something. Warn them to expect witches to manifest out of thin air at any moment. Rotate every hour.' He paused for a moment. 'That's all.'

'Sir!' This time Heidlor didn't dally.

Otto turned on his heel and marched back towards the steps leading down from the battlements. He didn't need to look to know that his bodyguard – Frantz and four hand-picked pistoleers, equally good with witch-gun or wheel-lock, and armed with cavalry swords besides – were falling into line behind him. The way the witches fought, by stealth and treachery, his own life was as much under threat as that of any of his soldiers, if not more so.

The corkscrewing steps (spiraling widdershins, to give the advantage to a swordsman defending the upper floor) ended on the upper gallery of the great hall. Otto looked down on the fishermen and their guards, as they hastily strung their close-woven net across the floor at ankle height. Spikes, hammered heedlessly into the wooden paneling, provided support for the mesh of ropes. The carpenters were busy assembling crude runways on trestles above the netting, so that the guards could move between rooms without touching the floor. At the far end, near the western door that opened onto the grand staircase, there was a carefully planned open area: a killing ground for the witches who would be unable to enter from any other direction.

Sir Geraunt, the royal courier, was standing directly below him, looking around in obvious puzzlement. 'Sir Geraunt!' Otto boomed over the balcony: 'Will you join me up here directly?'

A pale face turned up towards him in surprise. 'Sir, I would be delighted to do so, but this cat's cradle your artisans are weaving is in my way. If you would permit me to cut the knot – '

'No sir, you may not. But if you proceed through the door to your left, you will find the stairway accessible – for now.'

A minute later Sir Geraunt emerged onto the balcony, shaking his head. A couple of weavers also emerged, lugging a roll of netting between them, but Otto sent them a wave of dismissal. 'We are in less danger from the witches the higher we go, but the balcony must be netted in due course,' he explained, for the younger man was still staring at the work in the room below with an expression of profound bafflement.

'My lord, I fail to understand what you are doing here. Is it some ritual?'

'In a way.' Otto walked to the edge of the balcony, and pointed down. 'What do you see there?'

'A mess –' Sir Geraunt visibly forced himself to focus. 'Nets strung across the floor, and walkways for your men. The witches appear from the land of shadows, do they not? Is this some kind of snare?'

'Yes.' Otto nodded. It wouldn't do to let the witches retake the castle too easily – his majesty's little plan wasn't the kind of trick you could play twice. 'Observe the open area, and the position of the guards – who are free to move where they will. I am informed by an unimpeachable source that the witches cannot arrive inside another object: that is, they may be able to appear within the building, but if the exact spot they desire to occupy is filled by a piece of furniture or a tree or another body, they are blocked. The netting is close enough to prevent them arriving anywhere on the covered floor. Thus, if they wish to pay us a visit, they must do so on the ground I leave to them. Where, you will note, my soldiers are awaiting them.'

Sir Geraunt's eyes widened. 'Truly, his majesty chose wisely in placing his faith in you!'

'Perhaps. We'll see when the foe arrive. That was why I called for you, as a matter of fact: the witches have unforeseen resources. A most peculiar carriage just overflew us, carrying a man who is now, without a doubt, hastening to their headquarters with word of our presence. I had counted on having an entire day to prepare the defenses here, and the surprise outside. To make matters worse, my guards fired on the intruder – and missed. His majesty is still a day away. I therefore expect the witches to attack within a matter of hours.'

The knight's reaction was predictable: 'I stand before you. What can I do on your behalf?'

Otto managed to produce a thin smile. 'I expect to kill a fair number of witches, but they have better guns than my men, and probably other surprises beside. So I am moving things forward. A reinforced company will stay here to take the first attack. The survivors will fall back through the tunnel to the river. Hopefully the resistance will force them to concentrate in the castle, but our witch-guns on the curtain walls, pointing inwards, will bottle them up for long enough to execute his majesty's plan . . .'

*

It was shaping up to be a good day, thought Eric, as he twisted his left wrist with increasing effort to get the gyroball up to speed. A good day in a good week. Judith's report from the scene under Scollay Square was the second bit of really good news after Mike Fleming's remarkable reappearance. *Heads we win: Lucius punches in the PAL code and switches off the bomb. Tails we don't lose: we get to deal with a fizzle, but we keep Boston.* There were cover stories available to deal with a fizzle, to sweep it under the rug – it would be messy, but a whole different matter from losing the core of a city. 'I'm waiting on a definite match when they finish fuming for prints,' Judith had told him from the scene, 'but we got some good UV-fluorescence images of latent prints in the dirt around the lock, and it sure looks like GREENSLEEVES was here.' Eric gave the ball another flick of the wrist. *Which means we can take the kid gloves off now,* he thought, with a warm glow of satisfaction. *Just as soon as we've confirmed no other stock is missing.* And he went back to staring at his desk.

Back when telephone switchboards were simple looms of wires and plug boards, different networks needed different wires. You could judge how important an official was by how many phone handsets he had on his desk. Life had been a lot simpler in those days. Today, Eric had just the one handset – and it plugged into his computer instead of a hole in the wall. He glanced at the clock in his taskbar to confirm the call was late, just as the computer rang.

'Smith here.' He leaned back.

'Eric? Mandy in two-zero-two.'

'Hi Mandy, Jim here. Y'all had a good day so far?'

'I'll take roll call.' Eric grinned humorously. The list of names on the conference call was marching down the side of his screen. 'Looks like we're missing Alain and Sonya. I'd give them another five minutes, but I've got places to be and meetings to go to, so if we can get started?'

The field ops conference call was under way. Like any policing or intelligence-gathering operation, the hunt for the extradimensional narcoterrorists called for coordination and intelligence sharing: and with agents scattered across four time zones it couldn't be carried out by calling everyone into a briefing room. But unlike a policing job, some aspects of the task were extraordinarily sensitive and could not be discussed, and unlike a normal intelligence operation, things were too fluid and unstable to leave to the usual bureaucratic channels of written reports and weekly bulletins. So the daily ops call had become a fixture within FTO, or at least within that part of FTO that was focused on hunting the bad guys within the Continental United States. Each field office delegated a staff intelligence officer who could be trusted to filter the information stream for useful material and refrain from mentioning in public those projects that not everyone was cleared for. Or so the post hoc justification went. In practice, they gave Eric a chance to keep a finger on the pulse of his department at ground level without spending all his time bouncing around the airline map.

In practice, normally all it was usually good for was an hour's intensive wrist exercise with the gyroball and a frustrating ten minutes writing up a summary for Dr. James. But today, Eric could smell something different in the air.

' . . . Following up the cell phone thing via Walmart, we've made some progress over here.'

Eric snapped to full alert, glancing at the screen. It was Mandy, from the team in Stony Brook. 'How many phones?' He cut in.

'I was just getting to that.' She sounded offended. 'The suspects bought two hundred and forty-six over the past six months, all the same model, batches of ten at a time, right up until yesterday. Walmart has been very cooperative, and we've been going over their videotapes – they think it's some kind of fraud ring – and it looks like a Clan operation for sure. It's the same two men each week: if they follow the usual pattern –' the Clan had a rigid approach to buying supplies, always paying cash for small quantities at regular intervals '– we could lift them next week. We've also got a list of phone IMEIs and SIM numbers they bought and we're about to go to Cingular to see if – '

'Don't do that,' Eric interrupted again. He glanced around frantically, looking for a pen and a Post-it: he hadn't expected this much information, so soon. 'We have other resources to call on who are better at dealing with this angle.' To be precise, Bob and Alice at No Such Agency, who – given a cell phone's identifying fingerprints – could tell you *everything* about them. This was the trouble with ex-FBI staff: they did great investigative work, but they didn't know what external strings they could pull with Defense. 'E-mail me the list immediately,' he ordered. 'I'll take it from there.'

'Certainly, I'll send them right after – '

'No, I meant *now*.' The gyroball, unnoticed, wound down. 'If any of those phones are switched on, we can get more than a trace.' He took a deep breath. 'I'm going offline now, waiting on that e-mail, Mandy.' He hit the hangup button and shook his head, then speed-dialed a different number.

The phone picked up immediately. 'James here.'

'It's me. I assume you're in the loop over Lucius's little project? Well, Stony Brook has just hit the mother lode, too. Cells, numbers. I'm forwarding everything to EARDROP. If any of them turn out to be live I intend to put some assets on the ground and tag them – then it's time to turn up the heat. If Herz confirms that the gadget under Government Center was planted by GREENSLEEVES, and Dr. Rand's friends confirm that no other weapons of the same class are missing, I propose to activate COLDPLAY.'

'Excellent,' said James. 'Get started, then get back to me. It's time to hurt those bastards.'

*

Three coaches full of medieval weekend warriors drove in convoy through the Massachusetts countryside, heading towards Concord.

The coaches were on lease from a small private hire firm, and someone had inexpertly covered their sides with decals reading HISTORY FAIRE TOURING COMPANY. The passengers, mostly male but with some women among them, wore surcoats over chain mail, and the luggage racks overhead were all but rattling with swords and scabbards: the air conditioners wheezed as they fought a losing battle with the summer heat. They looked like nothing so much as the away team for the Knights of the Round Table, on their way to a joust.

The atmosphere in the coach was tense, and some of the passengers were dealing with it by focusing on irrelevancies. 'Why do we have to wear all this crap?' complained Martyn, running his thumb round the neckline of his surcoat. 'It's about as authentic as a jet fighter at the battle of Gettysburg.'

'You'll grin and bear it,' said Helmut. 'It's cover, is what it is. You can swap it for camo when we link up with the wardrobe department. And it'll do in a hurry, if it comes to it . . .'

'Consider yourself lucky,' Irma muttered darkly. 'Ever tried to fight in a bodice?'

Martyn blew a raspberry. 'Are we there yet?'

Helmut checked the display on his GPS unit. 'Fifteen miles. Hurry up and wait.' Someone down the aisle groaned theatrically. Helmut turned, his expression savage: 'Shut the fuck up, Sven! When I want your opinion I'll ask for it.'

The medieval knight at the wheel drove on, his shoulders slightly hunched, his face red and sweating. The lance members wore full plate over their machine-woven chain vests and Camelbak hydration systems – it was much lighter than it looked, but it was hellishly hot in the sunlight streaming through the coach windows. Heat prostration, Helmut reminded himself, was the reason heavy armor had gone out of fashion in this world – that, and its declining utility against massed gunfire. 'Hydration time, guys, everyone check your buddies. Top off now. Victor, make with the water cart.'

A police cruiser pulled out to overtake the coach and Helmut tensed, in spite of himself. Thirty assorted knights and maids on their way to a joust and a medieval faire shouldn't set the traffic cop's alarm bells ringing the way that thirty soldiers in American-style body armor would, but there was a limit to how much inspection their cover could handle. If the police officer pulled them over to search the baggage compartment he'd be signing his own death warrant: Helmut and his platoon of Clan Security soldiers were sitting on top of enough firepower to reenact the Vietnam war.

'Keep going.' The police car swept past and Helmut sent Martyn a fishy stare. 'Mine's a Diet Pepsi,' Martyn said, oblivious. Helmut shook his head and settled back to wait.

Some time later, the driver braked and swung the coach into a wide turn. 'Coming up on the destination,' he called.

Helmut sat up and leaned forward. 'The others?'

'Braun is right behind me. Can't see Stefan but I'd be surprised if – '

Helmut's phone rang. Gritting his teeth, Helmut answered it. 'Yes?'

'We see you. Just to say, the park's clear and we're keeping the bystanders out of things.'

'Bystanders?'

The voice at the other end of the connection was laconic: 'You throw a Renaissance Faire, you get spectators. Ysolde's telling them it's a closed rehearsal and they should come back tomorrow.'

Helmut buried his fingertips in his beard and scratched his chin. 'Good call. What about the –' he checked his little black book '– ticket seats?'

'They're going up. A couple of problems with the GPS but we should be ready for the curtain-raiser in about an hour.'

Helmut glanced at his book again to confirm that *curtain-raiser* was today's code word for *assault team insertion*. One of the constraints they'd been working under ever since the big DEA bust six months ago was the assumption that at any time their cellular phones (carefully sanitized, stolen, or anonymously purchased for cash) might be monitored or tracked by hostile agencies. Clan Security – in addition to fighting a civil war in the Gruinmarkt – had been forced to rediscover a whole bunch of 1940s-era communication security procedures.

'Call me if there's a change in status before we arrive,' Helmut ordered, then ended the call. 'Showtime,' he added, for the benefit of the audience seated behind him.

'It's not over until the fat lady sings,' Martyn snarked in Irma's direction: she glared at him, then drew her dagger and began to ostentatiously clean her already-spotless nails.

The coach turned through a wide gateway flanked by signs advertising the faire, bumped across loose gravel and ruts in the ground, then came to a halt in a packed-earth car park at one end of a small open field. A couple of big top circus tents dominated it, and a group of men with a truck and a stack of scaffolding were busy erecting a raised seating area. To an untrained eye it might easily be mistaken for a public open-air event, close by Concord: that was the whole idea. Real SCA members or habitual RenFaire goers weren't that common, and those that might notice this event would probably write it off as some kind of commercial rip-off, aimed at the paying public. Meanwhile, the general reaction of that public to a bunch of people in inaccurate historical costume was more likely to be one of amusement than fear. Which was exactly what Riordan had proposed and Angbard had accepted.

In fact, the strip mall on the far side of the open space was owned by a shell company that answered to a Clan council director – because it was doppelgängered, located on the identical spot occupied by a Clan property in the other world. And the supposed historical faire was one of several ClanSec contingency plans designed to cover the rapid deployment of military units up to battalion strength into the Gruinmarkt.

'Let's move those kit bags out,' Helmut barked over his shoulder as the driver scrambled to open the baggage doors on the side of the coach. 'I'll have the guts of any man who opens his kit before he gets it inside the assembly tent.' His troopers scrambled to drag their heavy sports bags towards the nearer big top: he'd checked that they'd been properly packed, and while any hypothetical witnesses would see plenty of swords and 'historical shit' as Erik called it, they wouldn't get even a hint of the SAWs and M16s that were the real point of this masquerade – much less the M47 Dragon that Stefan's fire support platoon were bringing to the party.

The setup in the tent would have surprised anyone expecting a show. Half a dozen men and women – officers in Clan security, comptrollers of the postal service, and a willowy blonde in a business suit who Helmut was certain was one of the duke's harem of assassin-princesses – were gathered around a table covered with detailed floor plans: three more, armed with theodolites, laser range finders, and an elaborate GPS unit were carefully planting markers around the bare earth floor. At the far side, a work crew was unloading aluminum scaffolding and planks from the back of a truck, while another gang was frantically bolting them together at locations indicated by the survey team. Helmut left his soldiers scrambling to pull camouflage surcoats and helmets on over their armor, and headed straight for the group at the table, halting two meters short of it.

The duke glanced up from the map. As usual, he was impeccably tailored, dressed for the boardroom: a sixty-something executive, perhaps, or a mid-level politician. But there was a feral anger burning in his eyes that was normally kept well hidden: Helmut suppressed a shudder. 'Third platoon is dismounting and will be ready to go in the next ten minutes,' he said as calmly as he could.

The duke stared at him. 'Good enough,' he rasped, then glanced sideways at his neighbor, whom Helmut recognized – with a surprised double-take – as Baron Oliver Hjorth, an unregenerate supporter of the backwoods conservative cabal and the last man he'd have expected to see in the duke's confidence. 'I told you so.'

The baron nodded, looking thoughtful.

'Is there any word from Riordan?' The duke turned his attention towards a plump fellow at the far side of the table.

'Last contact was fifty-two minutes ago, sir,' he said, without even bothering to check the laptop in front of him. 'Coming up in eight. I can expedite that if you want . . .'

'Not necessary.' The duke shook his head, then looked back at Helmut. 'Tell me what you know.'

Helmut shrugged. Despite the full suit of armor, the gesture was virtually silent – there was neoprene in all the right places, another of the little improvements ClanSec had made to their equipment over the years. World-walkers were valuable enough to be worth the cost of custom-fitted armor, and they hadn't been slow in applying new ideas and materials to the classic patterns. 'Stands to reason he's hit the Hjalmar Palace, or you wouldn't have called us out. Is there any word from Wergatsfurt or Ostgat?'

The duke inclined his head. 'Wergatsfurt is taken. Ostgat hasn't heard a whisper, as of –' He snapped his fingers.

'Thirty-seven minutes ago,' said the ice blonde. She sounded almost bored.

'So we were strung out with a feint at Castle Hjorth and the Rurval estates, but instead he's concentrated eighty miles away and hit the Hjalmar Palace,' summarized Helmut. He glanced around at the scaffolding that was going up. 'It's fallen?'

'Within minutes,' Angbard confirmed. He was visibly fuming, but keeping a tight rein on his anger.

'Treachery?'

'That's my concern,' said the duke, with such restraint that Helmut backed off immediately. The blonde, however, showed no sign of surprise: she studied Helmut with such bland disinterest that he had to suppress a shudder.

So we've got a leak, he realized with a sinking feeling. *It didn't stop with Matthias, did it?* 'Should I assume that the intruders know about doppelgänger defenses?' He glanced round. 'Should I assume they have world-walkers of their own?'

'Not the latter, Gray Witch be thanked.' Angbard hesitated. 'But it would be unwise to assume that they don't know how to defend against us, so every minute delayed increases the hazard.' He reached a decision. 'We can't afford to leave it in their hands, any more than we can afford to demolish it completely. Our options are therefore to go in immediately with everything we've got to hand, or to wait until we have more forces available and the enemy has had more time to prepare for us. My inclination is towards the immediate attack, but as you will be leading it, I will heed your advice.'

Helmut grimaced. 'Give me enough rope, eh? As it happens, I agree with you. Especially if they have an informant, we need to get in there as fast as possible. Do we know if they are aware of the treason room?'

'No, we don't.' Angbard's expression was stony. 'If you wish to use it, you will have to scout it out.'

'Aye, well, there are worse prospects.' Helmut turned on his heel and raised his voice. 'Martyn! Ryk! To me. I've got a job for you!' Turning back to the duke, he added: 'If the treason room is clear, we'll go in that way, with diversions in the north guard room and the grand hall. Otherwise, my thinking is to assault directly through the grand hall, in force. The higher we go in –' he glanced up at the scaffolding, then over to the hydraulic lift that two guards were bringing in through the front of the tent '– the better I'll like it.'

*

Motion sickness was a new and unpleasant experience to Miriam, but she figured it was a side effect of spending days on end aboard a swaying express train. Certainly it was the most plausible explanation for her delicate stomach. She couldn't wait to get solid ground under her feet again. She'd plowed through about half the book by Burroughs, but it was heavy going; where some of the other Leveler tracts she'd read had been emotionally driven punch-in-the-gut diatribes against the hereditary dictators, Burroughs took a far drier, theoretical approach. He'd taken up an ideological stance with roots Miriam half-recognized – full of respectful references to Voltaire, for example, and an early post-settlement legislator called Franklin, who had turned to the vexatious question of the rights of man in his later years – and had teased out a consistent strand of political thought that held the dictatorship of the hereditary aristocracy to be the true enemy of the people. Certainly she could see why Burroughs might have been exiled, and his books banned, by the Hanoverian government. But the idea that he might be relevant to the underground still struck her as peculiar. *Do I really want to get involved in this?* she asked herself. It was all very well tagging along with Erasmus until she could get her hands on her laptop again and zip back to the United States, but the idea of getting involved in *politics* made her itch. Especially the kind of politics they had over here.

'He's a theoretician, isn't he?' she asked Erasmus, as their carriage slid through the wooded hills. 'What's Lady Bishop's interest?'

He stared out of the window silently, until she thought he wasn't going to reply. Then he cleared his throat. 'Sir Adam has credibility. Old King George sought his counsel. Before Black Monday, he was a Member of Parliament, the first elected representative to openly declare for the radicals. And to be fair, the book – it's his diagnosis of the ailment afflicting the body politic, not his prescription. He's the chair of the central committee, Miriam. We need him in the capital – '

There was a sudden jerk, and Miriam was pushed forward in her seat. The train began to slow. 'What's going on?'

'Odd.' He frowned. 'We're still in open country.' The train continued to slow, brakes squealing below them. The window put the lie to Erasmus's comment almost immediately, as a low row of wooden shacks slid past. Brakes still squealing, the long train drifted to a halt. Erasmus glanced at her, worried. 'This can't be good.'

'Maybe it's just engine trouble? Or the track ahead?' *That's right, clutch at straws,* she told herself. Her hand went to her throat, where she had taken to wearing James Lee's locket on a ribbon: at a pinch she could lift Erasmus and land them both in the same world as the

Gruinmarkt, but . . . 'I can get us out of here, but I know nothing about where we'd end up.'

'We've got papers.' Now he sounded as if he was grasping at straws, and knew it.

'Don't anticipate trouble.'

'Get your bag. If they want a bribe – '

'Who?'

'How should I know?' He pointed at the window: 'Whoever's stopped the train.'

The door at the end of the compartment opened abruptly, and a steward stepped inside. He puffed out his brass-buttoned chest like a randy pigeon: 'Sorry to announce, but there's been a delay. We should be moving soon, but –' A bell sounded, ringing like a telephone outside the compartment. ''Scuse me.' He ducked back out.

'What kind of delay?' Miriam asked.

'I don't know.' Erasmus stood up. 'Got everything in your bag?'

Miriam, thinking of the small pistol, swallowed, then nodded. 'Yes.' It was stuffy in the un-air-conditioned carriage, but she stood up and headed over to the coat rail by the door, to pick up her jacket and the bulging handbag she'd transferred the notebook computer into. 'Thinking of getting off early?'

'If we have to.' He frowned. 'If this is – '

Footsteps. Miriam paused, her coat over her left arm. 'Yes?' she asked coolly as the door opened.

It was a middle-aged man, wearing the uniform of a railroad ticket inspector. He looked upset. 'Sir? Ma'am? I'm sorry to disturb you, but would you mind stepping this way? I'm sure we can sort this out and be on our way soon.'

Erasmus glanced sideways at her. Miriam dry-swallowed, wishing her throat wasn't dry. *Bluff it out, or . . . ?* 'Certainly,' he said smoothly: 'Perhaps you can tell us what it's about?'

'In the station, sir,' said the inspector, opening the door of the carriage. The steps were already lowered, meeting the packed earth of a rural platform with a weathered clapboard hut – more like a signal box than a station house – hunched beside it. Only the orange groves to either side suggested a reason for there to be a station here. The inspector hurried anxiously over towards the building, not looking back until he neared the door. Miriam caught Burgeson's eye: he nodded, slowly. *The Polis would just have come aboard and arrested us, wouldn't they?* she told herself. *Probably . . .*

As her companion approached the door, Miriam curled her fingers around the butt of her pistol. The inspector held the door open for them, his expression anxious. 'The electrograph from your cousin requested a private meeting,' he said apologetically. 'This was the best I could arrange – '

'My *cousin*?' Miriam asked, her voice rising as the door opened: 'I don't have a cousin – '

A whoosh of escaping steam dragged her attention up the line. Slowly and majestically, the huge locomotive was straining into motion, the train of passenger cars squealing and bumping behind it. Miriam spun round, far too late to make a run back for it. 'Shit,' she muttered under her breath. A steam car was bumping along the rutted track that passed for a service road to the station. Erasmus was frozen in the doorway, one hand seeming to rest lightly on the inspector's shoulder. Another car came into view along the road, trailing the first one's rooster-tail of dust.

'You don't?' The inspector looked confused.

'Who set this up?' Erasmus asked, his tone deceptively calm.

'I don't know! I was only following orders!' Miriam ducked round the side of the station house again, glancing in through the windows. She saw an empty waiting room furnished only with a counter, beyond the transom of which was an evidently empty ticket office. *It's not the station*, she realized, near-hysteria bubbling under.

'Into the waiting room,' she snapped, bringing the revolver out of her pocket. '*Move!*'

The inspector stared at her dumbly, as if she'd grown a second head, but Erasmus nodded: 'Do as she says,' he told the man. The inspector shuffled into the waiting room. Erasmus followed, his movements almost bored, but his right hand never left the man's shoulder.

'How long 'til they get here?' Miriam demanded.

'I don't know!' He was nearly in tears. 'They just said to make you wait!'

'*They,*' said Erasmus. 'Who would *they* be?'

'Please don't kill me!'

The door to the ticket office was ajar. Miriam kicked it open and went through it with her pistol out in front. The office was indeed empty. On the ticket clerk's desk a message flimsy was waiting. Miriam peered at it in the gloom. DEAR CUZ SIT TIGHT STOP UNCLE A SENDS REGARDS STOP WILL MEET YOU SOONEST SIGNED BRILL.

Well, that *settles it.* Miriam lowered her gun to point at the floor and headed back to the waiting room.

' – the Polis!' moaned the inspector. 'I've got three wee ones to feed! Please don't – '

Shit, meet fan. Even so, it struck her as too big a coincidence to swallow. *Maybe the Polis are tapping the wires? That would do it.* Brilliana had figured out where she was, which train she was on, and signaled her to wait, not realizing someone else might rise to the bait.

Burgeson was grim. 'Miriam, the door, please.'

'Let's not do anything too hasty,' she said. 'There's an easy way out of this.'

'Oh please – '

'Shut up, you. What do you have in mind?'

Miriam waved at the ticket office. 'He's not lying about my cousin: she's on her way. Trouble is, if we bug out before she gets here she's going to walk into *them.* So I think we ought to sit tight.' She closed the door anyway, and glanced round, looking for something to bar it with. 'I can get us both out of here in an emergency,' she said, a moment of doubt cutting in when she recalled the extreme nausea of her most recent attempts to world-walk.

The first car – *more like a steam-powered minivan,* Miriam noted – rounded the back of the station and disappeared from sight. Almost two minutes had passed since they reached the station. Miriam slid aside from the windows, while Burgeson did likewise. Boots thudded on the ground outside: the only sounds within the building were the pounding of blood in her ears and the quiet sobbing of the ticket inspector.

'Mr. Burgeson!' The voice behind the bullhorn sounded almost jovial: 'And the mysterious Mrs. Fletcher! Or should I say, *Beckstein?*' He made it sound like an accusation. 'Welcome to California! My colleague Inspector Smith has told me all about you both and I thought, why, we really ought to have a little chat. And I thought, why not have it somewhere quiet-like, and intimate, instead of in town where there are lots of flapping ears to take note of what we say?'

Across the room, Burgeson was mouthing something at her. His face was in shadow, making it hard to interpret. The inspector knelt in the middle of the floor, in a square of sunlight, sobbing softly as he rocked from side to side wringing his hands. The appearance of the Polis had quite unmanned him.

'Like this: *parlez-vous français, Madame Beckstein?*'

They think I'm a French spy? Either the heat or the tension or some other strain was plucking her nerves like guitar strings. Somehow Erasmus had fetched up almost as far away as it was possible to get, twelve feet away across open ground overlooked by a window. To get him out of here one or the other of them would need to cross that expanse of empty floor, in front of –

The ticket inspector snapped, flickering from broken passivity to panic in a fraction of a second. He lurched to his feet and ran at the window, screaming, '*Don't hurt me!*'

Erasmus brought his right hand up, and Miriam saw the pistol in it. He hesitated for a long moment as the inspector fumbled with the window, throwing it wide and leaning out. '*Let me –*' he shouted: then a spatter of shots cracked through the glass, and any sense of what he had been trying to say.

The bullhorn blared, unattended, as the inspector's body slumped through the half-open window and Miriam, seeing her chance, ducked and darted across the room, avoiding the lit spaces on the floor, to fetch up beside Burgeson.

'I think they want you alive,' he said, a death's-head grin spreading across his gaunt cheekbones. 'Can you get yourself out of here?'

'I can get us both out –' She fumbled with the top button of her blouse, hunting for the locket chain.

'After how you were last time?'

Miriam was still looking for a cutting reply when the bullhorn started up again. 'If you come out with your hands up we won't use you for target practice! That's official, boys, don't shoot them if they've got their hands up! We want to ask you some questions, and then it's off to the Great Lakes with you if you cooperate. That's also a promise. What it's to be is up to you. Full cooperation and your lives! Hurry, folks, this is a bargain, never to be repeated. Because you're on my manor, and Gentleman Jim Reese prides himself on his hospitality, I'll give you a minute to think about it before we shoot you. Use it carefully.'

'Were you serious about waiting around for your friends?' Burgeson asked. 'Is a minute long enough?'

'But –' Miriam took a deep breath. 'Brace yourself.' She put her arms around Erasmus, hugging him closely. His breath on her cheek smelled faintly stale. 'Hang on.' She dug her heels into the floor and lifted, staring over his shoulder into the enigmatic depths of the open locket she had wrapped around her left wrist. The knot writhed like chain lightning, sucking her vision into its contortions – then it spat her out. She gasped involuntarily, her head pulsing with a terrible, sudden tension. She focused again, and her stomach clenched. Then she was dizzy, unsure where she was. *I'm standing up*, she realized. *That's funny*. Her feet weren't taking her weight. There was something propping her up. A shoulder. *Erasmus's shoulder*. 'Hey, it didn't – '

She let go of him and slumped, doubling over at his feet as her stomach clenched painfully. 'I know,' he said sadly, above her. 'You're having difficulty, aren't you?'

The bullhorn: 'Thirty seconds! Make 'em count!'

'Do you think you can escape on your own?' Burgeson asked.

'Don't – know.' The nausea and the migraine were blocking out her vision, making thought impossible. 'N-not.'

'Then I see no alternative to –' Erasmus laid one hand on the doorknob '– this.'

Miriam tried to roll over as he yanked, hard, raising the pistol in his right hand and ducking low. He squeezed off a shot just as Gentleman Jim, or one of his brute squad, opened fire: clearly the Polis did things differently here. Then there was a staccato burst of fire and Erasmus flopped over, like a discarded hand puppet.

Miriam screamed. A ghastly sense of déjà vu tugged at her: *Erasmus, what have you* done? She rose to her knees and began to raise her gun, black despairing fury tugging her forward.

There was another burp of fire, ominously rapid and regular, like a modern automatic weapon. *That's funny*, she thought vacantly, tensing in anticipation. She managed to unkink her left hand, but even a brief glance at the locket told her that it was hopeless. The design swam in her vision like a poisonous toadstool, impossible to stomach.

Erasmus rolled over and squeezed off two more shots methodically. Miriam shook her head incredulously: *You can't do that, you're dead!* Someone screamed hoarsely, continuously, out behind the station. Shouts and curses battered at her ears. The hammering of the machine gun started up again. Someone else screamed, and the sound was cut short. *What's going on?* she wondered, almost dazed.

The shots petered out with a final rattle from the machine gun. The silence rang in her ears like a tapped crystal wineglass. Her head ached and her stomach was a hot fist clenched below her ribs. 'Erasmus,' she called hoarsely.

'Miriam. My lady, are you hurt?'

The familiar, crystal-clear voice shattered the bell of glass that surrounded her. 'Brill!' she called.

'My lady, *are you alone in there*?'

Urgency. Miriam tried to take stock. 'No,' she managed. 'I'm with Erasmus.'

'She's not hurt, but she's sick,' Burgeson called out. He shuffled backwards, into the shadowy interior of the waiting room, still clutching his pistol in his hand. He focused on Miriam. 'It's your girl, Brill, isn't it?' he hissed.

'Yes,' she choked out, almost overwhelmed with emotion. *He's not dead!* More than half a year had passed since that terrible moment in Fort Lofstrom, waiting beside Roland's loose-limbed body, hoping against hope. *And Brill –*

'Then I suggest we move out of here at once!' Brilliana called. 'I'm going to stand up. Hold your fire.'

'I'm holding,' Erasmus called hoarsely.

'Good. I'm coming in now.'

*

Another wild goose chase, Judith told herself gloomily. No sooner had she gotten back to the serious job of shadowing Mike Fleming like he was the president or something, no sooner had she managed to breathe a series of extended gasps of relief at the news – that Source GREENSLEEVES' fingerprints had been all over the casing and it *was* missing from inventory and Dr. Rand had punched in the PAL code and switched it off without any drama – than the colonel came down with his tail on fire and a *drop everything* order of the day: absolutely typical. 'Leave a skeleton team on site and get everyone else up here *now,*' he said, all trace of his usually friendly exterior gone. Crow's-feet at the corners of his eyes that hadn't been there the week before. *Something's eating him,* she'd realized, and left it to Rich Hall to ask what the rush job was and get his head bitten off.

Which was why, four hours later, she was sitting in the back seat of an unmarked police car behind officers O'Grady and Pike, keeping an eye on a strip mall and a field with a big top in it and a sign saying HISTORY FAIRE outside.

'What is it we're supposed to be *looking* for, ma'am?' Pike asked, mildly enough.

'I'll tell you when I see it.' The waiting was getting to her. She glanced once more at the laptop with the cellular modem and the GPS receiver sitting next to her. Seven red dots pocked the map of Concord like a disease. Updated in real time by the colonel's spooky friends Bob and Alice, the laptop could locate a phone to within a given GSM cell . . . but that took in the mall, the field, and a couple of streets on either side. 'There are tricks we can play with differential signal strength analysis to pin down exactly where a phone is,' Smith had told her, 'but it takes time. So go and sit there and keep your eyes peeled while we try to locate it.'

The mall was about as busy – or as quiet – as you'd expect on any weekday around noon. Cars came, cars went. A couple of trucks rumbled past, close enough to the parked police car to rock it gently on its suspension. O'Grady had parallel-parked in front of a hardware store just beside the highway, ready to move.

'We could be here a while,' she said. 'Just as long as it isn't a wild goose chase.'

'I didn't think you people went on wild goose chases,' said Pike. Then she caught his eye in the rearview mirror. He reddened.

'We try not to,' she said dryly, keeping her face still. Her FBI credentials were still valid, and if anyone checked them out they'd get something approximating the truth: on long-term assignment to Homeland Security, do not mess with this woman. 'We're expecting company.'

'Like that?' O'Grady gestured through the window. Herz tracked his finger, and stifled a curse. On the screen beside her, an eighth red dot had lit up in her cell.

'It's possible.' She squinted at the coach. Men were coming out of the big top to open the gate, admitting it.

The laptop beeped. A ninth red dot on the map – and another coach of HISTORY FAIRE folks was slowing down to turn into the field.

'Just what do they do at a history faire anyway?' asked Pike. 'Hey, will you look at that armor!'

'Count them, please,' Judith muttered, pulling out her own phone. She speed-dialed a number. 'Larry? I've got two coachloads that showed up around the same time as two more positives. Can you give me a background search on –' she squinted through her compact binoculars, reading off the number plates '– and forward it to Eric? He's going to want to know how many to bring to the party.'

'What's that they're carrying?' Pike grunted.

Judith blinked, then focused on a group of men in armor, lugging heavy kit bags in through the door of the marquee. 'This doesn't add up –' she began. Then one of the armored figures lifted the awning higher, to help his mates: and she got a glimpse at what was going on inside.

'Officers, we're not dressed for this party and I think we should get out of here *right now.*'

'But they –' began Pike.

'*Listen* to the agent.' O'Grady started the engine. 'Okay, where do you want me to go, ma'am?'

'Let's just get out of the line of sight. Keep moving, within a couple of blocks. I'm going to phone for backup.'

'Is it a terror cell? Here?'

She met his worried eyes in the mirror. 'Not as such,' she said, 'but it's nothing your department can handle. Once you drop me off you're going to be throwing up a cordon around the area: my people will take it from here.' She hit a different speed-dial button. 'Colonel? Herz. You were right about what's going on here. I'm pulling out now, and you're good to go in thirty . . .'

*

Rudi squinted into the sunlight and swore as he tried to gauge the wind speed. The walls of Castle Hjorth loomed before him like granite thunderclouds – *except they're far too close to the ground, aren't they?* He shook his head, fatigue adding its leaden burden to his neck muscles, and glanced at the air speed indicator once more. *Thirty-two miles per hour, just above stall speed, too high . . .* The nasty buzzing, flapping noise from the left wing was quieter, the ripstop nylon holding. He leaned into the control bar, banking to lose height. Small figures scurried around the courtyard below him as he spotted the crude wind sock he'd improvised over by the pump house. *Okay, let's get this over with.*

The ultralight bounced hard on the cobblestones, rattling him painfully from teeth to tailbone. He killed the engine. For a frightening few seconds he wondered if he'd misjudged the rollout, taking it too near the carriages drawn up outside the stables – but the crude brakes bit home in time, stopping him with several meters to spare. 'Phew,' he croaked. His lips weren't working properly and his shoulders felt as stiff as planks: he cleared his throat and spat experimentally, aiming for a pile of droppings.

Rudi had originally intended to go and find Riordan and make his report as soon as he landed, but as he took his hands off the control bar he felt a wave of fatigue settle over his shoulders like a leaden blanket. Flying the ultralight was a very physical experience – no autopilots here! – and he'd been up for just over three hours, holding the thing on course in the sky with his upper arms. His hands ached, his face felt as if it was frozen solid, and his shoulders were stiff – though not as stiff as they'd have been without his exercise routine.

He unstrapped himself slowly, like an eighty-year-old getting out of a car, took off his helmet, and was just starting on his post-flight check-list when he heard a shout from behind. 'Rudi!'

He looked round. It was, of course, Eorl Riordan, in company with a couple of guards. He didn't look happy. 'Sir.' He stood up as straight as he could.

'Why didn't you report in?' demanded the eorl.

Rudi pointed mutely at the remains of the radio taped to the side of the trike. 'I came as fast as I could. Let me make this safe, and I'll report.'

'Talk while you work,' said Riordan, a trifle less aggressively. 'What happened?'

Rudi unplugged the magneto – *no point risking some poor fool chopping their arm off by playing with the prop* – and began to check the engine for signs of damage. 'They shot at me from the battlements and the gatehouse,' he said, kneeling down to inspect the mounting brackets. 'Took out the radio, put some holes in the wing. I was two thousand feet up – they've got their hands on modern weapons from somewhere.' He shook his head. 'If anyone's going in – '

'Too late.'

Rudi looked up. Riordan's face was white. 'Joachim, signal to the duke: defenders at the Hjalmar Palace have guns. No, wait.' Riordan stared at Rudi. 'Could you identify them?'

'I'm not sure.' Rudi stood up laboriously. 'Wait up.' He walked round the wing – tipped forward so that the central spar lay on the ground – and found the holes he was looking for. 'Looks like some-thing relatively large. They were automatic, sir, machine guns most likely. Didn't we get rid of the last of the M60s a long time ago?'

Riordan leaned over him to inspect the bullet holes. 'Yes.' He turned to the messenger: 'Joachim, signal the duke, defenders at the Hjalmar Palace have at least one – '

'Two, sir.'

'Two heavy machine guns. Go now!'

Joachim trotted away at the double, heading for the keep. A couple more guards were approaching, accompanying one of Riordan's officers. For his part, the eorl was inspecting the damage to the ultralight. 'You did well,' he said quietly. 'Next time, though, don't get so close.'

Rudi swallowed. He counted four holes in the port wing, and the wrecked radio. He walked round the aircraft and began to go over the trike's body. There was a hole in the fiberglass shroud, only inches away from where his left leg had been. 'That's good advice, sir. If I'd known what they had I'd have given them a wider berth.' It was hard to focus on anything other than the damage to his aircraft. 'What's happening?'

'Helmut and his men went in half an hour ago.' Riordan took a deep breath. 'When will you be ready to fly again?'

Whoa! Rudi straightened up again and stretched, experimentally. Something in his neck popped. 'I need to check my bird thoroughly, and I need to patch the holes, but that'll take a day to do properly. If it's an emergency and if there's no other damage I can fly again within the hour, but –' he glanced at the sky '– there're only about three more flying hours in the day, sir. And I've only got enough fuel here for one more flight, anyway. It's not hard to get on the other side, but I wasn't exactly building a large stockpile. To be honest, it would help if we had another pilot and airframe available.'

Riordan leaned close. 'If we survive the next week, I think that'll be high on his grace's plans for us. But right now, the problem we face is knowing what's going on. You didn't see any sign of the pretender's army, but that doesn't mean it isn't out there. Get your work done, get some food, then stand by to go out again before evening – even if it's only for an hour, we need to know whether there's an army marching down our throat or whether the Hjalmar Palace is the focus of his attack.'

*

Brill was one of the last people Miriam had expected to meet in California – and she seemed to have brought a bunch of others with her. 'You're unhurt?' Brill asked again, anxiously.

The trio of Clan agents she'd turned up with – two men and a woman, sweating and outlandish in North Face outdoor gear – as if they'd just parachuted in from a camping expedition somewhere in the Rockies, in winter – had taken up positions outside the station. One of them Miriam half-recognized: *Isn't he the MIT postgrad?* Perhaps, but it was hard for her to keep track of all the convoluted relationships in the Clan, and right now – covering the approach track with a light machine gun from behind a bullet-riddled steam car – he didn't exactly look scholarly. Brilliana was at least dressed appropriately for New British customs.

'I'm unhurt, Brill.' Miriam tried to hold her voice steady, tried not to notice Erasmus staring, his head swiveling like a bird, as he took in the scattered bodies and the odd-looking machine pistols Brill and the other woman carried. The Polis inspector and his men had tried to put up a fight, but revolvers and rifles against attackers with automatic weapons appearing out of thin air behind them. 'Just got a bit of a headache.' She sat down heavily on the waiting room bench.

'Wonderful! I feared you might attempt to world-walk.' Brill looked concerned. 'I must say, I was not expecting you to get this far. You led us a merry chase! But your letter reached me in time, and a very good thing too. His grace has been most concerned for your well-being. We shall have to get you out of here at once – '

Miriam noticed Brill's sidelong glance at Burgeson. 'I owe him,' she said.

Erasmus chuckled dryly. 'Leave me alive and I'll consider the debt settled in my favor.'

'I think we can do better than that!' Brill glanced at Miriam. 'How much does he know?'

'How much do you think?' Miriam stared back at her. This was a side to Brill that she didn't know well, and didn't like: a coldly calculating woman who came from a place where life was very cheap indeed. 'They were lying in wait for us because they intercepted your telegram. The least we can do is get him to his destination. Leave him in this, and . . .' She shrugged.

Brill nodded. 'I'll get him out of here safely. Now, will you come home willingly?' she asked.

The silence stretched out. 'What will I find if I do?' Miriam finally replied.

'You need not worry about Baron Henryk anymore.' Brill frowned.

'He's dead; but were he not, the way he dealt with you would certainly earn him the disfavor of the council. He overplayed his hand monstrously with the aid of Dr. ven Hjalmar. The duke is minded to sweep certain, ah, events into the midden should you willingly agree to a plan he has in mind for you.' Her distant expression cracked: 'Have you been sick lately? Been unable to world-walk? Is your period late?'

Miriam blinked. 'Yes, I –' she raised a hand to her mouth in dawning horror. 'Fuck.'

Brill knelt down beside her. 'You have borne a child before, did you not?'

'But I haven't slept with –' Miriam stopped. 'That fucking quack. *What did he do to me?*'

'Miriam.' She looked down. Brill was holding her hands. 'Ven Hjalmar's dead. Henryk is dead. *Creon* is dead. But we've got living witnesses who will swear blind that you were married to the crown prince at that ceremony, and this was the real reason why Prince Egon rebelled. Ven Hjalmar, with the queen mother's connivance . . . it's unconscionable! But we're at war, Miriam. We're at war with half the nobility of the Gruinmarkt, and you're carrying the heir to the throne. You're not a pawn on Angbard's chessboard anymore, Miriam, you're his queen. Whatever you want, whatever it takes, he'll give you –'

Miriam shook her head. 'There's only one thing I truly want,' she said tiredly, 'and he can't give it to me.' The claustrophobic sense of losing control that she'd fled from weeks ago was back, crushingly heavy. She lowered one hand to her belly, self-consciously: *Why didn't I think of this earlier?* she wondered. *All those examinations . . .* Then another thought struck her, and she chuckled.

'What ails you?' Brilliana asked anxiously.

'Oh, nothing.' Miriam tried to regain control. 'It's just that being figurehead queen mother or whatever scheme Angbard's penciled in for me isn't exactly a job with a secure future ahead of it. Even if you get this rebellion under control.'

'My lady?'

'I was planning on bargaining,' Miriam tried to explain. 'But I don't need to, so I guess you want to know this anyway: it's too late.

I ran into an old acquaintance on my way out of the burning palace. His people had been watching it when the shit hit the fan. It's the U.S. government. They've got agents into the Gruinmarkt, and it's only a matter of time before – '

'Oh, *that*,' Brill snorted dismissively and stood up. 'That's under control for now; your mother's running the negotiations.'

Miriam held a hand before her eyes. *Make it stop*, she thought faintly. *Too much!*

'In any event, we have worse things to worry about,' she added. 'Sir Huw was sent to do a little job for the duke that I think you suggested – he'll brief you about what he found on the flight home. The CIA or the DEA and their friends are the least of our worries now.' Brill laid a hand on her shoulder. Quietly, she added: 'We need you, Miriam. Helge. Or whoever you want to be. It's not going to be the same this time round. The old guard have taken a beating: and some of us understand what you're trying to do, and we're with you all the way. Come home with me, Miriam, and we'll take good care of you. We need you to lead us . . .'

*

The treason room was a simple innovation that Angbard's last-but-two predecessor had installed in each of the major Clan holdings: a secret back door against the day when (may it never arrive) Clan Security found itself locked out of the front. Like almost all Clan holdings of any significance, the Hjalmar Palace was doppelgängered – that is, the Clan owned, and in most cases had built on, the land in the other world that any world-walker would need to cross over from in order to penetrate its security.

For an empty field, the location where they'd set up the HISTORY FAIRE had a remarkably sophisticated security system, and the apparently decrepit barns at the far end of the field, collocated with the palatial eastern wing, were anything but easy to break into.

The treason room in the Hjalmar Palace had once been part of a guardroom on the second floor of the north wing. That is, it had been part of the guardroom until Clan Security had moved everybody out one summer, installed certain innovative features, then built a false wall to conceal it. The cover story was that they'd been installing plumbing for the nobs upstairs. In fact, the treason room, its precise location surveyed to within inches, was an empty space hidden behind a false wall, located twenty feet above the ground. The precise coordinates of the treason rooms were divided between the head of Clan Security, and the office of the secretary of the Clan's commerce committee, and their very existence was a dark secret from most people.

Now, Helmut watched tensely as two of his men ascended towards the middle of the tent on a hydraulic lift.

'Ready!' That was Martyn. Big and beefy, he waved at Helmut.

'Me too,' called Jorg. He pulled the oxygen mask over his head and made a show of adjusting the flow from his tank, then gave a thumbs-up while Martyn was still fiddling with his chin straps.

'Move out when you're both ready,' Helmut called.

Martyn turned, lumbering, and switched on the tactical light clamped under the barrel of the MP5 he wore in a chest sling. Then he knelt down. Jorg climbed onto his back. The platform creaked and its motor revved slightly as he stood up, raising his left wrist to eye level before him. Silently and without any fuss, they disappeared from sight: a perfect circus trick.

Helmut nodded to the platform's operator. 'Take it down three inches.' The platform whirred quietly as it lowered. It wouldn't do for the returning world-walker to be blocked by the lift. He checked his watch. *Thirty seconds.* The drill was simple. Jorg would drop off Martyn's back, Martyn would swing round, and if there was any company he'd take them out while Jorg came right back over. If not, they'd inspect the room, plant the charges in the pre-drilled holes, set the timer to blow in half an hour, and then Jorg would carry Martyn back. After which, the next group through wouldn't need the masks – they wouldn't be entering a room that had been filled with carbon dioxide and sealed off behind a gas-tight membrane for fifty years.

Elapsed time, two minutes. Helmut shook his head, dizzy with tension. *If they've found the treason room and booby-trapped it . . .* He'd known Jorg as a kid. This wasn't something he wanted to have to explain to his mother.

'It's going to work,' a voice at his shoulder said quietly.

Helmut managed not to jump. 'I hope so, sir.'

'It had better, because this is the real treason room, not the decoy.' Angbard cast him a brief feral grin. 'Unless my adversary is a mind reader . . .'

The thud of boots landing on metal dragged Helmut's head round. 'Yo!' Jorg waved from the platform, which swayed alarmingly. He pulled his oxygen mask up: 'It's clean!' Behind him, Martyn staggered slightly, fumbling with the lift controls. The platform began to descend, and Helmut drew in a breath of relief.

'Stand down,' he told the guards who still stood with M16s aimed at the platform.

'Aw, can't I shoot him?' asked Irma. 'Just a little?'

'You're going in next,' Helmut said, deadpan. Now he was tense for an entirely different reason: anticipation, not fear. On the other side of the tent, Poul's couriers were already wheeling the siege tower forward. The aluminum scaffold on wheels didn't look very traditional, but with its broad staircase and the electric winch for hauling up supply packs it served the same purpose – a quick way into an enemy-held fortress. He looked up at Martyn. 'Time check!'

'Catch.'

Martyn tossed underarm and Helmut grabbed the grip-coated stopwatch out of the air. He stared at the countdown. 'Listen up! Eighteen minutes and thirty seconds on my mark . . . Mark! First lance, Erik, lead off at plus ten seconds. I want an eyeball report no later than T plus thirty. Second lance, Frankl, you're in after the eyeball clears the deck. Third lance, you idle layabouts, we're going in thirty seconds after that. Line up, line up! Take your tickets for the fairground ride!' He headed off around the tent, checking that everyone knew their assigned role and nothing was out of place.

Minutes passed. The siege tower was finally set up on the carefully surveyed spot below the treason room. The couriers were still hammering stabilizer stakes into the ground around it as Erik led his lance up the ramp to the jump platform. The medical team was moving into position, maneuvering stretchers into position next to the winch: an ambulance sat next to one of the side doors to the tent, ready to go. Helmut checked the stopwatch.

'Sir Lieutenant.' He glanced round, as Angbard nodded at him. The old man had a disturbing way of moving silently and unobtrusively. He straightened as the duke continued: 'I don't intend to jog your elbow. You have complete discretion here. However, if there is an opportunity to take the commanding officer of the attacking force, or one of his lieutenants, alive, without additional risk to yourself or your men, then I would be *most* interested in asking him certain questions.'

'Really?' He grinned in spite of himself. It wasn't an expression of amusement. 'I can imagine, your grace.' He glanced at the scaffolding. In a few minutes, it was quite possible that some or most of his platoon would be dead or injured. And right that moment, the idea of dragging the man who'd inflicted this shocking insult upon the Clan's honor up before his liege was a great temptation to Helmut. 'I shall do everything in my power to oblige you, my lord. I can't promise it – not without knowing what is happening within the castle – but I'd like to make the bastards pay for everything they've done to us.'

'Good.' Angbard took a step back, and then, to Helmut's surprise, raised his fist in salute: 'Lead your men to victory, knight-lieutenant! Gods guide your sword!'

Helmut returned the salute, then checked the time. *Minus one minute.* He raised a hand and waved at Erik, pointing to the stopwatch. 'One minute!'

On the other side of the wall between the worlds, the timer would be counting down towards zero. Martyn and Jorg had packed the pre-drilled holes with blocks of C-4 strung together on detcord, plugged in the timer, and synchronized it with the stopwatch in Helmut's hand. In a few seconds' time, the thin false wall would be blasted into splinters of stone, throwing a deadly rain of shrapnel across the guardroom. It was intended to kill anyone inside, clearing a path for the assault lance waiting on the siege tower above. *Any second* –

Helmut raised his hand. 'Time!'

Twelve pairs of boots shuffled forward above his head. The rattle of M16s and M249s being cocked, like a junkyard spirit clearing its throat: Erik's lance flipping out the knotwork panels beside their sights, squinting along their barrels and shuffling forward.

'Plus five!' called Helmut. 'Six! Seven! Eight! Nine! Ten!'

The platform juddered on its base as the soldiers flickered out of sight. Helmut took a deep breath and turned towards the map table where the duke was conferring with his officers. Raised voices, alarm. Helmut glanced at the sergeant standing with his men beside the ramp. 'Frankl, you know the plan. When the eyeball reports, go if it's clear. I'm –' the duke's raised voice made up his mind '– checking something.'

'Is this confirmed?' Angbard demanded: the signals officer hunched defensively before him. 'Is it?'

'Sir, all I have is Eorl-Major Riordan's confirmed report on Lieutenant Menger's overflight. If you want I can put you through to Castle Hjorth, but he's already redeploying – '

'Never mind.' Angbard cut him dead as he turned to face Helmut. 'They've got M60s,' he said conversationally, although his cheeks showed two spots of color. 'Your men need to know.'

'M60s?' Helmut blanked for a moment. 'The gatehouse!'

'More than that,' the duke added. 'It sounds like they captured a stockpile from one of the strategic villages. Eorl Riordan is redeploying his company. They should be arriving here within the next three hours.'

'Right, right.' Helmut nodded jerkily. 'Well, that puts a different picture on things.' He glanced at Angbard, anticipating the duke's dismissal. 'If you'll excuse me, sir, my men need me?'

He turned and trotted back towards the siege tower. Overhead, on the platform, the first lance's messenger was shouting excitedly, something about the room being clear. 'Listen up!' he called. 'Change of plan. We're going in *now*. Housecleaning only, new plan is to secure the upper floors, strictly indoors. Anyone who goes outdoors gets their ass shot off: the bad guys have got their hands on a couple of M60s, and until we pinpoint them we're not going to be able to break out. Lance three, follow me in. Lance two, follow after.'

He strode up the ramp as fast as he could, bringing his M16 down from his shoulder. The messenger was almost jumping from foot to foot. 'It's clear, sir! It went really well. Erik said to tell you he's moving out into the upper gallery and will secure the roofline. Is that right?'

'It was.' *Five minutes ago, before we knew they had machine guns on the bastions.* Helmut shook his head, an angry sense of injustice eating at his guts. Erik and his men were probably already dead. 'Okay, let's go to work.' He glanced over his shoulder, at Irma and Martyn and the others in the lance he, personally, led: they were watching him, trusting him to lead them into the unknown. 'For the glory of the Clan! Follow me . . .'

DOPPELGÄNGERED

Otto nearly didn't make it out of the castle. He was in the courtyard with Sir Geraunt and his personal guards, supervising the withdrawal of the body of his forces to the gatehouse and the prepared positions outside the castle walls, when there was a deafeningly loud blast from inside the central keep. 'What's that?' Geraunt asked, stupidly.

'Nothing I planned.' Otto turned to Heidlor, who was waiting for further instructions: 'Stations! As I ordered!' The hand-man hurried off, and Otto met Sir Geraunt's curious gaze. 'It'll be the enemy. Too damned early, damn them. Quickly, this way.'

'But the fighting – '

Otto bit back his first response. 'A commander who gets himself killed in the first engagement isn't terribly effective later in the battle,' he said. 'Come *on*.' He hurried towards the gate tower's postern door. 'You there! Stand by!'

A crackle of witch-gun fire echoed out of the central keep. On the top of the gate tower, and the tops of the four towers around the curtain wall, he saw the shields of the captured M60s swinging to bear on the keep.

More gunfire, and screams – this time, the flat boom of his own men's musketry, but far too little of it, too late. *Gods, they're good.* He could see it in his mind's eye: the witches appearing in the middle of a room, unable to enter in strength, surrounded by the cat's cradle of ropes while his men hacked at them desperately with blade and club, trying to keep them from advancing into the keep before the welcome mat was ready –

He paused at an arrow slit. A light blinked in one window high up in the keep, flashing a prearranged signal. He blinked, then swore. 'What is it?' asked Sir Geraunt.

'They had a back door,' Otto said tersely. Just as he had feared:

and they'd come through it hard and fast, hours sooner than his plan called for. 'Every man of ours in the keep is as good as dead.' He turned from the window and stopped: Sir Geraunt was between him and the staircase leading up to the top of the gatehouse.

'We must do something! Give me a score of men and I'll force an entrance – '

'No you won't.' Otto breathed deeply. 'Come on, follow me. It's premature, but.' A grinding roar split the air overhead and he winced: it stopped for a moment, then started again, bursts of noise hammering at his ears like fists as the machine gun battery opened fire on the roofline of the keep, scything through the figures who had just appeared there. 'Quickly!'

Up on top of the gatehouse the stench of burned powder and the hammering racket of the guns were well-nigh unbearable. Otto headed for the hetman he'd left in charge. 'Anders. Report.'

'They're pinned down!' Anders yelled over the guns. 'They keep trying to take the roof and we keep sweeping them off it.' The machine gun paused as two of his men fumbled with gloves at the barrel, swearing as they inexpertly worked it free and tried to slot the replacement into position.

'They seem to have learned to keep their heads down,' Otto said dryly. A spatter of gunfire from a window in the keep targeted the doorway to the northern tower: the heavy guns on the south and west replied, chipping lumps of stone out of the sides of the arrow slit. 'Keep them bottled up. Conserve your fire if you can.' He glared disapprovingly at the two other towers, whose gunners were pounding away at the enemy as if there was no shortage of ammunition. 'Carry on.'

He ducked back down the stairs towards the guardroom overlooking the gate tunnels. 'March,' he said, spotting a sergeant: 'What state did you leave the charges in?'

'The barrels are in position, my lord.' March looked pleased with himself. 'The cords were ready when I left.'

'Good!' Otto looked around: there was an entire lance of soldiers in the room. 'Then let's set the timers and fall back to our prepared positions.' He made the sign of the Crone behind his back, where the men couldn't see it: *If this fails* . . . It wasn't just the king's men who knew how to decorate the branches of a wise tree.

*

The duke was as tense as she had ever seen him: that worried Olga. Not that most of the junior nobility and officers scurrying between communications and intelligence tables would recognize the signs – Angbard was not one to fret obviously in public – but she had known him for years, almost as a favorite uncle, and had observed him in a variety of situations, and she'd seldom seen him as edgy as this. From the set of his shoulders to the way he held his hands behind his back as he listened to messengers and barked orders, the duke was clearly trying to conceal the extent of his ill-ease. *Is it really that bad?* she wondered.

It had started with the messenger who arrived just minutes after the vanguard of the raiding group crossed over into the treason room: she'd been close enough to hear the news of the machine guns, and she could hardly fault the duke for being disturbed by *that*. But as time went by, and the minutes counted on from the incursion, the duke had become even more unhappy. The brief message from Brilliana – she'd been standing right behind him when he received it – had brightened his mood momentarily, but the lack of courier reports was obviously preying on his mind. Clan security didn't have enough bodies to keep him supplied with a blow-by-blow account of the action, and he knew better than to micromanage a skilled subordinate, but his patience had limits. And so, she waited by the duke's command table, keeping one eye on Eorl Hjorth – who she trusted as far as she could throw him. Hjorth's testimony to the council might well decide whether the duke remained in charge of Clan Security. *So we'll have to make sure that his testimony is favorable, won't we?*

'Sir, I have the hourly report from Eorl Riordan.' The messenger offered Angbard a printout to scrutinize. The duke glanced up. 'Where's Braun?' he demanded.

'Sir.' Braun – a wiry fellow, one of the distaff side of the Hjorth-Wu side – saluted.

'Messenger for Helmut, or whoever's in charge, immediate: sweep the cellars for explosive charges.' The duke paused for a moment. 'He's not to attempt to sally from the keep until Stefan's unit is in place to take out the machine guns.' Olga glanced over her shoulder: the second platoon, with their heavy equipment, were already climbing the siege tower. 'Instead, he's to ensure there are no surprises in the cellars under the keep. I think the pretender's trying to be *clever*.' He delivered the final word with contemptuous satisfaction. 'What – '

There was some kind of disturbance going on at the perimeter. Even as Braun charged off to brief a courier, and the heavy weapons platoon climbed the tower and vanished from its top deck three at a time, a distant noise reached Olga's ears, like the throbbing growl of distant traffic. She glanced up. *Lightning Child! Not here, not now!* A pair of guards detached themselves from the group near the awning and trotted towards the table. Reflexively, she moved her right hand close to her jacket pocket, interposing herself.

The first of the guards stopped three meters short and saluted. Olga relaxed slightly, for a moment. 'Sir! We have hostiles in view. Sergeant Bjorg is calling a Threat Red.'

'How many hostiles?' asked the duke, as if it was a minor point of interest.

Olga cleared her throat. 'Sir, I think we should evacuate *now*.'

'Two choppers overhead at last sighting, sir, but it's not looking good on the ground, either: there've been no cars or trucks for a couple of minutes now.' The throbbing was getting louder. *Almost as if –*

The duke shook himself. 'Get everyone across immediately!' he barked. He pointedly refrained from looking up. 'Third platoon, provide covering fire if necessary. Olga!'

'Your grace?' She stared at him.

'You're going across right now, with the headquarters staff. Keep an eye on Hjorth – he's mostly got our interests at heart, if he's smart enough to understand where they lie.' The duke gestured at the siege tower. 'Get moving!'

'But they're –' The bass roar of rotor blades was unmistakable now: not just one set, but the throb of multiple helicopters. Olga set her jaw. 'After you, my lord!'

'You –' For a moment, the duke looked furious: then he nodded tightly, and stalked towards the tower. A squad from the third platoon raced to take up positions around the entrance and behind the low awning, as the duke's staff hurriedly grabbed their papers and equipment and trotted towards the platform from which they could cross into the treason room.

Olga ducked over to the side of the map table and retrieved her rifle and kit – a very non-standard item, more suitable for a sniper than a soldier – then followed the exodus towards the tower. The roof of the tent billowed beneath the thunder, and for a terrifying moment she wondered if she was about to see a SWAT team dropping right through the fabric roof on ropes – but no: *The cops won't do that: they'll go for a siege. Unless –*

The voice of an angry god battered through the walls. '*Come out with your hands up! You have ten seconds to comply!*'

Olga grimaced. *Bastards,* she thought absently. For a routine weekly briefing this was certainly turning out to be an interesting one. *I wonder how they tracked us?* It couldn't be the phone Mike had given her – that wasn't even in the same county.

The queue at the tower had backed up, bottlenecked at the foot of the stairs, but it was moving fast, the world-walkers jumping as soon as they reached the top step with reckless disregard for whatever might be waiting for them on the other side. Olga could see the duke up ahead, near the top step. He glanced over his shoulder as if looking for her, then reached the platform and disappeared. She took a deep breath, relieved. The throbbing roar of rotor blades and the flapping of the canvas roof were making it hard to think: *But we were negotiating: why attack now?* she thought. *Why?* It made little sense. *Unless they think –*

A punishingly loud blast of gunfire ripped through the side of the tent, slapping the fire team behind the main entrance into the ground. '*We can see you. Drop your weapons and come out immediately!*'

Olga stared at the mangled bodies for a fraction of a second, then forced herself to palm her locket open and focus. Some of the surviving guards were shooting blind, suppressive fire through the walls of the tent, while ahead of her half the bodies in the queue were doing just as she was – trying to cross over blind, heedless of hazard. Some of them would make it, some wouldn't, but at least the crush would clear. The design on the inside of her amulet spiraled and twisted, dragging her eyes down towards a vanishing point. Somewhere behind her, a concussive blast: and then she stumbled forward into a smoke-filled space, the air thick with suspended dust, her head pounding and her stomach coiling. *I made it*, she thought. Then: *We're mousetrapped.*

'Milady!' Her eyes widened as she turned towards the Clan soldier, lowering the pistol that had appeared in her hand before she consciously noticed his presence.

'Where's the duke?' she snapped.

'This way.' He turned and she followed him, nearly tripping over some kind of obstruction. *A fishing net?* There was a raised runway above it, and bodies. *Too many bodies,* some of them in Clan uniforms. She took a step up onto the rough-cut planks, bringing her feet above the level of the netting.

'What happened here?'

'Rope trap, my lady. It's a partial doppelgänger, if they'd had time to complete it they'd have locked us out, but we used the treason room instead – '

'I understand. Now take me to the duke. I'm meant to be guarding his life.'

Her guide was already heading up the servants' stairs, two steps at a time, and all she could do was follow. Behind her another body popped out of the air and doubled over, retching. *It's not all over yet,* she realized.

The former guardroom was a mess – one wall blown in, furniture splintered and chopped apart by shrapnel, the bodies of two de-fenders shoved into a corner and ignored – but at least it was in friendly hands. Angbard's staff clustered around in groups, exchang-ing messages and orders, and – *Where's the duke?* Olga headed for the biggest knot, who seemed to be bending over a table or something –

'Your grace?' She gaped.

Angbard glared at her with one side of his face. The other drooped, immobile. 'G-get –' He struggled to speak.

'My lady, please! Leave him to us.' A thick-set, fair-headed officer, one of the Clan Security hangers-on, Olga thought, struggling to recall his name, cradled the duke in his arms. 'Where's the corpsman?' he asked.

'Your grace,' Olga repeated, dumbly. The world seemed to be crumbling under her feet. *Sky Father, what are we going to do now?* The abrupt shift in perspective, to having to confront this mess without him, was far more frightening than the bullets and bombs outside. 'Try to rest. We made it across, and we hold the keep.'

'Corpsman!' the officer called. 'Milady, please move aside.' Olga stepped out of the way to let the medic through.

Eorl Hjorth, lurking nearby, looked at her guiltily. 'He was like this when I got here,' he said. Olga stared at him. 'I'm telling the truth!' He looked afraid. *As well you might,* she thought, looking away. *If this turns out to be anything other than Sky Father calling his own home . . .*

A loud 'Harrumph!' brought her attention back to the stocky officer who still supported Angbard's shoulder. He met Olga's gaze evenly. 'I have operational command here, while his grace is incapacitated. Previously he had indicated that you have your own tasks to discharge, although I doubt you were expecting to discharge them here.'

'That's true. You have the better of me, sir – '

'Carl, Eorl of Wu by Hjalmar. Captain of Security.' He glanced at the communications team, who were still wrestling with their field radio and its portable generator. 'You report directly to his grace, don't you? External Operations?'

'That is correct, yes.'

'Well. We could do with a few more of your friends here, for sure.' Carl grunted. 'It looks like a mess here, but nothing we can't break out of in a few hours.' A frown creased his face. 'Although whether his grace lasts it out is another matter. And I liked it better when we had no enemy at the back door.'

'He's –' Olga shut her mouth and looked back at the medic who, with the assistance of a couple of guards, was trying to make the duke comfortable. 'He needs an American hospital.'

'Well, he's not getting one until we break out of here.' Carl's mustache twitched. A messenger cleared his throat behind Olga. 'Report!'

'Sir! We got them!' The man held up a handful of yellow-sleeved wires.

'Yes, but did you get them *all?*'

'These were all the fuses first squad could find in the cellars – '

A distant thud, like a giant door slamming shut outside, took Olga's attention. 'What was that?' she demanded.

'Don't know.' Carl strode towards the nearest window. 'Damn.'

'What is it?'

The security officer turned back to her. 'That –' his thumb aimed at a rising plume of dust '– unless I'm mistaken, is the culvert to the river.'

'Oh.'

'My compliments to Sergeant Heinz, and you can tell him he did indeed find all the fuses in the cellar,' Carl told the messenger. 'He's to hold until the heavy weapons are in place, then proceed with task bravo.' The messenger ran off. 'Unfortunately he was in no position to check the pump house for charges,' Carl continued. 'Which is a problem. Because we're bottled up in here under those guns, we have no water, our doppelgänger location is besieged, and his grace is inconvenienced.' He didn't say *dying*, Olga noted. 'So if you have any suggestions, before I go and attempt to retake the curtain wall in the face of our own stolen heavy machine guns, I'd like to hear them.'

Olga dry-swallowed, trying to work some juice into her mouth.

'Have you radioed Eorl Riordan to warn him off the American trap?'

'Yes. But he has his own problems. He won't be able to relieve us in less than two days, and if the royal army is out there, that'll be too late.'

'But he has a flying machine.' Olga shook her head. Then she smiled. *Do I have to do all the plotting around here?* 'With your permission, I should like to talk to Eorl Riordan immediately. And you might ready such of your men as are ready to world-walk again. I think we might be able to deal with the enemy without mounting a frontal attack on those guns: and in the process, inconvenience the pretender mightily . . .'

Charles Stross was born in Leeds, England, in 1964. He has worked as a pharmacist, software engineer, and freelance journalist, but now writes full time. To date, Stross has won two Hugo Awards and been nominated twelve times. He has also won the Locus Award for Best Novel, the Locus Award for Best Novella, and has been shortlisted for the Arthur C. Clarke and Nebula awards. In addition, his fiction has been translated into around a dozen languages.

Stross lives in Edinburgh, Scotland, with his wife, Feòrag, a couple of cats, several thousand books, and an ever-changing herd of obsolescent computers.

ALPHARETTA
Atlanta-Fulton Public Library